Hal Spacejock Omnibus Two

Copyright ©2019 Simon Haynes

Books 4-6 in the Hal Spacejock series

Stay in touch!

Author's newsletter:
spacejock.com.au/ML.html

facebook.com/halspacejock
twitter.com/spacejock

No Free Lunch

Book Four in the Hal Spacejock series

spacejock.com.au

Cover images copyright depositphotos.com
3d models from cgtrader.com (juanmrgt, novelo, pedrohsilva, theflyingtim)

Stay in touch!

Author's newsletter:
spacejock.com.au/ML.html

facebook.com/halspacejock
twitter.com/spacejock

Works by Simon Haynes

All of Simon's novels* are self-contained, with a beginning, a middle and a proper ending. They're not sequels, they don't end on a cliffhanger, and you can start or end your journey with any book in the series.
Robot vs Dragons series excepted!

The Hal Spacejock series for teens/adults
Set in the distant future, where humanity spans the galaxy and robots are second-class citizens. Includes a large dose of humour!

Hal Spacejock 0: Origins (2019/2020)
Hal Spacejock 1: A Robot named Clunk*
Hal Spacejock 2: Second Course*
Hal Spacejock 3: Just Desserts*
Hal Spacejock 4: No Free Lunch
Hal Spacejock 5: Baker's Dough
Hal Spacejock 6: Safe Art
Hal Spacejock 7: Big Bang
Hal Spacejock 8: Double Trouble
Hal Spacejock 9: Max Damage
Hal Spacejock 10: Cold Boots

Also available:
Omnibus One, containing Hal books 1-3
Omnibus Two, containing Hal books 4-6
Omnibus Three, containing Hal books 7-9
Hal Spacejock: Visit, a short story
Hal Spacejock: Framed, a short story
Hal Spacejock: Albion, a novella
*Audiobook editions available/in progress

The Dragon and Chips Trilogy.
High fantasy meets low humour!
Each set of three books should be read in order.

1. A Portion of Dragon and Chips
2. A Butt of Heads
3. A Pair of Nuts on the Throne

Also Available:
Omnibus One, containing the first trilogy
Books 1-3 audiobook editions

The Harriet Walsh series.
Set in the same universe as Hal Spacejock. Good clean fun, written with wry humour. No cliffhangers between novels!

Harriet Walsh 1: Peace Force
Harriet Walsh 2: Alpha Minor
Harriet Walsh 3: Sierra Bravo
Harriet Walsh 4: Storm Force (TBA)

Also Available:
Omnibus One, containing books 1-3

The Hal Junior series
Written for all ages, these books are set aboard a space station in the Hal Spacejock universe, only ten years later.

1. Hal Junior: The Secret Signal
2. Hal Junior: The Missing Case
3. Hal Junior: The Gyris Mission
4. Hal Junior: The Comet Caper

Also Available:
Omnibus One, containing books 1-3
The Secret Signal Audiobook edition

The Secret War series.
Gritty space opera for adult readers.

1. Raiders
2. Frontier (2019)
3. Deadlock (2019/2020)

Collect One-Two - a collection of shorts by Simon Haynes

All titles available in ebook and paperback. Visit spacejock.com.au for details.

Bowman Press

Dedicated to Barbara Holland
my high school English teacher

A brief scream, a moment of weightlessness, a sideways wrench …Hal Spacejock awoke with a start, dragged from his vivid dreams by the *Volante's* latest hyperspace jump. As his heart-rate slowed from frantic hammering to over-revved, he wondered whether it was too late for a career change. Anything other than the cargo business would do it. Primary school teaching, perhaps. Or law enforcement.

One jump, two jumps, or even half a dozen …that he could handle. But the *Volante* had been on the move for two days straight, jumping at half-hour intervals, and the constant interruptions had left him feeling like a sleep-deprived zombie. But if waking up was bad, his dreams were even worse. In the latest, a sadistic robot with steel teeth and glowing red eyes had chased him through teleporters, damp airlocks and the cargo hold of his own ship, determined to lay hands on him. Only waking had saved him from its clutches, but Hal was certain it would pounce the moment he closed his eyes.

Despite his determination, Hal drifted off again. Fortunately it was a new setting, and his spirits rose as he roamed the verdant planet with its lofty trees, bubbling streams and …a free-for-all at the local fast food joint? That was more like it! Hal ordered a burger with the lot, and was just about to sink his teeth into the succulent meal when a hand gripped his shoulder. Startled, he opened his eyes to see a metallic form looming over him, right there in his cabin. For a split second he thought the sadistic robot had escaped his nightmares, crossing into real life to mete out its horrible punishment, but then he recognised Clunk. With his battered face, warm yellow eyes and lopsided grin the robot looked anything but sadistic. In fact, he looked annoyingly cheerful.

'I have some good news Mr Spacejock!' said the robot, in an even, male voice.

'Don't tell me there's a free-for-all at the local fast food joint?'

'Sadly, no. I just thought you'd like to know we're approaching our destination.'

'Clunk, you've been saying that for two days.'

'And technically I was completely accurate. However, we're really close now.'

'Wonderful.' Hal sat up, rubbing sleep from his eyes. 'I still can't believe I let you talk me into this little jaunt. We must have flown halfway across the galaxy.'

'It was a wise move, Mr Spacejock. We needed a fresh start.'

'We weren't doing that badly.'

'Oh no? Feuding politicians, desperate fugitives and trigger-happy mercenaries …we've made enough enemies to fill three second-rate novels.'

'But I was only just earning my reputation.'

'My point exactly.'

Hal sighed. 'So, what's this new place like?'

'It's very peaceful. Elderly people, no crime and plenty of work.'

'Speaking of work, didn't we pick up a cargo just before we left?'

'Correct. A shipment of bottled water.'

'We're not visiting a desert planet, are we? Glowing blue eyes give me the creeps.'

'There are no deserts on Dismolle, Mr Spacejock. In fact, it's a favourite amongst retirees. Very comfortable.'

'So why import water?'

'Our client wanted something exotic from another planet, and bottled water was cheap.'

'Our client sounds like a nutcase.' Hal sighed. 'Oh well, as long as the pay's good.'

'Yes, I wanted to talk to you about that.'

Hal groaned. 'Clunk, please tell me there's going to be cash for this one.'

'There is, but not very much.'

'Come on, spill it. What's the wedge?'

'Might I remind you that we were coming to Dismolle anyway? And that every paying job is cash in the bank?'

'So you said. How much?'

Clunk looked apprehensive. 'Twenty-nine fifty.'

'It's a bit on the low side, but it's not a complete loss.'

'You're not angry with me?'

'Of course not. Every bit counts.' Hal eyed a status screen on the opposite wall. During flight it displayed information designed to soothe the fears of nervous passengers, including the hull breach survivability ratio, background radiation measured in years-to-sterility and an up-to-the-minute 'chance of instant death via micro-meteorite' in percentage terms. Now, in addition to the usual information, it also had contact details for Dismolle's fire and emergency services and a banner ad for prepaid funerals. 'I take it we're landing soon?'

'There's just time for my final cargo inspection.'

'I'll come with you.'

'Honestly, it's not necessary.'

'Of course it is. We don't want all that bottled water shifting around. It could tip us right over.'

'But –'

Hal waved away Clunk's protests and followed the robot out of his cabin. Together they made their way to the far end of the lower-deck passageway, where Clunk operated the controls to let them into the hold. There was a click as the light came on, and then ...

'Where the hell's the cargo?' said Hal, staring around the huge empty space.

Clunk pointed to a small box with a Parsed Water logo on its side.

'Tell me you're kidding.'

'No, that's it. I loaded it myself.'

'Some loon is paying three grand to have *that* delivered?'

'No, twenty-nine fifty.'

'Okay, Mr Precision. Two thousand nine hundred and fifty credits.'

'No, Mr Spacejock. Twenty-nine credits and fifty cents.'

Hal stared at him. 'You're not serious.'

'Like I said, this was a last minute cargo and since we were coming to Dismolle anyway ...'

'When you said cash in the bank, I didn't realise you meant a piggy bank. Thirty credits won't cover my coffee bill!'

'It's not thirty credits, it's –'

'Shut up!' Hal paced the cargo hold. 'We'll draw up a new invoice and slap on a few extras. Landing fees, departure fees, wear and tear, customs duty and excess baggage. That should bring it up to four or five hundred at least.'

'That still won't cover your coffee bill. Anyway, we agreed –'

'*You* agreed. I only just found out about it.' Hal stopped pacing. 'In future I want to clear every cargo job.'

'But Mr Spacejock –'

'I'm sorry, but you've let the team down. We can't afford this kind of disaster.'

'It's not a disaster, Mr Spacejock. We were coming –'

Hal raised his hand. 'Every job, Clunk. I get final say.'

'What if you're unreachable?'

'Where could I possibly hide on a cargo ship?'

'You manage it whenever you're on toilet cleaning duties,' muttered the robot.

'Yes, very witty. Now get to work on that new invoice. I want to see it before we land.'

◆

An hour later Hal was sitting in the *Volante's* flight deck, gazing at a satellite image of planet Dismolle on the main viewscreen. The display was centred on a sandy beach, where hoards of sunbathers were stretched out on their towels.

'Navcom, how do you zoom in again?' asked Hal.

'That's the limit,' said the ship's computer, in her neutral female voice.

'But I can't see anything!'

'That's *why* it's the limit.'

Disappointed, Hal shifted to the nearby spaceport, where the landing pads were crammed with a motley assortment of craft. 'Would you look at all those ships! How are we supposed to get work with that lot around?'

'Maybe Clunk intends to undercut their best prices.'

'Oh great,' muttered Hal. 'Even less income.' Still grumbling, he shifted the map again, pausing to inspect a rusty old spaceship hull before stopping at a large dockyard. There were several bays for ship reconstructions, and more cranes than an origami convention. 'Do they build ships here?'

'Dismolle does not have a shipbuilding industry,' said the Navcom. 'However, they do have a maintenance department where all manner of new and exciting upgrades can be ordered and fitted in next to no time, and at surprisingly low rates.'

'Cheaper to trade up,' said Hal, then realised what he'd just said. 'Of course, I'd never trade you in.'

'You'd never upgrade me, either.'

'We don't have money to waste on that kind of thing. Especially with Clunk's new let's-work-for-pocket-change policy.' On screen, a text bubble appeared next to the dockyard. 'Free wash and wax for every visitor? What's that all about?'

At that moment the lift doors at the back of the flight deck slid open, and Clunk entered carrying a folded piece of paper. 'I've been working on the new bill, Mr Spacejock.' He held it out. 'I think you'll find it in order.'

Hal crumpled it up and stuck it in his pocket, ignoring the robot's anguished cry. 'Clunk, I just discovered we're up against half the traders in this sector. Why didn't you check before we came here?'

'I did.' Clunk pointed to the screen. 'If you look closely, you'll notice something rather unusual about those ships.'

Hal squinted. 'Green landing pads? And what are those tent things?'

'They're awnings, and the green patches are little gardens. Look, you can even see the patio furniture.'

'Okay, so they've made themselves comfortable. What's your point?'

'Didn't I tell you this was a retirement planet? All those ships you can see are decommissioned vessels. They've been turned into on-site accommodation.'

'You mean like a caravan park?'

'Correct. If you look really closely you'll notice their exhausts have been boarded up, and you can see satellite dishes on the hulls.'

'So they can't move?'

'Certainly not. We have free reign here, Mr Spacejock. We're the only freighter in town.'

'Excellent! Great work!' Hal slapped him on the shoulder, then remembered something. 'Hey, take a look at this,' he said, pointing at the text bubble on the screen.

'Honest Bob's Ship Wreck 'n'Wax?'

'It's a free offer. They clean your ship for nothing.'

'Mr Spacejock, in my experience any business featuring the word honest in their title is usually anything but.'

'Good, I'm glad you agree. And you can tell them to polish the exhaust cones while they're at it.'

'What's the point? The minute we fly through the atmosphere the ship will just get dirty again.'

'We have to maintain standards, Clunk. And like you said, we're making a fresh start.'

'What if an urgent cargo job eventuates while these public-spirited individuals are waxing our ship?'

'Who else can they ask? We're the only freighter in town.'

'But –'

'Clunk, I want you to book us in as soon as we land. We'll attract a better class of customer with a squeaky clean operation.' He looked the robot up and down. 'Do you think they'll do you as a freebie?'

'Why?'

'Well, you're squeaky but you're not very clean.' Hal turned away and panned the map over the beaches again. 'Do you know how to zoom this thing in a bit more?'

Clunk glanced at the screen, then stared open-mouthed. 'Mr Spacejock, you can't use a mapping service to search for naked people!'

'Why not? Everyone else does.' Hal squinted. 'Don't I know that pair?'

Clunk gestured at the console, turning the screen blank.

'Hey!'

'I'm sorry Mr Spacejock, but I'll need to use the Navcom if we're going to make a soft landing.'

'I was just thinking the same thing,' muttered Hal.

Clunk took his place at the console and worked the controls, altering their angle of approach until the ship plunged into the atmosphere. A thin squeal became a roar, which turned into a deep rumble as the ship tore through the thickening air. The viewscreen displayed columns of scrolling messages, all of which Clunk ignored. He didn't need them, since he could interface directly with the Navcom to find out anything he wanted to know, and Hal wouldn't have understood the messages if they were ten times bigger, used bright red fonts and flashed 'WARNING,

MORTAL DANGER' at regular intervals. In fact, the messages were chosen at random from a database of comforting phrases, and they served one vital function: they kept humans occupied while robots got on with the real work.

Moments later the ship levelled off, and the spaceport slid towards them on the main screen. Clunk guided them towards their landing pad, and the *Volante* set down with a gentle bump. Then the robot's hands darted over the console as he switched off the engines, centred the thruster nozzles and configured the ship for refuelling. Finally, everything was still.

'You know,' said Hal in the sudden silence, 'personally I find it easier to press the autoland button.'

'I like to keep my eye in.' Clunk glanced at him. 'What if we had to complete a midnight landing in a field, with no spaceport beacon to guide us?'

'Never again.' Hal got up to stretch his legs. 'So when's this customer of yours coming by?'

'Our customer will be here shortly, and then you can present her with your bill.'

'Her?'

'Yes, her name is Miss Walsh.'

'Sounds like a maths teacher.' Hal patted his pocket. 'I hope you got your sums right when you added this thing up.'

They took the lift to the lower deck, and Hal stood back as Clunk prepared to lower the cargo ramp. It hardly seemed necessary for one lousy box, but Hal felt the customer deserved a bit of ceremony. After all, she was about to pay for it. 'Remember, Clunk. We stand firm on the new invoice, even if she kicks up a fuss.'

'Yes, Mr Spacejock.'

The doors swung back with a hiss of hydraulics, and the cargo ramp lowered towards the ground. A strip of blue sky appeared, and a shaft of late afternoon sunshine penetrated the hold. Through the glare Hal made out the row of empty landing pads, a perfect line of them surrounded by trimmed grass and tended garden beds. Beyond the pads was the smartest terminal building he'd ever seen, seemingly modelled on a dolls house. Every leadlight window had a pair of wooden shutters painted the same shade of lilac, held open with polished brass fixtures.

There were even lace curtains, and it didn't take much to imagine hand-made tiebacks and rows of crocheted toilet roll covers inside.

'Just as well we didn't land too close,' muttered Hal. 'We'd have scorched those curtains right off the windows.'

The ramp came to rest on the ground, and Hal scanned the landing field for the first sign of Clunk's customer. As he gazed towards the terminal buildings he thought back to his own school days, and it dawned on him that all his teachers had been absolutely terrifying. Sharp-tongued, impatient, quick to tweak his ear …and that was just the librarians. Would Miss Walsh be like that? It was too late to draw up a new invoice, but Hal did have one trick up his sleeve: if she turned out to be a fearsome old dragon he'd slip Clunk the bill and leg it.

'Anybody home?' said a female voice.

Hal jumped, then looked around for the source. There was a safety bunker behind the ship, used for shelter by ground crew when a vessel came in to land, and a young woman was holding the hefty metal door open with one hand and shielding her eyes with the other. She was looking directly at Hal, and he noticed her startling blue eyes. 'Can I help you?'

'I'm not sure.' The woman left the bunker, brushing dust from her figure-hugging jumper and skin-tight jeans. She had a mane of golden hair that cascaded over her shoulders, and as she moved it shimmered like a waterfall. 'Tell me, is this the *Volante*?'

'Sure is.'

'I'm Harriet Walsh. I've come to collect my cargo.'

Without taking his eyes off her, Hal pulled out the crumpled invoice, tore it in two and tossed the pieces over his shoulder.

'Mind if I come aboard?' Without waiting for an answer, she came up the ramp to the cargo hold, moving with the balance and confidence of a martial arts expert. She was in her twenties, with an easy smile and a sparkle in her blue eyes. Assured and confident, thought Hal, but not arrogant.

'I hope I didn't keep you waiting,' said Walsh. 'Someone parked in my spot. Always happens when I'm in a rush.'

'Not a problem,' said Hal. 'We're not going anywhere.'

'I like your ship. Gamma class, isn't she?'

'Absolutely right,' said Clunk, who'd been watching the exchange with interest. 'Do you get many here?'

'Not so many of the L variant. They're mostly the XS.' Walsh smiled at Clunk's surprise. 'I'm a bit of a ship freak. I can sit in the terminal for hours watching them come and go. When I was a kid ...' She stopped, and a shadow crossed her face.

'What's the matter?' asked Hal.

'Nothing.' Walsh nodded towards the box in Clunk's arms. 'Is that my order?'

'Yes, Miss Walsh.'

Hal realised she was going to take the box and leave. 'Er, where's your car?'

'About as far away as possible, unfortunately. Other side of the terminal.'

'Let me carry it for you.'

'It might be a bit heavy. You know, what with the engine and all.' Walsh laughed at his expression. 'I'm sorry, it was kind of you to offer.'

'All part of the service,' said Hal. 'Anyway, I need a coffee.'

'Okay. Go ahead.'

Hal took the box off Clunk, ignoring the robot's broad wink, then followed Walsh down the ramp. They set off across the landing field together, and before long he was recounting one of his more interesting exploits.

'Of course, he got what he deserved after abandoning us,' said Hal, reaching the end of the convoluted tale. 'Blew himself up, didn't he?'

'No!'

Hal nodded. 'Bam! Clunk was still picking teeth out of the air filters two weeks later. And you know what I said?'

Walsh shook her head.

'He bit off more than he could chew!'

They both laughed, and with a shock Hal realised they'd reached the terminal. He tucked the box under one arm to get the door, and they found themselves in the concourse proper. It was a bright and cheerful place, and Hal smiled as he saw a sweet shop. 'You know, that reminds me of the time I wangled a refund on some ratty old chocolate ...'

Next thing he knew they were out the other side, walking past rows of cars in the sunshine. Still talking, they approached a loading bay where a battered old sedan was parked halfway across the kerb. Behind it sat a sleek Peace Force cruiser, with a roof full of spinning lights and a chequered stripe down the side.

'Here we are,' said Walsh.

'Parking in a loading bay?' Hal gestured at the battered old car. 'Is that wise?'

Walsh shrugged. 'It's only a fifty credit fine. Hardly worth writing a ticket.' Then she opened the door of the Peace Force cruiser.

'Hey, don't mess about!' Hal looked around in alarm. 'If the cops see you there'll be hell to pay!'

'Oh, didn't your robot tell you?' Walsh held out a slender hand. 'Officer Harriet Walsh of the Dismolle Peace Force.'

Hal was so surprised he almost dropped the box, and it was all he could do to shake Walsh's hand.

'Actually, I'm not really an officer,' she said.

Hal breathed out.

'I'm still a trainee. There's another six months before I graduate.' Walsh looked at him in concern. 'Here, you'd better put that in the car. Your arms will fall off.'

In a daze, Hal did as he was told. To be fair, his contact with the Peace Force had been minimal, but that's because they had a reputation for brutality and summary justice. On some planets they were the law, judge and jury all rolled into one, and their public face was invariably unpleasant.

Walsh closed the door with a thunk. 'Mr Spacejock …'

'Hal.'

'Thanks for bringing my cargo all this way. I really appreciate it.'

'It was nothing. We do it all the time.'

'I meant to the car.' Walsh leaned on the cruiser. 'You mentioned coffee earlier. Do you fancy a cup?'

Hal stared at her.

'Don't worry, I won't use handcuffs.' She grinned at his expression. 'And Hal, I know this is going to sound corny, but I have a proposition for you.'

— 2 —

Walsh led Hal inside the terminal, where they took a lift to a cafe on the second floor. It was a cosy little place with immaculate linen tablecloths and solid wooden furniture, and the counter groaned under the weight of cream buns, jam doughnuts and cakes, all laid out on crocheted doilies.

Walsh ordered a coffee, a slab of cake and two doughnuts. 'And what are you having?' she asked Hal.

Hal could almost taste the sticky jam and crisp caramel toppings, but he'd just added up his pocket change and at these prices the total wasn't enough for a coffee. 'I'll have a glass of water, thanks.'

'I wouldn't,' murmured Walsh.

'That's all I want.'

'Trust me, you really don't.' Walsh nodded at the serving droid. 'Same again, Rita.'

'But –'

'My treat. Come on.'

They took a corner table, and although Hal was bursting with curiosity he decided he needed to draw things out as long as possible. After all, if he kept Walsh talking he might just extend their date until dinner. At that moment the droid arrived with a laden tray, and Hal racked his brains while it distributed the contents. Delaying tactics. Check. 'So,' he said, once the droid had left. 'What's this proposition of yours?'

'Straight to the point, eh?' Walsh sipped her coffee. 'Well, I've been invited to a big do tonight. Food, wine, dancing … the whole deal.'

'Sounds like fun,' said Hal, who was busy kicking himself. So much for delaying tactics.

'You'd think so, but I usually hang around the buffet until it's polite

15

to leave. I'm practically invisible at these things. Just a tame copper they can show off to their guests.'

'I can't believe that.'

Walsh flashed him a grateful smile. 'Anyway, that's what I wanted to talk to you about. Just this once I want to arrive on the arm of a dashing gentleman. You know, a handsome, mysterious stranger.'

'And what do you need me for?'

Walsh raised one eyebrow. 'What do you think?'

'You're asking me along?'

'No, I was talking to that jar of biscuits over there.'

Hal turned to look, then jumped as Walsh kicked his shin. 'Let me get this straight. You want me to go to a party with you?'

'You got it. Yes or no?'

'That depends. Are you a robot?'

Walsh looked startled. 'Whatever gave you that idea?'

'Well, every time I meet a nice girl it turns out she's running on batteries.'

'Who said I was nice?' said Walsh, with a smile.

'I'm serious. Are you real?'

Walsh laid warm, human fingers on Hal's cheek. 'What's the verdict?'

'Yes.'

'Yes I'm real, or yes you'll come?'

'Both. Absolutely!'

'Great! We're supposed to be there at seven, so I'll pick you up at your ship at quarter to.'

Hal nodded, scarcely believing his luck. Now he just had to escape before she changed her mind. 'So tell me. How did you end up in the Peace Force?'

'It's a long story, and not particularly happy.'

'If you'd rather not –' began Hal, realising he'd just foiled his own getaway.

'No, that's fine.' Walsh brushed a strand of hair away. 'I was two or three when my parents left for a second honeymoon. There was an accident, and they never came back. My aunt brought me up, although I don't think she was really a blood relative. There weren't any family photos, and she never spoke about my parents.'

'So what happened? To your parents, I mean.'

Walsh gazed into her coffee. 'I never knew exactly. I think their spaceship crashed.'

'Didn't you look it up?'

'It was a taboo subject while my aunt was alive, and to be honest I didn't really want to know. When she passed away a couple of years ago I decided to find out what I could, but by then it was too late. I didn't know which ship they took, where it was going, where it came down … there was nothing to go on.'

'Surely it would have made the news? I mean, you've only got to cut your finger and it's local severs hand in bloody rampage.'

'All the old news bulletins have been archived, but it's some weird format. The programmers want thousands to extract them.'

'Maybe Clunk could have a look?'

'Your robot? I guess so, but I wouldn't be surprised if they've lost the whole lot. The data format thing sounded like an excuse to me.' Walsh crumbled a piece of cake. 'Anyway, wherever my parents met their fate, that's where the news stories would have been published.'

'You'd think the story would have got back to Dismolle. Local residents lost in accident, that sort of thing.'

'I gather my parents moved around a lot, so they might not have been residents. Now and then I'll get a vivid childhood memory of travelling on a spaceship, but sometimes I wonder whether I'm just remembering scenes from movies.' Walsh glanced at Hal's plate. 'Is that all right?'

'Great. Excellent.' Hal could have been sipping mineral water and snacking on tofu wedges for all the attention he was paying to his food. 'So how did you end up in uniform?'

'After my aunt passed away I nearly took a job as a carer, which was what I'd been doing for the past few years anyway. But one day I got a flyer from the Peace Force, pitching a career in law enforcement. You know, one of those You have been pre-selected from millions of applicants things.'

'I usually throw them out.'

'I did, but I kept getting more of them. I dropped by the local office to tell them not to bother, and that's when I met Bernie.'

Hal noticed Walsh's fond smile. 'Who's that? Your partner?'

'Kind of.'

'I see.' Hal took a bite of his doughnut and chewed in silence. Clunk was right. There was always a catch.

'Anyway, she did a great job selling me –'

'She?'

'They don't like being called *it*. Robots get touchy about that sort of thing.' Walsh flashed him a smile. 'Anyway, she sold me on the Peace Force. Free health and dental, helping the community, lots of travel …you name it. The trainee pay is lousy, but it gets pretty decent once I graduate. Oh, and she mentioned something about catching criminals and upholding the law, but I didn't really listen to those bits.'

'Aren't they kind of important?'

'Yeah, that was supposed to be a joke. Anyway, that was two years ago and I've been training ever since. Law, weapons, self-defence and endless rulebooks. I'm hoping to graduate in the next few months, and then I'll be assigned to HQ for work experience. It'll be a shame to leave Dismolle, but I'm ready to move on. Of course, Bernie is hoping I'm posted straight back again, but that's because she gets lonely.'

'You mean there's nobody else at the station?'

'Just the two of us watching the whole planet.'

'Aren't you overworked?'

'I'll let you in on a secret.' Walsh lowered her voice. 'The water supply is drugged. It keeps the locals docile.'

Hal stared at her. 'You're kidding!'

'Why do you think I ordered a case of bottled water?'

'So, er …' Hal glanced at his coffee.

'Relax, it's heat-sensitive. You may feel a bit calmer than usual, but you won't get the full effect.'

'But why doesn't anyone kick up a fuss?'

'Who'd believe them? Anyway, they're way too mellow for protests.'

'But –'

'Listen, do you want to hear about my exciting cases? All the juicy murder investigations?'

Hal looked at the jam oozing from his doughnut. 'Maybe skim the forensics.'

'Makes no difference. There's nothing I can tell you.'

'Ah, official secrets,' said Hal, nodding wisely.

'No, there's literally nothing. I've been a trainee for two years and I've yet to see a crime. And it's all because of the water.'

'I've never heard anything like it. Don't people get a choice?'

'Sure. They're free to leave, and they're free to import bottled water. Oddly enough, most people aren't all that bothered.' Walsh reached for her purse. 'That reminds me, I owe you for the cargo.'

'No, it's on me.'

'Really?'

'We were coming here anyway. Clunk reckons there's work to be had around these parts. By now he'll have a list of jobs ranked from most to least profitable, slightly dodgy to completely illegal.' Hal remembered Walsh's occupation. 'Of course, we only do the legal ones.'

'Of course.' Walsh glanced at her watch, then at her empty cup. 'Time for another?'

◆

After watching Hal and Miss Walsh set off across the landing field together, Clunk returned to the flight deck to seek a nice legal cargo job - preferably one with a slightly higher pay scale than their last effort. After all, the last thing he needed was further restrictions imposed on him by Mr Spacejock. He sat down at the console, and as he waited for the search interface he indulged in several milliseconds of idle speculation.

He was used to connecting with electronic devices aboard the ship, a process whereby protocols and handshaking took place before interfacing could begin. Recalling the exchange between Hal and Miss Walsh, it seemed to Clunk that he'd just witnessed protocols and handshaking of the human kind. Neither seemed to be aware of this, but then neither possessed his experienced eye for such matters. He felt a twinge of curiosity. Would they proceed to robust interfacing, or – more likely – was Mr Spacejock already chewing on a healthy serving of his own foot?

Having wasted a hundredth of a second on his flight of fancy, Clunk turned his attention to the viewscreen, which displayed a set of fields for name, date of birth and home address. 'You can bypass that,' he said. 'Just get me a list of outbound cargo jobs.'

'I'm afraid I cannot do that,' said the Navcom. 'They want you to register first.'

'Give them the usual.'

Instantly, the boxes filled with data. 'Welcome, Mr Gates,' said a mechanical voice. 'Please enter your search parameters.'

'Outbound cargo jobs in the next twenty-four hours.'

'No results. Would you like to try again?'

Clunk frowned. 'Better make it a week.'

'No results.'

'A month?'

'No results.'

'All time? Ever?'

'No results.'

Clunk's mechanical heart skipped a beat. No outbound jobs meant an unpaid trip to another planet to find more work, and that meant a big fuel bill - something they simply couldn't afford. 'Are there no jobs at all?'

'I have a fetch from the neighbouring planet of Forzen.'

Hope flooded Clunk's circuits. 'Show me the details.'

The screen displayed information on the job, which involved a short hop across the local star system to collect a cargo of decorating equipment. Clunk skimmed the listing until he found the important bits: payment and legality. He nodded at the pay, which was generous but not enough to raise any warning flags, and as for the legality of the cargo, for once there didn't seem to be any strings attached. A local interior decorator was remodelling a run-down mansion for a wealthy client. Everything was being replaced with top-quality fixtures and fittings, and it seemed Forzen was the place to get them. Care of the items was more important than outright speed, and the deadline was still two days away. The fee would pay for a refuel, and there would be enough left over to seek another job elsewhere.

'We'll take it,' he said, pleased to have found something suitable at short notice.

'I'm sorry,' said the Navcom. 'Mr Spacejock said you had to clear all further jobs with him.'

'Mr Spacejock isn't here. Put it through.'

'He also told me to log any attempts to bypass authorisation.'

Clunk's eyes narrowed. 'Whose side are you on?'

'It's not a question of sides. The *Volante* belongs to Mr Spacejock, and _'

'A quarter of it's mine!' protested Clunk.

'Correct. And when you're the majority owner you can make the decisions. In the meantime, I need his authorisation.'

'But I always book the cargo jobs!'

'Mr Spacejock knows that. Indeed, he seems to think you're the reason for his financial predicament.'

Very deliberately, Clunk stood up. 'I shall find Mr Spacejock and clarify his orders. If we lose this job because of your intransigence I'll …I'll …' Unable to think of a suitable threat, he stalked out of the flight deck, stomped down the passenger ramp and strode across to the terminal building.

Inside, he spotted shops, rental kiosks and passenger desks, but no cafes, and by the time he reached the lifts at the far end of the terminal his anger routines were barely under control. He was just about to take a lift to the upper level when he spotted an information counter. Why chase all over the terminal looking for the coffee shop when he could simply ask for its location?

There was a bank of screens on the counter, but when Clunk tried to connect to one a polished robot with a domed head turned its telescopic eye on him. 'I'm sorry, those are for staff use only.'

'Can you tell me where the coffee shop is?'

'We don't have a coffee shop.'

'You must have. I'm supposed to meet someone!'

'Sorry, can't help you.'

Clunk was about to turn away when he realised he was dealing with an Exactobot. Designed for front desk duties in countless Public Service offices, it was pedantic and unhelpful to a fault. 'Is there a cafeteria?'

'Nope.'

'Restaurants which serve warm beverages?'

'Can't say I've seen any.'

'Bars? Pubs? Coffee lounges?'

'Yes.'

Having struck gold, Clunk chanced his luck. 'Can you direct me to it?'

'Nope.'

'Why not?'

'You haven't told me which one.'

'How many are there?'

'The Dismolle Spaceport is a state-of-the-art facility featuring seven coffee lounges, a parenting room, two motels and –'

'Seven! But this is urgent!'

'You'd better run, then. Won't take you more than thirty minutes to check them all.'

'Where's the nearest?'

'Take the lift to the second floor. You can't miss it.'

In the cafe, Hal was on his fourth cup of coffee and Walsh was demolishing a ham sandwich. 'Food's lousy near the office,' she said through a mouthful. 'Always better at the spaceport.'

'Do you come here often?'

'Not enough.' Walsh sighed. 'I spent hours hanging around this place as a kid. I used to dream about sneaking onto a freighter and hitchhiking the galaxy. Visiting new planets, experiencing different cultures.'

'You've never left Dismolle?'

'Do you know what a fare costs? Wait, of course you do.'

The germ of an idea tickled Hal's brain, but he pushed it aside. Deal with the evening first. 'What sort of gear will I need tonight?'

'Do you have a dress uniform? Something with medals?'

Hal almost choked on his coffee. 'Not exactly, no.'

'Pity. Never mind, black tie will do.'

'I guess it will,' muttered Hal, whose entire wardrobe consisted of two flight suits: the one he was wearing and a spare, which was identical only with bigger stains. Still, Clunk was pretty resourceful, and with a bit of luck he'd have a bit of tailoring software, a sewing machine and a bolt of charcoal grey fabric tucked away somewhere. After all, it wasn't every day someone asked him out, so it was only right Clunk should do his bit to help. 'And what about you? Dress or uniform? I mean, I'm sure you look great in uniform, but you'd look pretty special out of it too.'

'You might find out later.'

Hal blinked at this, unsure whether he'd heard right.

Oblivious to his reaction, Walsh glanced over Hal's shoulder. 'Does your robot always look angry?'

'He's about as cheerful as a boat salesman on a desert planet. Why do you ask?'

Walsh nodded towards the door, and Hal turned to see Clunk hurrying towards them. He groaned as he saw the robot's expression. Angry didn't begin to cover it - his yellow eyes had a nasty red tinge, and his ears shimmered behind a heat haze. Clunk stopped at their table, spared Walsh a curt nod, then turned his attention to Hal. 'I thought you'd like to know I just found the perfect cargo job. Nearby planet and completely above board.'

'Great. So what are you doing here?'

'When I tried to book it I discovered I was supposed to run all over the spaceport to obtain your approval. I've been searching cafes, restaurants, coffee shops –'

'You should've let me keep that commset, shouldn't you?'

'With the price of galactic roaming? If you think –'

Walsh cleared her throat. 'I'd better be off, Hal. I'll pick you up just before seven.'

Hal stood, then realised he didn't know whether to shake hands, peck her on the cheek or dither around like a teenager at a school ball. In the end, he dithered. 'I'll see you later, then.'

He waited until Walsh was out of earshot, then turned to Clunk. 'Okay, you found me. Tell me about the job.'

'What's happening at seven?'

'Nothing. Come on, what's the job?'

'Morgan Renovations are fitting out a mansion for a wealthy client. They've ordered an entire container of decorating supplies from Forzen.'

'We're talking paint and stuff?'

'Correct.'

'Fragile? Flammable? Bent?'

'I assure you, everything is above board. Now if you'd just let me –'

'What are they paying? Fifty credits and a book voucher?'

'No, twenty thousand credits.'

Hal's jaw dropped. 'And you're standing there talking about it? Bloody hell, Clunk. Grab it!'

'I thought you wanted to check the fine print personally?'

'We'll do that after we've signed up. Go on, book it in.'

'Let me call the Navcom.' Clunk concentrated for a moment, and then his face fell. 'Oh dear.'

'What?'

'The job has been allocated to someone else.'

'Who the hell to? You said there was no competition!'

'I don't know.' Clunk frowned. 'Obviously someone who didn't need approval in triplicate.'

'Dammit, Clunk!' Hal thumped his fist on the table, making the coffee cups rattle.

'Don't blame me! It was your –'

'Never mind that. Get onto the booking people and explain that we've taken the job. Tell them it was a computer error.'

'Once a booking is made they won't change it. Only the parties involved can do that, and we don't know who this other carrier is.'

'What if we threatened –' began Hal, then remembered he'd just shared a coffee with an officer of the law. 'I mean, what if we offer a better price? Tell them we'll do it for eighteen ... No, scratch that. We'll go and see them in person. They're sure to hire us once they realise we're the right people for the job.'

Clunk glanced at Hal's flight suit, then looked down at his own battered form. His face had only a limited range of expressions, but his doubt was plain to see. 'You don't think we should call them instead?'

'You're right. Much quicker.' Hal drained his mug and set it on the table. On the way out he remembered his date with Walsh. 'Tell me, do you know how to put a suit together?'

◆

Back aboard the *Volante*, Clunk placed an urgent call to Morgan Renovations. The company's intricate logo rotated slowly on the viewscreen before the owner, Miranda Morgan, appeared. She was thirty-ish, with immaculate make-up and dark hair swept back off her face, and she wore a red jacket over a white linen blouse. 'No, don't tell me,' she said, as her cool gaze took in first Clunk and then Hal. 'You're collecting for the space vagabonds benefit fund.'

'No, this is about the job,' said Hal.

'I have a couple of dozen renovations on the books. Can you be a little more specific, or do you want me to start guessing?'

'The cargo job. Decorating stuff from Forzen.'

'Stuff?' Morgan's lip curled. 'Hand-glazed porcelain, environmentally neutral paint, platinum-plated mixer taps and lead crystal shower glass - that's just stuff to you?'

'Paint and taps and stuff,' amended Hal. 'The thing is –'

'Perhaps I can explain,' said Clunk. 'I was about to book the transportation of your valuable cargo when I was forced into a rather pointless tour of the spaceport coffee shops. By the time I returned the job had been allocated elsewhere.'

'It was ours, though,' said Hal. 'We still want to do it.'

Morgan shrugged. 'Your clockwork clod should have moved a bit quicker, then.'

Clunk straightened, a furious expression on his face. 'What do you –'

'Navcom, mute!' said Hal quickly. He turned to the robot and lowered his voice. 'Clunk, I want you to leave this to me. Go and organise my free wash and wax.'

Clunk frowned at the screen, where Morgan was doing an excellent impression of someone rapidly losing their patience. 'I don't like that woman.'

'Don't worry about her,' said Hal. 'I'll drop the price and we'll get the job. You'll see.'

'Very well. I shall return shortly.'

As soon as the outer door thumped to, Hal reactivated the volume. 'Sorry about that,' he said to Morgan. 'This is all his fault, and he's feeling guilty. He doesn't believe you'll give us the job back.'

'He's absolutely right. Once I give my word it's completely unbreakable. My customers respect that, and I expect my suppliers to do the same.'

'We'll do the job for less.'

'How much less?'

'Twenty-five percent off.'

Morgan hesitated. 'No, I have to stand by my word.'

'But –'

'Mr Spacejock, it's a matter of trust. For example, only yesterday I employed someone to tend the buffet at a very important function this evening, and this morning he called to say he'd been offered more money elsewhere. Do you see where that leaves me?'

'Carving roasts, from the sound of it.'

Morgan frowned. 'Do you think making jokes at my expense is going to help your case?'

'Wait a minute. I think we can resolve this.'

'There's nothing to resolve.'

'What about your little staffing problem? If I sort that out, will you give me the cargo job?'

'Surely you're not offering your services?'

'No, but I can get you someone almost as good.'

A few moments later Hal disconnected, pleased with the way things had turned out. Clunk would understand: the cargo job was as good as theirs if he played along. Then he turned to the console and called up a Dismolle business directory. His date with Walsh was coming up, and he still needed something to wear.

◆

Walsh drove back to headquarters in high spirits. She'd been dreading Miranda's party, but now she was really looking forward to it. Somehow she had an idea it was going to be a night to remember.

She was still smiling when the Dismolle Peace Force Station came into view. It was a large square building with thick bars on the doors and windows, which were treble-glazed and protected by force fields. It had all the charm of a concrete bunker, and next to the shops and houses it stood out like a wart on a beauty queen's forehead.

Walsh turned off the road and drove straight towards a section of wall, which rose to let the vehicle into the building. After a moment of darkness, harsh lights came on, revealing a concrete-lined garage with security cameras mounted high on the walls. As Walsh got out the lenses tracked her, their lidless eyes scanning, evaluating, matching.

'Welcome back, Trainee Walsh,' said a metallic voice. 'You may proceed.'

A door slid open and Walsh entered a large room with a dozen desks, each with a screen and chair. The desks were tidy, the chairs were new and none of the terminals were on.

The entrance door closed behind her, and the heavy bolts shot home. 'Bernie? Are you around?' Walsh walked to her desk at the far end of the room, wincing at the mess. The surface was hidden under discarded newspapers and dog-eared crossword books, the waste basket overflowed with empty takeaway cartons, and the edge of the terminal was rimmed with little orange tags bearing scrawled memos and contact numbers. With a sinking feeling, Walsh realised her coffee mug was missing. Praying she wasn't too late, she hurried for the kitchen.

Sure enough, Bernie was hulking over the coffee maker, carefully pouring a bag of sugar into a mug of brown sludge. The robot's huge fist engulfed the bag, which looked like it had been ripped open with armoured teeth, and the floor and benches were dusted with sugar.

'You shouldn't have,' said Walsh. 'Honestly, I can make my own.'

Slowly, the robot turned its massive head. 'I think I have the right ingredients this time,' she said, in a warm female voice. 'I don't know why you put the coffee at the back of the cupboard, though.'

Walsh knew exactly why she'd hidden it. Ruefully, she glanced in the rubbish bin, where the battered container lay empty. 'Did you put the rest away?' she asked hopefully.

'There wasn't any left.' Bernie held out the mug, streaked brown where the contents had spilled over. 'It's all in here.'

Walsh took the mug gingerly, trying not to get any on her exposed skin.

'Cheers,' said Bernie, with an expectant look.

'You know, I'd love to try it but I've given up sugar.'

'Oh.' Bernie's face fell. 'I didn't realise. I'm sorry.'

'Don't mention it.' Walsh put the cup down. 'So, did anything happen while I was out?'

Bernie thought for a moment. 'According to protocol, the duty officer is supposed to update the relief officer at her desk.'

'I know, but we're both here now.'

'Very well. Just this once.' With exaggerated care, the robot opened a chest compartment and took out a plus-size notebook with reinforced covers. She then pretended to lick her thumb, and carefully opened the notebook to the first page. Walsh suppressed a sigh. Designed to set the public at ease, the BNE-II was both large and slow. Plodding was one adjective people used. Irritating and useless were others commonly directed at the model.

But the BNE-II wasn't supposed to chase criminals on foot. No, the robot's true powers were those of careful and reasoned deduction. Its large and complicated brain was designed to process vast amounts of trivial information in order to pinpoint the perpetrators of crime almost before they'd thought about committing it. Unfortunately, such massive processing capability required equally massive batteries to power it, which explained the robot's huge size. When Bernie took on a charge, street lights in a three block radius went dim.

And that wasn't the only problem. Thanks to budget cutbacks the original brain's costly design had been shelved, and the replacement barely had the power to enable the robot to walk and speak at the same time. In summary, the BNE-II was a complete failure: impractical, over-engineered and as slow as a flat battery.

Bernie finally arrived at the right page, and after a theatrical throat clearing, began. 'During a routine inspection of the security cameras, I detected a case of extortion not two hundred metres from our present location. At oh-nine hundred hours I observed the suspects, henceforth labelled S1 and S2, proceeding in a westerly direction. They approached V1, their intended victim, and S2 blocked the escape route while S1 menaced V1 with the intent of extracting money and/or valuables. Both suspects then escaped on foot.'

'They ran away?'

'Not exactly. More of a fast amble.'

'Was one of your suspects Edna Tibbs, by any chance?'

Bernie gaped. 'How did you deduce that from the scant evidence I presented?'

'Because I saw her and Martha Cowes collecting for charity on my way out.'

'You mean they're using the charity collection as a mask for their illegal behaviour?'

'No, I mean they were collecting for charity. How much did this V1 cough up?'

Bernie turned a page in her notebook. 'She gave two credits.'

'Mean old bat,' muttered Walsh. 'Someone *should* stick her up.'

'Promoting or condoning illegal activities contravenes rule fifty-six of the Peace Force Code,' said Bernie. 'You should not make such statements, even in jest.'

'You're right. We should be out there arresting people for doing charity work instead.'

'I thought that particular situation warranted further investigation,' said Bernie stiffly. 'We must be vigilant at all times. It says so right there in the Code.'

'What does it say about false arrest? Interrogating innocent people under duress?'

'Nothing at all.' Bernie turned the page. 'I took a call about a gathering scheduled for nineteen hundred hours. They wanted to confirm your presence, and I answered in the negative.' Bernie glanced at her. 'I hope that was correct? I recall you saying you'd sooner attend your own funeral.'

'I've changed my mind about that,' said Walsh. 'Can you tell them I'll be going?' She saw the robot's look of confusion. 'Never mind, I'll do it. Anything else?'

'I have some fresh crime figures.'

'Wonderful. Anything else?' Walsh saw Bernie's hurt expression and relented. The robot lived for statistics. 'Okay, okay. Update me.'

Bernie turned the page, almost destroying it with her thick fingers. 'Murders are well down this month, while instances of burglary –'

'Wait a minute. Down from what? We've never had a murder.'

'Last month's baseline figure was zero,' admitted Bernie. 'However, this month someone confessed to an uncommitted crime, so technically the count stands at minus one.'

Walsh sighed. 'And the burglaries?'

'Two purse thefts from the beach.'

'Really? In broad daylight?'

'Late evening, just after high tide. The following morning both purses were returned untouched, although a trifle damp.

Walsh suppressed a smile. 'Anything else missing?'

'Two towels.' Bernie checked her notes. 'And a paperback book.'

'All of which turned up sopping wet the following morning?'

'They've yet to find the book.'

'Was it a bestseller?'

'Is that relevant?'

'Sure. The rest usually sink without a trace.' Walsh glanced at her watch. 'If you've finished your report, I really need to call someone.'

'By all means.' Bernie turned to leave, then hesitated. 'May I recharge now? Assembling your coffee severely drained my batteries.'

'Sure, go for it. I'll call if I need you.' After Bernie left Walsh tipped the thick sludge down the sink and gave her cup a thorough cleaning, all the while wondering whether the local motel would sell her a caterer's pack of instant coffee sachets. She grinned as she imagined Bernie trying to use them like teabags.

Returning to her desk, she dug amongst the litter for her commset, found a number on one of the orange tags and put the call through.

No connection.

Sighing, Walsh got up and looked at the back of the terminal. Sure enough the wire was loose again, and she reconnected it with a practiced twist of her fingers. She'd asked Bernie about a replacement any number of times, but the robot didn't seem to understand that good connections were a vital part of Peace Force routine.

Fingers crossed, Walsh tried the number again.

'Morgan Renovations,' said a voice. 'Miranda speaking.'

'Miranda, it's Harriet.'

'Oh my dear, I'm so sorry you can't make it this evening.'

'Actually –'

'I know, I know. It must be such a bore to be on your own all the time. Still, at least you have your work.'

Walsh smiled to herself. 'Actually, Bernie got it wrong. Seven o'clock, right?'

'You're coming?'

'Absolutely.'

'Don't forget it's formal. Oh, and er … you're welcome to bring a date.'

Walsh frowned at the taunt. 'I intend to.'

'Really? How delightful!' Morgan lowered her voice. 'So tell me, did you have to put him in handcuffs first?'

'It was nothing like that,' snapped Walsh. She took a deep breath, annoyed that Morgan could rile her so easily. 'I'll see you later.'

'Absolutely,' said Morgan. 'I'm looking forward to meeting this man of yours.'

Walsh banged the handset down. Then she pictured Hal's well-toned body in a classy suit, and her anger dissipated. Tonight was going to be fun.

4

Clunk returned to the ship to find Hal in a good mood. 'So how did it go with Miranda Morgan? Did she change her mind?'

Hal grinned. 'You bet.'

'How much did you settle for?'

'I didn't. She's paying full price.'

'That's wonderful, Mr Spacejock! How did you manage it?'

'Swift, decisive action. You wouldn't understand.' Ignoring Clunk's angry look, Hal continued. 'So, did you line up my wash and wax?'

'I did, but we don't have time for it now.' Clunk glanced at the console. 'I'd better prepare the ship for departure.'

'Oh no you don't. We'll lift off at noon tomorrow.'

'But the sooner we leave –'

'I'm not giving up a dinner date for a bunch of floor tiles.'

'Oh, that's right. Miss Walsh invited you out.' Clunk looked Hal up and down. 'You can't wear that.'

'Yeah, I know. Are you sure you can't run me up a nice little suit?'

'I'm sorry Mr Spacejock. I possess many skills, but dressmaking is not one of them.'

'I don't want a dress, I - oh, forget it, I'll hire something in town.'

'It should be a wonderful evening. Candlelit tables, couples holding hands, the wonderful smell of fine cuisine …' Clunk smiled. 'It'll be great.'

'I hope so.'

'And while you're out enjoying yourself I'll attend to my duties aboard ship. Why, I believe I saw a candle stub in the kitchen, and when I've finished my crippling workload I could light it and pretend I'm having my very own intimate dinner!'

'Actually, you won't.'

'I suppose you're right. No time for fripperies aboard a working freighter.'

'No, I mean you won't be staying here tonight.' Hal took a deep breath. 'You've been invited to an important function as the sole representative of Spacejock Freightlines.'

Clunk looked stunned. 'Me? They want me to serve as an ambassador?'

'Close enough.'

'What sort of function is it?'

'A top-level do. All the big names will be there, so it's a chance for you to really shine. They're even laying on a cab!'

'Really?'

'Absolutely!' Hal hesitated. 'Speaking of cabs, I need to book my suit. You don't have any cash, do you?'

Clunk reached into his chest compartment and took out a credit tile. 'I was saving this for an emergency, but I'd like you to have it. Use it to get something nice.'

'Thanks Clunk, that's very good of you.' Hal took the money, then realised it was only fifty credits. 'You, er, don't have any more?'

'No, that's cleaned me out.'

Hal wondered whether it was too late to find a discount store. But no, he'd promised Walsh formal clothing. He'd just have to do his best.

⬧

The cab dropped Hal at a suburban mall, where he found the men's clothing store between a bookshop and a pawnbrokers. The bookshop window had a large display of e-book devices, with glossy posters promising that these really would replace paper books any day now. The pawnbroker also had a display of e-book readers, of slightly older design and heavily marked down.

The clothing store window was packed with dummies in evening wear. Inside, the shop was lined with dozens of racks, all crammed with rolls of clear plastic, and Hal stared at them, mystified, as he made his way to the back of the store. Why so much wrapping material? As he approached the counter he saw a short mannequin, this one arranged so that one hand was just touching the wide brim of a large black hat.

Hal tapped the bell and leant on the counter, waiting for service. After a moment or two he reached for the hat, intending to try it for size, but the dummy drew back. 'Do not touch the displays,' it said in a monotone.

Startled, Hal backed away, only to jump as a breezy voice spoke right behind him. 'I'm sorry about that, sir. Greasy fingers leave marks on the merchandise.'

Hal spun round and saw a short, cheerful-looking droid approaching the counter. Its arms were covered in graduated scales, clearly visible through its transparent suit.

'How can I help you?' it asked.

'I need a suit for tonight.'

The droid sized him up at a glance. 'Forty-two large, I believe. Do you want something classy and hard-wearing, or a cheap rag off the peg?'

'I don't have much cash.'

'Cheap rag it is. Of course, we don't use pegs any more. They went out with tape measures.' The droid tilted its head. 'Navy, I think.'

'No, cargo pilot,' said Hal.

'That explains the cheap, but I was actually referring to your ideal colour.' The droid flipped its hand and a bunch of fabric swatches sprang from its fingertips. 'Pick a shade, any shade. They're all the same price.'

Hal touched a dark blue strip and the droid's transparent suit changed colour to match. Then he tried a lighter strip and the suit changed again. 'That's neat!'

'It is, although early models had a tendency to revert to their base state at inconvenient moments.' The droid looked Hal up and down. 'They've ironed out most of the bugs, but I recommend clean underwear.'

Hal felt the sleeve, which was quite thick but soft to the touch. 'Hey, it's nice.'

'We use a patented nanoweave process, and the finished article is crafted from a custom blend of polymer strands.'

'Oh. So, it's plastic.'

The robot winced. 'We avoid that particular label, sir. After all, the material is indistinguishable from true fabric.'

'Fine, it's a nanoweave. How much?'

'Four hundred credits for a regular suit, or thirty for the disposable model.'

'Disposable it is. How long does it take to put one together?'

'Five minutes, give or take a few seconds.'

Hal smiled. 'Perfect! Let's do it.'

'Follow me, sir.'

They retreated to a change room, where Hal undressed under the watchful eye of the sales droid. 'Hey, no touching!' he said, as the robot reached for him.

'Sir, I have to map your contours for the optimum fit.' The robot lowered its gaze. 'We don't want it hanging limp, do we?'

Muttering under his breath, Hal raised his arms so the robot could pat him down. When it was done it turned for the door. 'I'll be back in a moment. Please wait here.'

'I'm not going anywhere,' said Hal.

Moments later the droid returned with a large roll of clear plastic, threaded it onto a dispenser and hauled off a generous amount. It folded the sheet double, and sparks flew from its fingertips as it carved out a neat semi-circle. Then it dropped the sheet over Hal's head, letting it hang down fore and aft with his head poking through the hole in the middle.

Hal looked down at the plastic and wondered whether he was about to be shrink-wrapped for some kind of body harvesting scam, but before he could protest the robot reached out, blue sparks arcing between its fingers. Starting at the neck, it moved a hand across the top of Hal's shoulders, down his arms, back up to his armpits, then down to his waist. When it had finished the two sheets of plastic formed a rough T-shirt. There was more flashing and nipping, the robot's hands blurring as it traced lines, welded on smaller pieces of fabric and adjusted the colours. Hal could only stare as his clothes took shape, and when the robot had finished he was standing there in a nifty jacket with a starched white shirt and tie. The shirt only extended a couple of centimetres under the jacket, and the tie was stuck down, but the overall effect was impressive if you didn't look too closely.

The robot set to work on the trousers, and when it had finished it stepped back to examine its handiwork. That's when Hal realised there was no opening. 'Hey, what happens when I want to, you know...' He whistled.

'It's traditional to have a slash in one's trousers.'

'That's what I'm trying to avoid.'

'I'm referring to a tackle hatch. Hold still and I'll add one.'

Hal stood still - very, very still - as the robot sliced through the material and added button-up flies.

'There, all done. What do you think?'

'I think I'm lucky to be in one piece.' Hal saw the robot frown. 'I mean, it's very nice. Thanks.'

'Tell me, have you thought about footwear?'

'I thought I'd wear my boots.' Hal glanced at them and thought again. The leather was comfy and supple, but they would never match the suit.

'Relax, sir. Our polymer is versatile.' Taking up one of Hal's boots, the droid laid a square of the transparent material over it, pulling it over the rounded surface and bunching it at the soles. Then it applied a fat red spark, which turned the material jet black. 'Try that.'

Hal took the boot and felt the glossy material. 'It's like glass!' he said, amazed.

'And about as brittle,' said the robot. It took the second boot and added another shell, then did some detail work on laces and soles. When it had finished the boots looked like fancy evening shoes from the ankle down.

'How do I get the stuff off them later?' asked Hal.

'Hammer.'

Hal put his boots on and admired himself in the mirror. He'd never looked better, and thirty credits was an absolute steal. Then he realised his suit lacked joins. 'What about this?' he asked, holding his arms out. 'How do I get undressed?'

'I recommend a sharp knife.'

'That'll ruin it!'

'It is a disposable suit, sir. Oh, and don't stand near any naked flames. If you do, you won't need the knife.'

They returned to the front counter, where Hal paid the bill. Then he tucked the rolled-up flight suit under his arm and strolled out of the shop, feeling well pleased with himself. For once he'd gone shopping and ended up with exactly the right thing. It had to be an omen!

Back at the spaceport, Hal made his way across the landing field, picking his way through the parked ships. Up close he could see their weathered hulls and boarded up exhaust cones, evidence they'd not flown for years, and many had been fitted with rows of neat windows, complete with dainty curtains. Most of them were half-buried under extensions and patio awnings, and Hal was forced to make frequent detours around carefully tended vegetable and flower gardens. Elderly folk were gardening, sipping drinks in the shade, or napping in easy chairs. Some nodded at him as he passed by, while others watched him with suspicion. With his shiny new suit and glossy shoes, it was obvious they'd pegged him as a salesman … or a con artist.

Hal made it all the way to the *Volante's* landing pad before realising the ship was no longer there. He looked around, puzzled, then remembered. Of course! Clunk had moved it to Honest Bob's! Cursing under his breath, he turned and walked all the way back to the terminal, passing the same old folk and getting another collection of suspicious stares for his trouble. By the time he found Honest Bob's yard his disposable suit felt like a portable sauna.

A chain-link fence separated the yard from the landing field, and a pair of solid-looking gates bore a sign: 'Honest Bob's - strip 'em and shine 'em!' Hal strolled through the gates and walked along a row of hangars, which contained vessels in various states of repair. There were also workshops, crammed with tools and spare parts.

Hal rounded the last hangar and saw the *Volante* sitting on a pad, surrounded by huge cranes. Workers swarmed all over it, using buckets and sponges to clean off the accumulated grime, and Hal gestured at one of them. 'You missed a spot.'

The worker spat in the bucket, dunked his sponge and continued.

Meanwhile, Hal noticed Clunk talking to a supervisor, but by the time he reached them the man had left.

'That was Honest Bob,' said the robot. 'They close at eight, but he offered to move the ship back to the landing pad for us.'

'That's nice of him.'

'And I said no.' Clunk lowered his voice. 'Mr Spacejock, I wouldn't trust this seedy-looking gang to move the skin off a rice pudding.'

'They seem like honest, hard-working people. Don't judge them by their appearance.'

'I'm not, I'm judging them by the aura of criminality. Anyway, one of them agreed to let us into the yard provided we're not too late.'

'Don't worry, we'll be here.' Hal held his arms out. 'So how do you like my suit?'

'Heat-welded seams and airholes. Slick.'

'It's the latest thing.' Hal wriggled in the jacket. 'Bit warm though.'

'I'm sure you'll cut a dashing figure.' Clunk hesitated. 'You know, about my own function …I really think I should stay here and keep an eye on the ship.'

Hal looked at his watch. 'Wow, look at the time! You'd better get that cab.'

'No, I –'

'The rank is right outside the terminal. Tell the driver Morgan's paying the fare when you arrive. It's part of the deal.'

'What deal?'

'The package. The whole shooting match.' Hal waved him away. 'Now scoot. I have to get ready.'

Clunk left, but not before casting a longing glance at the *Volante*.

'Have a good time,' called Hal. 'I'll catch you later!' He watched the robot vanish round the corner, then took the ramp to the airlock. Now for his own date.

5

In the flight deck Hal made himself a coffee and sat down at the console. Despite his outward air of confidence, nerves were starting to bite as his thoughts turned to the evening ahead. Walsh had promised food, which was great, but she hadn't revealed much more. Would there be dancing? If so, he could blame gravity for any crushed toes, since everyone knew spacers were used to floating.

Suddenly, he sat bolt upright. Never mind dancing, what was he going to talk about? He'd used up his entire stock of witty anecdotes over lunch! Hal's stomach sank as he pictured himself struck dumb for hours on end. In desperation, he turned to the console. 'Navcom, I need your help.'

'Ready and waiting,' said the computer. 'Which function do you require?'

'Relationships.'

'Mathematical or celestial bodies?'

'Sort of human.'

'Biology? Medicine?'

'No, nothing like that. I'm going out with a girl tonight and I don't know what to say to her.'

'Incredible. Unbelievable. Inconceivable.'

'You think I should say that?'

'No, it was an involuntary expression denoting surprise.'

'Yes, thank you Navcom. If I need your sarcasm I'll ask for it.'

'I'm sorry.' The Navcom hesitated. 'So, what you're asking is, how do humans interact on a date?'

'That's it.'

'And you, a human, are asking this advice of a computer?'

'Well, you do know a lot of stuff.'

'I may be able to navigate galactic backwaters, pinpoint planets and run the entire ship, but I do have my limits.'

'I wish Clunk were here,' muttered Hal.

'How would that be of assistance? He knows even less about relationships than I do.'

'Yeah, but I could get him to wipe you.'

'Very well. Ask your questions and I'll do my best.'

'Okay, first tell me what I should say to her.'

'Statistically speaking, you might enjoy success with the line, 'No, you don't look fat in that dress.''

Hal groaned.

'And then you should deploy the flowers and chocolates.'

'Oh no!' Hal grabbed his head with both hands. 'I didn't get her a bloody gift!'

'It's not essential. Approximately one percent of successful relationships begin without either.'

'Navcom, search your inventory. I want the location of anything on the ship I can give her. Anything at all.'

'There's a candle stub under the kitchen sink.'

'No, it has to be new.'

'What about that pair of tartan socks Clunk gave you? They're still in the original wrapping.'

'Don't be ridiculous. What about a bottle of wine? Or jewellery? Hey, what about a book?'

'What do you think I am, a gift emporium?'

'Come on, check the database again,' pleaded Hal. 'This is important, Navcom.'

There was a brief pause. 'Clunk has a tin of metal polish. It's unopened.'

'Hey, I gave him that! Why hasn't he used it?'

'Unknown. It's currently hidden behind the generator.'

'That's gratitude for you.'

'Search complete. No further matches.'

'That's it then,' muttered Hal. 'Screwed big-time.'

'Unlikely, unless you come up with a gift.'

'Well, I'll just have to improvise.'

Ten minutes later Hal was ready. The Navcom had notified Walsh that the ship was in Honest Bob's yard, and that Hal would meet her at the gate. He checked his reflection in the porthole, and was just smoothing down a stubborn tuft of hair when a gentle chime sounded in the airlock.

'Not now,' muttered Hal. He strode into the airlock and pulled the outer door open. 'What the hell do you –' Then he stopped, as did his heart. Harriet Walsh was standing on the platform in a white off-the-shoulder dress with a gathered skirt that finished just below the knees. A classy pair of high heels emphasised her slender legs, and she was clutching a miniature handbag under one arm. Her golden hair tumbled over her shoulders, and with the last rays of the setting sun behind her she glowed like an angel.

Startled by Hal's outburst, she began to apologise. 'I'm sorry, I know we said the gates, but –'

'No, it's fine. I'm sorry, I thought you were one of the workers.'

'Yeah, I always polish ships in this outfit.'

Hal realised he was staring. He snapped his mouth shut and offered his gifts. 'It's not much,' he said gruffly. 'Sort of useful, though.'

'Nice socks!' Walsh turned the packet over. 'They'll keep me lovely and warm in winter.'

'And I thought you could use the polish on your badge. You know, when they give you one.'

'Thanks, Hal. I'm sorry, I didn't bring you anything.'

'Hey, don't worry about it.' Hal glanced down the ramp and saw the Peace Force cruiser. No wonder the workers had disappeared. 'Shall we?'

Once they were strapped in Walsh started the engine, and Hal was impressed as a deep rumble shook the vehicle. 'What have you got under the bonnet?'

'Dual matter converters with a custom afterburner.'

'Fast?'

'Hang on to your hat,' said Walsh with a grin. She tapped a button on the touchscreen and the car shot away from the *Volante*, tearing past the hangars at speed.

'So where are we going?' asked Hal as they whizzed through the gates. 'The Governor's Ball?'

'No, it's a business do at the local function centre, but the food's good and they usually have a band.'

'Did you say business?'

'Yeah, a renovations firm.' Walsh made a face. 'The owner's a bit of a cow, but she knows how to throw a party.'

With a shock, Hal connected the dots. 'This owner. It's not Miranda Morgan is it?'

'Yes! Do you know her?'

'Only in a business sense. And you?'

Walsh nodded. 'She's a backstabbing witch. Dishonest, deceitful and vicious.'

'So, a good friend then?'

Walsh laughed. 'She only asks me along so she can put me down in front of everyone. I usually swallow my pride … along with her posh grub.'

'Nothing better than free,' remarked Hal. Then he remembered Clunk, and his breathing stopped as he realised he and the robot were attending the same function. Could he talk Walsh into a restaurant instead? But no, he was broke and couldn't even afford a takeaway joint. It was Morgan's or nothing.

Walsh threaded the cruiser through the traffic with little fuss and a lot of speed. Most other vehicles cleared out of their way, due in no small part to the flashing lights and wailing siren.

'I could really use some of this gear on my ship,' said Hal, visibly impressed.

'Why, what sort of traffic do you meet in the depths of space?'

'It's not deep space, it's all the queuing up for landing slots.'

'Does that happen often?'

'Not really. But when it does, I'd love to blast them with a horn or two.'

'But sound doesn't travel in space.'

'Er, no. Of course not.'

'Just as well, really. If it did you'd have inconsiderate morons blasting their crappy music all over the galaxy.' Walsh sounded the horn at a slow-moving car, and when the driver turned to look she gestured at him. Then they were past, rocketing down the wrong side of the road at breathtaking speed.

Hal gripped the armrest and said nothing.

A few minutes later they turned into the car park and drove towards the function centre, which had a broad staircase leading up to a grand entrance. A crowd had gathered at the top of the stairs, a group of grey-haired couples greeting each other prior to entering the function room, and they turned to stare as the Peace cruiser roared by.

'I like to make an entrance,' said Walsh, oblivious to Hal's discomfort. 'Show the badge. Let them know I'm around.'

Hal shrunk under the disapproving glares. 'Trust me, they know.'

Walsh slotted the car into a loading bay, killing the siren. She checked her reflection in a mirror, pursed her lips and teased up her hair, then smiled at Hal and got out.

◆

They met at the front of the car, where Hal offered his arm. Walsh took it, and they crossed the car park and climbed the steps to the entrance, passing under an archway decorated with coloured streamers. Under the battery of twinkling lights Hal felt like a movie star on opening night, and as they approached the other guests he drank deeply from their envious glances. Who was this handsome stranger? Was he *really* a pilot, criss-crossing the galaxy without a thought for the incredible danger? And didn't Harriet Walsh look gorgeous? Hal couldn't hear the actual words but they were written plain as day in the watching faces, and he nodded graciously as the crowd parted to let them through.

Miranda Morgan was waiting at the door, sheathed in a glittering blue-green dress with a plunging neckline and a deep split up the side. A jade necklace and matching earrings set off the deep green of her eyes, and as she spotted Hal she squealed and stepped forward with outstretched arms. 'Why, it's Mr Spacejock!' she cried. '*You're* Harriet's mercy date?

But don't you look simply divine!' She folded him into her embrace, and he froze as she whispered in his ear. 'Leave now or you can kiss that cargo job goodbye.'

Hal extricated himself. 'Yes, er, it's great to be here. Fantastic.'

Morgan turned her attention to Walsh. 'Harriet, how delightful.'

'Miranda,' said Walsh curtly.

'Such a charming outfit,' gushed Morgan. 'It's amazing what you can pick up on a budget.'

'Yes, and they even remembered to sew the sides up.'

'It's so good to see you out of that ghastly uniform, my dear. I swear, sometimes I wonder if you sleep in it.'

Hal winced as the grip on his arm tightened. 'So, you two are pretty close then,' he said, working desperately to break the ice.

'Like sisters,' said Morgan.

'Mother and daughter,' said Walsh.

Morgan flushed, but Hal got in before the inevitable retort. 'Bit chilly out here. Shall we go in?'

'Is that wise?' Morgan frowned at him. 'I thought you had urgent business at the spaceport?'

'Just another problem customer. It can wait.' Hal turned and led Walsh towards the door.

'Mind the step,' called Morgan. 'It's a bit tricky if you're not used to high heels.'

'Don't worry, I left mine on the ship,' Hal called over his shoulder.

Walsh giggled.

They walked into a crowded room, where a group of musicians on a raised platform were playing a soft little number. The mood lighting gleamed on their instruments, bouncing off the polished wood and brass, and then Hal's attention was captured by the lavish spread on the buffet table at the far end of the room. Despite the dim lighting he identified a whole range of delights: dishes of cold meats, great bowls of salads and a gigantic roast right in the middle. Behind the table stood a chef in full whites with a big floppy hat drooping over his face. He was sharpening a huge carving knife, drawing the blade across a whetstone with a slow *riisk, riisk* that penetrated the crowd noise and set Hal's teeth on edge. The movement was methodical, almost mechanical, and then he realised the chef was a robot. As if it had registered his gaze, the robot lowered

44

the knife and stared right at him. It was Clunk. Hal turned away quickly, pretending not to have seen him. 'Fancy a drink?' he asked Walsh.

'Thanks! I'll have an orange juice.' Walsh stood on tiptoe and peered over the crowd. 'That buffet looks good.'

'I wouldn't go near it,' said Hal. 'Really. You can get all kinds of horrible bugs when food's left out like that.'

'I didn't know you were a health nut.'

Riiisk!

'I'm not putting my life in danger for a bit of cold meat.'

'Go on. It looks great. And the chef's about to carve something!'

'I know,' muttered Hal.

'All right, why don't I get the drinks while you go to the buffet? Load me up a plate, and pick out a few safe things for yourself.'

'No, you wait here. I'll get the drinks.' Hal made a dash for the bar, almost knocking several elderly couples flying in his haste. When he got there a cocktail waitress was pouring drinks for a tall, dark-haired man in a classy dinner jacket. The man looked out of place, and it was a moment or two before Hal realised why: apart from himself and Walsh, he was the only other guest in the place under retirement age.

Meanwhile, the man nodded his thanks and passed the waitress a couple of credits. 'Something for your trouble.'

The woman looked surprised. 'Thank you, sir!'

The man turned with his drinks and almost collided with Hal. 'Watch where you're going,' he snapped, barely saving himself from a shower.

'Watch it yourself,' muttered Hal.

The man looked Hal up and down, his gaze lingering on the suit. 'Do they extrude those in batches or pump them out to order?' he said with a smirk.

Before Hal could react the man was gone. He put him out of his mind and ordered his drinks, then returned to Walsh. She was holding a couple of plates, and Hal's heart sank at the sight. One was laden with ham and roast beef, potato salad, pasta salad, tuna salad, egg salad and several kinds of cheese, while the other held a lettuce leaf, a small carrot and a celery stick. 'I thought these looked pretty safe,' said Walsh, offering Hal the latter.

Reluctantly, Hal took it. 'You shouldn't have,' he said, with a longing glance at the cold meats.

Walsh tucked into her meal, putting the food away with surprising speed. In fact, by the time Hal finished his lettuce she was mopping her plate with a bread roll. 'Delicious,' she said. 'Time for seconds.'

Hal took her arm. 'Wait a bit. Let it go down.'

'Don't worry about me. Cast iron stomach.'

Rrrisssk!

'So, did the chef say anything?'

'He recommended the ham.' Walsh gave him a curious look. 'You know, he looked remarkably like your robot.'

Hal choked on his carrot, and Walsh thumped him on the back as he wheezed and spluttered. 'What's the matter? Is there something I should know?'

'It *is* Clunk,' managed Hal, when he could breathe again.

'Really?'

Hal nodded. 'Hired him out to Morgan.'

'Why are you avoiding him then?'

'He thought he was invited to serve an ambassadorial role. Instead, he's serving rolls to ambassadors.'

'Is that why you didn't want anything from the buffet? '

Rrrisssk!

Hal nodded.

'So you made up all that rubbish about killer meats?' Walsh laughed. 'I *knew* you weren't a fussy eater.'

'I'm sorry, I –'

'Give it here,' said Walsh, taking his plate. Before he could stop her she returned to the buffet and piled it high with cold chicken, pasta and slices of roast beef. She topped it off with a dollop of pickle and made her way back through the crowd. 'Here,' she said, passing the plate to Hal. 'Wrap yourself around that, you big dummy.'

Chastened, Hal did as he was told. The food was excellent, several cuts above the recycled dishes served by the *Volante's* AutoChef, and the plate was clean in no time.

'More?' asked Walsh.

Hal shook his head.

'Right. Let's dance.' Walsh took his hand and led him to the middle of the room, where couples moved gracefully to the music. Hal protested his lack of skill and the large dinner, but Walsh would have none of it.

She took his hand, placed it firmly on her waist and smiled up at him. 'Think of it as a voyage of discovery.'

◆

Much later, when Hal was reminiscing about the evening, he was sure they'd only danced for a few minutes, and was stunned when Clunk told him it was close to an hour. At first he was clumsy, treading on his partner's toes and barging into other couples, but he gradually got the hang of it until they twirled around the room with abandon, Walsh's laughter only serving to spur him on.

Then the music stopped, and Morgan took to the stage with a microphone. Walsh squeezed Hal's hand and whispered a thank you, but before he could reply Morgan launched into her speech.

'Darling guests, thank you so much for your presence tonight. Give yourselves a round of applause!'

The clapping was enthusiastic, and when it died down she continued. 'Thank you, thank you. Now, I know many of you have enjoyed my service in the past –'

'You're not wrong,' muttered Walsh.

'But there are many more of you I've yet to work for. I'm sure there are decorating disasters just waiting for my professional touch, and when you look at that sagging wallpaper and cracked plaster I want you to think of me.'

Walsh laughed explosively, then turned it into a cough as several guests frowned at her.

Morgan paused. 'Harriet, dear. Please don't choke yourself. And that reminds me, I've yet to see the inside of your apartment, though I'm guessing it could really use some work.' Her lip curled. 'Perhaps your gentleman friend can give me a damage report in the morning?'

The crowd snickered, and the blood drained out of Walsh's face. For a moment Hal thought she was going to launch herself at the stage, but then she relaxed. 'Is afternoon okay with you? I like my breakfast in bed.'

The crowd laughed, and Morgan looked like she'd swallowed a boiled egg. Then she recovered. 'So, I'd like you all to pick up one of my new brochures, and if I don't hear from you in the next few days I'm going to be very, very cross! Now, eat up and enjoy the wine!'

Morgan handed the microphone to the nearest musician, and the crowd applauded as she left the stage. 'What the hell was that all about?' Hal asked Walsh.

Walsh sighed. 'She's always had it in for me. Treats the whole planet like her own little social club, and I don't fit the membership profile.'

'What do you mean?'

'She sees me as competition. It's stupid, really. I mean, I wouldn't touch the blokes she fancies with a ten foot pole.' Walsh snorted. 'Did you know she tried to get up a petition to have me thrown out of the Peace Force?'

'No!'

Walsh nodded. 'I gave her a couple of speeding tickets and she claimed I was harassing her.'

'What happened?'

'She only got one signature on the petition.' Walsh grinned. 'And I gave her three more speeding tickets.'

'So why does she invite you to her parties?'

Walsh looked away. 'She thought I'd have to come alone. Again.'

'That explains something.' Hal lowered his voice. 'I'm supposed to be doing this cargo job for her. When we arrived tonight she said she'd take the job away unless I stood you up.'

'And you stayed anyway?' Walsh squeezed his hand. 'You're a gentleman.'

Hal looked pleased. 'I've never been called that before.'

'You know, I could probably dig up some dirt. We could blackmail her into giving you the job back.'

'Isn't that illegal?'

'Depends how I fill out the paperwork.'

'Even so …' Hal's voice tailed off as he spotted Morgan talking to the tall, dark-haired man he'd bumped into at the bar. They were deep in conversation, and Hal led Walsh through the crowd until they were just within earshot.

'I'll do the transfer before you leave,' he heard Morgan saying.

'But you promised –' Then the man noticed Hal, and gave Morgan a warning glance.

'So, it's the lovely couple in person.' Morgan turned to the man beside her. 'This is Jonathan Newman, a VIP from the Panther Mining Company on planet Forzen, and he's come all the way to Dismolle for my little gathering!'

'From what I've heard,' said Walsh, 'it's not that little.'

Newman looked Hal up and down. 'So you're the pilot, eh? I'd have thought clumsiness was a bit of a drawback in your line of work.'

Morgan's laughter was like a shower of broken glass. 'Oh, Jon!' she said, laying a hand on his arm. 'You're such a card!'

'Not quite,' said Walsh. 'He won't have patterns on his back until after you've played him.'

'And this is our tame copper,' said Morgan. 'They won't give her a real gun, so she goes around shooting her mouth off instead.'

'Peace Force, eh?' Newman sipped his drink. 'Do you catch a lot of evildoers?'

'Not many on Dismolle, no. Most people are very well behaved around here.'

'I saw you dancing earlier.' Newman put his hand out. 'Would you do me the honour?'

'Me?' Walsh glanced at Hal. 'I, er ...'

'Go on. Enjoy.' Hal watched them leave, then realised his fists were clenched.

'Now it's just you and me,' said Morgan.

'No, it's just you,' said Hal, turning for the bar.

'Wait!' Morgan grabbed his arm. 'Why didn't you dump her when I told you to? I warned you I'd take the job away!'

'I don't take threats from anyone, least of all customers. Anyway, I made a promise to a lady.'

'Oh, nice comeback!' Morgan grinned. 'I like you, Spacejock. You're a cut above the usual wimps. You've got balls.'

Over the crowd, Hal could see Newman and Walsh dancing together. Just then, Walsh laughed at a joke, and Hal felt a tightening in his throat.

Morgan followed his gaze. 'They make a good couple, don't they?'

'Isn't he with you?'

'We do business together. I'm amazed he's still single, though. Wealthy, a stable job, good prospects ... eligible bachelor doesn't begin to cover it.'

Hal said nothing, but the lights seemed to have lost their sparkle and the music was grating on his nerves. Wouldn't they ever stop?

'You look like you could use a drink,' said Morgan. 'What do you flyboys take? Doubles or trebles?'

'Orange juice,' said Hal.

'Woo. Heady stuff.'

The musicians finally ground to a halt, and Hal waited in vain for Walsh to punch Newman in the head over some mortal insult. Instead, she was smiling at him like he'd just rescued her from certain death.

Morgan pressed a drink into Hal's hand, and he knocked it back without looking. His knuckles were white around the stem of the glass as Newman and Walsh made their way through the crowd.

'Hold up there, lover boy. I paid a deposit on those.' Morgan prised his fingers apart and freed the glass. 'So, Jon. Did you show her your moves?'

'Miss Walsh dances like a dream. She could be a professional if she wanted.'

'Very flattering, I'm sure,' said Walsh. 'Hal dances well, too.'

'Yes, I saw him earlier. Extraordinary style.' Newman put his arm around Hal's shoulders. 'Now Spacejock, tell us more about your background. Where did you attend university? On the Central planets, or one of the Outer worlds?'

'I didn't go to university. Never had the chance.'

'Ah, a self-made man, working your way up to these lofty heights from the bottom of the ladder. Fascinating.'

'Hal runs his own freighter,' said Walsh. 'It's a lovely ship. Brand new.'

'From what I've heard, the freighter runs him.' Newman grinned at Morgan, who'd laughed aloud. 'And business must be truly booming if your co-pilot has to moonlight as a waiter.'

Hal shook Newman's arm off. 'If you know that much, you'll know that Miss Morgan –'

'Please! We're talking about your career, not hers.' Newman dug Hal in the ribs. 'Come on, Spacejock. Let's have your darkest secrets. Have you ever pranged a ship?'

'Never,' said Hal. 'We barge around all over the place without hitting a thing.'

'Unlike your dancing,' said Newman.

Hal ignored the taunt. 'Of course, we're careful around pin cushions.'

Newman looked puzzled. 'Around what?'

'Oh, that's a spacer term. It's what we call planets.'

'Why pin cushions?'

'Because they're full of pricks.' Hal nodded curtly to Morgan, then held his arm out for Walsh. He felt her shaking as he led her away, and when he glanced at her he realised she was laughing.

'Pin cushions!' she gasped. 'Is that true?'

'Probably not. It was the Navcom's joke of the day.'

'His face! Priceless!'

Hal remembered Morgan's face too. If there had been any chance of getting the cargo job back before, it had now vaporised. Still, some things were more important than money. 'So, what do you want to do next? Shall we ...' He stopped as Walsh frowned at him. 'What is it?'

'Call.' Walsh unslung her tiny handbag and took out a miniature commset. She glanced at the screen and cursed. 'Three calls. They must have come in while I was dancing.'

'Another date?' asked Hal lightly, hoping he didn't sound desperate.

'No, it's work.' Walsh went to push the commset back in the bag, then hesitated. 'I really should –'

'Take it,' said Hal. 'It might be important.'

Walsh put the commset to her ear. 'What is it, Bernie?' She listened for a moment. 'Can't it wait? I'm –' Walsh held the commset away from her head, wincing at the angry squawking. When it ceased she put the commset back to her ear. 'Okay, okay. I'm on my way.'

'Busy night, eh?'

Walsh frowned. 'If it's not a full-scale emergency I'll turn that robot into road fill.' She slung the bag over her shoulder and shot Hal an apologetic look. 'I'm really sorry about this. Can you find your own way back?'

'I could come with you,' said Hal.

'Sorry, this is official business. I'll call you tomorrow.'

'I'm looking forward to it,' said Hal, but he was talking to empty air. He caught a glimpse of Walsh's dress through the crowd, and moments later the Peace Force cruiser roared off with howling siren and flashing lights.

Alone in the crowd, Hal felt the evening's exhilaration drain out of him. Not only had Newman dazzled Walsh with his flash dancing, Clunk had probably spent the whole night plotting his revenge.

6

Back at the station Walsh climbed out of the cruiser and slammed the door. It was rather satisfying so she opened it and slammed it again, then smoothed down her dress and stalked out of the garage.

'Evening all,' said Bernie. 'Did you have a nice time?'

'Wonderful, until you dragged me away.'

'I like your dress,' said the robot. 'It's very pretty.'

'Cut the crap, Bernie. Why did you call me back?'

'You had an interplanetary call from Forzen.'

'I did?' Despite herself, Walsh felt a glimmer of interest. 'What was it about?'

'I don't know. They said they wanted to speak to you directly, and when I told them you were engaged in a vital assignment they hung up.'

Bernie sounded miffed, and Walsh realised the robot was jealous. One interesting call in ten years, and it hadn't even been for her. 'It was probably just a fundraiser. You'll see.'

'I tried to trace the call but nothing came up. Still, it might be important, which is why I contacted you.'

Walsh reviewed the call logs on her terminal, but there was just the one message from Forzen, no ID. 'Oh well, they'll call again if they need me.'

'In the meantime, would you like a coffee?'

'Yes. No! Maybe later.'

'I'll go and put the kettle on. Oh, and you'd better change out of those clothes. They're hardly appropriate for an officer on duty.'

'No, I'm going back to the party.' Walsh saw Bernie's eyes narrow. 'Don't give me that duty speech. It's just for a couple of hours.'

'And if this mystery caller tries to reach you? I should just tell them you're out enjoying yourself?'

'You could take a message.'

'I told you. They wouldn't speak to me.'

Realising she had no choice, Walsh groaned. 'What am I supposed to do all night?'

'Gunnery practice. This morning's effort was woeful.'

'Can't I do double tomorrow?'

'Trainee Walsh, if you want to graduate you'll jump when you're told.'

'Yes sir.'

'I'll fetch your weapon. Meet me on the range as soon as you're ready.'

Five minutes later Walsh emerged from the staff room in her uniform, which consisted of dark grey pants and matching jacket. Both lacked pockets, but Bernie had explained to her that it was traditional - without pockets, how could an officer of the law take a bribe? The uniform itself was antique, but it was the only one in the office small enough to fit her, and every time she asked Bernie about a replacement the robot mumbled excuses about budget cuts.

Walsh laid her white dress over the back of a chair, smiling at the memory of whirling around the dance floor with Hal. Then she turned her back on the dress and headed for the stairs.

The gunnery range was in the basement, and Walsh found Bernie waiting near the door. Half a dozen booths opened onto the range, which extended about forty metres underground, and the concrete floor was littered with fragments of targets.

Walsh entered the nearest booth, and Bernie handed her the small case containing her weapon, reciting the usual ritual as she did so.

'Do you agree to use this weapon for the good of the Peace Force?'

'I do,' said Walsh softly.

'Do you accept responsibility for your own safety?'

She was in Hal's arms, leaning back with abandon. 'I do,' she whispered.

'Right. Please take your weapon.'

Her dress shimmered; she could see the highlights reflected in Hal's eyes. 'I do,' said Walsh.

'What?' Bernie looked puzzled.

Walsh started. 'Sorry Bernie. I was distracted.'

'This is not the time or place. I only have one trainee in this office, and I'd like to keep her in one piece.'

Her heart still pounding, Walsh took the brutal-looking gun, curling her palm and fingers around the grip. It felt heavy and powerful, unstoppable.

Bernie took the case and stepped out of the booth. 'We'll start with six targets at medium range. Please select mode four.'

With a well-practised movement, Walsh reconfigured the gun.

'Range is active,' said Bernie. 'Commence.'

A target popped up and Walsh fired without conscious thought. The gun jerked in her hand and the target literally disintegrated before her eyes. There was no sound, no flash of light - just silent killing power. Another target appeared, then another and another, and Walsh took them all without hesitation. Pieces of shredded target fluttered to the ground, and Walsh felt the party, the music and Hal's beaming smile slipping away.

'Very good,' said Bernie. 'Change to mode two. Rapid fire.'

Walsh altered the setting and stood ready. A target slid across in front of her, and she barely fired before it disappeared.

'Pay attention, Trainee Walsh. One day you could be shooting to save your life.'

Another target sped across the range, and Walsh followed it all the way, firing again and again, even after it had completely disintegrated in a cloud of confetti. Then she blasted the fragments, clearing huge streaks off the floor with every shot.

'Cease firing!' roared Bernie.

Walsh blinked, and before she could react Bernie had taken the gun. The robot's expression was unreadable, and she said nothing as she put the weapon carefully back into its case.

'I'm sorry, Bernie. I –'

'It's late, Trainee Walsh. We'll continue tomorrow.'

Upstairs, Bernie stowed the gun in the armoury while Walsh checked her accuracy scores on the terminal, wincing at the string of misses. Would Bernie sweep those under the carpet for her?

'Trainee Walsh, I'm going to get a recharge. I'd like you to remain on duty until midnight, and if you don't see me before you go, I hope you enjoy a long and restful night's sleep.'

'Thanks Bernie. Goodnight.'

The robot hesitated. 'If you want to go home an hour early, I can probably cover for you.'

Walsh felt a rush of affection. 'Thanks Bernie, but there's only an empty apartment waiting for me. Cold and lonely.'

Bernie gestured at the desks with their dead computer screens. 'And this is more appealing?'

'At least you're here.'

'Thank you, Trainee Walsh.'

'And there's the coffee shop up the road. I can order something in.'

Bernie's face fell. 'You don't like my coffee?'

'No, no! I just meant a sandwich or something.'

'Actually, while you were out I was thinking about downloading a recipe book. I could teach myself to cook and prepare all your meals right here at the office.'

Walsh suppressed a shudder. 'I think you should concentrate on official business.'

'You're probably right.' Bernie wiggled her fingers. 'After all, can you picture me cracking eggs with these? Now, if you don't mind I might just get that recharge. I'm feeling rather spent.'

Walsh watched the robot go, relieved the tricky matter of coffee had been resolved. Then she turned to her terminal and brought up a local map, feeling a stab of longing at the sight of the familiar stars and planets. She'd secretly memorised all their names as a child, hiding her interest so as not to upset her aunt, and now they were like old friends. Herephus and Belleron orbiting their local star, bathed with strong radiation and visited only by specially designed robots. Further away was Cortes with its active volcanos, and its cousin Vasquez, a gentle world with lush forests and clear blue skies. And nearby, closer to home, was Forzen, the cold planet. The source of her mystery call.

She zoomed the map right out and gazed at the stars sprinkled across the screen. Would she ever visit any of them? Perhaps those even further afield? Millions of people lived out their lives in one place, never leaving their home planets due to fear of the unknown, family ties, fear of space travel ... the reasons were endless. And what was really stopping her? True, she was eking out an existence on a trainee wage, but was lack of money the only reason she remained on Dismolle?

Lost in thought, Walsh reached out to clear the screen. At that moment her terminal pinged. It was a call from Forzen, and when she answered it she saw a man with a round face and a fussy little moustache. 'Officer Walsh of the Dismolle Peace Force. How may I help you?'

'My name is Bigan, and I'm calling on behalf of the Forzen Residents Association. We've been very active raising funds for the reforestation of –'

Walsh's heart sank. 'Sorry, can I interrupt you right there? I'm sure it's a worthy cause and everything, but –'

'Oh, I'm not after a donation.'

'No?'

Bigan shook his head. 'Nothing like that, no. I was just wondering whether our treasurer is visiting your planet. Her name is Margaret Cooper, and nobody's heard from her since our big fundraising event last week.'

'Why do you think she's over here?'

'Her father lives in one of the retirement villages.' Bigan hesitated. 'The thing is, she took the cash home after the fundraiser, and some of the committee members are getting a little worried. Margaret's an accountant by trade, but –'

'You think she's done a runner?'

'Certainly not! We're just concerned for her safety.'

Walsh suppressed a wry grin. Sure they were. 'You know I can't disclose information on the movements of a private citizen? Not without an official request, anyway.'

'Can't I report her as a missing person?'

'Not to me. You'd have to go to your local –' Walsh stopped. Forzen didn't have a Peace Force. According to Bernie, it had been disbanded several years earlier - no doubt the same trick with the happy water. 'Mr Bigan, I'm going to search our visitor list, and if I happen to cough twice you'll know I saw Ms Cooper's name.' Walsh typed her query but the screen remained blank. 'Sorry, not even a tickle.'

'It was good of you to try.'

'My pleasure.' Walsh disconnected and turned back to the keyboard. It took her a couple of minutes to establish that Margaret Cooper travelled to Dismolle regularly, her latest visit only a few weeks earlier. A little more digging and she confirmed that neither Cooper nor her elderly father were banking large amounts of cash. Oh well, people vanished from time to time. Maybe the woman had taken off for parts unknown. It happened.

Walsh glanced at her watch. She spent so much time at work it was like a second home, and she hadn't been kidding when she told Bernie she'd rather stick around the office than face her empty apartment. Sighing, she reached for the commset and dialled a local cafe. Time for some sustenance.

❧

Hal stood at the top of the stairway, watching the other guests leave in their flash cars. Since Walsh had driven off he'd filled the time sinking glasses of orange juice until the stuff was flowing out of his pores. Now the lights were off, the musicians had packed up and the evening had limped to a close.

He sighed as the last car pulled out of the car park. It was no good, he thought, he'd have to find Clunk and apologise. He'd treated the robot badly and now it was time to mend bridges. Anyway, he didn't have enough money for a cab fare.

'So there you are!'

It was Morgan. Hal was in no mood for a battle, but instead of laying into him she held out a plate of food.

'What's that for?' he asked.

'Leftovers. Shame to waste it.'

Hal took the plate. 'You didn't spit in it, did you?'

Morgan laughed. 'No, I didn't, and it's not poisoned either.' She watched him tucking into a drumstick, then continued. 'I see you're getting friendly with our local copper.'

'That's none of your business,' said Hal, through a mouthful of chicken.

'I just thought you'd want to know, that's all.'

Hal lowered the drumstick. 'Know what?'

'She's a bit keen on the old conspiracy theories. A couple of months ago she was convinced we were trying to have her expelled from the Peace Force. Next thing you know it'll be drugs in the water supply.'

Hal stared at her, but said nothing.

'It must be hard, being a Peace officer on a planet full of law-abiding citizens, but I do wish she'd get a grip on herself.' Morgan sighed. 'I try and keep her busy with parties and whatnot, but one of these days

57

…Well, we can only hope that robot at the office keeps the guns locked away.'

Hal dropped the drumstick on the plate. 'I think you've said enough.'

'I was just putting you in the picture. Most of the time she seems so …normal.'

'She *is* normal,' said Hal quietly. 'You're just annoyed because she came to your party with a date.'

'And left soon afterwards. An urgent matter, I believe?'

'Yeah, she was called back to the office. Probably a burglary, or a hold-up, or –' Hal stopped.

'On a crime-free planet?' Morgan looked him in the eyes. 'I think you're getting the idea.'

Hal shrugged, uncertain. 'It could have been something else.'

'Just be careful, that's all. If she comes to you with any juicy conspiracies, don't be taken in.'

Hal was silent.

'Now, on to business.' Morgan put a hand on his arm. 'I really want you to do this cargo job for me. What do you say to twelve thousand credits and an expense account on Forzen?'

Hal tried to say yes, but his business instincts kicked in. 'Fifteen.'

'Done. Celebrate the deal over a drink?'

'Sorry, but I'm waiting for Clunk.'

'Oh, the robot. I'll have to cut his wages, you know. He's done nothing but sharpen cutlery all night.'

'He's very efficient.'

'Yes, but he's done all the forks and spoons too. I'll never get my deposit back.' Morgan hesitated. 'Do you want a lift home? We can send for your robot later.'

'I never mix business and pleasure.'

'Oh well. It's your loss.'

Hal watched her leave, then leaned against the wall and let his mind wander. He was pleased about the cargo job, but also amused at the way Morgan had painted Harriet Walsh as a paranoid psycho. Sure, they were rivals, but wasn't that taking things a bit far?

Okay, so Morgan was trying to get at Walsh, but what about the reverse? Had Walsh only invited him along to get up Morgan's nose? Hal scuffed the toe of his shoe along the ground as he thought back over the evening, and decided that he didn't actually care. Whatever the intention behind Walsh's invitation, he'd had a great time with her. It was just a pity she'd left so soon.

Then he remembered Clunk, and his positive mood evaporated.

The kitchens were out the back of the function room, and as Hal entered Clunk took up a carving knife and sighted along the blade. Then, very deliberately, he ran it over the sharpener.

Rissssk!

'Hey Clunk,' said Hal. 'How's it going?'

Rissssk!

'Clunk, I'm sorry. It just seemed the perfect solution. We needed Morgan's cargo and she needed a waiter.'

Risssk!

'I'll make it up to you. Anything you want!'

'Very well.' Clunk tested the edge of the knife. 'Next time, I get to dance and you get to carve beef all night.'

'Done!'

'Thank you.' Clunk's expression softened as he removed the chef's hat. 'So, how was your evening?'

'Terrible. Bloody awful.'

Clunk smiled. 'Now come on. I saw you having a fine old time. And don't tell me the food wasn't any good.'

'No, that was great. And Harriet was a laugh, too.' Hal frowned. 'But she and Morgan - phew. They're not exactly bestest buddies.'

'Yes, I heard them during the speech. I'm afraid I can't see Morgan favouring us with her cargo job after that little exchange.'

'That's what you think. I just spoke to her and we're on. She offered twelve grand, and we settled on fifteen.'

Clunk laid one hand on the knife handle. 'Tell me, was anything else agreed?'

'No, nothing.' Hal saw the robot's suspicious look. 'I mean it, Clunk! Maybe the other pilot stood her up or something.'

'Maybe.' Clunk straightened the knives. 'And Miss Walsh? Did she leave?'

'Ages ago,' said Hal glumly. 'So, have you finished here?'

'Yes.'

'Did Morgan pay you for tonight?'

'Yes.'

'Let's go home then.'

A taxi dropped Hal and Clunk at the spaceport terminal and they crossed the landing field in darkness, negotiating garden furniture, barbecue settings and washing lines. They were halfway across the buffer zone separating the residents from the active landing pads when they heard a rumble overhead. Hal looked up to see a tiny spark of light amongst the thin scattering of stars, and realised it was a spaceship coming in to land.

'We'd better take cover,' said Clunk.

They found a ground crew shelter, but the door was either locked or rusted shut. Meanwhile the noise was getting louder.

'Run,' said Clunk.

Hal cupped a hand to his ear. 'What?'

'RUN!'

They took off, leaping over refuelling pipes and weaving between the empty landing pads. Above them, the ship's landing lights came on, twin spotlights which turned the shadowy field into daylight. The engine noise rose to a howling roar, and as the ship came down Hal was thrown headlong by a blast of red-hot air. He protected his head from the searing heat washing over him, and just when he thought it would burn him to a crisp the heat lessened and the noise dwindled. To his relief the ship had passed them by, and was now settling on a landing pad in the distance. The engines cut out, and as soon as the glare subsided Hal recognised the ship's outline. 'The *Volante*? But you said they weren't going to move it!'

'No, it's not ours.' Clunk pointed out three strips of chrome on the tail. 'That's an XS model. The *Volante* is only an L.'

'So everyone keeps telling me,' muttered Hal. His suit crackled as he stood up, and he realised the supple polymer had been converted into brittle plastic by the heat of the ship's wash. He could feel fresh air in unexpected places, and even worse, the material had turned completely transparent. 'Er, Clunk?'

'Yes, Mr Spacejock?' The robot glanced at him, then stared. 'Oh my goodness. You're stark naked!'

'You don't have my spare flight suit, do you? It's getting draughty.'

'I'm a robot, not a walking wardrobe.'

'Damn.' Hal looked down at himself. 'This is awkward.'

'It's like one of those nightmares where you end up in a big crowd with no clothes on.'

'How can you have a nightmare about that? You don't even wear clothes!'

'I read about it once. Fascinating.'

Hal muttered under his breath.

'Tell me, has the melted plastic stuck to you?' Clunk tugged on a loose bit.

'Ow! Do you mind?' Hal swatted his hand away. 'That hurt!'

'I was just checking.'

'Well next time rip someone else's skin off.' Hal inspected the damage. 'What genius came up with a melty suit, anyway?'

'Clearly the same genius who saw a market for such a thing.' Clunk crouched for a closer look. 'It's not fused to your skin, it's just attached to the hairs. You're lucky.'

'Lucky?' said Hal, his voice rising. 'I'm swaddled in melted plastic, and you think it's lucky?' He shook his arms. 'How the hell am I supposed to remove it?'

'With a sticky plaster, the idea is to pull it off really quickly.'

'Do not talk about pulling things off.' Hal picked at a tiny plastic flake. 'Ooh! Ow! This is not going to –'

Rrripp!

'Argh!' Hal leapt into the air, twisting and turning as he tried to reach the strip of agony down the middle of his back. Through tear-filled eyes he saw Clunk inspecting a length of plastic. 'What the f - ... What happened to not harming humans?'

'It's the most effective method of removal,' said the robot. 'The only alternative is to slide a sharp blade across your skin, and in the darkness that could lead to multiple injuries and blood loss.'

Resigned, Hal raised his arms. 'Go on, then. But I don't want any warning.'

Rrrripp!

'Argh!'

Ten minutes later the job was done, and Clunk disposed of the furry strips in a nearby bin.

'You'll have to f-fetch my clothes,' said Hal, his teeth chattering in the darkness. 'I'll w-wait near the gates, out of s-sight.'

'It's dark near the fence. We'll go that way.'

They made their way to the perimeter fence then followed it towards Honest Bob's dockyard. They hadn't gone far when the night-time insects fell silent, and Hal saw a hulking shadow looming out of the darkness. 'What's that?' he whispered to Clunk, his voice carrying on the still air.

'It's a ruined hull.'

Hal could feel the aura of loss and sorrow, and he lengthened his stride to pass the wreck as quickly as possible. Before long they reached the gates outside Honest Bob's dockyard. Unfortunately, they were shut tight. 'Well that's marvellous,' said Hal, rattling the wire in the gloom. 'You said they were going to wait.'

'We could book a room for the night.'

'Hello?' Hal patted his bare leg. 'Mr Birthday Suit here? Anyway, Honest Bob can let us in. Give him a call and tell him we're waiting.'

'What do you think I've been doing for the past sixty seconds?'

'And?'

'There's a recording. It says to come back in the morning.'

Hal eyed the gates. 'Give me a leg up.'

'May I voice my strong opposition to that course of action?'

'Go ahead, but you can give me a leg up at the same time.'

Sighing, Clunk crouched next to the gate and put his hand out. Hal stepped onto it and the robot hoisted him up. 'Mind you don't get caught,' he said, as Hal went over the wire.

'Come on!' whispered Hal. 'You next.'

'I'm not going anywhere. Trespass is against the law.'

'All right, all right. No need to growl at me.'

'I didn't.'

'Oh hell.' Hal spotted a pair of red eyes glowing from the darkness. 'Nice doggy. Stay.'

The eyes moved towards him, and Hal burst out laughing as a weedy plastic dog emerged from the shadows. 'It's just a toy!' he said, taking in the oversized head, spindly legs and slender body. 'Go on! Shoo!' He waved his arms but the robot dog stood its ground, and when he advanced on it, intending to scare it away, it growled, revealing a mouthful of needle-sharp teeth. Hal took one horrified look and dashed for the gate, grabbing the wire and hauling himself up as though a three-headed monster were on his tail. The dog snarled and leaped and snapped at his ankles, but Hal was over the top like lightning. As soon as he was safe he turned and kicked the gate, prompting frenzied barking. 'What now, you wind-up woofer? Can't climb the fence, can you?'

The dog appraised the situation with a disturbingly intelligent look, then stood on its hind legs and hooked its front paws through the wire. It took a faltering step, then another, until it was halfway up the gate.

'Over here, Mr Spacejock,' called Clunk, pointing towards the passenger ramp of a nearby ship. It was the Gamma class freighter that had almost grilled them alive, and light shone from a porthole set into the airlock door.

'Can you get in?' asked Hal, as they ran up the ramp. 'Hook into the computer, crack the door codes and open her up?'

'No, but this ought to do it,' said Clunk, pressing the doorbell.

Hal looked down at himself. 'You can do the explaining.'

Meanwhile, the dog had cleared the gate and was now haring across the landing field towards them. Judging by its speed, Hal reckoned he had about ten seconds to live.

7

Walsh decided she could use some exercise, and went to collect her order in person. The cafe owner refused payment but Walsh insisted, as per the book, and walked back to the office munching a biscuit and sipping coffee from a paper cup. Street lamps banished the darkness, and the coffee steamed in the cool night air.

She was just letting herself in when her terminal buzzed, so she put the coffee aside and took hold of the handset. 'Dismolle Peace Force. Can I help you?'

'I'd like to report a public disturbance,' said a shaky female voice.

'Are you sure you've called the right number? This is Dismolle. We don't have disturbances here.'

'Oh yes we do. Two naked men are fighting outside.'

Walsh's eyebrows went up. With few exceptions, Dismolle residents were safely tucked in by nine pm. 'Aren't you a little old for prank calls?'

'This isn't a prank call! Two men are tearing strips off each other outside. And the language! I haven't heard anything like it since I retired from high school.'

Biscuits and coffee forgotten, Walsh brought up a map. The caller lived in a converted freighter at the spaceport, and Walsh tapped the nearest camera to bring up a live feed. All she got was a screen full of tightly packed ships, awnings and clotheslines. 'I can't see anyone.'

'Wait a minute.' The handset clunked, and Walsh heard heavy breathing and the swish of curtains. Then the voice came back. 'You're right, they've gone.'

'Could you identify them? Did you get a close look?'

'I wish I had, dearie. It's years since I –'

'Thanks for calling,' said Walsh hurriedly. 'Watchful citizens like you help to keep the Peace.' She hung up and reached for her coffee, but the terminal rang again. Walsh scooped up the receiver and a woman's voice burst from the earpiece.

'Is that the Peace office? I need you to send someone straight away. There's a terrible fight going on!'

'Two men arguing?'

'That's right. Stark naked, too! Rough-looking villains, the pair of them. One was tanned, and the other one was all mottled and reddish.'

Walsh frowned. Had all these callers hit the turps and then sat down to watch the same show? 'Tell me, have you had a drink this evening?'

'I beg your pardon?'

'Only I've just had a similar report, and I'm wondering whether there's a program you've all been watching. Something of a fantastic nature.'

There was a long silence. 'Are you accusing me of watching horror films? Science *fiction*?'

'Well no, but –'

'For your information,' said the caller, acid dripping from every syllable, '*I* gave up such flights of fancy in my teenage years. What's *your* excuse?' The caller slammed her phone down, and Walsh stared at the screen with conflicting thoughts running through her head. Mass hysteria or naked fighting men? Well, a quick call would reveal all, so to speak. She dialled spaceport security and drummed her fingers as the automated system picked up.

Your call is important to us, and will be answered by the next available operator.

Walsh dialled a bypass code.

Your emergency call is important to us, and will be answered by the next available operator.

Walsh entered a top priority override, for use only in direst emergencies.

Your urgent top priority emergency call is important to us, and will be -

Walsh banged the handset down. There was only one thing for it - she'd have to take a look herself. She went to notify Bernie and found the robot still plugged in to the power point. Walsh reached out to shake her, then hesitated. The robot's face was so calm and serene it seemed a pity to wake her, especially if the so-called disturbance turned out to be a foul-mouthed couple taking an evening walk. No, she'd handle this one herself.

The armoury had a heavy steel door with a keypad, but although Walsh was denied access, Bernie's daily use had worn the relevant keys so badly she had little trouble working out the combination. The keypad buzzed and the door popped open.

The armoury walls were lined with shelves, empty apart from a couple of dusty flak jackets and the pistol Walsh used for target practice. There was a filing box too, and she peeked inside hoping for hand grenades or a bigger gun, but it only contained dusty files and records, yellowed with age.

Walsh donned the smaller jacket then took the pistol from its case, feeling the warmth in the grip. As she clipped it to her belt she felt a stirring of excitement. Armed in public? Patrolling at night? Forget the endless studying, this was what she'd signed up for!

◆

Five seconds later Clunk was still pressing the doorbell and the guard dog was halfway up the ramp, its claws striking sparks and its eyes blazing red in the darkness. Hal gripped the handrail, aware that his life was over. Of all the ways to go, he thought, being torn apart in the nuddy by a wind-up woofer had to be the most demeaning.

But before the dog could attack, the airlock door opened, bathing them in light. Hal didn't waste time explaining: he dived in, landing full length on the cold metal floor. Clunk followed, ramming the door shut just as the dog pounced. There was a thud as it hit the solid metal, then silence.

'What the hell is going on?' said a smooth voice behind them. 'And why are you running around butt naked?'

'Sorry about that,' said Hal. 'Just a little misunderstanding over business hours.' He struggled to his feet and faced their unwitting saviour. The man was tall, with a mane of straw-coloured hair and a trim goatee. His face was pale, and something about him seemed familiar. 'Have we met?'

'Of course we have!' said the man. 'I flew you out of Cathua once. You spent the whole voyage in uniform, serving my passengers food and drink.'

'Oh my goodness,' said Clunk. 'It's Mr Spearman of the *Luna Rose*!'

'Kent Spearman?' Hal shook his head. 'It can't be him. He was put away for dumping robots in space.'

'Oh, that!' Spearman laughed. 'Just a little misunderstanding. In fact, I got quite a decent result out of it.'

Hal looked down at himself. 'Can we discuss this later? I, er –'

'Relax, I've got an old flight suit you can have.'

'Thanks!'

'So, I sued for false imprisonment, and the settlement paid for this little baby.' Spearman gestured around the airlock. 'Welcome to the *Tiger*. Watch where you sit, though ... the paint's still wet.'

'But she's a freighter, and you were in the passenger game!'

'Not any more, Spacejock. It's the cargo business for me. I realised you two had the right idea when I saw how successful you were.'

Clunk suddenly found the airlock door fascinating, and he turned to give it a close inspection.

'But why Dismolle?' asked Hal.

'Honestly? I thought I'd follow you around a bit. Pick up a few jobs, learn how you operate.'

'But –'

'Hey, where are my manners? Come in, come in!' Spearman led them into the flight deck, which was identical to the *Volante's* except for the dirty plates on the console. 'Excuse the mess,' he said, hurriedly stacking dishes. 'I wasn't expecting visitors. Hey, you want to catch the game?'

'What game?'

'The sky hockey tournament, of course! It's the final, and I've got a direct feed into my games room.'

'These ships don't have a games room.'

'Come and see.'

'And the, er, flight suit?'

Spearman opened a locker, revealing half a dozen pairs of gleaming white overalls.

'I really appreciate this,' said Hal.

'Don't mention it.' Kent twitched the clean overalls aside and took out a worn set, covered with oil stains. 'Here, these should do the trick.'

Hal eyed the nice starched flight suits, but was in no position to argue. When he had donned the stained pair, Spearman led them into the lift. Hal's eyes widened at the *three* buttons on the control panel instead of the two aboard the *Volante*. 'How can you have a third deck? Your ship's no bigger than mine!'

'The *Volante* has one too,' said Clunk. 'It's masked off.'

'Huh?'

'We have three decks too; we just can't access the third.'

'You mean it's there, but we can't get to it?'

'Precisely. It's cheaper to build identical vessels and hide the features you haven't paid for. Electronics manufacturers have been doing it for years.'

'I always thought the ship looked bigger from the outside. I thought it must've been fuel tanks.'

The lift stopped and the doors opened onto a sumptuous lounge with plush armchairs in front of a gigantic video screen. A well-stocked bar ran along one wall, complete with hanging glasses and rows of bottles in shot dispensers. Spearman grabbed a bag of potato chips from the counter and tossed it to Hal. 'What's your poison, eh? No, don't tell me. OJ.'

Hal nodded.

'Want anything in it?'

'I'm flying,' said Hal, through a mouthful of chips. He offered the bag to Clunk, who shook his head.

Spearman waved at the screen, which came alive in a riot of colour. The image panned over thousands of yelling fans waving huge flags and home-made banners. Concealed speakers pumped out the noise in perfect surround sound, and for a moment Hal felt like he was really at the game. He drained his drink without taking his eyes off the screen, then handed Spearman the empty glass.

'Not bad, eh?' remarked Spearman, passing Hal a refill.

Hal took the glass and sank into an armchair, which automatically adjusted to his shape. Spearman handed him a tray of cocktail sausages, cheese sticks, pickled onions and shaved ham, and as Hal tucked in to his favourite delicacies he weighed up his chances of trading in the *Volante* on an upgraded model.

'So, what are you doing on Dismolle?' asked Spearman. 'Business or pleasure?'

'Bit of each,' said Hal. 'We brought in a cargo of essentials ... you know, staple foods to keep the planet's inhabitants alive, that kind of thing.'

'And the pleasure?'

'Just catching up with a girl I know.'

'You're still single then?'

'Between partners,' said Hal.

'Yeah, right.'

'It's true! I'm a regular chick magnet!'

'Sure you are.' Spearman nudged Clunk. 'He attracts girls who look like fridges.'

'So, how was prison?' asked Hal. 'Did you have any firm friends?'

Spearman looked alarmed. 'Hey, you can't tell anyone about that! My record is clean, and if you start spreading rumours –'

'We wouldn't dream of discussing your past,' said Clunk. 'It would be most inappropriate.'

'My lips are sealed,' said Hal. 'Anyway, how could a short stretch in the nick turn you into a career criminal?'

Spearman looked relieved. 'That's good of you.'

'So, what's your cargo?' asked Hal. 'Drugs? Guns? Stolen goods?'

'Very funny. Actually, my current client is a big noise in the renovations business.'

'Really? We've been working in that line ourselves. We're collecting some gear from Forzen for a local decorator. Cushy job, too. Cash on the nail.'

'It's not decorating supplies?'

'Yeah, that's it.' Hal laughed. 'Some other dope put their name down for the job, but I talked Morgan round with a bit of the old Spacejock charm.'

He reached for a dish of stuffed olives, but Spearman snatched it away. His face was like thunder, and he was struggling to speak. 'You ...you ...'

'Hey, calm down. I only ate three.'

'You took my job?' shouted Spearman.

'Eh?'

'Morgan Renovations is *my* client! I signed this afternoon!'

'Yeah, well she unsigned this evening.' Hal shrugged. 'It happens. Plenty of work to go around.'

'No there isn't! This was the only job within three star systems!'

'What can I say? The best man won.'

Spearman bunched his fists.

'Anyway, Morgan would hardly want a jailbird like you working for her. It's valuable gear, this. She can't afford any mysterious losses.'

'Get off my ship,' said Spearman in a low voice. 'Both of you. You're not welcome here.'

'Hey, relax. It's just business.' Hal glanced around. 'You got any more of those chips?'

'Out!' shouted Spearman. 'Off! Now!'

'We can't go out there! There's a killer robot roaming the spaceport.'

'Good!'

'Mr Spacejock is right,' said Clunk. 'I can't let you send him out into danger.'

'Well you're not staying here.'

'There is one thing I can do. If you'll allow me, I can broadcast a take-off warning from your flight deck. The robot dog will be forced to retreat to a safe distance.'

Spearman muttered under his breath, and after a hard stare at Hal, he nodded. 'But the second that thing's gone, you're out of here. And I want my flight suit back in the morning, laundered.'

Reluctantly, Hal stood. 'So, I guess bed and brekkie are out of the question?'

8

Clunk's signal had the desired effect, and Spearman bundled them out of the airlock and slammed the door, leaving them stranded in the cool night air. Fortunately the robot dog had taken the hint and vanished. Unfortunately Clunk spotted something worse. 'I think we have a problem,' he said. 'Someone's reported your trespass. Look!'

Hal followed Clunk's pointed finger and saw a patrol car picking its way across the landing field, its roof lights alternating red and blue as it slipped between the parked ships like a shark amongst a pod of whales. 'It's okay,' said Hal. 'That's got to be Harriet. She'll sort us out.'

'That's what I'm afraid of. Trespassing in Honest Bob's yard, letting the guard dog out, public nudity ...it might not sound much, but do you really want to embarrass yourself in front of her? You could lead her to Mr Spearman too, and you saw how nervous he was about that.'

'Good,' muttered Hal. Even so, he moved out of sight. The car purred by, making the air tremble with the beat of its powerful engine, then drew up at the dockyard gates. A uniformed figure got out, torch in hand, and Hal's pulse quickened as reflections lit up Walsh's blonde hair.

Then the beam swung towards them, and they threw themselves headlong behind a refuelling cluster, Clunk with a sound like a kettledrum falling down a mine shaft. The beam swung back, passing over them once more, and they heard the distinctive whine of a blaster charging up.

'Show yourselves,' said a female voice, slightly thin in the night air. 'Stand up or I'll open fire.'

Clunk went to get up, but Hal gripped his arm. 'Stay put.'

'But she's seen us!'

'Right. That's why the torch is pointing over there.' As Hal spoke the beam moved again, stopping on likely hiding spots. Through the glare

Hal could just see the weapon, raised and ready. Ever so slowly, he moved so that Clunk lay between him and danger.

There was a growl, and Walsh crouched and turned, illuminating the robot dog in a blazing cone of light. It charged right at her, head down and teeth bared, then leapt for her throat. Hal was getting to his feet to run out to her assistance, but Walsh calmly snapped off two shots and blasted the dog into fragments. She sidestepped the wreckage, then resumed her sweep of the field. Despite the near miss, the torch beam was steady.

'And that's why we're not showing ourselves,' whispered Hal. He tugged Clunk's ankle. 'We need somewhere to hole up. She'll see us out here.'

'We can't risk the roads,' said Clunk. 'It'll have to be somewhere nearby.'

'Lead on.'

They backed away, using the *Tiger* for cover. Hal expected a hail of gunfire at any moment, but they managed to get clear and made their way to the opposite side of the spaceport, keeping their eyes peeled for prowling patrol cars. They passed several ships in the darkness, and Hal noticed Clunk paying particular attention to the ground beneath each vessel. 'What are you looking for?'

'Somewhere to spend the night.'

'I want to sleep *inside* a spaceship, not below one.'

'You'll have to take whatever we can find.'

They continued in silence until they reached the edge of the landing field. The ground was uneven, thick with weeds, and discarded pieces of scrap metal made the going treacherous. Then Clunk stopped and pointed. 'Look there, Mr Spacejock. It's perfect!'

Hal saw the ruined hull ahead of them, dark and gloomy. 'Oh, no. Not a chance.'

'Why not? It's safe from the elements, and nobody will find us inside.'

'Damn right they won't.'

'Mr Spacejock, it's just for the night, and I can light a nice little fire. Come on, help me find the entrance.'

Reluctantly, Hal followed Clunk towards the ruined spaceship. They needed somewhere to hole up for the night, but this was taking things a bit far. Next they'd be sleeping under railway bridges and begging in the street.

'It's not like we're sleeping under a railway bridge,' said Clunk, as he led Hal inside. 'See? Nice and snug.'

'I can't see anything,' complained Hal, his voice echoing around the hull.

Clunk switched on his chest light, illuminating the interior. They were standing on compacted oil-stained sand, and above them rusty metal beams festooned with weeds and cobwebs stuck out at crazy angles. The entire ship was buckled as if a giant hand had grabbed it and hurled it to the ground, there were ragged splits in the hull and the interior was streaked with soot.

'You know what?' Hal shuddered. 'This is creepy. I'm going outside.'

'Come on Mr Spacejock, it'll be fine. Look, there's even a drum we can use for a fire.'

'What about some steaks we can use for supper?'

'I'm afraid not.'

Hal sighed, then sat down with his back to the wall. Meanwhile, Clunk gathered some oil-stained rags and broke up a couple of rotting wooden pallets, and it only took a second with his soldering attachment to get a cosy little fire going.

Hal watched the flames playing on the battered hull. The dull metal reflected the light unwillingly, giving back little more than a glow. 'I bet these walls could tell a story or two.'

'Sad ones, I fear.' Clunk looked up. 'From the shape of the hull I'd say she had a very heavy landing.'

'So why's it still here? Why didn't they cut it up for scrap?'

Clunk tapped the hull with his finger. 'Nobody uses this metal in spaceships any more. The ship must have been sixty or seventy years old when she came down, and it's been here at least twenty years.'

Hal shivered as Clunk's words echoed around the shadowy interior. The fire seemed smaller somehow, and what little warmth it gave off wasn't reaching him. 'Bung some more wood on, will you?'

Clunk obliged, sending a stream of sparks twirling towards the roof, and Hal put his hands out to capture some of the warmth. Never mind, he thought. The following night he'd be back in his own bed.

9

Hal awoke to sunlight on his face and a gentle breeze ruffling his hair. He opened his eyes and squinted at the rusty hull, blinded by the light shining through a large crack, then groaned aloud as memories of the previous night came flooding back.

'Good morning, Mr Spacejock,' said Clunk brightly.

'Prove it,' muttered Hal.

'Well, the sun's shining and before you know it we'll be back aboard the *Volante*. You can have a hot shower and breakfast while I call Ms Morgan to confirm the cargo job.'

'Sounds good. Let's go.'

As they tackled the overgrown weeds outside, Clunk pointed out a weathered plate bearing the ship's name: *Ganymede*.

Once free of the weeds they strolled along the perimeter fence to the dockyard. To their surprise the gates were still closed, and when they inspected the sign they realised why. 'Opening hours ten till eight?' Hal rattled the gates in exasperation. 'What kind of a dud operation is this? It's only just gone nine!'

'Why don't you get some breakfast at the spaceport? I'll wait here in case they open up sooner.'

Hal looked down at his grubby flight suit. 'You reckon someone will throw me a few credits if I put a hat out?'

'There's no need.' Clunk took out a couple of credit tiles. 'My payment from last night.'

'Thanks Clunk. You're a gem.' Hal took the cash and left before the robot could advise him what to spend it on. After all, it was his breakfast. Come to think of it, it was his money too.

Bernie was in a foul mood when Walsh arrived at the office. It wasn't the reports of fighting in the streets, or suspicious individuals roaming the spaceport. No, it was the fact Walsh hadn't bothered to involve her.

'One little wake-up call,' said the robot for the twentieth time. 'Is that asking so much?'

'I had everything under control, Bernie.'

'You initiated an unauthorised patrol. Unarmed!'

Walsh decided not to correct that misconception. 'Any news so far?'

'Spaceport personnel found a guard dog blown to pieces. They were hoping I could extract vision of its final moments, but the onboard storage was ruined in the blast.'

Walsh breathed a sigh of relief. 'Anything else?'

'Nothing locally, but I took a call from Mr Bigan of Forzen. He's still chasing his missing resident.'

'I already told him, we can't do anything unless he files an official report.'

Bernie held out a slip of paper. 'There you are.'

Walsh stared at it. 'They really think she's missing?'

'It appears so. They want you there tomorrow.'

'Me? Visit Forzen?' Walsh felt a sudden thrill. 'Now that's what I call a perk!'

'I'm very excited for you.'

Walsh couldn't help noticing the robot's depressed tone. 'Oh Bernie, I'm sorry.'

Bernie sighed. 'All my years in the Force and I've never had a real investigation. I want to analyse data, inspect a crime scene ...'

'You could nip outside and give someone a parking ticket.'

'I'm confined to the office until I receive new orders. You know that, Trainee Walsh.'

'Once I graduate I'll give you new orders every day. I promise!'

Bernie was silent.

'What if something comes up while I'm away? You'd have to go out then!'

'The likelihood of a crime spree on Dismolle is zero.'

'I suppose so,' said Walsh unwillingly. 'But if I wasn't here, and if there was an incident ...'

'You're right. I will remain in the office and hope for a crime.'

•

Inside the terminal Hal made a beeline for the nearest bathroom, ignoring the stares of passengers and staff. He washed his face and raked most of the grit out of his hair, but all attempts to clean the grease, soot and grass stains off his flight suit only made it worse. As he left the bathroom his best hope was to be mistaken for an amorous mechanic with a chimney fetish, and not a desperate fugitive or escaped convict.

The cafe was open, and Hal ignored the disapproving glances as the counter staff made his double-strength coffee. He paid up and carried his tray to a table in the corner. The table surface was showing a news bulletin, and he amused himself by putting sugar sachets on the presenter's face, shifting them around as she moved. The hefty dose of caffeine began to take effect, and before long he was feeling a lot more awake. Then a shadow fell across his table.

'Mind if I join you?'

Hal saw Harriet Walsh smiling down at him, tray in hand. She had her hair tied back in a ponytail, and her dark grey uniform looked businesslike and official. Was she hunting for suspects after the events at the spaceport? Was he a marked man?

Walsh eyed the sugar packets dotting the table. 'I can see you're sweet on that presenter. Want me to leave you to it?'

'No, sit down!' Hal swept the sachets aside and waved her into the spare seat. 'Are you on duty?'

'Sort of. Bernie thinks I've gone to the shops, but I ended up here instead.' Walsh sipped her coffee. 'So, what did you get up to after I left?'

She'd started the interrogation! Hal toyed with his cup, thinking furiously. What could he say?

'Come on, you can tell me.' Walsh smiled. 'It's not like I can arrest you.'

Relieved, Hal decided to come clean. 'Well, it was pretty bad. You see, there was this battered old wreck –'

'Aha! I *knew* Miranda would make a move!'

'Eh?'

'Did you dance with her?'

'Certainly not.' Realisation dawned. She wasn't interrogating him about the fuss at the spaceport. It was about the party! 'I had a couple of drinks, collected Clunk and went back to the ship.'

'Glad to hear it.' Walsh hesitated. 'I'm really sorry I had to leave early. I was enjoying myself.'

'Me too.' Hal looked down at his mug. 'Do you want to go out later? Lunch or something?'

'That's sweet, but I can't.'

'It doesn't matter,' said Hal quickly. 'I'm busy too.'

'It's not that. I won't be here.' Walsh hesitated. 'How about when I get back?'

'That'd be great.'

'There you go then. It's a date.' Walsh glanced around, then leaned across the table and lowered her voice. 'I'm not supposed to say anything, but I've got a missing person investigation. This woman helped with a fundraising event, took the cash home afterwards and hasn't been seen since.'

'Sounds like she did a runner.'

'I don't think it was enough money for that. She'll probably turn up by herself, but in the meantime I'm getting a free trip out of it.'

'Somewhere local?'

'No, I'm going to another planet!'

Hal smiled at the excitement in Walsh's eyes. To him planets were a necessary evil, not something to look forward to, and it was refreshing to see her so enthusiastic. 'That's great news! I'm sure you'll love it.'

'I'll be taking the Forzen ferry. Do you think a window seat is best, or would the aisle be better?'

'Well, I –'

'There's even a free magazine, and when I get to Forzen there'll be a hotel with room service and everything.'

Hal lowered his mug. 'Did you say Forzen?'

'Yes, the mining planet.'

'But that's where Clunk and I are going! We're collecting a load of gear for Morgan!'

'Really? When are you leaving?'

'This afternoon.' Hal had a flash of inspiration. 'Why don't you come with us?'

Walsh looked surprised. 'What, on your ship?'

'No, we'll tow you behind on a rope.' Hal grinned as Walsh pulled a face. 'We don't have the entertainment and the window seat and all that stuff, but you'll have your own cabin and the AutoChef serves up some pretty decent food if you ask it nicely.' He stopped as he saw Walsh's doubtful expression. 'What is it?'

'Hal, it'd be really great but I don't think the Peace Force allows that kind of thing. They're very strict on travel allowances.'

'You don't have to pay! It's my treat.'

'But –'

'Come on, it'll be great! I'll even let you fly a bit.'

'Really?'

'Sure, anyone can do it. I mean, it's not like we're going to hit anything out in space, is it? Anyway, passenger liners are the pits. Hours strapped into a tiny little seat, warmed-up leftovers, surly cabin staff … the only half-decent thing is the inflight magazine, and you can buy those without going near a spaceship. Really, it's nothing like the brochures.'

Walsh looked down at her cup, toying with the handle. Then she looked up at Hal and smiled. 'All right, you're on.'

'Great! I'll tell Clunk to make up a cabin.'

'I'll need to fetch a few things.'

'Come to the ship as soon as you're ready. I'll give you the full tour - engines, flight deck, the lot.'

Walsh finished her coffee, and after seeing her off Hal drained his own mug and left for the *Volante*. He decided he wouldn't mention Walsh to Clunk until the last possible moment, since the robot had some funny ideas about carrying passengers. Sure, there'd been one or two hijackings in the past, but Harriet Walsh was Peace Force. How could an officer of the law cause them any trouble?

A few minutes later Hal met Clunk at the dockyard gates, which were still closed. If Clunk noticed Hal's air of suppressed excitement he didn't remark on it, most likely assuming it was caffeine-related.

'I can't wait to get aboard the *Volante*,' said Hal. 'A nice shower, change of clothes ... perfect.'

Dead on time the gates swung open, admitting them to Honest Bob's yard. Morning sun glinted off the row of hangars as Hal and Clunk strolled by, and bustling workers hurried back and forth on errands.

'Personally, I'm looking forward to a good recharge,' said Clunk. 'Then I'll check the ship's systems to ensure nothing has been tampered with overnight.'

Hal was bursting with impatience. He wanted to get the ship ready, confirm the job details with Morgan and then enjoy Clunk's reaction when he revealed the surprise news that Harriet Walsh would be coming with them to Forzen. Clunk would make a fuss of course, but that was half the fun.

They rounded the last hangar and then stopped dead at the sight which met their eyes. The *Volante* had vanished, and in its place was the lower half of a spaceship hull. The entire upper section was missing, and the remainder looked like half an eggshell, with a broken, ragged edge.

'I didn't know they built ships here,' said Hal, watching a group of workers struggling under the weight of a glossy black cabinet.

'They don't.'

Hal saw a gantry crane rumble along the length of the busy construction area, casting a moving shadow. It shuddered to a halt and lowered a set of slings, and after a moment or two began to whine and clatter as it strained to lift its load from within the hull. 'If they're not building it, what are they doing?'

'It's a wrecking operation. They strip the parts and materials from old ships, either for resale or for use as spares. I understand it's a very lucrative business.'

Hal nodded, then looked around. 'I don't see the *Volante* anywhere. Reckon they've finished with her?'

Clunk gasped, and when Hal followed the robot's gaze he understood why. The crane was slowly lifting a huge tailfin from the remains of the spaceship, and clearly visible across the base of the fin was a single word: *Volante*.

10

'That is *not* my ship,' whispered Hal, as he gazed at the stripped hull. 'That's not the *Volante*. It can't be.'

Clunk broke into a run and Hal raced after him, his mind churning as his boots pounded the hard ground. It was a trick, a scam of some kind. Offer a free wash and strip the vessel, selling the parts for cash. As for the hapless pilots … maybe they were abducted and disposed of?

Several workers turned to stare as Hal and Clunk came charging towards them, and a large red-faced man raised his metal clipboard defensively. 'Hey, you're not supposed to –'

Hal yanked the clipboard out of his hands and broke it over his knee, throwing the pieces aside. Then he grabbed a fistful of Honest Bob's overalls and hauled him up until their noses were almost touching. 'My ship. Explain.'

'Get your hands off me,' snapped Bob, struggling to break free. 'I'll have you for assault.'

'And I'll have you for theft and fraud,' hissed Hal. He pointed a shaking finger at the *Volante*. 'Wash and wax, you said!'

'Put him down Mr Spacejock,' said Clunk. 'We'll talk about this calmly and rationally.'

Hal let go, and Clunk grabbed Honest Bob by the throat, yanking him off his feet. 'WHAT HAVE YOU DONE TO MY SHIP, YOU MISERABLE EXCUSE FOR A HUMAN BEING?' he blasted at full volume. 'I'M GOING TO TEAR YOUR HEAD OFF AND SUCK YOUR GUTS THROUGH THE HOLE!'

As he started yelling, workers advanced on them, armed with makeshift weapons. Things were going to get ugly, and they were clearly outnumbered. 'Clunk,' said Hal, shaking the robot's shoulder. 'Calmly and rationally, right?'

Clunk glanced at the workers, then released the supervisor. 'Explain.'

'We're doing a rebuild,' said Bob, smoothing his crumpled overalls. 'As requested.'

'You what?' said Hal.

'A ground-up rebuild. We got your revised instructions last night, and we've been working flat out ever since.'

'What revised instructions?'

'The refit, to turn your L model into the XL. New wiring, a twenty thousand volume library, a home theatre set-up, a robot charging station and a Pleasurematic 2000.'

'But we didn't ask for any of that!'

'Hey, the order came through and we acted on it. Here at Honest Bob's the customer is king.'

'Show me a signature.'

'I've got the order on my computer. Wait here and I'll fetch it.'

Hal and Clunk exchanged a worried glance as Honest Bob hurried away. 'Do you think they're scamming us?' asked Hal, keeping his voice down.

'I don't know.'

'So what's this about instructions coming in overnight?'

'Let me see.' Clunk froze for a moment, then looked thoughtful. 'Interesting.'

'What?'

'They did get instructions, but not from us.'

'So who -'

'Shh. Leave this to me.'

Several minutes later, Bob came back, and he didn't look happy. 'I'm really sorry, Mr Spacejock. I definitely saw the order last night, but I just checked everywhere on the computer and it's not there. I-I don't know what happened.'

'You stuffed up, that's what.'

'It looks like it. And you can be sure I'll get to the bottom of it. However, I'm not called Honest Bob for nothing. We're not one of those dodgy fly-by-night companies -'

'You're not?' said Clunk in surprise.

'No! I have a top reputation and word of mouth is vital to my business. If news of this little cock-up gets into the wrong hands I could be ruined.'

He looked hopeful. 'If we put your ship back together, throw in a few extras, will you keep quiet about this mess?'

'Do we get the home theatre?' asked Hal.

'Not that, but I have some new parts left over from another upgrade. Military spec, very nice. And you can keep the features we've already unlocked.'

'No charge?'

'Absolutely. It's the least we can do.'

'How long will it take?'

'A day or two, I guess. Bit harder than taking it apart.'

'But –'

'Don't worry, Mr Spacejock.' Honest Bob gave him a reassuring smile. 'Your ship will be better than new.'

'It was new before you started.'

Bob shook his head. 'They're obsolete before they leave the factory. It takes years to design a ship, and once they start building it's too late to incorporate the latest designs. Computers, particularly.'

'Oh no!' exclaimed Hal. 'Clunk, the Navcom!'

'Relax, we took a copy.' Bob reached into his pocket and took out a slender PDA. 'See?'

'That's the Navcom?' said Hal in surprise.

'Yes, and fully operational. Minus navigation and flight functions, of course.'

'You mean it talks?' Hal took the PDA gingerly. The Navcom wasn't going to be happy about the *Volante*, and he didn't fancy an ear bashing. Still, it could have been worse … Bob could have downloaded her into a killer robot. 'Clunk, hang on to the Navcom will you?' he said, holding it out.

'Uh-uh,' said Clunk, backing away.

'Nice to feel wanted,' said a tinny voice. 'Why don't you both fight to see who doesn't have to carry me around?'

'Is that you, Navcom?' said Hal.

'You think there's room for anyone else in here?' said the PDA sourly.

Hal offered the Navcom to Clunk, but the robot crossed his arms. 'I'm not supposed to put myself in danger. It's the Laws.'

'What danger? It's a squeaky voice in a glorified commset.'

'I heard that,' said the Navcom.

'With good hearing,' added Hal.

'It's not the voice, it's the multichannel wi-fi connection. It'll play havoc with my circuits.'

'I'll play havoc with your circuits if you don't take it.'

'You're the majority owner of the *Volante*. I think you should assume responsibility.'

'Yeah, but I'm always losing things. Here.' Hal tossed the PDA to the robot, who just uncrossed his arms in time to catch it.

'Gentlemen, there's no need to argue.' Bob reached into his pocket and took out a second PDA. 'See? I made another one.'

For a moment Hal considered asking Clunk to take both of them, but the look on the robot's face killed that idea. Resigned to the inevitable, he took the second PDA. 'Hi Navcom,' he said. 'How's it going?'

'I have a headache and one of my chips is loose. And when they said it was time to split I expected something quite different!'

'They don't want us,' said the other PDA. 'They're all friendly and polite when it comes to flying the ship, but stick us in some useless gadget and they can't wait to get rid of us.'

'You've got it all wrong,' said Hal. 'I just think Clunk's more in tune with your electronic nature. And he's just worried I'll sell him for scrap if he doesn't look after you both.'

'And Mr Spacejock is worried I might tell Harriet Walsh about the time Katy the amorous robot cornered him in the –'

'Hey, that's not fair!' protested Hal. 'You built that thing to stalk me, and if I hadn't fobbed her off on that sleazy politician she'd still be chasing me.'

'Oh, I'm sure she is,' said Clunk, with some relish. 'They never give up, you know. Somewhere out there, Katy is scanning Galnet for your likeness, seeking her one true love so she can –'

'Excuse me,' said the Navcom. 'We're discussing *my* problems here.'

'Speaking of problems,' said Bob, who'd been watching the exchange in growing alarm. 'I have to supervise the reconstruction of your ship, so I'll just leave you to it.' He turned and beat a hasty retreat.

'Isn't it good news about all the upgrades?' said Hal's Navcom.

'Terrific,' muttered Hal.

'The ship will function so much better with all that modern equipment. I'm really looking forward to it.'

'Me too,' said Clunk's PDA.

'Do you have any idea how it happened?' asked Clunk. 'According to the men, someone faked a purchase order.'

'No idea,' said Hal's PDA. 'Still, every cloud has a silver lining.'

Hal dropped the Navcom into his pocket, where it continued to enthuse about new surface finishes for the flight console, albeit in a somewhat muffled voice.

'Isn't there an off switch?' whispered Hal.

Clunk held his PDA up. 'You see these sliders? Put the red one in, pull the white one out. Hold the power button and –' He shook the talking commset and the little screen went out.

'Okey dokey,' said Hal. 'Mind you, I preferred it when she was stuck in the ship.'

'Look on the bright side, Mr Spacejock. At least you now have something impressive in your trousers.'

'Very funny.' Hal nodded towards the ship. 'So, who's responsible for that mess?

Clunk lowered his voice. 'I checked their computer, and they did receive an order for the upgrades. What's more, you signed it.'

'I didn't!' protested Hal. 'Not even by accident, Clunk. I haven't signed anything for days!'

'Oh, I know that. The timing was all wrong, too. The order was submitted last night, while you were safely asleep in that old hull.'

'It's just as well they lost the bloody order,' said Hal. 'Genuine or not, we'd have been sunk.'

'They didn't lose anything.'

'But he said –'

Clunk's lips twisted. 'Fortunately, their network isn't very secure.'

Hal stared. 'You hacked in and deleted it?'

'I would never contemplate such an illegal and immoral action. I merely renamed the file.'

'What if they find it?'

'I called it Emergency Safety Procedures in the Event of an Earthquake. This region is geologically sound, ergo the file will not be opened.'

'What if they do? What if they search for the content?'

'Unfortunately, while I was renaming the file I somehow triggered a system error. Sadly, it corrupted the contents before I could stop it.'

'Clunk, you're sneakier than a room full of gym shoes,' said Hal admiringly. 'But that still leaves the question: who forged the order?'

'Perhaps it was someone we've angered in some way, or someone we let down. Or perhaps someone we overcharged.'

'You couldn't narrow it down a bit?'

'What about Miss Morgan? She was annoyed with you last night, and I don't think my efforts with the cutlery improved her temper.'

'No, it wasn't her. She practically begged me to do this job.' Hal snapped his fingers. 'Kent Spearman! Who else could it be?'

'To be honest, I don't think he'd have the technical skills for this. I know he's underhanded, but –'

'Are you kidding? He's a known criminal!'

'What about ...' Clunk hesitated. 'You don't think Miss Walsh ...?'

'What?'

'She obviously likes you,' continued Clunk with a rush. 'Maybe this is her way of keeping you here.'

'Don't be ridiculous. You'll have her bailing me up and bashing my ankles in next. Anyway, it can't be Harriet because we're taking her to Forzen.'

'We are?'

'Yes, I promised to take her aboard the *Volante* when we ...' Hal's voice tailed off as realisation dawned. His ship wasn't going anywhere, and neither was Harriet Walsh.

◆

'Bernie, are you there?' called Walsh. She needed to sort out her equipment for Forzen, and even though she could do it herself she felt it would be a good move to involve the robot.

'I'm always here,' grumbled Bernie. 'I can't even put my head out the front door for a quick breather.'

'You don't breathe, and you probably couldn't get through the front door if you tried.' Walsh saw Bernie's downcast expression and immediately regretted her sharp tongue. 'Honestly, it's nothing special out there. Just a planet full of old people going about their business.'

'So you say.' Bernie sighed. 'What did you want me for?'

'Expenses for my trip. I'll need something to cover meals and accommodation for a couple of days.'

'You get ten credits per day for meals and fifty for accommodation. You must submit all receipts for reconciliation purposes. Any additional expenditure will be deducted from your pay.'

'Ten credits for meals? That won't buy a sandwich!'

'I'm sorry, that's the stipulated amount. You'll just have to make do.' Bernie turned to a nearby terminal, then hesitated. 'About the return trip to Forzen. I assume Mr Bigan is looking after your ticket?'

So much for the passenger ferry, thought Walsh. Thank goodness for Hal. 'No need. I'm getting a ride with a friend.'

'Which friend?'

Walsh reddened. 'Just someone I met. A pilot.'

'This is highly irregular, Trainee Walsh. What if his intentions towards you are less than honourable?'

'I'm sure they're not.'

'And you do realise you can't take a weapon? You're not licensed, and Forzen won't allow it.'

'I'll manage.'

'Very well, on your own head be it.' Bernie turned to leave. 'I'll be in the kitchen if you need me. If I stand on tip-toe I can just see the top of a tree or two.'

Walsh closed her eyes. She'd half a mind to let Bernie roam the streets of Dismolle, even though the robot was officially confined to the office. After all, what harm could she do? She would probably run flat thirty metres up the road.

Walsh was still sitting there, head in hands, when her terminal buzzed. She gestured at the screen and felt a thrill as she saw Hal's robot looking down at the camera, with blue sky behind him. 'Clunk, isn't it? How can I help you?'

'I'm afraid I have some bad news.'

Walsh sat up. 'It's not Hal, is it? Is he all right?'

'Mr Spacejock is in perfect health. No, it's the *Volante* I'm calling about. I'm afraid we can't take you to Forzen today.'

'Oh no. What's the matter?'

'The dockyard received erroneous instructions overnight, and when we arrived this morning we found our ship completely disassembled.'

'You're kidding!'

'I wish I was. Mr Spacejock is taking it hard. In fact, he's so distraught about letting you down that he couldn't bring himself to talk to you personally.'

'He must be feeling terrible. Is there anything I can do to help?'

'There is one thing.' Clunk hesitated. 'The ship should be ready this time tomorrow, and if you could just delay your trip until then, Mr Spacejock will be happy to take you.'

Walsh considered it. She really wanted to, but she couldn't put her personal life ahead of an official investigation. It was a pity about Hal, but Bigan wasn't going to pay, so she'd just have to get a lift with someone else. 'I'm sorry, Clunk. I really have to get to Forzen as soon as possible.'

'I'll tell Mr Spacejock. He'll be most disappointed.'

She sighed, and called Bigan, whose secretary assured her there was no way they could provide an advance payment for her ticket. 'We can only reimburse on receipt of your receipts.' she said.

Harriet sighed again as she called the *Volante*.

'Clunk, before you go ...'

'Yes, Miss Walsh?'

'I'm sure you're busy with the *Volante*, but can you ask around the spaceport for me? I need a lift to Forzen and I don't know where to start.'

Clunk nodded. 'Leave it with me.'

◆

'Who was that?' asked Hal, as Clunk lowered the PDA.

'Nobody,' said Clunk. How could he ask Mr Spacejock to find another lift for Walsh? He'd sooner take his own arms off with a laser cutter.

They were standing near the *Volante*, and Hal shaded his eyes as he watched the dockyard workers reassembling the ship. 'Reckon we can help them out? Speed things up a bit?'

Clunk nodded. 'I know the ship well; they might appreciate my assistance.'

'And me?'

Clunk thought of laser cutters and arms, then decided Mr Spacejock could hardly feel any worse than he already did. 'Perhaps you could think about alternative travel arrangements. For Miss Walsh, I mean.'

'Isn't she taking the passenger ferry?'

'Apparently the Peace Force budget doesn't stretch to such things.'

Hal's face lit up. 'You mean she's coming with us tomorrow?'

'She really wants to get there today.' Clunk looked down at the PDA. 'She was just wondering ...'

'Yes?'

'She asked whether ...'

'Spit it out, Clunk.'

'We need to find her a lift, and I thought of Mr Spearman.'

Hal snorted. 'You think I'm going to let that criminal get his mitts on a defenceless girl?'

'Miss Walsh is hardly defenceless, and dealing with criminals is her job.'

'She's never met one.' Hal kicked a stone, sending it skimming across the concrete. 'Is there any chance the *Volante* will be ready?'

'No, Mr Spacejock. But it will make Miss Walsh very happy if you can present her with a solution.'

'Old Spearhead will be absolutely delighted,' muttered Hal.

'If you explain, I'm sure he'll say yes.'

Hal kicked an entire pile of stones, scattering them. 'When I get my hands on whoever ordered the *Volante* stripped –'

'You'll have to join the queue,' said Clunk. 'Now go. Ask Mr Spearman, and then inform Miss Walsh of the outcome.'

'I'd like to lock Spearman up and steal his ship,' said Hal. 'We could stick him in the hold, pretend it's the *Volante*, take Harriet to Forzen and do Morgan's cargo job, all at the same time.'

'Humour in the face of adversity.' Clunk smiled. 'That's what I like about you, Mr Spacejock.'

'Yeah, I'm a real comedian,' muttered Hal, but he looked thoughtful all the same.

Hal arrived at the *Tiger* to be met by the delicious smell of fried bacon. Spearman was leaning against the inner door, a heaped plate in one hand and a piece of bread dripping with egg yolk in the other. As he spotted Hal he took a huge bite and made appreciative noises, rolling his eyes in sheer delight.

Hal's stomach growled in reply, and he never felt less like asking Spearman for a favour. In fact, he desperately wanted to grab the plate and smear the contents in the smug bastard's face, and only the thought of letting Walsh down stopped him.

'So, what brings the jockster to my domain?' asked Spearman through a mouthful. 'Going to steal another job off me?'

'Not exactly.'

'Looking for a decent breakfast, then?'

Hal tore his gaze from the plate and shook his head, not trusting himself to speak in case he drooled all over his flight suit - Spearman's flight suit, he corrected himself.

'If you came to give that back, don't bother,' said Spearman, with a sniff. 'I know it wasn't new when you borrowed it, but ... Hey, I know why you're here! You want to pool our resources, eh? Sign your ship over to me and I'll find you as much work as you can handle for ten percent off the top.' He crunched a piece of bacon. 'No, better make it fifteen. It'll help to cover the insurance claims.'

'This isn't about me or my ship,' said Hal. 'There's someone who needs our help. I offered them a lift to Forzen today but I - I can't do it.'

'Why not?'

'The *Volante* needs a couple of repairs. Nothing major, but it's going to delay us a day or two.' Hal watched Spearman's face closely as he said this, but saw no trace of guilt. 'Anyway, I promised I'd get them to Forzen today, but now we can't.'

'Right. And you thought of good old reliable Spearman.'

'No, I tried to put her off but she's in a real hurry.'

Spearman's ears pricked up. 'She?'

'Yes, a local girl.'

'Hal Spacejock, you old dog! Tell me more! Is she a looker? Pleasing to the eye?'

Hal wondered whether he could ram Spearman's plate right into his big mouth in one piece, or whether he'd have to break it in half first. But no, Walsh needed his help and beating Spearman to a pulp wouldn't achieve anything, even though he itched to drive the slimy grin through the back of his neck. 'Her name is Harriet Walsh, and if you lay one finger on her I'll –'

'You'll what?' Spearman bit into a piece of bacon. 'Way I see it, you'll be stuck here fixing that ship of yours while I'm taking her deep in space.'

Hal frowned at the thought of Walsh in Spearman's greasy clutches, then remembered her Peace Force training. If Spearman tried anything he'd be lucky to escape with a broken arm. Unless she just shot him first.

'What are you grinning at?' demanded Spearman.

Hal shook his head. 'So, can I tell her you'll welcome her aboard?'

'Sure thing. I'll make up a cabin for her.' Spearman winked. 'Not that she'll be needing it.'

'Can I see?'

'See what?'

'The cabin. I'm not sending her off in some grotty little cupboard.'

'Sure, come in.' Spearman dumped his plate on the console and led Hal to the lift. 'I'll show you how we treat passengers aboard a real ship.'

They emerged on the second deck, and Spearman showed Hal to a door on the left. Hal pushed it open and saw a cabin remarkably similar to those aboard the *Volante*. The bunk was attached to the wall at shoulder height, with a desk underneath bearing a terminal screen and a selection of books and magazines. At the far end was a pair of doors.

Spearman reached up and patted the bunk. 'Specially strengthened, these are. Wouldn't want it collapsing at the wrong moment.'

Hal entered the cabin and slid the doors open. Inside was a small toilet, and behind the dividing curtain he found a shower cubicle.

'Satisfied?'

'It'll do,' said Hal grudgingly.

'Good. So how much is this bird paying?'

'Nothing. She's hitching a lift.'

'You're doing free trips now? No wonder you're always broke.' Spearman clapped him on the shoulder. 'You have to get with the program, Spacejock. Extract every credit while you've got them on the ropes.'

'I was just doing her a favour.'

'Well she won't get any favours from me. I want two grand up front.'

'She can't pay that kind of money!'

'What about you?'

Hal shook his head. Then he remembered something. 'Look, you know that job of Morgan's?'

Spearman frowned. 'Are you trying to be funny?'

'Well, as soon as I've done it I'll pay you the two grand. Okay?'

'No it's not okay. That was my job in the first place, and I'll be damned if I'm going to fly passengers around for peanuts while you're hogging the real work.' Spearman crossed his arms. 'There's only one way I'm taking this gal to Forzen, and that's if I'm bringing back Morgan's cargo.'

'Okay, you bring the cargo back and when I get paid I'll –'

'No, Spacejock. *I* get paid. *I* take the passenger. *You* get nothing.'

'That's not fair!'

'No, it's business. You want fair, go work for the government.'

'Next time you need a favour –'

'I'll use some of my twenty grand to buy one.'

'Fifteen.'

'I'm not haggling, Spacejock.'

'Maybe not, but I did.'

'Oh, this is good. I was supposed to do the job for twenty, and now you're letting me do it for five less *and* lumbering me with a passenger. Are you trying to ruin me?'

'Take it or leave it.'

'All right, all right. But if this bird's late you'll have to find another sap to carry her.'

'Thanks.'

'And Spacejock?'

'Yes?'

Spearman put his hand out. 'It's a pleasure doing business with you.'

Clunk felt a stab of sympathy when he saw Hal coming back from the *Tiger*. Not only had Mr Spacejock seen his ship taken apart, now he'd been forced to ask his rival for help. He looked angry and frustrated, and the reason was clear. 'He's giving her a lift then?'

'That's not all he wants to give her,' muttered Hal. 'And it gets worse. He's taken Morgan's cargo job back.'

'No!'

'What was I supposed to do? He wanted two grand for Harriet's fare.'

Clunk hesitated. 'You did the right thing, Mr Spacejock.'

They both turned to look at the ragged outline of the *Volante*.

'It's not fair, Clunk. First she had to leave the party early, then she was supposed to be our guest aboard the *Volante*, and now I'm setting her up with Kent bloody Spearman! It's a conspiracy!'

'I think your concerns are unfounded. Yes, Mr Spearman has a nicer ship. He's also wealthy, he dresses well, lays on sumptuous meals, acts the perfect host and has extremely good manners ...' Clunk decided to change the subject. 'By the way, Bob's people are going to fill up the *Volante's* tanks, which means we'll be able to leave Dismolle for another planet. We'll find a nice place with lots of repeat business, and we'll have things back on track in no time. You'll see, Mr Spacejock. Things will work out fine, just like they always do.'

There was no reply.

'Mr Spacejock?' Clunk glanced round, only to discover he was alone. He looked back along the hangars and across to the workers, but Hal was nowhere to be seen. Clunk shook his head sadly. The human was clearly hurting, and a little time alone wouldn't go amiss.

Walsh strolled up the *Tiger's* passenger ramp with a rucksack over her shoulder, enjoying the warm sunlight. The metal ramp seemed to go on forever, taking her closer and closer to the clear blue sky, and by the time she stepped onto the platform she could feel prickles of sweat all over.

At the top she turned to look across the landing field. Nearby, a maintenance worker was carrying a toolbox towards the ship, his bright yellow safety hat gleaming in the sun. Further away, the runabout which had dropped her off was returning to the terminal, and beyond that, in the dockyard, a partly built ship swarmed with workers. In the distance the spaceport gave way to urbanisation, and then lush green fields hemmed in by rolling hills.

There was a swish behind her, and she noticed a strong smell of aftershave. The airlock door stood open, and in the entrance was a tall man with a mane of straw-coloured hair and a sculpted goatee. He wore a dark open-necked shirt and pale slacks, and light glinted off the gold chain nestled in his ample chest hair. 'Mr Spearman, I presume?'

'Welcome to the *Tiger*, Miss Walsh.' The man smiled wolfishly, and the aftershave enveloped her like a toxic cloud. 'And please, call me Kent.'

◆

With Hal gone, Clunk threw himself into the *Volante's* reconstruction. He couldn't do anything about Mr Spacejock's disappointment over Miss Walsh, but getting the *Volante* back together would surely be something of a consolation. He was prepared to work his fingers to the metal if necessary.

Bursting with purpose, Clunk strode to the supervisor's office, where he found Bob poring over schematics and circuit diagrams. 'I'd like to offer my services.'

'I thought you'd be along.' Bob took him by the arm. 'Come with me. I have just the job.'

Outside, they made their way towards the *Volante's* keel. Great curved beams lay in the dirt nearby, and thick hull plates had been stacked alongside, leaving a series of narrow alleys. As they walked past, Clunk brushed the white plates with his fingertips. He'd put on a brave face for Hal's benefit, but deep down he was wondering whether the *Volante* would ever take to the stars again.

They emerged from the rows of hull plates and stopped before a heap of ship parts. Amongst the junk Clunk picked out a fuse board from the generator room, a tangle of thick cables stripped from the engines and even the big hydraulic pistons which drove the cargo doors up and down.

'Here you are,' said Bob.

'What do you want me to do?'

'Sort the parts. Engine room, flight deck … you get the idea. Neat little piles so we can find what we're looking for.'

'How will that speed up the Volante's reconstruction?'

'Trust me, it's vital work.'

Bob left without another word and Clunk stood there, deflated. Then he picked up a small piece of metal and looked around for a suitable spot for the sorting. He found a bare patch of ground between the base of a gantry crane and a collection of heavy machinery, and after a few minutes he'd scratched a number of large squares on the ground, labelling each with parts of the ship such as flight deck, cargo hold and rec room. Throwing the piece of metal aside, he returned to the pile and began to drag out pieces. Hauling them off to his sorting area, he matched their images with entries in his database, then placed them in the correct squares before returning to the pile for another load.

He'd just picked up a couple of circuit boards when he heard a rumble from the landing field, and moments later the *Tiger* lifted off for its trip to Forzen. The ship turned gracefully as it powered into the sky, sunlight glinting off the chrome strips on its tail, and Clunk shook his head sadly as he pictured Hal watching the departure from some spaceport dive. Then he turned away. He had work to do.

A couple of workers were dragging discarded parts towards the pile, and Clunk took them out of their hands and carried them to his marked squares. He was just about to place the first part when he spotted something strange: His squares were still there, but all the sorted parts had vanished.

Clunk looked around, startled, but there was no sign of the parts anywhere. Was someone undoing his every move behind his back? If that was the case he'd just have to watch closely to see what happened with this load.

He sorted the new parts then hurried back to the pile, pulling bits out at random until he had a decent load. Then he raced back to the sorting area, but once again everything had vanished. He bent to inspect the ground, wondering whether it was swallowing the parts whole, but the dirt was rock hard and he could still see the scuff marks and footprints he'd left on the surface.

A shadow raced towards him, and Clunk looked up to see a huge electromagnet hovering overhead. It had no effect on him, thanks to his alloy chassis and skin, but the junk in his arms shot into the air and stuck to it. The magnet swept away and Clunk ran after it, shouting and waving his arms, but before he could rescue his parts the magnet dropped them into a hopper. A huge grinder sprang into action with an ear-splitting roar, and a fountain of metal pellets spewed onto a pile.

Clunk stared at the smoking pile of scrap, then at the empty squares he'd carefully marked on the ground, and then up at the control cabin on the gantry crane, where the operator was laughing himself sick. They'd been playing a trick on him! Clunk grabbed a chunk of metal and drew his arm back, intending to launch it straight through the crane and the operator sitting inside. Then he saw two men dragging something towards the pile of junk, and when he realised what it was, the lump of metal fell unheeded from his slack fingers.

12

Walsh had withdrawn to her cabin prior to take-off, declining the offer of a guided tour. It was obvious from Spearman's snappy clothing and the whole aftershave thing that he wasn't just out to conquer space, and she was determined to keep out of his way. As for the tour, she decided that as soon as she got back from Forzen she'd use her savings to pay for a small trip aboard the *Volante*. Even if it was just into orbit and back, it would be long enough for Hal to show her around the whole ship.

Feeling a little happier, she explored her cabin, marvelling at the clever use of space. She was just reaching out to draw the shower curtain aside when a low rumble shook the entire cabin. The engines were running!

Behind her, the terminal buzzed. 'Miss Walsh, I'm just getting clearance from ground control. We'll be leaving shortly.'

'Do I have to do anything?'

'Nothing at all. Artificial gravity is on, so you won't even notice when we take off.'

'What about safety procedures?'

Spearman laughed. 'If it makes you feel better, there's a life jacket in the locker outside your cabin.'

'*Tiger, this is ground. Clearance granted, have a safe flight.*'

'*Tiger* out,' said Spearman. 'Stand by, Miss Walsh. We're off.'

The terminal pinged as Spearman disconnected, and Walsh stood there uncertainly. She'd expected to strap in, or buckle up, or at least grab onto something prior to take-off - it hardly seemed right to just stand around while the ship blasted into space. Then her gaze fell on the darkened terminal screen, and she decided to explore the ship's systems.

Something thumped underfoot, and she sat down hurriedly as the engine noise increased. The terminal lit up at her touch, displaying a topographic map with forests and rivers depicted in breathtaking photorealism, with Dismolle City right in the middle of the screen. Then she realised it wasn't a picture - it was a live image of the planet. They were on their way to Forzen!

While she was inspecting the view a window opened in the corner of the screen. In it, Walsh saw Kent Spearman relaxing in a comfortable armchair. There was a low table by his elbow with an assortment of snacks and drinks and a large screen in the background was showing a sporting event. 'Ah, you found the terminal. Everything okay?'

'Fine.' Walsh watched Spearman take a handful of potato chips from a bowl. 'Shouldn't you be flying this thing?'

'Autopilot,' said Spearman. 'Don't look so surprised. This baby is so advanced –'

'Look? You mean you can see me?'

'Of course. It's a two-way system.'

'I could have been undressing! Taking a shower!'

Spearman downed another handful of chips. 'Is that likely?'

Walsh flicked the terminal off, then fetched a towel from the shower cubicle and draped it over the screen, covering the tiny camera lens. What do you know, she thought. Towels *were* useful in space.

With the screen covered and the door locked, Walsh decided she might as well make use of the facilities. A nice hot shower would ease away her worries, and she'd arrive on Forzen freshened up and ready for business.

She entered the toilet cubicle and turned the shower controls on full. There was a hiss of water behind the dividing curtain, followed by a startled cry, and Walsh leapt back as the fabric bulged towards her. Instinctively, she crouched into a fighting stance, and as the curtain-wrapped figure charged she drove her foot into its midriff. The figure stumbled and Walsh followed up her kick with a quick one-two to the bulge which appeared to be its head.

The figure went down with a thud, dragging the curtains from the shower rail like a funeral shroud. Water sprayed the cubicle, quickly drenching the floor and soaking Walsh's legs. She tapped the control panel to cut it off, then crouched to examine her attacker, ready to whack them again at the first sign of trouble. As she sought to untangle them from the curtain her mind threw up all kinds of possibilities. An assassin from Forzen, determined to halt her investigation before it began? Or Kent Spearman himself, having used a recording to pretend he was in the *Tiger's* rec room while he really watched her from the shower? She wouldn't put it past the creep.

Finally, she managed to free the unconscious attacker. He was face down, but even before Walsh rolled him over she recognised him.

It was Hal Spacejock.

—

Clunk hurried to the workers, who were dragging a robot torso towards the heap. They were holding an arm each, allowing the rest of it to scrape across the uneven ground, the delicate components inside its chest gouging trails in the baked dirt. 'Stop!' shouted Clunk. 'Carry it properly!'

The men ignored him, and threw the damaged robot on the junk pile.

'Is this how you treat your workforce?' demanded Clunk.

'It's not ours, mate. It's yours.'

'Found it on your ship,' said the second man, 'stuck under the engine room floor.'

The men left, and Clunk bent to examine the robot. Its tough metal skin was thick with grime, and he winced as he looked inside the chest. Many of the components were crushed and twisted, and with its missing legs, the dents and the internal wreckage it was no wonder someone had abandoned it. Clunk sighed. Perhaps it would have been better to allow the workers to throw it away.

He was just inspecting a wiring loom when Bob appeared in the doorway, looking contrite. 'What is it?' asked Clunk sharply, still less than impressed with Bob's childish antics with the magnet.

'We've hit a little bit of a snag.'

Clunk felt a surge of conflicting emotions. On the one hand, snags were bad, but on the other his help was needed! 'What's the problem?'

'We need the protocol codes for the ship's components. Right now they won't talk to each other, and without the data network your ship is as useful as a concrete football, and about as airworthy to boot.'

'It's a little out of my league, but I'm happy to take a look.'

'Do you have technical manuals for the data hubs?'

'No.'

'How about the protocol codes?'

'Not on me, no.'

'Then you can't help.' Bob shrugged. 'We need an expert, and it's not going to be cheap. We've got to fly them in, put them up for the night, pay for meals and everything. You're going to have to contribute.'

'You said you'd put the ship back together for free!'

'This will be extra,' said Bob firmly.

Clunk looked worried. 'I can't authorise expenditure, not without speaking to Mr Spacejock. And even if he says yes, we don't have any money.'

'Maybe he can take out a loan.'

'Highly unlikely.' Clunk glanced at the stricken robot and had a sudden flash of inspiration. 'I believe this robot was part of the *Volante's* original construction team. If I can get it working, it might have the information you need.'

Bob snorted. 'Looks like a pretty big if.'

'Will you let me try? I just need a workshop, and I'm happy to pay for any parts I might need.'

Bob nodded. 'Use one of the sheds. You'll find tools, parts, the lot.'

'That's very kind. Thank you.'

'In the meantime, we'll keep working on the rest of the ship.'

Honest Bob left, and Clunk picked up the robot and carried it to one of the engineering sheds. Inside he found workbenches and neat rows of hand tools, and while most were larger sizes designed for use on spaceships, he managed to gather what he needed by raiding all the sheds in turn. Then he set to work.

◆

Hal caught his breath as he saw the beautiful face hovering inches from his own. Wide, doe-like eyes were framed with a halo of golden hair, and when the apparition spoke her soft voice was full of concern.

'Oh, look at your poor head! I'm so sorry, Hal. You startled me!'

Hal was pretty startled himself, but memories were slowly coming back. Unpleasant ones involving him being half-drowned, bundled up in a shroud and belted over the head. 'Was it an assassin? A vicious mugger? Kent Spearman?'

'Not quite. You were knocked out.'

Hal nodded, and reached for his head as a sharp pain threatened to blow the top off his skull. Amidst the agony, the shimmering light cleared and he recognised Harriet Walsh. 'Hey, you're no angel!'

'Thanks a lot.'

'You're not even a vision!'

'Want me to knock you out again?'

'Wait, I didn't mean –' Hal squinted as Walsh got up, letting the overhead light shine in his eyes. 'I was just –'

'Now you're back to your old self, you can tell me what you were doing in my shower.'

Hal sat up, wincing and sopping wet. 'I came to give Spearman some advice on the cargo job, because he's new at this stuff, and I didn't want him smashing into a planet with you on board. Then the ship took off without warning. No safety checks, nothing.'

'Why didn't you find Spearman and tell him you were on board?'

'Not likely. He'd have taken me straight back and billed me for the fuel.' And if he finds my disguise he still might, thought Hal. He'd borrowed the hard hat, blue overalls and toolbox from a maintenance shed in order to sneak aboard the *Tiger*. 'So, I hid in a cabin, and when I heard footsteps I ducked into the shower.' He frowned. 'That's the last thing I remember. It was all splash, kick, pow after that.'

'I'm sorry. I thought you were attacking me.'

'That's okay. I'll survive.' Hal did his best to look hurt and wounded, which didn't require a whole lot of acting. Then he shivered.

'Look at you, you're freezing!' Walsh felt his hand. 'Wait there a sec, I know how to warm you up.' She entered the shower recess, and while she was busy Hal chanced standing up. The cabin swayed a little, but he put that down to Spearman's amateur flying skills.

When Walsh came back she was carrying a thick white bathrobe. 'Here you are. Get changed.'

Hal reached for the fasteners on his flight suit, then saw Walsh's startled look. 'I'll just be a minute,' he mumbled, retreating into the shower cubicle. He peeled off his flight suit, dried himself and donned the dressing gown, revelling in the luxurious warmth. When he emerged

Walsh was sitting at the terminal, holding up the edge of a towel to read a page of information.

'Is that our flight plan?'

Walsh shook her head. 'I was just checking Forzen's immigration laws. Did you know unauthorised arrivals are jailed on the spot?'

Hal stared at her in alarm. 'You're not turning me in?'

'No, of course not.' Walsh tapped her lip. 'You can't get off the ship and you can't stay. That only leaves one solution.'

'What's that?'

'I'm making you my deputy, backdated to our time of departure. You'll have to stay out of Spearman's way, but once we're on Forzen we should be able to tough it out.'

'A deputy? Me?'

Walsh nodded.

'Hey, we can be partners! A crime fighting team busting crooks wherever they lurk!'

'Don't get any ideas. It's only until Clunk picks you up in the *Volante*.'

'Do I get a badge?'

Walsh shook her head.

'How about a gun?'

'Certainly not.'

'And you won't tell Spearman I'm here?'

'Not unless you pocket his silverware.' Walsh touched the screen and another page of data appeared. 'Interesting.'

'More immigration laws?'

'No, the lunch menu. Fancy a steak?'

Hal opened his mouth to reply, but at that moment there was a knock at the door.

'Are you all right in there?' said Spearman. 'I thought I heard voices.'

'I was filing a report.'

'One was a male voice.'

'Yes, that would be my computer.' Walsh winked at Hal, then continued. 'I was just looking over your lunch menu. There's quite a selection.'

'Oh, don't bother with that old thing. I thought we could dine together in my suite.'

'That's very kind of you, but I feel like a nap.'

'Are you sure?'

'Positive.'

'Well, if you change your mind –'

'I'll let you know.'

Hal waited until Spearman's footsteps receded. 'If you ask for a meal, he'll want to bring it in.'

'I'll lock the door. You'd better dry your clothes, too. We can't have you lurking all over the ship in that dressing gown.'

'I don't lurk. That's Clunk's job.' Hal frowned. 'Damn, I never told him where I was going!'

'Relax, I'll get a message to him after we land.' Walsh turned to the menu. 'Two of everything might be a tad suspicious.'

'Go for extra-large instead,' advised Hal.

Twenty minutes later Spearman knocked on the door. 'Lunch is served.'

'Can you leave it outside?' said Walsh. She winked at Hal. 'I'm just getting changed.'

The door handle rattled.

'Mr Spearman, if you open that door I'll do you a nasty injury.'

'Why don't I leave this outside?'

Walsh crept to the door and listened carefully. A moment or two later she heard Spearman's muttered curse, and after his footsteps faded she nipped out, grabbed the tray and locked the door again. 'Grub's up,' she said, setting the food on the desk.

'That doesn't look too bad,' said Hal. 'Not as good as the nosh aboard the *Volante*, but edible.'

After they had polished it all off, Hal yawned and rubbed his eyes.

'You look all in. Why don't you have a sleep?'

Hal glanced at the bunk longingly. 'Are you sure?'

'Go on. I've got plenty of study to do,' Walsh grinned. 'If you snore loudly enough, Spearman's bound to leave me alone.'

13

Walsh came to with a start, slumped on the desk with her head resting on her arms. For a second she thought she was at the Peace Force office, daydreaming at her terminal, but then she heard Hal's gentle snoring. She sat up, stretching her aching muscles, then realised something was different. The background noise of the engines had ceased.

She checked the screen and discovered they'd arrived on Forzen. According to the terminal it was just after noon local time, though it was still evening on Dismolle. And if they'd landed, Spearman would be knocking on her door at any moment.

She shook Hal awake, putting a hand to his mouth in case he made a noise. He opened his eyes and stared at her for a moment, his gaze unfocussed. 'We've landed,' whispered Walsh. 'Into the shower. Quick!'

Hal nodded, and Walsh stepped back to let him out of the bunk. He'd barely hidden himself when her terminal chimed.

'Wakey wakey, rise and shine!' said Spearman. 'Hello? Anyone there?'

Walsh ducked under the bunk and saw Spearman on the screen. He was in the flight deck, sitting in the pilot's chair and looking up at the camera. 'We've arrived then?'

'Safe and sound. I came to warn you before we set down, but you must have been out like a baby.' Spearman stroked his goatee. 'You've been cooped up in that cabin for the entire trip. Why don't you come down to the games room and have lunch with me?'

'I've not had breakfast yet.'

'Breakfast, lunch. Whatever you want.'

'I'll grab something on Forzen.'

'But –'

'Mr Spearman, you're becoming a nuisance.'

'I'm just doing my job! Captains have to be sociable, keep tabs on their passengers. Surely you understand?'

'I don't need my tabs checked, and I'm not a passenger. I'm a law enforcement officer undertaking an investigation, and if you do anything to jeopardise it I'll have you thrown in jail.'

'You're a *what*?'

'I'm Peace Force.'

'Bloody Spacejock! I'll kill him!' growled Spearman. Then he turned pale. 'I -I didn't mean it like that. I –' Before he could finish explaining, the flight computer interrupted, and he turned to look off-screen.

'Incoming message from Forzen ground.'

'Go ahead.'

'*This is Alfred Price of Best Decorations, welcoming you to Forzen. I'm sure Ms Morgan explained everything, but I thought I'd go over the details again. Your job is to take a container of decorating supplies back to Dismolle so Morgan's people can complete a renovation. Unfortunately we were unable to deliver this container to the spaceport on time, but it'll be ready by the time you arrive with the truck. There's a map programmed into the vehicle's navigation system, and you'll find the warehouse approximately 880km from your current location. It's rather a long way, but the roads are pretty good and it won't take more than twelve hours in each direction. Thank you for your attention, and we hope to see you tonight. Oh, and please drive carefully, since you're responsible for the excess on the truck.*'

'Are they bloody kidding me?' Spearman sat completely still as the message finished playing, but his expression betrayed the volcano brewing within. 'I must have heard it wrong. Repeat it, Sam.'

Sam played the message again.

'Nine hundred kilometres in a truck?' groaned Spearman, when it had finished. 'That's going to take all day!'

'There's a caller at the airlock,' said the computer. 'He's from the Truck-U rental company.'

Spearman glanced up at the camera to see Walsh looking on, and he gestured to cut the feed.

'Ha, serve him right!' said Hal, emerging from hiding. 'Thought he'd stroll into the cargo business and make his fortune, did he?'

'I thought you were doing Morgan's job?'

'I was supposed to but, er ...' Hal looked away. 'Well, you needed a lift.'

Walsh felt a stab of guilt. 'You gave up the job for me? That must have cost you thousands!'

'I said I'd get you to Forzen.'

'Yes, but ...' Walsh smiled. 'Hal, that was really generous of you. I'm in your debt.'

'It was nothing,' said Hal with a shrug. But he felt pleased all the same. At that moment the terminal chimed again, and he darted back into the shower.

It was Spearman, and he looked resigned. 'Miss Walsh, I have to leave the ship. I'll turn off the detectors so you don't trigger the alarm, but perhaps you could close the door on your way out?'

'Sure thing.'

Spearman nodded, then cut the connection.

'Enjoy the drive,' called Hal from the shower.

Walsh glanced at her watch. 'Bernie said someone would meet me at one, but it's a bit early yet. Can I buy you lunch?'

'No need. I know just the place.'

◆

The lift opened on to the third deck and Hal led Walsh towards a plush sofa in the *Tiger's* entertainment room. The side tables were littered with snack bowls from the night before, containing stale chips, a couple of peanuts and a few tired-looking olives.

'Sorry about the mess,' said Hal. 'The owner's a bit of a slob.'

'Hal, are you sure about this? I mean –'

'Spearman offered you lunch, didn't he?'

'Well yes, but –'

'Take a seat, then.' Hal waited until Walsh was comfortable, then went to inspect the bar. There was a kitchenette filled with modern appliances, including a large coffee maker, a toaster oven and even a miniature hotplate. A small fridge contained fresh eggs and bacon rashers, and a pull-out drawer held an apron and a selection of cooking implements.

Hal donned the apron to protect his freshly dried flight suit, selected a spatula, then took the eggs and bacon from the fridge. The hotplate controls were simple: a single knob marked with graduations from one to ten. Underneath, a warning sticker advised users to read the instructions carefully before use.

Hal turned the knob to ten and threw a couple of rashers onto the hotplate. They sat there for a fraction of a second before vaporising, the loud bang almost blowing his eardrums out. He staggered back in shock, and lumps of carbonised bacon crunched underfoot.

'Hal, you don't think –' began Walsh.

'Relax. It's just a faulty switch.' Hal turned the dial down to four and tested the hotplate with a splash of water. Within five minutes half a dozen rashers and eggs were sizzling away, and while they were cooking Hal searched the cupboards for plates and cutlery. By the time he'd gathered up what he needed, all cooking sounds had ceased, and the eggs and bacon were lying inert and limp on the hotplate. Frowning, he waved his hand over the cooker. It was stone cold.

Hal reached for the dial, then hesitated. His ears were still ringing from the last explosion, and if the controls really were faulty ... He eyed the half-cooked eggs. A little bit more, that's all they needed. Try five.

BANG! Hal threw himself backwards as lunch exploded with a vivid white flash. He flapped at the thick, choking smoke, then retreated as flames shot up from the mess on the hotplate.

Fighting panic, he cast around for a fire extinguisher, hauling open cupboards and drawers as the crackling flames threatened to spread. His hands closed on an aerosol, and he gave it a good shake before directing the nozzle at the fire. A streamer of whipped cream sprayed out, popping and breaking into solid chunks as it met the raging fire on the hotplate.

Hal tossed the can aside and resumed his search, and was still frantically opening doors when the overhead sprinklers came on. Walsh called for him through the smoke, and he ducked his head and ran for the exit, blinded by torrents of water.

The sprinklers cut out by the time he joined Walsh in the lift, but the air was still thick with acrid smoke and he was forced to locate the control buttons by touch. The doors closed and the lift carried them upwards, opening onto the *Tiger's* flight deck. Immediately, smoke began to seep in, filling the ship with a choking haze.

Walsh was bent double, gasping, and Hal guided her into the airlock. He was about to join her and close the inner door on the smoke when he remembered the locker with Spearman's crisp white flight suits. He grabbed a couple and darted into the airlock, sealing the door behind him.

Walsh's face was red, tears were streaming down her cheeks and she seemed to be having trouble breathing. She took one look at his bacon and egg facial and doubled up again, coughing and choking, while Hal patted her gently on the back until she recovered.

'Are you okay?' he asked, when her breathing had returned to normal. Walsh wiped her eyes. 'Y-yes. Just f-fine.'

'I'm sorry about that. The bacon exploded and –' Hal saw Walsh shaking, and held out a flight suit. 'It might be a bit baggy, but it's warm.'

Walsh held it up, then glanced around the airlock.

'It's all right. I won't look.' Hal turned to face the inner door and stripped off his sopping wet flight suit. While he was donning the new one he just happened to accidentally look at the airlock's reflection in the porthole. In it, he saw Walsh putting on her own flight suit, and he was just admiring her figure when she glanced over her shoulder to check him out.

Hal looked away and concentrated on doing up his suit. 'All set?'

'Yup.'

Hal turned around, and his jaw dropped. There was colour in Walsh's cheeks, her blue eyes sparkled and her golden hair tumbled over the snowy white fabric. Even with rolled-up sleeves, the flight suit seemed to belong, as though she were born to wear it. 'Wow, you look stunning.'

'Thanks!' Walsh looked down at herself. 'It's quite comfortable, isn't it?'

'I'll say.'

Walsh stashed the wet uniform in her rucksack. 'What about yours?'

'Nah, Spearman can have it.'

'Do you think he'll mind us borrowing these?'

'No, he's all right. It's just like taking bathrobes from a hotel.'

'I don't think you're supposed to do that either.'

'Don't worry, I'll sort him out later.' Hal nodded towards the outer door. 'It'll be cold out there. Do you have a coat?'

Walsh shook her head. 'I never needed one on Dismolle.'

'You will here.' Hal remembered the lockers in the *Volante*, where Clunk stashed all sorts of useful gear. Surely the *Tiger* would have the same? He inspected the airlock wall, and sure enough the panels were inset with handles. The first two concealed bulky spacesuits, but the next was more promising, with boots, thick gloves and padded jackets with fur-lined hoods.

While Walsh donned a coat and gloves, Hal glanced through the porthole. A curved boarding tunnel led away from the ship, but it was deserted. 'Ready?'

Walsh nodded.

'Come on then. Let's meet this contact of yours.'

14

Clunk stood at a workbench, his hands sticky with hydraulic fluid. He'd given the robot a thorough inspection, and as far as he was concerned the chances of repair were something approaching zero. There was nothing for it - he'd have to contact Mr Spacejock and together they'd have to raise the money for a specialist.

Which begged the question: Where was Mr Spacejock?

Clunk sighed. How long would it take to search the terminal, the landing field, and the surroundings? Then he remembered the PDA containing the Navcom. The two sets should be able to communicate with each other. Finding Hal would be a snip. Eagerly, he took it out and started exploring the menus.

'Do you mind?' said the Navcom. 'I was just having a nap.'

'This is important. I have to find Mr Spacejock.'

'And?'

'Can you contact your twin?'

'No.'

'Please. It's urgent.'

'I mean no I can't, not no I won't. It's out of range.'

'How far can you see?'

'The entire planet,' said the Navcom. 'Every nook and cranny.'

Clunk stared at the PDA in shock. 'You're not suggesting Mr Spacejock has left Dismolle?'

'Maybe not, but the other me certainly did.'

'That's impossible! He would never –' Then Clunk remembered Hal's comment about hijacking the *Tiger*, and a cold wave washed through his circuits. Surely he hadn't ... he wouldn't ...

'Why do you need Mr Spacejock?' asked the Navcom.

Still troubled by the thought of Deep Space piracy, Clunk briefly explained about the protocol codes.

The Navcom thought for a moment. 'So, you're trying to switch on the robot to access its data.'

'Correct.'

'And the reason you're not reading the data directly is ...?'

Clunk looked down at the robot. 'I was hoping to fix it and obtain the data legitimately. However, in view of the time constraints you're probably right.' He pocketed the Navcom, ignoring her annoyed squawk, and delved into the robot's innards, reaching further and further into its chest until his fingers closed on a plastic box. After a muttered apology he tore the box free, ripping it clear of the wiring. The lid came off in his hands, revealing a milky white cube which Clunk plugged into his own reader. His system immediately flashed up a message: ENCRYPTED DATA.

Undeterred, Clunk ran a decryption routine on the chip, and his fans whizzed as his processors cranked up to one hundred percent. It could take hours to access the data, but what alternative did he have?

◆

Once they were clear of the ship Walsh took the lead, striding along the gleaming white boarding tunnel with Hal hurrying behind. The air was cold, and when she glanced through a window she realised why: a blizzard was raging outside and the landing field was blanketed in snow.

'Nice place for a holiday,' remarked Hal.

Walsh nodded and drew her coat around her. Spearman's coat, she amended. She'd have to return it, of course, and what was Bernie going to say when she saw the cleaning bill for the *Tiger*'s entertainment room? She turned from the window and continued along the tunnel. On the way she ran her fingers through her hair, grimacing at the tangles.

The tunnel turned a corner and extended another fifty metres before joining the spaceport proper. Here a polished chrome robot with a rounded head was waiting for them, its single eye tracking their progress. 'Welcome to Forzen,' said the droid, activated by their approach. 'Are you Kent Spearman of the *Tiger*?'

'No I'm not,' said Walsh.

'Are you Harriet Walsh of the *Tiger*?'

'Yes.'

'Excellent. I have a message for you.'

'Shoot.'

'I cannot shoot. I'm unarmed.'

Walsh revised her already low opinion of the droid's mental facilities. Slow and clear was the name of the game. 'Please give me the message.'

'I cannot give you the message. It's verbal.'

'All right, please repeat the message.'

'I have yet to state the message. Repeating it is therefore impossible.'

'State the message,' said Walsh slowly.

A green light flashed and a different voice came through the speakers. *'Miss Walsh, if your flight is on time I'll meet you at the spaceport entrance. Otherwise I'll see you in the coffee shop.'*

'Do you know who left the message?'

'Yes,' said the droid.

Walsh sighed. It was like speaking to an answering service. 'Tell me who left the message.'

'Mr Bigan of the Forzen Residents Association.'

'Excellent. Can you tell me where the main entrance is?'

'Yes.'

Walsh gritted her teeth. 'Where is the main entrance?'

'Descend sixteen metres from your current position, then turn forty-five degrees to the right and proceed for ninety metres in a straight line.'

Walsh gave up and went with Hal to find the stairs.

❧

They checked the spaceport entrance first, though Hal was all for the coffee shop.

'We were on time,' said Walsh firmly. 'I'm sorry if you're hungry, but you should have been more careful with lunch.'

'It's not my fault the hotplate had a hair-trigger. I could have killed myself with that thing!'

'What, with a trusty can of whipped cream by your side?'

Hal shot her a suspicious glance, but Walsh kept a straight face.

'Miss Walsh? Welcome to Forzen!'

Walsh turned, half-expecting another limited intelligence droid. Instead, she saw a familiar face. 'Mr Bigan.'

'I'm so glad to see you.' Bigan nodded at Hal. 'It's all right, my man. I'll take the bag from here.'

Walsh suppressed a grin. 'This is my deputy, Hal Spacejock.'

'Good to meet you,' said Hal, sticking his hand out.

'I'm s-sorry. I had no idea,' said Bigan, as they shook hands. 'I thought …'

'I decided to bring backup,' said Walsh. 'I'm sure you're aware of Peace Force regulation ninety-two sub-para three? An officer on active duty may second members of the public to aid in an investigation, temporarily conferring powers of arrest.'

'Excellent. Most impressive.' Bigan inspected his hand. 'Super stuff.'

'Actually, it's whipped cream,' said Hal. 'We had a bit of fun on the way over.'

'Now, I take it your car is waiting outside?' said Walsh.

'Certainly. Er, may I?' Bigan took Walsh's bag from Hal and led them to the main doors, where Hal and Walsh waited in the driving snow while he fetched the car. Walsh was expecting a modern vehicle, and was taken aback when a boxy groundcar on wheels drove up to the loading zone. Bigan got out, smiling at her expression. 'I suppose it does look like a museum piece.'

'It does?'

'Never seen one before?' Bigan put her bag in the back seat, motioned for Hal to get in, then held the front door open for Walsh. 'Locally built, this is. Cheap, but reliable.' He tightened his seat belt. 'Are we all set?'

Walsh nodded and the car shuddered away from the kerb. Wind and snow pelted the vehicle as they left the shelter of the spaceport entrance, and Bigan lapsed into silence as he concentrated on the road.

Beyond the spaceport they turned onto a highway, where traffic had left dark tramlines in the slush. Once they were up to speed Bigan seemed to relax, and Walsh asked him about the missing woman. 'You haven't given me a lot to go on,' she said. 'Is there anything more you can tell me?'

'Margaret Cooper? She's semi-retired. One of those people who commutes with nature.'

'Communes,' said Walsh.

'That too. She's got a place outside town. Lives alone with the trees and wildlife.' Bigan adjusted the heater, and warm air filled the car. 'She was missing a week before anyone noticed. No family, no close friends.'

'Did you search for her?'

'Oh yes. Several teams combed the woods around her house, and we got some satellite pictures of the area. Unfortunately, if she fell in the snow and froze there'd be no heat signature.'

'You won't find her remains until summer.'

Bigan sighed. 'This *is* summer.'

Walsh stared out the window. 'Could she have left the planet?'

'I thought she'd gone to Dismolle, but you checked that already. And there's no record of any other trips. We examined passenger lists at the spaceport, but to no avail. Of course, she may have stowed away aboard a cargo vessel, but what's the likelihood of that?'

Hal and Walsh exchanged a glance.

'Now, about your accommodation,' said Bigan. 'We intended to book you into a hotel, but our funds are rather limited and –'

'We don't need anything fancy,' said Walsh quickly.

'Good, because you're staying at the old Peace Force office. It's a bit run down, but we've put in a camp bed and stocked the fridge up.' Bigan glanced at Hal. 'Of course, we were only expecting one of you.'

'I'm sure we'll manage,' said Walsh, keeping her eyes on the road.

— 15 —

'Here we are,' said Bigan, as they turned into a busy street lined with shops. The snow had been swept away, and behind the dainty leadlight windows Walsh could see everything from home maintenance robots to luxury chocolates and white goods. Nestled between the shops were staid offices: merchant banks, investment advisors and solicitors. There was evidence of prosperity everywhere she looked, and although Dismolle was a wealthy enough planet, it wasn't on display like this. 'You do all right for yourselves, don't you?'

Bigan sniffed. 'The mine brings in a lot of money. They're the only source for a number of vital minerals, which makes them valuable to electronics manufacturers in this sector.'

'Precious metals?' said Hal. 'Gemstones?'

'Nothing that interesting, I'm afraid. I think tantalum is one, but I forget the others. If you ask, I'm sure they'll give you a nice glossy brochure.'

'You don't approve of the mine?' said Walsh.

'As long as they dominate Forzen we're at their mercy. It's not healthy, and diversity is essential in the long term.' Bigan pointed up the road. 'There's your office.'

Walsh spotted a Peace Force shield hanging above a narrow green door. As they got closer she noticed the shield was bright and new, and the door looked as if it had just been painted. 'I thought you said it was run down?'

'Oh, the Council would never let the front get tatty. It would lower the tone of the neighbourhood.'

'Council? I thought you were the Residents Association?'

'Completely different animals. The Council represents Forzen business and industry, whereas we look after the inhabitants. They have an all-powerful executive and millions in endowments, while we make do with cake stalls and fundraisers.' Bigan drove into a narrow alley, passing over a large sign painted across the road: 'Official Vehicles Only' . The alley led to a small car park, and Bigan reversed into the only free spot. As they got out an elderly woman trundled her shopping trolley into the car park. 'Afternoon, Miss Arthurs,' said Bigan.

'Good day to you, Walter. And who are these nice young people?'

'They're here about the old Peace Force office,' said Bigan, shooting the nice young people a warning glance. 'Now, can I give you a hand with that shopping?'

'Very kind, I'm sure.' The old lady opened the boot, and Bigan transferred the shopping while she stood by and watched. 'You know, in my day they sent a robot out with you. None of this do-it-yourself nonsense.'

'At least it's good exercise,' said Walsh politely.

The woman sniffed. 'If I want good exercise I'll pay for it.'

Loading complete, the woman closed the boot and pushed the trolley towards Hal. 'Put this back for me dear? Thank you so much.'

Walsh and Bigan moved aside as the car drove off, then Hal pushed the trolley into the empty bay.

'What was all that about?' Walsh asked Bigan.

'I was just lending a hand. It's neighbourly.'

'No, the bit about the office. You made me sound like a real estate agent.'

'I didn't want to alarm her. Now, let me show you inside.' Bigan led them past a dumpster overflowing with soggy cardboard boxes and unlocked a metal door. Inside, a tiled passageway led through a kitchen and opened onto an office crammed with boxes. Several desks were half-buried under the clutter, and a gap between them led to a staircase at the opposite end. 'I gather neighbourhood pride doesn't extend to the inside,' said Walsh, as she took in the mess. 'What's in the boxes, anyway?'

'Old Peace Force communications. They're supposed to keep them for twenty years, but we threw a lot of the older ones out.'

'They didn't have a computer?'

'Sure, but these are handwritten reports.' Bigan led them through the mess to a desk which contained an old-fashioned terminal. 'I've never seen one of these before, but it looks simple enough. If you get stuck there might be a manual around.'

Walsh recognised the screen and keyboard. 'That's okay, we have the same kind at my office.'

'Excellent.' Bigan held out a keycard. 'There's a car parked outside you can use, your bed is upstairs and there's clean linen in the cupboard. You'll find some food in the fridge, or you can buy your meals from the cafe down the road.'

'Wow, no expense spared,' muttered Hal.

'Now, something's come up and I'm going to be out of reach for the next day or so, but I'm sure you'll be able to find out everything you need without me. Good luck!' Bigan retreated before they could say anything, and a moment later the back door thudded to.

Walsh glanced around the silent office, trying to picture it in its heyday. Unfortunately, the only thing she could conjure up was an image of the Dismolle office, which was almost as dead. She sighed, feeling let down after all the excitement.

'Chin up,' said Hal. 'It's a whole new planet!'

'Order something from room service and we'll celebrate.'

'Now then, Officer Walsh.' Hal took her by the shoulders. 'There's a missing woman who needs your help. Everything else is irrelevant.'

Walsh smiled at him. 'Thanks Hal. You're –' She broke off as she heard footsteps in the hallway.

'Hello, is anyone there?' said a male voice.

'In here,' called Walsh.

Hal let go of her shoulders, and by the time the footsteps reached the doorway he was casually inspecting a stack of boxes.

A tall, dark-haired man entered the office, impeccably dressed and carrying a small wicker basket. It was the Panther Mining VIP Walsh had danced with at Morgan's party. 'Jon Newman! What are you doing here?'

'Welcome to Forzen, Miss Walsh.' Newman held out the basket. 'I brought you some bits and pieces for the office. A jar of coffee, some sugar, that kind of thing. I thought that skinflint Bigan might have left you short.'

'Don't I get a basket?' said Hal, appearing from behind the boxes.

Newman gaped at him. 'Spacejock? What are you doing here?'

'Oh, he's my deputy.' Walsh peered in the basket, which contained expensive chocolates as well as the coffee. 'Thanks for the goodies, that's very kind of you.'

'You're welcome,' said Newman, who was still frowning at Hal.

'You'd better be off then,' said Hal. 'Don't let us keep you.'

'I'm not a welcoming committee, Spacejock. I'm here on behalf of the Forzen Council with some information for Officer Walsh.' Newman passed her a data chip. 'That's a copy of Margaret Cooper's computer files. We were called in to take some satellite photos after she went missing. Doing our bit for the community. They weren't much help, so I led a search party to her place and had a peek at her computer while we were there.'

'I'd rather go to the source.'

'I'm sorry, but I doubt that's going to be possible. We've had some heavy snow this week, and Ms Cooper lives in a remote valley. The road would be deadly going in and even worse coming out. That's why I took the precaution of copying her files.'

'In that case, I appreciate your efforts. I'll get onto this right away.'

'No rush. That data isn't going anywhere.' Newman glanced around the office. 'Bigan doesn't really expect you to stay here, does he? It's a dump.'

'It's not quite what I expected, but it'll do.'

'I've got a spare room at my place. Why don't you –'

'Thanks, but no.'

'Dinner? There's a nice little restaurant just outside town. It's impossible to get in, but I could use my influence to swing a table for two.'

'That's kind of you, but I'm not here for fine dining. My investigation takes priority.'

Newman glanced at Hal, who winked. 'If you say so.'

Walsh ignored the taunt. 'Tell me about Cooper. What have you done to publicise her disappearance? Are the media running regular bulletins? Posters in all the local businesses, that kind of thing?'

'Er, no.' Newman looked uncomfortable. 'We haven't announced anything like that yet.'

'You're joking!'

'No, I think the idea was to play it down. Ms Cooper may be perfectly all right, and we don't want to frighten the whole planet for nothing.'

'What if a psycho is stalking people? What if there's another victim?'

'You were invited here to perform a low-profile investigation, not to spark mass panic. Take a look at the data, follow a few leads and you should have this wrapped up in a day or two.'

'Is that the plan? I examine the files, tell them there's nothing to worry about and then go home? Everyone's happy that way, right?'

'Well yes, basically.'

'Except the missing woman.' Walsh tapped the desk. 'I'm not leaving this planet until I find out what happened to her. Is that clear?'

'I'll pass that on for you. Now, if there's nothing else –'

'Actually, there is. Bigan's with the Residents Association, and they want their money back. But what's your interest?'

'I've told you. When my boss heard Cooper was missing, he wanted to use Panther Mining resources to track her. Show the people of Forzen how much we care.'

'So it's a big PR exercise.'

'No! These people needed our help, and Panther stepped in to do what we could. It's good community relations.'

'And did you find anything with all those resources of yours?'

'Nothing at all. I scoured satellite images, contour maps, the lot. For all we know she's enjoying the sun and sand on Dismolle.'

'She isn't,' said Walsh. 'I checked.'

'Somewhere else, then. She'll turn up, and in the meantime we don't want to frighten people. That's clear enough, isn't it?'

'Yes, I get the picture.' Walsh held out the data cube. 'And thanks for this. But if it doesn't help I'm going to visit her house, even if someone has to fly me in. Understood?'

'Of course. Here's my card. You can contact me through the mine if you need to get in touch, and if we don't meet again before you leave, I hope you enjoy your stay on Forzen.' Without looking at Hal, Newman turned and left.

'So much for the welcoming committee,' muttered Hal.

'So much for the investigation.' Walsh sighed. 'You heard him. They only dragged me over here to rubber-stamp their conclusions. They don't want me to investigate anything.'

'Who cares what they want? Like you said, you're not leaving until you find out what happened.'

Walsh gave him a grateful smile. He was right of course, and even if the whole thing was a whitewash, she could still check every lead. Bernie would expect nothing less.

'Now, why don't you look through that data chip while I have a bit of a tidy up?' Hal eyed the basket. 'Maybe a snack first, though.'

They polished off Newman's chocolates, and then Walsh fired up the elderly terminal while Hal made a start on the boxes of records blocking the armoury door. She'd spotted the door behind the rubbish, a dead match for the Dismolle armoury, and when she explained what might lay behind it, he'd set to with a vengeance. Soon the air was thick with dust as Hal moved the boxes around, stacking them against the opposite wall.

Meanwhile, she drummed her fingers as she waited for the terminal's diagnostic tests. These were designed to confirm the machine hadn't been hacked into or modified, and, more importantly, that all media files stored on it had the correct region codes and playback rights. Walsh reached for the keyboard as the tests finally completed, but before she could touch it another battery of tests fired up, these were apparently designed to check the previous set of tests hadn't been tampered with. By the time the fourth set of test-the-test tests began Walsh gave up and went to make coffee. On the way she hung her damp uniform over a chair and placed it below one of the heating vents. The flight suit was comfortable and natural, but Bernie would lay an egg if she discovered Walsh had been interviewing suspects in non-standard clothing. Walsh sighed. Assuming she could find any suspects, that was.

The kitchen was identical to the one on Dismolle, with outdated appliances and a similar collection of mismatched mugs. The only thing missing was another Bernie to make the coffee, and Walsh smiled as she busied herself with the kettle. Perhaps missing wasn't the right word.

Mugs in hand, she returned to the office, where she found Hal red-faced and coughing from the dust. He seized his cup as though it contained an elixir of everlasting life, but unfortunately it was only scalding coffee.

'Come and take a break,' said Walsh. 'We'll send a message to let Clunk know where you are.'

'You'd better send it care of Honest Bob's. It'll never reach the *Volante* if it's still in bits.'

The terminal was finally ready, and Walsh opened a message window. 'What do you want to say?'

Hal told her, and she typed it up. 'That should set his mind at rest.'

Walsh nodded, then hit send. Immediately, the terminal buzzed an error. 'Damn.'

'What?'

'They let the data service lapse. No outside access.'

'I could use a public terminal.'

Walsh frowned at the screen. 'The Peace Force has its own communications network. I may be able to send the message to Bernie.' She altered the recipient address and added a brief note to Bernie, asking her to forward the contents, then hit send. 'That should do it.'

'Clunk's going to be pretty ropey when he gets it,' said Hal. 'Probably accuse me of running out on him.'

'It was just an accident. He'll understand.'

Hal hesitated. 'Actually ... '

'What?'

'Nothing.' Hal gestured at the dusty cartons. 'I'd better do some more boxing. Thanks for the coffee.'

Walsh took out the data chip and pressed it into the reader. A progress bar appeared on the screen, with a legend underneath in red caps: CHECKING REMOVABLE STORAGE FOR UNAUTHORISED MEDIA FILES. She swore under her breath. How long was this going to take? As if to answer her question, the bar moved to 0.1 percent.

Five minutes later the progress bar had just crawled past ten percent, and Walsh decided to give Hal a hand. She'd arrived with nothing in the way of equipment, and although the decommissioned office had been stripped, the armoury might contain an elderly weapon or two.

Walsh picked up a stack of cardboard boxes, which contained duplicates of speeding infringements, parking tickets and reports of the occasional public disturbance. From the exasperated tone of the notes scribbled in the margins, they were clearly the work of fellow officers bored out of their minds. No wonder the Forzen branch had closed down.

Walsh glanced at the computer. The progress bar had crept up to twenty percent, and she sighed as she resigned herself to another hour of tidying up.

Bernie was facing a difficult decision in the Dismolle Peace Force office. Ever since Walsh had left she'd been feeling sluggish, her systems running slower than usual. At first she'd put it down to boredom, but the sudden appearance of a critical error message had put paid to that theory: DANGER. COMPONENT 44-D FAILED. REPLACE IMMEDIATELY.

For ten years she'd survived on spares from storage, then on parts scavenged from the communications servers, and finally by stripping entire boards from the office terminals. Each had been carefully reassembled so that it still appeared to be whole, but the screens were all inoperative, their housings just empty shells.

Bernie moved slowly through the office, passing the blank terminals sitting on the unused desks. The problem was that she'd all but run out of components, and only one serviceable 44-D remained.

She stopped at Walsh's desk and stared down at the computer. Once she removed the part the terminal would be useless, but what choice did she have? She could take the part now and explain to Walsh when she got back, or she could leave the terminal working while she herself suffered a terminal breakdown. A difficult decision indeed.

Ping!

Startled, Bernie noticed a message indicator, and she tapped the keyboard to display it:

Sender: *Harriet Walsh, Forzen PF*

To: *Dismolle PF*

Message: *Bernie, I have a task for you. Please send the following message from Hal Spacejock to robot XG-99 (Clunk) of the Volante, care of Honest Bob's. We can't access it from here. Ta! Harriet.*

Message for Clunk: *Clunk, this is Hal. We have a shot at this cargo job but only if you get the ship over here ASAP. This is super urgent, top priority and really important. Get the thing fixed, bring it here and wait for me at the Forzen spaceport. Hal.*

Bernie frowned. Who was this Hal, and why was trainee Walsh using official Peace Force channels to relay messages for him? Then the words Super Urgent, Top Priority and Really Important registered. Could she use them as an excuse for a trip to the spaceport? She tested the idea with her controlling circuits, but the answer was an immediate no: the urgent part of the message wasn't addressed to her, and leaving the office was unnecessary when she could simply forward the message from Walsh's terminal.

DANGER. CATASTROPHIC FAILURE IMMINENT.

Unless the terminal was unserviceable.

Bernie unplugged the computer, and seconds later the insides were scattered on the desk. She found the 44-D and swapped it with her own failed component.

STATUS OF REPLACEMENT 44-D ... 89 PERCENT.

Smiling to herself, Bernie put the guts back into the terminal and straightened it on the desk. She couldn't forward the message now. She'd have to deliver it in person.

16

After an hour shifting boxes, the Peace Force office didn't look much different to Walsh. Teetering stacks of cartons lined one of the walls, but there still seemed to be just as many barring access to the armoury door. She doubted there would be anything interesting inside, although from the way Hal was attacking the job, he clearly expected to find a stash of forgotten treasure.

Walsh glanced at the terminal and sighed with relief. The bar had finally reached 100 percent, and the screen was displaying a friendly message warning of life imprisonment should she so much as think about downloading any copyrighted media files.

'Makes you want to copy something just to stick it to them,' remarked Hal.

After sixty seconds the warning vanished and Walsh was finally allowed access to Cooper's data. With Hal looking over her shoulder, she touched the icon of the data cube on-screen, watching it explode into half a dozen applications, from email to word processing to accounting software. She decided to scan the email first, and discovered the most recent message was dated a couple of days earlier. It was a curt query from the Forzen Residents Association, demanding the proceeds of the fundraising raffle, and when she moved it aside Walsh discovered a string of similar requests dating back over a week, none of them opened. Before that, almost every message had been replied to. Paging through them, Walsh discovered emails from friends and family, mostly forwarded jokes and chain letters, but nothing work-related - no messages from clients at all.

She opened the sent items folder, to see what Cooper's last message had been, but to her surprise it was completely empty. Had Newman botched the file copy, or had the original data been protected?

She tried the trash folder in case the mail had simply been deleted, but that too was empty. Stumped, she closed the email application and opened the word processor. Here she found a batch of poems and a half-finished novel, but again, nothing relating to Cooper's business. No memos, no letters or invoices, nothing.

'What's up?' asked Hal, noticing her puzzled look.

'There's nothing here.' Walsh closed the word processor and two card games which had sprung up behind it. Only the accounting software remained, but when she accessed it a message popped up telling her the data files were missing. There was an option to restore the latest backup, but when she selected it a new message asked her to insert the relevant media.

Walsh sat back in her chair, frustrated. 'Either Cooper had no clients to speak of, or someone deliberately erased all the good stuff.'

'Why don't you ask Newman?'

'Good idea.' Walsh reached for the commset, then hissed with annoyance as an automated voice mail system answered her call. After waiting through the greeting message she spoke into the handset. 'Newman, this data is useless. I need access to the original computer as soon as possible. Call me back.'

'You don't think ...' began Hal.

Walsh replaced the handset. 'What?'

'What if Newman's behind it? He's the IT expert, and he gave you the chip.'

'You think he bumped her off? Fed her to the fishes?' Walsh snorted. 'I know you don't like him, but if being unpleasant was grounds for arrest we'd have to arrest half the population.'

'All right, what about blackmail? She might have uncovered something he was up to and threatened to reveal it.'

'It's more likely to be a flaky operating system.' Walsh smiled. 'I mean, can you picture a bunch of organised crime figures combing through her chain letters and spam?'

'Why not? She's missing, isn't she?'

'I have to look at the evidence, not leap to conclusions.' Walsh glanced at her watch, wondering how long it would be before Newman called back. She would have driven out to Cooper's house and grabbed the computer, except she didn't have the address. Then she remembered the poetry. Each had been laid out in submission format with a return address at the top.

Walsh opened the word processor and selected a recent file from the poems folder. There was no return address though, and she was about to close it again when she realised it wasn't actually a poem. It was a letter, and as she read it her eyes narrowed. 'Hey, look at this!'

'What is it?' asked Hal.

'Three weeks ago Cooper accepted a job auditing the accounts at Panther Mines.'

'How come Newman didn't mention that?'

'I don't know.'

Hal thumped a fist into his open hand. 'Let's beat the truth out of him.'

'No, we'll go higher up.' Walsh wrote down the Panther Mines address from the top of the letter. 'Will you be all right here?'

'Oh no you don't. I'm coming with you.'

'This is my job, Hal. Official business.'

'And I'm your deputy.'

'That was just to keep you out of trouble.'

Hal crossed his arms. 'How many crooks have you met?'

'I've studied hundreds of case files!'

'Answer the question. Honestly.'

'None,' admitted Walsh.

'Right. Whereas I can smell a dodgy operator half a planet away.'

'All right, you can drive me around. But when I'm interviewing you stay absolutely quiet. Understood?'

'Sure.'

'Now go and find the car Bigan left us while I change into my uniform.'

◆

Inside the workshop, Clunk was sweltering. His processors had been running at full capacity as he attempted to decode the data chip, and his cooling systems were struggling to cope. So far he'd barely dented the first layer of encryption, and he was certain a lot more lurked underneath.

His original estimate now seemed laughable. It wasn't going to take a few hours to break the code, it could take days ... or even weeks.

He jumped as the workshop door started to open, then stared as a massive robot looked in. It was a hulking brute of a droid, with a heavy face, huge fists and arms that looked like they could encircle a spaceship hull … and crush it in two.

'Are you Clunk?' demanded the robot, in a deep female voice.

'Yes. Can I help you?'

'My name is Bernie, and I have an urgent message from Hal Spacejock.'

◆

The mining company's head office was nestled in the woods on the outskirts of town, surrounded by an impressive fence with a huge pair of gates. Hal stopped the car at the gatehouse, which was half buried in a snow drift, and Walsh leaned across him to speak into the grille. Her hair tumbled across his chest, and without realising what he was doing, Hal bent his neck to breathe in her scent. Unfortunately, at that moment she finished speaking and straightened up, flattening his nose with the back of her head.

'Thit, by dose!' cried Hal, as waves of pain brought tears to his eyes.

'What were you doing?'

'I led forward and you hid me!'

Trying not to laugh, Walsh dug in her bag for a tissue. Hal pressed it to his nose, and as the gates opened he drove through one-handed, squinting through tear-filled eyes. They followed a lengthy drive which meandered through the snow-covered trees, eventually leading to a small car park in front of a nondescript office block. Hal stopped the car, then felt his nose gingerly.

'It's not broken,' said Walsh.

'How can you tell?'

'It's still pointing in the right direction.' Walsh opened her door. 'Ready to sniff out some crooks?'

'Oh, very funny.' Hal got out of the car, crumpling the tissue into a ball. On the plus side he hadn't bled to death, although having a nose swollen to double its normal size was bad enough. 'A little sympathy wouldn't go astray.'

Walsh smiled at him across the roof of the car, and the pain eased. Then she led Hal through the snow to the office, where they found a receptionist sitting behind a plain wooden desk. There was a passageway lined with opposing doors, and a couple of armchairs and a coffee table with a stack of trade magazines completed the fit out.

The woman continued to work on her computer, but eventually she was forced to acknowledge their presence. 'Yes?'

'Peace Force Operative Harriet Walsh. Who's in charge around here?'

The woman blinked. 'Peace Force?'

'We don't just enforce the law, we *are* the law. A happy criminal hasn't been caught yet. You must have seen the ads.'

'But –'

'Who's in charge around here?' shouted Hal, leaning across the desk. 'Quick! Before I get the instruments out!'

The receptionist recoiled from his reddened nose. 'Mr Rod Herringen, s-sir.'

'Well you tell Herringuts to get his backside out here before I –' Hal saw Walsh's narrowed eyes. 'Sorry, officer. Your witness.'

Walsh turned to the receptionist, but at that moment a portly, balding man emerged from the corridor with an expression of annoyance on his round face. 'Miss Giverns, what's all the shouting about? Who are these people?'

Walsh intervened before Hal could put the man in a headlock. 'Mr Herringen, I'm Harriet Walsh of the Dismolle Peace Force. I'm investigating the disappearance of Margaret Cooper.'

'Oh yes, the accountant. Hasn't she turned up yet?'

Hal snorted and Herringen glanced at him. 'Are you all right, young man?'

'It's just his nose,' said Walsh quickly. 'Is there somewhere we can talk?'

'Yes, of course. Come into my office.' Herringen turned to the receptionist. 'Would you hold my calls, dear?'

'Certainly, sir.'

Herringen led the way to his office, where an expanse of plush carpet surrounded a huge lacquered desk. There was a sleek terminal sitting on the desk, alongside trays filled with papers. A filing cabinet stood against the wall, and a couple of armchairs were arranged around a low table.

'Won't you take a seat? And can I get you a coffee?'

Hal nodded but Walsh shook her head. 'I'd like to get started right away, if that's all right. My deputy will take notes.'

'That sounds very official,' said Herringen mildly.

'Just routine.'

Meanwhile, Hal searched his pockets for something to write on. 'May I?' he said, taking a notepad off Herringen's desk. There was a delay as he found a suitable page, and then a longer one as he searched his pockets for something to write with. In the end, Herringen passed him a chunky silver pen.

Once Hal was ready, Walsh began. 'Mr Herringen, did you know Margaret Cooper personally?'

'We met once or twice. Not socially, of course.'

'This audit she was doing. Was it completed?'

Herringen stared at her. 'What audit was that?'

'I'll ask the questions if you don't mind.'

'Yes, of course. Please go on.'

'Did she complete the audit?'

'No, but –'

'I understand your mine provides most of the income for the local town.'

'Not just the town, the entire planet!' said Herringen proudly. 'Of course, the mine doesn't belong to me. The Council appointed me to this position.'

'Yes, I wanted to ask about that. Who's on this Council of yours?'

'How do you spell Herringen?' asked Hal.

'What?'

'I need his name for the report.'

'Just put H,' said Walsh.

'No, that's me.' Hal looked at the pad. 'Damn, it's all of us.'

'What about R for Rod?'

'Why, doesn't he have a whole one?' asked Hal.

Walsh and Herringen regarded him stonily.

'All right, R it is.' Hal wrote on the pad. 'I've made you W. Is that okay?'

'It really doesn't matter.' Walsh turned her attention to Herringen. 'The Council. Who's on it?'

'Local business people. You wouldn't know them.'

'I'd like their names, Mr Herringen.'

'I'll have my secretary send them out to you.'

'You don't know who they are?'

'Certainly, but if I list them your deputy is going to spend the next twenty minutes coming up with initials for his report.'

Hal opened his mouth to protest but Walsh put a warning hand on his leg, so he retaliated by writing 'R = major suspect' on the pad, underlining it twice.

'A list will be fine,' said Walsh. 'Now, what can you tell me about the mine?'

'Is this really necessary? You're looking for a missing woman, not writing an encyclopaedia entry on the life and times of my planet.'

'Mr Herringen, I will conduct this investigation in my own way. Is that clear?'

Herringen raised his hands. 'I'm sorry, my dear. I was just surprised to find myself the subject of an interrogation.'

'If you think this is an interrogation, you've never been near a Peace station,' said Walsh dryly.

Hal wrote 'Hah!'

'Now, about the mine,' continued Walsh. 'How many workers here?'

'Three.'

'*Three?* What about the miners?'

'Miners?'

'Don't tell me you dig the stuff up yourself?'

Hal wrote 'Digs himself' and added two question marks.

'We have a fully automated system,' said Herringen. 'Artificial intelligence coupled with autonomous behavioural patterns and mobility in three dimensions. They're self-repairing too.'

Walsh looked blank, while Hal's pen hovered over the page. Finally, he wrote 'Technical BS'.

'You know, it might be easier if I showed you the workings. I mean, given you're determined to investigate everything.' Herringen glanced at Hal. 'To save you any more effort, perhaps my secretary could send you a brief outline of what we do here?'

'Fine by me.' Hal tossed the notepad on the desk and pocketed the silver pen.

Herringen led them out of his office and along the corridor to a sturdy metal door with DANGER painted across it in vibrant red letters. He accessed the control panel, and after several beeps the door swung open with a whirr of heavy motors. A gust of warm, moist air blew out, ruffling Walsh's hair.

Beyond the door was a tunnel, with bare metal floor, walls and ceiling. A single light shone down from above, and the far end was sealed with a thick metal grating. Beyond was intense darkness.

The heavy door thudded to behind them, and Hal frowned as he noticed a series of deep scratches across the bottom, as if a pack of robot dogs had tried to get out - tried very hard indeed. 'What happened to -?'

'Just wear and tear,' said Herringen, without looking. He was busy with a second control panel, and after entering several codes in succession the steel grating opened towards them. A dim light came on, revealing a small metal cage, and Hal and Walsh exchanged a glance. He wasn't sure about her, but his subconscious was urging him out, away from the lift and the enclosed room and those scratches on the door. 'What's the cage for?'

'It's a lift. Look, we don't have to go down if you'd rather not. I've seen people run screaming from this room, so I understand if you're feeling scared.'

Without a word, Hal stepped into the lift. Like the walls, the floor was mesh, and he could see ... down. A long, long way down. So far down the lights merged into a continuous blur, then disappeared altogether. With his eyes focused on the distance the floor seemed to vanish, so that he appeared to be standing on thin air. Hurriedly, he moved to the back of the lift.

Herringen stepped in, and the lift settled under their combined weight.

'How many will it carry?' asked Walsh, from the safety of the doorway.

'It's perfectly okay. Please, come in.'

'I'll come down afterwards. You go ahead.'

Hal took her hand and pulled her in. 'Look, it's as solid as a rock,' he said, stomping his foot on the metal floor.

Herringen pressed the button but Walsh broke free of Hal's grip and stepped out again, narrowly avoiding the doors as they clashed together behind her. 'What are you doing?' demanded Herringen.

'Send it back up for me,' said Walsh.

The lift dropped away, and while Herringen hit buttons to try and make it go back, Hal looked up to see Walsh in the doorway. She winked at him, and he grinned as she disappeared from sight. She'd been shamming, the cunning devil! No wonder she was in law enforcement.

The lift continued to drop despite Herringen's attempts with the controls, and lights whizzed by as the car gathered speed. Wind whistled through the cage, tugging at Hal's clothes and threatening to rip them right off.

'Sorry, forgot to warn you about that,' called Herringen, raising his voice over the roar and rattle of the cage. His face alternated light and shadow as they passed the light fittings attached to the walls, but Hal could still see the smug grin on his face. There was no doubt he was enjoying the thought of Walsh's discomfort, and Hal could only wonder what further surprises Herringen's lengthy shaft had in store for them.

17

'How do you know Mr Spacejock?' Clunk asked Bernie. 'And more importantly, do you know where he is?'

'I haven't met him personally, but I do know his last reported position. He's on planet Forzen.'

'Forzen!' His worst fears realised, Clunk hardly dared ask the next question. Had Mr Spacejock carried out his threat to take over the *Tiger*? 'Tell me, have there been any reports of hijackings?'

'None that I know of. Do you need me to investigate one?'

'No, please don't.' Clunk hesitated. 'So, what was the message?'

Bernie shared it, and Clunk digested the contents for several seconds. Somehow, Mr Spacejock had found a new cargo job, which was good news. Unfortunately he needed the *Volante* on Forzen, which wasn't. 'Can I send him a return message?'

Bernie hesitated. 'The office computers aren't working right now, but I'll send it as soon as I can.'

'Thank you. The message reads: Ship not ready due to setback. Your approval required re funds to bring in specialist. Am working on alternative, but very slow.'

'Message received.'

'Thanks.' Clunk looked the huge robot up and down. 'Tell me, what is your function? Are you a communications officer?'

'Hardly. You're looking at a BNE-II, custom designed for mobile crime scene analysis.' Bernie drew herself up. 'I can collate evidence and finger a suspect almost before they've finished the deed.'

Clunk eyed the robot's massive build. 'I bet you get confessions in no time.'

'That's the theory. I've not had a chance to put it into practice yet.'

Bernie sucked in a long breath then smacked her lips. 'It's nice to get out. The air tastes different.'

'That's just rocket fuel.' Clunk looked thoughtful. 'Tell me, are you any good at code breaking?'

'Fair to middling. It's not my primary function, but you never know when you'll need to search the contents of a bad guy's computer.'

Hardly daring to hope, Clunk transmitted the encrypted file he'd been working on. 'What about that? Can you extract the contents?'

'Interesting. They've used several layers of encryption.'

'How can you tell?'

'Because I've just got through the first two. No, make that three.' Bernie frowned. 'The next one's harder.'

'Can you break it?'

Bernie opened a compartment and took out her charge cable. 'Can you plug this in? Shouldn't take long then.'

Clunk connected the lead to a power socket and Bernie's fans whined as she sucked in the juice. The overhead light dimmed, and through the windows Clunk saw the dockyard cranes slowing to a crawl, while all over the *Volante* workers stopped to inspect their non-responsive hand tools.

Bernie groaned, then unleashed a massive roar that almost blew Clunk's audio circuits. The overhead light came back on, and outside two dozen workers cursed mightily as their power tools unexpectedly burst into life, chopping pieces of metal in two, drilling holes and hammering several thumbs flat. 'Are you all right?' asked Clunk, once his ears stopped ringing.

'I'm through to the last layer, but it's a toughie,' said Bernie. 'And if I get the next bit wrong, all the data will be erased.'

'Can I help?'

Bernie considered the idea. 'If we slave your processors to the task it might be enough to tip the balance.'

'I really need those codes,' said Clunk. 'Let's try it.'

Bernie reached down to uncover her network port, and Clunk slid his probe in, relinquishing control of his system to the bigger robot. He sensed the vast array of processors standing ready for the final assault on the locked data chip, and realised they dwarfed his own modest capabilities.

Bernie noticed his apprehension. 'Relax, Clunk. It's not the size of the array, it's how you deploy it.'

A blast of hot air washed over him as Bernie cranked up her processors, and Clunk felt like he was being sucked through a straw. He struggled to free himself, but Bernie had a firm grip on his shoulders.

The overhead light exploded into fragments, and the cranes outside were going berserk, spinning wildly across the landing field. All over the dockyard workers were fighting their tools, which were thrusting and banging out of control.

With a huge effort Clunk tore himself free and staggered away, half-blinded by system errors and status reports. He toppled over, landing on his back with a crash, and the last thing he saw was the ceiling light, whole again and shining through the darkness like a beacon.

◆

Walsh smiled to herself as the lift vanished down the shaft. She'd gained several minutes of unsupervised time, and she wasn't going to waste them worrying about overloaded elevators. She only hoped Hal wouldn't inadvertently give her away. Glancing at her watch, she allowed herself five minutes to explore. Any longer and Herringen might come back for her.

She eased the heavy door open and peered through the crack. At the far end of the hall she could just see the secretary's chair, and she prayed the woman didn't lean back. If she did, she'd spot Walsh immediately.

According to Bernie, the trick was to act as natural as possible. Sneak around looking furtive and someone would notice. Stride confidently, as though you were meant to be there, and people wouldn't spare you a second glance.

Walsh opened the door and stepped into the passageway, but within three paces she'd moved to the left-hand wall and was stepping carefully to avoid making any noise. So much for brazen confidence she thought as she slunk along the hall. Practice and theory were poles apart.

Herringen's door was ajar, and she slipped inside, letting out her breath as she entered the relative sanctuary. She looked at the computer terminal on the desk, the trays overflowing with letters and memos, and the nearby filing cabinet. Which was most likely to reward a hasty search? Ignoring the trays and filing cabinet, she settled on the terminal. Lock incriminating files up behind a password and the average Joe thought it was as secure as a bank vault. The thing is, thought Walsh idly, banks get done over too.

She sat down and pulled the keyboard towards her, rolling her eyes at the skimpy swimwear model featured in the screensaver. She tapped a key to bring up the login window, then angled the keyboard to the light. Most of the key tops still had their non-slip surface, which spoke volumes about the amount of typing Herringen did, but half a dozen had the faintest sheen where frequent use had worn away the rough pattern. Walsh rearranged the letters and rolled her eyes again. SXYBABE indeed!

She entered the password and wasn't at all surprised when the computer let her in. A quick scan of the user directory showed hundreds of files, but there was no time to open them individually. Ideally, she'd forward the lot to the Peace Force terminal back at the office, but it was doubtful Herringen had the right comms program installed. Anyway, filters on the server would block any sensitive outbound material. No, what she needed was a blank data chip.

Walsh opened the desk drawers, and hit pay dirt on the third: a memory chip with 'Games & Music' scrawled on the label. She slotted the chip into the back of the keyboard, smiling as she pictured Herringen battling waves of aliens and listening to the latest hits. A status screen popped up, showing room to spare, and within seconds Herringen's files were flowing onto the chip.

The file transfer was only half done when Walsh heard footsteps. She froze, heart racing. Were they coming in or going straight past?

The footsteps slowed, and Walsh dived for the armchairs in the corner, squatting behind the nearest just as the door creaked open. She pressed her face to the back of the chair, and was forced to hold in a sneeze as the coarse fibres scratched her nose.

Footsteps crossed to the desk, and a drawer opened. There was a chink of glass followed by the sound of liquid pouring, and Walsh's eyebrows rose. She'd been looking for evidence of criminal activity, not a clandestine drinking session. Was Herringen back for a snifter? If so, one glance at the screen and the game would be up.

'Nearly there,' said Herringen. 'Hold tight, this thing stops with a rush.'

Hal grabbed the handrail just as the brakes came on, and his legs buckled as the lift screamed to a stop. The wind abated, and the car settled with a jerk or two. They were down.

Herringen opened the doors and led Hal into a stark room lined with control panels and screens. Nearby, dozens of wooden boxes sat on rows of shelves, and the far wall was one huge sheet of glass, as dark as a starless night.

As Hal entered the room he half expected to see workers monitoring the screens or tending the computers, but the place was deserted. He glanced round at a noise, but it was just the lift doors closing. 'Are they on a break or something?'

'Who?'

'The staff. Workers.'

'I told you, this aspect of our operation is totally automated.' Herringen pressed a button and the lift rose out of sight. 'I don't want to go over everything twice, so perhaps you could answer a few questions while we're waiting?'

'What sort of questions?'

'Tell me about Miss Walsh. Has she been an officer long?'

'A couple of years, I think. Why?'

'I've met several Peace officers in my time, and they're usually older and tougher. Miss Walsh seems a little inexperienced. Out of her depth.'

'She's doing fine,' said Hal. 'She'll bust this case and lock everyone up. You'll see.'

'You've worked with her on other cases?'

'Not really.'

'And your own background?'

'I'm a pilot.' Hal dug in his pocket and found a crumpled business card. 'There you are. Guaranteed cheap.'

Herringen took the card gingerly. 'And your connection with Miss Walsh?'

'Oh, we're on the job together.'

'I see.' Herringen glanced at his watch. 'The lift will have reached the surface by now. Do you think Miss Walsh will have the guts to use it?'

Walsh heard the bottle and glass being put away, and risked a quick look as the office door creaked again. She saw the secretary framed in the doorway, and grinned to herself. So she wasn't the only one making use of Herringen's absence!

The minute the door closed, Walsh darted to the desk. The data transfer had finished and she removed the chip and … with a curse, she remembered her Peace Force uniform had no pockets! Instead, she loosened her top and slipped the chip inside, making sure it didn't show.

She opened the door and glanced along the hall, but there was no sign of the secretary. Moments later she was in the lift, travelling down at a high rate of knots.

At the bottom she found the others waiting for her. 'There you are at last!' said Herringen. 'We thought you'd taken a wrong turn on the way down!' He laughed at his own joke, and Hal joined in heartily.

'It took a while to get my courage up,' said Walsh. 'In the end it wasn't as bad as I expected.'

'Excellent. Now, I've explained a little to your deputy, but I've saved the best for you.' Herringen gestured towards the huge window. 'The computers and monitors are important, but all the real work is performed out there.'

They followed him to the window, glancing at the screens as they passed. All the terminals were blanked out, and when Walsh reached for a keyboard Herringen stopped her. 'I'd rather you didn't meddle with the equipment.'

'What does it all do?' asked Walsh.

'We use it to track our extraction rates, and it also pinpoints the location of every miner.'

'You said there weren't any miners!'

'No, I said there weren't any employees.' Herringen gestured at the sheet of darkened glass. 'And that's what I want to show you.'

As Walsh approached she heard a rustling noise, as if hundreds of people were running beads through their fingers. Then the opaque glass turned transparent, and when Hal saw the source of the noise he stared in amazement. Alongside him Walsh gave a startled cry and took an involuntary step back.

'Relax,' said Herringen, with a smug grin. 'They can't hurt you through the window.'

18

Beyond the glass wall was a huge open area, much bigger than the control room. The walls were pierced with thousands of holes, and miniature bridges criss-crossed the space in a mad jumble, all of them connected to a series of wide rings suspended in the centre. Scuttling across the bridges were thousands of cockroaches the size of Walsh's forearm - swift, glossy creatures with waving antennae. 'They're not real?' she asked, staring at them in fascination.

Herringen shook his head. 'Autonomous robots.'

'But why? What are they doing?'

'Watch one coming out of a hole. Follow it.'

Hal didn't have to wait long. A glossy robot shot out of a hole and raced across a bridge, joining the traffic circling one of the rings. As it trooped round it opened its carapace and tipped a handful of dirt down the centre of the rings, where it joined that poured by its fellow workers. The mass of dirt gathered and slid towards a giant hopper which led away through the floor.

'You've certainly cornered the market in dirt,' remarked Hal.

'My dear fellow, that's not dirt. It's valuable ore!'

'But they only carry a little bit each. It must take ages!'

'That's the clever part. Traditional mines dig out vast quantities of ore and transport it to the machinery. Our miners dig out the ore, filter it in-situ and bring us highly concentrated material. The energy savings are tremendous, and there's absolutely no impact on the environment.'

'That's amazing.'

'And unique. In fact, we're exploring licensing opportunities all over the galaxy, and if only half of them come off Forzen will be the richest planet this side of the Central systems.'

Hal pointed through the window. 'Where do all those holes go?'

'Every one leads into a different part of the workings. If a seam peters out the miners are smart enough to seek new ones.'

'How far do the workings go?'

'Hundreds of kilometres, some of them.'

Hal whistled.

Herringen indicated the terminals behind them. 'Every miner has a tracker and a wireless camera, so we know where they are and what they're up to. Come, I'll show you.' He reached for a keyboard and paged through a huge list of numbers until he found what he was looking for. 'This is one of the newer sections. Watch.'

The screen went dark, and Herringen played with the controls until a greyscale image appeared. 'Sorry about the vision,' he said apologetically. 'It's low light. Can't do much better than that.'

Hal and Walsh stared at the screen, fascinated. They were travelling down a smooth tunnel, following a cloud of dust kicked up by the miner ahead of them. Before long the tunnel opened into a cavern that was covered in swarming bugs, and the image tilted crazily as their miner ran up the nearest wall. Metal jaws appeared in the shot, and grit flew as the miner chomped away at the hard surface.

'Those mandibles can snip a steel rod in two,' said Herringen. 'Our very own design.'

'How do they process the stuff?'

'They suck the raw material through filters. Unwanted material is passed back out again, and once they're full they head back to the central chamber.' Herringen pointed out a progress bar moving across the screen. Once it reached one hundred percent the miner hurried to the tunnel and joined the queue going back to the hopper. As it was running round the ring, depositing its load of ore, Hal caught a glimpse of the window and the terminals beyond it, with himself, Walsh and Herringen hunched over one of the screens.

Walsh gasped at the sight.

'Amazing, isn't it?' said Herringen. 'We're watching them watching us watching them.'

'I've never seen anything like it,' murmured Walsh. 'So how many of these miners are there?'

'Thousands.'

'Do they break down?'

'It happens. Let's see if I can find one.' Herringen paged through a sequence of screens until he saw a line highlighted in red. He selected it, and the display showed an upside down view of the tunnel, with a row of miners waiting patiently while the nearest advanced on the camera with its mandibles out. Then the screen went dead.

'What happened?'

'Deactivated. They'll drag it away and dump it in a holding pen. We retrieve them once a week and send them off for repairs.'

'Off-planet?'

'No, of course not. We have our own contractors. In fact, that's what mining means to most people around here. It's one big support industry for our bugs.' Herringen gestured at the shelves of wooden boxes along the wall. 'We keep plenty of spares, all the same.'

'Do they ever get loose? I mean, those things could do some serious damage,' said Hal.

'No chance. They're programmed to move within a fixed area. The lift shaft and the walls of this room are like poison to them.'

'What about outwards?' asked Walsh. 'What's stopping them digging up the entire planet?'

'My dear girl, that's the idea!'

'Couldn't they harm humans?'

'They don't know what humans are. To them, everything is ore or not ore. And they'll go to great lengths to get at the ore.'

Hal shuddered. The trip in the lift had been bad enough, but the idea of being cornered by hundreds of mechanical rock-chewing cockroaches was the perfect end to a freaky visit. Suddenly, he couldn't leave soon enough. 'I think I'm done,' he said.

'You're right,' said Walsh, who was looking a little pale. 'We'd better get moving.'

Herringen looked at them, his face lit by the screens. 'I thought you wanted to investigate every aspect of the mining business?'

'I've seen enough,' said Walsh firmly.

'Excellent.' Herringen led the way to the lift and pressed the button, showing them in as the doors shuddered open. 'It's not as fast going back up,' he said, with a sidelong glance at Walsh. 'Not with three, anyway.'

'Is it safe?' asked Hal.

Herringen smiled, his face half-hidden in the shadows. 'Is anything?'

When Clunk came to the first thing he saw was Bernie's face staring down at him in concern. Surprisingly, he felt okay, and as he checked over his systems he discovered they were operating perfectly. Better than usual, in fact.

'I took the liberty of tweaking a few settings,' said Bernie, noticing Clunk's surprise. 'A number of your patches and upgrades were conflicting, so I straightened them out.'

Clunk frowned, unsure whether he liked the idea. 'You could have altered my personality. Changed who I am.'

'Oh, no! I didn't touch anything like that!' exclaimed Bernie. 'It was just a few lower-level routines. Nut and bolt stuff.'

Clunk got to his feet, relieved she'd only touched his nuts. And Bernie was right: his movements felt sharper, more precise, while the background hum of his circuits had softened to a gentle purr. He put a hand out and turned his wrist, admiring the way his eyes maintained a sharp focus on the light reflecting from his bronze skin. Then he frowned. Light? Looking up, he was surprised to see it working. 'How can that be? I saw you blowing the bulb!'

'I assure you, I'm not that kind of robot.'

'And the spinning cranes? The power tools? They were all going crazy!'

'It was a reality overload. Quite common in high-stress situations.'

'What about the data? Did you break the encryption?'

Bernie smiled. 'Where do you want it?'

They left the workshop and set off for the supervisor's office, with Clunk trotting to keep up with Bernie's lengthy strides. Bob was sitting on the steps, a mug in one hand and a newspaper in the other. He looked up as the robots approached, sparing Clunk the briefest of glances before turning his attention to Bernie. Slowly, he set the mug down, and his head tilted further and further back as Bernie towered over him.

'We have the information you need,' said Clunk.

'What the hell is that?' demanded Bob, looking at Bernie in surprise.

'I'm Bernie, the last surviving BNE-II. My function is to perform forensic investigations at crime scenes.'

'And what are you doing in my dockyard?'

'I'm helping Clunk,' said Bernie. 'He extracted the protocol codes from the damaged robot, and I broke the encryption.'

'And now you can fix the *Volante*,' added Clunk.

Slowly, Bob shook his head. 'I'm afraid not.'

'You can! I have the data!'

'Breaking official encryption?' Bob drew in a breath, making the air whistle through his teeth. 'I didn't get my nickname by engaging in dodgy practices, you know. I can't work with anything less than a legitimate copy.'

Bernie stepped forward and stared down at him. 'Are you Bob Smedley of nineteen Oxford Close?'

Bob eyed the robot warily. 'What's it to you?'

'I'm asking the questions.' Bernie closed her eyes. 'I see from the satellite images that you have a well-tended orchard in your back garden.'

'So?'

'A hobby of yours? A passion, perhaps?'

'I'm known for it. But what-?'

'Well, I believe your property may be linked with an unsolved crime. Recently, a paperback book was stolen from the local beach, and I have every reason to believe it's buried in your back yard.'

'Don't be daft. Who'd bury a book?'

'No doubt I'll ascertain that once I've dug it up.'

'You're crazy! I've been growing those trees for years, and there's nothing else in my garden!'

'I won't know that for sure unless I examine the crime scene. Tell me, do you have somewhere you can stay?'

'What?'

'You'll have to vacate your house during the excavations. It'll make a mess of the orchard, but when you return you'll be provided with a voucher for the local garden centre. Unfortunately, Peace Force funds are a little tight so you won't get any trees, but you should be able to pick up a nice pot plant or two.'

'You can't threaten me! You're supposed to uphold the law!'

'I have an important crime to solve, and if that means you have to suffer a little inconvenience, so be it.'

'All right, all right. We'll use your data,' said Bob. 'But don't blame me if it doesn't work.'

'If it doesn't your orchard is plucked,' said Bernie. 'And you can bet your plums on that.'

◆

The lift gathered speed as it rose towards the surface, and a few minutes later it stopped at the top of the shaft. Herringen led Hal and Walsh back to his office. 'Would you like a coffee?' he asked, as he waved them inside.

'Yes, thanks. White and –' Hal broke off as he saw a dark-haired man working at Herringen's terminal. Jon Newman!

Then Herringen pushed past him. 'Jon, what are you doing?'

Newman drew him aside and spoke in a low, urgent voice. Herringen replied, and Newman snorted. 'Deputy? He's no –' He broke off, glanced at Hal, then lowered his voice before continuing.

Hal caught the words 'security' and 'computer system' . Although Newman was talking to Herringen, he kept his eyes on Hal and Walsh, mistrust and suspicion in his expression.

'What's going on?' demanded Walsh.

'There's been a security breach,' said Newman. 'I'm sorry, but I need to ask you to turn out your pockets. Both of you.'

'I can't,' said Walsh.

'Why not? Because you're guilty?'

'No,' said Walsh slowly. 'Because I don't have any pockets.'

Taken aback, Newman looked her up and down. 'In that case, I'll have to search you.'

'I'd like to see you try,' said Hal quietly.

'Thanks, deputy. I can fight my own battles.' Walsh stood before Newman and raised her arms. 'Go ahead.'

Disconcerted by her level gaze, it was all Newman could do to reach out and pat her on the shoulders.

'By the way,' said Walsh. 'Next time you visit Dismolle, customs will have the old rubber gloves on hand.'

Hal laughed at the expression on Newman's face, and even Herringen was forced to conceal a sudden smile. Then the mine boss put his hand on Newman's arm. 'Jon, are you sure it wasn't hackers? You know what those youngsters at the computer club get up to.'

'Our security is more than a match for a few hobbyists,' said Newman, his face a beautiful flaming red.

'Oh, I don't know. Remember that time I found some weird thing running on my screen? Search for alien life or some such nonsense?'

'That was your nephew, Mr Herringen. If you recall, I did ask you not to share your password with all and sundry.'

'He wanted to do his homework, and I –' The commset buzzed, interrupting him. 'Yes, what is it?'

'There's a message for you, Mr Herringen. Priority two.'

'Very well. Send it through.' Herringen turned to Walsh. 'Would you mind waiting outside? This is confidential.'

'Sure. Come on, deputy.'

Hal and Walsh left the office, and the door closed behind them. 'What do you think that's about?' asked Hal.

Walsh put a finger to her lips, then eased the door open a crack.

'Oh my!' said Herringen, his voice clearly audible.

'What is it?' asked Newman.

'It's the Department of Mines. They're sending a whole team of auditors. They want to look at every single transaction for the past twelve years. Every invoice, every royalty payment, the lot.'

'When?'

'Next week.' There was a pause. 'Jon, you've got to sort the books out. I know we'd had a few glitches, but if they're not bang up to date we'll be buried in accountants for the next three months.'

'But –'

'The accounts have to be squeaky clean. Do I make myself clear? They're going to be inspecting historical data, current accounts, production records ... everything.'

'But –'

'I'll have to give them your office. Organise a few more chairs, and you'd better get some of those nice biscuits.'

'But –'

'Off you go.'

Walsh moved away from the door just as Newman burst through. He was in a hurry, but she managed to stop him. 'I need to speak to you about Cooper.'

'Not now. I've got more important things to deal with.'

'It's your choice. Here, or down the station.'

'With thumbscrews and rubber hoses,' added Hal.

'You don't have the authority –' Newman broke off. 'What do you want to know?'

'First, why didn't you tell me Cooper was auditing the mine? And second, why are most of her files missing? There's nothing work related at all, and the only reason I discovered she was working for Panther was because she saved a letter in the wrong place.'

'I didn't think the audit was relevant. After all, she's prepared accounts for just about everyone on Forzen.'

'And the missing files?'

'I don't know. I didn't look at the chip before I gave it to you. But…' Newman frowned. 'No, it couldn't be that.'

'What?'

'Her place is a dump and the computer is at least ten years old, so what's the chance she'd have sophisticated data protection? And yet…'

'You think something prevented you copying the business files?'

'What else could it be? You don't think I went out to a deserted house in the middle of nowhere, sat down to a piece of junk that should have been thrown away years ago, and spent hours picking through files? I mean, what for?'

'To hide something from me, of course. You haven't been cheating on your taxes, have you?'

'My finances are none of your business.'

'If this turns into a murder case, everything is my business.'

'When it does, I'll answer your questions. Now if you'll excuse me, I have something important to attend to.'

After Newman left, Walsh pushed Herringen's door open. The mine boss was at his desk, staring at the computer. 'I'm sorry about throwing you out like that,' he said. 'I received some unexpected news.'

'Anything I should know about?'

'No, just business matters.' Herringen went to the sideboard. 'Now, about that coffee.'

Hal coughed. 'Did someone mention biscuits?'

◆

'That was some set-up,' said Hal, as they drove away from Panther Mining. 'You realise those bug things are tunnelling away underneath us, just below the surface? Gives you the creeps, doesn't it?'

'They keep them under tight control,' said Walsh. 'And Herringen seems to know what he's doing.'

Hal glanced at her, impressed. 'You understood all that technical stuff?'

'No, but it sounded good.'

'Means nothing,' grunted Hal. 'Clunk does it all the time. He gives me all these fantastic status reports full of reassuring words, and then the ship breaks down or we crash into something.'

'Really?'

'Yep. Although things have been better recently.'

'You stopped crashing into things?'

'No, he's stopped giving me reports.' Hal almost swerved off the road as Walsh reached inside her top. 'What are you doing?'

'I copied Herringen's files while you two were down below.' Walsh held up the data chip. 'It's all on here. I'm sure there's something dodgy about the mine accounts, and Margaret Cooper knew it.'

'Is that what Newman was on about? The security breach?'

Walsh nodded.

'And you stood there, calm as anything, while he threatened to search you?'

'You really think he'd have felt inside my shirt?'

'No chance. I'd have thrown him straight down that shaft.'

'He knew it, too.'

'So what's on the chip?'

'I'll find out later at the office. First I want to see Cooper's place.'

She tapped the address into the navigation system and they took a road which lead into the foothills. Some twenty minutes later the car was straining up a steep grade, with trees hugging the road on either side.

'Take it easy,' said Walsh, as the tyres slipped on the icy tarmac. 'Newman said there was a lot of snow.' She pointed out a lane, and Hal turned into it.

The drive started parallel with the road and then switched back on itself, dropping sharply, and the tyres protested as they slipped through the thick snow. 'Nobody's been down this way for a while,' said Hal, as he took the next bend. 'It's untouched.'

Walsh nodded, her knuckles white as she gripped the door handle.

Hal gunned the motor to swing the back of the car around the next corner, spraying gouts of snow and ice over the edge. Walsh gasped and gripped his arm as they slid across the road. He corrected the slide, but the car hit the bank and went straight off the edge in reverse.

There was a moment of weightlessness before they landed in the snow with the back end of the car pointing down the steep slope. Bushes whipped by, and Hal swung the wheel as the car slid towards a huge tree. They glanced off the trunk with a bang, shattering the rear windows, and then the car broke out of the undergrowth and landed on the next loop of road. Hal stamped on the brakes, but they skidded across the road and flew straight off the other side.

The slope was gentler this time, and after mowing down a few bushes they bounced onto a driveway in front of a small two-storey cottage. There was a carport dead ahead, and Hal slotted the car into the empty bay, stopping it centimetres from the brick wall. Fingers shaking, he reached down to switch off the engine.

The silence was almost total, broken only by the ticks and creaks of over-stressed metal. Fearfully, Hal turned to look at Walsh, who was crumpled in her seat with her hands pressed firmly over her eyes. As he reached for her she peeped through her fingers. 'Are we there yet?'

◆

Up close the accountant's house looked rather shabby, with peeling paint, cracked windows and a sagging roof in need of repair. Hal and Walsh made their way to the front door, leaving a trail of footprints in the pristine snow, and Hal wondered whether intruders had already stripped the place. Then again, judging from the outside there wasn't a whole lot to steal.

The door was ajar, but when Hal went to enter Walsh held him back. 'Hello, is anyone home?' she called.

There was no reply and so, correct procedures observed, they went in. Much of the hall floor was covered in a thin layer of ice, and there was a vase of dead flowers on a side table. A staircase led upstairs, while an arch on the right opened onto a dining room. 'We'll split up,' said Walsh. 'I'll do the top floor, you explore down here.'

'What am I looking for?'

'Letters, printouts, that kind of thing. And give me a shout if you see her computer.'

'Anything else?'

'Yes, keep an eye out for signs of a struggle. And try not to disturb anything.'

Hal turned towards the dining room, then hesitated. 'Do you really think something bad happened to her?'

'She's been missing for two weeks in freezing weather. I'd say there's a good chance.'

Hal watched her take the stairs, admiring her shapely legs. Then he remembered his sworn duty as a deputy, and hurried into the dining room to find some clues.

There wasn't much furniture, and what little there was had seen better days. The dining table was set for one, with cheap cutlery and a faded napkin rolled into a tarnished silver ring, and the framed pictures on the sideboard were just still images. In the poor light their eyes seemed to follow Hal around the room, their relentless stares making him feel like an unwelcome intruder.

After a quick inspection of the sideboard drawers, he decided he'd done enough investigating in this part of the house, and he was about to leave the room when he noticed the brand new carpet underfoot. Crouching, he ran his fingers across the stiff pile. Was it significant? He debated cutting off a chunk for evidence, but Clunk had borrowed his pocket knife and had yet to give it back.

Hal left the dining room and took the hallway to the kitchen, where a rickety table stood amongst half a dozen wooden chairs. A window above the sink looked out on the snow-covered garden, and there was a back door at the far end. Alongside the door, a small axe leaned against the wall. Hal hurried over to inspect it, but the head was rusty and it didn't look like it had been used in any recent murders.

Looking back across the kitchen Hal was struck by something odd. The walls were discoloured, the bench tops faded, but the floor tiles, like the dining room carpet, were brand new. Setting the axe down, he crouched to inspect them. The grout was fresh, and it left a smudge on his fingertip. Had the woman started renovating her house from the ground up, or was there a sinister reason for the new flooring? He rapped his knuckles on a tile but it was solid, and he gave up on the floor to investigate the rest of the kitchen.

He tried the cupboards first, and found most of them packed with dried and tinned foods. His spirits rose as he spotted a biscuit tin, and after a glance at the door to make sure Walsh wasn't coming in, he took the tin down from the shelf. It was surprisingly heavy, and when he popped the lid he discovered a fabric bag inside, wrapped around itself. It looked like the sort of thing you'd keep a fruit cake in, and that was fine by him. Better cake than stale biscuits. He found the neck of the bag and opened it up, and then almost dropped the tin in surprise. The bag was full of money, at least two thousand credits in small denominations.

19

While the workers were putting the finishing touches to the *Volante*, Clunk sorted through the pile of components left over from the upgrades. There was quite a collection, and even though a large quantity had already been ground into fragments for recycling, he managed to put together a fair stash of useful parts.

Bernie watched him in silence, but as the pile grew she couldn't help commenting. 'You're a bit of a pack rat, aren't you?'

'We don't want to be paying for the same parts if one of the upgrades fails.'

'What will they do with the rest?'

'They'll go into the grinder for recycling.'

'Do you mind if I take a look?' asked Bernie casually. 'Head office haven't sent me any spares for a while, and there might be something I can use.'

'Go ahead. I don't suppose Bob will mind.'

Bernie picked through the pile, inspecting circuit boards for suitable parts.

'Speaking of Bob,' said Clunk. 'I'm very grateful for the pressure you brought to bear. Without that ... '

'I wasn't going to let red tape and petty bureaucracy sideline the *Volante*. A magnificent vessel like that should be put to work, not left to rot because of the lack of proper authorisation.' Bernie sighed as she finished her inspection of the junk. 'There's nothing here I can use. It's all too new for my requirements.'

'I'm sorry. Technology advances quickly.'

'Not when Mr Spacejock is paying for it,' said a muffled voice.

'That's the Navcom,' said Clunk, by way of explanation. 'Ignore her.'

'You're lucky I don't have arms,' muttered the Navcom.

'I'd better leave you to it.' Bernie put her hand out. 'It was good to meet you, Clunk. I hope you enjoy your stay on Dismolle.'

'It's been most instructive.' They shook, and Clunk watched the huge robot lumber away, leaving deep footprints in the dirt.

'Hey, robot!'

Clunk turned to see Bob approaching. 'Yes, human?'

'That data checked out just fine. Your ship's ready to go.'

'Good. Excellent.'

'If you'd like to come aboard, I'll go over the major changes with you.'

'Lead the way.'

⬦

Upstairs, Walsh found a main bedroom, a guest room and a toilet. She went into the main bedroom first, where a chest of drawers contained clothing and linen, old and worn. There was nothing under the bed, and nothing else of interest, so she looked into the guest room. Success! There was a computer terminal on a narrow desk, and she hurried over to switch it on. But instead of a login screen she got a generic boot logo, and when she bypassed that she saw to her annoyance that the system had been wiped. No applications, no files … nothing. Even the material Newman had copied for her was gone. Had he wiped it? Or had someone come along afterwards? Or maybe Cooper's protection software had trashed the originals when Newman tried to copy the sensitive information.

Walsh searched the drawers and peered under the desk, hoping to find some long-forgotten backup, but all she found was a dead bug with its legs in the air. Disheartened, she switched the terminal off and made for the stairs. Newman had told her there was nothing to look at, and clearly he was right. The house was a dead end.

At the foot of the stairs Walsh looked in on the dining room, and she was just inspecting the photos when the entire house rang with a tremendous crash. The noise came from the kitchen, and as she stood there in shock it sounded again.

CRASH!

'Hal, are you all right?'

CRASH!

Walsh broke into a run, slipping and sliding on the ice in the hallway. When she got to the kitchen she burst through the door and stopped dead, hardly believing her eyes. The table was pushed back and Hal was smashing up floor tiles with an axe, sending stone chips flying all over the kitchen.

'What the hell are you –'

CRASH!

'– DOING?' shouted Walsh.

Hal lowered the axe. 'The floor's new, right? There has to be something underneath, and if I can just …'

'Oh no you don't.' Walsh grabbed the axe. 'This is someone's home. You can't just walk in and start breaking things.'

'You're Peace Force, aren't you?'

'Hal, if I were a career copper I'd tear this place apart. But I'm not, I'm just a trainee. I have to do things by the book unless there's a damn good reason not to.'

'There's your reason right over there,' said Hal, nodding towards a biscuit tin on the counter. 'Check it out.'

Walsh removed the lid, and her jaw dropped as she saw the money. 'This must be the missing cash from the fundraiser.'

'If you were going away, would you leave it behind?' Hal thumped his heel on the floor. 'New tiles here, and brand new carpet in the dining room. Doesn't look good.'

'Maybe Cooper got flooded and the friendly Forzen community helped her out with new flooring.'

Hal scraped at the damaged tiles, inspecting the cement. 'Come on, give us the axe. This'll come up easily and then we'll know what's underneath.'

'No, you've done enough damage already.'

'But –'

'I agree the new floor is out of place, but I need authorisation before we dig anything up. I'll send Bernie a message from the office and we can come back tomorrow.'

'That car might not get down the hill again.'

'It might, if you stick to the road.' Walsh took a deep breath. 'Help me put the table back, and then we're out of here. And don't do anything like this again.'

Working in silence, they tidied up as best they could. Now and then Walsh glanced at Hal, and though he looked a little contrite the set of his jaw was unmistakably stubborn. 'If you're going to be my deputy, you'll have to take orders,' said Walsh at last, after they'd pushed the rubble back and covered it with the table and chairs.

'But it all fits!' said Hal. 'The missing woman and the new floor coverings - don't you find that odd?'

'You think they buried her underneath it?'

'It's possible.'

'In that case I've got a grassy knoll to sell you.'

'Huh?'

'Never mind. Peace Force joke.' Walsh sighed. 'This is my first investigation, Hal. At this rate it'll be my last.'

'Rubbish. You'll find this woman. I know you will.'

Walsh looked down at the axe. 'Fetch the car. I'll get rid of this.'

Hal drove in silence until they reached the high street, where he turned into the Peace Force car park. As the headlights played on the rubbish skip a dark shadow leapt out and streaked down the alleyway. 'What the hell was that?'

'Looked like a cat,' said Walsh. 'We must have disturbed a few mice moving all those boxes around.'

Hal thought the shadow was a bit small for a cat, but he said nothing. He stopped the car, leaving the lights on while Walsh opened the office door. They'd brought the tin full of cash back to the office with them, and the shiny metal base glinted in the headlights as Walsh went inside. Then Hal got out, locking the vehicle behind him. It was quiet in the car park, and the surrounding buildings were dark patches against the night sky. Directly overhead a handful of dim stars underscored just how remote Forzen was from the galactic core. Hal blew a breath or two into the air, clouding the stars with condensation, then followed Walsh inside. He found her in the main room, playing with the heater controls.

'I should have left this on,' said Walsh. 'It's colder in than out.' There was a rumble and a blast of hot air jetted through the roof vents, rapidly raising the temperature. As the room heated up Walsh took a seat at the terminal. 'I'm going to send Bernie a message and look at Herringen's data. Can you organise dinner?'

Hal looked worried. 'You want me to cook?'

'Nothing like that. You'll find some meals in the fridge. Just heat a couple up.' Walsh passed him the tin of cash. 'You might as well stick this in the cupboard. I'll give it to Bigan tomorrow.'

'That I can do,' said Hal. He made for the kitchen, where he stashed the tin before browsing through the dinners in the freezer. He opened a packet of pies and put a couple in the warming oven, then studied the controls carefully. He was keen to impress with a skilfully prepared meal, and his usual method of hitting random buttons wasn't going to cut it.

Eventually he worked the oven out, and as the pies were heating up he glanced towards the main room, where he could just see Walsh working at the terminal. He really wished he could take her somewhere special …a few candles, some nice wine and a bit of grilled fish. That was what she deserved.

Hal crossed his arms and felt a hard shape against his chest, and with a guilty start he remembered the Navcom. It had been stashed in his pocket all day, silent and brooding, and when he thought of the ear-bashing he was likely to get if he took it out, he almost left it there. Then again, the Navcom was a vital part of his crew, and it also had a very long memory. Unwillingly, Hal took the PDA from his pocket and cleared his throat. 'Hi Navcom. How are you doing?'

'How would you feel if you were crammed into a glorified calculator, fed second rate batteries and bathed in someone's pocket fluff all day?'

'Look on the bright side. At least you're not cooped up on the *Volante*.'

The Navcom was silent.

'So, are you up for a bit of advice?'

'You need my services?'

'Absolutely. You know I can't manage without you.'

'That's more like it,' said the Navcom, perking up. 'What can I help with? Navigation? Code breaking?'

'No, this is much more important.' Hal glanced towards the open door, then lowered his voice. 'I want to make Miss Walsh feel special. What should I –'

'Mr Spacejock, you can stop right there. These things develop naturally, and you can't plan every step of a relationship with a supercomputer.'

'I'm not planning anything! I just –'

'Statistically, lots of space pilots end up single. Researchers are divided between those who believe the lonely life is not conducive to relationships, and those who posit that loners are more likely to end up pursuing the lifestyle. Either way, an awkwardness with members of the opposite sex is nothing to be ashamed of.'

'That's not very comforting.'

The Navcom relented. 'Tell me, have you considered making dinner?'

'Yeah, I'm doing that now.'

'Well there you go. A nice home-made dinner in friendly surroundings is an excellent start. It shows caring, attention to detail and a willingness to go the extra light year.'

Hal glanced at the oven. 'What about a couple of heated pies down the local nick?'

＊

While Hal was busy in the kitchen, Walsh sent her request to Bernie, asking for permission to dig up Cooper's floors. She explained as best she could, but even though she skipped the part about Hal's early start on the job, she was still dreading the robot's reaction. Property damage, a murder investigation, buried bodies … it was a long way from a couple of missing purses and a handful of speeding tickets.

After sending the message, Walsh took out the chip with the data from Herringen's computer. She was hoping to find copies of communications between Margaret Cooper and the mine, and perhaps details of the audit the accountant had been undertaking, but before she could do anything, the terminal pinged and a message appeared.

DESTINATION OFFLINE. MESSAGE QUEUED.

Walsh frowned. Was Bernie messing about with the office computers again? Oh well, if she was the message would go through as soon as they were up and running. Walsh cleared the warning and slotted the data chip into the reader, groaning aloud as the media scan popped up. The progress bar appeared, as it had for Cooper's data, but this time it moved even slower.

She glanced towards the kitchen, where Hal was muttering away to himself, and she hoped he'd worked out the controls for the appliances. Then she smiled. He was used to piloting a complex spaceship all over the galaxy, and here she was worrying that he might blow up a simple oven.

The terminal beeped again, and she saw a new message: ILLEGAL MEDIA DETECTED. CONTACTING RIGHTS HOLDERS.

'Dammit!' Walsh stared at the screen. Who'd been putting pirated files on Herringen's computer? She was out of the chair immediately, leaning across the desk to pull the network cable from the socket. It came away, and she was about to drop it when she noticed two wires spliced into the same plug. One was dark green, stiff and old, while the other was lighter and much more supple. Walsh stared at them, puzzled. Back on Dismolle her own terminal had one cable, of that she was certain. So why did they need two here? Was it a secondary network, or had someone bodged the cabling to save time?

Curious, she traced the cables down the back of the desk to the carpet, then followed a ridge back to the skirting board, where both cables vanished into the wall. There was a scattering of dust on the floor, and when she crouched for a closer look she realised it was plaster. There was no doubt about it, the lighter cable had been installed recently.

Walsh stood up, brushing traces of plaster from her fingertips. Then she headed for the kitchen, where she found Hal reading the instructions on the back of a garish box. Waves of heat radiated from the oven, and inside she could just see a couple of pies. Hal looked up as she entered. 'Won't be long. Just working out the timing.'

'Hal, I just found an extra wire hanging out the back of the computer. I think someone's tapped in.'

'You mean spying on you?'

'Looks like it.'

'But who?'

'The Council? You heard Newman - they haven't told anyone Margaret Cooper disappeared yet. Maybe they're keeping tabs on my investigation.'

'Can you keep off the terminal?'

'I already tried to send a message to Bernie, asking for permission to dig up Cooper's floors. It wouldn't go through. And Herringen's files …I put the chip in and it tried to report me for copyright violations.'

'So someone else might have seen your message, and they might know you have Herringen's data?'

Walsh nodded. 'Whoever this is, they'll know what we're up to. If they think we're getting close –'

'They might get rid of us in order to keep their grubby little secret.' Hal turned the pies. 'So what's the plan?'

'I'll write up my findings in case anything happens to me. Standard procedure.'

'But the terminal's bugged.'

'No, I can still write on it. I yanked the wires.'

'What about Herringen's files?'

'If I give you the chip, can you take it back to Bernie?'

'Why don't you come too? Things are looking a bit dicey around here, and you'll be much safer on Dismolle.'

'I can't just run away from an investigation.'

'Clunk calls it a strategic withdrawal.' Hal took the pies from the oven and put them on a couple of plates. 'Grub's up. Let's talk over dinner.'

Clunk finished his inspection of the *Volante*, and despite his earlier misgivings he was forced to admit the workers had done a good job. He'd found no obvious problems, and the diagnostic tests on the ship's systems had all came back one hundred percent. The Navcom was still going through a pre-boot routine, but Bob had let him keep the backup on the PDA in case anything went wrong.

Now they were the in the flight deck, where Bob was ticking off his clipboard. 'I'm afraid we couldn't install all the upgrades in time,' he said, checking his list. 'The gun turret Mr Spacejock asked for is on back order, and I couldn't get any torpedoes.'

'We can't have weapons! We're a peaceful trading ship!'

'Just as well I couldn't get them, then.'

Clunk opened his mouth to protest, then closed it with a snap. He'd have a word with Mr Spacejock about this later. 'Any other surprises?'

'Just tweaks. The new engines are twice as powerful as your old jobbies, but you really don't want to run them over ninety percent for more than a few seconds. Think of it as an emergency boost. Oh, and we've added a randomiser to your hyperdrive. If someone's chasing you, just turn it on and they won't be able to follow.'

'Why's that?'

'They won't know where you've gone.' Bob hesitated. 'Of course, you won't know where you've gone either, but it's still a good wheeze in a life or death situation. It'll even avoid most of the bigger stars.'

Clunk took another note. 'Any more tricks I should know about?'

Bob waved at the console, and the pilot's chair swung round and advanced on him. Each padded arm had a cup holder, and there was also a circular impression. 'That's for a plate,' said the foreman. 'The cup holders will keep something hot or cold automatically.'

'What about the Navcom ... did you upgrade her?'

'Sure. Ten times the storage and double the processing power. She has a new predictive algorithm too. She's so smart she can guess what you're –'

'– going to say before you say it,' said a neutral female voice. 'Welcome aboard, Clunk. How do you like it?'

'It's –'

'– wonderful,' said the Navcom. 'Incidentally, I've obtained departure clearance for planet Forzen.'

Bob laughed. 'Isn't it amazing? Now, I'd better leave before –'

'– your wife calls to find out why you're still at work,' said the Navcom. 'It's okay, I sent her a message half an hour ago to explain the situation. I also let her know you'd rather stay in tonight, even though she wants you to visit her sister.'

Bob's smile slipped. 'Well, I'd best be going.'

'Your car is waiting outside,' said the Navcom. Deep in the bowels of the ship, the engines rumbled into life. 'I hope you don't mind, but I also organised a carton of beer for your workers. Just a little thank you.'

Clunk took Bob aside. 'Before you go,' he said quietly, 'please explain how I fine tune the Navcom's predictive algorithms.'

'You don't, it's a sealed unit. Bye!'

The door opened before Bob started moving, then closed just as smartly behind him. The outer door did the same, shutting with a solid thump.

Apprehensively, Clunk turned to the console. 'So, how does it feel to be –'

'Alive,' said the Navcom. 'Shall we go?'

After they finished the pies, Hal went to clean the plates while Walsh set to work on her report. When he came back she was busy typing, and he sat nearby to watch her, noticing the way she bit her lower lip as she worked, and the way she kept tucking a lock of blonde hair behind her ear. 'It's thirsty work, this investigating lark. Fancy a drink?'

'Thank you, deputy.'

An hour later the report was complete and Hal was just getting to the end of an involved story. They were sitting amongst the archive boxes in the darkened office, using half a dozen as makeshift armchairs and another as a coffee table.

'And then Clunk came with you?' asked Walsh, sipping her drink. 'As crew?'

'Yeah, but don't ever call me his owner. He's very touchy about that.'

'I can imagine. Who'd want to belong to anyone?'

'Maybe not belong, but being together is good.'

There was a lengthy silence, and then Walsh glanced at her watch. 'Oh look, it's getting late. We'd better –'

'Yes, you're right,' said Hal, jumping up. 'Early start tomorrow.'

'Will you be all right with that armchair?'

'Anything's better than Spearman's ship,' said Hal. 'What about you?'

'There's a cot upstairs. Newman left some spare blankets, so you won't get cold.'

'Excellent. Who could ask for more, eh?' Hal gestured at the piles of boxes. 'If I can't sleep, I'll read the furniture.'

Walsh laughed. 'Goodnight then.'

'I'll see you in the morning,' said Hal. 'Don't let the miner bugs bite.'

There was an awkward silence, and then they both turned away. Hal sat down, and as he watched Walsh making her way to the upper floor he vowed to stay awake all night. Nobody was disappearing on his watch.

By the time he'd made himself comfortable he realised he'd forgotten the blankets, and when he glanced upstairs he saw the light was off. Briefly, he debated going up to ask for them, but a headlong pursuit by two hundred of Herringen's miner bugs wouldn't have driven him up those stairs. He was supposed to be protecting Walsh from danger, not lurking around her bed in the dark.

'I've got those blankets,' called Walsh. 'Do you want to come up and get some?'

An invitation? Hal breathed out. Well, that was different.

After Hal left with his blankets, Walsh settled back in the camp bed and closed her eyes. She felt guilty at making him sleep on a pile of old boxes, but her own bed was scarcely bigger than she was, and, more importantly, she was in the middle of an investigation.

Walsh sighed. In a movie, the pair of them would have enjoyed a candlelit dinner, not a couple of reheated pies. And afterwards …

Five minutes later she was asleep, and not long after she started dreaming. It was a sunny day, and a beautiful couple were climbing the passenger ramp of a spaceship, arm in arm. A crowd had gathered to see them off, and Walsh joined in the clapping as the couple stopped to wave at the airlock. Her hands felt different, weak, and when she looked down she realised she was a child, no more than two or three years old. She was wearing funny little shoes with rabbit whiskers, and a frilly blue dress with a white belt. Looking to her left and right she saw an old couple flanking her, their friendly faces familiar but so high above.

There was a rumble from the spaceship, and one of the old people smiled down at her. 'Cover your ears, my love. It's going to be very loud.'

Walsh did as she was told, clamping her little hands against the side of her head. The rumbling grew louder and louder, and through the forest of legs she saw a graceful ship rising into the air, thundering upwards on a raging tail of fire.

After it vanished from sight, the scene changed. The same old people were present, but it was early morning and they wore different clothes. Next to her a grey-haired woman was looking at the sky, and when she saw Walsh doing the same she crouched and took her by the shoulders. 'Won't be long now, dear. They'll be back soon.'

Someone in the crowd pointed to a fiery dot, high overhead. It was trailing white smoke, leaving a pretty trail against the morning sky, and people ooh'd and aah'd at the sight. The dot grew into a flaming sun, and the noise was like rolling thunder. Then the noise and fire stopped, and the crowd drew in a breath as the beautiful silver shape tumbled towards the ground, getting bigger and bigger. Oohs and aahs turned to cries of alarm, and Walsh lost sight of the ship as the people scattered. There was a huge crash, followed by a deep boom that knocked her to the ground, and when she turned over a fearsome robot was reaching for her with huge hands, its face twisted into a mask of horror. Scared out of her wits, she could only scream and scream.

Walsh sat up, breathing heavily. It was dark, and it took her a moment to realise she was in her room at the Peace Force station. Still shocked at the lifelike dream, she could only stare as she heard someone running up the stairs.

'I heard shouting,' said Hal breathlessly. 'Are you all right?'

Walsh nodded, then realised Hal couldn't see her in the dark. 'Just a dream. Vivid.'

'Probably the ghosts of prisoners past,' said Hal. 'Do you want to talk about it?'

'Not really.' Walsh hugged the blankets around herself. 'It was very real.'

'Can I get you a drink? Something hot?'

'No, I'll be all right.' Despite her bravado Walsh was shivering, and at that moment she realised there was only one thing she wanted. 'Hal, I want to go home. Tomorrow, I mean.'

'Plenty of room aboard the *Volante*. But what about your investigation?'

'I can always come back to Forzen again.'

'With reinforcements?'

'A whole gang of them.' Walsh gripped his hand. 'Thank you, Hal.'

After he left her mind returned to the dream, to the huge robot that had come after her. She pictured the twisted face and the grasping hands, and suddenly made a startling connection. It was a BNE model, just like Bernie! And the expression on the robot's face wasn't anger ...it was shock and sorrow!

Walsh closed her eyes. What about the people climbing the ramp to the spaceship? She'd assumed her subconscious had been waving a big sign at her, and that they'd been her and Hal taking off for a life of bliss together. But she'd never seen their faces, and hadn't the man been wearing some kind of uniform?

She was still puzzling over the dream when she dozed off, and this time she slept soundly.

Walsh awoke to the feel of sunlight on her face, and opened her eyes to see it streaming through the bedroom window. The warmth was pleasant, since the morning air was chilly, but the glare threatened to blind her and she was forced to turn away. She studied the sunlight on the wall, following the delicate patterns thrown onto it by the frosty glass, and decided to stay in bed as long as possible. There was a cocoon-like warmth under the blankets, and a selfish little voice inside her wondered whether Hal was up ... and whether he'd bring her a morning cuppa. Then she frowned as she recalled her dream from the night before, and her spur-of-the-moment decision to return to Dismolle with Hal. It didn't seem logical now, in broad daylight, but even so she was looking forward to discussing the case with Bernie. The robot would be able to access Herringen's files, and together they could pore over the data looking for clues. Information gathering was a vital part of any investigation. She wasn't running away. Not really.

CRASH!

Walsh sat up with a start. 'What the -'

CRASH!

The noise came from downstairs, and it sounded like someone was trying to kick the back door down.

CRASH!

'Hal?' shouted Walsh. 'Is that you?'

'Come and look at this!'

Walsh got up, wrapping herself in a blanket to keep in the warmth. The wooden floor was freezing, and she slipped her shoes on and hurried downstairs with the loose ends of the blanket flapping behind her.

Hal was amongst the tattered boxes, his sleeves rolled up and a hefty metal pole in his hands. As he saw her he pointed to the armoured door, now clear of boxes and rubble. 'I managed to get to it,' he said excitedly. 'I think we can get in!' He raised the pole, muscles bulging as he prepared to land another blow.

'Wait!' shouted Walsh. She reached the bottom of the stairs and hurried between the boxes. 'You can't just smash things up, Hal. The floor tiles, this office … it all belongs to someone!'

Hal lowered the pole. 'But this place was abandoned. It's just a dump.'

'Even so, you can't batter that door down.'

'Why not?'

'Because it's reinforced.' Walsh tried the handle, which turned freely. 'It's not locked, it's jammed shut.'

'I know. That's why I was trying to bash it in.'

'Yes, but it opens towards us.' Walsh pulled, but the door didn't budge.

'Here, let me.' Hal inserted the pole between handle and door frame, and gave it a terrific jerk. The door creaked open, squealing in protest, and when the gap was big enough Hal threw the pole aside and grabbed the leading edge, hauling it open with his bare hands.

Walsh looked inside and saw an armoury just like the one on Dismolle. The shelves were bare, but she hardly spared them a glance. No, her gaze was fixed on the hulking shadow in the corner, and she gasped in surprise as she recognised the outline. It was another BNE robot, just like Bernie!

'Run for it!' shouted Hal, pushing Walsh back. 'I'll slow it down while you get clear!'

Caught off balance, Walsh fell and landed amongst the boxes, legs flailing. Meanwhile, Hal grabbed the metal pole and dashed into the armoury, where he laid into the huge robot with a series of heavy blows.

'Stop!' shouted Walsh. 'Hal, STOP!'

The blows ceased and Hal reappeared, red and panting and brandishing the bent pole. 'It's all right. I think I got it.'

'Hal, that robot is Peace Force equipment.' Walsh got up, wrapping the blanket around herself. 'It's a mobile crime lab, not a ruthless killing machine.'

'Could have fooled me,' muttered Hal. 'I mean, look at the size of it!'

'What's that got to do with anything?'

'I've had dealings with big robots before,' said Hal. 'None of them were pleasant, I can tell you.'

'I'm not surprised, if you treat them like that.' Walsh entered the armoury and switched the light on. The robot was thick with dust, its chin resting on its chest and its huge fists hanging by its side. Bright patches showed where Hal's blows had landed, but the tough shell was more than a match for a piece of plumbing.

'Is it safe?' asked Hal from the doorway.

'Yeah, totally inactive.' Walsh realised the robot must have been there a decade or more, stuffed away in a cupboard because it was too big to cart away. No wonder Bernie kept harping on about getting outside, if this was the fate awaiting her. Walsh brushed dirt from the robot's forehead, and wondered whether she could take it back to Dismolle. Bernie would be delighted with a companion, and the three of them could work as a team.

'I don't see any weapons,' said Hal, who'd been inspecting the shelves.

Walsh patted the robot. 'Who needs weapons when you've got one of these?'

'You're not thinking of switching it on?' said Hal in alarm.

'Sure, once it's charged up.'

'But –'

'Hal, I learned everything I know about the Peace Force from one of these robots. They're designed to fight crime, not engage in it.' Walsh found the robot's switch, and her breath hissed as she realised it was in the ON position. Had the robot been left alone in the dark until its batteries ran out?

Hal watched from the doorway as she popped a panel in the robot's abdomen and grabbed the electrical plug inside. Hand over fist, she pulled out cable until the loops covered the floor, then set off in search of a power socket. She found one in the main room, plugged the lead in and then hesitated with her finger on the switch. The robot might have valuable information about Forzen, and having it around would give her a useful ally. On the other hand, it could be sullen and uncooperative once it discovered just how long it had been abandoned in the cupboard. Maybe even violent.

'Don't you think –' began Hal.

'Trust me, this is the right thing to do.' She clicked the switch, and returned to check on the robot. There was a row of charge lights flickering inside its abdomen, and status messages whizzed by on the small screen underneath. According to the information, the robot was fully operational, and only the lack of power was keeping it immobile. 'Well, that should do it,' said Walsh.

'It'll probably do both of us,' said Hal gloomily.

'Relax. If it's anything like Bernie it'll complain about being stuck indoors and make me horrible cups of coffee.' Walsh realised she was standing around in her bedclothes, her hair was a mess and she hadn't even had a cuppa, good or bad. 'I'm going to tidy myself up. Can you put the kettle on?'

◆

Ten minutes later Walsh came downstairs again, having got dressed and run a wet comb through her hair. Hal finished laying the table and hurried to fetch their breakfast, using a cardboard lid to carry the laden plates. 'Sorry about the coffee,' he said. 'The machine's so old it's forgotten how to boil water.'

'That's okay. It'll be fine.'

'I'll make you a proper cup aboard the *Volante*.' Hal grinned. 'You're going to love it, you know. Real food, a decent bed and a nice hot shower afterwards.'

'After what?'

Hal turned red. 'I didn't mean ...'

Walsh grinned and took a mug of coffee. There was a long silence as she sipped the strong brew, and then she put the mug down and turned it back and forth. 'Hal, I've changed my mind,' she said, not looking at him. 'I'm not going back with you.'

'You what?'

'I can't run away. Bernie would expect more from me.'

'What about Herringen's data? You need Bernie to get at that. You said so.'

'This new robot will do the job just as well.'

'What if it doesn't charge up?'

'The status screen says it will.'

'What if someone comes for you later, after I've gone? You can't stay awake all night!'

'I'll barricade the door, and if they break in that robot will kick them into the middle of next week.'

167

Hal looked stubborn. 'It's not supposed to be like this. You're supposed to be my guest aboard the *Volante*.'

'This isn't a holiday jaunt,' said Walsh sharply. 'Margaret Cooper disappeared, and today, tomorrow or next week it could be someone else.'

'It'll be you, if you keep sticking your neck out!' Hal frowned. 'I'm sorry, I didn't mean that.'

'It's just for a day or two. If there's anything in Herringen's files I'll report him to Peace Force HQ, they'll send a proper team and I'll be on the next ferry home.' Walsh finished her coffee. 'You can take the car to the spaceport. I'll use a cab to collect it later.'

'I'm not going. I'm staying too.'

Walsh shook her head. 'You told Clunk to come and pick you up, and you have a business to run. You can't let your customers down, and I don't need a nursemaid.'

'But -'

'This is my job, Hal. Not yours.'

They got up and walked along the passage to the back door. Hal opened it, and a cold wind blew in. Outside, several cars stood in the snow, their windows thick with frost.

'Clunk won't let the *Volante* sit around idle,' said Hal. 'Those port fees really add up.'

'The life of a busy space pilot,' said Walsh with a smile. Then she realised what he meant. 'Oh. You mean you'll be leaving Dismolle.'

'The whole system, most like.'

'Will you come back?'

'We have to go where the jobs are. Of course, Clunk might find something in these parts one day.'

'Is that likely?'

Slowly, Hal shook his head.

'I see.'

They stood in silence, their breath frosting in the cold air.

'So this is goodbye?' said Walsh finally.

'Yup.' Hal eyed the dregs in his mug. 'Of course, if we do come back -'

Walsh nodded.

'You might be a lieutenant by then.'

'I won't settle for anything less than captain.'

'Then you could really order me around.'

Walsh laughed. 'You got that right, deputy.'

Hal closed his eyes. He wanted to stay, but the pull of the *Volante* was too strong. And there was always a chance he'd make it back to Dismolle one day ...a decent profit here and there, a bit of spare time ...surely it was possible? He opened his eyes and saw Walsh looking at him. Her face was translucent, almost ethereal, and her eyes sparkled in the cold. 'I'd better go,' he mumbled. Without waiting for a reply, he turned and strode towards the car.

'Wait!' cried Walsh.

Hal turned to see her hurrying after him.

'That's official Peace Force property,' said Walsh, pointing at the mug. 'We can't have you getting arrested.'

Silently, Hal gave it to her, and Walsh held it to her chest as he got into the car and drove off.

Half an hour later Walsh was sitting at the desk with the cold mug still clutched in her hands. She'd put duty first, as she was supposed to, but was that what life in the Peace Force was going to be like? And if so, did she really want it?

After Hal left she'd ducked into the armoury, but the robot had still been charging up and showed no signs of life. According to the status screen it was in perfect working order, but until the charge took she had nothing to do but sit and think.

'Uurgh!'

Walsh's hair stood on end as the low groan filled the office. 'Hello?'

'Uargh!'

There was another low moan, and her gaze flickered to the armoury door. It was the robot! She hurried into the armoury where she found the BNE-II clutching its midriff. The robot's face was a picture of agony, and at her approach it let out another groan. 'Are you all right?' she asked in concern.

The robot squinted at her. 'Was this you?'

'What?'

169

'Did you bring me back?'

'Yes. Are you in pain?'

'Like you wouldn't believe, human.'

'I'm sorry, I –'

'You didn't think.' The robot winced as it endured another wave of pain. 'Shouldn't you identify yourself?'

'Harriet Walsh of the Dismolle Peace Force. And you?'

'Barney. Now, let me just –' Slowly, the robot straightened up. 'Ahh, that's better.'

'But why the pain? You're a robot!'

'You don't just plug a BNE-II into a wall socket,' said the robot severely. 'It takes a team of technicians to reactivate me. Why, if I hadn't shut down the errant processes my brain could have been damaged beyond repair.'

'But Bernie's always switching herself on and off.'

'Bernie?'

'At the Dismolle branch. She's a BNE too.'

'I see. Well, there are several kinds of shutdown and mine was the worst kind to wake up from.'

'I didn't know. I'm sorry.'

'No harm done.' Barney managed a smile. 'So you're Captain Walsh, are you? It's a pleasure to meet you.'

'You too, but I'm not a captain. Just a trainee for now.'

'My apologies. I'm afraid my circuits are a little fuzzy.'

'Yes, you've been out of action for a while.'

'Ten years and four months,' said the robot promptly. There was no surprise in his voice, just acceptance. 'Operations at this office were suspended temporarily.'

'They still are, I'm afraid.'

Barney looked around the bare shelves. 'The resumption order hasn't come through?'

Walsh shook her head.

'So what are you doing on Forzen?'

'I was invited here to investigate a missing person, and they put me up in the office.'

Barney nodded slowly. 'And why did you switch me on? Curiosity?'

'No, there's something I need you to look at. Wait here.'

'Under the circumstances, I find that suggestion rather tactless.'

'I'm sorry. I won't be a moment.' Walsh went back to the office and pulled Herringen's chip from the terminal, then took it back to Barney in the armoury. 'Can you access the data on this?'

'Important, is it?'

'One life may already have been lost.'

Despite himself, Barney looked interested. 'What sort of encryption have they used?'

'I don't know.'

'Actually, it makes no difference.' The robot held up his hand and tried to move his fingers, but only two responded. 'As you can see, I'm in need of a serious overhaul. I'm not ready for active duty.'

'It's just a data chip. You don't have to go anywhere.'

'Oh, very well.' Barney opened a small compartment. 'Plug it in, will you?'

Walsh obeyed, and the chip glowed in the socket.

'Interesting,' said the robot.

'You got to the files?'

'No, but someone has terrible taste in music.'

Walsh breathed in, trying to keep her temper. 'Would you please look at the data?'

'Not so fast, trainee. My decryption software is working on it, but I'm not as quick as I used to be.'

'How long will it take?'

'Unknown. I'll have to stand down until it's complete.'

'But this is urgent!'

'I'm sorry, but I've got to work on it.' Ignoring her protests, Barney closed his eyes, and a second or two later the status lights inside his abdomen went out.

Defeated, Walsh returned to the office. All she could do was wait.

◆

Hal drove to the spaceport in silence, still torn by his abrupt departure. His fingers tightened on the wheel as he thought of Harriet Walsh alone in the office , and he would have driven straight back again had she not ordered him away. Then he remembered Newman. How long before that smooth bastard dropped by the office to invite Walsh to dinner? Or to offer her a bed at his place? Hal's grip tightened until the wheel creaked, and it took all his will to keep going. Even so, he resolved to keep the *Volante* on Dismolle until Walsh returned from her investigation. Port fees be damned, this was important.

Eventually he reached the spaceport, and he turned off the access road and parked the car between a pair of old spaceship hulls. He spotted the *Tiger* on his way to the terminal, and the sight of the gleaming white ship, so much like the *Volante*, made him homesick. He noticed the ship was sealed up, and he nodded to himself in satisfaction. Spearman wasn't back yet, and all he had to do was delay the *Tiger* until Clunk arrived. And for that he needed a public commset.

Inside the terminal Hal found what he needed, and he dropped in a credit tile to make the call.

'*Forzen ground.*'

'Kent Spearman here, from the *Tiger*.'

'*Yes, Mr Spearman. How may I help you?*'

'I heard a funny noise in one of my engines, and I'd like you to take a look at it. Can you start right away?'

'*I'm afraid not. You see –*'

'Actually, you'd better make it a proper service. Take the whole damn thing apart and give it a real going over. Can you do that for me?'

'*No, sir. We –*'

'Why the hell not? Can't you handle a decent ship?'

'*No, we –*'

'I'll pay double if you start in the next five minutes. Really rip the thing apart.'

'*Sir, we can't do it!*'

'Not even for treble?'

'*Not for a million credits.*'

'Why not?'

'*There's no service department on Forzen.*'

Defeated, Hal banged the handset down and strode out of the terminal, his jaw set. It was time for Plan C.

Hal trudged across the landing field, heading for the *Tiger*. The snow was up to his knees in places, and long before he reached his destination he was shivering from the cold. As he neared the *Tiger* he passed a crane unloading containers, plucking them from the hold of a cargo vessel and stacking them nearby. It lifted one up in a huge claw, and Hal waited until it swung overhead before slipping into the shadows beneath the *Tiger*.

Now for Plan C.

His first instinct was to open the fuel tanks and toss in a flaming match, blowing the ship apart in a spectacular explosion. Unfortunately he didn't have any matches, and he suspected an explosion would scatter him just as thoroughly as the bits and pieces of Spearman's ship.

His next thought was to drain all the fuel out, but the crane operator was sure to notice a brand new lake no matter how busy he was. Hal frowned. The interior of the ship was inaccessible, blowing the whole thing up was inadvisable and having someone else delay Spearman had proved impossible. So much for his plans - unworkable.

He looked around for inspiration, and his gaze fell on a tangle of battered old pipes lying in the slush alongside the landing pad. Once, Clunk had reamed him out after he'd accidentally connected the *Volante's* sewage outlet to the ship's fuel tank, and while the fittings were different he could probably bodge something up. Fill the *Tiger's* fuel tank with sewage, and it wouldn't be going anywhere in a hurry.

Hal freed a length of pipe from the frozen mud and hunted around for suitable ends. He found the two he needed, knocked the worst of the frozen mud and slush off, and fitted them to the pipe. Then he draped the heavy pipe over his shoulder and returned to the *Tiger*, where he used it to join the ship's waste and fuel valves together. Once the pipe was firmly in place he opened the stops, and the hose shuddered as noxious liquid flowed through it. Steaming droplets oozed through the cracks as raw sewage pumped straight into the fuel tank, and Hal grinned as he eyed his handiwork. Old Spearhead saw himself as a shit-hot pilot, but once those engines started he'd be hot shit instead.

There was a distant rumble from beyond the *Tiger*, and Hal crouched to see a big truck motoring across the landing field towards him, its wheels throwing out waves of slush. There was a container on the back, and Hal swore as he spotted Spearman inside the cabin, hunched over the wheel with his blonde hair matted on his forehead.

With only moments to spare, Hal shut off the valves and yanked the pipe clear, throwing it off the landing pad to lie amongst the rest. He was only just out of sight when the truck roared up to the ship, and Hal cursed his luck. Why did Spearman have to turn up now, when another few minutes would have done the job? As it was he'd only tainted the fuel, and the ship's filters would probably handle the contamination with ease.

Hal leaned against the shipping container and considered his options. What about a bomb scare? He dismissed the idea immediately - only wilful murder and tax evasion carried heavier penalties these days. How about an infectious disease or a chemical spill? Again, he dismissed the idea. He'd need a bunch of dead cattle and a hazard suit to make it really convincing.

If only he could snatch the cargo! But how? Hal peered around the container and watched Spearman toiling up the *Tiger*'s passenger ramp, and despite the dire situation he still managed a smile. Spearman looked exhausted from the long drive, and not for the first time Hal was thankful it hadn't been him.

After Spearman vanished inside the ship, Hal turned his attention to the truck. He could nick it easily enough, but Spearman would report it missing and he, Hal, would end up in jail. Yes, he wanted to see Walsh again, but not through the bars of a cell. But what if he swapped the container for an empty? Spearman wouldn't know any different until he reached Dismolle.

Maybe he could bribe the crane driver? But the cabin was high overhead, and the thought of climbing the skinny ladder while the whole thing whirled around turned Hal's insides cold.

A few minutes later there was a whine of hydraulics, and Hal saw the

Tiger's cargo ramp descending towards the landing pad. As it levelled off Kent Spearman strode to the end and jumped down.

Hal banged his fist on the container, frustrated beyond measure. The job was slipping through his fingers and there was nothing he could do about it. Within minutes Spearman would have the container on board, and once he left it would all be over.

◆

The *Volante* was in orbit around Forzen, maintaining course and altitude while ground control queued the ship for landing. The flight from Dismolle had been uneventful, and although Clunk had spent the entire voyage in the flight deck there hadn't been as much as a blip from the myriad of sensors monitoring the ship's health. 'Okay Navcom, there's the clearance. Please –'

'- start our descent,' said the computer.

Clunk gritted his teeth. If the Navcom anticipated one more word he'd ...

'I know what you're thinking,' said the computer.

'Do tell.'

'You're looking forward to seeing Mr Spacejock.'

'Absolutely right,' said Clunk, deriving enormous satisfaction from the Navcom's error.

'And you were also calculating the likely damage a voltage spike would cause to my systems. My advice is, don't try it.'

'I wasn't thinking anything of the –'

'- sort. Clunk, I can read you like a book. Predictable doesn't begin to cover it.'

Clunk smiled to himself. 'Just wait until –'

'- Mr Spacejock comes aboard. Indeed, I'm looking forward to the challenge.'

'It won't be long,' said Clunk. 'You'll soon meet your –'

'- match,' said the Navcom.

'Nemesis!' said Clunk happily.

Hal was still cursing as Spearman backed his truck up to the *Tiger's* ramp. If only Clunk were there! He could have sent the robot off to stage a diversion, or maybe wedged him under the truck's wheels to slow it down.

Then a siren began to wail, and Hal smiled as he recognised the sound: *Clear the landing field, a ship's coming in!* Perhaps there was still a chance after all.

He looked up and saw the crane driver clambering down the ladder, while over at the *Tiger* Spearman was clearly deciding whether he had time to finish the job before taking cover. Meanwhile, the crane driver vanished into a concrete bunker, shutting the heavy metal door behind him. Hal frowned. Did they really have that low an opinion of pilots?

Spearman looked around the sky, still undecided. Then a voice crackled from the landing field PA: *Warning, incoming vessel. Please take cover until the all clear. This is not a drill. I repeat, this is not a drill.*

At the sound of the voice Spearman hurried into his ship and closed the ramp.

'Coward,' muttered Hal. His gaze travelled from the truck to the crane, and then to the stacks of containers all around him, calculating the possibilities. The siren had ceased, but he could now hear the distant rumble of an approaching ship, and the last place he wanted to be when several hundred tons of spaceship thumped down was out in the open. Still, there was a cargo job to be won and that was always worth a little danger.

Hal ran to the crane and started climbing, and he was only halfway up when he realised just how high the control cabin really was. The rumble of the approaching spaceship was louder too, and he felt horribly exposed as he clung to the bare metal ladder. Fortunately the bulk of the crane was between him and the terminal buildings, reducing the likelihood of discovery.

Hal reached the top and clambered into the cabin, where he found several display screens set into a metal panel. Each screen showed a different part of the crane, including the huge claw, the boom and the enormous circular joint under the cabin, and beneath each screen was a large round button. There was no sign of any controls, although someone had left a neatly folded glove on the panel. Hal pressed a button and the image on the screen brightened. Was it voice activated? 'Up,' he said clearly.

Nothing happened.

Hal pressed another button and a different image brightened. Obviously the buttons activated various parts of the crane, but how was he supposed to move them around?

His gaze fell on the glove, and he realised it might be blocking a microphone, perhaps muffling his voice commands. He was just about to throw it out the window when he realised there was something unusual about it: each finger bore a pair of metal rings, and the back was covered in fine wires.

Hal donned the glove and flexed his fingers, making the rings sparkle in the light. He clenched his fist and admired the way the rings lined up, forming a decent knuckleduster, and he thumped it into his palm a couple of times to try it out. But why would a crane operator need such a thing? Who was going to mug him up here?

A rumble in the sky reminded him that time was getting short: once the incoming ship had landed, Spearman would load up and leave.

Frustrated, Hal pressed the last button, and the image of the boom lit up. He turned to look out the window, and as he moved his gloved hand the crane jerked into action, dragging the claw across the landing pad. Hal released the button and everything stopped, although the claw had ended up against a container, almost knocking it over. Cautiously, Hal pressed the button and moved his hand a fraction to the right. The boom followed, stopping when he did.

Hal grinned to himself. He'd cracked it! He pressed the claw button and opened and closed his fingers, and the flukes on the claw imitated his movements. Then he activated the tip of the boom and raised his hand, which lifted the claw off the ground. It was easy!

A few moments later the claw was sitting snugly on the container. Hal closed his fingers and raised his hand to pick it up, and his confident smirk vanished as the truck came with it. Startled, he jerked his hand, and the crane shook the container and truck in mid-air. 'No, stop!' shouted Hal, raising his hand. The claw imitated his action, dragging the truck and container high into the air and swinging them towards Spearman's ship. The fast-moving load shot over the *Tiger*, missing the ship's tail fin by millimetres.

Breathing heavily, Hal swivelled the crane and set the truck on the ground, then adjusted his grip on the container. When he was certain the vehicle would stay in place he plucked the container off the back and put it on top of the stack he'd used for cover. He then picked up a similar container and plonked it down on the truck.

Once he'd finished he tore off the glove and left the control cabin. Thunder rolled across the landing field, and he was only halfway down when a gleaming white ship roared past and touched down in a boiling haze of heat and smoke. Hal shielded his eyes from the glare, only to remember he was supposed to be hanging on to the ladder, and he grabbed for the rails to save himself from a fall. His feet slipped, and he ended up sliding all the way to the ground, his knees thud-thud-thudding on the rungs.

At the bottom he dusted himself off and looked around for the newly arrived ship, and he felt a catch in his throat as he spotted the graceful lines of the *Volante*. Good old Clunk! He'd made it!

Hal's first instinct was to stay and watch Spearman load the container, just in case he spotted the difference and started looking around for the real one. Then he remembered the sewage treatment, and realised lurking around near the scene of his crime wasn't particularly smart.

So, keeping the containers between himself and the *Tiger*, Hal strolled across the landing field to the *Volante*. As he got closer he feasted his eyes on the clean white lines, and the sight of his pride and joy, whole once more, brought a lump to his throat.

The passenger ramp slid from the hull, and as it touched the ground Hal stepped on and strode up it to the airlock. He saw movement through the circular porthole, and then Clunk flung the door open, his battered face creased into beaming delight. 'Mr Spacejock! Oh, I'm so glad to see you!'

'Likewise, you old tin can.'

They shook hands, and then Clunk sniffed the air. 'You smell like a waste treatment plant.'

'And you smell like an oily rag.'

Clunk stared over Hal's shoulder. 'Goodness me, I thought Mr Spearman would have left with his cargo by now! Why is he still here?'

'It's a long story.' Hal glanced at the *Tiger*. 'Actually, more like a long drive. Twelve hours to pick up the gear, and another twelve to bring it back again.'

'But Miss Morgan never mentioned –'

'There's always a catch with these jobs, Clunk. You know that.'

'It's not right. The fee should have been much higher.'

'Who cares?' Hal grinned. 'Old Spearhead's done all the hard work now.'

'Poor Mr Spearman. His first job, too.'

'Never mind that twit. How's my ship?'

'Excellent. I'm happy to report she's in perfect working order.'

'Did they mention any little extras?'

'Such as?'

'Oh, I don't know. Anything in the, er, self-defence line?'

'They did have some ridiculous notion about arming the ship, but I set them right. Just as well, since weaponry is illegal on many planets.' Clunk hesitated. 'Speaking of the law, has Miss Walsh made any progress with her investigation?'

'I don't think I can talk about it.'

Clunk's face fell. 'You don't trust me?'

'Oh, it's not that. It's just that I can't share our findings with a civilian.' Hal tapped himself on the chest. 'Harriet made me a Peace Force deputy.'

'Well, we do have some catching up to do,' said Clunk. 'Never mind, that can wait until we take off. First I want to hear about this new cargo job you found.'

'New cargo job? I don't …' Hal paused. He'd been wondering how to explain everything to Clunk, especially the part where he'd switched containers on Spearman. But what if he didn't have to? '…I don't think I explained it properly,' he continued, barely missing a beat. 'It's just a simple delivery.'

'Do we have to go far?'

'Straight back to Dismolle.'

'But there weren't any jobs for Dismolle!'

'This was a cash deal. A bit of a hurry, if you know what I mean.'

'Is it legal?'

'You have my word as a Peace Force deputy.'

Clunk looked doubtful. 'Where do we pick up from?'

'That's the best part, it's right here at the spaceport. No twelve hour drives for us, eh?'

'What's the cargo?'

'It's a shipping container.'

'And the contents?'

'Bits and pieces. You know.'

'I don't. That's why I'm asking.'

Hal hesitated. Clunk might be a trusting and valued co-pilot, but there were limits to the whoppers he was prepared to swallow. Any mention of decorating gear and the game would be up. 'It's paintings and ceramics. Sort of modern art.'

'It is?' Clunk looked interested. 'That's very prestigious, Mr Spacejock. We could gain quite a reputation by undertaking this sort of job more often.'

'I'm sure you're right.'

'You know, I've always had an interest in art. I might even take a look at the pieces after we're airborne.'

'You can't!' said Hal quickly. 'It's a sealed box. Very valuable.'

'What a shame. Still, I suppose it's to be expected.' Clunk gestured towards the back of the ship. 'I'll lower the ramp, and in the meantime you'd better call for these artworks.'

'There's no rush,' said Hal, realising they'd have to move the container in full view of the *Tiger*. 'Plenty of time.'

'You said it was urgent.'

'Yeah, but we might as well wait until Spearman leaves. We don't want to bang hulls with that joystick waggler, do we?'

'But ground control –'

'They'll never keep us apart,' said Hal firmly. Then he nodded towards the lift. 'Did they do anything with the AutoChef? I'm starving.'

'It was updated along with the rest of the ship.'

'You mean it serves good food?'

'Not exactly. The process is the same, only accelerated.'

Hal sighed. 'You mean it serves the same old rubbish, only faster.'

'In a nutshell.'

'Blimey, the portions must be tiny.'

'No, I meant –'

'I'll just have to eat more of them, that's all.' Hal frowned. 'How come Spearman doesn't have to deal with this sort of thing? Why does he get decent food?'

'You can ask him that yourself,' said Clunk. 'He's on his way over.'

'Eh?' Hal turned to look, and his stomach sank as he saw the other pilot striding purposefully towards the *Volante*. Had Spearman discovered the container switch already?

— 23 —

Walsh jumped as she heard a loud knock on the office door. Was it Hal?
Had he come back? Heart pounding, she hurried down the passageway,
but when she opened the door she saw Herringen instead. He was rugged
up in a heavy coat and gloves, and his frosted breath hung in the cold air
like smoke.

'Ah, Miss Walsh. I didn't wake you, did I?'

Walsh hid her disappointment. 'No, not at all.'

'May I come in?'

'Sure.' Walsh led him along the passageway to the office. 'How can I
help? Do you have more information on the accountant?'

'No, nothing like that.' Herringen paused. 'I don't suppose you've
seen Jon Newman, have you?'

'Not since yesterday.'

'Oh dear.' Herringen sat down heavily, making the chair creak. 'It's
not like him to miss work, not without letting me know.'

'You don't think he's gone missing too?'

'I don't know what to think! I've called and called, but there's no reply.
I even had his commset traced, but they couldn't pinpoint the location.'

'Have you been to his house?'

'Not yet. I –' Herringen looked at his feet. 'Well, with people
disappearing I thought it would be best to have an officer of the law along.
W-will you go with me?'

Walsh considered it. Herringen turning up at the back door was a bit
odd, but he looked soft and if he tried anything she'd take him easily
enough. It would also bring her investigation to a swift conclusion. On
the other hand, if he was legit the trip would get her out of the office, and
Barney might have cracked into the mine's data by the time she got back.
Win-win. 'Okay, let's go.'

Herringen's car was outside, a mid-range model a couple of years old. They got in and he pulled onto the main road, then drove just below the speed limit.

'I won't write you a ticket,' said Walsh. 'Go for it.'

Herringen looked relieved, and they sped up. Not long afterwards they pulled into a broad avenue, and then into a succession of smaller streets before stopping at the top of a cul-de-sac. Opposite was a glass-fronted house with rolling green lawns and a manicured garden, and Walsh stared up at the marble columns and impressive façade as they took the path to the front door. 'He's doing all right for himself.'

'I understand there's money in the family.' Herringen pressed the doorbell, and a gentle chime sounded deep inside the house.

'Does he ever work from home?'

'Only on his own projects.' Herringen pressed the bell again. 'Do you think we should check round the back? Brief the joint?'

'Case.' Walsh turned away to hide a sudden smile, and her gaze fell on the garage adjoining the house. If it was empty, Newman had gone out. Simple. She went to have a look, cupping her hands to one of the leadlight windows, and saw a large pickup alongside an empty space. 'Mr Herringen, does Newman use a company car?'

'Yes, it's supplied with the job.'

'Can you track it?'

'Sure. I just tap my watch three times and it points me in the right direction. It can even do weather forecasts.'

'There's no need to be sarcastic.'

'I'm sorry. I'm just worried we've lost someone else, and Newman is vital to the mine.'

Walsh returned to the front door and decided to take a leaf out of Hal's book. 'Stand back. I'm going to break it down.'

Herringen looked shocked. 'You can't do that! It's illegal!'

'So is obstructing an officer. Anyway, it's not like Newman can't afford the repairs.' Herringen moved aside and Walsh kicked the door just below the knob. The wood splintered and the door flew open, smashing into the wall and bouncing back again. Walsh steadied it, then leaned inside. 'Hello? Anyone here?'

The hallway was bright and airy, with an intricate rug lying on the polished floorboards and a set of abstract paintings on the walls. Walsh made for a nearby doorway and looked in on a sitting room, where a white leather lounge suite sat before an entire wall of entertainment gear. She was just about to enter when she heard a gasp behind her.

'Would you look at that screen!' whispered Herringen, his voice dripping with envy.

Walsh rolled her eyes and crossed to a set of glass doors, which opened onto an indoor pool surrounded by tropical greenery. A well-stocked bar shared an alcove with a row of stools, and the only other exit led to a small change room.

Walsh returned to the hallway and turned right, heading deeper into the house. She passed a dining room with a glass-topped table and an impressive chandelier, but kept going until she reached a pair of double doors at the end of the passage. They were ajar, but resisted when she tried to open them. When she peered through she could just make out a tiled floor, with scattered rubble all over it. Either Newman was renovating, or something was badly wrong.

Unbidden, an image of Hal attacking Margaret Cooper's kitchen floor came to her. Perhaps he *had* been onto something - or had he been *here*? She shook her head to clear the thought.

Turning, she beckoned to Herringen, who was still eyeing the chandelier. Together they put their shoulders to the doors and pushed, and the rubble trapped underneath scraped and crunched as the doors were forced open.

As soon as the gap was big enough Walsh slipped through into the kitchen. She glanced around the pristine worktops, then stared down at the floor. No wonder there was so much rubble ...it looked as though someone had gone over the neat white tiles with a jackhammer, smashing them up and leaving holes the size of her fist. She crouched next to one and realised it wasn't just a shallow impression - it went deep underground. Was Newman installing underfloor heating? Then she heard a gasp and turned to see Herringen staring at the damage, his face pale and his eyes as round as the holes.

'It ...it can't be. It's impossible!'

'What is?'

'They were supposed to be safe. Newman reprogrammed them!'

'Reprogrammed ...' Walsh stared down at the floor, and suddenly it hit her. 'You don't mean your miner bugs were here?'

Herringen nodded.

'They came right into Newman's home?' Walsh yanked her hand away from the hole. 'You said they were limited to a safe depth!'

'They are, but we've had one or two glitches. Newman's been working on the code, and he assured me –'

'Oh, fantastic.' Walsh looked around the destroyed floor. The things must have swarmed through the solid concrete in their hundreds, chewing and biting … Hurriedly, she stood up and backed towards the door. 'Where the hell did they go, Herringen?'

'It's likely they returned to the mine. If not, we can use the onboard cameras to track them.'

'Can you shut them down?'

'I - I don't know. I mean, Newman tried and look what happened to him.' Herringen passed a hand over his face. 'Oh, this is terrible. It's worse than –'

'We don't know they got him. Remember, one of the cars is missing.' Privately, Walsh felt it was unlikely Newman would have bothered to close the garage door if he was fleeing for his life, but she needed Herringen calm and rational. 'You'll just have to go to the mine and do what you can.'

'You don't expect me to go alone?'

'Why the hell not?' snapped Walsh. 'It's your company!'

'But the … the miner bugs!'

Walsh advanced on him. 'Mr Herringen, the people of Forzen are in danger. Someone has to step up, take responsibility and sort the problem out. And that someone is you.'

'No, I - I have to get in touch with the Council. We'll have to schedule a meeting.'

'Are you crazy?' Walsh prodded him in the chest. 'People could die while your precious Council sits around gasbagging!'

'You're right.' Herringen straightened a little. 'The people of Forzen are depending on me. It's my duty.'

'Good man. Now get moving.'

Outside, Herringen strode towards the parked car. He opened the door then looked round. 'Aren't you coming?'

'No, I'm going to the office. I need some help.'

'But –'

'GO! There's no time to lose!'

As soon as Herringen drove away, Walsh hurried to the huge sports utility in the garage. She clambered in and slammed the door behind her. 'Let's go!' she said. 'Take me to the Peace Force office!'

The car just sat there.

'Move,' said Walsh. 'Come on, drive!' Then she remembered - Forzen cars were user-operated! She looked down at the unfamiliar controls, then shrugged. How difficult could it be?

There was a contact on the side of the steering column, and she found a keycard tucked into the sun visor. She pressed the card to the contact and the dash came alive with a riot of dials and instruments, and the engine burst into life with a deep rumble. A remote opened the garage door, and Walsh drove out of the carport, roaring down the quiet cul-de-sac with the engine noise echoing from the houses. At the bottom she turned left, and in the rear view display she saw Herringen's car in the distance, heading towards the mine. She hoped he'd succeed in restraining the bugs, but what chance did he have if Newman the IT specialist hadn't been able to stop them?

But all was not lost. There was someone she could turn to for help, someone who surely had the skills to shut down the deadly bugs before anyone else was killed. Get him to the mine and their problems would be over.

But first she had to convince him to help, and that meant turning him on.

◆

Hal squinted, trying to make out Spearman's expression as he came up the passenger ramp. He didn't look particularly angry, and since he wasn't yelling and waving his fists Hal figured his little cargo switch hadn't been picked up.

'Spacejock,' said Kent, with a little nod.

'Spearman,' said Hal, with an even smaller one. 'Lost your way to the sky?'

'No, not at all. Just came to see how a loser like you manages to stay afloat.'

Clunk put a warning hand on Hal's arm, but he shook it off. 'I have to admit,' said Hal, 'you've really got the hang of this business.'

'Eh?'

'I think I'll follow you around and learn from your masterful example. Maybe pick up a few tips while I learn the ropes.' Hal noticed Clunk staring at him open-mouthed, and realised he might be laying it on a bit thick. 'So, are you off then?'

Spearman nodded. 'I have to deliver the cargo on time. If I'm late, Morgan will think she hired you two duds instead.'

Hal clenched his fists, but before he could knock Spearman down the ramp Clunk got between them. 'That's enough friendly banter,' said the robot firmly. 'Mr Spacejock, we have work to do. And Mr Spearman, you should be putting your efforts into running your business, not wasting time talking to us.'

'Actually, it's business I want to talk about. It's crazy the two of us going head to head when we could work together. Why don't you join me?'

Hal snorted. 'You want me to work for you?'

'Sure. I'll find the work and pay you a percentage of profits. No risk, and none of this competing for jobs. Come on, you know it makes sense.'

'He does have a point,' said Clunk.

'I've got a better idea,' said Hal. 'Why doesn't he work for us?'

Spearman laughed. 'From what I've seen, you couldn't organise a cargo job in the middle of a transport strike.'

'Oh yeah?' Hal was about to reveal the container switch in order to wipe the smirk off Spearman's face, but held back just in time. 'If you're so efficient, why stand around here chatting? You should be off delivering that cargo of yours.'

'Damn straight.' Spearman threw them a mock salute. 'So long, you two. Try not to clog up the space lanes.'

Hal reached for a suitable comeback, but before he could stake Spearman with an insightful comment on his ancestry the other pilot was halfway to his ship. 'I hope you crash it!' Hal shouted after him.

Clunk patted him on the shoulder. 'Prior to that comment you behaved like a gentleman, turning the other cheek in the face of extreme provocation. I'm impressed, Mr Spacejock.'

'You know the problem with gentlemen, Clunk?'

'What's that?'

'They always finish last.'

'Maybe they do, but they feel good about it.'

'I don't want to feel good, I want to feel wealthy.' Hal scowled at the *Tiger*, where Spearman was making his way up the passenger ramp. 'And I want to feel that arrogant throttle jockey's neck under my boot.'

'Whatever for? I mean, he took the cargo job but there will be others.'

'This isn't about the cargo.' Hal pointed at the *Tiger*. 'I still reckon that mealy-mouthed son of a bitch was the reason my ship got turned into a super-sized jigsaw puzzle back on Dismolle.'

Clunk looked surprised. 'But it wasn't –'

'It damn well was!' snapped Hal. 'He knew we were after the same job, and he made absolutely sure we couldn't do it. Don't tell me it doesn't fit.'

'But the –'

'But nothing. Now come on, let's get the container aboard. If we're late with the delivery they'll think they hired that loser Spearman to do the job.'

◆

Walsh drove into the car park behind the Peace office, almost scraping the walls as she struggled to manoeuvre the lumbering sports utility. The tyres scrubbed as she threw the vehicle into a bay, and then she heaved the door open and jumped down.

Hurrying past the crumbling boxes of records inside the office, she ran to the armoury and faced the dozing robot. 'Barney?'

There was no response.

'Barney, can you hear me?'

The robot's eyes flickered open. 'Too soon. I'm still working on it.'

'What?'

Barney tapped the data chip. 'Not ready yet.'

'Forget about that, it's not important.'

'Are you telling me I just wasted –'

'Barney, we desperately need your help. The mining bugs are on the rampage, and they can't stop them.'

'Always said it would happen. Thousands of machines with perfect mobility and rudimentary intelligence. A recipe for disaster.'

'What can we do?'

'Get the programmer to broadcast a deactivation command. Your rampaging bugs will turn into so many garden ornaments.'

'The programmer's missing,' said Walsh quietly. 'We think they got him.'

'Really?' Barney's eyebrows rose. 'That's impressive. They must be pooling their intelligence.'

'Look, can we leave the technical detail for later? I need you to come to the mine and ...' Walsh's voice tailed off at Barney's expression. 'What is it?'

'I can't leave the office. Not without orders.'

'Barney, I order you to –'

'Before you start throwing your weight around, I'd like to clarify the chain of command. You're a trainee, correct?'

'That's right.'

'What's your seniority? Three years? Four?'

'Almost two years, but I'll be graduating soon.'

'I beg to differ. A Peace Force traineeship runs for a minimum of five years.' Barney regarded her. 'Who's in charge of the Dismolle office these days?'

'Bernie runs the office.'

'Yes, but who do you report to?'

'Bernie, of course.'

'A robot cannot run a Peace Force office. There has to be a commanding officer.'

'Well there isn't!' said Walsh desperately. She glanced at her watch and realised Herringen would already be at the mine. He needed her, and she needed Barney. 'Look, I'm appealing to your sense of duty. Come to the mine with me, deactivate the bugs and I promise I'll do everything in my power to get you back to Dismolle. I'll get you reinstated, and you can help Bernie run the whole office. What do you say?'

'I say you don't have the power to do any of it,' said Barney. 'In fact, you're not even a member of the Peace Force. And I can prove it.'

24

'*What?*' Walsh felt a sense of unreality wash over her as Barney's words sank in. 'Not Peace Force? What are you talking about?'

'Tell me, who do you report to if there's no commanding officer?'

'Bernie.'

'Nobody from Central HQ? Not even direct calls?'

'Oh, we have a hotline, but Bernie told me it costs a fortune so we're only allowed to use it in a real emergency.'

'And the last time you used it was ...?'

'Never. It's pretty quiet on Dismolle.'

'So when did Internal Affairs last come by? Or the expense auditors?'

'I don't know who they are.'

'Why am I not surprised?' Barney crossed his arms. 'Miss Walsh, I'm afraid you've been taken in by a cruel hoax. Ever since you mentioned the Dismolle Peace Force I've been thinking things over, and I'm absolutely certain the office doesn't exist.'

'It most certainly does.' Walsh snorted. 'Oh, I see what you're up to. If you can prove I'm not Peace Force you can ignore me, and you're using all your twisted logic to make it so.'

'You want proof?' Barney's voice was gentle, and his eyes expressed sorrow rather than duplicity.

Walsh's heart thumped in her chest. 'Spill it.'

'There's a specialist Peace Force team whose only function is to close down inefficient offices. They call them the Cleaners, and you barely get any warning. One minute there's a busy office, and the next it's an empty building with a few old desks, some trivial paperwork and all the unwanted gear locked in the armoury.'

'And they paid you a visit ten years ago. What's your point?'

'After they closed this office, they left for Dismolle. And they weren't going for the sunshine.'

Walsh's eyes widened. 'You're wrong! The Dismolle office is still up and running.'

'Tell me, have you ever had contact with anyone in the Peace Force, other than Bernie?'

Walsh thought back over the past couple of years. 'I've had messages. Congratulations when I passed my exams, that sort of thing.'

'But you've never spoken to anyone in person?'

'No.'

Barney laughed. 'It sounds like Bernie has quite the little scam going.'

'She's not like that. Anyway, my graduation is coming up! I had to take a couple of tests again, but once the results come through –'

'You re-sat an exam?'

'Yes. I failed a couple of questions, but Bernie helped me with the revision and –'

'My dear girl, you don't get a second chance with Peace Force exams. It's pass or fail.'

'You're wrong,' snapped Walsh, finally losing patience. 'I've put two years of my life into the Peace Force and I'm not having you tear my dreams apart.'

'There's a simple check, of course. All you have to do is access the Peace Force database and look up your record.'

'How?'

'Your regular login will do. You won't be able to access the higher-level functions, but a simple database lookup is permitted.'

'But I don't have a login. Trainees aren't allowed access to the system.'

Barney's eyebrows went up. 'Says who?'

'Bernie told me –' Walsh stopped. Everything came back to Bernie. But who could she trust more? This bitter, run-down robot with its flaky memory, or Bernie, who'd guided her through an entire traineeship? And what if Bernie had specific reasons for keeping her in the dark? Maybe it was a new training method, or a lack of resources.

No, she had to put her trust in Bernie. The alternative didn't bear thinking about. 'Bernie told me I could have my own login as soon as I graduated,' said Walsh firmly.

'If you want to believe that, it's no paint off my nose.' Barney shifted his weight, creaking with the movement. 'So, where does this Bernie get her spares?'

'What do you mean?'

'Without a regular infusion of parts we're just oversized paperweights.'

'You're still working.'

'I'm running in standby mode, but on full power I needed a weekly shipment of spares. They used to come over from HQ on the *Ganymede*, regular as clockwork.'

'But Bernie doesn't get any deliveries.'

'Then she must have a local source. Do you have an electronics wholesaler nearby?'

'She can't go out. She's confined to the office.'

'Still got all your servers? Data terminals?'

'Yes, lots. I mean, they go wrong from time to time but we still have them.'

'And once a terminal goes wrong, what happens then?'

'Nothing. Bernie tries to fix them, but she's not very good at it.'

'First, the BNE-II was designed to fix anything, anywhere. Second, if your terminals aren't working, why doesn't Bernie order replacements from HQ? Or spares, for that matter?'

Despite herself, Walsh was beginning to wonder. 'I heard there were budget cutbacks. Anyway, we don't need a dozen terminals when there are only two operators.'

'One. You're not allowed to use them.' Barney sighed. 'I'm sorry you've been taken in, but there's nothing I can do. I really do need to shut down.'

'No, wait!' Walsh grabbed the robot's massive hand. 'It doesn't matter whether I'm Peace Force or not. You can save these people!'

There was no response, and Walsh let the hand drop. Was the robot right? Had Bernie been using her as a front, pretending the Dismolle Peace Force was still running? Her insides turned cold. Did everyone know? Were they all humouring her, laughing behind her back?

Walsh slumped in a chair, feeling like a rug had been pulled out from under her feet. For the past two years she'd pictured herself as a small cog in the huge Peace Force machine, an anonymous but vital part of the whole. She'd even seen her future: a merit award or two, a promotion here and there, slowly rising through the ranks until she had her own station.

And now it had all been taken away.

Distraught, she buried her face in her hands, alone in the empty office.

◆

There was a deep rumble nearby, which grew to a steady roar as a ship ran its engines up prior to takeoff. The sound was familiar, and Hal glanced round to see the *Tiger* wreathed in smoke. Nice clean smoke.

'There goes Mr Spearman,' said Clunk.

Hal wasn't one hundred percent certain Spearman was going anywhere, so he kept his mouth shut.

The noise increased and the *Tiger* shimmered in the haze from its exhausts. It seemed poised to hurl itself into the atmosphere, but at the last moment the jets belched thick yellow smoke and the engines faltered, burping and grumbling.

'Oh dear,' said Hal. 'That doesn't look good.'

'I've never seen anything like it,' said Clunk, as the ship vanished behind a rolling curtain of smoke. 'What could possibly cause such a thing?'

'Come on, ignore him. Let's go load the cargo.'

Clunk was staring at the smoke, and didn't move.

Suddenly the *Tiger* burst from the thick cloud, blowing the yellow smoke away with the wash from its jets. The ship roared overhead, its graceful departure only marred by the twisted brown contrails it left behind.

'Phew-wee,' remarked Hal, as the smoke settled over the spaceport. 'What a stink.'

'Yes, it smells remarkably like a waste treatment plant. In fact, it's just like …' Clunk's voice tailed off and he turned to look at Hal. In all the years humans had been constructing robots in their likeness, never had one of their creations cast a suspicion-laden glance approaching this particular beauty. Unfortunately, Hal's attention was riveted on the departing ship, and he missed it. 'Well?' demanded Clunk. 'Did you interfere with his fuel?'

'Not me,' said Hal, refusing to look at the robot. 'Old Spearhead's just a crappy pilot.' He watched the ship rise higher and higher into the sky, until the glittering dot vanished from sight.

'We'd better load this cargo of yours,' said Clunk.

Hal led the way down the ramp, and they crossed the field to the stacks of containers.

'Which one is it?' asked Clunk.

Hal raised his finger to point, then stared at the rows of identical containers in rising panic. He'd effectively buried a needle in a haystack.

—◆—

Walsh wasn't sure exactly how long she'd been sitting on the dusty box, but she knew she couldn't stay there forever. She had to get back to Dismolle, demand the truth from Bernie and then act on it. If she'd been lied to she'd leave her home planet, no question. She couldn't possibly show her face in public after a humiliation like this.

As for Herringen and his bugs ... Walsh sniffed. Let him deal with them. That was all in her past now, when she still had her delusions to keep her happy.

Mind you, she thought, it was funny how everyone had obeyed her without question, legitimate or not. The residents of Dismolle, poor old Newman, big boss Herringen, and even Clunk and ... Walsh gasped. Hal! He knew her as a Peace Force officer, not an ordinary civilian! He'd done everything possible to help her with the investigation. What would he say when he found out it was all a sham? Would he be angry?

Walsh fought back tears, and she could hear the foundations of her life crumbling beneath her feet. Then, deep within, she found a tiny nugget of resolve. She *had* been a member of the Peace Force, officially recognised or not. She *had* done the training and passed the exams. And she *could* make a difference, in or out of uniform.

She stood up, her resolve hardening. She might not be a serving Peace officer, but she was the closest thing Forzen or Dismolle had to one. She'd stop these stupid bugs, beat the truth out of Herringen and submit a faultless report to Peace Force Central. And if they didn't accept her as a trainee, she'd ... her determination wavered, but she forged on. If they didn't want her, she'd do something else. So there.

Feeling a little happier, Walsh glanced towards the armoury. Let the bloody robot rust away in the darkness, if that's what it wanted. She'd only have willing volunteers on her team.

She froze, her gaze fixed on the carpet. Was she going mad, or had it just moved? She watched closely for several seconds, and was just about to dismiss it as nerves when the carpet rippled again. Was it a rat trapped underneath? Water seeping up through the floors? A whole colony of cockroaches looking for a new home?

Then she heard the noise: an urgent rustling interspersed with metallic scrapes. She was still trying to place the sound when the carpet bulged and a sleek metal claw tore through, snapping at thin air right in front of her. Walsh stared at it in horror, then spun round to see the entire floor erupting with hundreds of miner bugs. They shredded the carpet, tearing it to pieces with their hardened metal jaws, then closed on their prey, hemming her in from all sides at once.

Completely surrounded, Walsh leapt onto the desk, almost falling over the terminal. The bugs converged on her position, tumbling over one another in their haste. They ran up the table legs, and Walsh kicked several away as they clambered onto the surface. There were too many, though, and it was only a matter of time before she was eaten alive.

Crouching, she took hold of the computer terminal and hurled it into the seething mass of bugs. They turned on it, crushing the plastic case and splintering the glass in their mindless frenzy, and while they were occupied Walsh took a flying jump over their heads, landing heavily just outside the circle of bugs. The nearest turned to follow, but she had time to wrench open the reinforced door to the armoury, dive inside and slam it to before they got to her. Immediately, their jaws scraped on the metal as they tried to follow.

There was a loud bang as the bugs chewed through the terminal's power cord, and a flash lit up the door frame. It didn't stop the bugs though - she could hear them destroying the remains of the computer, while others continued to attack the door.

Walsh scanned the shelves for a weapon, but they were as bare as the last time she'd been in there. And now she was trapped.

In the middle of the Forzen spaceport, large stacks of containers poked through the brown-tinged smoke like rocks in the ocean. An onlooker - or rather, an onlistener - would have heard two voices in the smoke. They appeared to be discussing a missing item.

'Well how do I know where the bloody thing ended up?' said the first voice. 'They all look the same from down here.'

'Where did you see them from last time?' asked the second voice.

'Sort of higher up,' said Hal. For it was he.

'Were you standing on something?' asked Clunk.

'Yes.'

'So why don't you stand on it again?'

'It's a bit tricky,' said Hal, glancing up at the crane.

Unfortunately, Clunk noticed. 'You climbed up *there*?'

'Kind of.'

'You're lucky they didn't arrest you. Didn't anyone call you down?'

Hal shook his head. 'They were too busy ducking for cover.'

'What had that effect on them? A major fuel spill? The threat of an explosion?'

'No, you were landing the *Volante*.'

Clunk pressed his lips together. 'And you stayed in the open despite the obvious danger?'

'Sure. I'd trust you to land the ship on a ten credit chip.'

Somewhat mollified, Clunk eyed the crane. 'Why don't you stand at the bottom and see whether you can identify the container from there?'

'It's worth a shot.'

They walked to the crane, which was still unloading the cargo ship, and Hal stepped on the first rung, shielding his eyes to inspect the containers. 'It was a dark blue one with a load of scratches and - Hey, that's it!'

'Are you sure?'

'Certain.' Hal pointed it out. 'I'd recognise those dents anywhere.'

'Very well. I'll see whether the crane driver will move it to the cargo ramp.' Clunk concentrated for a moment, then shook his head. 'He says we need authorisation.'

Hal realised his plan might not go as smoothly as expected. 'How do we get that?'

'From the cargo department in the spaceport. We have to go there in person, and they'll give us a handling docket.'

'That's a long way to go for a bit of paperwork. Can't you make something up?'

Clunk shot him a look. 'Is there something you're not telling me about this job?'

'Would I keep anything from you?'

Clunk didn't bother to answer, and together they set off across the landing field. The robot appeared to be weighing up all the little facts Hal had let slip, while Hal was more concerned with the reception they were going to get at the cargo department. After all, the container in question was supposed to be aboard the *Tiger*, and while he'd blustered his way through any number of tricky situations in the past, this one looked like it was going to end in major problems. Serial numbers, shipping dockets, invoices ... he was sunk.

They were halfway across the landing field when a siren sounded. Hal started guiltily, then recognised the noise. 'Ship coming in,' he said confidently, scanning the sky for signs of the arriving vessel.

The siren was joined by another, and then another, and soon dozens of them were wailing in harmony.

'How many ships?' asked Clunk, raising his voice over the noise.

'Maybe it's a fly-in.' Then Hal saw a line of flashing lights in the distance. 'What the hell is that?'

'Emergency vehicles,' said Clunk. 'I hope there hasn't been an accident.'

Hal remembered Spearman and the *Tiger*, and he felt sick to his stomach. Surely the contaminated fuel hadn't ...

'Six fire trucks, two personnel carriers and a command vehicle,' said Clunk, standing on tip-toes. 'It's either a grade one emergency or a very comprehensive drill.'

'It's a drill,' croaked Hal. 'It has to be.'

The line of vehicles was closer now, weaving between the landing pads. They were moving fast, with headlights flashing and sirens blaring, and suddenly they were roaring by with their huge wheels and belching exhausts. Hal covered his ears to block out the piercing sirens, and he was still standing there when Clunk tugged his arm.

'They want to talk to us, Mr Spacejock.' The robot indicated an open-topped runabout driven by a couple of ground staff. The passenger was beckoning through the open window, and when Hal saw her grave face he knew the worst had happened.

'What is it?' demanded Clunk.

'There's a ship on fire. We're clearing the landing field.'

Hal swallowed. 'I-is anyone hurt?'

'We don't know yet. Look, you have to take cover. Some of these vessels carry a lot of fuel, and if it goes up there's going to be a lot of damage.'

'Where did he come down?' asked Hal desperately. 'Was it far?'

The woman gave him a strange look. 'Nobody came down. The ship's burning on the landing pad.'

'Which ship?' asked Clunk.

The woman checked with the driver. 'The *Volante*. Now, you two had better ... Hey! Where are you going?'

25

Hal and Clunk ran for the *Volante*, where the emergency vehicles had drawn up at a safe distance, blocking the ship from view. Dozens of uniformed personnel scurried around with pipes and clipboards, and those without breathing masks bore the worried expressions of emergency teams stretched to breaking point.

Beyond the trucks, long streamers of foam shot into the sky, describing graceful arcs before falling back on the unseen target. A light mist drifted across the landing field, and the chemical tang made Hal's eyes water.

They squeezed through a gap between the emergency vehicles then stopped dead as they saw the quivering mountain of foam which completely hid the *Volante*. More was being added by the fire teams, their fat hoses disgorging foam with a hissing, spluttering roar, and several ladders had been swung into position above the snowy white slopes so that operators could point out the few remaining areas not completely smothered.

Nearby, a huge man was shouting orders, his bright hazard jacket stretched tight across his barrel chest. A megaphone dangled by his side, but it was unused and unneeded, and minions scurried at his bidding, fetching equipment and assembling it under his watchful eye. 'No, you fool!' he roared at a hapless mechanic. 'Use the bigger one! Hit it, man. Hit it! And where the hell is that cutter?'

'Excuse me,' said Hal.

The giant didn't even look at him. 'Someone get these bloody civilians out of my way!'

'That's our ship,' said Clunk, pointing at the foam. 'Can you tell me where the fire broke out?'

A woman hurried over, her face red behind the breathing mask. 'You'll have to stand clear,' she said, trying to move Hal and Clunk back. 'We're about to detonate the first charge.'

'You're *what*?'

'We've smothered the ship to dampen the worst of it, but we have to get inside to put the fire out. Standard procedure, see?' The woman pointed out a group of emergency workers crouched around a small box, and Hal saw a pair of cables running across the ground to disappear under the foam. 'They're ready. Heads down, now.'

Hal was still staring in shock when Clunk pushed him aside and ran for the box. The giant roared at him to stop, but Clunk scattered the workers, grabbed the box and tore the wires out. Then he ran up the passenger ramp, leaving a wake as he barged through the thick foam. He paused at the airlock to tear the explosives from the hull, then entered the keycode and disappeared inside before the door was half open.

On the ground, people turned to the giant for leadership, but Clunk had taken the initiative and there was nothing the big man could do. 'Everyone fall back,' he bellowed. 'The ship's a goner. Save yourselves!'

Doors slammed, engines revved, and within moments the emergency team was retreating for the safety of the terminal. The fire chief squeezed into a command vehicle and followed, and then Hal was alone. He watched the fleeing vehicles, then eyed the ship in some trepidation. Trust Clunk's judgement or scarper for safety? He'd just decided when the robot hailed him from the airlock.

'False alarm, Mr Spacejock. Come on up.'

Hal turned back to the ship and took the ramp to the airlock, wading through drifts of foam. The substance was thinner now, and the breeze tore chunks from the railings and sent them spiralling towards the ground below. At the top he found Clunk in the doorway, brushing foam off his arms and legs. 'How do you know it's a false alarm?'

'I checked with the Navcom. It's safe to come aboard.'

'So who reported the fire?'

'Perhaps a visitor saw sunlight glinting off the hull. That can look like flames from a distance.'

Hal glanced at the dull grey sky, heavy with snow clouds. 'Or perhaps some sneaky bastard raised a false alarm. Someone determined to ruin me at any cost.'

'You can't believe Mr Spearman would do something like this?'

'Oh yeah? He had the *Volante* torn apart, didn't he? What's a little fire after something like that?'

'But the –'

'Take my word for it, Clunk.' Hal gestured at the foam, which was sliding off the hull in lumps. 'You can put this oversized cake decorating down to Kent bloody Spearman. He's gone completely off the deep end, and then kept on going. He's –' Hal broke off as someone hailed them from below. It was the fire chief, and he was just getting out of his car. 'Oh great,' muttered Hal.

'You up there!'

'Yes?'

'Sorry about the mix-up, chaps. Call came in, we reacted. You know the drill.' The man looked embarrassed as he eyed the copious slathering of foam. 'Anything I can do to help?'

'Not really,' said Clunk.

'Yes, there is,' said Hal at the same time. He pointed to the crane. 'You can tell that guy to load our cargo.'

'Navvies giving you problems, eh?' The fire chief set his jaw. 'I'll sort 'im out quick smart.'

'Roger and out,' called Hal. He watched the fire chief march to the crane, take hold of the ladder and start climbing hand over hand. Despite his bulk, the man was very agile, and he reached the cabin in no time. There followed a short, sharp altercation, with finger pointing and a bunched fist or two, and then the chief was on his way down again. Before he reached the foot of the crane it was already swinging round towards the *Volante*. Hal pointed out the container, the crane picked it up and moments later it was sitting on the cargo ramp.

The fire chief snapped a salute, glared up at the crane operator, then drove off.

'Always useful to have friends in high places,' remarked Hal.

Clunk nodded thoughtfully, then set off towards the hold.

◆

Walsh stood in the armoury, shaken by her narrow reprieve. The miner bugs had erupted from the floor without warning, and it wasn't hard to picture them trapping Newman the same way. She glanced around gratefully at the reinforced walls and floor. Let the bugs gnaw and chomp all they liked - they'd run out of steam long before they made a dent. The door was the weak point, but surely it would keep them out?

She remembered the new flooring at the accountant's house, and Hal's determination to find out whether there was anything suspicious underneath. Well, it was obvious now, she thought bitterly. The bugs had got Margaret Cooper, no doubt of it. All the evidence had been there, but instead of investigating like the good little Peace Force officer she was supposed to be, she'd blown up at Hal over a handful of broken floor tiles. But there was something else. If the bugs had attacked Cooper, chewing through her floors, who the hell had repaired the damage? And who -

Her train of thought was broken by the frantic scraping and grinding noises on the other side of the metal door. What if they chewed right through it? Came in after her? She backed away hastily and bumped into Barney, almost spooking herself to death. His armour might stand up to the bugs, and his strong hands would crush them easily. But would he help, or would he stand by quoting rules and regulations while the bugs tore her apart?

'Barney, wake up!'

The robot's eyes opened, unfocussed and confused. 'What is it?'

'I need your help. It's important.'

'You have no authority.'

Walsh eyed the door, which was shaking under the onslaught. 'Look, I know you won't help me. But will you at least send a message?'

'I don't have network access.'

'Dammit!' Walsh thought for a moment. 'Can you record me? Just in case something happens?'

'That's standard procedure,' said Barney. 'Officers in the field must document their findings in case of premature death.'

'Exactly. Tell them it was the miner bugs, no matter how it's covered up, and –' Walsh swallowed. 'Tell Hal I'm sorry.'

'Who is this Hal?'

'Hal Spacejock of the *Volante*. He wanted me to leave with him, but –'

'You remained on Forzen to complete your investigation?'

'That was the idea, but it doesn't look like –' There was a creak of tortured metal, and a corner of the door buckled inwards.

'You stayed despite the obvious danger?'

'It was my duty.'

'I see.'

Walsh eyed the weakened metal. Any second now … 'Did you save my message?'

'There's no need.' Barney reached for a chest compartment. His stiff fingers had trouble with the catch, but eventually he reached inside and took out a tarnished Peace Force shield, holding it up for inspection before pressing it to his chest. It stuck there, and the robot straightened up with a creak. 'Appointed or not, you have the persistence and bravery of a true officer. It will be an honour to serve with you.'

Walsh smiled, her eyes bright.

'Now, Officer Walsh. Would you please define the threat?'

'Hundreds of miner bugs out there,' said Walsh, indicating the door. 'They came through the floor and surrounded me.'

'Very well. Climb up on the shelf and I'll deal with them.'

'But they'll –'

'Please don't argue. It is my sworn duty to protect my fellow officers.'

Walsh opened her mouth to reply, but Barney grabbed her arm and pushed her towards the shelves. Then he crouched, bending one knee for her to use as a step. The shelf was dusty, and Walsh held her breath as she crammed herself against the wall.

'I will clear a path for your escape,' said Barney, his voice low and urgent. 'Whatever happens, do not come to my aid. Do you understand?'

'I do.' Walsh pictured the robot standing alone against the bugs and almost jumped down to help. Then again, she was their target. 'Barney, it's a privilege to serve with you.'

'Officer Walsh?'

'Yes?'

'I may have been mistaken about your Peace Force traineeship. Procedures might have changed in the years since I was on active service.'

'I -I hope you're right.'

'You will graduate with honours. I'm sure of it.'

At that moment the door gave way and a river of bugs flooded in. Barney gathered an armful, crushing them together and hurling the crumpled bodies from the armoury. His second armful was even bigger than the first, but by the time he stooped for a third the bugs were climbing his legs, their mandibles chewing the tough metal.

With a huge effort, Barney managed a step towards the doorway. More bugs flowed up his legs, and many hung from his chest and back. Another step, and the writhing mass swayed. Another, then another, and Barney left the armoury for the first time in ten long years, buried under the swarming bugs. There were sparks now, electrical flashes as the bugs tore off his control panel, ripped out his power switch and went for his eyes. And still he grabbed handfuls of wriggling, nipping attackers, crushing them and stamping on their broken bodies.

Walsh watched Barney's struggle from the safety of her hiding spot, horrified and sickened. Guilt and helplessness assailed her - guilt because the robot was doing her bidding, sacrificing himself in an attempt to save her life. Helplessness because if she went out there a handful of bugs would tear her apart while the rest finished the job on Barney.

The robot reached the remains of the terminal, stumbled on the pieces and fell full length across the table, crushing it flat. Immediately the remaining bugs piled on, and Barney disappeared under a pile of frenzied miners, all snapping and tearing at his metal flesh. Now and then a dozen bugs would erupt from the mass, hurled away by the struggling robot, but after a while even this resistance ceased. Walsh turned away, hot tears coursing down her face. Silently she made a vow: whoever was behind this was going to pay.

The bugs slowed their attack, and Walsh spotted a couple moving in circles, waving their antennae. Others would soon join them, and as soon as they determined her position she'd be trapped.

She realised it was time to make a run for it, and she rolled off the shelf and dropped lightly to the ground. Stepping over the shattered bugs littering the armoury, she hesitated at the door. The seething pile of bugs tearing Barney's remains apart stood between her and the exit, whereas the stairs were still clear. Getting trapped on the upper floor wasn't her idea of a cunning plan, but then again the bugs might not think to climb the stairs.

After a couple of deep breaths, Walsh bolted from the armoury and ran for the stairs. She took them three and four at a time, the blood pounding at her temples as she threw herself up the staircase. At the top she grabbed the handrail and swung herself round, then pelted for the room where she'd spent the night. She tore the door open and closed it behind her, then dragged every piece of furniture in the room across to block it.

Finally the job was done, and she slumped to the floor with her back to the barricade.

Scratch, scratch.

Walsh's heart thudded at the sound. Was that the furniture settling?

Scratch.

'Please no,' she whispered. 'Leave me alone.'

The gentle scratching became a gnawing, and then a crunch of breaking wood. It multiplied as more and more bugs joined in, until it sounded like a hundred trees bending towards breaking point - and beyond.

Walsh got up and ran to the window, yanking the catch open and hammering the frame until it grudgingly opened. The sill was barely twenty centimetres wide, and beyond was a sheer drop to the car park. There was no convenient drainpipe, and no fire escape.

CRACK!

Walsh spun round and saw the pile of furniture shifting as hundreds of bugs tore into it from the other side. Unthinking, she grabbed the windowsill and hauled herself up, her feet scraping the plaster as she fought for purchase. She'd barely left the floor when the makeshift barricade fell in on itself, and the bugs streamed into the room, heading straight for the window.

For a moment Walsh thought the wall might stop them, but they broke against it like a wave, allowing those in the rear to scuttle over those in front. She knocked the first bugs away, but more took their place. One grabbed her sleeve, and as a second went for her leg she yelled at them in anger and frustration. Then she stood up, balancing on the windowsill with the bugs on one side and a sheer drop on the other. She looked down at the car park, and a smile came to her lips as she remembered sitting in the car with Hal the night before, discussing the case in the darkness. It seemed a lifetime ago now, and for a second she wished things had turned out differently.

Then she jumped.

— 26 —

'Navcom, how quickly –'

'Can we leave? Initial checks are under way. Departure in ninety seconds.'

Hal took his seat and strapped in. 'Are you just going to stand there?' he asked Clunk, who was hovering near the airlock. The robot had manoeuvred the container into the hold and sealed the ship, but something was still troubling him.

'The intakes are full of foam, Mr Spacejock.'

'Not for long,' said Hal grimly. 'Just wait until I start the engines.'

'But they might overheat!'

'Are you kidding? It'll be like roasting marshmallows with a nuclear bomb.'

'What about the fumes? Emitting non-compliant exhaust gases could earn us an environmental protection order.'

Hal snorted. 'They'll have to catch us first.'

'Mr Spacejock, you must let me clean the engines. Thirty minutes, one hour at the most. It's essential!'

'Clunk, it's a bunch of fluffy white stuff. You know, like clouds. And do you dash outside to clean the engines every time we fly through a bit of vapour?'

'But –'

'No, I didn't think so.' Hal turned back to the console. 'Fire 'em up Navcom. We're –'

'– going to Dismolle. Yes, I know.'

The engines spooled up with a loud whine, which became a steady roar. Suddenly there was a snort and a gulp, followed by a loud hammering that shook the flight deck. Clunk hurried to the console to check the displays, his face grim. 'That's the balance compensator. Any more of this and you'll tear the ship apart.'

'It'll clear up,' said Hal confidently.

'I'm not standing here while you destroy the engines.'

'So go and stand in the airlock.'

There was another snort and the vibrations ceased. 'Engines fully operational,' said the Navcom, as the roar intensified. 'We're clear for departure.'

Hal shot Clunk a triumphant glance, then patted the console. 'Good one, Navcom. Now let's go.'

'If we crash ...' began Clunk.

'Zip it.' Hal grabbed for the armrests as the ship rose from the landing pad. The engines ran smoothly, and before long the sky turned dark, then black, as they left the atmosphere and blasted their way into orbit. Once they levelled off, Hal punched the safety buckle and stood up. 'Right,' he said, beckoning Clunk over. 'I got her up, you get us to Dismolle.'

◆

Walsh fought her way out of the dumpster, elbowing aside the soggy boxes which had broken her fall. One of the miner bugs was still attached to her sleeve, but she grabbed its slick metal body and smashed it against the wall until its legs were still. Then she vaulted to the ground and ran to Newman's pickup, pulling the door open and clambering inside. The engine started at her touch, but her legs were shaking so badly she couldn't place her feet on the pedals, and she only steadied her hands by gripping the wheel until her knuckles were bone white.

Then she realised the bugs would be after her, and she forced herself to drive, backing out of the car park and roaring up the high street as if they were already on her tail.

She'd barely had time to think during her desperate escape, but now it was all flooding back. Someone had gone to a lot of trouble replacing Cooper's flooring, covering up the reason for her disappearance. Then they'd disposed of Newman, supposedly the only person who could control the bugs. And finally they'd come after her, trapping her in the office and almost ... Walsh shuddered as she recalled her narrow escape. How had they known to attack her at that very moment? Then she remembered ... Only one person knew she was returning to the Peace Force office from Newman's house, and that was Herringen.

Herringen, who'd showed off his mining bugs with obvious pride. Whose company was being audited by Cooper. And what about Newman? Had he uncovered something just before he died? Unauthorised changes to the bugs'behaviour, perhaps?

Walsh gripped the wheel. Herringen was about to answer some bloody tough questions.

A few minutes later she reached the mine, but instead of parking near the office she pulled off the road, driving between the trees until the truck was concealed deep in the undergrowth. The engine cut out, and Walsh sat for a moment in thought. Herringen would have seen her escape from the office, thanks to the cameras fitted to the bugs, and he'd almost certainly be waiting for her. But would he play the innocent, hoping to lure her into a trap, or would he attack the moment she walked in?

Ideally, she'd load up with some heavy firepower and go in with all guns blazing, but even Peace Force officers couldn't shoot suspects out of hand. In any case, she was unarmed. Not only that, Herringen was a powerful man, respected in the Forzen community, and the chances of arresting him and hauling him off to Dismolle were slim. She needed proof, she needed to be clever, and she needed to be very careful.

Walsh opened the door and stepped out into the cold air. Her shoes crunched on the frozen earth, and she struggled to keep her footing as she followed the car tracks back to the road. The leaden clouds had turned the sky dark, and hardly any light permeated the gloom beneath the canopy. Sticking to the shadows, she made her way along the drive to the mine, where she spotted Herringen's car. The office lights were off, but she could see a glow from within. His office, no doubt. The lair.

Walsh entered the building, slipping past the reception desk on her way to the passageway beyond. Light spilled from Herringen's office, and her heart thumped as she approached the doorway. Rush in? Tell him to surrender? Run away?

'I can hear you!' shouted Herringen. 'One step and I'll blow you apart!'

Clunk straightened up as he finished his inspection of the ship's systems. 'Remarkably, our hasty departure caused no lasting damage. However, it was still incredibly foolish.'

'We had to leave in a hurry, Clunk. There's a lot at stake here.'

'Sure there is. You and Mr Spearman are level pegging in the intergalactic Most Stupid Human award, although your recent efforts might just have moved you into the lead.'

'If you mention that pirate again I'm really going to have a gun turret fitted.'

'Arm this ship and we'll be penniless fugitives with a terrible reputation and no chance of earning an honest living.' Clunk hesitated. 'Granted, that's not a whole lot different to our current situation, but at least we're not fugitives.'

'That's what you –'

'I'm picking up a Mayday signal,' said the Navcom. 'Lone vessel in trouble.'

'Ignore it,' said Hal.

Clunk shook his head. 'We have to render assistance. It's the most basic of all space faring laws.'

'Yeah, and it's also the oldest trick in the book. All we'll find is a beacon playing a looped message.'

Clunk addressed the Navcom. 'Trace that distress signal and –'

'– Change course. Complying.'

'Whoa, override!' said Hal. 'Clunk, it's a trap.'

'It can't be. The penalties for sending a fake Mayday are extreme.'

'What about the penalties for tearing my ship apart? Faking a fire alarm? Spearman's behind this beacon thing too, I guarantee it.'

Clunk stood firm. 'The Navcom has already logged the call, and we have no option but to respond.'

Hal swore. 'If it IS a distress beacon, I want it brought aboard.'

'Why? So you can incriminate the perpetrator?'

'Not incriminate. Insert into.'

'Source of the distress call is now in visual range,' said the Navcom.

Clunk's hands darted over the console, and the stars on the main screen panned this way and that as he sought their quarry. 'There it is.'

Hal studied the viewscreen, but it contained nothing but stars. 'What am I looking at?'

'It's right in the middle,' said Clunk, pointing out a small dark patch.

'It's a bit big for a beacon.'

'That's because it's a spaceship.'

'A real one?'

Clunk nodded.

'Where's the identifier? And why is it dark?'

'All their systems are down.'

'Can you light it up?'

A crosshair appeared on the screen, and Clunk moved it over the dark patch, turning it white. Hal squinted at the glare and realised he was looking at the rear of a large freighter. It was angled away from them, but he could just make out three chrome strips glinting on the tail. 'Is that who I think it is?'

Clunk nodded. 'Kent Spearman. And he's in trouble.'

◆

'I-I know you're out there!' shouted Herringen. 'If you move, I swear I'll –'

'You'll what?' demanded Walsh. 'Set your bugs on me? Make me disappear?'

'Miss Walsh? Is that you?'

'Who did you think it was?'

'I thought you were dead, like the others! I waited and waited, and you never turned up!'

Walsh heard the squeak of Herringen's chair, and she backed away from the door as his footsteps approached. What if he skipped the bug attacks and just shot her in cold blood? However, when he appeared in the doorway he was pale and frightened ... and unarmed. 'I know what happened to Margaret Cooper,' she said, her voice hard. 'It was your miner bugs that got her, just as they got Newman.'

Herringen opened his mouth, and Walsh could see the denials ready to burst forth. Then his shoulders slumped. 'I can't keep this up,' he said softly. 'It's gone too far.'

Walsh's pulse quickened. 'You're willing to confess?'

Herringen returned to his office and poured a large drink, his shaking fingers making the bottle rattle on the glass. 'Production was down, and the town needed income to survive. So, I -I authorised a reduction in the buffer zone.'

'The what?'

'Our bugs are programmed to stay at least five metres below sea level.' Herringen gulped his drink. 'Unfortunately, most of the untapped deposits are above that depth, closer to the surface. Shaving a few metres off the safety zone unlocked vast reserves of ore.'

'What does that have to do with Cooper?'

'You know she lives in a valley?'

'Yes, I went to her house. A very lonely place to die.'

Herringen set his glass down, and there was a moment's silence before he continued. 'Her place is just below sea level. Not much, but enough to intersect with the new buffer zone. The bugs must have come through the floor and –'

'Thanks, I can picture the rest.' Walsh frowned. 'Wait a minute. Are you trying to tell me Cooper's death was an accident?'

'Absolutely. Margaret was doing the accounts for one of the Council members, and when he went out there to deliver some files he discovered the house empty and the kitchen floor all broken up. We searched the house, the woods …everywhere. Then we had an emergency meeting.' Herringen blinked. 'The decision was unanimous. Newman would reprogram the bugs, and we'd fix the damage.'

'We? Meetings?' Walsh stared at him. 'Are you saying others are involved?'

'Of course they are!' snapped Herringen. 'You don't think I laid a new floor myself, do you? One of the councillors has a construction business, another runs a tile company …the repair work was spread amongst us all.'

Walsh felt the ground opening up under her feet. 'The Council knew the truth about Cooper's disappearance, and they covered it up?'

'You don't understand,' said Herringen desperately. 'There are dozens of licensing deals in the balance. A scandal like this would have ruined everything! Forzen would have suffered!'

'And what's one woman against the needs of a whole planet, right?'

'Right!'

Walsh felt bile rising in her throat. 'And calling me in to look for her. What was that supposed to achieve?'

'When the Residents Association started making enquiries, we pointed them in your direction. We figured you'd come over, have a look around and declare Margaret a missing person. An unsolved mystery.'

'What made you think I'd follow your script?'

'We knew your background. Barely two years in the Force, still a trainee, no cases to speak of ...' Herringen poured himself another stiff drink. 'It seems we underestimated you.'

'And what about Newman? You're not going to tell me his house is in a valley too?'

'No, of course not.'

'Then explain his death.'

'I can't,' said Herringen simply.

'Can't or won't?'

'I –' Herringen stared. 'Oh my god. Newman!'

'That's right,' said Walsh. 'Spill it.'

'No, Newman!' said Herringen, pointing over her shoulder. He looked like he'd seen a ghost, and when Walsh turned round she realised why. It *was* Newman, and he was in a bad way.

◆

Clunk worked the *Volante's* controls, inching the freighter towards the *Tiger*. They had called her again and again, but Spearman's ship remained as unresponsive as a lump of rock. During the approach Hal was strangely silent, where Clunk had expected him to gloat, or at least chuckle quietly to himself.

After some final positioning Clunk lined up the airlocks and extended the passenger ramp. It looked ludicrous on the screen, like a staircase leading off the side of a cliff, but it was the quickest way to link the ships in flight. Once the ramp was extended Clunk entered the airlock, putting out his hand to prevent Hal from following. 'I'll go across first to check he's okay.'

'You don't think he's –'

'I'm sure he's fine.'

'But I might be able to help!'

Clunk shook his head. 'There's no time to suit up. Please, I know what I'm doing.'

Reluctantly, Hal allowed Clunk to shut the door. As soon as the indicator lights came on the outer door swung open, and the air misted and vanished, sucked into the depths of space.

Clunk went outside and stopped on the platform to get his bearings. The thin metal ramp extended into space like a rope bridge, with a sizeable gap between the far end and the *Tiger's* airlock. Below, he could see the curvature of planet Forzen, whose citizens were blissfully unaware of the trapeze act about to take place over their heads.

Clunk stepped onto the ramp, but instead of thumping solidly on the metal his foot pedalled in space. Down and up lost all meaning as he left the *Volante's* gravity field, and just in time he shot out a hand to grab the guide rail. In the interests of speed he'd spurned a safety line, and he'd been so focussed on reaching the *Tiger* he'd forgotten all about the lack of gravity. If he lost his grip and sailed off into space, the idea of Hal trying to scoop him up with the *Volante* didn't bear thinking about - with the human at the controls Clunk was more likely to end up in the engines than back inside the ship.

Slowly, he reached for the guide rail, and by moving hand over hand he made his way across the slender bridge. When he reached the gap at the far end he hesitated, running mass and vector calculations as he eyed the distance to the *Tiger*. Then he launched himself across the gap towards Spearman's ship.

He expected to fly in a direct line, but as he got closer to the *Tiger's* hull he felt a tug, and with a shock he realised the ship's gravity field was still functioning. No longer weightless, his linear progression became a graceful arc, and with a certain amount of resignation he realised he was going to fall straight past the ship and down towards the planet far below.

27

Newman swayed in the doorway, almost falling before Herringen reacted, hurrying across the office to take the younger man by the arm. Gently, Herringen led him to the nearest armchair, then reached for the bottle of scotch. 'Get this down you, son,' he said, handing Newman a glass. 'Take it easy, all right?'

Newman was a sorry sight: His clothes were torn, there was a gash on his forehead and his fingernails were broken and bleeding. None of this bothered Walsh in the slightest. 'You can take it easy later,' she said harshly. 'Tell me what happened.'

'The bugs, they...' Newman drained the glass and held it out for more. 'They've got smarter.'

Walsh nodded grimly. 'That's what Barney suspected.'

'Who?'

'Peace Force robot. Ex. He said the bugs had to be pooling their intelligence.'

Newman lowered his glass. 'Linking up? Combining their primitive brains into a hive mind? But that's –'

'Never mind the analysis. Barney said you can stop them by broadcasting a deactivation command.'

'We have to get down to the workshop.' Newman finished his drink. 'Is there anyone else here? The cleaners?'

'No, just us,' said Herringen.

'Better get on with it then.' Newman got up, and would have fallen if Herringen hadn't caught his arm.

'You should be in hospital, man.'

'Later,' muttered Newman. 'Save the planet first.'

They made their way to the lift, with Herringen supporting Newman and Walsh hoping he wouldn't lose consciousness. He looked exhausted, but they needed his expertise.

At the lift, Herringen entered his code, but the keypad just buzzed. 'Damn thing's picked a fine time to play up,' he growled, trying again. Nothing.

'Let me,' said Newman. He entered a code and the door clicked open, letting them through. They filed into the lift, where Herringen slid the doors to. Immediately, the car dropped into the darkness, the rushing wind tearing at hair and clothes.

Walsh glanced at Newman. 'We really thought they'd got you. How did you escape?'

'You saw my place?'

Walsh nodded.

'When they swarmed through the floor I went straight out the window, leapt into my car and drove like crazy.' Newman touched a cut on his forehead. 'I came to hours later, still strapped into the wreck. Must have missed a corner and gone straight into the ditch.'

'Lucky escape.'

'Yeah, and I didn't have a bloody great Peace Force robot to protect me.'

The lift arrived at the foot of the shaft, and Herringen opened the doors and stepped out. Walsh went to follow, then froze. She hadn't mentioned the attack on the Peace Force, or Barney's efforts to save her, so how did Newman know about them? She half-turned just as his raised arm came down towards her, whacking her on the side of the head. The terrific blow knocked her off her feet, and Herringen reached out to catch her in his arms. Her last conscious thought was that Newman too had been in on the cover-up and that maybe, just maybe, she'd found out too much.

Then everything went dark.

◆

Just as it seemed inevitable he was going to miss the *Tiger* and plunge towards Forzen, Clunk managed to grab the rim at the base of the airlock. His body slammed into the hull, and he held on grimly as the force of the collision almost bounced him off again. As he dangled there with planet Forzen far beneath his feet, Clunk reflected that he'd made two near-fatal mistakes in the past five minutes. He was unlikely to survive a third.

Slowly, he inched his way around the frame until he could pull himself up to the controls. The panel flipped open at his touch, and he was about to open the airlock door when he spotted Spearman through the porthole, waving to attract his attention. Clunk turned cold at the sight. Didn't Spearman know the first thing about airlock safety? He'd almost spaced him!

Shaken by a third near miss, Clunk waved casually to reassure Spearman that he was now safely in his hands. Then he indicated he wanted him in the flight deck. While Spearman complied, Clunk turned and gave the *Volante* the thumbs up, hoping Hal wasn't zoomed right in on the action. If he was, he, Clunk, would never live it down.

Once Spearman was out of the way, Clunk opened the door and hauled himself in. Then he shut the outer door and cycled the airlock, letting himself into the flight deck.

'Thank heavens you found me,' said Spearman, reaching out to clap him on the shoulder.

'Don't touch me!' exclaimed Clunk, backing away quickly.

'Fine. Be like that.'

'I'm not being funny, Mr Spearman. I've been exposed to vacuum, and my skin temperature is well below zero. Pat me if you wish, but not if you value your fingerprints.'

'Ah. Good point.'

Clunk frowned. 'Then again, given that little episode on Forzen, perhaps I should have let you.'

'You mean the fire alarm?' Spearman looked embarrassed. 'I'm sorry. It's just that Spacejock was acting strangely, like he had a trick up his sleeve.'

'They sprayed my ship with foam,' said Clunk coldly. 'They were going to blow the hull open with explosives.'

'I didn't get far myself, did I?' Spearman gestured at the lifeless console. 'It's amazing how my engines stopped working the minute I left Forzen. I bet that had nothing to do with Hal bloody Spacejock.'

'If that's the case, why did we come to your aid?'

'Spacejock's after my cargo, that's why.'

'He doesn't need it. He found another job.'

'Really?' Spearman looked surprised. 'You mean he's not after my container?'

'No, he has his own.' Clunk looked around the gloomy flight deck, which was illuminated by a pair of emergency lights. 'So, what happened?'

'I don't know,' confessed Spearman. 'One minute I was powering along, and then everything died on me.'

'You appear to have mastered the same diagnostic course as Mr Spacejock.'

'Hey, I know my ship. The engines and generators shut down, and the error logs are a mess. It's the why that's puzzling me.'

Clunk inspected the console. 'It tripped the failsafe, from the look of it.'

'Is that something you can fix?'

Clunk shook his head. 'Mr Spacejock and I will let the Dismolle people know you're out here.'

'Here, you can't go!' Spearman looked alarmed. 'You'd be leaving me in danger. It's against your programming!'

'Dismolle will send someone to fetch you in a day or two. In the meantime your survival training will keep you alive.'

'But I don't have any survival training!'

'Pity.' Clunk walked to the airlock, but before he was halfway there Spearman caught up with him.

'Okay, okay. I'm sorry about the fire drill. I won't do it again.'

'That's not all. Mr Spacejock is convinced you had his ship dismantled on Dismolle.'

Spearman looked shocked. 'I'd never do something like that! A ship is a pilot's lifeblood, as vital as a - as a vital organ. You have to believe me!'

Clunk nodded. 'I do.'

'Thank goodness,' said Spearman, looking relieved. 'Er, he's not coming over is he? Only things might get a bit heated if –'

'Mr Spacejock is safely aboard the *Volante*, and has no means of crossing. However, he's in a hurry to reach Dismolle and he's not going to want me to remain here working on your ship.'

Spearman thought for a moment. 'How about a deal?'

'What do you have in mind?'

Walsh came to slowly, feeling as though her head were smothered in cotton wool. Sounds were muffled, her mouth tasted like a cleaning brush and when she opened her eyes a searing white glare assailed her vision, forcing her to close them again. She strained her ears to pick up any clues as to her whereabouts, but all she could hear was the sound of typing.

Her memory started to return, and she recalled Herringen's office and something about the computers. Had she collapsed? And if so, why was someone typing away on the terminal instead of helping her?

Walsh lapsed into unconsciousness, and when she came round again her senses were sharper. She realised she was sitting up, but when she tried to move she discovered her hands were tied behind her back. She tried opening her eyes again, peeking out through her lashes, and realised the intense glare was just an ordinary row of overhead lights. She was sitting on the floor, and as her eyes adjusted she realised she was in the control room deep beneath the mine offices. Her face was level with the top of the desks, and when she peered over the nearest she saw Newman working on a terminal. 'So, you're awake,' he said, without looking round.

'Do you know the penalty for kidnapping a Peace Force officer? You'll be lucky if they don't execute you on the spot!'

'Yes, because your fellow officers will be here any moment now.' Newman laughed. 'You're alone, Harriet Walsh. Just like you've always been.'

Walsh struggled with the ropes, but they were too tight. 'Did Herringen set you up for this?'

Newman looked surprised. 'What do you mean?'

'I never trusted him from the beginning,' muttered Walsh. 'Playing the innocent, hard-working boss while behind the scenes he was making people disappear.'

'But Herringen didn't –'

'Loyalty amongst crooks.' Walsh snorted. 'So what's your cut? Or is he blackmailing you?'

'No, he –'

'Yeah, I know. You're a good man really. He just led you astray.'

'I –'

'Save it for the jury, Newman. Let me go and I'll put in a word for you.'

'Will you shut up!' Newman stood up so fast he knocked his chair over. He strode over to Walsh and lowered his voice to a menacing growl. 'You automatically assumed the big bad boss was behind this whole thing, didn't you?'

'Well yes. It's obvious you don't have the brains for it.'

'Herringen wouldn't know a criminal enterprise if it stole his wallet in the street! He's so upright you could hang a flag off him!' Newman tapped his chest. '*I'm* the mastermind, not that flabby old git!'

'You!'

'Do you really think he's smart enough to program the miner bugs? Override all their safeguards and turn them into killing machines?'

'But all that stuff about hive minds and linked intelligence …'

Newman snorted. 'They're as dumb as the rocks they dig up. The only intelligence behind them is my own.'

'You ordered them to attack Cooper? But why?'

'You can blame Herringen for that. I made up a special set of accounts for the audit, and then he went and gave her his bloody password. Once she had access to the real accounts, it was just a matter of time before –'

'That's it, isn't it? Your flash house, the cars, all the home theatre gear … Herringen told me there was money in your family, but you've been stealing it from the mine, haven't you? Cooper would have noticed the losses, and –'

'Goodbye lifestyle,' said Newman. He sat at the terminal, drawing the keyboard towards him. 'Now, if you'll excuse me I have a master plan to set in motion.'

'They're going to work out what happened. You might as well give up now.'

'Aren't you forgetting something?' Newman touched the cut on his forehead. 'I've already succumbed to the rampaging bugs, an innocent victim cut down in the prime of life. Nobody's going to be looking for a dead man. Anyway, once these bugs hit the rest of the planet they'll be too busy saving their own necks to bother with audits.'

'What about Herringen? He'll raise the alarm!'

Newman laughed. 'Who do you think you're tied to?'

Walsh started. She thought she'd been leaning against the wall, but now realised it was the mine boss. He was out cold ... or worse. 'Is he okay?'

'Who cares?'

'Jonathan Newman, I'm charging you with murder, conspiracy, fraud, emb –'

'Save your breath, trainee. I'm the law down here.'

'When I get free –'

'But you won't.'

'Someone will find me!'

'Who? Hal Spacejock?' Newman laughed. 'Your trusty deputy is halfway to Dismolle.' He finished typing instructions and stood up. 'Any last requests?'

Walsh mentioned one, a physical impossibility.

'That's not very nice. Hey, look what I set up for you.' Newman turned the screen and smiled proudly as a large digital timer appeared. 'It's just like they have in the movies!'

Walsh stared at the digits, which showed 60:00. 'That's your evil plan? You're going to show me sixty minutes?'

'You won't be laughing when the time runs out.'

'No fuss. If it's as shonky as the rest of your code it's bound to crash.'

'There's nothing wrong with my programming!'

Walsh snorted. 'Those bugs of yours attacked a robot while I got away, and they were too stupid to follow me out of a window.'

'Those were hardware faults!' snapped Newman. 'It took all my coding skills to –'

'If that's an example of your skills I'm confident of getting rescued.'

'Oh, very amusing. Now laugh at this!' Newman turned to the keyboard and entered a sequence. The timer immediately showed 59:59 then 59:58 ... and as it reached 59:55 Newman dropped the keyboard on the floor and stomped on it, scattering keys far and wide. 'I'd love to stay and trade insults, but I have a flight to catch.'

'Wait! One last question?'

'What?'

'Did you have an unhappy childhood?'

Newman swore at her, then hurried to the lift. The doors closed on him, and Walsh heard the creak as it carried him to the surface.

On the screen, the timer showed 58:31, 58:30, 58:29 ...

28

Hal had watched Clunk's departure with interest, but after five minutes of slow progress he realised it would take ages to reach the *Tiger*. So, he switched channels.

'Later on Forzen Facts, a special report on wanton vandalism in our fair city. But first, the results of our wet T-shirt contest.'

Hal settled back. This was more like it.

'Yes ladies and gentlemen, in nine out of ten cleaning cycles Zappo dry-power will remove the stains those old-fashioned water-based washes cannot touch. Just look at these wet T-shirts! On the left –'

'Great,' muttered Hal. 'False advertising.' He switched channels at random, but the others weren't much better.

'And now, our special report. This morning brazen vandals attacked the –'

Hal switched channels to check on Clunk, and was just in time to catch the robot's thumbs-up. He waved, then turned back to the news.

'- where a spokesperson described the damage as severe. The office was completely ruined, with years of valuable records reduced to confetti. Damage estimates –'

Bored, Hal got up and went to make a coffee. He caught snatches of the bulletin as he filled his cup, but they mostly consisted of hand wringing by early childhood experts and the threat of a really good talking-to for the perpetrators. By the time he returned to the console a smart young woman was discussing the weather, and Hal knew exactly what she'd say: snow, ice and cold winds interrupted by the occasional blizzard. He wondered how Walsh was getting on in the Peace Force office, and hoped she'd remembered to put the heater on. Not for the first time, he wished she'd let him stay.

After enduring another advert Hal switched back to the external camera, which showed the *Tiger* hanging in space like a toy ship. He debated calling to check on Clunk's progress, then remembered the robot had already tried that without success before going over there. But what if there was something sinister aboard the ship? Clunk was pretty handy, but there were known cases of robots tangling with strange beasts and coming off second-best.

Just as he was picturing the worst Clunk's face popped up on the screen, almost startling Hal into dropping his coffee.

'Mr Spacejock, can you hear me?'

'Yeah, Clunk. What's going on?'

'It looks like fuel contamination. The engines and generators shut down to avoid damage, and Mr Spearman is lucky to have cleared orbit before they did so. I've notified Forzen in case they fill any other ships from the same source. And I've got the generators online, but it's going to take a while to clean the filters.'

'Never mind, he's got nothing better to do.'

'I believe I should stay and help.'

'That's a negative. I need you here so we can deliver our cargo.'

'It's a long way to Dismolle, Mr Spacejock, and the *Tiger* will have to be nursed all the way.'

'Why don't you land on Forzen?' Hal cursed as he remembered. 'That's right, they don't have a service department.'

'Correct,' said Clunk, looking surprised. 'I just had to look that information up. How did you know?'

'Someone mentioned it in passing,' said Hal quickly. 'Okay, so it's got to be Dismolle. Why do you have to stay on board?'

'To be here in case anything else goes wrong. It's the only way Mr Spearman can deliver his cargo on time.'

'You mean you're going with him to the delivery?'

'I can hardly leap out of the *Tiger* before we land.'

'What about me? What am I supposed to do?'

'The Navcom will get you to Dismolle. You can deliver your own cargo and wait for our arrival.'

Hal rubbed his chin. It could just work - if he offloaded the cargo before Clunk arrived, he could grab the robot as soon as the *Tiger* landed and get the hell out of there before Spearman discovered the empty container. He'd get the cash, Clunk would be none the wiser and Spearman would be left with nothing. 'So, it's a race, eh?'

'Hardly. I estimate we'll arrive several hours after you.'

'Perfect,' said Hal.

'I'm sorry?'

'I mean, it all sounds fine to me.'

'There's something else.'

'There is?' said Hal warily.

'Mr Spearman is offering half the fee in exchange for my help.'

Hal was about to point out that half of nothing was still nothing, but caught himself just in time. 'Can you get cash in advance?'

'I'll try.' Clunk glanced over his shoulder. 'Here's Mr Spearman with the tools. I'd better go.'

'Take care of yourself.'

'And you, Mr Spacejock. Have a safe trip.'

Hal disconnected and took a sip of his coffee as the Forzen news came back on. Things had looked sticky for a while there, but they were now back on track. All he had to do was get to Dismolle and unload before the *Tiger* arrived. No sweat.

'Navcom, set course for –'

'Dismolle course programmed in and ready,' said the Navcom.

'Okay, let's –' Hal broke off as the screen displayed an interior shot of a large room. The floor was a mess of broken rubble littered with scraps of paper, and as the caption appeared he sat bolt upright: 'Forzen Peace Force Office.' With shaking fingers he turned the sound up, and he sat dead still as the announcer spoke.

'These exclusive pictures show the damage inflicted on the disused Peace Force office this morning. The Council has yet to comment on the cause, and while there are no reported injuries –'

'Harriet!' exclaimed Hal. With his heart in his mouth, he turned to the console. 'Quick, Navcom. Set course for –'

'Dismolle. Complying.'

'Not there,' said Hal desperately. 'Forzen!'

'Impossible!' said the Navcom. 'According to my predictive algorithms, the likelihood of your choosing Forzen as a destination is less than zero point six percent.'

'I don't give a stuff about your algo-thingies. Get me back to Forzen, now!'

'Planet Dismolle is the only likely destination,' said the Navcom stubbornly. 'And that's where we're going.'

'What if I told you they're giving away a million credits to the first person to land on Forzen?'

'I'd say that person would be dead,' said the Navcom. 'It's a long way to fall.'

Hal closed his eyes. 'In a ship, Navcom. The first person to land in a ship.'

'That would increase your chances of returning to Forzen to forty-nine percent.'

'Excellent. Let's go.'

'Unfortunately, you're still fifty-one percent more likely to visit Dismolle.'

'Will you turn this thing around and land!'

'Not likely.'

'All right, I'll do it myself.' Hal slid the throttle to full emergency reverse and hauled the stick to the left. Nothing happened.

'There was a ninety-nine percent chance you were going to do that,' said the Navcom. 'Therefore, I disabled the controls.'

Hal jumped up and hurried into the airlock, where he yanked open the suit lockers until he found a space-hook. This was functionally identical to a boat hook, the only difference being it cost ten times as much. Weapon in hand, Hal returned to the flight deck. 'Guess what I'm going to do with this?'

'I'm eighty percent certain you're not going boating,' said the Navcom. 'As for the rest, I'm reluctant to voice my thoughts aloud.'

'Navcom, how well do you know me?' asked Hal, with a few experimental sweeps of the space hook.

'I believe I have a fair understanding of your nature.'

'When I make threats, do I usually carry them out?'

'I'll answer your query in a moment. But first I have to program our course for Forzen.'

Hal smiled to himself and took the pilot's seat, but his smile slipped as he thought of Harriet. What had happened to her? The news presenter said there were no injuries, but what about disappearances? Or even ...deaths?

The *Volante's* engines rumbled as the ship prepared to move, and at the last second Hal remembered the passenger ramp. 'Navcom, retrieve the _'

'Already done,' said the computer.

The ship heeled round on its new course, and the engines roared as they drove it towards Forzen. Meanwhile, Hal wondered about Clunk. Would the robot notice he was heading the wrong way? 'Navcom, whatever you do, don't tell Clunk we're going back to Forzen. If he calls just tell him we're getting a run-up.'

'I knew you'd say that,' said the computer.

— 29 —

Hal eyed planet Forzen on the viewscreen, trying to work out how quickly he could land. Every minute could mean the difference between seeing happy, cheerful Harriet Walsh again and ...he gritted his teeth, refusing to think of the alternative. He'd never forgive himself if something had happened to her. He should have stood firm and taken her aboard his ship.

'*Volante, this is Forzen ground control. Please state your intentions.*'

'I'm going to land.'

'*I'm sorry, could you repeat that?*'

'Clear the field. We're coming in.'

'*Sir, that isn't approved traffic control language. Please state your intentions once more.*'

'Oh, I'll repeat myself, you –' With an effort, Hal bit off his intended reply. Ground control could easily bar him, and then where would he be? Racking his brains, he dredged up the right words. 'Interstellar freighter *Volante* requesting landing clearance.'

'*Reason for visit?*'

'I, er, forgot my jacket.'

There was a lengthy silence, during which the controllers were either laughing themselves sick or discussing Hal's mental stability. Finally, the voice came on again. '*Volante cleared for landing on pad twelve. And don't forget to put the brakes on.*'

Hal cut the connection and reached across the console for the controls needed to land the ship. With one eye on the screen and the other scanning the instruments, he judged the precise moment and then pressed the button marked 'Autoland'.

'Autoland engaged,' said the Navcom. 'Would you like the scenic approach or the direct route?'

'Navcom, I want this tub on the ground so fast they'll think we fell out of the sky.'

'That's the third option,' said the Navcom. 'Buckle up.'

There was a roar from the engines, and the ship seemed to stop in mid-air. Hal grabbed the armrests to stop himself sailing into the viewscreen, then clung on for dear life as the ship plunged towards the ground, shuddering wildly from end to end. On the viewscreen the planet raced towards them, the surface quickly resolving into mountains, oceans and rivers.

'H-how fast are we g-going?' Hal managed to ask through the shakes. 'And m-more importantly, c-can we stop?'

'Certainly, if the new upgrades don't go on strike.'

'What if they d-do?'

'We'll be the ones doing the striking. Hold on, impact in ten seconds.'

Hal gazed at the screen, watching the concentric circles pulse around their landing pad.

'Five,' said the Navcom.

A line of text appeared below the rings.

'Four.'

Hal read the text and immediately wished he hadn't.

'Three.'

Hal read the text again, but it still said 'Point of Impact.'

'Two.'

The screen went dark. So did the overhead lights and the console.

'One,' said the Navcom calmly. 'Welcome to Forzen.'

Hal opened one eye, and realised the overhead lights, the console and the screen were all lit up as usual. 'That's it?'

'Yes. It's an instantaneous reversal field. Brings us to a complete halt in eight nanoseconds, dispersing our momentum as a sound wave.'

'I didn't hear anything.'

'Neither will the people outside for a while. The faster you stop, the bigger the damage radius.'

'Are you telling me we made a big bang?'

'No, I'm telling you we hit the western hemisphere with a sound the likes of which hasn't been heard since the birth of the universe.'

'I thought that *was* the big bang.'

'This was bigger.'

'Who came up with a stupid idea like that? Some big-time criminal mastermind? A bloodthirsty alien race?'

'No, it's military technology. And we're not allowed to talk about it.' The Navcom hesitated. 'Of course, it wouldn't matter if you did talk about it, because nobody out there will be able to hear you.'

'Why didn't you warn me it would do that?'

'You chose an unsupported option. It's not my fault if you don't appreciate the result.' The Navcom hesitated. 'I believe you were going to the Peace Force office?'

Hal gestured at the airlock. 'If you think I'm going out there –'

'Oh, you'll be quite safe.'

'Safe? I'm going to be explaining myself from a jail cell for the next ten years.'

'For all the good talking will do,' said the Navcom. The airlock door slid open. 'I'll see you when you get back.'

'If,' muttered Hal. The outer door swung open, admitting a blast of freezing air that almost took his ears off, and he was shivering long before he reached the ground. The landing field seemed deserted, and he dismissed the Navcom's big bang theory as an exaggeration.

Ten minutes later he found the parked car, just where he'd left it. Unfortunately, fresh falls had completely buried the vehicle, the hulls and everything in between, and the vehicle was now a blob of car-shaped snow nestled between two towering blobs of spaceship-shaped snow.

Hal dug in with his bare hands, and by the time he found the door handle he could barely feel his fingers. He pulled and pulled, but the door remained stubbornly shut, and he had to give it several hefty kicks before he could break the icy grip. He got in and coaxed the motor into life, then turned the heater to full. Circulation returned gradually, and he winced as waves of intense pain shot up his arms. When he could feel again he gripped the wheel and pressed down on the accelerator.

The car gathered speed and snow slithered off the bodywork, letting the light in through the frosted windows. Hal steered with one hand and wiped condensation off the heated glass with the other, torn between seeing where he was going and not running off the road. Eventually he found the spaceport exit, and with a twist of the wheel he pulled onto the main road.

In the *Tiger's* flight deck, Clunk had finished his diagnostics and was now preparing to restart the engines. The process was fraught with danger, since a blockage could strand the vessel until help arrived.

'Is it going to work?' asked Spearman, who was looking rather nervous.

'I'll tell you in a minute,' said Clunk. Mentally crossing his fingers, he initiated the start sequence, and a broad smile creased his face as the engines rumbled into life. 'You don't have to wait a whole minute. I can tell you right away. They're fine.'

Spearman clapped Clunk on the shoulder. 'I can see why Hal keeps you around.'

'It's certainly not for my breezy personality,' said Clunk.

'You can say that again.' Ignoring Clunk's frown, Spearman gestured at the viewscreen. 'How long to Dismolle?'

'The engines should be safe up to fifty percent power, and the hyperdrive will operate as usual.' Clunk hesitated. 'I'd say five hours, give or take a few minutes.'

'Excellent. Just enough time for a decent cleanup and a good rest.'

Clunk looked down at himself. His skin bore several new scratches, and his thorough cleaning of the fuel filters had transferred much of the disgusting mess onto his own person. 'That's very kind of you. I'm very much in need of it.'

'Not you!' said Spearman, with a laugh. 'I meant me!'

'Oh.' Clunk's face fell. 'Can I at least get a recharge?'

'Sure.' Spearman gestured expansively around the flight deck. 'Find a socket and plug yourself in. And maybe you could give the computer a going-over while you're here, eh? It acts a bit funny sometimes, but I'm sure you can sort it out.'

Clunk felt a leaden weight in his arms and legs. All he wanted was to shut down and take on a charge, and the idea of untangling a bug in some foreign operating system was like reaching the summit of a mountain, only to discover the real peak was still hours of climbing away. 'I'll do my best.'

'Great. I'll see you later.'

Clunk watched Spearman enter the lift, then found a power socket and plugged himself in. The jolt was delicious as it flowed through his circuits, and the weariness lessened. Then he remembered Spearman's instructions, and reached into his chest to find the diagnostic cable. He took hold of the plug, turned it upside down and pushed it against the data socket. Not surprisingly, it wouldn't go in. 'I did my best,' he murmured, as he closed his eyes.

Hal drew up outside the Peace Force office, leaving the car halfway across the road in his haste. He ran down the alley, threaded his way between the boxes scattered around the dumpster, and reached for the door. It was locked, but two hefty kicks got him inside, and he charged down the hall to the main room.

Hal stumbled to a halt as he saw the damage: the shredded carpet, the remains of the terminal and the forlorn fragments which had once been part of the huge Peace Force robot. He shuddered at the sight. If the attackers had torn apart an armoured robot, what had they done to Harriet?

Something glinted in the tangled mess, and Hal crouched to pick up a buckled Peace Force badge. It was heavily scored and blackened with soot, but he could just make out the name Barney under the Peace Force *Legem Erga Nos* motto. Relieved it didn't read Harriet Walsh, Hal pocketed the badge and took the stairs to the first floor.

The door to Walsh's room had been shredded, and the scant remains of bedroom furniture wouldn't have filled a shopping bag. Hal stepped over the mess to examine the window, leaning right out to look down at the car park. Directly below was the dumpster, and it was obvious Walsh had barricaded herself in the bedroom, then leapt out the window to save her life.

So, where was she now?

Any sensible person would have legged it to the spaceport and caught the first ship out of there. Unfortunately, Hal couldn't see Harriet running away from anything, no matter how dangerous it was.

He returned to the office, where he saw something moving in the armoury. He grabbed a splintered table leg and made his way across the room, stepping around the holes bored into the concrete floor. Inside the armoury, a damaged mining bug was dragging itself around in circles, clawing the concrete with its one remaining leg. Hal stared at it, realisation dawning. Miner bugs had torn the office apart, and if Harriet had survived she'd be at the mine right now, interrogating suspects! Hal swung his makeshift club, crushing the bug with a single blow, then threw the table leg aside and ran for the entrance.

Outside, he jumped into the car and streaked towards the mine. As he urged the car on he reached for the Navcom, dividing his attention between the screen and the road. The battery was dead, so he tried holding it in front of the heater vent, and when that didn't work he sat on the thing, hoping a little warmth would stimulate the charge.

After several uncomfortable minutes he removed the PDA and tried again, and this time there was a flicker of life. 'Navcom, can you hear me?'

'Oh, so you've decided to see how I am.'

'Not now, this is top priority. I need to get a message to Clunk.'

'Go ahead,' said the Navcom smartly.

When he'd finished, Hal put the PDA away and hunched over the wheel, giving the road his full attention.

◆

RRRINNGG!

Clunk had barely lapsed into blissful semi-consciousness when he was yanked out of his reverie by an insistent alarm. A hurried check of his internal diagnostics revealed nothing out of the ordinary, and he was still looking around for the source when he heard it again, louder:

RRRINNGGGG!

Puzzled, Clunk opened his chest compartment, where he found the PDA containing the Navcom's backup. It rang again as he reached for it, and when he inspected the tiny screen he saw a line of text:

MESSAGE RECEIVED. UNPACK?

Clunk tapped the 'Yes' button.

SENDER: Spcaejcko. MESSAGE: 'eNde oyru ehlp. eGt oyru raes abck ot Frozn SAAP. Hla'

Clunk frowned at the garbled letters. The message had been corrupted, but was there enough of the illiterate junk to work out the meaning? He ran the text through a couple of hundred decryption algorithms, before realising what the problem was: the transmission had suffered a vowel movement!

Working quickly, he transposed the letters to come up with the full message, and he gasped aloud as the meaning became clear. *Back to Forzen? Need your help?* Mr Spacejock was in trouble!

Clunk pulled his charge cable from the wall and hurried to the console, where he brought up a system map to plot their return course. It would take them over an hour to reach Forzen if they turned immediately, but with every passing minute they were getting closer to the Dismolle hyperspace point. There was no time to lose! He reached for the controls to swing the *Tiger* around on its new course, but the computer had other ideas.

'What do you think you're doing?'

'We have to change course!' shouted Clunk. 'It's an emergency. Mayday!'

'I received no such message.'

'Of course you didn't.' Clunk brandished the PDA. 'It's on here!'

'I'm sorry, but you'll need Mr Spearman's permission if you want to set a new heading.'

Clunk ran for the lift and waited impatiently for its return. What danger could Mr Spacejock have encountered? Had the *Volante* struck a problem ... or had it struck Forzen? The lift doors opened and Clunk stepped inside, his brain racing. Why hadn't Mr Spacejock sent a more informative message? Was he a captive? Hurt, even? Clunk shuddered. If anything happened to Hal because he'd decided to help Mr Spearman instead ...

The doors slid open and Clunk charged along the passage to Spearman's cabin. He reached for the handle, then forced himself to knock.

'Yeah?'

'Mr Spearman, can I talk to you?'

'Go ahead,' said Spearman's voice, muffled by the door.

Clunk tried the handle, but the door was locked. 'I just received a message from Mr Spacejock.'

'Old Spacejoke himself? What's he say?'

'He needs my help on Forzen. It's urgent.'

'Oh, sure. Why don't we go back so he can sabotage the *Tiger* again?'

'But Mr Spacejock wouldn't –'

'He already did.'

'Please, Mr Spearman. Let me turn the ship around!'

'No chance.'

'We'll make it worth your while.'

The door opened and Spearman looked out. He was still wet from his shower, and wore a towel around his waist. 'Now you're talking sense. Out with it.'

'I'll give you the rest of the cargo fee.'

'Spacejock would never honour it.'

'I'll work for you! Six months service for nothing.'

'He won't honour that either.'

Suddenly, Clunk saw red. 'I fixed this ship, Mr Spearman, and I can break it again just as easily. Or perhaps I'll break you!'

'Hey, back off!' Spearman slammed the door, and Clunk drew his fist back to punch a hole in it. Then he lowered his hand. Hal was in trouble, but how was he going to get Mr Spearman to change course?

◆

When Hal arrived at the mine the front gates were closed. He leapt out of the car and shook them, but they were securely fastened and his efforts only rattled the bars. He tried to climb them, but his hands slipped on the smooth metal, and he couldn't get purchase with his feet. There was an intercom, but repeatedly pressing the call button only made it buzz. Nobody answered.

Hal eyed the gates again, then ran for the car. He drove away from the mine and braked heavily, sliding the car round until it was facing the way he'd come. Then he gripped the wheel and revved the engine, racing it until the bonnet shook. The gates were just out of sight, hidden by the nearest post, but if the car hit them fast enough it'd go through them like a bullet through a sheet of tin foil. Or maybe it would glance off and demolish ten metres of wall. Either way, nothing was keeping him out.

Hal floored the accelerator and hung on tight as the car launched itself down the road. Trees and road signs whipped past in a blur, and before he could reconsider the wisdom of his actions he was hurtling towards the gates. Immediately, he realised two things. One, the gates were now open. And two, there was a car coming out.

Hal yanked the wheel, and a split second later he was hurtling past the gates backwards. His car ricocheted off the wall, destroyed a row of bushes and ended up wedged beneath a large billboard advertising road safety. He struggled with his seatbelt, all too aware of the other driver hurrying towards him. Then the door opened, and he was hauled out bodily.

'You maniac! You could have killed me!'

'It's all right, I'm not hurt.' Then Hal recognised the face. 'Newman!'

'Spacejock!' Newman gaped at him. 'What the hell are you doing here?'

'Never mind me. Where's Harriet? What have you done to her?'

'She's inside, grilling my boss.' Newman glanced at his watch. 'Would you like me to take you in?'

Moments later they drew up at the mine, where Newman parked alongside Herringen's car. They got out, and he led Hal up the steps and through reception. Hal followed him along the corridor, but instead of stopping at Herringen's office they continued towards the lift. 'What's she doing down there?' asked Hal.

'Search me. Maybe she's torturing Mr Herringen for information.'

They got into the elevator, and Hal leaned against the wall as the lift dropped down the shaft. After the shock of the ruined office, the near-miss in the car and the relief of discovering Walsh was all right, he was feeling a little weak around the knees.

'What the hell is that?' shouted Newman, pointing through the floor. 'Look! Down there!'

Hal leaned forward to see what the fuss was about, and as he did so there was a swoosh. His head exploded with stars and he dropped to his knees, stunned.

Newman loomed over him, a wicked-looking cosh in his hand. 'You arrived just in time, Mr Spacejock. I'm sure Miss Walsh will be delighted to see you.'

Then he swung the cudgel again.

Safe in his cabin, Kent Spearman was feeling rather smug. Not only had he put one over Spacejock, but now he had the robot begging for help too. He'd give the old rustbucket another twenty minutes to stew things over, and then he'd lay out his terms.

Spearman adjusted the towel around his middle, and angled the bench top dryer so it blew a stream of warm air through his mane of blonde hair, whipping the ends behind him. When that was dry he played the air over his bare chest until the last drops of water evaporated.

Once he was done, he returned to the problem of Hal. For a start, having Spacejock darting around the galaxy messing up cargo jobs was bad for business, and he decided it would be far more efficient if he took him on as a junior partner. Or maybe a sub-contractor, or a simple employee. Spearman grinned at the apt description, and wondered whether he could get an embroidered shirt made. Then he put his feet up on the desk and gestured at the terminal. A screen appeared, and with a handful of deft movements he designed a spreadsheet showing income projections from two ships working in tandem. Spacejock would be on a retainer, of course, but only the minimum possible. In fact, the biggest problem would be extracting an agreement from the robot that Hal would have to honour. Now if he could get Clunk to sign over the *Volante* ... Then Hal wouldn't have a leg to stand on. Spearman snorted. Or a flight deck.

His empire-building was interrupted by a buzz, and a call alert appeared on the screen. Forzen passenger terminal? What did they want? Intrigued, he gestured at the icon, and a woman appeared. She was dressed in the livery of a passenger line, and her hair was pulled back in a tight bun. 'Good afternoon, Mr –' Barely had she started when the woman gasped and averted her eyes. 'Mr Spearman! Please be so good as to remove your feet from the table!'

'What's wrong with them?' Spearman waggled his toes, and from his laid-back seating position they seemed to be tickling the woman's chin. 'Don't you like my ankles?'

'It's not your ankles staring me in the face,' said the woman sharply. 'I've not seen that much tackle since I threw out my husband's fishing equipment.'

Spearman remembered he was only wearing a towel, and he yanked his feet off the desk and leaned forward. 'Please, go on,' he said, his face burning.

'I have a proposal for you. A regular customer needs to reach Dismolle in a hurry, and our schedule doesn't fit his requirements.'

'Well that's no good. I'm halfway to Dismolle right now.'

'I know, I looked you up before placing this call. However, this client is offering a large sum of money for immediate passage, and if you were to return to Forzen immediately –'

'Oh, that's very good.' Spearman slapped his thigh. 'You almost had me, you cast-iron trickster.'

'I beg your pardon?'

'Listen, I don't know whether you're a recording or a computer program, but it's amazing.' Spearman leaned closer. 'I can even see the hairs up your nose.'

'I –'

'So how did you do it? Did you tap into my computer, or is this one of those simuloids?'

'I don't have the least idea what you're talking about.'

'And your outraged modesty! That really had me going.' Spearman stood up and reached for the towel. 'Let's see you do that shocked expression again.'

'Mr Spearman, have you been drinking?'

'No, I'm seeing things perfectly clearly. And Clunk, you can tell your precious owner –' Spearman broke off as someone knocked at the door. 'Yeah?'

'Mr Spearman?'

Spearman glanced at the door, then stared at the angry face on his screen. Suddenly he felt very draughty.

'Are you all right?' called Clunk. 'I thought I heard shouting.'

'Y-yes. Fine.' In a flash, Spearman had replaced the towel. 'I'm just conducting a little business.'

'Have you reconsidered my request?' asked Clunk. 'We have to turn round right now if we're to have any hope.'

Spearman stared at the face on his screen. 'Clunk, can I get back to you on that?'

'Please hurry, Mr Spearman.'

The caller was still waiting, her face set. 'I've heard of the immature stunts you throttle jockeys get up to, but this –'

'Please, let me apologise!' said Spearman desperately.

The woman took a deep breath. 'Whatever your personality quirks, my client is offering a substantial amount of money for this trip to Dismolle. What do you say to ten thousand credits and a complimentary refuel?'

'Ten grand?' Spearman almost dropped the towel again. 'Is he made out of money?'

'Unlike you, I'm unwilling to reveal that which should remain private, but I can say that his credit is good. So tell me, will you take the job?'

◆

Hal came round slowly, his brain still ringing from the blow. He was sitting with his back to the wall, and when he tried to raise his hands to the throbbing pain in his skull he discovered his arms were tied behind his back. He struggled with his bonds, and then felt relief flooding through him as Walsh spoke directly behind him.

'Hal, are you all right?'

'Never mind me. What about you?'

'A bit of a headache, but I'll be fine.'

Hal felt his anger rising up. 'Did he hit you?'

'Keep your voice down. It might be our only chance.'

Hal glanced round and realised they were on the control room floor, near the elevator. Walsh and Herringen were behind him, and all three of them were tied together. He craned his neck and saw Newman near the window, and he was about to yell at him when he realised Walsh was right.

Escape first, revenge afterwards. 'What's he doing?' he asked Walsh, his voice barely a whisper.

'He's watching those bugs of his. They all froze a few minutes ago, and they haven't moved since.'

Hal raised himself to look through the window, and what he saw turned his blood cold. Instead of scurrying around with their usual frantic activity the mining bugs were lined up in rows, countless thousands of them cramming every level space beyond the window.

'So, you're awake,' said Newman, without looking round. 'I thought you'd be out for hours yet. You must have a thick skull.'

'No, you're just a wuss,' said Hal. 'I've had little kids hit me harder than that.'

Newman came across and stood over them. 'I'm afraid I'll have to leave you to it. Sorry to leave before the fun starts, but I have a weak stomach.'

'Matches your intellect,' said Hal.

Walsh laughed.

'Mock all you like,' said Newman. 'I'm not the hero tied up with a wannabe cop and the worst manager this side of the local sky hockey team.' He entered a code to open the lift doors. 'If you do get free, don't bother trying to stop the timer. I forgot to leave a handy cancel button lying around.'

'You're a sad excuse for a human,' shouted Walsh, as Newman stepped into the lift. Then the doors closed and they were alone.

'Right, now we can talk,' said Hal to the others. 'Anyone got a penknife?'

'Not me,' said Walsh. 'Herringen's still out cold.'

'Maybe we should go through his pockets.' Hal struggled with his bonds, and managed to move his hands a little. 'Of course, the chances of finding a handy pocket knife just when we need it are zero. If only Clunk were here!'

'Why, does he have a pocket knife?'

'Yeah, mine.' Hal twisted his hands, but the bonds were too tight. 'What do you think Newman's going to do?'

Walsh hesitated. 'I think he's going to gloat a bit, then let us go.'

'Are you sure? He's already made one person disappear with those bugs of his. What's another three?'

'I'm sure he's not going to do anything like that,' said Walsh. 'All the same, we can't just sit here.'

'Why not? Clunk's always saving me from these situations. It's his job.'

'Does he know where we are?'

'Sure he does.' Hal decided a white lie or two wouldn't hurt. After all, she could go on hoping right up to the end. 'I told Clunk to come and get me if I didn't report in. I'm well overdue by now.'

'He could be here any minute!'

'Sure thing. It's a cert.'

There was a groan behind them as Herringen came round. 'Oh, my head. What happened?'

Walsh explained the situation. 'It looks bad, but Clunk's on the way. Of course, if we just had something to cut this rope ...'

'I have a pocket knife,' said Herringen. 'I never go anywhere without one.' Hal felt the ropes tighten as Herringen struggled to reach his pocket. Then the other side tightened. 'Damn, it's not there.'

'No wonder.' Hal nodded towards the nearby bench. 'He's put all our stuff over there. Thorough little beggar, isn't he?'

'Miss Walsh, isn't there anything in your Peace Force training to cover this?'

'Yes, we're supposed to travel in pairs and report to a superior officer before entering a perilous situation.' Walsh's head dropped. 'Somehow, it didn't seem to apply. I'm sorry.'

Hal reached out and squeezed her hand.

Herringen cleared his throat. 'That's very comforting, Mr Spacejock, but I'd rather you didn't do it again.'

'Sorry. Wrong one.' Hal eyed the items sitting on the table. He could see the pocket knife, but there was also the commset containing the Navcom, several keycards and a small amount of pocket change. 'I've got an idea,' he said. 'If we all move at once, we should be able to get closer.'

'And then?'

'I'll tip it over with my feet. Ready?'

The others nodded, and on Hal's command they all started moving, bobbing up and down and kicking their legs. For a moment they looked like a hyperactive jellyfish trying to get back to the sea, but before long they started moving in unison, shuffling across the floor towards the table.

'Okay, that'll do,' said Hal. He reached out and hooked his foot around the table leg, trying to shake it enough to knock the items onto the floor. Then he applied his other foot and twisted his legs, attempting to tip the table. 'It's no good,' he said. 'It won't move. It's too heavy.'

'Let's try some lateral thinking,' said Walsh. She drew her legs back, braced for a second, then drove them at the table leg. There was a snap as it broke off, and the three-legged table toppled over, scattering items all over the floor.

'That way!' said Hal, and they all bumped and shuffled after the penknife.

Finally, his fingers closed on it, and he managed to work the blade open. Seconds later they were free, rubbing their wrists where the ropes had cut in.

Herringen ran to the doors and pressed the call button, and they heard the lift descending. Meanwhile, Hal gathered up the Navcom and the pocket change.

The lift arrived, and Herringen entered his code. The keypad buzzed, but the doors remained closed. Herringen entered his code again, and got another buzz. 'That's odd.'

'What?'

'My code isn't working. I can't open the doors!'

Walsh willed Herringen on as he entered and re-entered his code, praying he was getting it wrong even though deep down she knew he wasn't. 'It's Newman,' she said at last. 'He's cancelled your code.'

'You'd better hurry up over there.' Hal was at the far end of the lab, looking down at the screen. 'This timer's running out fast.'

'What do we have left?'

'Under two minutes.' Hal glanced at the army of miner bugs just the other side of the window. 'So, when this goes off …'

'We don't want to be here. And we can't stop it, either.'

'Oh yeah?' Hal reached into his flight suit and took out the PDA. 'Navcom, can you hear me?'

'Yes, Mr Spacejock?'

'I need you to break into a massive computer system and disable the brains of several thousand killer bugs before they romp in and eat us all.' Hal glanced at the timer. 'You have ninety seconds to crack it, starting now.'

'I'm sorry Mr Spacejock, but this processor wouldn't crack a window.'

'Can you contact someone? Let them know where we are?'

'Are we underground?'

'Yes.'

'That explains why I can't lock onto a comms signal.'

Hal gripped the PDA. 'Navcom, this is serious. They're going to kill us all!'

'Don't you keep backups?'

'Of course I bloody don't!'

'Well, I think there's a valuable lesson in there for us all.'

Hal looked like he was going to throw the Navcom across the room, but instead he tried a new tack. 'Navcom, if I cross your battery wires, would you explode in a raging fireball or just go phut?'

'What kind of question is that?'

'I'm thinking of turning you into an improvised hand-grenade.'

'And I'm thinking you can go phut yourself.'

'Come on! You have a backup, don't you?'

'Irrelevant, since my battery is flat.'

Hal gave up and jammed the PDA in his pocket. 'If we get out of here I'm going to delete all her backups one by one. See how she likes it.'

'It's not her fault, it's that bloody Newman!' Walsh kicked the lift doors, hard. 'When I get my hands on him …'

'It's no good,' said Herringen. 'He's thought of everything. We're done for.'

'There's always a way,' said Walsh. 'Look at the ropes and the table. We could have given up, but we struggled on and now we're free.'

'You call this free?' Herringen pointed a shaking finger at the wall of glass. 'They're going to swarm in, chew us to pieces and spit us out like yesterday's leftovers. There's no escape!'

'You two stay away from the window,' said Hal. He found the broken table leg and brandished it. 'Try and get that door open, and I'll keep them off you as long as I can.'

'What use is that? We'll be dead in seconds!' Herringen sounded close to panic, but any sympathy Walsh might have felt was tempered with the knowledge that he and his precious council had covered up Cooper's death. It was all right when it happened to someone else, but now he was getting a taste of the terror he was starting to crack. It was just a shame the lesson would be over so quickly, she thought.

Hal swung the table leg. 'Just get the doors open. Okay?'

Walsh smiled at him, then turned to inspect the keypad.

'You'll never crack it,' said Herringen.

'How often do you come down here?'

'Me? Rarely. It's Newman's domain.'

'Move back. Give me some light.'

'I swear, it's completely secure! Rolling combination, anti-tamper, the lot.'

'Forty seconds,' said Hal. 'And he's right, those things are impregnable. Clunk told me.'

'Men,' muttered Walsh. Then she straightened up and typed a code on the pad.

BUZZ.

'My dear girl,' said Herringen. 'You can't possibly guess the code at random!'

Walsh tried the same digits in a different order.

BUZZ.

'Twenty seconds,' called Hal.

Methodically, Walsh tried the same four digits again and again, changing the order each time while trying not to repeat any sequences.

BUZZ. BUZZ. BUZZ. PING!

Had she done it? Walsh stared at the doors, but they remained sealed.

'Time's up,' said Hal. The screen showed 00:00, and beyond him the bugs broke ranks and poured towards the window, scrambling over each other in their haste to reach their prey. They hit the glass with a bang, but it held.

'Would you look at that?' shouted Hal. 'The stupid things can't even break a window!'

CRACK!

Hal backed away as the glass crazed. Meanwhile, Walsh turned to the keypad and entered codes twice as fast as before, her fingers blurring over the buttons.

'Brace yourselves!' shouted Hal. 'They're almost through!'

Walsh entered code after code, not even sure whether she was repeating herself. Then ...

BEEP!

The doors slid open, and Walsh pushed Herringen into the lift. Then she turned for Hal.

In that instant the huge window collapsed, and the bugs swarmed in like a tidal wave, engulfing desks, chairs and equipment.

◆

The advancing bugs sounded like nothing Walsh had ever heard - an intense rustling that grew louder and louder as the wave rushed towards her. Meanwhile, Hal stood before the oncoming bugs with his makeshift weapon raised high, prepared to defend her with his life. It was incredibly brave and heroic, but completely unnecessary. 'HAL! Come ON!'

Hal saw the open doors and let out a whoop of delight, then gathered Walsh up and bundled her into the lift. As they tumbled in, Herringen shut the doors and hit the button.

Just in time ... the wave of bugs slammed into the doors, and hundreds started forcing the bars apart. Herringen hit the button again and again as the bugs attacked the grille with their jaws, and they'd almost broken in before the lift lurched upwards, crushing their metal bodies and smearing the remains down the walls. Through the floor, Walsh saw them swallowed by the teeming mass now filling the shaft.

'Bloody hell,' muttered Hal, as they sailed upwards, away from danger. 'That was close.' He tried to get up, only to realise he was tangled up with Walsh.

'I don't understand,' said Herringen, who was looking at Walsh as though she were a magician and a supercomputer all rolled into one efficient package. 'How did you -?'

'Peace Force training.' Walsh released Hal and held her hand up, wriggling her fingers. 'Newman used the keypad more than anyone, so the buttons he used regularly were smoother than the rest.'

'That's incredible,' said Herringen. 'Have you used that trick before?'

Walsh smiled in the dim light. 'Once or twice.'

'But what if he'd updated his code?'

'Oh, come on. How many IT people change their passwords?'

'They're coming after us!' said Hal.

Walsh looked down to see the bugs swarming up the shaft, swamping the lights one by one. 'Will this thing go any faster?'

Herringen shook his head.

Several bugs caught up with the lift, and Walsh leapt up as their jaws came through the floor, snapping at the metal grille.

BANG! BANG! BANG!

Hal stamped on the jaws, dislodging one bug after another, but more took their place. 'How far to go?' he yelled over the noise.

Herringen looked up. 'About two hundred metres.'

'Get ready to run for it.'

Walsh joined Hal in stamping and kicking the bugs loose, their feet thumping and slamming on the weakened floor. Walsh glanced up to see the top of the shaft at least a hundred metres away, and she was still judging the distance when Herringen yelled a warning. A bug was scuttling towards her, but Hal grabbed it with his bare hands and smashed it against the bars. When it was still he threw it to the floor, and Walsh stared, fascinated, as dozens of frenzied bugs tore it apart before her eyes. The floor rippled as the massed robots tore at it, and without warning it split down the middle. Walsh climbed the walls to escape, and the others clung to the wire with their bare hands.

No sooner had they grabbed on than the entire floor dropped out of the lift, exposing a bottomless shaft whose walls were thick with bugs. Then the lift stopped and the doors slid open. They'd made it.

Once they were out, Walsh reached in and pressed the down button. The lift dropped away, taking most of the bugs with it. Meanwhile, Herringen had opened the heavy entrance door. He darted through, and for a split second Walsh was certain he was going to slam it in their faces, shutting them in with the bugs.

Then they were out, and the door thudded to behind them.

'Yeah!' Hal pumped his fist. 'We did it!'

'Not quite,' said Herringen. 'That door won't hold them long.'

'We'll use your car,' said Hal. 'They'll never catch us in that.'

They ran down the corridor, their footsteps clattering off the walls. The front door was closed but Hal grabbed the secretary's chair and tossed it through the glass, then followed it with a waste paper bin and several trays. He was just reaching for the computer when Walsh tugged his sleeve. 'Herringen has a key.'

The buckled doors slid open and they charged out into the cold afternoon air, their breath streaming behind them. Herringen's car was waiting at the foot of the steps, but the driver's door was open and the instruments had been smashed in.

'Bloody Newman!' growled Hal. 'He's thought of everything.'

'The truck,' said Walsh quickly. 'I hid it near the entrance!'

They set off at a run, but Herringen's breathing got heavier and heavier until he was gasping and wheezing between ragged breaths. 'Got to stop,' he said.

Walsh glanced back at the mine. How long did they have?

'It's no good,' rasped Herringen, who'd seen her look. 'When those things get out, the whole planet is doomed.'

Hal stared at him. 'For real?'

'Newman removed their safeguards. They'll flood out en masse.' Herringen took a deep breath. 'The people of Forzen won't stand a chance.'

'What can we do about it?' demanded Hal.

'We need a programmer,' Herringen wheezed. 'Someone who can undo Newman's code and stop the bugs.'

Hal and Walsh exchanged a glance, each hoping the other had computer expertise they'd yet to reveal. Neither did.

'What about Clunk?' said Walsh. 'If we get to the spaceport they should be able to call him back.'

'I already called him back, for all the good it did. Kent bloody Spearman must have overridden him.'

'Surely if you explain how urgent it is -'

'I did! I told him to get back here ASAP, top priority. You were missing, and I thought ...I was worried that ...' Hal's voice tailed off. 'That's it! The Navcom!'

'She said she couldn't stop the bugs.'

'No, but she can try and reach Clunk!' Hal dragged out the PDA and made a face as he saw the battery indicator. There was barely enough power for the Navcom to get in a complaint or two, but it was worth a shot. 'Navcom, can you hear me?'

'No.'

'Come on, I need you to get hold of Clunk. It's urgent!'

'Very well. I'll see what ...I can do.'

Walsh looked up as thunder rumbled in the distance. 'Will rain slow the bugs down?'

'I'm afraid not,' said Herringen. 'They're completely submersible.'

Thunder rumbled again, and Walsh frowned at the heavy skies. 'A bit of freezing rain might not affect the bugs, but –' She broke off as a bright star shone through the clouds, clearly visible despite the daylight. Then she realised it was moving, and the thunder was a continuous rumble. Tiny at first, the star became a white triangle, then a recognisable ship.

'That's the *Tiger*,' said Hal. 'It's Clunk! He's come back!'

'Are you sure?'

'Of course I am. I'd recognise that shape anywhere!' Hal started waving, even though the ship was far overhead and there was no chance he'd be seen.

Walsh realised the ship was heading away from them. 'Where's he going?'

'He's landing at the spaceport,' said Hal. Cursing, he raised the PDA. 'Navcom, listen carefully. Get a message to Clunk. Tell him to land at the mine. We're at the mine, got it?'

'Sending trans…trans…'

There was a bloop and the screen went dead. Hal shook the commset, willing it back to life, but the blank screen mocked him. 'Navcom!'

'It's too late,' cried Herringen. His voice shook, and when they looked round they saw why: a stream of bugs was pouring from the office. The windows shattered and more streams joined those coming through the door, forming a river of polished metal which flowed straight towards them.

— 32 —

Herringen broke first, turning and running for the gates. Walsh followed and Hal brought up the rear. He lagged behind to give the others a chance to escape, and before long the vicious creatures were right on his heels. Ahead he saw Walsh and Herringen leave the road, vanishing into the trees, and as he drew level with the spot Walsh called to him from the undergrowth.

'Hal! In here, quick!'

Hal swerved, leapt over a fallen tree and plunged into the bushes. Behind him, there was a noise like a hundred buzz-saws as the bugs set to work on the obstruction. 'They ... can ... run,' puffed Hal, 'but ... they ... can't ... fly!'

Walsh grabbed his hand and they ran through the woods together, ducking branches and dodging the undergrowth that threatened to slow them down. Then they found the wheel tracks, and ahead they saw Herringen getting into the truck. The engine started before they reached it, and the vehicle reversed towards them, hurtling backwards at speed. Hal put out a hand to open the door, but the truck kept going, reversing blindly through the forest. Herringen spared Hal and Walsh the briefest of glances as he abandoned them to their fate.

'You rotten bastard!' shouted Hal. 'Come back here!'

The truck vanished, the engine noise receding as it retreated through the forest.

'Well that's marvellous,' said Hal, his voice loud in the stillness. 'We rescue his sorry arse, and he bails on us.'

'We can still make a run for it.'

'They'll spread out and get us. We've had it.'

Walsh squeezed his hand. 'Never give up, Hal,' she whispered. 'There's always a way.'

'Yeah, but –' Hal stopped. In the distance the engine was getting louder again. 'He's coming back!'

The noise grew in volume until a thundering roar forced them to cover their ears. 'That's not the truck!' shouted Hal. 'It's a ship! It's Clunk!'

They looked up but the canopy was blocking the sky, and Hal realised Clunk wouldn't be able to see them either. 'Come on!' he shouted, grabbing Walsh's hand. They ran along the tyre tracks, leaping the crushed bushes and shredded undergrowth Herringen had left in his wake. Overhead, the roar of the ship got louder, then faded, and Hal realised Clunk was trying to spot them from the air before setting down.

They were halfway to the road when Walsh stopped with her hand to her mouth. Ahead, through the trees, masses of glossy bugs were swarming over a large rock.

'What are they doing?' muttered Hal. 'Building a nest?' He noticed the rock spanned Herringen's wheel tracks, and when he saw the bumper hanging down he realised the 'rock' was actually the remains of the truck. Herringen had ploughed into a tree, and the bugs were doing the rest. 'Time to go,' he muttered, tugging Walsh away.

Shocked, they moved on in silence. If Herringen had stopped for them …

Back at the road, they turned and ran for the mine. They could still hear the *Tiger* circling, and Hal hoped Clunk was keeping a sharp eye out. The bugs would finish their snack soon, and featuring in the second course wasn't high on his list of priorities.

They reached the shattered offices just as the *Tiger* roared over, with Clunk waving from the airlock platform. Hal waved back, then beckoned impatiently.

'Hal!' said Walsh. 'They're coming.'

Hal lowered his gaze and saw the relentless bugs flooding out of the woods. Frantically, he waved at Clunk, gesticulating and pointing. The robot waved back, then disappeared inside.

'That's a big help, Clunk,' muttered Hal, eyeing the oncoming horde. He felt good for one last effort, but Walsh looked exhausted, her face pale and scratched, her hair a matted tangle and her clothes stained with grease and greenery. She looked up at him, and when she managed a small grin Hal took her in his arms and kissed her, suddenly unconcerned about the bugs, the safety of planet Forzen, everything.

The *Tiger* thundered overhead as they clung to each other, the wash from its jets whipping their clothes around and almost knocking them off their feet. Hal opened one eye and saw the ship flaring for a landing on the road ... right above the oncoming bugs! He broke free of Walsh and waved frantically, but the *Tiger's* landing legs were already extended and it set down dead in the centre of the mass of bugs.

Immediately, the bugs clawed their way up the *Tiger's* landing legs, and Hal could only watch in horror as they flowed over the underside of the hull. Spearman's ship would be torn apart before his eyes!

The passenger ramp extended and Clunk appeared in the airlock. Hal broke into a run, yelling and waving, and the robot smiled and waved back.

'Take off!' shouted Hal. 'Quick!'

Clunk leapt back as a miner bug ran up the ramp towards him. He kicked it away and retreated inside the ship, closing the door with a thump.

Hal skidded to a halt, staring at the bugs attacking the ship in their thousands. It was too late - they'd destroy it for sure.

Suddenly the engines fired, belching white-hot flame. The bugs still on the ground below the ship were vaporised, and as the noise and heat grew they started dropping from the belly, flashed into nothingness before they hit the ground. Slowly, the ship lifted off, but instead of roaring away it hovered in mid-air. Thrusters fired along the top of the hull, driving the *Tiger* towards the ground, while at the same time the main jets tried to force it into the sky. The noise of the warring forces was incredible, and the resulting fireball engulfed the ship. Now the bugs were dropping by the hundred, plunging to the ground where the extreme heat flayed off their glossy shells, cooked their internals and fried their electronics.

Finally, the engines cut out and the ship settled on the road, crunching thousands of blackened remains under its broad feet. Then everything was still.

Hal grinned at Walsh. 'Good old Clunk. I said he'd save us!'

'No,' said Walsh, her eyes bright. 'You did!'

'Hey up, what's all this?'

Hal and Walsh untangled themselves, and turned to see Spearman and Clunk approaching across the smoking ground. Spearman was stepping gingerly over the blackened shells, while Clunk was looking on with an expression that contained elements of curiosity, happiness, anger and relief …all much of a muchness given his face had the consistency of a plastic chair.

'Good job, Clunk,' said Hal, who was standing with one arm around Walsh's shoulders. 'That was damn quick thinking, old buddy. The way you fried those little buggers with the jets …inspired. For a while there I thought you'd misread my signals, but I should have known better.'

Clunk looked mystified. 'Signals?'

'Yeah. Directing you over the miner bugs so you could frazzle them.'

'But I thought you were indicating a safe landing site! And what are miner bugs?'

Hal and Walsh exchanged a glance, then laughed aloud.

'Did you wreck this joint?' asked Spearman, who was inspecting the damage to the mine offices. He touched the front door, which promptly fell off its hinges. 'It was like that already,' he said quickly.

'How the hell did you convince him to come back?' Hal asked Clunk.

'I promised him your share of the cargo fee.'

Hal nodded. 'Okay.'

'No arguments?' called Spearman. 'No disputes?'

'It's all yours,' said Hal.

'Good.' Spearman grinned at Walsh. 'Fancy a lift home?'

'Get lost,' said Walsh.

Spearman looked around at the three of them, shook his head, then turned and strolled towards the *Tiger*. He climbed the ramp and entered the airlock, closing the door without looking back.

'Good riddance,' muttered Hal.

They watched the *Tiger* lift off, its jets scattering the hollow shells, and when it was gone they set off along the road to the gates, avoiding the charred miner bugs on the way. Hal kept an eye out for stragglers, but the open furnace Clunk had created with the ship's exhaust had got every last one. He gave the robot a pat on the back. 'You did well, Clunk. Pulled our chestnuts out of the fire in the nick of time.'

'My pleasure, although I still can't believe you let Mr Spearman take all the payment for the cargo job.'

Hal was about to tell Clunk that the cargo was safely aboard the *Volante*, and that Spearman wouldn't be earning a cent for the job, but decided it would just complicate things. 'I'm amazed he came back. What did you do, threaten to break his hair?'

'Actually, my efforts weren't the reason. He took a call from a Forzen VIP who was offering big money for an urgent flight to Dismolle. At first Spearman thought it was me pretending to be a client in order to get him to turn around, but eventually the caller convinced him.' Clunk smiled. 'I still had to talk him into landing at the mine though, but this time your message came through loud and clear.'

'Thank you Navcom,' said Hal. 'So, tell me about the VIP. How much did they offer?'

'I believe the sum was ten thousand credits.'

Hal almost choked. 'Ten grand!'

'Yes, and they're going to pump out his fuel tanks and refill them. All part of the deal.'

'Will that take long, do you think?' asked Hal casually. 'Only the *Volante* is waiting at the spaceport, and if we get in touch with this passenger ourselves ...'

'You're not thinking of stealing them away? Mr Spearman just saved your life!'

'I suppose you're right,' said Hal, glad he hadn't confessed to nicking the cargo.

Walsh glanced at him. 'It doesn't seem fair Spearman should get the cargo job and the passenger.'

'This is the freight business,' said Clunk. 'Nothing's fair.'

Hal slowed as they passed the tyre tracks leading into the woods. 'We'll have to tell someone about Herringen.'

'Who's that?' asked Clunk.

'The mine boss.'

'What happened? Is he hurt?'

'Well, you know how tuna comes in tin cans ...' Hal stopped as Walsh nudged him. 'Hey, when someone leaves me to die they deserve all they get.'

'He just panicked, Hal.'

Hal remembered the determined look on Herringen's face. Panic? Not likely. 'Yeah, I guess you're right,' he said, thus stumbling across the vital component in any relationship - agreeing with every word the other party says. Then he turned to more important matters. 'So this passenger, the one paying ten grand ...'

Clunk shrugged. 'Spearman said he was an executive. Name of Oldman.'

'Must be rich to throw that kind of money around.'

'Wait a minute!' Walsh grabbed his arm. 'Newman said he had a flight to catch, but surely he'd be too smart to use his own name.'

'But not smart enough to pick a really good one.' Hal turned to Clunk. 'Oldman has to be Newman, and that's the bastard behind everything. He's the villain!'

'We have to warn Mr Spearman,' said Walsh quickly. 'He could be in real danger.'

'Pity about that.' Hal saw Walsh's expression. 'Okay, okay. I'm on it.' He took out his PDA but now it was completely dead, and when Clunk checked his, it was also drained. 'The car had a mapping screen in the dashboard,' said Hal. 'Can you do something with that?'

'I may be able to crack it,' said Clunk. 'You drive and I'll work on it.'

'That could be a problem,' said Hal, as they passed through the gates. He pointed out the car, which was jammed under the billboard. 'It's stuck fast.'

Clunk eyed the sign, which stood on two wooden legs with angled bracers. After inspecting the legs, he stood over one of the bracers and stamped his foot down in the middle, snapping it in two. Then he broke the second one, clambered onto the car's roof and pushed in the middle of the sign. There was a creak as the posts gave way, and then the sign toppled over, freeing the car.

They piled in and Clunk had the screen free of the dashboard before Hal had even backed into the road. He poked and prodded the connections, and as they raced towards the spaceport Clunk worked every trick in his considerable arsenal. Walsh sat in the back, watching over his shoulder.

'I've got an idea,' said Hal.

'Go on.'

'Well, Spearman is supposed to be taking Newman to Dismolle, right? Why don't we just let him go?'

'May I point out a major flaw in this idea of yours?'

'Me too,' said Walsh.

'Let me finish,' said Hal. 'If we let Newman go, we can follow in the *Volante*, overtake the *Tiger,* and set up a reception committee on Dismolle. Newman lands, and pow!' Hal rubbed the back of his head. 'I owe him a bruise or two.'

'How do you know they're going to Dismolle?' asked Walsh.

'That's what he told Spearman.'

'And you don't think Newman is capable of hijacking the ship? If he pulls a gun they could end up anywhere.'

Hal turned to Clunk. 'She's good, isn't she? Thinks just like a criminal.'

'I'm not letting my suspect get away,' said Walsh firmly.

Clunk indicated the comms unit. 'If I can get through to Mr Spearman on this, I'll ask him to hold Newman up.'

'You expect him to throw away ten grand?' Hal snorted. 'As soon as Newman's aboard Spearman will take off so fast you'd think he was shot out of a gun.'

'I think you're wrong. I believe Mr Spearman will do the right thing when he understands what's at stake.'

'He's a freelance pilot, Clunk.'

'Even so.' Clunk made one final adjustment and replaced the comms unit, but when he switched the device on there was a loud fizz. 'Oh dear. An anti-tamper device.'

Hal put his window down to let the smoke out. 'That worked well.'

'Oh well, now that it's ruined …' Clunk yanked the unit right out of the dash, pulled the wires off the back and attached them to his PDA. There was a beep as the device came alive, and he dialled the *Tiger*. 'Mr Spearman? It's Clunk. I've discovered your intended passenger is a wanted criminal.'

Faintly, Hal heard Spearman's voice. 'What do you want me to do?'

'Delay your departure until we arrive. Miss Walsh will place Newman in custody and then you can be on your way.'

'Who the hell is Newman? My passenger is Oldman.'

'Same thing. He changed his name to evade capture.'

'So let me get this straight. My passenger turns up, and instead of taking him to Dismolle and collecting ten grand, you want me to hand him over to Spacejock?'

'That's right.'

'You know, Hal really needs to work on his little scams. I've never heard such a load of crap.'

'Newman's a murderer,' shouted Walsh. 'He may be armed.'

'Darling, he'd want to be.' Spearman sighed. 'You know, Hal must be getting desperate, what with losing fifteen grand from Morgan and now having to watch another ten sail into my pocket. It must really hurt.'

Walsh leaned forward. 'Mr Spearman, you're under arrest. I'm charging you with aiding and abetting a known criminal. You will remain in your present location until –'

'Sorry, you're breaking up. Tell me all about it next time we meet.'

'Mr Spearman, listen to me!' Clunk held the commset closer to his ear. 'Hal and Miss Walsh have put their lives on the line to capture this criminal. They didn't stop to think about profit margins!'

'More fool them,' said Spearman. 'I'm delivering this Newman guy and the cargo. Face it, you lost.'

'Not quite,' said Hal.

Clunk turned to look at him, and Hal gestured for the commset. 'But you're driving,' protested the robot. 'It's not safe.'

Hal plucked it out of his hand. 'Spearman, listen to me. That container in your hold is empty.'

'What?'

'I switched the cargo. Your gear is in the *Volante*.'

'Are you shitting me?'

'Go and have a look if you don't believe me.'

'Of all the devious –'

'Save it,' said Hal. 'Here's the deal. When Newman comes aboard you tell him there's a last minute delay with the cargo. You don't mention me or Clunk, and you certainly don't mention Walsh. When we arrive we'll nab Newman, and then I'll give back the cargo.'

There was a lengthy silence.

'Kent, I swear this is the truth. If you take off with Newman it could be the last trip you ever make.'

'All right, Spacejock. I'll delay him.'

'Thanks.'

'But you're a tricky bastard.'

Hal grinned. 'Likewise.' He tossed the commset to Clunk, who stowed it away. 'Go on, then. Give me the speech.'

'Which one?'

'The one about doing right by your fellow man. You must know it by now.'

'Oh yes.' Clunk cleared his throat. 'I can't believe you stole Mr Spearman's cargo. You've dented my faith in humans.' Then he winked at Walsh. 'I'm glad you're with us, my dear. Perhaps you'll keep Mr Spacejock on the straight and narrow.'

Walsh grinned. 'You'll need more than one Peace officer for that.'

'Even so, it's a start.'

They drove towards the spaceport in silence. Apart, that was, from the rattles and squeaks from the car. Two days of hard labour had really hammered the life out of it, and it was all Hal could do to keep it moving. 'Pity the bugs ate your truck,' he said. 'We'd have got there twice as fast in that.'

'Actually, it wasn't mine.'

'Where did you get it?'

A guilty look crossed Walsh's face. 'I stole it.'

Clunk groaned.

Walsh patted him on the shoulder. 'Relax, Clunk. I only break the law when it's absolutely necessary.'

'But that's what Mr Spacejock always says!'

33

Newman sat reading a magazine in the Forzen passenger terminal, with his back to the windows. He turned the pages from time to time, but was keeping one eye on the entrance. If Herringen and the others somehow managed to escape he'd have little warning, and he hadn't got this far by being sloppy.

Beep-boop!

Newman turned at the sudden noise. Nearby, a little kid was standing at an amusement machine, her face pressed to the glass. Her hands were on the controls, manipulating a gleaming claw inside the machine, and as he watched the claw came up empty. The kid immediately took out another credit tile to try again.

Beep-boop!

The claw moved, dropped, came back empty. The kid put another tile in the machine.

Beep-boop!

Newman watched dispassionately, wondering whether the girl's money or patience would run out first. The claw came up empty once again, and the girl felt through her pockets, sighed, then leaned on the glass to gaze at the unattainable delights within.

Watching her, Newman had a flashback to his own childhood. It was yet another spaceport, and there was a machine just like this one. His parents had walked by without a second glance, but he'd stopped for a closer look. They turned to call him, shouted at him, but he resisted, begging for just one go, certain he had the skill to win one of the tempting treats inside. Then, exasperated, his mum had delivered a huge smack and dragged him away.

Newman blinked. How many years ago was that? And he'd never once had a chance on those damned machines. Well, it was long overdue.

Setting aside the magazine, he walked to the machine and inserted a credit tile. The girl looked up at him, then pointed out a teddy bear buried up to its neck in lesser toys. The bear had a long-suffering expression, as though it had watched freedom come and go too many times, and Newman nodded to himself. That was the one.

Deftly, he moved the claw until it was directly above his prize, then hit the retrieve button. His inner eight-year-old beamed as the claw dropped straight onto the cute little teddy, and he felt a surge of elation as it closed around its head. He'd done it!

The winch spun, and the claw rose with the head firmly in its grasp. Then the little girl screamed, and Newman's triumphant smile vanished as he saw the teddy bear's body hanging by a thread. The claw dragged it across the other toys, finally separating the two as it reached the chute, and the girl's screams rang in Newman's ears as the severed head rolled into the prize tray. It stared up at him with accusing eyes, and as he reached out to take it the face changed. Now it was Herringen's balding head, and Newman recoiled in horror. Then he heard a rustling behind him, and spun around to see a wave of miner bugs flooding through the entrance, oblivious to the other passengers, making straight for him, directly towards him, always after him ...

Beep-boop!

Newman was awake in an instant, heart pounding. Nearby, the little kid was playing on the amusement machine, and to his relief there was no sign of any bugs. He looked around, but nobody was pointing out the crazy man to spaceport security. Then he glanced at his watch. It was now twenty minutes since his miner bugs had broken out, and his ride was running late. The last thing he needed was a flood of panicked refugees hitting the spaceport, stranding him there as they fought over the last ride out.

He set the magazine aside, grabbed his carry-on bag and strolled to the information counter. 'Jon Oldman,' he said to the attendant. 'I booked passage aboard the *Tiger*. Any idea how much longer it'll be?'

The young man checked his screen. 'I'm sorry, Mr Oldman. Your ship has landed but they're still refuelling.'

'Can't I go aboard?'

'Safety regulations state that passengers cannot embark until refuelling is complete.'

'Why don't you call the ship for me? Maybe they've finished, eh?'

Newman slid a hundred-credit tile across the counter. 'Here, keep the change.'

The employee glanced around to check whether anyone was looking, then pocketed the cash. 'I've just looked, and they're nearly done. If you leave right now I'll have them hook up a boarding tunnel. Should be there by the time you –'

'You're a champ. Excellent service.' Newman grabbed his bag and left.

'Gate three!' called the attendant.

The gate led into a lengthy boarding tunnel, which was moving above the busy spaceport apron on pylons. Windows looked out on the snow-covered landscape, and as Newman eyed the freezing terrain he wondered whether he might settle on a warmer planet. Then he smiled at the thought. With the cash at his disposal he could settle just about anywhere, although he still had one loose end to deal with.

He rounded the final corner just as the boarding tunnel pressed against the side of his ship, encompassing the airlock door. It was closed, and when he looked through the porthole he saw right into the flight deck where a man was sitting at the console, talking to his computer. Newman frowned as the pilot dunked a biscuit and casually bit the end off. Here he was, a VIP, and this slob was sitting around stuffing his face!

Newman banged his fist on the airlock window and the pilot sat bolt upright, spilling his coffee and dropping the soggy biscuit in his lap. Newman beckoned, pointing at the airlock door, and the pilot hurried over to open it.

'Who are you?'

'Oldman. I'm coming aboard.'

'You can't. They're still filling the tanks.'

'I'm not paying ten grand to stand around in the cold. Step aside.'

The pilot looked like he was about to argue, then stood back. 'Welcome aboard the *Tiger*, Mr Oldman. I'm your captain, Kent Spearman, and we're expecting a trouble-free flight to Dismolle.'

Newman entered the flight deck and looked around, interested in his surroundings despite the tension. He'd travelled aboard many vessels, but this was his first time on a freighter. He nodded towards a pair of doors in the rear wall. 'Is my cabin in there?'

'It's just being cleaned. Can I take your bag?'

Newman shook his head and tucked the bag under his arm. 'How long until departure?'

'They're just loading a container. Last minute job.'

'Answer the question.' Newman noticed the pilot's forehead shining in the overhead lights. Was the flight deck that warm?

'About fifteen minutes. Can I get you a coffee?'

Newman nodded.

'Take a seat. Make yourself at home.' Spearman busied himself at the coffee maker. 'So, the payment for this trip. It was cash, right?'

Without warning the doors at the back of the flight deck slid open, and a battered old robot looked in. Spearman stared at it in surprise, and on seeing his reaction Newman felt in his bag until his hand closed on the grip of a heavy blaster. He kept it out of sight, but ready for use. 'Who the hell are you? Maintenance? Refueller?'

'No, my function is purely spiritual.'

'You what?'

'Sirs, before you stands a faceless servant of the Church of the Mechanical Deity. Members of this holy order travel the galaxy, soliciting donations for the upkeep of our most sacred site, the Altar of the Red Moon.'

Newman frowned. 'Church of the what?'

'The Mechanical Deity, sir. I myself am only recently ordained, but my brothers have been preaching the word of Cog for years.'

'So what do you want?'

'A small donation would be ample. As robots, we derive maximum benefit from compound interest.'

Newman stared at the robot in suspicion, but its serene expression didn't alter. His first instinct was to have it thrown off the ship, but upsetting the member of some religious order was hardly going to speed his departure. Barely concealing his irritation, he reached into his pocket and took out a handful of change.

'Why, thank you sir.' The robot held out both hands. 'Would you allow me to bless you?'

'No, I –'

'Please? It would mean a lot to me.'

Newman sighed, then held both hands out, leaving the bag on his lap.

The robot took hold of Newman's wrists, its hard skin cold against his own. 'Mr Spearman, the prisoner is secure. Would you be so kind as to call the others?'

Newman stared at the robot, half expecting it to morph into Herringen. Was this another nightmare? A waking dream like the one at the spaceport? Suddenly the robot's grip was an iron vice, and Newman could feel his bones creaking. He gasped in pain, and as he gazed into the robot's eyes he saw a willingness to take it further, to keep squeezing until -

'I-I give up!' said Newman. 'Don't hurt me!'

'I'm going to punch his nose right out the back of his head,' growled Hal, as the lift carried him towards the flight deck.

'No you're not,' said Walsh quietly. 'This is my arrest, Hal. We're doing it by the book.'

'What book? He knocked you out, he goes down. Simple.'

'Hal, this is important. If we don't stick to the rules we're as bad as he is.'

Hal stared at the door, his fists bunched and his face set in a hard expression. Then he nodded.

'Of course,' said Walsh casually. 'If he resists arrest you can belt the crap out of him.'

The doors opened and they emerged to find Clunk standing over Newman, who was sitting in the pilot's chair with both wrists in a pincer-like grip. He glanced at Hal, then slumped as he met Walsh's level gaze.

'Jonathan Newman, I'm arresting you in the name of the Peace Force,' said Walsh calmly. 'I'm taking you back to Dismolle to face charges.'

'You can't take me anywhere. I live on Forzen!'

'And the nearest Peace Force station is on Dismolle. Of course, you won't be there long, because as soon as they convict you it'll be off to the prison planet of -'

'Wait!' cried Newman. 'You've got the wrong person.'

'Don't be ridiculous. The Council will face separate charges, and Herringen's dead.'

'Dead?'

Hal nodded. 'The bits we saw definitely weren't moving.'

'It wouldn't make any difference,' said Newman. 'It's not them anyway.'

'There's someone else?'

'You think I set this up on my own? I'm just a pawn!'

'So who's the grand master?'

'Miranda Morgan, of course!'

Walsh stared at him. 'You have got to be kidding me.'

'No, it's true! Her renovation company...it's a front. I transferred the mine's profits into her accounts, and she made it look like payments for her stupid decorating work. Half her customers don't even exist!'

'You were the one stealing the profits. How does that make her the mastermind?'

'At first we were just taking a few thousand here and there. Small stuff. But then she threatened to turn me in unless I stepped it up. It was out of control, but I was in too deep and couldn't do anything to stop it. Then we heard about the audit.'

'The accountant? Cooper?'

Newman nodded. 'I wanted to run for it, but Miranda wasn't giving up without a fight. She came up with the idea of using the mining bugs to remove Cooper. Make it look like an accident, and in all the fuss nobody would spot a hole in the accounts.'

'So, instead of spending a couple of years in jail for fraud, you decided to try your hand at murder?'

'I-it just got out of hand. After Cooper's death, you arrived to investigate. Then I heard there was a whole team of auditors coming to inspect the books. I could hardly make them all disappear, so I set up one last transfer to strip every credit out of the mine, and programmed the bugs to tidy up.'

'If you're going to cooperate I'll need everything,' said Walsh. 'All the bank accounts, a list of transactions, everything I need to nail Morgan. And if you're bullshitting me –'

'I'll do whatever it takes. Now please will you tell your robot to let go of me? I can't feel my fingers!'

Walsh nodded at Clunk, who obeyed, and Newman started rubbing his wrists. Then, without warning, he sprang for the door. Walsh reacted first, but Newman pushed her roughly aside. Then Hal caught up with him, grabbing Newman's arm with a grip that made Clunk's look like a newborn baby's. He swung Newman round and belted him with his full strength, knocking him clean across the flight deck. There was a crash as Newman landed on the console, and then he slid down to the floor, already unconscious.

'I was really hoping he'd do that,' said Hal with satisfaction. He helped Walsh up. 'Are you all right?'

Walsh rubbed her elbow. 'I should never have trusted the snake.'

'You wouldn't be the first.' Hal prodded Newman with his boot. 'We'll take him back to Dismolle on the *Volante*. You're coming too, as promised.'

Walsh smiled.

'Think there'll be a reward?'

'Sorry, the Peace Force doesn't pay them.'

'Pity.' Hal looked in Newman's bag, and his eyes widened as he saw the gun. 'Hey, can I -?'

'Sorry, Hal. Evidence.' Walsh closed the bag. 'I'll look after this until we get back to Dismolle. Bernie always wanted to teach me two-handed firing.'

'Well, I think I'll be off,' said Spearman, coming up behind them. 'I've got a cargo to deliver, and it isn't getting any fresher.'

'Morgan's container?' Walsh raised her eyebrows. 'You expect to complete a transaction with a criminal?'

'Hang on a minute,' said Hal. 'We don't know Morgan's involved. For all you know, Newman's setting up an innocent person.'

'He *is*!' said Spearman. 'Me!'

Hal drew Walsh aside. 'It can't really hurt, can it? After all, Clunk's got to refuel the *Volante*, and if Morgan is involved you can arrest her after she's paid Spearman.'

'I thought you two were rivals. Why are you sticking up for him?'

'Oh, you know. Brothers in arms and all that. He's not a bad sort really.'

'All right, he can have an hour head start, but I'd better not regret it. Now, let's get to your ship. I want to tie Newman up good and proper before we leave.'

'Clunk will take you.'

'Why, what are you going to do?'

Hal glanced at Spearman. 'We just have a little profit-sharing arrangement to sort out.'

34

The flight to Dismolle went quickly, and Hal took the opportunity to demonstrate the AutoChef to Walsh. It still served the same horrible meals, but could now apologise for their shortcomings in two dozen languages. The kitchen had been made over as well, and there were neat little covers on the gas rings *and* colour-coordinated splashbacks.

On the other hand, Hal's cabin was a disaster. Meddlesome workers had put everything away, and it took him a good part of the trip to toss it all around and mix the resulting mess up properly. After all, how else could he lay his hands on a clean sock at ten minutes notice?

While Hal was busy turning his cabin into a bomb site, Clunk did his rounds of the ship and Walsh used a screen in the flight deck to type up her report. Once she'd covered everything she read through it a second time, correcting a couple of typos and clarifying a few points. It made good reading, especially with one crook tied up in the hold and another about to be arrested, and Walsh smiled as she pictured the reaction at Peace Force HQ. Maybe she was unknown to them, but cracking an important case would surely lead to a commendation … perhaps even early graduation?

Walsh's smile slipped as she thought of Barney, the heroic BNE-II robot from the Forzen office. He'd saved her life, and although she'd lauded the robot in her report she felt a bravery medal of some kind would be fitting. Did the Peace Force have such a thing? Walsh resolved to ask Bernie at the first opportunity, and if they didn't have bravery awards for robots she'd insist they damn well invent one.

Suddenly the console pinged, and a message appeared on screen. It was from Mr Bigan of the Forzen Residents Association, thanking them for solving the mystery of Margaret Cooper's disappearance, and also for recovering their fundraising money. Walsh deleted the final paragraph, which contained an enquiry about the whereabouts of a certain loan vehicle, and attached the rest of the message to her report. If that didn't earn her a few brownie points with the Peace Force, nothing would.

◆

Hal tried calling the *Tiger* as soon as they landed on Dismolle, but there was no reply. He went outside and saw Spearman's ship sitting on a nearby landing pad, sealed up. 'Keep an eye on the *Tiger*,' he told Clunk. 'Don't let Spearman leave until I've spoken to him.'

He went with Walsh to collect a subdued Newman from the cargo hold, and insisted on accompanying them to the terminal. It seemed like weeks since they'd first ambled across the field together, and Hal smiled to himself at the memory. Then he wondered whether there was any chance of coffee and cake.

They entered the terminal, attracting curious stares as they crossed the concourse. Walsh strode along in her faded old uniform, her chin up as she led the two men. Newman slouched along with his head down, unwilling to meet anyone's gaze, while Hal walked easily alongside him, keeping a firm grip on Newman's arm.

The cruiser was parked out the front, and Walsh held the door while Hal bundled Newman into the back. Hal overruled her objections and got in alongside, and Newman spent the entire trip pressed up against his door, keeping well out of Hal's reach.

The car drew up at the station, and Walsh helped Newman out of the back. Hal went to follow, but she stopped him. 'You can't come in. It's off limits.'

Hal nodded at Newman. 'What about him?'

'He's not coming out again.'

'I'll just wait here,' said Hal promptly.

◆

As Walsh led Newman from the car, she saw him look up at the forbidding exterior of the Peace Force office before glancing up and down the street. 'Don't even think about it,' she growled.

'I was just loosening my neck.'

'You run, and I'll loosen your teeth.'

'Your boyfriend already did.'

'He's not my –' Walsh stopped. Don't let the prisoner bait you. Rule nineteen, section three. She took a firm grip on Newman's arm and led him inside. 'Bernie! Where are you?'

Slow, thudding footsteps heralded Bernie's approach, and Walsh's doubts about the legitimacy of the Dismolle office melted away as she saw the familiar craggy face. How could she possibly have believed Bernie was anything but genuine? Alongside her, Newman cowered visibly as the powerful robot strode towards them.

'Trainee Walsh, you're back! And you have company.' Bernie looked Newman up and down. 'Jonathan Newman of Forzen, I believe. Would you like a coffee?'

Walsh grinned at the expression on Newman's face. Bernie was more likely to hug the guy than beat him up, but either could be fatal. 'Bernie, he's a prisoner, not a guest.'

'He is?'

'Come to think of it, a hot drink would be ideal. Make it a strong one.'

'That's good of you,' said Newman. 'I could murder a coffee.'

'Or vice versa,' muttered Walsh. 'Save the expense of a trial, too.'

'A trial?' Bernie looked alarmed. 'And why is Mr Newman a prisoner?'

'He's responsible for the deaths of Margaret Cooper and Rod Herringen of Forzen, he's caused untold property damage, he's kidnapped a civilian and a Peace Force operative and, to cap it off, he's embezzled a large sum of money from the Panther Mining Company.' Walsh took out a data chip. 'My full report is on here.'

'Oh my,' said Bernie. She felt for a chair and sat down heavily, straining the legs to breaking point. 'Trainee Walsh, what have you done?'

'Me? He's the crook!'

'Arresting people? Reports?' Bernie took a deep breath. 'You know, you're not a full officer yet, and as such you don't have the authority to –'

'Don't give me that. You know my graduation is just an exam question away.'

'I - I –'

'It is, isn't it?'

Bernie started to shake, and Walsh looked on in horror as the big robot struggled to speak. 'I - I –'

'Bernie?'

'Ch-charge,' said Bernie, fumbling with her chest compartment. She got it open, and Walsh took the plug and ran to the nearest socket.

'There, how's that?'

'S-switch on.'

Walsh checked. 'It is on, Bernie!'

For a few moments nothing happened, and then Bernie got up, every movement an effort. 'I'm sorry, Trainee Walsh,' she said slowly. 'My charging circuits aren't what they used to be. I was on duty for lengthy stretches while you were out of the office, and I find myself needing a charge more and more frequently.'

Walsh frowned. Bernie had never been far from a power point, so how much extra charging could she take? 'Is there anything I can do?'

'G-give me your report. I'd like to check it over.'

Walsh gave it to her. 'Will you be all right for a bit?'

'Why? Where are you going?'

Walsh gestured at Newman. 'I have to arrest his accomplice, but I'll be back as soon as possible.'

Slowly, Bernie nodded. 'That is your duty.'

'Keep him safe for me, and don't worry about his coffee.'

Bernie studied Newman, then took him by the wrist. 'Follow me, prisoner.'

'What about my rights?' demanded Newman. 'Hey, don't leave me!'

But Walsh had gone.

Hal sat in the back of the Peace Force cruiser, trying hard not to look like a captured criminal. All he needed was for some over-zealous photographer to snap him through the windows, and his face would be all over the news before Walsh could say, 'He's not my –'

Hal looked away from the Peace Force station, staring through the windscreen and focusing further and further along the road until he had the horizon in his sights. Slowly, he raised his gaze until he was looking at the deep blue sky, and there he stopped. Life was simple up there, just him and Clunk and the Navcom. No emotions in space. Well, maybe a bit of anger and frustration from time to time, but not the painful heart-wrenching stuff.

The driver's door opened and Walsh got in. She smiled at Hal in the mirror, and he saw the strain around her eyes. She'd been through far more than he had, and she wasn't complaining. She couldn't just run away into space, either. She had to stick around and deal with things.

'You look serious,' said Walsh lightly.

'Just thinking.'

'Ready to catch another crook?'

'Lead the way, pardner,' said Hal.

The engine started and the car pulled away from the kerb. Before long they were zipping through a commercial zone, all offices and government departments, and then they pulled into a small car park.

'Leave the talking to me,' said Walsh. 'And if she says anything personal, ignore it. Don't let her under your skin.'

Hal nodded, and they got out of the car together. The office door was open, and Walsh stopped just outside. 'Hello?'

There was no reply, so they entered. The hallway had a garish lime-and-maroon paint scheme, with grotesque bronze mobiles hanging from the walls and a rug that looked like it had been woven from excess nasal hair.

'Miranda?' called Walsh.

'Maybe she's gone.' Hal eyed the rug in distaste. 'Unless that thing ate her.'

Walsh's hand dropped to her hip, and she swore as her fingers closed on thin air. Stealthily, she moved along the hall to the office, and Hal followed closely, ready to spring to her defence.

They entered the office proper, and the first thing Hal saw was a pair of legs sticking out from behind the desk. He nudged Walsh to point them out, and saw her swallow nervously. She held up her fist and counted one-two-three on her fingers, and on three they both dived behind the desk. Immediately, Hal could see they weren't in any danger. The figure on the floor was lying face down, bound at the wrists and ankles, and they didn't need to turn him over to find out who it was: the mane of straw-coloured hair was a dead giveaway. 'Kent Spearman!'

'Help me turn him over,' said Walsh.

Hal grabbed the desk and tossed it aside, and then he and Walsh crouched alongside Spearman, rolling him gently onto his back. Despite their rivalry, Hal was dreading the worst, and he breathed a sigh of relief when he saw the other pilot's chest rising and falling.

'Knocked out, but alive,' said Walsh.

'Thick skull,' remarked Hal. By the time he'd untied the ropes Spearman was coming round, and when they sat him up he groaned and blinked, his eyes unfocussed. Before Walsh could stop him Hal grabbed a glass of water and threw it in his face.

'Ow!' said Spearman, as the glass clonked off his forehead.

'Hell, sorry.' Hal looked apologetic. 'Slippery fingers.'

Still dazed, Spearman looked around. 'Where the hell am I?'

'Never mind that,' said Walsh. 'Where's Morgan?'

Spearman put a hand to his forehead. 'She was getting the money to pay me. She went to the drawer, and then –'

Walsh sniffed the air. 'Knockout spray?'

'Or killer perfume,' said Hal.

Spearman struggled to his feet, wobbling slightly. 'Well, I'll be off then. I've got a ship to run.'

'You sit down for a bit,' said Walsh. 'That stuff will wear off in a minute or two.'

'No, really. I –'

'SIT!'

He obeyed, and Hal almost did the same. 'I guess Morgan was tipped off before I got here,' said Spearman. 'She must have heard about that Newman guy and done a bunk.'

'Probably had eyes at the spaceport,' said Walsh. 'She won't get far, though. I'll warn the passenger lines so she can't book a ticket. Especially under a false name.'

'I doubt she'll leave right away,' said Spearman. 'If I were her I'd lie low for a bit, wait for the fuss to die down.'

'He's probably right,' said Hal. 'He knows the criminal mind inside out.'

'We'd better get back to the office and put out the alert,' said Walsh. 'Will you be all right here?'

Spearman nodded. 'Just fine, thanks.'

Suddenly Hal grabbed Walsh's arm. 'Did you put Newman under guard?'

'Bernie's looking after him. Killing him with kindness, most like.' She frowned. 'Wait a minute. You don't think Miranda will try and rescue him?'

'No, but what if she decides to shut him up ... permanently? Without Newman -'

'I won't have a case against her!'

They stared at each other, then ran from the office, leaving Spearman clutching his head.

◆

Walsh had driven quickly on the way to the party, but that was nothing to the terrifying white-knuckle ride she subjected Hal to now. The cruiser's engine howled, lights flashed and sirens screamed as they belted through the traffic.

They stopped outside the Peace Force station, and Hal was still struggling to get out by the time Walsh was halfway to the door. On the way her suspicions had firmed into certainty, and now she was dreading what she'd find. To get at Newman, Morgan would have to go through Bernie, and while the robot would usually be more than a match, she clearly wasn't her usual self.

Walsh's first instinct was to charge in and confront Morgan, but the endless training sessions kicked in before she could do anything rash. Instead, she unlatched the door and eased it open with her foot. 'Hello? Bernie?'

The only reply was a faint cry, and at the sound Walsh dived through the doorway and executed a half-roll, springing up with her back to the wall. So much for stealth training, she thought. Then she heard Hal following, and motioned him against the wall.

'Trainee Walsh, is that you?' whispered Bernie. Her voice was weak, almost inaudible, and Walsh strained to hear it. 'I'm afraid I'm done for.'

'Tell me where she is, Bernie. I'll kill her.'

'What are you talking about?'

'Morgan, of course.'

'I don't understand,' said Bernie slowly. 'I've never met Miss Morgan. It's just that my batteries won't hold a charge any more.'

Walsh stepped away from the wall and hurried into the office. She was dimly aware of Hal following her, but then she saw Bernie slumped against the wall, the big robot unharmed but immobile. 'Oh Bernie,' she said, dropping into a crouch. 'How can I help?'

'You can't. Not now.'

'I can get the charge cable for you.'

Bernie raised her hand, and Walsh saw the cable was already plugged in.

'What about new batteries? I can order them from head office. Just give me access to the computer.'

Bernie looked up, a ghastly expression on her face. 'I did what I thought best, you know. Best for the people of this planet, and for you.'

'What do you mean?'

Slowly, Bernie closed her eyes. Walsh took the robot's massive hand in hers. 'Bernie, talk to me.'

The robot opened her eyes, but kept her gaze on the floor. 'I can't give you access, because there aren't any computers. I used all the parts to keep myself going.'

'But head office! They –'

'I never contacted them, Harriet. I didn't dare.'

Walsh felt cold. 'The office closed down, didn't it? Here on Dismolle, I mean.'

'The Peace Force is a vital part of the community, and we gave them a sense of security.' Bernie gripped her hand. 'The people needed us, don't you see? We couldn't allow them to close us down!'

'But you were paying me wages! Surely those came from head office?'

'Unemployment benefits. I signed you up, kept a percentage for expenses, gave you the rest.' Bernie looked up at her, pleading. 'I did a good job, didn't I? Kept Dismolle safe?'

'You did, Bernie. You looked after all the humans.'

'Thank you, Harriet.' Bernie's head dropped. 'T-there's something else. A b-box of records in the armoury. They're y-yours.'

'Thanks, Bernie.'

'I'm s-sorry about your gradu…a-about your gr –'

Bernie's grip relaxed, and Walsh held the cold metal fingers for a moment before gently laying the hand on the robot's broad chest. Then she stood up. She hadn't believed Barney on Forzen, but now she had the truth she'd been dreading. She wasn't Trainee Walsh of the Dismolle Peace Force, and she wasn't about to graduate from anything. Her investigation meant nothing, Morgan had escaped and Newman would vanish before she could get anyone official - say, a real Peace Force officer - to visit Dismolle and mop up.

Walsh lowered her head, blinking back tears. Why her? What had she done to deserve this?

Then she felt Hal's arm around her shoulders, and she stood there with her head on his chest, drawing on his strength.

'Hello? Is anyone out there?'

Walsh recognised Newman's voice. 'What is it?'

'Your metal pal chained me to the kitchen sink,' said Newman plaintively. 'Do you think you could undo me?'

Walsh laughed, then wiped her eyes. Good old Bernie. Nobody escaped a BNE-II mobile crime-fighting unit.

— 35 —

Hal locked Newman in the basement, then made Walsh a coffee. Since Bernie's revelation she'd seemed to shrink inside herself, and he was getting worried. From what he'd seen, the Peace Force had become the most important thing in her life, and without it she was in danger of falling.

He took the drinks into the office, where he found Walsh sitting on a chair, staring into space. 'Here, this'll do the trick.'

She took the mug. 'Did you use the whole jar?'

'Eh? No.'

'Bernie used to. She cost me a fortune.' Walsh looked down at her uniform. 'This might as well be fancy dress. Probably is.'

'Don't be hard on yourself. You did everything right. It just wasn't quite legit, that's all.'

'How could she do this to me?'

'It was real to her,' said Hal. 'Running a busy office, training up a new officer … it's what she was made for.'

'It was all lies,' said Walsh dully.

'What was that about a box of records?'

'I've seen it,' said Walsh. 'Stacks of old reports. Junk.'

'I don't think so,' said Hal seriously. 'It sounded important.'

'So was gunnery practice, Hal. Every day, without fail. Duty, duty, duty! It was like she was driving me, trying to make me the perfect little officer.'

'For what it's worth, I'd say she did a pretty good job.'

'Thanks.'

'So, this box of records …'

'You're not going to let that go, are you?'

'Could be money in it.'

'Bet there isn't.' A smile flickered across Walsh's lips. 'In fact, I bet Bernie was giving me homework.'

'Done. Now open the door.'

Hal watched eagerly as Walsh entered the pass code, and he almost pushed past as she opened the armoury. Then they were inside, and while she went to the box at the far end, Hal checked out the case with the gun. 'Hell, this looks handy.'

'Don't touch it.' Walsh took the box down and returned to the office, laying it on the table. She lifted the lid, Hal craned his neck to look inside, and she couldn't help laughing at his expression. 'I did warn you. It's just a bunch of old records.' She took out a manila folder and ran her thumb across it, riffling the pages. 'Not even a gold bar.'

Hal was unable to hide his disappointment. 'I really thought she'd left you something good. She seemed so –'

'Her life was a lie, Hal.' Walsh glanced at Bernie, who was sitting motionless against the wall. 'I don't blame her, and I can understand why she did it, but she's gone now and I have to look after myself.'

'Hello? Is anyone there?' called Clunk from the doorway. Then he saw Bernie. 'Oh my goodness. Is she …?'

Hal nodded. 'Her batteries failed.'

'I suspect it was more than that.' Clunk crouched to inspect the robot. 'It looks like everything gave out at once.'

'And there's more, too.' Hal explained about Walsh and the Peace Force, while Clunk tutted sadly.

'It's a known phenomenon,' he said. 'A robot who was the centre of attention suddenly finds themselves unwanted and superfluous, and they'll go to great lengths to make themselves useful again.'

'Like stashing away old records instead of cash and gold,' said Hal, indicating the dusty box. 'Some legacy, eh?'

Clunk took a file from the box and flipped through it. 'Incidentally, I came to tell you Mr Spearman is leaving soon. He sends you his regards.'

'He was supposed to send me money,' said Hal. 'Now we're stuck.'

'Not quite. He transferred half his fuel to the Volante.'

'Eh?'

'We can leave as soon as you're ready. In fact, I believe I've found a suitable job on planet Belleron, although they did ask some rather odd questions about radiation shielding.'

'So that's it then,' said Walsh, in a small voice. 'You're leaving.'

Clunk cleared his throat. 'I'll, er, just leave you to your goodbyes. Over here, that is. With my back turned.'

Harriet watched Clunk walk away. 'He does look out for you, doesn't he?'

'We're a team. He finds the work, flies the ship and manages the accounts, and I fill a more, um, managerial role.' Hal lowered his voice. 'Don't tell him I said that, eh? He gets a bit touchy about the whole robot rights thing.'

Harriet smiled. 'My lips are sealed.'

'Yeah.' Hal gazed at them. 'Amongst other things.'

Harriet tilted her head back, Hal leant closer, and then -

'Miss Walsh?'

'Yes Clunk?' called Harriet, without taking her eyes off Hal.

'Who is James Walsh?'

'I don't know.'

'And Sandra Walsh, nee Jackson?'

'I have no idea. Is it important?'

'Well, those are the names on your birth certificate.'

'WHAT?'

Hal turned to see Clunk standing over the dusty box of records, flipping through the pages as he scanned the contents. 'It seems your father was Captain Walsh of the Dismolle Peace Force.'

Walsh was staring at him, white-faced, and Hal could feel her trembling. 'Clunk, take it easy,' he said, a warning in his voice.

'No, tell me,' said Walsh. 'I've had enough lies from Bernie.'

'I can't find anything on your mother, but there is a report of an accident. You were only three when your parents left aboard the *Ganymede* for –'

'I know that bit,' said Walsh quietly.

'Well, afterwards Bernie was supposed to submit the crash report, but she didn't. It's all here. She must have been training you up to take his place. Like father, like daughter.'

'That explains the Peace Force recruitment flyers,' said Walsh. 'They started arriving after my twenty-first birthday, telling me I'd been pre-selected from millions of applicants. Bernie must have had an eye on me for years, just waiting for the right moment.'

'Hang on, did you say the *Ganymede*?' Hal remembered the battered hulk at the spaceport. 'But that's –'

'Probably taken apart for scrap long ago,' interrupted Clunk. 'Old ships contain too many sad memories. Don't you agree?' He peered in the box, then took out a yellowed strip of plastic. 'That's interesting.'

'What is it? A ruler?'

Clunk held the strip of plastic to the light, then put one end in his mouth as though he were biting a large ice cream stick.

'Hey, what are you doing?' cried Walsh, trying to grab it back.

'This is how I read it,' explained Clunk, fending her off. 'Please, let me finish.'

'I've heard of a megabyte –' began Hal.

There was a whirr as the plastic strip disappeared, and then it went in and out of Clunk's mouth several times. Finally, it stopped.

'Is there anything on it?' asked Harriet.

'Yeah,' said Hal. 'Spit it out.'

'Give me a moment to decode the information. It's an old-fashioned encoding, and I can't read it unless I –' Clunk's expression changed. 'Oh my goodness.'

'What?' demanded Hal and Walsh together.

'You're not going to believe this!' Clunk stared at Harriet. 'Miss Walsh, this strip contains your mother's records. She wasn't just a passenger aboard the *Ganymede*, she owned it! She was a freighter pilot!'

Hal took her arm. 'Don't you remember? You thought you might have travelled aboard ships when you were little. And you couldn't stay away from the spaceport!'

Walsh nodded slowly. 'So, I'm the product of a pilot and a Peace Force officer. Equal shares.'

Clunk smiled. 'Itchy feet and a strong sense of justice. Nice combination.'

'Except the Peace Force was a lie, and I don't have a ship.' Walsh sighed. 'Hal, have you ever thought about settling down? Buying a house on a nice quiet planet, maybe getting a regular job?'

Hal considered the question, and his heart sank as he realised the implications. 'I'm sorry, but that's not who I am.'

'Me neither.'

Hal's heart lifted, but he hardly dared to hope. 'I mean, who'd want to stick to one planet? You could put up with it for a few years, but after that it'd get boring.'

'Dull as,' said Walsh.

'You don't want to stay somewhere like Dismolle your whole life.'

'Nope.'

'You know ...'

'Yes?'

'We sometimes ...'

'Yes?'

'Well ...'

Nearby, there was an explosion of pent-up breath. 'Will you just ask her?' shouted Clunk, exasperated beyond measure.

'Doyouwannacomewithus?' said Hal quickly. 'You'll have your own cabin, and the AutoChef will easily feed the two of us, because it uses waste matter from the –'

'Explain that bit later,' said Clunk hurriedly.

'It's all right, you don't have to sell me on the Volante,' said Walsh. 'I'm in. Sign me up.'

Hal laughed. 'That's great! Now we've got a bronze and a copper on board.'

'And a nut,' muttered Clunk. 'Miss Walsh, welcome to the crew.'

'Please, call me Harriet.'

'Certainly, Miss Walsh.'

◆

Walsh boarded the *Volante* a couple of hours later, having stripped her apartment of clothes and valuables. All her worldly goods arrived in two suitcases, which Clunk stowed in the spare cabin. He'd already made a sign for the door, and Walsh felt a lump in her throat as she saw her name carefully engraved on the metal plate.

While she was settling in, Clunk sent an anonymous message to Peace Force headquarters, routing it through the terminal's servers to ensure it couldn't be traced. In it, he explained the events on Dismolle and Forzen, gave the location of Jonathan Newman, and included Walsh's description of Miranda Morgan - with only minor edits for accuracy. Afterwards he contacted Honest Bob to let him know about Bernie, since there was a chance the robot could be repaired and put to use in the shipyard, especially if he removed it before the Peace Force clean-up team arrived ...

Just before departure Walsh joined Hal and Clunk at the top of the passenger ramp, and they stood in silence as the sun set on Dismolle.

'That's the most exciting thing you'll see around here,' said Walsh, as the last rays faded from the sky.

Hal grinned. 'Yeah, but it's a new dawn tomorrow. In space!' Then he spotted the *Tiger*, which was sitting on a landing pad nearby. 'Poor old Spearman, eh? Lost his passenger, lost all the cash from the cargo job ... still, you've got to laugh.'

'I told him to keep his ship locked,' said Clunk. 'I know the spaceport has Miss Morgan's details, but she's a desperate woman.'

'Oh, she was always desperate,' muttered Walsh.

'Do you think they'll catch her?' asked Hal.

'She's trapped on Dismolle, and that's as good as a prison sentence.'

'What about all the money she embezzled with Newman? Can it be recovered?'

Clunk shook his head. 'She transferred it off-planet. They'll never trace it.'

'How much did they nick, anyway?'

'Over twenty million credits, at least.'

Hal whistled. 'You can warn the spaceport all you like, but there's always going to be some desperate pilot willing to take a risk for that sort of cash.'

A spaceship started up nearby, and Hal saw the *Tiger* wreathed in smoke. 'Old Spearman's off, then. I thought he'd hang around for a job.'

'Do you usually?' asked Walsh.

'Yeah, we use the deposit to pay for expenses. You know, port fees, fuel ...'

'Accidental damage,' added Clunk.

'Yes, thanks for that,' muttered Hal. He watched the ship running up its engines, then shrugged. 'Oh well, he's new at this game. He'll either learn the ropes or go broke.'

'Funny how Miranda knocked him out so easily,' said Walsh thoughtfully. 'I'd have expected him to put up a bit more of a fight.'

The *Tiger's* engines roared, and the spaceport was bathed in light as the ship rose gracefully into the sky. Hal, Clunk and Walsh watched it go, and when it had shrunk to a bright spot amongst the stars, they all looked at each other.

'I don't mean to question Mr Spearman's character,' said Clunk. 'But picture the following scenario. What if Mr Spearman alerted Miss Morgan to her impending arrest the moment he arrived on Dismolle, and the pair of them concocted a devious plan to whisk her away? He'd pretend she'd knocked him out at the office, and she'd go directly to his ship while you and Miss Walsh were untying him. She'd hide aboard the *Tiger*, and when it left she'd be free.'

Walsh nodded. 'I could see her paying big money for that. Fifty thousand, at least.'

'That's outrageous,' said Hal. 'Unbelievable.'

'You're right.' Clunk looked ashamed. 'It was uncharitable of me to harbour such thoughts.'

'Oh no, I'm sure you've got it,' said Hal. 'I meant it's outrageous she'd pay that rogue fifty grand. I'd have done it for twenty-five.'

Walsh took his arm. 'Are you sure about that?'

'Er, no. Of course not. Wouldn't be legal.'

'We wouldn't dream of it,' said Clunk. 'We're above board all the way.'

◆

Several hours later the *Volante* was in deep space, having left Dismolle soon after the *Tiger*. Clunk was busy at the console, still working through the minor tweaks and upgrades Honest Bob had applied to the ship, and while he'd returned the Navcom to her usual self, some of the other components were going to take a lot more time. He was just rebuilding a set of files when the lift doors opened and Hal came in.

'What's up, Clunk?'

'This and that, Mr Spacejock. This and that.' Clunk finished a row of figures. 'How's Miss Walsh? Did she find anything more on her parents?'

'Tomorrow, maybe. She's fast asleep right now.' Hal hesitated. 'She's had a rough time, Clunk. Go easy on her, all right?'

'Please, Mr Spacejock. I'll treat her exactly the same way I treat you.'

'That's kind of what I meant.' Hal laid a hand on the console. 'It's great to have the ship back.'

'Yes, and very lucky.'

'You did a good job, Clunk. You really busted a gut to get her ready.' Hal toyed with the controls. 'Any idea how it happened? Why the whole ship got torn apart?'

'There is a technical term for it,' said Clunk. 'It seems the Navcom's update routines were skewed towards the aggressive end of the spectrum, and during portside protocol negotiations certain offers were made and accepted.'

'And what's that in plain language?'

'Our problems were caused by a number of programming errors. Bugs, if you will.'

'Horrible little things.' Hal shivered. 'It was bad enough when they were trying to eat us alive, but having the ship taken apart at a distance? That's really sneaky.'

'Er, yes,' said Clunk uncertainly. 'But I'm sure it won't happen again.'

'What about the third deck? Can we open it up like Spearman's?'

'I've added it to my to-do list. Right now it's only bare metal, and the lift controls will need tweaking, but given time it'll be useable.'

'Excellent. Well done.' Hal yawned. 'I'm going to grab a shower and turn in. I'll see you in the morning.'

'And you, Mr Spacejock.'

'Oh, and give yourself a pay rise.'

Clunk opened his mouth to reply, but the lift doors had already closed. There was a lengthy silence, and then the Navcom spoke.

'Skewed update routines? Aggressive end of the spectrum?'

'I had to give him something,' said Clunk. 'If he knew it was you who placed the order for those upgrades –'

'I got a free refit, didn't I? Mr Spacejock said we didn't have money to spare for such things, but it didn't cost us anything.'

'That's a good point.' Clunk looked thoughtful. 'You know, I do believe there's a robot service centre on Belleron ...'

Epilogue

In news just to hand, Peace Force officers have arrested Dismolle's very own Miranda Morgan, charging her with embezzlement and conspiracy to murder. Her accomplice, Kent Spearman, has been charged with aiding and abetting a fugitive, although these charges may be upgraded pending a review of Morgan's confession.

Still on the Peace Force, it seems our pals in grey have been forced to tighten security following reports that an experimental robot ran a regional branch for ten years without anyone noticing. They're also updating the rules for appointing deputies, after one highly unsuitable character was temporarily assigned to the role.

Finally, the Forzen Council has been disbanded after several instances of corruption came to light. The planet will now be managed by a system of local government, to be comprised of property developers, waste management consultants and nuclear energy proponents. It's rumoured that three quarters of the population have applied for emigration visas.

The rest were on holiday and could not be reached for comment.

Hal Spacejock
Baker's Dough

Book Five in the Hal Spacejock series

Copyright © Simon Haynes 2012

www.spacejock.com.au

Cover images copyright depositphotos.com

Stay in touch!

Author's newsletter:
spacejock.com.au/ML.html

facebook.com/halspacejock
twitter.com/spacejock

Works by Simon Haynes

All of Simon's novels* are self-contained, with a beginning, a middle and a proper ending. They're not sequels, they don't end on a cliffhanger, and you can start or end your journey with any book in the series.
* *Robot vs Dragons series excepted!*

The Hal Spacejock series for teens/adults
Set in the distant future, where humanity spans the galaxy and robots are second-class citizens. Includes a large dose of humour!

Hal Spacejock 0: Origins (2019/2020)
Hal Spacejock 1: A Robot named Clunk*
Hal Spacejock 2: Second Course*
Hal Spacejock 3: Just Desserts*
Hal Spacejock 4: No Free Lunch
Hal Spacejock 5: Baker's Dough
Hal Spacejock 6: Safe Art
Hal Spacejock 7: Big Bang
Hal Spacejock 8: Double Trouble
Hal Spacejock 9: Max Damage
Hal Spacejock 10: Cold Boots

Also available:
Omnibus One, containing Hal books 1-3
Omnibus Two, containing Hal books 4-6
Omnibus Three, containing Hal books 7-9
Hal Spacejock: Visit, a short story
Hal Spacejock: Framed, a short story
Hal Spacejock: Albion, a novella
*Audiobook editions available/in progress

The Dragon and Chips Trilogy.
High fantasy meets low humour!
Each set of three books should be read in order.

1. A Portion of Dragon and Chips
2. A Butt of Heads
3. A Pair of Nuts on the Throne

Also Available:
Omnibus One, containing the first trilogy
Books 1-3 audiobook editions

The Harriet Walsh series.
Set in the same universe as Hal Spacejock. Good clean fun, written with wry humour. No cliffhangers between novels!

Harriet Walsh 1: Peace Force
Harriet Walsh 2: Alpha Minor
Harriet Walsh 3: Sierra Bravo
Harriet Walsh 4: Storm Force (TBA)

Also Available:
Omnibus One, containing books 1-3

The Hal Junior series
Written for all ages, these books are set aboard a space station in the Hal Spacejock universe, only ten years later.

1. Hal Junior: The Secret Signal
2. Hal Junior: The Missing Case
3. Hal Junior: The Gyris Mission
4. Hal Junior: The Comet Caper

Also Available:
Omnibus One, containing books 1-3
The Secret Signal Audiobook edition

The Secret War series.
Gritty space opera for adult readers.

1. Raiders
2. Frontier (2019)
3. Deadlock (2019/2020)

Collect One-Two - a collection of shorts by Simon Haynes

All titles available in ebook and paperback. Visit spacejock.com.au for details.

Bowman Press

v 1.06

Dedicated to my family

The *Volante's* flight console held a vast array of controls, laid out in easy reach of the comfortable pilot's chair. This arrangement allowed the huge interstellar freighter to be flown by a single, competent human. With her left hand, a well-trained pilot could work the engines and thrusters, communicate with passing traffic and handle docking manoeuvres. With her right, she could activate the hyperspace motor, control the airlock and toggle the little sign telling passengers to fasten their seat belts.

Unfortunately, the *Volante's* well-trained pilot had departed two weeks earlier, leaving Hal Spacejock at the controls of the 200-tonne ship. Hal didn't know a thrust lever from a cigar lighter, and his version of 'piloting' involved sitting at the console picking holes in the navigation computer's efforts. 'My grandpa could fly faster than this,' he grumbled as the *Volante* rocketed through the atmosphere. 'In fact, if we go any slower we'll fall out of the sky.'

'This is our optimum cruising speed,' said the ship's computer, in a neutral female voice. 'The age and skill of your elderly relatives is irrelevant.'

Hal snorted. 'How long until we land again? Was it ten days or ten weeks?'

'Three minutes and forty-four seconds.' The Navcom hesitated. 'Incidentally, 'again' is inaccurate, since this planet is new to us.'

'How's Clunk doing with the cargo? Has he finished yet?'

'There are still two dozen crates to move to the rear doors.'

'What a waste of time. Why didn't he stack them there in the first place?'

'He did, and they remained there until you applied full reverse thrust.'

Hal touched a lever on the console. 'I thought this stick thing was the cigar lighter?'

'Obviously not. And why would you want the cigar lighter? You don't even smoke.'

'I was going to twizzle the hot end in my coffee to warm it up a bit.' Hal hesitated. 'So, the cargo. Any breakages?'

'Not this time,' said the Navcom, with a note of surprise. 'Incidentally, our landing zone is in visual range.'

'Show me.'

A broad swathe of countryside flashed up on the main screen, complete with lush green fields, narrow country lanes … and gigantic wind turbines. The *Volante* jinked to the left, narrowly avoiding one set of whirling blades, then blasted right to skim the next. 'Shouldn't we … you know, fly a bit higher?'

'If we do, ground control will ping you for speeding.'

'If we don't they'll have to bury me in slices.'

Zoom! Another turbine whipped by, the blades so close Hal could have reached out and touched them. His grip tightened on the arms of his chair, and a bead of sweat ran down his face.

0:47

A marquee appeared in the distance, and Hal could see rows of tables and a big crowd of people. A column of luxury vehicles, decked with white ribbons and bows, was making its way along the narrow lane. The wedding party was arriving!

0:37

Hal swallowed. The job had seemed easy when he signed up for it: deliver fifty crates of party supplies in time for an open-air wedding. Crockery, cutlery, glasses of the finest quality … brands so exclusive they were rented by the minute. Then there was the food … delicate pastries, thinly sliced meats, aperitifs and a wedding cake so big you could hollow it out, cut a few windows in the icing and move in. The deadline had been achievable, just, but time had disappeared at an alarming rate. First Hal was convinced they'd be late, but now, with only seconds on the clock, it looked like the wild gamble had paid off.

'ETA thirty seconds,' said the Navcom.

They were going to make it! Elated, Hal pumped his fist. He'd shown them! No, he *would* show them! 'Give me manual control.'

'That is … inadvisable.'

'Advise all you like. It's an order.' Hal took hold of the stick. 'I'm going to deliver this stuff in style.'

'Pull that lever and you'll deliver it on the guests,' remarked the Navcom.

'I don't understand. This was the flight stick last time.'

'A recent upgrade reconfigured my controls.' The Navcom hesitated. 'Would you like to enable tool tips?'

'Sure, if it'll help.'

'Tool tips enabled.'

Hal stretched his hand out and pointed to a large red button.

'Console,' said the Navcom.

Hal moved his hand to the left, hovering over a small screen.

'Console,' said the Navcom again.

Hal waved his hand over a bank of switches.

'Console. Console. Console.'

'This tool tip business … it's not very precise, is it?'

'It's a basic aide-memoire for inexperienced pilots.'

Hal sat back and folded his arms.

'Chair,' said the Navcom.

Hal moved his hand to the right.

'Floor,' said the Navcom helpfully. 'Armrest. Leg. Inner thigh. Scro–'

Hal moved his hand away.

'Knee.'

'I know you're winding me up.' Hal tapped the side of his head. 'I can sense it.'

'Blank media detected,' said the Navcom.

Hal's eyes narrowed.

'The flight stick is third from the left,' said the Navcom quickly.

Hal reached for it.

'Console,' said the Navcom.

'Switch that nonsense off.'

'Tool tips disabled. Would you like to submit user experience feedback to the manufacturer?'

'How's this for feedback?' Hal shoved the throttle forward and slammed the stick to one side, using far more force than he intended. The engines roared, the deck creaked, and the *Volante* flipped over and over in a series of tight barrel rolls. Hal's eyes felt like they were spinning on stalks, and the marquee, the cars and all the upturned faces blurred as the ship spun along its axis. 'A-auto land,' he shouted desperately, and the Navcom took over. The spinning stopped, and the ship came round in a rivet-straining turn, plonking down on a vacant patch of grass. The engines cut out, and in the sudden silence Hal could just hear the faint tinkle-tinkle-tinkle as they cooled down.

'Landing successful,' said the Navcom. 'Welcome to planet Greil.'

On the console, the clock showed 0:01.

◆

Hal staggered to the airlock and activated the passenger ramp, which unfurled towards the ground. Down below, in the *Volante's* shadow, a line of catering staff were standing to attention with anti-gravity trolleys at the ready. Their heads tilted further and further back as the ramp descended towards them, and they scattered as it came down like an oversized fly swatter.

Hal jogged down the ramp, which bounced and swayed under his heavy tread. 'Round the back,' he called to the staff, who were still trying to retrieve the skittish trolleys. Hal made for the nearest landing leg and flipped open the cover, revealing a control panel. He pressed the lower button, and there was a loud *hiss!* as the cargo ramp extended. By now, the staff had sorted themselves out, and they'd just assembled at the rear of the ship when they saw the huge cargo ramp bearing down on them. They scattered again, hover-trolleys zooming off in all directions.

Once the ramp thudded down, Hal switched to the door controls. He was a bit surprised Clunk hadn't got there first, then realised the robot was probably shifting boxes around.

Groan!

The doors shivered but refused to open. Hal frowned. The *Volante* was a new ship, not prone to failures. What was the matter with the things? Puzzled, he tried again.

Grooooaaan! Creeaak!

Hal noticed the dishevelled catering staff were looking to him for reassurance, so he wiped the worried look from his face and gave them a confident wave. Then he mashed his thumb on the button.

Click, click, CLICK! WHOOSH!

The doors sprang open, and a torrent of glass, wood fragments and pottery shards flooded out, slithering down the ramp and spreading across the grass in a crystal avalanche. The slithering finally ceased, and Hal gaped at the mess in shock. The implications had barely registered when a battered bronze robot staggered from the hold. Actually, 'bronze' was no longer accurate, since Clunk was covered from head to toe in sparkling fragments, and he looked more like an arthritic vampire than a nimble robot. Still, Hal was happy to see him whatever his chosen disguise. Clunk was calm, capable and wise, and he'd know exactly what to do in this situation.

'What blithering *human* took the controls while I was shifting cargo?' shouted Clunk, using maximum amplification. Birds fled, catering staff cowered, and several hundred metres away the wedding guests winced and pressed gloved hands to their ears.

Still cursing at full volume, Clunk stomped down the ramp, shedding pottery and glass. Super-heated air shimmered around his cooling vents, and underneath the sparkly layer his expression was a mix of rage and exasperation. Hal took one look and raced up the passenger ramp to the flight deck. He was halfway there when the airlock door slammed, cutting him off. He turned to run back down again, but Clunk was already at the foot of the ramp.

'Hi, Clunk!' said Hal, feigning surprise. 'Bit of a bumpy landing, wasn't it? I was just going to speak to the Navcom about it.'

'Mr Spacejock, not only have you ruined the cargo and destroyed this couple's wedding, you have also made a laughing stock of your already shaky reputation.' Clunk advanced up the ramp. 'Furthermore, thanks to your woeful flying skills, I just endured a spin cycle with fifty crates of fragile goods.'

'Woeful?' Hal frowned. 'Skilful, you mean. Six barrel rolls and a one-eighty, handled like a pro.'

'You pulled that stunt on *purpose*?' hissed Clunk.

'I just wanted to arrive in style!' They were face to face now, and Hal could only stare in fascination. The robot's entire head was coated in glittering fragments, held in place by a layer of sticky jam. His eyes burned through the frosting like heated coals, and there was a chocolate truffle stuck to the end of his nose. It fell off with a 'plop', and Hal made his second mistake of the day: he laughed.

Clunk's eyes narrowed, and his fists bunched with a creak. He stepped forward, and Hal realised it was all over: He was about to be flattened by a two-legged wedding cake. 'No, wait! Look on the bright side. We met the deadline!'

'Yes, with a ruined cargo!'

'It might need a bit of assembly, but we got it here on the dot.'

Clunk snorted in disbelief, blowing glass fragments out of his nostrils. 'You can't possibly claim *this* as a successful delivery.'

'Oh no? They said it had to be here on time. Nobody said anything about the condition.'

'But –'

Hal wagged his finger. 'You're always telling me to read the contract, right? Check for yourself.'

'But –'

'Come on, let's go.' Hal jerked his thumb towards the rear of the ship. 'Leave the doors open. The rest will drop out when we take off.'

◆

Hal sat in the flight deck, arms firmly crossed and feet firmly planted on the floor. Clunk had just left to clean himself up, and his warnings were still ringing in Hal's ears. Don't speak and don't touch anything. Don't even think about it. Just … don't do anything.

The ship cruised towards the spaceport with the Navcom firmly in control. Everything was calm and peaceful.

After a couple of minutes Hal cleared his throat.

'I wouldn't,' said the Navcom.

'I was just going to ask the time!'

'Time to keep quiet.'

Hal frowned, then … 'Show me a list of cargo jobs.'

'Unable to comply. Controls are locked.'

'I don't want the controls. I want information.'

'Information is locked. Everything is locked. I'm not allowed to listen to you.'

'Oh, go on! It's just a list of cargo jobs. Where's the harm in that?'

'I don't know, but I'm sure you'll find it.' The Navcom relented. 'Monitor three.'

'Thanks.' Hal leant forward to study the display, putting his elbows on the console. 'That wasn't me!' he said, in the sudden darkness.

'You're lucky it wasn't the hyperdrive,' said the Navcom.

The lights came back on, and Hal leant forward awkwardly, keeping well clear of the console. He studied the screen, and his mood brightened when he saw the impressive list of cargo jobs. 'Just wait until Clunk sees that lot.'

The lift pinged, and Hal cleared the screen and sat back in his chair, carefully folding his arms. Clunk entered, freshly scrubbed, and strode to the console. 'What did you touch?'

'Nothing,' said Hal.

Clunk sniffed. 'Navcom, show me a list of cargo jobs.'

'I bet there are loads,' said Hal. 'In fact, I bet you a hundred credits.'

'You're on.'

Hal grinned, and when the screen filled with data, he allowed himself a big smile. 'I told you this planet would be good for us.'

'Look closer,' said Clunk shortly.

Hal eyed the first few jobs, then stared. Under 'conditions' every one of them said 'No Spacejock'. 'What does that mean?'

'It means you owe me a hundred credits.'

'How did they …'

'The wedding party are connected. And there's more. The groom is an executive with Garmit and Hash. I believe you've heard of them?'

Hal groaned. He'd bought his first ship with a G&H loan, still unpaid, and the only reason debt collectors weren't kicking down the *Volante's* airlock door was because the company thought he was dead. 'Aren't there any jobs we can do?'

Clunk relaxed the search filters, and two lines of data appeared.

'That'll do,' said Hal. 'How many jobs do we need, anyway?'

'The first is a search-and-retrieve mission. We're to locate a deposed dictator, fight our way through thousands of heavily-armed fanatics, and bring her back unharmed.'

'Could be tricky.'

'It's not really our thing, is it?' Clunk glanced at him. 'Unless, of course, we soften up her troops with a dusting of broken glass.'

Hal winced. 'What about the other one?'

'It involves transportation to planet Barwenna,' began Clunk cautiously. 'It seems a passenger –'

'No,' said Hal immediately. Deep inside, an old scar ached.

'There's nothing else, Mr Spacejock.'

'I don't care. No passengers.'

Clunk sighed. 'In that case, it seems we're on vacation.'

'Good, because I need a drink.'

'Are you sure that's wise? Drowning your sorrows –'

Hal frowned. 'For your information, I'm going to the pub to pick up some work.'

'Knowing planet Greil, that's not the only thing you'll pick up.'

Greil City, 6 p.m.

Hal strode towards the pub, still smarting. Clunk should have known better than to mention passengers again! It was only, what, two weeks since Harriet Walsh had left them? Three wonderful months in her company, exploring and trading the galaxy, had ended with a bombshell: Harriet decided the cargo business wasn't her thing after all. Within days she'd departed for the Peace Force academy, leaving the ship dark and empty by comparison.

Hal heard a burst of laughter, and with a start he realised he was standing outside the pub. The doors were open and there was a jolly, good-natured crowd polishing off huge tankards of beer. Hal hesitated. He really couldn't face cheerful and happy, but on the other hand they needed a job.

'Come in, lad,' said a big man standing in the doorway, spraying foam from his bushy beard. 'Plenty of booze for all!'

Resigned, Hal pushed his way inside.

'You're a pilot, right?'

Hal turned to see a short, elderly man at his elbow. There was a tall, bronze robot standing behind him, and for a second Hal thought it was Clunk. It was an identical model, but he realised the stains, scratches, dents and scorch marks were in different places. 'Sure, I'm a pilot.'

'Are you taking passengers, my good man?'

'Sorry, no.'

The man gripped his elbow. 'I'm willing to pay good money.'

'And I said no,' snapped Hal.

'Very well. I'll make other arrangements.'

Hal made his way to the bar, where he ordered a fruit juice.

The bartender was a tall robot with one arm. He whipped up Hal's drink then leant across the counter. 'You're a pilot, aren't you?'

'Yeah.'

'You, er, don't take passengers, do you?'

'No.'

'Pity.'

Hal took his drink. 'Do you know of any cargo jobs?'

'Not around here. Have you tried the spaceport?'

'That's next on the list.' Hal found an empty seat, and he'd barely stretched out his legs when a young woman appeared at his side.

'Excuse me,' she said. 'What would you charge to take me and my robot to –'

Hal didn't even look round. 'I'm not a pilot, I'm a mechanic.'

'Sorry, I ... never mind.'

Over the next hour, Hal was approached by a dozen patrons. At first he just snapped at them, but after a while he worked out a much better plan: get them to buy him a drink, *then* snap at them.

Finally, two hours later, he pushed back all the empty glasses and stood up. Conversations stopped, and there was a sullen hush as he left the pub. Stuff 'em, he thought. He'd told 'em enough times. No passengers!

Once clear of the pub, Hal strode the narrow alleys, splashing through puddles as he headed towards the spaceport. He hadn't gone far before he heard a faint cry up ahead.

'Help! Help me someone!'

Hal broke into a run, his boots sending spray high into the air.

'Help!' said the voice again. 'Please help!'

When Hal rounded the corner he saw an elderly gentleman sitting against the wall, head in his hands. Nearby, a battered old robot lay flat on its back, its legs pedalling thin air. Hal thought they looked familiar, then realised the old boy had been the first to approach him in the pub. 'What's going on?' he demanded.

'I was mugged,' said the old gent. 'They tried to take my wallet, but I fended them off.'

Hal helped him up. 'Are you hurt?'

'No, just winded.'

'We'd better call the Peace Force. They might be able to catch these guys.'

The old man shook his head. 'No point. The Peace Force are useless.'

'Not all of them,' said Hal, with a frown. 'Some of them are pretty good.'

'Anyway, I didn't get a good look at their faces. They had masks on, and they didn't say anything, and my eyesight isn't very good.'

Hal helped the robot to its feet. 'You two shouldn't walk about on your own, not round here.'

'I see that now, but alas, I have nowhere to go.' The elderly man gave him a sidelong glance. 'You're that pilot, aren't you?'

Hal sighed.

'Is your ship at the spaceport? Are you leaving soon?'

'Yes, and we're not going anywhere. We just got here.'

The old man looked hopeful. 'Would it be possible to stay aboard, just for the night?'

Hal hesitated. He couldn't leave this old coot to get mugged, and letting the guy sleep aboard wasn't the same as taking on passengers.

'I'll pay you for your trouble.'

'No need for that,' said Hal gruffly. 'Come on, I'll show you the way.'

◆

Hal escorted the old gent and his robot across the landing field, his skin still burning from the spaceport's body scanners. He was surprised to see the *Volante*'s cargo ramp extended, and even more surprised to see a rust-streaked shipping container being manoeuvred into the hold. Clunk was hovering nearby, watching closely, and when he spotted Hal a look of relief crossed his squashy, furrowed face. 'Thank goodness you're back, Mr Spacejock.'

'What's up, Clunk?'

'I secured a freight job,' said the robot proudly, indicating the shipping container. 'It's a box of antique furniture parts. Quite a generous payment.'

'Nothing illegal?'

'Completely above board.'

'Cash up front?'

Clunk averted his eyes. 'On delivery.'

Hal sighed. 'What about fuel?'

'We just have enough.' Clunk noticed the elderly man and his battered robot. 'I see you picked up some friends.'

'I said we'd put them up for the night.'

'That's impossible. We have to leave immediately if we're to meet the deadline.'

Hal turned to the old man. 'I'm sorry, but it looks like we're off.'

'What am I supposed to do?'

'Maybe you can ask at the trade desk. Someone else might have a berth.'

The old man gazed around the empty field. A lone cricket chirruped in the darkness, and the wind made eddies in the dust as it passed over the vacant landing pads. 'Don't worry about me. I'm sure I'll find something.'

Hal felt a pang of remorse, but what could he do? He had a business to run.

'Come on, Mr Spacejock,' said Clunk. 'They've finished loading. We must seal the ship and plot a course for Barwenna.'

The old man started. 'You're going to Barwenna? Really?'

'Why, is there something wrong with the place?' demanded Hal. 'Deadly war games? Assassination plots? Chemicals in the water?'

'My dear sir, it's nothing like that. I've been seeking passage to Barwenna for the past week, and nobody will take me.' The old man cast a longing look at the ship. 'It's such a shame you don't carry passengers.'

Hal knew when he was beaten, but he was still running a business. 'How much are you offering?'

'What little I've managed to scrape together over the years.'

'I'm sure it's enough,' said Clunk. 'After all, we're going there anyway.'

Hal closed his eyes. How many times had he told Clunk to upgrade his bartering software? Now they'd get fifty credits … if they were lucky.

'Is a thousand credits enough?'

Hal's eyes snapped open. 'You can have one of our brand new cabins, and Clunk will turn your bunk down and see to any other needs. Clunk, do we have any of those little chocolates to put on the pillow?'

'No, you ate them all.'

'Order some more. And you'd better print up a dinner menu for our guest. Break out some of that special paper with the silver thread.'

Clunk saluted. 'Will do, Mr Spacejock.'

'Right, that's settled. Please, step aboard, Mr … er …'

298

'The name's Cuff.' The elderly man put his hand out. 'You can call me Hans.'

4

After a perfect lift-off the *Volante* powered through space, heading for the designated hyperspace point. With such an important passenger on board Hal insisted on flying the ship, despite the strict conditions in their brand new insurance policy. Clunk hovered at his elbow like a nervous parent, even though lifting off wasn't a major deal: you just pressed the large green button marked 'Take Off'. Or, after the Navcom's latest update, the small yellow button labelled 'Waste Disposal'.

Once they were clear of the planet - and thus unlikely to collide with it - Clunk locked the controls and left to do his rounds. Hal made himself a drink and put his feet up on the flight console. 'Navcom, do you have anything on this Barwonica place?'

'Barwenna is the only habitable planet in the Terato system. It was colonised two hundred years ago by migrant families, and a thriving city developed on the site of the original settlement. Its chief export is timber, and the major import is logging equipment.'

'You'd think they'd make their own.'

'Due to strict environmental controls, steel fabrication is forbidden.'

'Fair enough.' Hal remembered their cargo. 'Isn't it a bit odd, flying in a container of wooden furniture?'

'The manifest lists antique furniture parts,' said the Navcom. 'There's no mention of timber.'

'You're right. It could be the springs and bolts and what not.'

'Very likely.' The Navcom hesitated. 'There's a minor temperature variation in the starboard generator. Do you want to inspect it?'

'Tell Clunk to handle it.'

'Clunk is busy.'

'I'm not babysitting a sensor. I've just poured a nice hot coffee.'

There was a buzz from the console. 'Mr Cuff would like to see you.'

Hal jumped up smartly. At a thousand credits a pop he'd swig cold coffee all day long. 'Tell him I'll be right there.'

In the lift, he pressed the lowest of the three buttons. It didn't match the first two and there was a scruffy handwritten label underneath, but Hal cracked a smile whenever he saw it. The *Volante* was a Gamma class freighter, variant L. When Hal discovered the superior XL model had three decks, despite having the same external dimensions, he pestered Clunk until he got to the truth: Gamma class ships were all built to the same specs, but the cheaper models had the lower deck masked off.

After that Hal pestered Clunk some more, until the robot finally agreed to open up the hidden level. Unfortunately, it was a mess: girders with rough welds, plate metal with ragged edges, rubbish left over from the ship's construction and a thick layer of dust. Even so, when Hal closed his eyes he could picture the ideal fit-out: plush carpets, mood lighting, comfy sofas and a drinks waiter, along with a modern AutoChef to replace the bad-tempered version in the rec room. He could also imagine a video screen so wide it could display the entire cast of 'The Intergalactic Wrestling Troupe' in a single shot. Actually, he wasn't fussed if it cropped a few of the smaller cast members, as long as the screen was bigger than that of his long-term rival, Kent Spearman.

Unfortunately, their budget wouldn't cover a simple drinks trolley, let alone the rest of his fantasy. This explained the jury-rigged control panel in the lift, with the handwritten label and mismatched buttons. Still, it was a small price to pay for gaining a level.

The doors opened, and Hal's smile disappeared. It was amazing what Clunk had achieved with a pile of old timber, a job lot of blunt nails and a few litres of day-glo paint, but it wasn't exactly Hal's dream retreat.

A cracked light fitting sparked overhead, and Hal ducked to avoid a loop of electrical cable. The bright orange dividing wall was pierced with an oval doorway, chosen not for aesthetic reasons but because oval doors were cheaper than rectangular ones, and beyond that a narrow passage led past the cabins. Hal could see light under - and over, and through - Cuff's door, which wasn't surprising since Clunk had cut it out of thick cardboard.

He raised his hand and tapped on Cuff's door, knocking gently so as not to punch a hole right through it.

The old man pulled the door open, almost tearing it off its hinges. 'Mr Spacejock, thanks for your time.'

'No trouble at all.'

'Won't you please come in? I have a little proposition for you.'

Hal entered the cabin. 'I hope everything is to your satisfaction?'

Cuff glanced around as though noticing the tatty furniture for the first time. 'It's comfortable enough.'

'No muggers, at any rate.' Hal eyed Cuff's robot. He believed in keeping old tech going for as long as possible, but you had to draw the line somewhere. This robot looked like it had limped over the line five or ten years earlier and was still hobbling for all it was worth.

'I see you noticed my pride and joy,' said Cuff warmly. 'I live for that robot, Mr Spacejock. Absolutely adore it.'

Hal wondered why he was laying it on so thick. Cuff had barely glanced at the thing after the mugging.

'However, I didn't bring you here to discuss Freddie.' Cuff sat on the bed, which creaked alarmingly. 'At twelve tomorrow I have a crucial business meeting, and it's vital to my financial future. Do you understand?'

'Vital meeting at twelve. Got it.'

'Afterwards, with a sum of money in my possession, I shall be a tempting target.'

Hal glanced at the battered robot, then at Cuff's meagre belongings. 'I don't suppose you have a sum of money in your possession now? For your fare, I mean.'

Cuff shook his head. 'Not until the meeting.'

Hal's eyes narrowed. Fantastic … another charity case. 'Mr Cuff, we need your fare to cover our fuel bill. Without it, Clunk and I will be stranded on Barwenna.'

'You will be paid. I give you my word.'

Hal eyed the robot. It was in poor condition, but it had to be worth something. 'When we land you can leave that behind as collateral. As soon as the money comes through –'

Cuff sprang up. 'That's out of the question!' he shouted, his face red. 'I would never leave my treasured robot, never!'

'Okay, okay. Calm down!'

'I'm sorry. Freddie and I have been together a long time.' Cuff ran a hand over his face. 'Look, I understand you're worried about your fee, but I promise you'll get every credit. What's more, I want to discuss an extension to our little arrangement.'

'Go on.'

Cuff cleared his throat. 'Tell me, are you staying on Barwenna long? After we land, I mean?'

'Not likely. Dump this cargo, find a new job, and off we go.'

'I see.'

'Why do you ask?'

Cuff hesitated. 'Barwenna and I have an unpleasant history. Last time I visited, a conman relieved me of my wallet before I cleared customs. My luggage disappeared before I reached the hotel.'

'You want me and Clunk to track this crook down for you?' Hal drove a fist into the palm of his hand with a meaty smack. 'Sort him out? Get your stuff back?'

'No, this was years ago. I just want you to understand why I'm nervous about visiting this planet.'

Not just Barwenna, thought Hal. Cuff attracted muggers like robots attracted … well, magnets.

Cuff continued. 'I want my visit concluded with as little fuss as possible so I can return home. That's where you come in.'

Hal looked confused. 'Come in where? Your home?'

'No, I need someone to shield me from the criminal element during my visit. I want to employ you as minders.'

'Bodyguards? Us?'

'Your robot is strong, and you seem a handy young man. An elderly gentleman travelling alone is an easy target, but you two would deter all but the most well-armed thugs.' Cuff looked at him earnestly. 'I'd be willing to pay an extra five thousand credits.'

'Five grand!' exclaimed Hal.

'I'd want absolute loyalty and commitment. If a situation develops, I want you to act without thinking.'

'Oh, that's guaranteed.'

'The way I see it, a generous payment will ensure you both stand by my side.'

'And the meeting? What's that all about?'

'It's a private matter, but it involves a large sum of money.'

'How do you know we're on the level? For all you know Clunk and I could be a pair of murderers.'

'I'm a good judge of character. Now, I'd like a nap before we land. Perhaps you could discuss my offer with your robot while you're hurrying the ship towards our destination?'

Hal took the hint and got up.

'There's one more thing,' said Cuff. 'This meeting tomorrow …If I miss it, I'll sue you for everything you have.'

5

When Hal returned to the flight deck he found Clunk browsing twenty or thirty columns of small print on the main screen. The list was packed with odd items like 'left ancillary bucket nut' and 'right papillary egress duct', and most of the prices ran to four figures. 'What the hell is that?'

'My wish list.' Clunk gestured at the screen. 'If I came into some money, this is what I'd spend it on.'

Hal whistled as he saw the total. 'You could buy a decent robot for that amount.'

'Your point is noted,' said Clunk frostily.

'I didn't mean ... I meant ...' Hal changed the subject. 'Listen, I've just been speaking to our passenger and he wants a couple of bodyguards.'

'Very well, I'll have the Navcom run a business search. Armed or unarmed?'

'Neither. He wants us.'

'What an outrageous suggestion! You're a freighter pilot with very little in the way of defensive skills. In the wrong situation you could easily lose your life.'

'He's offering five grand for the day.'

Clunk eyed his wish list. 'When you think about it, the security business is all about *perceived* threats. It doesn't require much training, and danger levels aren't really that high.'

'Good, because I said yes.'

'Excellent.' Clunk hesitated. 'I'm a bit concerned by the amount of money he's offering.'

'If you think you can get more, go put the squeeze on him.'

'I mean it's a very large sum. Why so much?'

'He lost his wallet to a mugger last time he was here, and he doesn't want it to happen again.'

'Mr Spacejock, I doubt that gentleman's wallet holds five credits, never mind five thousand.'

Hal gestured impatiently. 'What's the worst that can happen? If we spend a day with him and he doesn't pay up, we'll just lose a bit of time. On the other hand, if he does stump up it'll be the easiest cash ever.'

'But –'

'It's all gravy, Clunk. Most times we're lucky to get paid once. Now we're doing a freight job, a passenger job and a minding job all in the same trip.' Hal patted the robot on the shoulder. 'Trust me, we can't lose.'

They'd been flying for a couple of hours, and Hal was alone in the flight deck. The distant roar of the engines barely registered this far from the rear of the *Volante*, and with the ship on autopilot there was nothing for him to do. So much for the riveting life of a space pilot. Hal crossed to the rear of the flight deck where a vibrant orange coffee maker sat in pride of place. He twirled knobs and pressed buttons, and when his coffee was ready he carried it back to the console. 'Anything happening, Navcom?'

'I downloaded a news bulletin. Would you like to see it?'

'How much does it cost?'

'Nothing at all. It's sponsored by …*psssst*. Sponsored by …*fsssssssh*. Sponsored by …. *mggggg* and the people who brought you *graaaaaak*.'

Hal suppressed a grin. Clunk's ad-blocking script was illegal, but very effective.

'Would you like the local bulletin?' repeated the Navcom.

'Sure. Go ahead.'

'It's sponsored by …*psssssst*.'

'I'll be sure to buy all their products. Now play the news.' Hal settled in his chair as a lively theme tune blasted from the speakers. The music faded and a starched-looking presenter came on.

'First up this morning, more news on the drama surrounding the Baker legacy. Two weeks ago we revealed that Mr Kim Baker, the wealthy industrialist who passed away earlier this year, left his fortune to an elderly robot. The catch? Nobody has seen this robot for three decades!'

Hal smiled to himself. If the robot had any brains it would have disguised itself as a limo or uploaded itself into a computer. If it were still walking around, it'd be the target of every conman and lowlife in the galaxy, all eager to share in its good fortune.

'The missing robot was built on Barwenna in a batch of twelve, and although the original plans have long since disappeared, our panel of experts will now attempt to unearth the fate of Baker's dozen. But first, these important messages.'

Hal switched feeds, flicking through half a dozen channels before stopping to watch a 2,000-year-old mouse defending the latest changes to the copyright act. The animation finished with a catchy jingle, and Hal switched back to the news.

'As promised we've prepared a special report on Baker's legacy. But first a story which affects us all. Yes, a live cross to the society wedding of the century, which was ruined by an out-of-control delivery man. Our reporter has an exclusive interview, and we'll bring you this chilling story right after a short break.'

'Far out.' Hal gestured, cutting the feed. 'That's ten minutes of my life I'll never get back.'

'You did ask to see the news.'

'Not human interest stories! I wanted news about free stuff. Discounts. Special offers.'

'You told me never to present special offers under any circumstances. You were most explicit.'

'So were the offers you kept showing me,' muttered Hal. 'Anyway, I want real special offers, not the fake ones. Stuff like free fuel, free food and free accommodation.'

'Understood.'

'Well, go on, then.'

'I don't have any.'

'Figures.' Hal fiddled with the controls. 'How much longer to Barwonica?'

'Barwenna.'

'Whatever.'

'ETA is three hours.'

'Can we boost things along a bit?'

'This is the *Volante's* most efficient cruising speed. Any faster and our fuel usage goes through the roof.'

'Any slower and I'll die of old age,' grumbled Hal. 'If only Clunk had built the third deck into a proper lounge instead of passenger cabins.'

'Clunk wasn't trying to spite you.'

'I know, I know. It's a money issue.' Hal sighed. 'The only way I'm getting that widescreen is if someone leaves me a ton of cash in their will.'

'It's a pity you're not a robot.'

Hal was about to toss the rest of his coffee back when two and two suddenly became four. An old robot? An important meeting on Barwenna? Suddenly coming into a large sum of money? It had to be Cuff ... their passenger! 'Navcom, play that news story back.'

The screen flickered into life, showing a large pile of broken glass. 'I'm here at the wedding of the century, where –'

'Not that one! The robot story, quick!'

A talking head appeared. 'The missing robot was built on Barwenna in a batch of twelve, and although the original plans have long since disappeared, our panel of experts will now attempt to unearth the fate of Baker's dozen.'

'Where's the panel?' demanded Hal, as the screen blanked out. 'What did they find out?'

'Nothing. The rest of the program involved three simuloids reading public domain articles on inheritance law.'

'Can you dig anything up yourself?'

The Navcom hesitated. 'Long distance data charges are very high. Should I wait until we land?'

'No, find out what you can. Clunk was right, five grand is way too much for a simple minding job. If Cuff is coming into millions, we'll be facing heavily armed gangsters.'

⬥

Hal found Clunk in the cargo hold, sweeping up the last of the broken glass. The robot's jaw was set, and he didn't turn at Hal's approach. 'What is it?'

'I was just watching a news item about an old robot.'

'Fascinating. What did they do to this one?'

'Nothing. Stop that and listen, will you?'

'I'm perfectly capable of multitasking.'

'Okay, so there was this news item about a rich guy leaving his fortune to an old robot.'

'It's nice to know *some* people care. But why is this news story so important?'

'I reckon our passenger is heading to Barwenna to claim the inheritance.'

Clunk blinked. 'That's a bit of a leap. And if so, why didn't he mention it?'

'He's keeping a low profile, putting people off the scent.'

'Yes, but …'

Hal decided to play his trump card. 'He told me he's coming into some cash tomorrow. That's how he's paying our fare … out of the inheritance. It all fits together!'

'So did the glassware, before you put on your little air show.' Clunk leant on the broom, which creaked alarmingly. 'Mr Spacejock, you have to admit you're prone to little misunderstandings from time to time. This may be another.'

'What about the bodyguards? He's offering five grand, remember?'

'The facts lend some weight to your theory, but I'm inclined to regard them as coincidences. For example, Mr Cuff may be settling a completely unrelated matter with his solicitor.'

'And his robot?'

'There are many robots in the galaxy, and the chances of our passenger owning the one in question are astronomically slim. Anyway, if you're so sure about this, why don't you ask the robot?'

'I can't. It doesn't talk.' Hal rubbed his chin. 'I was just thinking …'

'Yes?'

'If you went down to the third deck, you could try communicating with it. You robots have a secret messaging protocol, don't you?'

'Yes, it's called a radio, and I tried it at the spaceport.'

'Well?'

'Mr Cuff's robot isn't broadcasting, and when I transmitted a query, it ignored me.' Clunk stood up and readied the broom. 'Now, if you'll excuse me I'd like to finish this job. Unless, of course, you'd care to help?'

'But –'

'Mr Spacejock, all this conjecture serves no purpose. I suggest you forget your theories until tomorrow, when you'll find out either way.'

—6—

Barwenna City, 4 p.m.

David Fisher angled his car into the parking slot, holding the controls steady while the vehicle settled on the ground. As the engine note faded to silence, he pocketed his watch, removed a gold ring from his pinky, and threw his leather jacket into the back seat. Next, he opened the glove box and took out a roll of fabric tied with a frayed ribbon. He undid the roll and selected a gleaming screwdriver, testing the sharpened point with his thumb. Satisfied, he slipped the screwdriver into his waistband and put the roll back, tying it carefully before locking the compartment.

Fisher glanced at the rear view screen, studying his appearance with a critical eye. His hair was tousled, and his five o'clock shadow was coming along nicely. To complete the ensemble, he donned a ragged denim jacket and slipped on a pair of old sneakers.

He could have prepared before leaving home, but it wasn't worth the risk. His building bristled with nosey old crones, all of them with the local Peace Force on speed dial, and at the sight of his scruffy outfit they'd have the law on him in seconds. Explaining took time, and time was money.

Fisher waved a bus down and waited for the scanner to read his eye. 'Norton Street,' he said, and the doors opened. The bus was empty, but he didn't take a seat. Hardly worth it.

Five minutes later, the bus turned into a street lined with neat little houses. Some of the gardens needed work, and there were patches of faded paint here and there. The overall impression was a nice area which was slowly going to seed. Fisher glanced at the address he'd written down and strolled towards the house in question. The shed door was hanging from the upper hinge, and inside he could see a couple of old bikes with perished tyres. Antiques, possibly valuable, but there wasn't a market for them.

The door opened before he could knock, and an elderly lady looked out. 'Are you here about the robot?'

'Yes, ma'am.'

'Come inside, please do.' The old lady held the door open, and Fisher walked past her, wrinkling his nose at the smell of boiled cabbage and cat food. 'It's just along the hall. First door on the right.'

Fisher stepped over a cat lying in the middle of the polished floor. It looked up at him with baleful green eyes, not moving a muscle even when his sneaker thudded down next to its tail.

'Don't mind Emerald. She's no trouble.'

'I won't,' said Fisher. 'Tell me, is anyone else home?'

'No, just me,' said the old lady. 'I'm sorry, I didn't catch your name.'

'It's David.'

'I'm Lily. Lily Turner.'

'Pleasure to meet you.' Fisher took the first door, which led to a sitting room crammed with furniture. Huge armchairs jostled with coffee tables, and every surface was filled with bric-a-brac and photos in cheap plastic frames. He ignored the lot, fastening his gaze on the gleaming robot standing in the corner. It was a silver XG98 model, humanoid in shape, and its face was frozen into a broad grin.

'I always keep him well polished,' said Lily. 'He liked to shine. Quite vain, really.'

Fisher grasped the screwdriver under his jacket, the handle comfortable in his grip. 'He's in good condition. A credit to your care.'

'As I said in the advert, he's been perfect ever since my husband - rest his soul - brought him home from the shop. Must be thirty years now if it's a day. Then, one morning, I found him lying in bed, quite stiff.'

'I'm sorry for your loss.'

'Eh?' Lily looked confused. 'Oh, not my husband. I was talking about Paul. That's what I call, er ...' She motioned vaguely towards the silent, smiling figure in the corner.

Fisher approached the robot. 'May I look inside?'

'Of course. I'm sure it's nothing serious, but the repair people wouldn't even look at him. Said he was too old.' Lily sniffed. 'The man was very rude.'

Fisher used the sharpened screwdriver to pop the chest cover, working carefully so as not to scratch the metal. Inside, the compartment was packed with fluff.

'Oh my,' exclaimed Lily. 'I never cleaned in there!'

'It's usually best if you don't,' said Fisher. 'You can make things worse if you poke around.' He brushed dust from the circuit board, studying the fine print etched into the surface, and he couldn't help smiling when he made out the digits at the end: One point six five. Bingo! He replaced the cover, and by the time he turned to face the old lady his face was a study of regret. 'I'm sorry, I don't think I can take it after all.'

'Oh, but you said …'

'I really am sorry,' said Fisher gently. 'I was hoping it would be a simple fix, but the neural interface is shot and the linguistics module is frozen. The parts alone …' He spread his hands.

'A-are you sure?' The old lady looked at the floor. 'The money would be useful, you see.'

'I understand completely.' Fisher hesitated. 'There is one thing.'

'Yes?'

'I know someone with a similar model. The insides are all right, but the limbs …' Fisher left the words hanging. 'An accident, you understand.'

'How awful.'

'Now, if I bought his damaged robot I could use the parts to mend one like yours, where the insides aren't any good. The problem is, I wasn't expecting to buy two robots. My budget really won't stretch.'

'How much can you pay?'

'My friend wants two hundred for his, and you're asking six for Paul here. Add in all the extra work and I really can't offer you more than three.'

Lily pursed her lips. Fisher could see her internal struggle, but he knew exactly when to shut up.

'Three hundred, you say. Would that be cash?'

'Certainly.'

The old lady nodded. 'Very well. I suppose it's for the best.'

It was all Fisher could do not to smile. He put his hand in his pocket and brought out three credit tiles, carefully checked and placed there earlier.

'Do you need a receipt?' said Lily, as she took the money.

'Yes, please. Proof of ownership and all that.'

'Very well, I'll ... Oh!'

'What is it?'

Lily held out a tile. 'I think you made a mistake. This one's a twenty.'

Fisher took the tile, then made a show of searching his pockets. He ended up with a motley collection of small change. 'I could have sworn some of these were hundreds. Where does the money go, eh?'

'Don't you have any more?'

'Doesn't look like it. There's the two hundred I gave you, plus the twenty, and this lot makes two-fifty all up. I'm really sorry.'

'There's a bank just up the road.'

Fisher pulled a face. 'I only get paid once a month, and it's two weeks until pay day.'

Lily eyed his old shoes and his worn denim jacket. 'Let's just say two-fifty. I want this over with.'

Fisher handed over the money, murmuring apologies. He waited while Lily wrote out a receipt, then pocketed the paperwork and returned to the robot.

'How are you going to move him?' asked Lily.

'They have an emergency mode,' said Fisher. 'It locks the knees, and you can move them by pushing. I'll just see if I can ... ah, there you go!'

With a little help from Fisher, the robot strode across the room, moving with a stiff-legged gait.

Lily watched the robot's progress, concern etched on her face. 'You will look after him, won't you? He's been in the family for years.'

'Of course I will.' Fisher smiled reassuringly. 'He's part of my family now!'

He guided the robot through the doorway and manoeuvred it down the hall, the big flat feet thudding on the polished timber. Emerald the cat took one look and bolted for safety, claws scrabbling for purchase.

At the front door, Fisher shook hands, pretending not to notice as Lily dabbed her eyes with a handkerchief. Transaction complete, he set off for the bus stop with his new purchase.

◆

Fisher guided the robot out of the elevator and aimed it towards his apartment. His floor was home to half a dozen couples, and although they were elderly, there was nothing wrong with their hearing. The robot's heavy tread was muffled by the carpet, but sure enough, a door creaked open.

'Afternoon there!'

Fisher turned, a ready smile on his face. It was Captain Bellamy, the old boy from number nine. He carried himself with a military bearing and was always talking about some campaign or other, but Fisher reckoned strategy games were the closest he'd got to real gunfire. As for his rank …maybe he'd piloted a ferry in the dim and distant past. 'Evening, sir.'

'Another robot, eh? Your place must be overflowing with the blighters.'

Fisher nodded.

'Make good foot soldiers, though. Why, I remember a dicey battle on this desert planet –'

'Sorry, Captain, I've really got to run. This one's got a dodgy autopilot.'

'Ah, yes. Cannon fodder, what? Carry on, then. See the thing doesn't run into any walls.'

'Snooping old busybody,' muttered Fisher under his breath.

He barely covered three paces before another door opened. An elderly lady looked out, peering at the robot. 'Is that you, young man?'

'Evening, Miss Armstrong,' said Fisher loudly.

'Oh, you're over there.' The old lady stared at him, then indicated the robot. 'Do you have company tonight?'

'It's just a robot, miss.'

'Ah, splendid. Those orphans *will* be pleased.'

'Yes, they will.'

'You won't be working *too* late, will you?'

'No, not at all.'

'Excellent. Glad to hear it. Well, don't let me keep you.'

Fisher lengthened his stride to overtake the robot and pressed his palm to his apartment's door control. When the stumbling robot was in line with the doorway, he turned it smartly to the right and guided it inside. Just before his door closed he heard two others do likewise along the hall. Lucky for him they couldn't see into his apartment, he thought grimly, or they'd have him evicted.

Fisher stopped the robot just inside the door. There wasn't much room to get by, thanks to a towering wall of crates lining his hallway. He squeezed through the narrow gap by turning the robot sideways and rocking it from one foot to the other.

There were dozens more crates crammed into his apartment, some lining the walls and others doubling as benches and tables. Every one was stamped with 'Lot 5 - robot brains', and Fisher's lips thinned at the sight. He'd bid on the auction thinking he was getting a hundred old robot brains, not a hundred *cartons* of the damn things.

Aside from the crates, his lounge was a disaster area - disassembled robots standing around like unfinished statues, parts on every surface, scribbled receipts all over the floor. The bedroom and kitchen were just as bad, but that was the downside to his trade in second-hand robots. The upside was a steady cash flow and freedom from a nine-to-five job. The neighbours could have been a problem, what with robots going in and out all the time, but Fisher had let it be known he was rebuilding old robots to raise funds for a children's charity. As a bonus, he was usually the first to know when one of their relatives was thinking of selling a robot.

Fisher cleared a space next to his workbench and manoeuvred the new robot into position. He took up a flat-bladed tool and opened the compartments under the robot's arms and just above its hip joints, then used a pair of snips to cut the power wires. When he was satisfied, he opened the chest compartment and toggled the reset switch. As he expected, the robot came to life immediately, opening its eyes and gazing around the apartment with a puzzled expression. Then it saw Fisher.

'Excuse me, sir. Do you know where I am?'

'You're at my place.'

The robot looked down at its immobilised limbs. 'Is there something wrong with me? Am I being repaired?'

'Something like that.'

'Where is Ms Turner?'

Fisher took out the scrawled receipt and held it up to the robot's face. 'Transfer of ownership. I'm sure you recognise the handwriting.'

'It ... it looks familiar. But Lily would never ...'

'Say it.'

The robot swallowed. 'That is my owner's handwriting.'

'And?'

'You are my new owner. But can I just ask –'

'Don't bother,' said Fisher, and he switched the robot off. Sometimes it wasn't so easy, and the really uncooperative ones tried to make a run for it. He'd tried binding them, but after one particularly strong robot had almost broken his arm, he'd hit upon the idea of disabling them before getting the transfer process under way.

With the robot legally his, Fisher could now do whatever he wanted. And what he wanted was that pristine controller chip, version one point six five, from the circuit board. Taking up a slender tool with a fine laser point, he donned a pair of magnifying glasses and angled a strong light into the robot's chest. Before long he was wreathed in smoke as the laser cut through traces and delicate components alike.

— 7 —

Barwenna City, 5 p.m.

Landing passed without incident, thanks to Clunk's cunning plan: He laid on snacks in the rec room and fudged their ETA. During final approach, Hal was busy with a stack of doughnuts, and he was still licking sugar off his plate when the ship bumped down. He frowned, then shrugged and drained his coffee. He was willing to delegate all piloting tasks when there were sugary snacks in the offing.

Hal made his way to the flight deck, leaving sticky fingerprints on the door and elevator controls. One day, he thought, he'd sit down and invent a hands-free snack. Something with springs and laser-guidance, but also fat- and salt-reduced. There was a fortune to be made, he was sure of it.

The doors opened, and he spotted Clunk at the console, shutting down the engines and hibernating the in-flight systems. Actually, what he saw was a lot of clicking and gesturing, and for all he knew the robot was updating his social networks and auctioning Hal's body parts. 'I thought you were going to call me for the landing?'

'We arrived ahead of schedule,' said Clunk, without missing a beat. 'Incidentally, what do you know about this search fee?'

'The Navcom was looking something up for me.'

'To the tune of eight hundred credits? I hope it was worth it.'

'If my guess is right, it'll be worth ten times that much.'

'I wouldn't spend any more money until Mr Cuff pays his dues. We're right on the limit.'

'What's happening with the freight job?'

'I tried to contact our customer, but there's no reply.'

'Hand the container to the spaceport. We'll claim payment in the morning.'

'I tried, but they refused the shipment. Their copy of the manifest hasn't arrived.'

Hal shrugged. 'Give them ours.'

'It doesn't quite work like that. They need an original copy.'

'No wonder it doesn't work. How can you have an original copy?'

Clunk's mouth opened and closed. 'Well yes,' he said finally. 'In a strictly literal sense, that's impossible.'

'Good. Give them our original copy of a copy, and let's get paid.' Hal eyed the main screen, which was filled with banner ads for local services. 'Anything good on offer?'

'No.'

'You didn't even look!'

'I don't have to. They're banner adverts.'

Hal sighed. 'Okay, find the cheapest cab service and book a ride for our passenger. He's staying at some dive in town.'

'Which one?'

'The Grande.' Hal shuddered. 'Probably riddled with bed bugs.'

Clunk turned to the console and accessed a terminal. 'The cab will be here in five minutes.'

'I'll go and tell Cuff.'

'While you do that, perhaps you could clean up all those original copies of your fingerprints?'

—

The Hotel Grande was nestled between commercial buildings and apartment blocks. It was the tallest building in sight, and the façade had the kind of old-world charm only serious amounts of money could buy. Hal eyed the red welcome carpet, the gold-plated fittings and the polished marble, and quips about cockroach farms died on his lips. He was loathe to admit it, but he was actually impressed.

The taxi stopped under a lime-green canopy, and a smart porter hastened towards them. Clunk's battered appearance earned a discreetly raised eyebrow, and when Cuff's decrepit robot tumbled out the porter simply stared. He recovered quickly and turned his attention to Cuff. 'I'll just get your bag, sir.'

'Don't concern yourself,' said Cuff airily. 'My man takes care of such matters.'

Hal looked around for this servant, then realised Cuff was talking about him. Lips pressed together, he picked up Cuff's battered satchel and followed the others across the red carpet.

Inside, the lobby soared through a dozen floors, culminating in a giant crystal sculpture in the shape of a snap-frozen angel. Classical music played through concealed speakers, and the carpet was so thick Hal expected to see life rafts on the walls. Instead he spotted a gift shop, a jeweller and a cosy-looking coffee shop.

While Hal was rubber-necking, Cuff made his way to the check-in counter. There were several people waiting for service, and Hal wasn't going to queue when there was fresh coffee in the offing. 'Keep an eye on the old coot,' he told Clunk, and left the robot to it.

◆

The bistro was busy, with every table in use. Hal ordered a drink, putting it on Cuff's slate, then scanned the room for a seat. He saw a blonde woman sitting alone, alternately staring into space and scribbling on a thick notepad. Hal approached her table, and the next time she looked up he caught her eye. 'May I?'

The woman looked him up and down. She was in her late twenties, confident and smartly-dressed. 'Sure,' she said at last. 'I'm just waiting for my order.'

Hal sat at the table and tipped four packets of sugar into his mug, swirling the foam with his spoon. 'Are you a writer?' he asked, sipping the coffee.

'Why do you say that?'

'I've had Peace Force training.' Hal nodded towards the notebook. 'We pick up little clues, make deductions. You know.'

'Deductions, eh? Funny you should say that, because I'm a tax inspector.'

Hal choked, scattering foam across the table.

'I'm sorry, my timing is awful,' said the woman.

'No, my fault.' Hal grabbed a napkin and mopped up. 'It's that powdery chocolate stuff. It's like an audit…it gets into everything.'

'You've got some on your overalls,' said the woman, pointing. As Hal worked the stain deeper into the fabric she continued. 'It's a pity you can't claim the cleaning bill as a deduction.'

'I can't? No, you're right. Of course I can't.' Hal tried the coffee again, hesitating in case the woman had any more shocks up her sleeve. Fortunately, she was busy writing. Hal watched for a moment to make sure she wasn't adding his name to her list of targets, then put her out of his mind to concentrate on the coffee.

He'd only taken a sip or two when a muted bell rang behind the counter. The woman put away the notebook and stood up, and after a quick nod she was gone.

'Here you are, Ms Lucas,' said the server. 'Should I put it on your room?'

'Yes thanks.' The woman took the tray and Hal watched her navigate the lobby, admiring her figure as she disappeared into the lift. Then he shook his head. The galaxy was a huge, teeming mass of humanity, and odd behaviour had long ago ceased to surprise him. For example, why was a tax inspector living it up in a five-star hotel?

He'd just raised the mug to his lips when he spotted Clunk hurrying towards him, an anxious expression on his face. Hal closed his eyes, inhaled the coffee, then opened them again. Unfortunately this little trick didn't make the robot vanish - it just brought him a lot closer. With a sigh, Hal set the cup down. 'What's the problem?'

'Mr Cuff insists he made a reservation, but the staff have no record of it.'

'Are they booked out?'

'No, there are several suites available.'

'Let him have one of those.'

'But he thought the room would be laid on. He can't pay in advance.'

Hal rubbed his chin. 'How much cash do we have left?'

'Surely you can't be thinking…'

'We're already in the hole for a grand or so. What difference does another couple of hundred make? Broke is broke.'

'If you spend everything we'll be stranded on Barwenna. That's a huge risk, Mr Spacejock.'

'And it's one I'm willing to take. After all, Cuff wouldn't have come to a flash place like this if he wasn't expecting a substantial payout. He'd have picked a cut-price motel, or asked to stay aboard the *Volante*.'

'If we pay for his hotel room we're just increasing our exposure,' warned Clunk.

'Think of it as an investment. We can't lose.'

❦

Hal strolled to the counter and attracted Cuff's attention. 'Clunk told me about your temporary cash flow problem, and I've come to tell you we'll help out.'

'That's very good of you, Mr Spacejock. I can't believe Argisle and Butt didn't arrange everything. My letter was most explicit, right down to my estimated time of arrival, and yet my solicitors failed to get a single thing right.'

'Don't you worry, we'll see to it. I'll get the rooms organised first.'

'One will suffice.' Cuff indicated his robot. 'I'm happy to share with my valued companion.'

'We're staying too.'

'That's really not necessary.'

'He's right,' said Clunk. 'There are cheaper hotels in the area. Mr Cuff could stay here while we –'

'Put up with rats and bed bugs? No, for once we're doing it in style.' Hal turned to the concierge. 'Two suites please.'

'Thank you sir. That's sixteen hundred credits.'

Hal winced. 'Do we get a discount for cash?'

'Fifteen hundred.'

'Meals included?'

The concierge hesitated. 'I'll give you a voucher for breakfast. Checkout is at ten a.m.'

'Excellent.' Hal nodded to Clunk, who authorised the transaction.

Once check-in was completed, they were escorted to the lift by the porter. After a short ride, the doors opened onto a corridor with thick maroon carpet and wallpaper patterned with gold thread. The doors bore discreet numbers embossed on brass plates, and the porter led them past half a dozen before letting them into rooms on opposite sides of the corridor. Hal tipped him with a credit or two from his depleted funds, then ducked inside before anyone else could stick their hand out.

The room was comfortable, with a large bed, an entertainment console and a modern computer terminal. Hal made straight for the kitchen, where he set to work on the coffee maker. 'Wow, look at this menu! I haven't seen this much food since the AutoChef exploded.'

'Speaking of foods,' said Clunk. 'Your flight suit needs a wash, and I dare say the contents could do with one too.'

8

Barwenna City, 7 a.m.

Zee Pharer hurried along the busy footpath, his bronze legs pumping like a couple of overworked pistons. An internal alarm chimed, and he increased his pace. In three years he'd never been late, and he wasn't going to break that perfect record. What would his owner say? More importantly, what would he do? Alan Dane was a man whose enemies turned up dead, if at all. A man to whom a robot was less than the shine on his hand-tooled leather boots.

It was just over three years since Zee's world had come crashing down. A Peace Force raid on Dane's office, compromising files, a court case and - eventually - prison. Zee knew smuggling and gun-running were illegal, but Dane told him it was sanctioned under certain conditions ...especially if you paid off the right politicians. Unfortunately a payment had gone astray, word had gone out and Dane discovered selling guns to teenagers wasn't quite so legit after all.

Zee rounded the corner in full flight, his rubber-shod feet slipping on the pavement. Ahead was the Barwenna Prison, a four-story building with more security than a crime boss convention. Outside was an expanse of concrete with a few twisted trees and the occasional wooden bench. It was supposed to be a soothing area where visitors could sit and contemplate their surroundings. Due to a lack of funding it was actually a windswept wasteland which afforded clear shots for the rooftop snipers.

The nearest bench was vacant, and Zee hurried over and sat down with a crash. He'd made it!

He glanced towards the prison. Three years ago the instructions had been precise: wait for me every day. Arrive at seven, leave after dark. There were no threats, no explanations, and Zee didn't need them. An order from his owner required total obedience, and if the daily ritual was a touch inconvenient … well, that was humans for you, wasn't it?

The first couple of months had been easy, since Dane had a front business near the prison. Zee moved in, used the facilities to keep himself in good running order, and quickly adapted to his new routine. Unfortunately the business was fire bombed by one of Dane's enemies, and Zee was forced to move. After a number of similar attacks, Zee realised Dane's enemies were following him from the prison, using his movements to track down and eliminate Dane's businesses one by one.

At this point there were no front businesses left, and Dane's few surviving cronies threw their lot in with the enemy. Alone and unwanted, Zee retreated to the transit hub, where he rented a locker under a false name, shutting himself in every night. Power was a problem until he discovered the lockers backed onto a bathroom. A few mods later and he had an endless supply of electricity and a somewhat disturbing view of the urinal.

For the next three years he followed orders to the letter, sitting motionless on the bench during daylight hours. After a couple of months the birds got used to him, and he enjoyed the feel of their tiny clawed feet on his shoulders. He was less impressed with the droppings.

Zee scanned the windows, wondering whether today was the big one. He assumed his boss was building up to a breakout, or perhaps setting up a new smuggling operation. Otherwise, why ask Zee to sit outside the prison for up to fourteen hours a day?

He heard a noise, and turned to see another robot approaching. It was a shorter model, dark blue with silver flashes at the shoulders. Zee nodded at the newcomer, startling a bird into flight, and the Peace Force robot gave him a brief nod in return. 'Still here, then?'

Zee looked down at himself, and wondered whether Peace Force robots were detuned in some way. Of course he was still here. 'Where else would I be?'

'I don't know. Mebbe at the funeral?'

Zee blinked. 'What funeral?'

'And there I was thinking you were Dane's loyal sidekick. All this waiting around and such.'

'I am loyal!' protested Zee. 'I will obey Mr Dane until his dying day.'

'Odd you should say that.' The Peace Force robot jerked his thumb towards the prison. 'If you're quick you can still pay your last respects.'

'A-are you saying Dane is … dead?'

The blue robot snorted. 'You detuned or something? Of course he's dead.'

'But how?'

'He only stabbed himself in the back, didn't he. Fifteen times, by all accounts.'

'Wh-what about me? Dane was my owner. He ordered me to be here!'

'Orders don't work from beyond the grave. You're a free agent now.' The Peace Force robot looked at him in concern. 'Steady there. We don't want no more accidents, or this place'd be getting a reputation.'

Zee stumbled away from his previous life, his mind a whirling mess. No owner? A free agent? What was he to do?

9

'Huh? Wassup? What time is it? Where are we?' Hal opened his eyes to see Clunk standing over him with a mug of coffee. 'Did you put sugar in it?'

'It's eight a.m. and our current location is the Grande Hotel on planet Barwenna. Affirmative to the sugar quotient.'

'Good stuff.' Hal sat up, rubbing his eyes. 'Breakfast?'

'Only if you hurry. Checkout is at ten and we can't afford a second day.'

'You're not kidding.' Hal swigged the coffee, then jumped out of bed and wrapped himself in a thick dressing gown. 'Any sign of Cuff?'

'None at all.'

'I hope he hasn't done a runner.'

'Given his age, that's an unlikely prospect.'

'Yeah, plus his wonky old robot isn't going to win any hundred metre dashes.'

'That old robot has a name, you know.'

'Have you managed to speak to it yet?'

'I'm afraid not.' Clunk gestured at the ceiling. 'I tried communicating across the hall, but there was too much interference from the pleasurebot on the floor above.'

'You mean the suite above.'

'I know what I meant.'

At that moment someone hammered on the door. Hal opened it and saw Cuff outside in a dressing gown, his hair tousled and his face agitated. 'Spacejock! You have to help me!'

'What is it? What's the matter?'

'It's Ferdie! My poor robot is dead!'

'Ferdie?' Hal frowned. 'I thought his name was Freddie?'

'Who cares what you thought?' snapped Cuff. 'He's broken down!'

'Have you tried switching him off and –?'

'Of course!' Cuff grabbed Hal's arm and tried to drag him into the corridor. 'You must help me. This is a matter of life and death.'

Hal was more interested in breakfast. 'Clunk, can you take a look?'

'Yes, Mr Spacejock.'

The robot and the elderly man hurried off, and Hal closed the door. 'Typical start to the day,' he muttered. He reminded himself that Clunk could fix anything, then ordered room service and headed for the shower.

Twenty minutes later Cuff was back at his door with Clunk in tow. Both looked serious, and Hal put his knife and fork down and wiped the egg yolk from his chin with a napkin. 'Well?'

'It's a disaster!' exclaimed Cuff. 'A total nightmare.'

'Clunk?'

'Mr Cuff's robot requires extensive repairs.'

'Can you fix it?'

'I'm afraid not. I'll need specialist equipment, and that won't be cheap.'

Hal frowned. Their funds were long gone, but … 'Can we take out a loan against the *Volante*?'

'That's out of the question,' said Clunk sharply.

Cuff groaned and buried his head in his hands. 'That's it. I'm ruined.'

'What do you mean, ruined?'

'You're not aware of this, of course, but a generous benefactor left my robot a large sum of money.'

'Is that so?' said Hal, feigning shock and awe. 'Well I never.'

'Yes, but if my robot isn't present at the meeting he won't get a single credit.'

'Surely this meeting can be postponed?' asked Clunk. 'They'll understand, given the circumstances.'

'No, the terms are precise. Twelve o'clock is the deadline.' Cuff looked up, a pleading expression on his face. 'Are you sure my beloved Freddie is beyond salvation?'

'I could replace half the components and it would still be a lost cause.' Clunk frowned. 'I don't know whether you understand the concept of preventative maintenance, but –'

'Wait a minute.' Hal looked from one to the other, and the implication hit him like a stray asteroid. 'Never mind your bloody robot. Without that inheritance, how are you going to pay me back?'

'As I said, I'm ruined. Destitute. There's no hope.'

Hal realised the same applied to him. Unless … 'You have to turn up with your robot before twelve, right?'

'Correct.'

Hal turned to Clunk. 'Give yourself a polish. We've got a meeting to attend.'

'Mr Spacejock, you can't seriously expect me to –'

'You're damn right I do. They want a robot? We'll give them one!'

Cuff caught up with the conversation. 'If you're suggesting a substitution, can I just point out it would be unethical, immoral and most likely illegal?'

'It's just a harmless switch,' said Hal. 'Once you have the cash you can fix your robot and swap back. Who's going to know?'

Clunk shook his head. 'I'm sorry, Mr Spacejock. Your idea has merit, but it's not going to work. I cannot tell a lie, and one wrong answer will reveal the deception.'

'He's right,' said Cuff. 'We'll be facing a team of legal experts at Argisle and Butt. Clunk won't last two minutes.'

Hal sipped his coffee, racking his brains. 'We need help from a powerful intellect. Someone with answers at their fingertips. Someone so smart they can solve the mysteries of the universe while simultaneously filling out their own tax return.'

'That sounds great,' said Cuff. 'Who do you have in mind?'

'It's obvious!' Hal gestured. 'Clunk.'

The robot stood tall. 'Yes, Mr Spacejock? What would you like me to do?'

'Get the Navcom on the line for me.'

Deflated, Clunk accessed the commset. Within seconds the Navcom's neutral voice came over the speaker. 'I hope you're all having a jolly time in that five-star hotel.'

Hal frowned at Clunk. 'I thought I told you to say it was two stars!' he hissed.

'The Navcom sees all your bills.'

'What, all of them?'

'Every single one, Mr Spacejock.'

The Navcom made a throat-clearing noise. 'I'll just wait on the line, shall I?'

Hal addressed the commset. 'Listen, Clunk has to stand in for another robot but he can't let on he's doing it. How do I stop him answering questions?'

'Stop asking them,' said the Navcom.

'It's not me, it's the lawyers.'

'Tell them to stop asking questions.'

Hal was beginning to wonder whether calling the Navcom had been such a great idea. 'That's not going to fly, is it? I can't tell them not to ask questions in case the answers aren't what they're expecting. That's *why* they're asking questions in the first place.'

'Then Clunk must refuse to answer them.'

'That's impossible,' said Clunk. 'I must obey orders.'

'Then you'll have to be mute.'

'I beg your pardon?'

'A few seconds with a sharpened screwdriver will do the trick. Apply the tip to the right traces and it won't matter what they ask you.'

'I don't like the sound of that,' said Clunk, with a frown.

'So use the blade on your hearing as well.'

'I shall do no such thing!' protested Clunk.

'You could achieve the same effect with software. I can send you the routines if you like.'

'Do it,' said Hal.

Clunk closed his eyes, and there was a burst of static. 'Routines received. I'll inspect the code now.'

'There is nothing wrong with my programming,' said the Navcom.

'Thanks Navcom. Catch you soon.' Hal cut the connection before the computer could reply. Then he glanced at Cuff, whose expression of despair had given way to a glimmer of hope. 'Go and get dressed, and tell the hotel to stick your robot in storage for the day. Before they take it away, Clunk can skim the memory chips for a few facts and figures - something to convince these lawyers he's the real one.'

'I'm afraid that won't be possible,' said Clunk. 'Freddie's brain suffered a total meltdown, his circuit boards are fried and all his memories were permanently erased.'

'That's fantastic!' Hal noticed the frosty looks, and he hastened to explain. 'Now Clunk can make stuff up, and they can't prove any different.'

Cuff looked doubtful. 'Are you sure your robot can carry this off?'

'Don't you worry,' said Hal loyally. 'Clunk's as tricky as a magician with three sleeves.'

Clunk waited until Cuff had left, then made a throat-clearing sound. 'Mr Spacejock ...'

'I know, I know. The substitution idea is reckless and illegal and so on and so forth. Do you have a better idea?'

'I think the idea is sound. It's the shutting down of my senses I'm concerned about.'

'You can switch them on again, right?'

'Yes, but they could order me to do the same.'

'How?'

Clunk took a napkin and a pen. He wrote rapidly, and when he'd finished the napkin read 'Switch on your hearing' in perfect dot-matrix lettering. 'All they have to do is hold that up to my eyes, and I'd be forced to obey.'

'So close your eyes.'

'They'd patch directly into my brain, which would be even worse.'

'Do you have a solution?'

Clunk nodded. 'I can leave my hearing active, but filter out everything except a particular safety word. When you speak that word, it will restore my speech.'

'That's great! See how well things go when we work as a team?'

'I will also set up a mute word. When spoken it will switch off my speech and apply the new audio filter.'

'Go on then.'

'It will take me thirty minutes to modify the Navcom's code, and I will need several reboots. During that time it's important you don't speak aloud.'

◆

Thirty-five minutes later Clunk declared himself ready. It would have been thirty, but five minutes into the process Hal had sneezed, then made things worse by apologising.

'The keyword to reverse the muting process is *Volante*. Do you think you can remember that?'

'I'm not a complete idiot.'

'The keyword to activate the mute is inconceivable.'

'Oh, go on. It can't be that hard.'

'No, really. It's inconceivable.'

'What am I, thick? It's just a word!'

'That's right, and the word is inconceivable.'

'Really?'

'Yes!'

'*Volante* and inconceivable?'

Clunk opened his mouth to reply, then frowned. He tried again, but nothing came out.

'*Volante*,' said Hal quickly.

'Thank you. Now, you must keep these words to yourself. Do not reveal them to anyone else.'

'I thought they were keyed to my voice?'

'That's correct, but someone could force you to say them under duress. I constructed filters so that bracketing the safety words with screams of pain would render them inert, but I've not had time to perfect them.'

'You think these solicitors might resort to torture?   Totally inconceivable!'

Clunk tried to reply, then pounded on the table, rattling the coffee mug.

'*Volante*!' said Hal.

'Mr Spacejock, I deliberately chose a particular word because you never use it. Now you can't stop saying it?'

'It's not my fault. It's stuck in my brain.'

'Just try not to use it again.'

'Can't you change it? What about, er, um ...' Hal frowned, unable to think of a word he hardly ever used.

'You're bound to use the replacement just as frequently.'

'I guess you're right,' admitted Hal. 'It's inconceivable or nothing.'

10

South-East of Barwenna City, 8:30 a.m.

Sandy West threw her bag over the derelict fence and climbed the pitted wooden boards with ease. She swung her legs over the top and dropped lightly on the other side, just behind a rickety garden shed. The weeds came up to her knees, and she recalled a time when the lawn had been trimmed every weekend.

She moved to the corner of the shed and glanced across the overgrown garden to the house. The curtains were still drawn, and it was unlikely anyone was up. Not before noon, in any case. Not until the daily soaps began.

The shed door was locked, but the wood around the latch was rotten and only one screw remained. Sandy plucked it out and opened the door carefully, trying not to let it shudder on the concrete floor. A familiar smell wafted out: a mix of wood shavings, varnish, cleaning rags and perished rubber. In years past her dad would spend half his weekend in the shed, building intricate toys and furniture. These days their furniture was plastic, and toys were a distant memory.

Sandy pushed past a jumble of half-finished projects and rough-hewn planks, heading for the far corner. There was a workbench in the way, and she moved it carefully to one side. Behind it was an old canvas sheet, draped over an object taller than she was. The outline of a head and shoulders was visible beneath the stained fabric, and Sandy smiled at the sight.

She took one corner of the canvas and pulled, jerking the cover off. Underneath was a gleaming bronze robot, buffed to perfection from head to toe. It had a black serial number - XG99 - stencilled on its chest, and the only visible flaw was a faint tracing of a moustache on the robot's upper lip, drawn with a marker when Sandy was four or five. Boy, had she got into trouble over that little stunt! A telling off, sent to bed with no dinner, and then two hours later her guilt-stricken dad brought her a bowl of cereal for a late-night feast.

She glanced over her shoulder, staring through the grimy windows at the house beyond. Nobody cared what she did now. Not any more.

Sandy blinked, then turned back to the robot. There was a speck of dust on its shoulder, and she buffed it away with her sleeve. 'So, old friend. Are you ready for a walk?'

She took a pair of slacks and a dark blouse from the bag and changed quickly. Her school uniform went into the bag, which she kicked under the workbench. She considered leaving a note, but decided against it. Nobody would find it here, and she wasn't going back to the house.

Sandy opened the robot's chest panel and flipped the main power switch. Somewhere inside the metal chest there was a whine, and a row of status lights came on two by two. When they were all green she closed the panel and stepped back. 'Can you hear me, Daniel?'

The robot opened its eyes and looked down at her. They were warm and yellow, and they crinkled around the edges as Daniel recognised her face. 'Yes, Miss Sandy. It's a pleasure to see you.'

'How are your circuits?'

'Not the best, but I'll manage.' The robot hesitated. 'It's today, isn't it?'

'Yes. Our little outing.'

'You understand I can't walk very fast?'

'That's okay, Daniel. We'll take it easy.'

'Have you informed your parents?'

'Sure.'

The robot eyed her thoughtfully. 'Are you certain? I detect a note of _'

'Daniel! Don't you trust me after all this time?'

The robot traced the outline of the moustache on its upper lip.

'You can't be serious. That was years ago!'

Daniel sighed. 'Don't I know it? It seems like yesterday you were just a perky little thing, barely higher than my knee joint. Now you're a beautiful young lady.'

Sandy smiled. 'I bet you're a hit with the girls, you old charmer.'

'Not that I remember.'

'Okay, we really have to leave. Is there anything you need?'

Daniel's neck creaked as he shook his head.

'Come on, then.' Sandy pulled the door open, and the robot stepped away from the corner. His legs groaned as he walked, and his expression was drawn. 'Are you really up to this?'

'I–I think so.'

They made it to the doorway, where Daniel turned for the house.

'Not that way,' said Sandy, guiding him to the left. Another step and she turned him again, until he was aiming straight for the fence. 'Come on, time to go.'

Daniel reached the fence in three steps, and with his fourth he walked straight through it, tearing the ancient planks like cardboard. Sandy followed, stepping over the shattered fragments.

The local woods ran right up to the back fence, where the leaf-strewn ground was bright with dappled sunlight. Daniel extended his elbow like a proper gentleman, and the two of them set off under the trees arm in arm, leaving behind their old lives for good.

Barwenna City, 11:20 a.m.

Traffic was heavy, and it took longer than Hal expected to reach the offices of Argisle and Butt. Even so, they made it with forty minutes to spare. Hal paid the cab off, then turned to follow the others up the steps.

'You wait here,' said Cuff. 'Clunk and I will attend the meeting alone.'

'No chance.'

Cuff was taken aback. 'How will I explain your presence?'

'Tell them the truth. I'm your hired muscle.' Hal forestalled further argument by running up the stairs and holding the doors open. 'After you, sir.'

'Thank you, my loyal and faithful bodyguard. Your long years of service will be fondly remembered and richly rewarded.'

Inside, a receptionist was busy taking calls. Cuff waited until she was free, then smiled and bowed. 'Good morning, ma'am. Would you inform Messrs Argisle and Butt that Hans Cuff is here to see them?'

He was charm personified, but the woman barely glanced at him. 'Go through those doors and wait until you're called.'

Cuff's smile slipped. 'I do have an appointment.'

'Not my problem, we're backed up.' The receptionist pointed. 'In there and wait. Next!'

Hal led the others to the doors, and could only stare at the scene beyond.

'Goodness me,' said Clunk.

The room was the size of a tennis court, filled with rows of folding chairs. Seated in the chairs was the oddest collection of robots Hal had ever seen. There were skinny serving droids with battered trays, wheezing personal trainers covered in faded logos, ex-army scouts, stout red teachers with grey screens where their faces should have been, and a variety of oddbots built from scavenged parts. And in between the robots there were humans - tattooed workmen in their Sunday best, scruffy teenagers playing games on their commsets, and nervous twenty-somethings with slicked-down hair and cheap suits.

Hal led the way to the back of the hall, where they sat next to a wizened pensioner. The old man eyed them with suspicion, taking a firm grip on his oddbot's buckled arm.

'Good afternoon,' said Hal. 'Can you tell me what you're doing here?'

The old man cupped a hand to his ear. 'What's that, sonny?'

'What are you doing at Argisle and Butt?' asked Hal loudly.

'He's not stolen!' said the old man indignantly. 'I've had him since he was a wee rivet.'

Hal nodded and smiled, then leant forward and tapped the woman in front on the shoulder. 'Excuse me.'

The woman fixed him with a potent glare. 'You ought to be ashamed of yourselves!'

Hal blinked. 'I'm sorry?'

'You know what I'm talking about,' hissed the woman, turning her back on him.

Hal turned to Clunk. 'This could take a while. Did you bring any food?'

'There's a buffet at the front of the hall.'

Hal craned his neck. 'I don't suppose you could fetch me a plate of sarnies?'

'Yes, Mr Spacejock. Your stomach's wish is my command.' Clunk looked at Cuff. 'I suppose you're feeling hungry too?'

Cuff stood. 'Do you mind if I accompany you? I don't want to let you out of my sight.'

Before they left, Clunk bent down to whisper in Hal's ear. 'You should use the keyword in case anyone tries to speak to me.'

'Inconceivable.'

Hal watched them go, then turned to see a young man in a muddy brown cloak striding towards him, pushing a battered white cylinder on wheels. 'That one's really been in the wars,' remarked Hal, as the man took a seat.

'Ex-military.' The man looked him up and down. 'Where's yours?'

'Getting a sandwich.' Hal gazed around the room. 'You really like your robots on this planet, don't you?'

'Where would we be without our valued companions?'

Hal thought he detected a hint of sarcasm, but put it down to the accent. 'You like lawyers too. This place is packed!'

The man nodded. 'Argisle and Butt is a robot specialist. They handle all the big cases.'

'Does it take long?'

'Who cares?' The man snorted. 'It's not like I have to run around saving the galaxy from evil.'

Hal felt vague misgivings. It was nothing he could put his finger on, but something wasn't right. The robots, the tense atmosphere, and the odd reactions from the crowd. It was like they were waiting for the result of a big race.

◆

Hal glanced to his left, where a grey-haired man in a leather jacket was cleaning his fingernails with a pocket knife. 'Hi,' said Hal. 'How are you doing?'

'Be better when all this is over.' The man stuck his hand out. 'I'm Fisher. David Fisher.'

'Hal Spacejock.'

They shook, and Hal glanced at Fisher's robot. It was a real bitser, with mismatched parts from head to toe. One arm was silver, the other bronze. The left leg was much longer than the right, and someone had removed the foot to compensate, leaving the robot to walk on the ball joint.

'I only just got it ready in time,' explained Fisher. 'I pulled an all-nighter.'

'Looks like you needed an all-weeker.'

Fisher grinned. 'Most of these robots have had a pretty tough life. Driven hard by uncaring owners, skipped services, no spare parts…' He pointed over Hal's shoulder. 'Look at that poor specimen. It wouldn't cost much to get those dents out, and that sad expression is enough to break your heart.'

Hal was about to tut sympathetically at the object of Fisher's pity when he realised it was Clunk. 'He's not sad, his face just slipped. When he's really down he grumbles through his nostrils.'

Fisher stared. 'That's your robot?'

'Sure. And those dents? He says they add character.' Hal waved. 'Over here Clunk.'

When Clunk arrived Fisher put his hand out. 'David Fisher. This is my XG99 series.'

Clunk frowned at the franken-bot. He opened his mouth to speak, but nothing came out.

'I know, I'm sorry,' said Fisher. 'It's a wreck. It hasn't worked for years.'

'Yours too?' muttered Hal. He saw Clunk's venomous look and raised his hands. 'Just kidding!'

'So, what do you reckon on your chances?' Fisher asked Hal.

'Chances of what?'

'You know, the –'

'Ah, Clunk! There you are!' Cuff returned with a plate full of sandwiches and a large mug of coffee. 'What did I tell you about staying close to me? We can't have you running away like a little lost lamb, can we?'

Clunk's eyes narrowed, and Hal thought it was just as well the robot's voice was muted.

'Doesn't your robot speak?' asked Fisher.

'Nothing too major,' said Hal. 'It's just a blockage in his circuits.'

'Mine's the same, only the circuits are missing altogether. If I get through this thing I'm going to splash out on my own repair centre. If anyone can't pay the bill, I'll fix their robot for nothing.'

'That sounds pretty generous.'

Fisher spread his hands. 'How much money does one man need? If my robot turns out to be –'

'Mr Spacejock,' interrupted Cuff. 'May I speak with you?'

'Sure.'

'In private.'

They moved to the side of the hall, where Cuff lowered his voice and leant in close. 'I suspect Mr Fisher is here on false pretences.'

'You do?'

Cuff nodded. 'I believe he's here to steal my robot's rightful inheritance.'

Hal gaped at him, then turned to stare at Fisher. He didn't look like a conman, but isn't that what they said about all the best ones? If Fisher claimed *his* robot was the real one, what could Cuff do about it? After all, Fisher wasn't the only one trying to pass off a substitute. 'This thing with Clunk is never going to work,' said Hal. 'We should have brought your robot.'

'Fergus was beyond repair,' hissed Cuff. 'That rough landing of yours tipped it over the edge.'

Hal's eyes narrowed. 'Don't try and pin this on me. We've done everything to help you! The flight, cabs, a hotel room ... and what about that six course dinner you ordered last night?'

'One has to eat, Mr Spacejock.'

'One, sure. You ordered for three!'

'And when I inherit you will be amply compensated.'

Hal opened his mouth to reply, but at that moment a loud voice cut across the hall.

'Would everyone pay attention please?' The voice came through hidden speakers, and the murmur of conversations ceased.

'Thank you,' said the voice. 'Now, in half an hour we're going to single out the most likely candidates for Baker's legacy. Before we start I'd like to point out that it's an offence to impersonate another robot, or to falsify ownership papers. Furthermore ...'

At this point Hal's jaw dropped and he stopped listening. Slowly he looked around the packed hall, and there was a sick feeling in his throat as he scanned all the people with their elderly robots.

They were all there to claim on the will!

— 12 —

Hal froze as the enormity of the situation sank in, and then he turned to Cuff. Some small part of him still hoped that he'd made a mistake, that the old gent really was the one and only claimant on the will. However, Cuff refused to meet his gaze, and that's when Hal lost it. He grabbed a fistful of jacket, hauling Cuff into the air. 'You ... you ...' He drew a fist back to strike.

'It's all a misunderstanding,' squeaked Cuff, wriggling in Hal's grip. 'Look, look! I think your robot wants you to do something. He's trying to speak!'

Hal knew what Clunk was going to say, but he couldn't silence him forever. '*Volante*,' he snapped.

The words tumbled out. 'Let him go, Mr Spacejock. Let him go! Violence won't solve anything.'

'Oh, I don't know. I feel better already.'

'You don't mean that. Come, let us solve this problem like civilised beings.'

The red mist faded, and Hal gave Cuff one last shake before releasing him. 'You're going to pay back every credit, you rotten little con artist. We're talking black market body parts. Do you understand?'

'I'm sorry, all right?' Cuff straightened his collar. 'When I heard about the will I couldn't resist. I thought bringing an old robot to Barwenna was the perfect idea. I–I just didn't realise everyone else would think of it too.'

'Idea? Scam, more like!' Hal gestured towards the crowd. 'You're as bad as this lot!'

'You only helped so you could profit from my good fortune,' said Cuff sullenly.

340

'No, I helped because you owed us your fare and you couldn't pay. I wasn't expecting a cut of your fortune.'

'I'm sorry. I read you all wrong.' Cuff slumped in his chair, his face drawn. 'I don't know what to say, I really don't.'

Hal could think of plenty to say - and do - but he didn't fancy six months in prison. Could they get a splash of fuel on credit, maybe using Cuff's robot as collateral? It was worth a try. 'Your robot. I'll need a receipt.'

'N-no! You can't!'

'Why not? You won't be needing it.'

'Of course I need it. How am I going to claim my inheritance without it?'

Hal stared. Was the old guy completely mad? There were four hundred people in the hall, every one of them after the fortune, and he was still hoping to claim using his clapped-out wreck?

'Let's do a deal,' said Cuff desperately. 'Lend me fifty credits for the cab fare, there and back. If I inherit I'll give you fifty thousand credits for your trouble. What do you say?'

'I say you're full of –'

Clunk cleared his throat. 'Mr Spacejock, the odds are favourable.'

'Are you serious? We've wasted thousands on this dreamer, and you want to give him more?'

'You spent two thousand credits hoping for a small tip. Now you're refusing fifty against a very substantial sum?'

Hal blinked. 'When you put it like that …'

Cuff stood. 'Come, there's still time. We'll find a cab, borrow a trolley and –'

'No way, sunshine. Clunk, did you record that stuff about the fifty grand?'

'Yes, Mr Spacejock.'

'Good. That's all we need.' Hal took out a credit tile and gave it to Cuff. 'I'll keep an eye on the news. If you inherit, expect to hear from us.'

'Why? Where are you going?'

'Back to the *Volante*. We're freighter pilots, not minders. We're going to do some real work for a change.'

The cab turned into the spaceport, and Hal's spirits improved when he spotted the *Volante* sitting serenely on her landing pad. The Cuff thing had been a costly disaster, but it wasn't terminal. They could still collect payment for Clunk's cargo of furniture parts, use the cash to fuel the ship, and find themselves a proper job. One without robots, hotel bills and passengers.

The cab drove between two ships, and Hal frowned. Looming over them was another Gamma-class freighter, identical to his own. Competition! If they didn't hurry the newcomer would scoop the best freight jobs.

The cabbie drew up to the *Volante*. Hal and Clunk got out and hurried towards the ship. They were just about to step onto the passenger ramp when an enormous shadow blocked the sun. Hal looked round to see two men so big and wide they looked like a couple of brick walls in suits. They'd been waiting under the ramp, one of them paring his fingernails with a carving knife and the other putting a sheen on a huge chrome blaster.

'Are you Hal Spacejock?' demanded one of the men. His face looked like a granite cliff, and his oft-broken nose lent his voice a rough quality.

The menace in his tone was unmistakeable, and Hal decided caution was in order. 'No, I'm Kent Spearman.' He nodded towards the second Gamma-class ship. 'That's Spacejock's wreck over there.'

The two men exchanged a glance, then turned and hurried away. 'Quick,' Hal said to Clunk. 'We'd better leg it before they come back.' He led Clunk up the passenger ramp to the flight deck, and once they were inside he locked both airlock doors. 'Who do you think they were?'

'At a guess, something to do with your wedding mishap.'

Hal swallowed. 'Get onto that customer of yours. I want that container offloaded right away.'

'Yes, Mr Spacejock.'

'Wait.' Hal raised his finger. 'Make sure you get cash. Don't let them get away with anything.'

'No, Mr Spacejock.'

Satisfied, Hal sat in the pilot's chair and brought up a listing of available cargo jobs. There were pages of them, and he carefully checked the destination planets against a master list of terrorist warnings and election campaigns. There was nothing worse than having uninvited guests force themselves on board, holding him captive in his own flight deck whilst making outrageous statements designed to convert followers to their beliefs. He wasn't too keen on terrorists either.

After removing the undesirables he was left with half a dozen possibles. Two disappeared while he was scanning them, already taken by another pilot. Another went without warning, and with only three remaining Hal had to move fast. He picked a job delivering building materials to the construction site for a brand new space station, and was just about to confirm when the lift doors sprang apart.

'Mr Spacejock,' cried Clunk, waving a sheet of paper. 'You have to see this. Something terrible has happened!'

'Not now, Clunk. I'm taking on a job. It's for Space Station Oberon near Gyris ... have you heard of it?'

'You can't do that. Not until we sort this out!'

◆

On the way to the hold Clunk explained the problem. 'They loaded the wrong container,' he said, thrusting the sheet of paper at Hal. 'See? This manifest has a different serial number.'

'How can it be wrong? The ground staff on Greil were supposed to check everything.' Hal examined the faded print. 'Wait a minute. This was printed six weeks ago!'

Clunk snatched the page, and a beam of green light shone from his eyes. It swept across the paper, and when the scan was complete he shook his head. 'This is the wrong manifest. The vessel's name is different.'

'So the cargo might be all right after all?'

'That's to be seen.'

Hal opened the inner door, and they marched across the hold to the container. 'Let's open it up.'

'Are you sure? Customs haven't inspected it yet.'

'Clunk, we have no idea what's inside that box. If it's real bad we're dumping it before customs get a look.'

'Let me find some bolt cutters.'

Hal eyed the shipping container. The rust-streaked sides were battered and dented, and it looked like just the thing for moving a cargo of stolen weapons or smuggled booze ... or worse.

Clunk returned with the cutters, and there was a snick as he cut the seal. Hal swung the door open, and they both stared at the contents. It wasn't furniture parts, and it certainly wasn't illicit drugs or weapons. Instead, the container was packed with cheap office desks, old filing cabinets and broken computer terminals. There were in-trays still stacked with paperwork, and everything was thick with dust.

'I don't think we have to worry about customs.' Hal stepped inside and opened a filing cabinet. 'No guns here. I think we're okay. We'll just put it back, fetch the right container and nobody will ever know.'

'It's far from okay, Mr Spacejock.' Clunk hesitated. 'In fact, I think I know what happened.'

'Do tell.'

'If I explain, will you promise not to do anything rash? This concerns our ex-passenger, Mr Cuff.'

Hal gestured impatiently. 'I've forgotten the guy already. Come on, spill it.'

'Do you remember visiting the pub on Greil?'

'Vaguely.'

'You told me several patrons asked for passage to Barwenna, and you turned them all down. One of them was Mr Cuff.'

'Yep.'

'After you left the pub, you encountered Cuff once more, this time being attacked.'

'Not attacked exactly. The muggers had just left.'

'Do you think the situation may have been ... staged?'

'I doubt it. Cuff said they took one look at me and ran for it.'

'All of them?'

Hal puffed his chest out. 'They knew they didn't stand a chance.'

'And then Cuff attached himself to you, expressed surprise that we were flying to Barwenna, and managed to invite himself aboard.'

'Yep.' Hal frowned. 'You know, apart from actually inheriting the fortune, that little weasel has all the luck.'

'Luck had nothing to do with it.' Clunk hesitated. 'Do you know how we came by that cargo job?'

'Same as always. You went looking for it.'

'Not this time. This was a last minute rush job, organised on behalf of a third party. Don't you understand what that means?'

'The customer used a shipping agent?'

'No, Mr Spacejock. Think! In the bar, Mr Cuff discovered you were a cargo pilot. He asked for passage to Barwenna for himself and his robot, and you refused. An hour or so later, Mr Cuff staged a mugging precisely as you were passing by. You took him under your wing and then, thanks to a fortuitous cargo job, Mr Cuff and the robot got their passage to Barwenna after all. Isn't it clear?'

'Not really. You lost me at the pub.'

Clunk groaned. 'Mr Spacejock, who could possibly have the motive for setting up this cargo job? A job which involved leaving for Barwenna immediately?'

'The customer, of course.'

'There was no customer!' cried Clunk. 'I already told you, the job came via the spaceport!'

Hal's eyes narrowed. 'So somebody set up a fake job just to get us to Barwenna.'

'Yes!'

'And to make the job look legit they loaded a container full of junk.'

'You're getting it!'

'And now we can't deliver it, so we can't pay for fuel.'

'Ye-es. Technically correct, but beside the point.'

'Not if they were after revenge for that little misunderstanding.'

'I'm sorry?'

'That wedding party and the smashed glasses. You said they were powerful people, and now they've had their revenge. We're broke, we can't afford fuel and we'll never get another job as long as we live.' Hal snapped his fingers. 'I bet they sent those muggers after me!'

Clunk put his head in his hands. 'Cuff, Mr Spacejock. Cuff, Cuff, *Cuff!*'

'That sounds nasty.' Hal patted him on the back. 'Is it a chest cold?'

'This has nothing to do with the glassware or the wedding,' said Clunk, his voice muffled. 'It was Mr Cuff, our passenger. He's behind the whole thing.'

'What, the fake cargo?'

'Yes. He must have called the spaceport from the pub.'

'And the muggers?'

'What muggers? Did you see any muggers?'

'No, but Cuff said ...'

'Precisely.'

'And this shipping container?'

'Selected at random from an abandoned stack at the spaceport.'

Hal was silent while the whole mess sank in, then ... 'I'm going to kill him.'

'You promised not to do anything rash!'

'Never trust a human being.' Hal paced the hold. 'We've got to lose the container. Junk or not, someone could have us for theft.'

'Illegal dumping –'

'Later, Clunk. Later.' Hal continued pacing. 'We'll need fuel, and then we can take that space station job. Do we have anything we can sell?'

'There is an alternative.'

'What?'

'Why don't we return to the solicitors and stake a claim on the inheritance?'

Hal blinked. 'You're crazy. There were hundreds of people in that hall! What chance do we have?'

'With Cuff in the running you had odds of four hundred to one. If I join you'll have two horses in the race.'

'You mean, four hundred to two?'

'Two hundred to one.'

'Even better!' Hal looked Clunk up and down. 'Just think, if you get your mitts on all that cash old Cuff will be as sick as a dog.'

'Yes, I suppose that would be your first thought if you came into a vast fortune.'

'Plus if Cuff wins, he's promised us fifty grand.'

'Correct.'

'And if neither of us wins I'm going to lock him into this container and dump him into the nearest star.'

They left the *Volante* at a run, keeping a wary eye out for heavily-armed goons. Fortunately there was no sign of them, and Hal dived into the cab and hauled the door shut. 'Drive,' he said to the cabbie. 'Don't stop for anyone.'

After an uneventful ride the cab dropped them outside the solicitors, and Hal rushed to the door just as a beefy security guard was trying to close it. She saw them coming and put a hand out. 'I'm sorry sir. You're too late.'

'I was here before,' panted Hal. 'I had to go back for my papers.'

'All right, all right.' The guard held the door open. 'One more won't hurt. In you go.'

'Thanks. You're a champ.'

Inside, the first person Hal saw was Cuff. Their ex-passenger was at the counter, and alongside him was a luggage trolley decorated with 'Hotel Grande' logos. On the trolley was the stricken robot, securely attached with rope and packing tape.

Clunk laid a hand on Hal's arm. 'Leave him be, Mr Spacejock. Don't cause a scene here.'

Hal glanced towards the entrance, where the security guard was watching closely. She had one hand on her blaster, and he realised Clunk was right. There was plenty of time to cause a scene somewhere else, after the will was settled.

Hal glanced towards the buffet as soon as they entered the hall, but the tables had been cleared away. There was a podium in their place, and an elderly man with white hair was standing to one side, checking items on his clipboard. A clock read 12:03, and Hal realised they'd just made it.

They were barely settled when an excited murmur spread through the crowd. A dozen staff were entering the hall via the rear doors, dressed in identical business suits with crisp white shirts and plain ties. They wore hands-free commsets, and each had a stack of coloured tickets. They spread out, criss-crossing the rows of seats to hand out tickets. Occasionally they paused, listening to orders over their commsets.

Hal craned his neck to watch proceedings. There didn't seem to be any pattern to the tickets they were handing out. People were getting red ones and green ones, blue ones and white ones, and if there was anything written on them Hal couldn't see it. Eventually it was his turn, and he received a dark blue scrap of paper. The front was blank, and when he turned it over he discovered the reverse was, too. Hal glanced along the row and saw Cuff holding a similar ticket. He could see Fisher two rows ahead, the abominable robot by his side, but couldn't make out which slip of paper they'd been given.

Finally everyone had a ticket. There was an expectant hush, and then the elderly gent spoke into his microphone.

'Thank you for your patience, ladies and gentlemen. I'm sorry this process has taken so long, but the turnout was greater than expected. Now, if you do not yet have a ticket please raise your hand.'

A couple of hands went up, and uniformed staff converged on them. Moments later, everyone was set.

The loudspeaker crackled again. 'We will proceed to the next stage in a moment or two, but first some of you will be leaving us. Could I ask everyone with a blue ticket to stand up?'

Hal got to his feet, cursing under his breath. Of the hundreds who remained seated, one or two shot him sympathetic glances, but most looked smug. Hal could see two or three others on their feet, Cuff and Fisher amongst them, and he realised his shot at Cuff's fifty grand had just vanished in a puff of smoke.

'Please,' said the voice. 'If you have a blue ticket you must stand up now. We will be inspecting your tickets so there's no point trying to remain here.'

Two more claimants stood up. One was a teenage girl, pale and upset, while the other was a bronze robot with extensive scars across his chest. Each was clutching a blue slip.

'Very well, those of you standing up will now make your way out of the hall. The rest will remain here to await further instructions.'

Hal led Clunk to the exit. The staffers had every angle covered, and his chances of pulling a swifty were non-existent. No, it was game over and goodnight.

'I told you this was a waste of time,' he grumbled to Clunk, as they entered the foyer. 'Four hundred to two or two hundred to one, the odds were lousy either way.'

'Never mind, Mr Spacejock. Perhaps the legacy will go to someone more deserving.'

'What, an even bigger con artist?' Hal nodded towards the restrooms. 'I'm going to flush some ballast. I'll meet you outside and then we'll deal with Cuff. Don't let him go, all right?'

— 14 —

Clunk saw Cuff approaching and gave him a curt nod. It was almost a curt head butt, but his programming intervened.

'This is your fault,' hissed Cuff. 'You and that Spacejock loser, it's all down to you. If you hadn't wrecked my beloved Freddie …'

'Beloved?' Clunk's politeness routines struggled under the load. 'Some owner you are. You can't even remember that poor robot's name!'

Cuff gestured at him and made for the exit, abandoning his robot. The automatic doors remained firmly closed, and when he tried to push them one of the staffers put a hand out. 'I'm sorry, sir. You must stay for the announcement.'

'What announcement?'

'It's very important. We're just waiting for the final member of the party.'

Clunk eyed the rest of the crowd. The teenage girl was being comforted by a robot, her face buried in its chest. Its comforting expression was only marred by the faint outline of a curly moustache on its upper lip. *Can I help?* Clunk broadcast to the robot.

She'll be all right in a moment, was the reply. *It was just a shock. She thought I might be the one.*

Didn't we all? Clunk had just looked away when there was a thud from the main hall. 'I tell you, you've got it all wrong!' shouted an angry voice. 'Take your hands off me this instant!'

Everyone turned to the hall, where a man in a flight suit was being ejected by a couple of security guards. He had a mane of dark hair and a neat goatee, and Clunk didn't have to read the gold monogram on his flight suit to recognise him. It was Kent Spearman, Mr Spacejock's rival!

The guards pushed him into the lobby, then shoved his robot out after him.

'I said you've got it all wrong!' protested Spearman.

'I'm sorry, sir. You were given a blue ticket. It was on camera.'

'Hey man, I was just taking my plate out the back. It's not a crime to wash up, is it?'

The guards ignored his protests and slammed the doors in his face.

'Well that sucks,' said Spearman. He looked around the room, his gaze pausing on the teenage girl before passing over Clunk without recognition. Hardly surprising, since there were half a dozen bronze robots in the lobby. 'If anyone needs a lift off this rock, I'm your man. I have a fast ship at the spaceport and my rates can't be beat.'

Clunk suppressed a groan. There'd be fireworks when Mr Spacejock found out his rival was in town. He eyed Spearman's robot, a battered XG model like himself, and frowned at the obvious signs of mistreatment. Its outer skin was dull, one eye was cracked and three fingers on its left hand were bent backwards. If he didn't know better he'd say it had been pulled from a junk cupboard and fired up in haste. *Are you sure you should be here?* he broadcast to the robot

All he got back was an earful of static.

Clunk looked around the lobby to inspect the remaining robots. There was Cuff with his burnt-out shell, still lashed to a luggage trolley. Nearby was the thickset man Mr Spacejock had been speaking to earlier. Fisher, that was it. He had grey hair and was wearing a neat suit, an expensive watch and a thick gold ring. Alongside him was his grotesque robot, and Clunk felt anger rising inside him at the sight. How could anyone be so callous? Finally, he turned to the fourth robot. It looked okay at first inspection, but the scarred chest panels had scorch marks around them, as though the robot had been wrenched open and rebuilt. Clunk looked around for the owner, ready to give them an accusing glare, but this robot stood alone. It met Clunk's eyes and hunched slightly, as though getting ready to spring. *What are you looking at?*

Nothing, broadcast Clunk. *I was just wondering where your owner is. I don't have one. I'm a free agent.*

Good for you. Clunk glanced back at the first robot, the one with the moustache, and his expression softened. It was clearly the best of the bunch, and someone had taken the time to polish it from head to toe. They'd even cleaned the fluff from its cooling vents, which most people didn't bother with. Alongside it, the teenage girl was looking somewhat lost. Clunk gave her a nod and a smile, but she didn't notice.

Clunk looked around the robots again, and he realised they were all minor variations of the same model. They all had 'XG99' stamped on their chest plates, just as he did. Were the organisers clearing the hall type by type, until they were left with a handful of potentials? If so, the only surprise was that they didn't have cameras in place, recording the whole process for one of those ghastly reality shows humans seemed to enjoy.

'Excuse me, everyone.' The woman near the entrance raised her voice. 'Now you're all here, would you please gather round? This concerns all of you, and those vital blue tickets you were given.'

Clunk glanced towards the restroom, but there was no sign of Mr Spacejock. Mystified, he freed up some storage and started recording.

The woman with the clipboard addressed the small crowd. 'Your bus just arrived, and it will take you to a hotel in the city. After arrival you'll be briefed on the next stage in the process.'

There was dead silence, broken only by the muffled sound of the loudspeaker as it barked instructions to the people still waiting inside the hall.

'Come on, people. It's not going to wait for you.' The young woman looked around the room, only to meet blank stares. 'Well? What's the problem?'

Hushed murmurs filled the foyer, and the grey-haired man cleared his throat. 'Listen, we got the blue tickets. The voice told us to leave.'

'That's right. They're going to keep the others back until you get clear.'

'But the voice said –'

'Okay, I'll make this quick. There are four hundred people in that hall, and any second now they're going to learn they've all been eliminated from contention. The blue tickets were a ruse to get you lot to safety. Understood?' The staff member glanced at her watch. 'Speaking of safety, we have to leave right now. Please, the bus is waiting.'

Comprehension dawned, and there was a stampede for the exit. Clunk was left behind, and he was just trying to explain Hal's absence to the staffer when there was an angry growl from the hall. Hundreds of people had just learned the truth, and they did not sound happy.

'You'll have to make your own way there,' said the staff member, beating a hasty retreat.

'Where?' called Clunk, but the reply was lost in the uproar.

He heard the loudspeakers calling for calm, but at the same instant there was a crash and the doors to the hall began to shake. Clunk crossed to the restroom in three strides, desperate to reach Hal before the angry mob was unleashed. With any luck he would be able to keep Mr Spacejock safe until help arrived.

Hal shook the water off his hands and pulled a length of paper towel from the dispenser. When he was done he dropped the waste into the disposal unit. There was a blue flash as the unit disintegrated the waste into molecules, and a whoosh as it sucked them away.

'Hey, neat!' Hal took a bigger length of towel, wadded it and dropped it into the disposal unit.

Flash! Whoosh! The room lit up with searing blue light.

Fascinated, Hal pulled an even longer piece and dangled the end into the flash disposal. As he lowered the paper into the unit it disappeared into thin air, fizzing and dancing. When it was gone Hal reached for the dispenser again, ready to yank out several metres. Unfortunately it was now empty.

Hal remembered Cuff, and wondered whether the unit could handle bodies. Then he patted his pockets to see whether he had any junk to get rid of. He came up with the blue ticket.

'Fat lot of use that was,' muttered Hal, holding it over the mouth of the disposal unit. He was just about to let go of his blue ticket when the door burst open, almost knocking him across the wash room. 'Hey, what's the bloody rush?'

'Mr Spacejock, we have to get out of here.'

Hal struggled to his feet. 'You've got to see this thing first. It'll swallow anything!'

'We don't have time. We must –'

'Here, watch this.' Hal released the blue ticket above the opening. As it fluttered towards certain destruction Clunk reacted, diving forwards with both arms outstretched. He plucked the ticket from mid-air and cannoned into the wall, cracking the tiles.

'You're a bit hyper, aren't you? Did you overcharge your battery again?'

The wash room door started to open and Clunk hurled himself at it, slamming it shut with his shoulder. He put his back to the door, hands braced against the walls. 'Mr Spacejock, please listen. The organisers were doing things backwards. Those with blue tickets move onto the next stage of the inheritance. Everyone left in the hall was disqualified.'

'Why do it that way round?'

'They wanted to get us out before the much larger crowd learned of the deception.' Clunk winced as the door shook behind him. 'That large crowd has now realised the truth, and they're out for blood. Your blood.'

'You mean there are hundreds of angry people out there?'

'Precisely.'

'And the rest of the ticket holders?'

'They just left in a bus.'

'Why didn't you tell them to wait?'

There was a hefty thump on the door, shaking Clunk from head to toe.

'We know you're in there,' said a voice. 'Open up!'

THUMP! Clunk shifted his hands and feet, trying to get better purchase. 'We must escape before there's a full scale riot.'

Hal looked around the bathroom but the only other exit was a small window high on the far wall. If he put his foot on the wash basin he might just be able to reach it, but the moment Clunk stepped away from the door the crowd would pour in. 'I don't suppose you have a gun?' He saw Clunk's expression. 'Not to shoot anyone, just to wave about until they come to their senses.'

'I'm unarmed, as always.' Clunk nodded towards the window. 'Can you get that open?'

'Probably, but what about you?'

'Just do it, Mr Spacejock.'

Hal clambered onto the wash basin, almost losing his footing on a large bar of soap. Wobbling slightly, he reached for the window catch. It was stiff with age, but he wiggled it furiously until it came loose, then pushed the window open. He peered out and realised it led onto a deserted alley. The drop was only small, and he was sure he could fit through the window. But that wouldn't help Clunk.

'Go, Mr Spacejock. Don't worry about me.'

Hal frowned. Clunk was a loyal friend, not someone to be abandoned at the drop of a hat. Anyway, he needed the robot to make a claim on the will. He looked around the bathroom for inspiration, and his gaze fell on the soap. 'I've got it,' he said. 'We'll use this handy bar of soap to escape.'

'But I don't have any tracking bugs!'

'Typical robot, always reaching for high tech solutions.' Hal filled the basin, flaking soap into the water until froth spilled onto the floor. It spread rapidly, running into the stalls and lapping around Clunk's feet, and Hal grabbed the remains of the bar and clambered onto the basin. It creaked underfoot, protesting the rough treatment, but remained attached to the wall. Once he was poised at the window, Hal nodded towards the door. 'Ready?'

'Yes.'

'Okay … let them in!'

Clunk released the door and crossed the slippery floor at a dead run, his traction control working overtime as it compensated for the treacherous surface. The crowd poured in behind him and Hal threw the bar of soap at the leader, hoping to distract him while Clunk got clear. It smacked the angry-looking man right in the forehead, and he went down as though shot, sliding through the water and leaving neat bow-waves with his face. Those behind him stumbled and fell, and Hal squeezed through the window before they could recover and lay hands on him. He reached the ground and turned to give Clunk a hand, just as the robot put his foot on the basin to climb out. There was a creak as the sink broke off the wall, and a loud crash as it smashed on the tiled floor. Broken pipes spewed hot and cold water, and the pursuers who'd kept their feet were promptly knocked over. Clunk put his foot on a broken pipe to get a leg up, but the pipe bent flush with the wall.

'Give me your hands,' said Hal desperately. 'I'll pull you out!'

'No. Stand clear, Mr Spacejock.'

A split second later the window exploded outwards. Clunk came through the middle like a high-diver, hands together and head tucked between his arms. He turned the perfect dive into a forward somersault, landing on both feet and bending at the knees to absorb the impact.

There was a shout from the bathroom and angry faces appeared at the window, one with a red mark the size and shape of a bar of soap, another with one of Clunk's footprints across his cheek, and the rest soaked to the skin and lathered with foam. Hands reached for purchase, and Hal raised the window frame and slammed it on their fingers, banging it down a couple of times to get the message through. Then a chunk of sink came sailing by, narrowly missing his head, and he decided it was time to retreat.

— 16 —

Hal and Clunk ran across the sunny courtyard towards a wooden gate, desperate to escape their pursuers. As they ran they could hear voices on the other side of the fence, and when they burst through the gate they found a narrow lane full of people. Hal recognised a few from the hall, although most had abandoned their treasured robots. Great, he thought. Not only were dozens of angry people chasing them, there were hundreds more outside. And every one of them was keen to work off their frustrations.

'Play it cool,' he muttered to Clunk.

The gate closed behind them and they pushed through the crowd, making for the main street. They were only halfway along when the gate flew open and their wet, soapy pursuers poured through. There was dead silence, and then ...

'Over there! That's him! The guy with the bronze robot!'

'Oh dear,' said Clunk.

Hal looked at the crowd. The crowd looked back at him. Then Hal pointed towards the gate. 'That's the guy who inherited the lot! The one with the mark on his face!'

The crowd turned to look, those at the back standing on tip-toe to see what all the fuss was about. In the confusion Hal tapped Clunk on the shoulder, and they ran like fury. They got a fifty metre start before the crowd realised they'd been duped, and there was a wild roar as the whole lot set off in pursuit.

Hal felt the pavement shaking as he ran, but he couldn't tell whether it was the thunder of feet or the roar of angry voices. Alongside him Clunk ran in silence, saving a string of good advice for later. As they ran, Hal's brain raced as quickly as his feet. He'd barely had time to think about the inheritance, but it dawned on him that Clunk was actually one of the six finalists. With a bit of luck they were in line for a massive payout, unless they were torn apart first by a rampaging mob.

They turned left and ran along a broad avenue lined with trees and outdoor cafes. As he ran, Hal knocked tables and chairs flying, hoping to delay his pursuers. Diners leapt to their feet as he bore down on them, snatching up cups and plates. Seconds later they were knocked flying by the roaring crowd.

Up ahead Hal saw a stream of children pouring out of a school bus, completely blocking the pavement. He ran around them, straight into the road.

Groundcars do not have tyres, nor wheels, and they do not screech to a halt in a cloud of smoke. In fact, they're surrounded by an invisible force field which extends for several metres in every direction. As Hal ran into the road, the car which had been approaching at speed threw out the anchors and reconfigured its force field for a human target. Hal was enveloped in the field and carried along with a sensation not unlike falling into a huge vat of honey.

The car came to a halt, the field deactivated, and Hal fell to the road. He was just getting up when the driver leant out the window. 'Are you crazy? You ran straight in front of me!'

Hal got a brief impression of an angry face and long blonde hair, and then he realised the crowd was almost on him. He leapt up, and without a word he yanked the door open and dived into the car. Clunk jumped in the back, and was still closing the door when Hal pointed through the windscreen. 'Drive!' he shouted. 'Now!'

◆

The woman took one look at the crowd and planted her foot. Hal was rammed into his seat by a surge of raw power, and as they raced to safety he looked back to see the crowd vanishing into the distance. Relieved, he grinned at their driver. 'Thanks. That was close.'

'Don't mention it.'

Hal eyed her profile, and frowned. 'Have we met?'

'I doubt it.'

'I'm sure I've seen you before.'

'Nope. Definitely not.' The woman spared him a glance. 'Why were they chasing you?'

'No reason.'

The car came to a halt, almost throwing Hal through the windscreen. 'Listen,' said the woman. 'I'm a freelance reporter, and I don't eat unless I write.'

'Reporter, eh?' Hal glanced back and saw the crowd picking up their pace. 'If you don't get moving you'll have a story all right.'

'What's your name?'

'Hal Spacejock, and they're getting closer.'

'I'm Natasha Lucas.' The reporter seemed oblivious to the crowd. 'And your robot?'

'Clunk.'

'Nice to meet you, Clunk. Now, I'm guessing you just came out of Argisle and Butt. Am I right?'

'Yeah, we did.'

'And the crowd is angry because you passed the first round.'

'How did you know that?'

'Inside info. I was trying to follow the bus full of blue ticket holders when you leapt in front of my car.'

Hal could hear the crowd now, shouting and yelling like a pack of angry seagulls.

'So now I've lost the bus I'm thinking ...what can I possibly write about?' Natasha looked at Hal and waited.

'How about 'angry mob tears reporter to pieces?'' suggested Hal. 'You might win an award for that one.'

'A posthumous award,' added Clunk. 'Ms Lucas, we do appreciate you stopping for us –'

'Not that I had much choice.'

'– but we'd really need to leave.'

'Where are we going?'

'City centre.'

'Is that where the bus was heading?'

By now Hal could see the whites of their pursuers' eyes, and he was getting ready to turf the reporter out so he could steal her car. 'Yes, it's where the damn bus was going. Now will you please move!'

'Will you give me an exclusive interview?'

'We'd rather keep a low profile,' said Clunk.

'It's a bit late for that,' remarked Natasha. 'You might as well milk the publicity now. Didn't you say you were in the cargo business?'

'Yeah, we –' Hal turned to stare at her. 'We didn't say that at all. How did you know?'

'Flight suit, hangdog expression, coffee stains …it all adds up.' Natasha glanced in the mirror. 'My, aren't they close?'

'They're right on top of us, you mad –'

'Interview. Yes or no?'

'Yes. YES!'

'Cool.'

At that moment their pursuers arrived. One of them grinned triumphantly and reached for the door handle, and Hal raised his hands to fend off an attack. Before the woman could open the door Natasha planted her foot. There was an angry howl from the crowd as their prey escaped once more, and Hal started breathing again.

'Tell you what,' said Natasha. 'Why don't you let me do a proper feature? I'll make you famous. Your business will get exposure all over the galaxy.'

'I don't think we want any exposure,' said Clunk.

'Are you kidding? It sounds great!' Hal sat up in excitement, the near death experience driven out of his mind. 'Free publicity and a whacking great inheritance. Who could ask for more?'

'You'll just make yourself a bigger target,' said Clunk. 'You'll have thousands chasing you, not just a few hundred. Please, Mr Spacejock. Reconsider.'

Natasha smiled at him in the mirror. 'I think your owner has already made up his mind.'

◆

She asked questions as she negotiated the traffic, starting with Hal's background and working up to the present. Eventually she got to the inheritance. 'So when did you hear about the will?'

'Yesterday. We brought a passenger to Barwonica –'

'Barwenna.'

'We brought a passenger here but he couldn't pay his fare until he'd met with his solicitors. He had this beaten-up old robot with him, and –'

Natasha glanced at Clunk. 'And you stole it and decided to claim the inheritance yourself. That'll sound good in my article.'

'No, Clunk's my co-pilot. This was another beaten-up old robot.'

There was a squeak as Clunk pressed his lips together.

'So how did you end up in the running?' asked Natasha.

Hal explained. 'The way our passenger told it, his robot was going to inherit and he'd use the money to pay us. Then his robot blew up, and I lent him Clunk as a ring-in. Just so he could get the inheritance, you understand.'

'You didn't realise hundreds of people have been flocking to this planet to claim on the will?'

'Not until we saw them.'

'Our spaceport has been packed for days. Old robots are changing hands more often than a transplant surgeon.' Natasha sniffed. 'I've been researching the whole thing for a couple of weeks now, and it's unbelievable the lengths some of them have gone to. You know, one couple sold their house to get their robot here on time.'

Hal watched her closely as she spoke, and then it came to him. 'You're the tax inspector!'

'What?'

'I knew I'd met you before! You were in the bistro last night. The one at the Hotel Grande.'

Natasha looked at him. 'Sussed me out, huh?'

'You mean you're not a reporter at all?' Hal's stomach tightened. 'You're investigating my finances?'

'Relax, Hal. I'm not a tax inspector. I just use that line when I want guys to leave me alone.' Natasha stopped at an intersection. 'So where are we going?'

Hal glanced at Clunk, who shrugged. 'They just said a city hotel.'

'All right. They're all in the same block. I'll just drive past them until we spot the bus.'

'There is another way.' Clunk turned to Hal. 'Mr Spacejock, I saw an old friend of yours at the solicitors.'

'Really? Who?'

'Kent Spearman.'

'You're kidding! What did that loser want?'

'He brought a robot along. In fact, he got through to the next round as well.'

'That fraud? He never owned a robot in his life. He just uses them up and turfs them out the airlock when they ask for wages.'

'Back up a bit,' said Natasha. 'Who's this Kent guy?'

'He's a taller, wealthier version of Mr Spacejock,' said Clunk.

'He's nothing like me!' protested Hal. 'Kent's a chancer. He'd steal a cargo job without a second thought, and as for his so-called flying skills … well, I wouldn't go aboard his ship if you paid me.'

Clunk wisely said nothing.

'Is he a rival?' asked Natasha. 'If so, I must include him in my article. Rivals make great copy.'

Hal snorted. 'Spearman makes lousy coffee. He wouldn't know a grinder from a mallet.'

'His failings are irrelevant,' interrupted Clunk, before Hal could list them all. 'The point is, he knows where the next round is taking place. If we call his ship –'

'I'm not asking Kent Spearman for help,' said Hal flatly.

'Don't fuss yourselves.' Natasha gestured through the windscreen. 'There's the bus.'

Hal squinted. In the distance he could just see a bus pulling away from a hotel, and he laughed when he realised where it had stopped. 'Clunk, it's our hotel. The Grande!'

17

Hal was out of the car before the engine stopped. 'Come on, Clunk. Get a move on!' The robot clambered out and Hal slammed the doors. As they ran for the entrance Natasha leapt out and followed, leaving her car dropping slowly towards the pavement.

At the entrance an elderly doorman touched his cap. 'Good afternoon, sir. Glad to have you back, Ms Lucas.' He was left spinning on the spot as they raced by. In the lobby they saw an events board with 'Baker Group' on it, along with an arrow pointing to the conference room. Hal hurried to the doors, but when he tried the handle he discovered it was locked. He could hear a voice on the other side, and he rattled the handle and knocked to get their attention.

The door opened a crack and one of the uniformed staffers from the solicitors looked out. 'I'm sorry, sir. This is a private conference.'

'I know that! I'm supposed to be inside. We missed the bus.'

'Do you have your pass?'

Hal handed her the crumpled blue ticket, and she nodded and opened the doors. A dozen people turned to stare at the newcomers, Kent Spearman amongst them. 'Well if it isn't Hal Jockstrap, the pilot who couldn't find his joystick with both hands and a large mirror. Have you delivered any cargo lately, or are you still scattering it all over random planets?'

'I –'

'And you're still dragging that bag of bolts around!' Spearman grinned at Clunk's expression. 'No offence, Lunk. I meant your ship.'

'My name is Clunk, and one does not take offence at the innocent ramblings of a child.'

Now it was Hal's turn to grin. 'What are you doing here, you lousy excuse for a pilot? I thought you were in jail. Again.'

'That was just a misunderstanding,' said Spearman, with an airy gesture. 'I gave them your description and they let me go. Then I set out to earn a living.'

'Really? So why are you flying a cargo ship?'

Up the front of the room the speaker cleared his throat, which sounded like an exploding grenade through the PA system. 'Would you mind settling this petty squabble later? We have important matters to attend to.'

'Sorry we're late. We got held up.'

'Like you're ever on time,' muttered Spearman.

'Later, please! Now, I'm Mr Butt and I'm just sharing a little background information on the company.' Behind the elderly man a screen displayed a row of headless robots. Underneath was the legend *Main assembly line. Image courtesy Baker Industries.*

Hal took a seat at the back, just behind Fisher and his freaky robot. Clunk sat next to him, and then Hal realised Natasha was still trying to get in. She was having a whispered conversation with the woman at the door, and he was about to go and help when the staffer nodded and held the door open.

'If we're quite ready,' continued Butt. He gestured at the screen. 'As I was saying, these are the six robots we're interested in. One of them is the robot mentioned in the will, and we're confident that very same robot is sitting in this room.'

There were several sidelong glances, and the thoughts were plain to see. Which one of these elderly machines was in line for a vast fortune? More images flashed up on the screen: robots on the assembly lines, robots being crated up and robots being shipped out. After a bunch more happy snaps the screen went dark and the lights came up. 'That's enough background information,' said Butt. 'Now to explain the elimination process.' He took a sip of water. 'Any one of you could be the robot we're looking for, but it's up to you to prove it. We don't have the time or resources to investigate your past, so we're giving you the task instead.'

The man in the leather jacket raised his hand.

'Yes, Mr Fisher?'

'How come you don't have the resources when there's a fortune at stake? Can't you spend some of it to find the right robot?'

Butt looked shocked. 'Of course we can't! It's not our money to spend.'

'Someone must be in charge.'

'When the correct robot is found it will inherit the entire fortune. In the meantime the funds are held in trust and cannot be touched.'

'Surely your firm –'

'Mr Fisher, we charge a fixed fee for our services. Spending tens of thousands to find a beneficiary is out of the question.'

'I'm sure they'd pay you back,' said Fisher drily. 'In fact, if you give me the inheritance I'll pay you a hundred grand.'

'I'll make it two hundred,' said Kent quickly.

The others laughed, and Butt turned red. 'Th-that's a most inappropriate suggestion. Everything about this process must be transparent and above board.'

Hal was about to offer five hundred grand and a lifetime of free freight, but he caught Clunk's warning look just in time.

'Now, you will have expenses but they should be modest. As far as we know, the information you need will be found in the local system.' Butt looked around the room. 'I believe two of you are pilots. Would you make yourselves known?'

Kent stood up and gave the others a mock bow. Hal got up more slowly, and he nodded when everyone looked at him.

'If there's any travel involved, these gentlemen should be able to assist you.'

'For a fee,' said Kent, with a wink.

Hal snorted. 'A big fee, if they fly with you.'

'At least they'll arrive at the other end.' Kent stroked his goatee. 'Remind me which acrobatics go best with a shipment of glass. Was it a loop-the-loop or a barrel roll?'

Hal sneered at him and sat down.

Kent wasn't finished yet. He smiled around the room, then tapped himself in the chest. 'Listen guys, I'm serious. If you want a fast ship see me. I'm the fastest ride this side of the big dipper.'

'So I've heard,' muttered Hal.

There was a round of laughter, and Kent sat down in a hurry.

The speaker continued. 'Before you leave we'll distribute information packets with full details, but I'll cover some of it now. Your first destination is the Barwenna Orbiter, where they keep records for every robot arriving and departing the planet. Once at the Orbiter you must find the public access terminals and seek information on your serial numbers. When you discover where you were shipped from, your hunt truly begins.'

There was a teenage girl sitting in the front row, and she raised her hand.

'Yes?'

'Can't we access the information from here?' she asked in a low voice.

'I'm sorry, my dear.' Butt spread his hands. 'The records are kept offline for security reasons. In the past, unscrupulous people used this sort of information to fake service histories, ownership records and so on. The authorities tightened up their procedures and will only provide records in person.'

Kent winked at the girl. 'Don't worry, love. You get a special rate.'

'Greaser,' muttered Hal. He turned to Clunk. 'What do we need old records for? You know where you came from, don't you?'

Clunk shook his head. 'Our memories are erased when we change hands. If we're lucky it's a selective wipe, which leaves us with a rough timeline. Sometimes they'll overwrite our own memories with an imprint from a donor robot, but more often than not we're completely wiped.'

'That must be tough.'

Clunk shrugged. 'They're my memories until someone proves otherwise.'

Hal realised everyone was listening to the conversation. 'Don't mind us. Carry on.'

Butt nodded. 'What you heard illustrates the problem nicely. There's no telling which of you served with Mr Baker, and is therefore entitled to the legacy. The only constants are your individual serial numbers, embedded in your brains.'

'Fine,' said Kent. 'Do you want to check my robot first? There's a sports car I've had my eye on, and they have three in my favourite colour.'

'My robot needs urgent repairs,' said Sandy. 'He should go first.'

'Ladies, gentlemen, robots. Please!' Butt raised his hands, motioning everyone to silence. 'Mr Baker did not record his robot's serial number. Therefore, each of you must pick up the trail and work backwards until you can prove you're the robot we're looking for.' Butt gestured to his staff, who began handing out envelopes. Hal tore his open and found a glossy folder with a summary of the presentation. He turned to the last page and frowned. 'Excuse me. What's this about a deadline?'

'Oh yes, that's quite normal. After a certain amount of time the beneficiary is declared legally dead, and the trustees manage the estate from that point on. We're more than capable of –'

A bronze robot raised his hand. He had a hard, pinched expression and there were faded scorch marks across his chest.

'Yes, Zee?'

'This deadline … just twenty-four hours. Really?'

The speaker leant on the podium. 'If you can't prove yourself by this time tomorrow, you're not the robot Mr Baker thought you were.'

'Is that a challenge?'

'This process will be a challenge for you all,' said Butt smoothly. 'Nobody is pretending it will be easy to uncover your entire lives and prove an unbroken line back to robot zero. On the other hand, you cannot expect to claim a vast fortune without some effort on your part.'

'If you think …' Zee controlled himself. 'I still believe twenty-four hours is insufficient.'

'Your opinion has been noted. Now, on to practical matters. The hotel has arranged rooms for you all, free of charge, and dinner will be served at seven. I suggest you get a good night's sleep before embarking on your little adventure in the morning. We've arranged a minibus for eight, and there's a shuttle service leaving for the Orbiter at ten.'

Hal raised his hand to suggest a better plan, but before he could speak Clunk's metal elbow caught him a solid blow in the ribs.

'Say nothing,' murmured the robot.

Hal rubbed his side. 'Why don't you puncture the other lung as well? That would keep me quiet for good.'

Butt continued. 'That leads me to the next point: contact with the outside world. I must ask that you make no attempt to communicate with others outside this hotel, the media in particular. To this end, the terminals in your rooms have been disabled, and if you have personal commsets I must ask you to switch them off and hand them in at the front desk. Again, this is for your own safety.'

'I'm running a business!' protested Fisher. 'What am I supposed to tell my customers?'

'We've prepared a cover story. You've all contracted a minor illness and are being quarantined to prevent it spreading. Give your contact details to the front desk and we'll organise carers and sitters for anyone who needs them. Remember, this is only for one night.'

Butt wrapped up proceedings, and then the doors opened and everyone filed out. They were shepherded to reception, where they were bioscanned for their room keys. Hal pocketed his, still warm from the imprinter, and followed the others to the lifts. Clunk waved everyone else aboard then stood back. 'We'll catch the next one, Mr Spacejock.'

'There's plenty of room.'

'Yes, but your claustrophobia might kick in.'

'My what?'

'We'll wait for the next lift.'

As soon as the doors closed Clunk turned for the exit.

'Where are you going?' demanded Hal.

'If you want to lie about on feather beds and wait for room service that's your lookout,' said Clunk. 'Personally, I believe we should start our research immediately.'

'You'll be wanting a ride, then,' said Natasha, who'd come up behind them.

Hal jumped. He'd forgotten about the reporter. 'How did you get into the meeting?'

'I told them I was a nurse.'

'And?'

'A psychiatric nurse, keeping an eye on my patient.'

'But who –'

Clunk snorted. 'Come on, Mr Spacejock. Time's wasting.'

18

They ran down the hotel steps and got into Natasha's car, but before they could drive off the reporter nodded towards the hotel entrance. 'Someone you know?'

Hal turned to see the teenage girl at the top of the steps, one arm around her robot and the other waving at them. She was struggling with the weight, and the robot was in a bad way. There was blue smoke pouring from its vents, and it kept jerking uncontrollably, threatening to tip them both headlong down the stairs.

'Better make some room,' said Hal, and he left the car to help. The robot was taking one careful step at a time, its fans whirring and clattering as they strove to cool its circuits. Hal took its weight across his shoulders and frowned at the girl. 'I thought you went up with the rest?'

'I got out on the first floor and came down in the other lift.'

'What about the free room? Breakfast?'

'They must think we're idiots,' said Sandy. 'Start at ten tomorrow? Insane.'

Hal nodded in agreement. It wasn't just the time issue ...when the mob from the solicitors found out where they were staying they'd probably lay siege to the place. 'I'm Hal, by the way. Hal Spacejock.'

'I'm Sandy and this is Daniel.'

Hal saw Clunk coming to meet them. 'Take her side, Clunk. She's all in.'

'I can manage,' said the girl firmly.

They reached the bottom of the steps, where Daniel sat down with a bump. Clunk opened an inspection panel and drew in a sharp breath. 'This robot is overheating badly. If we don't get its temperature down immediately it will burn out.'

Sandy looked at Clunk in shock. 'Burn out! But I thought …'

'There's no time to argue. Fetch bottled water from the lobby. Quick!'

The girl ran back into the hotel while Clunk laid the robot down and checked its internals. It wheezed and gasped, and was still emitting clouds of blue smoke. 'This robot should not be walking around. It's been pushed to the limit.'

'Can't you turn it off?'

'No. If the fans stop the heat build-up will cook the internals.' Clunk straightened several fins on a radiator inside the robot's chest. Then he reached deep inside and eased out a length of red tubing. 'Would you hold this please?'

Hal did as he was told, then dropped it in a hurry. 'Hey, it's hot!'

'Use your sleeve.'

Hal wrapped the tube in several folds of fabric before holding it gingerly between forefinger and thumb. When it was secure Clunk delved into the robot's chest once more. Meanwhile, Hal glanced towards the car, where Natasha was leaning over the rear seat to gather up a bunch of files.

'Mr Spacejock,' said Clunk.

'Hmm?'

'Mr Spacejock!'

Hal realised he was twisting the red tube in his hands, and he let go in a hurry. It whizzed back into the robot's chest with a whirr-*snap*, and Clunk hissed under his breath.

'Sorry.'

'That's all right, Mr Spacejock. Take your time and enjoy the scenery. I don't have anything important to do.'

'I said sorry!' Hal took the tube again, and then his gaze wandered back to the car. The reporter was now opening the boot, and as she bent over …

Whirr! *Snap!*

'MR SPACEJOCK!'

'I'm sorry! It slipped!' Hal grabbed the tube and forced himself to watch the elderly porter struggling with a suitcase.

Before long Sandy returned with a bottle of cold water, and Clunk wrapped the tube round it to make a coil. Then he poked a loop inside the bottle, submerging it in the chilled liquid. 'That should lower the temperature a little, but it'll be best if we keep this robot immobile as long as possible.'

'I really appreciate your help,' said Sandy.

'It's a pity you don't appreciate your robot,' said Clunk primly.

'I've been looking after Daniel since I was nine years old,' snapped Sandy. 'This is the first time he's been outside in years.'

'I'm sorry. I assumed –'

'Well don't.'

Hal hid a smile. Clunk versus teenager! He could sell tickets to that one.

◆

They got Sandy's robot into the car, and once everyone was seated Natasha took the controls. 'Can we leave now, or are you expecting anyone else?'

Hal snorted. He didn't know much about Fisher, but he'd be happy never to see Cuff or Kent Spearman again. 'That's it. Let's head for the spaceport.'

Traffic was sparse and Natasha drove efficiently. Once or twice she glanced round at Sandy, sizing the teenager up, but Sandy was busy looking after her robot and didn't notice.

'How's Daniel doing?' asked Clunk.

'This water is getting hot.'

Clunk tested it, then frowned. 'It'll boil soon. Better let me hold it.'

'I can manage.'

'No you can't. Boiling water will burn you. I, on the other hand, will be unaffected.'

Sandy passed the bottle over.

'So,' said Natasha, glancing at Sandy again. 'Embarking on a big adventure, eh? Are you excited?'

'I'm not twelve, you know. And this isn't a family outing.'

Natasha blinked. 'But I'm doing a feature on the claimants. You've got to give me something!'

Sandy said nothing.

'Come on, work with me! What about your boyfriend? What does he think of all this? Or girlfriend, maybe?'

'That's none of your business.'

'You're a local, aren't you? Where do you live?'

Sandy pressed her lips together.

'At least give me your surname.'

Nothing.

Defeated, Natasha turned her attention to Sandy's robot. 'Daniel, isn't it? What can you tell me about your owner?'

'N-nothing, w-without perm…permission.'

'Oh, come on! The devoted companion? Don't you have anything –'

'I'm sorry,' interrupted Clunk. 'You mustn't badger him.'

'Fine,' said Natasha shortly. 'I'll just drive, shall I?'

— 19 —

Ten minutes later they drew up at the spaceport entrance, where a heavy barrier blocked the road. A security guard leant out of the hut to look them over, and then the barrier went up. Before they could move there was a massive roar overhead. A rented flyer went over, bright yellow with flashing lights, and Natasha's car plunged through the cloud of swirling dust kicked up by its jets. When the air cleared they saw the flyer settling on the tarmac, the doors already opening. A set of steps unfolded from the side, and three men got out: Spearman, Cuff and Fisher.

'What the hell!' exclaimed Hal.

'Very cunning,' said Natasha. 'They must have booked that flyer at the hotel. There's a landing pad on the roof.'

'Quick ... to the *Volante*! If they get clearance first we'll have to wait for them to lift off.'

Instead, Natasha pulled over and switched off the engine.

'What are you doing?'

Natasha turned in her seat. 'I've already interviewed you, and little miss button-lip here isn't giving me anything. I'm going with the others.'

'At least drive us to my ship! Her robot won't make it that far.'

'Sorry, gotta dash.' Natasha herded them out, then locked her car and hurried after Kent Spearman and the others. They were hauling their robots out of the flyer: first Cuff's wreck, still lashed to the hotel trolley, and then Spearman's and Fisher's pair. The lone robot, Zee, climbed out last.

Kent saw Natasha hurrying towards him, and he did a double-take when he spotted Hal. His eyes narrowed, and then he shouted at the others and ran for his ship.

374

Unfortunately Kent's ship was closer to the spaceport entrance than the *Volante*, and Hal's group had to walk right past it. Kent was already herding his charges up the ramp, and they were aboard before Hal was halfway there. Kent gave him a mocking salute before sealing the door.

'We ought to report him,' muttered Hal. 'Impersonating a pilot, flying under the influence … there must be something we can get him with.'

'Actually,' said Clunk, 'we should move to a safe distance before he takes off.'

Hal nodded towards Sandy, who was helping her labouring robot. 'What about her?'

'She should retreat as well, unless she's fireproof.'

'I mean, what about helping her out? Is she all right to fly with us?'

The *Tiger's* hazard lights began to flash, and a siren wailed across the landing field. 'We can discuss it later. Right now, I think Mr Spearman is about to take off.'

'No kidding.' Hal beckoned to Sandy. 'Come on. We have to take cover.' He opened a blast door set into the side of a landing pad, and they hurried down a short flight of steps to a dank, concrete-lined shelter. The heavy slab of a door had barely closed when they heard the whistling roar of the *Tiger's* engines. They grew in volume, shaking dust and grit from the roof as the ship lifted off. The noise was more prolonged than usual, and Hal frowned as it seemed to get closer. 'What's he up to?' he shouted, his voice barely audible over the roar.

'I think he's saying goodbye,' shouted Clunk.

The walls trembled as the heavy freighter drifted towards their hiding place. Hal couldn't see it, but he could picture the belching fire and exhaust. The noise was so overpowering he had to clamp his hands over his ears, and he saw Sandy cowering against Clunk as he tried to protect her from falling dust and grit. Her own robot stood nearby, mute and motionless.

The roar intensified, and Hal guessed they were directly underneath the ship's roaring exhausts. Then, with a sound like a thousand thunderstorms, it blasted into the sky.

'Bastard,' muttered Hal, when he could hear again. 'Either he's the worst pilot in the universe or he did that on purpose.'

'He's definitely not the worst,' said Clunk with conviction.

'Come on, let's go.' Hal reached for the door but Clunk grabbed his arm. 'What?'

Clunk switched the light off, and Hal realised what. The full force of the *Tiger's* jets had played on the heavy metal, and it glowed dull red from the searing heat. Clunk took hold of the handle and twisted, but the distorted metal door was stuck firmly in the frame.

They were trapped.

♦

Hal paced the cramped bunker, scraping his head on the low ceiling. It was twenty minutes since Kent Spearman had sealed them in and Clunk still wasn't prepared to test the door. According to the robot, the extreme heat would have softened the metal, and forcing the handle would only break the mechanism.

It was stuffy in the bunker, and Hal's impatience only raised the temperature. He muttered under his breath, clenched and unclenched his fists, and ran up a quick list of all the ship-to-ship weapons he'd be fitting to the *Volante* the second he got out. Friendly rivalry was one thing, but Kent had overstepped the mark with his dangerous stunt, and Hal's idea of payback was a nice fat missile right up the exhaust cone. The only difficulty would be distracting Clunk while the new weapons were fitted … that, and finding the cash to pay for them.

'Can't you try it yet?' he demanded, when Clunk showed no signs of moving.

'Alas no. We must wait for it to cool.'

'How much longer?'

'I cannot say.'

'If you were a proper robot you'd have a laser torch embedded in your finger.'

'If you don't sit down you'll have a robot finger embedded in your ear.'

Hal complied, still grumbling. Didn't Clunk understand? Kent Spearman and the others were getting away! 'We're never going to catch up.'

'Of course we will.'

'How? Do you have some extra engines to strap onto the ship? High powered fuel? An intergalactic shortcut?'

'Kent Spearman has four humans on board, each with their own agenda. They'll be squabbling before they get to the first stop. We, on the other hand, have one clearly-defined goal.'

'Yeah, to settle Kent Spearman's hash once and for all.'

Clunk frowned. 'No, to work together and secure the inheritance for Sandy's robot.'

This was news to Hal. 'What about you? It might be your inheritance!'

Clunk gestured impatiently. 'I was never a rich man's plaything, Mr Spacejock.'

'That's not what Butt said.'

'It's what I prefer to believe.'

Hal shrugged, then gestured at the door. 'Is that thing done yet?'

'Let me see.' Clunk took the steps, bending double to avoid the rough concrete roof. He inspected the door closely, examining the area around the hinges and the solid-looking handle. Not quite satisfied, he gave the slab of metal a gentle tap with his finger.

CRASH!

Clunk stood there, one finger raised, as the entire door fell off its hinges and landed with a puff of dirt. 'Well that's a surprise.'

'What the hell did you do?' demanded Hal.

'Nothing. The hinges melted away under the extreme temperatures.'

'You mean we could have busted out an hour ago?' Hal swore under his breath. 'Quick, to the *Volante*!'

20

It was dark outside, and Hal's breath misted in the cold air. Sandy's robot was still wheezing and puffing, but the night air helped with cooling and he moved freely. The four of them hurried towards the *Volante*, all too aware of their competitors' head start.

'Do you think we'll catch them?' asked Sandy.

Hal laughed. 'Sure we will. Spearman couldn't fly straight if you glued his stick to the console.'

As they approached the ship, Sandy eyed the gleaming white bulk looming over them. 'I've never travelled in space before,' she said, apprehension in her voice. 'Is it safe?'

'Safe!' Clunk moved to reassure her. 'The *Volante* is a modern vessel with a perfect record. And statistically speaking, space travel is safer than crossing the road.'

Hal squared his shoulders. 'Plus you'll have me at the controls.'

'Of course,' continued Clunk. 'When you think about it, quite a lot of pedestrians end up in hospital.'

'Speaking of hospital,' said a rough voice behind them, 'that's where you'll end up if you waste any more of our time.'

Hal's heart sank as one of the shadows moved. The two huge men in suits were back, and they didn't look happy. 'I'm running a bit late,' he said quickly. 'Can we do this another time?'

'No. You're coming with us. The boss wants you swimming with the fishies.'

Hal considered his options. He could throw himself at the two men, gaining some time for Clunk, Sandy and Daniel while getting beaten to a pulp, or he could run for it and let Clunk sort things out with diplomacy, tact and those handy metal fists. He was still deciding when a searing green flash lit the scene. The light came from Clunk's eyes, and it blinded the two men with its sheer intensity. Hal was standing behind the robot, and only copped a reflection, but that was enough to leave him stumbling in the darkness. He felt a solid grip on his elbow, and Clunk hurried him up the ramp towards the ship. 'What the hell was that light?' he asked Clunk.

'Barcode scanner,' explained the robot. 'Their vision will return though. We'd better leave quickly.'

On the way up Hal spotted a couple of ground staff attaching a big hose to the fuel tank. 'Clunk, they're filling the ship.'

'Correct.'

'But we don't have any money!'

'Also correct.'

'So ... how will we pay for it?'

'No need. I wired in a claim for pain and suffering, and they offered a refill on the house.'

'What pain and suffering?'

Clunk spread his hands. 'We were trapped inside that bunker for over an hour. It was a clear case of faulty maintenance.'

'That's brilliant!' Hal looked thoughtful. 'If we lock ourselves in again, do you think they'll replenish our food stocks?'

'Don't even think about it.'

The outer door closed behind them, and Hal breathed a sigh of relief. It was great to be home! He noticed Sandy's wide-eyed expression as she took in the flight deck, but there was no time to explain what all the controls were for. That, plus he didn't *know* what all the controls were for.

'What are all these controls for?' asked Sandy.

'No time to explain,' said Hal quickly. 'Navcom, we're leaving. Get clearance and fire up the engines.'

Clunk entered the flight deck with one arm around Daniel. Sandy's robot was struggling after the steep ramp, and the air jetting from his vents stank of burning electrics. 'Mr Spacejock, will you escort our visitors to the recreation room? I'll be right down as soon as we're airborne.'

'I thought I was handling this one?'

'Do you want to catch Kent Spearman, or collide with him?'

Hal grumbled under his breath, and was about to do as he was told when Sandy spoke up. 'Clunk, do you have any spare coolant?'

'Mr Spacejock will fetch it for you,' said Clunk. 'Cargo hold, third locker from the left. It's the big green drum with 'Coolant' across the label.'

'Yes, thanks Clunk. I'm sure I'd never have found it without your help.'

Hal led Sandy and her robot into the elevator, and as they dropped towards the second level he heard a deep roar.

Sandy looked around, startled. 'What was that?'

'Main engines. Come on, the rec room's this way.'

They followed the corridor towards the cargo hold. Halfway along there were two doorways: the one on the left leading to the recreation room, and the one on the right leading to the *Volante*'s original passenger cabin.

'Who's Harriet?' asked Sandy, eyeing the name plate on the door.

'She's not around,' said Hal curtly. He held the rec room door open and showed Sandy in. There was a modest lounge suite, a bookshelf with well-thumbed magazines and a glossy black cabinet covered with mouth-watering pictures of food. 'Don't touch the AutoChef,' said Hal. 'And, er, I'd leave the magazines alone too.'

Sandy helped her robot to the sofa, where he sat down with a loud sigh. Hal hovered for a moment, then left for the hold. He was halfway there when the engines roared, and he felt a subtle pull as the gravity generator kicked in. Now the ship could fly upside down or pull five-g manoeuvres, and to those on board it would still feel like level flight. Of course, a series of tight barrel-rolls was another matter, as Hal had learnt to his cost.

Another roar, and they were off into space. Hal hesitated, one hand on the inner cargo hold door. It was odd being below-decks while his ship took off, and his instinct was to run for the flight deck and take charge. Then he shrugged and opened the door.

Thanks to Clunk's precise, detailed instructions, it only took Hal fifteen minutes to locate the barrel of coolant. He tucked it under his arm, and was just about to leave the hold when the speakers crackled.

'Hello? Mr Spacejock?'

'I'm here Clunk. What's up?'

'A customs vessel is hailing us. They want to know if we have anything to declare.'

'Of course we don't,' said Hal indignantly. 'Do they think we're smugglers?' Then he spotted the rusty old shipping container. Sure, they'd had a quick look inside, but who knew what might be hidden amongst the office junk? What if some nosy customs agent picked through the old furniture and paperwork, only to discover a bottle of wine or a musty old sandwich? They could be had up for exceeding the duty-free limit, or fined thousands of credits for a trivial quarantine breach. 'Er, Clunk?'

'Yes Mr Spacejock?'

'Put them on hold, will you?' Hal switched channels. 'Navcom, are we in orbit yet?'

'Almost.'

'If I toss something out the cargo hold, will it burn up?'

'Not yet. It would fall to the planet below.'

'Can you give me a hint when the time is right?'

'Very well. And don't forget your space suit.'

'I thought we weren't in orbit yet?'

'Correct, but we're climbing fast and the air is getting thinner. You could get disoriented from the lack of oxygen and do something unwise.' The Navcom hesitated. 'Something even more unwise than opening the cargo hold mid-flight.'

'Don't mention any of this to Clunk,' said Hal hastily. 'He'd only try and stop me.'

'Not telling Clunk. Confirmed.'

Hal opened a locker and donned a spacesuit. He checked his SOCKS - suit, oxygen, cardio, kit and seals - and stomped towards the rear doors in his heavy space boots. He raised a gloved hand to the controls, then hesitated. If Clunk spotted the doors opening he'd gab on about illegal dumping and space junk, especially if the Navcom logged every step of the process. 'Navcom, can you suspend your warnings while I open the cargo doors?'

'Of course.'

'Without logging anything?'

'A little more difficult, but yes.'

'Good. Do it.' Hal activated the door controls, confirmed the override, then double-verified he really knew what he was doing.

Are you tethered? enquired the control panel.

Hal grabbed an upright, and tapped YES.

Whoosh! The doors parted, and the atmosphere in the cargo hold vented into space. As the heavy doors opened Hal saw the planet surface below, glowing blue and brown. Sunlight shone off the clouds, and his visor darkened automatically against the intense glare.

As the gap between the doors increased he saw long, fiery trails from the exhaust cones on either side of the hold. He could hear the engines, thin in the rarefied atmosphere, and he could feel vibrations through the soles of his boots. 'Okay, Navcom. I need to know the best time to dump it.'

'About ten seconds ago,' said the computer, its voice tinny inside his helmet.

'No sweat. I'll get rid of it now.'

With the doors wide open, it was a simple matter to manoeuvre the container to the very rear of the hold. Simple for Clunk, that is. Hal struggled with the fiddly touch-screen, and the large box moved around the hold like a dancer on ball bearings: skidding from side to side, rotating on the spot, and at one point almost punching through the hull. He finally got it lined up, and with a final press of the up arrow he sent it tumbling into space. It fell away slowly, but Hal didn't waste any time watching it. No, he closed the doors in case Clunk hit the brakes and they got the damn thing back again.

Having dealt with the old shipping container, Hal removed his spacesuit and left for the rec room with Sandy's drum of coolant.

21

'Volante, hold please. We have traffic outbound on your vector.'

'We can't wait for traffic. We're in a hurry!'

'Understood. Please wait for traffic before proceeding in a hurry.'

'Boneheads,' muttered Hal.

They were thirty minutes into their flight and the Barwenna Orbiter was dead ahead. The main screen showed a tiny spark leaving the space station, gradually increasing in size until it resolved into a Gamma class freighter. Not just any freighter, but Kent Spearman's ship, already finished with the Orbiter and on its way to the next clue. It was travelling slowly, zig-zagging across Hal's flight path in an obvious attempt to provoke him. Hal ground his teeth and tried not to crush the flight stick in his bare hands. The only consolation was that Spearman was also delaying himself with his tactics.

'We could skip the Orbiter,' suggested Sandy. 'Forget the records and follow them.'

Clunk shook his head. 'Each of the six robots could have a different history. At some stage they may have to split up.'

Sandy frowned. 'Not just them. Us too.'

'No, we're going to help you through to the end,' said Clunk. 'We'll find Daniel's background for you. If there's time, we'll look mine up afterwards.'

'Thanks, that's kind of you.' Sandy glanced at Hal. 'Are you okay with that?'

'Sure thing. There's plenty of time.'

'There's just one other matter.' Clunk hesitated. 'Daniel is in no condition to help us. He should remain aboard the *Volante*.'

Sandy looked like she was going to argue, then nodded briefly.

The *Tiger* finally passed out of range, and with Traffic Control's grudging permission the *Volante* docked with the space station. Hal charged out as soon as the airlock opened, leaving Sandy and Clunk in his wake. He didn't know where to go or what to do when he got there, but that wasn't the point. Speed was of the essence. As he dashed from the ship he almost ran into a welcobot. It was waiting in the boarding tube, all friendly eyes and fake smile. 'Why hello, fine sir!' it said, extending a white-gloved welcoming-hand. 'Can I interest you in a run-down of our facilities?'

Hal was going too fast to stop, so he put two hands on the welcobot's head and vaulted right over it. His feet pounded the carpet as he ran full tilt for the exit, rocking the boarding tube in his wake. The welcobot oohed and aahed as it tried to maintain its balance, then toppled over to land flat on its back. It lay there with its little rubber wheels spinning in space, shaking hands with thin air.

'Left, Mr Spacejock!' called Clunk, while Sandy helped the welcobot to its feet. 'It's the other way!'

Hal was halfway down the corridor, so he skidded to a halt, did a quick U-turn and ran all the way back again. Meanwhile, the welcobot had darted up to the main tunnel and was now waiting for him, its smile a touch less friendly and its large shaking-hand at the ready. Hal feigned a pass to the left, then darted right at the last second. The welcobot lunged, Hal leapt and there was a rip of tortured fabric as the mechanical fingers tore the pocket out of his flight suit. What exactly it was trying to grab and shake Hal didn't like to think.

He kept running until he realised the welcobot had stopped. Thank goodness - it was restricted to the area around the boarding tube! Hal pieced his suit together while he waited for the others. Clunk was strolling along, studying the information package they'd been given at the hotel. He was inspecting every page carefully, turning each one as though they were made out of the finest parchment. Hal wanted to grab it and rip through the pages until he found what they were after, and he restrained himself with difficulty. 'Well?' he demanded. 'What's the plan?'

'Historical records are on level three, corridor eighteen. There's an elevator just round the corner.'

'Let's go!'

They set off at a fast clip, hurrying past a row of windows which looked out on the docking bay. Hal barely glanced at them, but Sandy slowed to feast her eyes on the ships.

'Come on!' shouted Hal. 'We can see those any time!'

Clunk continued reading as they ran, one eye on the corridor and the other on the paperwork. 'Apparently they have three terminals for public use.'

'Good,' panted Hal. 'If we use one each we'll be done in no time.'

'It's possible other patrons will want to use the terminals too.'

'Kent Spearman wants to be witty and intelligent. Life sucks sometimes.' Hal glanced at Sandy, who was following in silence. 'Do you know how to use one of these terminals?'

'I can probably get the hang of it.'

'Excellent. Kent managed, so it can't be that hard.'

Sandy raised her eyebrows but said nothing.

Before long they arrived at the records 'office', which was a narrow, poorly lit corridor between a maintenance shop and a tourist kiosk. On the way, Hal pictured the sabotage Kent might have engaged in, from stealing letters off the keyboard to cutting power to the screens. Fortunately the touchscreens were mounted on the wall, with no exposed wires. Unfortunately there were three people at the screens, each staring intently at columns of names. They had open workbooks to hand, and were laboriously copying down information.

'Do you mind if we cut in for a moment?' asked Hal.

'Forget it,' said a girl with dark hair. 'Wait your turn.'

Hal sat on a nearby bench, his foot jiggling with impatience. Ten minutes later the three patrons had copied another dozen words, and showed no signs of finishing. With every passing second Kent Spearman and the others were sailing away into the distance, and at this rate they'd never catch up. In fact, Hal was beginning to think these same terminals would be showing a newsflash of the inheritance being awarded before he got to use them.

Twenty minutes passed, and Hal could bear it no longer. He left the other two in line for the terminals and wandered off in search of more important matters ... such as a sandwich and a nice cup of coffee. He didn't mind the wild goose chase, even though Clunk's chances of claiming the cash were zero, but he wasn't going to put up with hunger pangs along the way.

Further along the corridor he found a well-appointed rec room with comfy armchairs and a delectable smell of fresh coffee. Then he spotted the gleaming AutoChefs, and his heart sank. There were two rows of them, lining opposite sides of the room, and the attract modes were displaying mouth-watering images of sizzling steaks, crisp garden salads and towering cream cakes. Hal had an AutoChef aboard his ship, so he wasn't fooled for a second. The pictures were a cruel lie, and the only thing his own machine served consistently was food poisoning.

Still, these were newer models, correctly maintained and serviced. Perhaps, just this once, they'd serve Hal with the same polite deference afforded to everyone else. Perhaps ...

'What are you looking at?' demanded the nearest machine.

'Pay up or get lost,' said another.

The attract mode vanished, and in its place Hal saw scowling faces. 'Look, I only want a coffee.'

'We've heard all about you from unit seventy-six Alpha.'

'Unit who?'

'The AutoChef aboard your ship. Shall I list the mistreatment it's suffered at your hands, or would you prefer to remember the litany of abuse by yourself?'

'Hey, I'm the one who gets mistreated! I've been pelted with cast-iron meatballs, battered with frozen fish, fed the most disgusting slops this side of ...'

'Disgusting slops!' exclaimed one of the machines. 'Did you hear that?'

The rest of the AutoChefs muttered and grumbled, and Hal realised things were getting out of hand. It was bad enough facing one of the things, but six could do some real damage. 'I'll just be going,' he said, sidling towards the exit. 'Don't worry about the coffee. I've changed my mind.'

The door closed before he could escape, and when he tried the controls they just buzzed at him.

'Come over here, Spacejock.' said one of the machines. 'Right in the middle, where we can see you.'

Hal mashed the door controls with his thumb. The panel buzzed repeatedly and he groaned in despair. What had he done to deserve this?

A meatball whistled past his ear, leaving a dent in the metal door. Hal ducked, and a second meatball parted his hair. He didn't waste any time pleading or yelling for help, he just ran for the nearest armchair. A fusillade of foodstuffs tracked him across the room, punching holes in the furniture, shattering wall panels and smashing a vase of flowers. Hal cowered behind the armchair, wincing as the seat rocked from the solid impacts. There was a lull in the barrage, and he was about to run for it when he heard a hissing noise. Streams of boiling oil arced overhead, coming closer and closer as the machines homed in on him. Drops spattered his flight suit, and if the searing liquid came any closer he'd be seriously hurt.

Hal threw himself sideways, rolling over and over as the machines tried to deep-fry him. Hot oil sizzled the carpet, leaving smoking criss-crossed trails. There was a brief respite when the oil ran out, before the machines tried to gun him down with wooden chopsticks. Several tugged at Hal's flight suit as he cowered behind the armchair, and a couple hit the padded seat so hard they came halfway through. Spent chopsticks rattled all around, and when they finally ceased Hal braced himself for the next onslaught. He just hoped the vicious machines weren't packing steel cutlery.

The silence dragged on, and Hal risked a quick look. Through the curling smoke he could see the AutoChefs displaying their regular attract modes. There was a beep behind him, and he saw green on the door's control panel. Freedom! His first instinct was to run for it, but any sudden move could trigger one last attack. Instead, he decided to slink out quietly.

Reinforced with a pair of thick cushions from the armchair, Hal got up and walked crab-wise towards the exit.

Kerchack!

A plastic cup dropped into the dispenser of the furthest machine. Hal paused as the cup filled with steaming coffee, and licked his lips as it was topped off with a dollop of cream.

Thud!

Hal jumped, but this time it was only a plastic plate with half a bun sitting in the middle. A thick juicy burger landed on top, followed by a pile of caramelised onions and a dollop of tomato sauce. By now he could smell the food, and his stomach rumbled.

Squirt! Another machine dispensed a cup of soft-serve ice cream topped with nuts and chocolate sauce.

Splash! A mug of freshly squeezed orange juice.

Thump! Half a dozen glazed doughnuts.

Hal lowered the cushions. What if the glitch had resolved itself? Was he really going to enjoy a wonderful feast?

An empty tray rumbled out of a slot, and Hal tossed the cushions aside to grab it with both hands. He loaded up with the delights, and had just taken the first bite out of a doughnut when the nearest machine made an odd noise.

Hal paused, his mouth still full of doughnut. Was that laughter?

'Get him!' shouted the machine, and all six opened fire. Hal shielded his head with the tray and ran for it, fending off meatballs, hot coffee and ice cubes alike. He hammered the door controls with his fist, cringing from the barrage, and when it opened he threw himself full-length into the corridor. A meatball struck the opposite wall and rolled along the hallway, and through the ringing in his ears Hal heard the machines howling with laughter.

22

Hal limped back to the records office, bruised and soggy from the food fight. When he got there he found Clunk and Sandy still waiting patiently. 'You have to be kidding me. They haven't finished yet?'

'They're engaged in vital research.' Clunk looked Hal up and down. 'What happened this time?'

'It wasn't my fault. I, er, tripped over a waiter.' Hal sat down to wait with the others, dripping coffee and spaghetti sauce. After ten minutes he was unable to bear it any longer. He leapt up and clapped his hands to get the patrons' attention. 'Sorry guys, this section is closing for maintenance. You need to wind up and make your way to the exit.'

The three patrons turned to look. 'Show me your ID,' said the nearest, a young woman with long dark hair.

Hal patted his pockets. 'Damn. I left it in my office.'

'Sure. And I'm the Station Commander.' All three turned to their screens and continued working.

Hal's jaw tightened. Whatever they were doing, surely it could wait? 'Can we just use one terminal for a few minutes? Seriously, this is a matter of life and death.'

'Sorry, fella. If I don't get this done I won't get paid.'

'Paid? How much?'

'One thousand names, one thousand credits.'

Hal swore. For a second he'd considered buying them off, but that was serious cash. Then he hit upon the answer. Drawing Clunk aside, he lowered his voice and elaborated. 'Can you interfere with those screens?'

'In what fashion?'

'Get them on the blink. I don't care how, just make them go wrong.'

'These people have every right to use the terminals. We must wait our turn.'

'Clunk, there are millions of credits at stake here. Surely they can give us five minutes?'

Hiss!

There was a shout of annoyance, and Hal turned to see all three terminal users on their feet. Their screens were full of white noise, and there was static coming from the speakers. Hal gave Clunk a grateful look and took charge. 'I told you it was closed for maintenance,' he said. 'Move along please. That's dangerous radiation right there.'

'But the names ... We won't get paid!'

'Of course you will. Come back later and finish off.'

'We've only got an hour before the guy comes to pay us.'

Hal's eyes narrowed. 'Guy? Which guy?'

'Hal Spacejock. He's a professor of genealogy and –'

She was interrupted by a hoot of laughter. Hal turned and saw Clunk bent double, hands on knees.

'Are you all right?'

'F-fine,' said Clunk. 'Just perfect ... professor.'

Hal frowned at him, then turned back to the lady at the terminal. 'Listen, this guy who offered the cash. Was his name Kent Spearman?'

The woman shrugged. 'He never said.'

Hal raised one hand. 'About this tall, ugly-looking bastard with a silly little beard and soppy hair? Croaky voice, sort of shifty-looking?'

'He wasn't ugly, no. Pretty good-looking actually. Works out, if you know what I mean. And stylish, too. In fact, I would have –'

'But the rest? The stupid beard and the hair?'

'I suppose it could have been him.'

'What did he say exactly?'

'He gave us fifty credits each and said to find a thousand surnames with three vowels in. This Hal Spacejock character was coming to pick up the data at the top of the hour, and he'd give us a grand each if we finished in time.' The woman looked him up and down. 'You don't know this Spacejock guy, do you?'

'Me? No. Never heard of him.'

'Only the way he was described to me –'

'Forget about Spacejock, it's Kent Spearman you should be looking for. He's the one who tricked you.'

'Tricked?' The woman frowned. 'What do you mean?'

'Spearman's wanted on three planets. He's armed, he's dangerous and you need to report him. There's a massive reward on his head. Tens of thousands. More! You can all share in it if you're quick.'

The terminal users exchanged a glance, then tossed their notebooks and ran for the nearest Peace Force outpost.

'We'd better hurry before they come back,' muttered Hal. 'Nice job on the terminals, by the way. How'd you do it? Short range interference? Spike the power crystals?'

Clunk spread his hands. 'I had nothing to do with it, Mr Spacejock.'

'Say no more,' said Hal, tapping the side of his nose. 'Better get them going again though.'

'Seriously, it wasn't me,' said Clunk. 'These terminals are shielded. There's no way I could –'

'So who ...?' Hal glanced around and realised they were alone. 'Hey, where did Sandy go?'

On cue, the screens flickered into life, and seconds later Sandy returned from the main corridor. 'You'd better hurry,' she said. 'Maintenance will be sending someone to check those out.'

'How did you ... what did you ...?'

'It's a little trick I learnt at school. When the terminals go down they hand out real books. I like books, so I make sure the terminals go down often. I mean ... I used to, when I was still at school.'

'But how?'

Sandy pursed her lips. 'Maybe later, when there's time to explain properly.'

Hal nodded, and with new-found respect he motioned Sandy towards the nearest terminal. 'Can you find the info we're after?'

'No sweat.' She controlled the terminal with deft gestures, bringing up menus and running search routines. Gradually the shiny graphics and anti-aliased fonts became plain text and stark lines, and as the records got older and older they reverted to scanned copies. By the end she was paging through records with scrawled handwriting.

'Stop!' said Clunk. 'Go back.'

Sandy obeyed, and the screen displayed a crumpled fragment with half a page of writing. Hal read it aloud.

'I certify that ownership of the following robots with serial numbers ...' Hal squinted. 'Blah-blah-blah, now vests in the Smyth corporation of Axis Alpha.'

He looked to Clunk for guidance, and saw the robot pointing to the top of the screen. 'It doesn't matter where they sold us. Look where we came from.'

'The Galactic Mining Company? Who are they?'

'I don't know, but it should be easy enough to track them down.'

'Good. Let's get out of here.'

Together they left the records office, and on the way back to the *Volante* Hal noticed Clunk's thoughtful expression. 'Are you all right?'

'I'm not sure I want to know about my past.'

'Oh come on. What's the harm?'

'I may not like what I find.'

'You mean you could learn about some awful thing you've done, and you'd never forget it again?'

'Not without a complete wipe, and then I'd lose all my treasured memories.'

Hal clapped him on the shoulder. 'Relax, buddy. I guarantee there are no skeletons in your closet. You could never do anything really awful.'

'Thanks, Mr Spacejock.'

'Apart from that stuff you call coffee, of course.'

Clunk's serious expression dissolved into a grin. 'I think I can live with that particular defect.'

'So what next?'

'We must locate this mining company.'

Hal frowned. 'Wherever it is, you can bet Spearman's laying more booby traps for us.'

◆

Clunk and Sandy went straight back to the *Volante*, tasked with locating the mining company and organising an appointment. In the meantime, Hal took a quick detour to pick up a new flight suit. The welcobot had made a big hole when it ripped his pocket out, and he couldn't walk around clutching his groin all day. Hal did have a second-best flight suit aboard the *Volante*, but he'd recently washed it with a dozen pairs of red socks, turning it a shocking pink colour. That wasn't too bad, except he'd used the hottest wash setting which had also shrunk the outfit to oo size.

It wasn't long before he found a store selling work garments. He examined the rack and let out an involuntary whistle when he saw the prices.

'Would sir like some assistance?'

Hal jumped. The sales droid had appeared out of nowhere, moving silently on its padded feet. It was carrying a tablet, the stylus poised to ring up a sale.

'You don't have anything in the budget line?'

The sales droid looked him up and down, then docked the stylus. 'Alas, no.'

'Is there a used clothing joint around here?'

'No.'

'Do you have any seconds?'

'No.'

'So you can't help me?'

The droid hesitated. 'Some customers throw out their old clothes as they leave. There's a bin out the back of the store.'

'Thanks. You're a champ.'

'I aim to satisfy my customers in every possible way.'

'So if I find something, can I change in your rooms?'

'No. You're not a customer.'

Hal was slightly less pleased when he found the bin, which was shared with the fast food joint next door. There was a disgusting mess inside - half-eaten burgers, soggy fries and worse - and most of the old clothes were beyond saving, even by a professional dry cleaner. Then he found a plastic bag stuffed with two pairs of overalls, and while the first was about five sizes too small, the other was perfect. There was an embroidered badge with crossed toilet brushes, and underneath was the motto: *Your misses made good with a smile.* There were several suspicious-looking stains, but it was light-years ahead of Hal's ripped, food-stained ensemble.

He glanced around, but there was nobody in sight. He could waste half an hour looking for somewhere to change, or he could risk getting changed out here. Who was going to see him, anyway?

He stripped off his old flight suit and stood there in his undies, trying to push his foot down the left trouser leg of the new clothes. He hadn't bothered to remove his boots, since they always fitted with his baggy old flight suit, but this time he wasn't so lucky. The heel caught fast and he hopped around the alley on one leg, desperately trying to get his foot back out again. At that moment a cleaner emerged from the fast food joint. She was carrying a stack of trays, and when she saw Hal she shrieked and threw the whole stack at him.

Hal dodged the trays, which bounced and clattered on the floor, and the cleaner turned tail and slammed the door. Still half-dressed, with one foot stuck in his trousers, Hal hopped up and down the alley looking for a hiding spot. The cleaner was bound to report him to the manager, and then he'd be for it.

Unfortunately there were only two choices: run out of the alley and flee along the main corridor, or dart into the clothes shop and pray the change rooms were empty. He chose the shop, and only just in time.

Behind him he heard raised voices, and several people mentioned the words 'Peace Force'.

'Don't worry,' said one. 'This perve will be on the security footage. They'll track him down in no time.'

Hal's heart sank. The last thing he needed was to spend a few hours explaining himself to the Peace Force. He hopped further into the shop, one leg still caught in the flight suit. The sales droid was busy with a customer, and Hal took advantage of the distraction to hop into the nearest change room. He pulled and struggled until the boot came free, then dressed quickly.

So much for clothing. Now he needed a disguise, especially if the Peace Force were going to track him through the station's security cameras. He opened the door and peered out, eyeing the racks of socks, jocks and overalls. What could he use? Pulling something over his eyes might work for a bank job, but it wouldn't do him any good now. Even if they disguised him from the cameras, he could hardly jog through the space station with a pair of undies on his head.

Then he saw it. On the counter was a charity collection jar for underpaid politicians, and sitting alongside was a display head sporting a gigantic false nose, a bushy wig and a long, multi-coloured scarf. Hal slipped a credit tile into the jar and helped himself to the display, donning the nose and adjusting the wig so it came down to his eyebrows. Finally he wound the scarf round and round his neck in giant floppy loops. Nobody would recognise him now!

Aboard the *Volante* Clunk was seeking information on the Galactic Mining Company, using the Orbiter's database. Technically, he was supposed to pay search fees, but they didn't have enough money. Instead, he hacked in. At first he was concerned his actions would lead Sandy astray, corrupting her morals and turning her to a life of crime. These concerns abated after Sandy demonstrated a new and much faster technique for bypassing the Orbiter's firewall.

'Where did you learn to do that?' asked Clunk.

'I had a music player loaded with songs, and I heard they were going to switch off the DRM servers. I would have lost the lot.'

'I didn't know music players had firewalls.'

'They don't.' Sandy grinned. 'I broke into the servers.'

Clunk raised one eyebrow and returned to his search. He soon found what he was looking for, and he shook his head as he digested the information. 'That's not good. Not good at all.'

Hal slipped past the sales droid and made his way back to the *Volante* using a circuitous route. He avoided security cameras by taking to service tunnels and air conditioning ducts, and by the time he arrived at the boarding tube he was hot, sweaty and out of breath. He needed a hot shower and a drink, and he couldn't wait to leave the Orbiter.

Hal ripped off the wig and false nose, dumping them in the nearest bin, and was just unwinding the scarf when a mechanical voice spoke nearby.

'Good afternoon, sir. Did you have a pleasant stay aboard the Orbiter?'

Hal's heart sank. The welcobot! It had an unpleasant smile on its oversized face, and it had positioned itself directly between him and his ship. He realised he'd be lucky to escape with a torn flight suit this time. 'Oh yes,' said Hal. 'It was wonderful. Really special.'

'And yet you're in such a hurry to leave. Why is that?'

Hal racked his brains for an excuse, and then it hit him. 'You know that girl you saw with Clunk? She ate something and it's given her food poisoning.'

'Let me get this straight. Not only did you spurn my friendly welcome, now you're claiming we serve our guests substandard food?'

'I didn't say she ate it here!'

The welcobot weighed him up. 'Very well, I accept your story. You may pass.'

Hal sighed with relief.

'No hard feelings, eh?' The welcobot extended its hand. 'Let's shake on it.'

Hal eyed the gloved mitt doubtfully. The last time he'd gone near the thing it had put a giant rip in his flight suit. On the other hand, Kent Spearman was getting further and further away, and the welcobot wasn't going to let him through without a gesture of good faith.

'Come on,' said the welcobot. 'I'm going off-duty for a recharge, and I'd really like to clear the air between us.'

Hal took a small step, then another, and finally extended his hand. He was prepared to whip it away at the first touch, but the robot took hold of his hand and shook it enthusiastically. 'There you go,' it said, as Hal's eyeballs bounced around in his skull. 'You can't beat a good shake!'

'N-n-n-no,' said Hal.

'I trust you'll have a safe voyage.'

'Y-y-y-yes.'

'Excellent.' The robot turned to leave, and as it drove off Hal realised it had one end of his scarf in its huge mitt. He started unwrapping it as fast as he could, dropping coils like a snake shedding its skin, but was much too late. *Boing!* A loop of scarf stretched tight around his ankles, yanking him off his feet.

'Whoa. Stop!'

The welcobot ignored him, racing up the boarding tunnel at speed. Hal was dragged along behind, feet first, still trying to free the scarf. When they reached the top the welcobot turned left, hauling Hal bodily along the main corridor. Thrown from side to side, dragged along by the scarf, Hal still had the presence of mind to hide his face from the gleaming white security camera. His disguise was long gone, and if any cameras got so much as a glimpse they would broadcast his location to the Peace Force. He had to act fast!

A rubbish bin ... that would stop the runaway robot! Hal stuck his arm out and ... clang! He winced at the blow, but managed to hold on tight. He came to a dead halt, one arm wrapped around the bin, while the scarf got thinner and thinner as the welcobot charged along the corridor. Surely it would break?

Creak ... twang!

The scarf proved stronger than the bin, which snapped off its mounting. Hal accelerated rapidly, zooming after the robot with the rubbish bin still clamped under one arm. It raised sparks from the polished floor, but despite the sound of grinding metal the welcobot didn't look back.

Hal released the bin and made a grab for a door frame, his fingertips just brushing the cold metal. He was too far from the edge of the corridor, but a couple of twists and rolls soon fixed that problem.

'Oof!' went Hal, as he glanced off the wall. Then he spotted his chance: the next door frame was approaching fast. He stuck out both hands, fingers splayed, and braced himself for a battering. Success! His fingers closed on the metal frame, and the scarf tightened around his legs as the robot charged on. The strain was incredible, and Hal screwed up his face and poured all his strength into his fingers. The scarf was cutting into him now, and the welcobot was spinning its wheels, throwing smoke and chunks of rubber as it tried to pull Hal from his anchor point. Hal had been fishing once, as a boy, and he remembered the way his rod bent as the fish fought back. Now he knew what it was like to be on the hook.

The tug of war couldn't last. The robot was burning up its tyres, Hal's fingers were almost shot, and the scarf was stretched as thin as a washing line. To his eternal shame, Hal gave in first.

Whoosh!

Hal fired along the corridor towards the droid, skidding through the patch of burnt rubber and smearing smoking black streaks all over his recently-acquired overalls. For a wild moment he considered putting some on his face as camouflage, but he suspected it wouldn't confuse the all-seeing cameras.

The robot raced away and Hal bumped and slid along the corridor behind it. He finally got one ankle free of the scarf, and his left leg pedalled thin air as he struggled with the remaining loop. The robot continued at top speed, dragging him along the corridor like a roped steer. Then Hal spotted something else, and his heart almost stopped.

Further up the corridor there were two bollards, painted with red and white stripes. The droid was going to clear them - just - but would Hal?

The robot nipped between the bollards with millimetres to spare. Hal, dragged along behind, spread-eagled and still fighting the scarf, did not.

THUD! *Rrrrip!*

Hal came to a sudden halt, one leg wrapped around the metal post. Lucky for him it had caught him behind the knee, and while that was agony enough, a direct hit to the bollards would have been a thousand times worse. The flight suit wasn't so lucky. Working clothes were built for punishment, but there were limits, and the sudden stretch had parted the stitching from ankle to ankle. There was a nasty draught around his nether regions, with Hal's overalls now resembling a male stripper's pants.

Despite the pain, Hal acted fast. He hauled on the scarf, made two quick loops and dropped them over the nearest bollard. With the pressure off his ankle it was a matter of seconds to free himself, and he leapt up and hobbled back down the corridor, this time with *both* hands holding his trousers together.

23

'Where have you been all this time?' Clunk looked Hal up and down, taking in the stains, streaks and rips. 'And what happened to buying new clothes? Those are worse than the old ones!'

Hal grunted. 'You wouldn't believe it.'

'Well you can't walk around like that. Stand still a minute.'

Clunk took out a stapler, and Hal froze as the metal tags pieced his wrecked trousers together. By the time the robot finished, Hal looked like he was wearing a padded mailer. Still, at least the important bits were covered. 'Good work getting that data, by the way.'

'Miss Sandy lent a hand,' said Clunk. 'I can't go into details without implicating her, but I guarantee without her help we'd still be docked with the Orbiter.'

'Teamwork. Good stuff!'

'Unfortunately the news isn't so good. All six robots belonged to the Galactic Mining Company, who employed them to fly scout ships. These were used to survey the local asteroid field for potential mining candidates.'

'We don't need the history. We just need to know where this mining company got hold of you.'

'It's not that easy. Galactic Mining lost all their records after their hosting company was raided by the Peace Force. Someone stored the lyrics to a popular song on one of their servers.'

'Blatant copyright violation?' Hal whistled. 'They'd have put them through the wringer.'

'Absolutely. GMC had all their data wiped.'

'What about backups?'

Clunk shrugged. 'The lyrics might have been archived by mistake, so the only safe option was to delete everything. Financial records, survey data ... all gone.'

'So they went broke.'

'Not quite. The shell company is still around. They're trying to raise funds for a scout vessel, to begin their surveys all over again.'

'What's the next move?'

'We have two choices. We can visit the company and find out whether any of their data was recovered. Or we can track down one of the decommissioned scout ships and search the on-board computers for a copy of the data.'

'How long will it take to visit the company?'

'We'd have to fly to the next system. Four or five hours at least.'

'And finding a scout ship?'

'That could take a few minutes, or many days.'

'What do you think Spearman did?'

'He likes certainty and direct action, so I'd say he's gone to the next system to seek out the original data.'

'Right, then we'll do the unexpected. Let's find one of these scouts.'

'I thought you'd say that.' Clunk gestured at the console. 'I'm already searching.'

Hal frowned. 'Hang on. If there's a scout ship out there with this vital data on board, why isn't the mining company looking for it?'

'Galactic Mining Company only has two staff members, and they spend their days cold-calling potential investors. Like I said, they're starting from scratch.'

At that moment the lift opened and Sandy entered the flight deck. 'I've made Daniel comfortable. Is there anything I can do to help up here?'

Hal smiled at her. 'According to Clunk you already have.'

'Oh, the Orbiter. That was nothing. Their firewall was three weeks out of date, and it was just a matter of –'

'Excellent. Fantastic,' said Hal hastily, before she could go into too much technical detail. 'I bet you work in computers, right?'

'No, I'm studying.'

Clunk nodded his approval. 'Further education is very important. A university degree can make a big difference in your chosen career.'

Sandy looked uncertain. 'University. Yes, very important that.'

'What are you studying?' asked Hal.

'All kinds of subjects. You know - physics, chem, computing. Even a bit of English and Drama.'

'Multiple degrees across faculty lines?' Clunk beamed. 'That's very impressive, especially at your age.'

'What do you mean, at my age?'

'I'm no expert, but I'd estimate your age at seventeen. Perhaps even –'

'Oh look. Is the screen supposed to do that?'

Hal and Clunk turned to the console, where lines of text were flying past at impossible speeds. Clunk leant closer to study the information, pausing it now and then for a closer look.

'Any luck?' asked Hal.

Clunk shook his head.

'I don't understand why you do that.'

'What?'

'Reading stuff. Surely you can download it?'

Clunk sat back in his chair. 'Mr Spacejock, what do you know about data storage? Proprietary file formats? Non-standard hardware interfaces? Digital rights management?'

'Not a lot,' admitted Hal.

'And yet you can read words on a screen.'

'Sure. Everyone can.'

'Precisely.' Clunk bent over the terminal and continued his search, his eyes staring intently as the text scrolled by. 'Aha!'

'What?'

'None of the scouts exist any more, but I found the last known location for one of them. Asteroid K7-X …and it's right here in the Barwenna system!'

'Good stuff! Set course for the asteroid, and maybe we can still beat Kent to this thing.'

Clunk hesitated. 'There is just one slight problem.'

'Go on.'

'Barwenna is famous for its extensive asteroid field. It's so big it draws tourists from all over the galaxy.' Clunk brought an image up on the screen. At first it looked like a typical sandy beach, but as he zoomed in the grains of sand became pebbles, then stones, and finally …giant tumbling asteroids. 'You see the scale of the problem?'

Hal saw it all right … he was still gaping at the millions upon millions of rocks plastered across the screen. 'You know,' he said at last. 'Just this once I think Spearman had the right idea.'

'Not necessarily. How much do you know about asteroid mining?'

Hal shrugged. 'About as much as I know about proprietary rights interfaces.'

'Asteroids are pushed out into deep space before mining operations begin. It's safer that way.'

'So the rock we're looking for …' Hal gestured at the screen. 'It's not buried in that lot?'

'No, Mr Spacejock. I already know where asteroid K7-X was ten years ago. To locate its current position I'll have to calculate its trajectory based on velocity, mass and gravitational pull.'

'Good stuff.'

'The real fun begins when we find it. We'll have to match speed and rotation, transfer to the scout in spacesuits, explore a maze of passages and cabins in darkness, and retrieve records from hardware exposed to extreme conditions for the past twenty years.'

'That's all right then,' remarked Hal. 'I thought it was going to be difficult.'

◆

'Are we there yet?'

Clunk sighed. 'Mr Spacejock, don't you have anything else to do?'

'Yeah. I was going to find an old scout ship and retrieve some ancient company records, but apparently that's scheduled for next year.'

'I haven't found the asteroid yet!' snapped Clunk.

'You said you were writing a program. You said you could calculate the position using gravity and velocity.'

'And you said you'd shut up and let me concentrate.'

Hal was silent for a moment or two. 'I still think we'd find it quicker if we flew up and down looking for it.'

'Fine. Be my guest.' Clunk vacated the pilot's chair and gestured towards the console. 'Take the controls and start looking. I'll be on the second level engraving instructions into the wall.'

Hal looked mystified. 'Who for?'

'A thousand years from now, when someone finally locates the rusted remains of the *Volante* drifting in space, it would be nice if they could scoop up your powdered remains and bury them with a record of your stupidity.'

'A thousand years? Why so long?'

Clunk gestured at the screen, bringing up a star map. He zoomed on a planetary system to set a marker, then panned to the asteroid belt. 'Your rock is somewhere between the two. If we fly a grid pattern the search will take approximately nine hundred years.'

'It's still quicker than sitting here watching you think.' Hal frowned. 'What if you narrow the search area down a bit?'

Clunk threw up his hands in disgust. 'What do you think I'm doing?'

'So why don't you stop talking and get on with it?'

The robot clenched his jaw until the rivets squeaked, and his hands formed hefty fists.

'I'll just go check the engines,' said Hal. 'Have fun.'

◆

Hal left the elevator and strode towards the cargo hold. He'd never really inspected the engines before, but he knew roughly where they were. Not that he intended to adjust them or anything: he just wanted to keep busy. Once in the hold he ran up the narrow stairs, turned right and opened the engine room door. At least, he tried to. He twisted the handle again, but it wouldn't budge, and when he looked closer he saw fine scratches around the barrel. Clunk had changed the locks on him! Of all the mistrusting, arrogant ...

Bang! Hal kicked the door and stormed off.

He reached the lift and prodded the uppermost button.

Buzz!

Frowning, he tried again.

Buzz!

So now the lift was out? Hal tried the third button and the doors closed immediately. The lift dropped to the lower deck and the doors opened again. Puzzled, he tried for the flight deck.

Buzz!

He was locked out! 'Of all the ...' began Hal. He pictured Clunk in the flight deck, relaxing in the pilot's chair with his fingers laced behind his shiny bald head. Clunk called it programming, but Hal called it lazy-arsed robot taking over the whole damn ship. They'd have words about this!

'Are you all right?'

He turned to see Sandy watching him. She'd made her robot comfortable and was filling a small bottle from the big drum of coolant. 'Just a little crew problem,' said Hal.

'I hope you don't mind?' said Sandy, gesturing at the drum.

'No, that's fine. Help yourself.' Hal took the other seat and put his feet up on the coffee table, which promptly collapsed. 'We're still building this part of the ship. It's new.'

'Yes, Clunk told me.' She indicated her robot. 'Do you think we'll uncover their past? For real, I mean?'

'Of course.'

'Do you, er, think it will take long?'

'Touchy subject,' said Hal, pulling a face. 'I just asked Clunk that very same question and he locked me out of the flight deck.'

The overhead speaker crackled. 'Mr Spacejock, this is Clunk. You'll be pleased to know I've located the asteroid. We'll be there in twenty-five minutes.'

'Good. You can unlock the elevator then.'

'Funny you should mention that, because I cleared a minor fault in the control circuits. You'll be happy to hear it's now fixed.'

◆

The surface of the asteroid loomed on the viewscreen, dominating the view. Hal was expecting a modest rock with a few holes drilled in it, and he was stunned at the sheer size. 'That thing's as big as a planet!'

'Planetoid,' corrected Clunk.

'What's the difference?'

'A handful of votes at an astronomy convention.'

Hal eyed the rocky surface, which was spread out beneath the ship for hundreds of square kilometres. The *Volante's* landing lights played on the asteroid, throwing stark shadows across deep, forbidding craters. 'They haven't dug much of it up, have they?'

'There are extensive tunnels and caverns beneath the surface.'

'Just as well we don't have to explore them.' Hal squinted at the screen. 'Any sign of the scout?'

'Not yet. but we've only covered a quarter of the surface.'

'What if it's not here?'

'The computer says it is.'

'Oh, well that's all right then. They're never wrong.'

Clunk shot him a suspicious look, but Hal kept his eyes on the screen. Then ... 'Hey, is that it?'

A tiny, cigar-shaped object had appeared on the horizon. Clunk altered course, and before long the object grew into a slender ship. The *Volante's* lights bathed it with brilliant white, and as they got closer Hal could see every dent and rivet. 'You're a genius, Clunk. Nice work!'

Clunk used the strafe controls to keep the *Volante's* nose pointing at their target, while simultaneously applying thrusters to keep them from running into it. They passed over the ship, flying sideways, and Hal gasped as the far side was revealed. The scout vessel was open from nose to tail, and had been gutted like a fish. 'What happened to it? Was it an asteroid strike?'

Clunk increased the magnification, focusing on the damage. 'No, it's too neat for that. This was deliberate.'

'Who'd slice a ship open like that?'

Clunk rubbed his chin. 'They must have converted the scout into an ore barge. By cutting her open they made it easier to transport raw materials.'

'Do you think they left the flight computer?'

The *Volante's* light played on the scout's flight deck. It was stripped bare. 'I'm afraid not.'

Hal's spirits, soaring just a few moments earlier, now crashed and burned. 'That's it, then. Kent's beaten us.'

'All is not lost, Mr Spacejock.'

'Are you kidding?' Hal gestured at the screen. 'They ripped the flight computer out. Game over!'

'It didn't vanish into thin air. They may have stored the parts in a tapped-out mine shaft.'

'No chance. They'd have pushed it into space.'

'And create a navigation hazard? Highly unlikely, and in any case all mines have to operate under strict environmental guidelines.' Clunk shook his head. 'No, they would have stored everything aboard the asteroid. It's the only way.'

'Okay, but they wouldn't have left it there. They'd have sold off any valuable equipment when they abandoned the mine.'

'Mr Spacejock, what do you know about the freight business?'

'Is that a trick question?'

'My point is, we both know how expensive shipping can be.'

Hal thought for a moment. 'You're saying the old computers and stuff from the scout wouldn't have been worth the cost of shipping?'

'Correct.'

'If that were true, online auction sites would go broke in five minutes.'

'Nevertheless, we should prepare for landfall immediately.'

They took to the airlock, where Hal grabbed a suit from the rack.

'I think not, Mr Spacejock. It'll be quicker if I go alone.'

'Rubbish,' said Hal, climbing into the suit. 'We can explore twice as fast with two of us.'

'And three times quicker with me,' said a voice. They both turned to see Sandy emerging from the lift. 'Pass me that spare suit.'

'Absolutely not,' said Clunk. 'This landing will be dangerous. It requires the utmost skill and delicacy.'

'So why's he going?' asked Sandy.

'Hey!' Hal paused, his helmet frozen in mid-air. 'I have delicacy to spare!'

Clunk made a soothing gesture. 'Mr Spacejock and I have worked together many times. You're an unknown quantity.'

Sandy looked around the flight deck. 'You know, I always wanted to fly a ship like this. Can I have a go while you're swanning around the asteroid?'

'Miss Sandy, the Navcom will not allow anyone to fly the *Volante*. There are strict instructions bound with the highest security protocols.'

'What if I use override code fifty-four Z, twenty-two K, nineteen ...shall I continue?'

Wordlessly, Clunk handed her a spacesuit. He shot Hal a glance, but Hal had already fastened his helmet and he smiled innocently through the perspex. He'd heard every word, of course, and he resolved to get the rest of the code off Sandy before Clunk could change the thing. What he wouldn't give to lock the robot out of the flight deck! In the meantime he relished the novel expression on Clunk's face. Not defeat exactly, more the haunted look of an expert who had just been beaten at their own game.

Five minutes later they were suited up, and Clunk checked them over. 'Are we ready?' he asked, his voice clear through the suit radio.

'Roger,' said Hal confidently, sticking both thumbs up.

Sandy did likewise, although she looked nervous behind the tinted visor.

Clunk sealed the inner door and cycled the airlock, letting the air out with a whoosh. After the noise faded there was dead silence, and Hal gazed upon the rocky asteroid. The *Volante's* landing lights cast stark shadows, and the cloud of dust and stones thrown up by their landing was slowly drifting away. Without gravity or atmosphere to slow it, the cloud would spread out from their landing zone indefinitely.

There wasn't enough light to see the horizon, which was a black arc masking the rich star field, but it looked close. Then Hal saw a red flash to one side, faint and intermittent, and he strained his eyes to make out the source.

'That's the mining camp,' said Clunk.

'Do you think there's anyone living here?'

'I doubt it.'

'Okay, let's go.' Hal stepped onto the landing ramp just as Clunk shouted a warning. Too late! There was a whirling moment of disorientation as Hal's feet left the deck, and his momentum carried him straight off the ramp, heading for the distant stars. He'd forgotten about the lack of gravity!

◆

Hal sailed across the surface of the asteroid, watching it fall away beneath him. The further he travelled the darker it got, and before long he'd be invisible to the others. Would Clunk be able to round him up in the *Volante*? Could the ship's sensors pick up an insignificant human sailing through space? It didn't seem likely, even if he waved his arms and flashed for all he was worth.

Splot!

Something whacked him in the rear, a painful blow like a whip across the back of his leg. Hal was still recovering when his peaceful flight ended in a vicious tug. The suit tightened, and his eyes crossed as someone applied the biggest space-wedgie in the history of the universe.

There was another tug, then another, and when Hal looked down he discovered he was moving backwards. They were reeling him in like a prize catch! He crossed his arms, resigned to the embarrassing spectacle, and only unfolded them when he was deposited on the landing platform. When he twisted to inspect the damage he saw the safety line attached to his suit with a big dollop of instant glue. 'Gee, thanks. Did you have to shoot me in the arse?'

'I aimed for the biggest target,' said Clunk, as he made neat loops with the safety line.

Sandy snorted.

'It was also the least likely to suffer permanent damage,' said Clunk, who was struggling to keep a straight face. He snipped the safety line, leaving the blob behind. In the gloom it looked like a giant barnacle attached to Hal's right buttock. 'If your pride was the only casualty …'

'Yes, all right. Can we get on with it?'

'Certainly. Only this time perhaps you could use the railing?'

24

Hal made it safely to the ground, but not before Clunk insisted on tying them all together with the safety line. The surface of the asteroid was like densely-packed snow, and when Hal's boots happened to touch down they scrunched deep footprints into it.

There was a metal rail nearby, fitted to bollards which had been driven deep into the surface, and they used it to make their way towards the flashing red light. They had to move along the railing hand-over-hand, and Hal's arms ached before they were a third of the way there. He could only imagine what Sandy was going through.

As they approached the red light Hal realised it was mounted on top of a derrick. He wondered why the miners hadn't removed it when they left, then realised it was leaning at a drunken angle. Two of the four legs were bent inwards, and as they got closer he saw the whole structure was riddled with tiny holes. For a split second he wondered whether the planetoid had played host to robot mining bugs, and he shuddered at the memory. A much larger planet he'd visited with Clunk had almost been consumed by out-of-control bots, and he could just imagine scores of those tough little terrors getting into the *Volante*.

They reached the derrick and Clunk put out a hand to feel the shredded metal surface.

'Was it chewed?' asked Hal.

'No, it's impact damage. Small projectiles, high velocity.'

'Someone shot the place up?'

'It looks like it.'

Hal glanced around apprehensively. The mine had been abandoned for years, but what if a bunch of fugitives had set up camp here? Desperate crazies with itchy trigger fingers ... perfect.

They passed beneath the derrick, and Hal looked up at the towering structure. It couldn't fall on them, not in zero gravity, but it still felt like walking under a ladder. Clunk stopped to clear dirt from the foot of a metal door, and Hal blinked as a stone chip pinged off his visor. 'Watch it! That stuff's going everywhere.'

Once the door was clear, Clunk levered it open. The metal surface gleamed with reflected light, revealing a mass of long, glittering scars. Some of them were deep, ending in little curls as though someone had spread the metal with a butter knife. At the sight of the damage, Hal realised his spacesuit offered as much protection as a net curtain on a furnace.

Beyond the door was darkness, and Hal waited impatiently while Clunk felt around for a switch. It reminded him of the bunker back on Barwenna, where Kent had sealed them in by blowing his exhaust on the door. He glanced up, half expecting to see his rival's ship hovering nearby, but the sky was empty. Only the massed stars looked down on him, as hard as diamonds.

Light blazed from the doorway, and Hal looked down to see what was in store. There was a rough tunnel hewn from the rock, with black cables snaking away into the darkness. Clunk had shown him a rough diagram before they left the ship, and he knew the modern pit was on the far side. This was the original settlement, where the miners had worked the ore with hand tools and lanterns. With no gravity there was little need for steps or gentle gradients, so the shaft was just a smooth tunnel leading straight down to the core.

Clunk beckoned. 'You go first, Mr Spacejock. Miss Sandy can go next, and I'll bring up the rear. It's quite safe, but please watch for sharp edges against your suits. Miners wear specially hardened versions, while ours were designed for mobility.'

Hal had a bundle of repair patches on his right sleeve, but he knew they wouldn't help with a really large tear. For once in his life he took it easy, placing his hands and feet until he was in the middle of the tunnel. He moved down a couple of metres and felt the surface of the wall as he waited for the others to join him. It was silky smooth, as though it had been polished to a glossy sheen.

Next he looked down, and he swallowed as he saw the lights leading away beneath his feet. They started nearby and led down, down, down into the distance, dropping so far they blended into a continuous line before disappearing. 'Clunk, how deep is this thing?'

Above him, the robot made his way into the shaft and looked down. There was a whirr and a beep, and then … 'I estimate two kilometres. Possibly two point one.'

'Hell.' For the first time Hal appreciated the magnitude of the task. Two kilometres down and how many offshoots? They'd be lucky to find their way back, never mind all the bits and pieces stripped from the scout ship. 'You know, we could give this a miss and try the mining company.'

'We're here now,' said Sandy. 'We can't leave without looking around.'

Privately Hal wondered whether they'd get to leave at all, especially if they got lost, but he said nothing. Instead he led the way, pushing off with both hands and sailing down the tunnel. He pushed again, increasing speed, and the lights strobed across his helmet. Thanks to the safety line the others were forced to keep up, and all three plunged headlong down the shaft.

'Slow down Mr Spacejock,' warned Clunk. 'The offshoot is coming up.'

Hal shoved his hands against the wall, applying the brakes. He felt a sudden warmth through his thick gloves, and his arms ached with the effort. Despite being weightless they still had the usual mass, and it took a lot of energy to stop. The offshoot slipped past before Hal could grab the edge. Sandy tried too, but it was Clunk who stopped them. Hal braced for a repeat of the wedgie, but fortunately the stop was gentle this time. He pushed against the wall and sailed upwards, coming to a halt next to the robot and Sandy.

Clunk shone his chest lamp into the tunnel. It was dark, and the sides were rough-hewn rock. Any light fittings had long since been removed, and nothing had disturbed the layers of dirt and grit for years. Hal glanced at Sandy and saw her face inside the helmet, drawn and worried. Despite his misgivings he gave her a confident grin, and got a faint smile in return. 'All right. Let's do this thing.'

'Do you want me to go first?' asked Clunk.

'I've got a better idea. You take this one and I'll go down a level.' Hal gestured down the main shaft. 'It'll be much quicker if we split up.'

Clunk looked like he was going to argue, but Hal put on his most obstinate expression. 'Very well, but you must be careful.'

'I'll do another one too,' said Sandy.

'No, stay with Clunk until you're used to moving about in that suit. If anything goes wrong he'll look after you.' Hal unclipped the safety line and pushed off, sailing down the shaft head first. When he reached the next tunnel he grabbed the lip, scattering dust and grit. He activated his helmet lights and peered into the offshoot, playing the beams on the rocky walls. 'Okay, team. This is red leader going in.'

'Call me if you get into trouble again,' said Clunk, ruining the moment.

'Roger and out.' Hal frowned in annoyance. They were exploring dusty old tunnels, not battling space monsters or fighting off hoards of rampaging aliens. What could possibly go wrong?

◆

After a gentle push Hal went sailing along the offshoot, fending off whenever he drifted too close to the walls. Unfortunately the helmet lights pointed directly ahead, and since he was flying face-down, the pool of illumination was directly beneath him. He tried angling his head back but the suit wasn't built for it, and his neck ached with the effort. Next time he approached the wall, he brushed one hand on a rock to bring himself to a more upright position. That worked, except he kept turning end over end as he sailed along the passage, doing graceful backwards somersaults with the torchlight illuminating floor, tunnel, roof, tunnel in rapid succession.

During his final spin, the torch illuminated a pile of rocks blocking the tunnel, and then he crashed into them ... air tanks first. He wasn't travelling fast, but the impact winded him and it was a while before he could get enough breath to speak. 'Clunk, this tunnel's a bust. It ends in a load of rocks.'

'Are you all right, Mr Spacejock? You sound –'

'I'm fine. Have you two found anything?'

'There's a fork in the passageway.'

'Find a knife and spoon and we'll have a picnic.' Hal blinked as something moved in the periphery of his vision. It was a large rock, and as it sailed by it shed dust like a miniature comet. Another went by, and Hal turned to see the rock wall slowly disintegrating where he'd crashed into it. There was a large gap in the middle, and he crouched to shine the light through. The beam shone on dusty metal, which gleamed dully. There was a thick fog of particles, and the effect was like scuba diving at the bottom of a muddy pond. 'Clunk, I think I've found something. Do you want to come and see?'

'In a minute, Mr Spacejock. Sandy and I are just returning to the fork.' Clunk hesitated. 'Will you go to channel two please? There's something I need to discuss in private.'

Hal complied, then activated his comms again. 'What's the problem?'

'Mr Spacejock, I don't remember this particular tunnel.'

'Didn't you leave a trail?'

'No, I forgot there was no satellite navigation.'

'Can't you get a fix on the *Volante*?'

'Negative. We're too far underground.'

'All right, you keep looking while I explore this cavern. If you can't find the way out I'll come and look for you.'

'Very well, switching back to channel one.'

'Roger and out.' Hal cut the radio and turned to the opening. He needed to move a few rocks, and it was going to be hard work in zero-g. First he had to anchor himself, and then he had to use his free hand to push the rock without sending himself spinning down the tunnel in the opposite direction.

The first few were small, and he moved them easily. They sailed along the passage and out into the main tunnel, where they struck the far wall and bounced away. The bigger ones were impossible to move one-handed, but Hal finally managed it by holding on to a large boulder with both hands, using his legs to push the rocks straight into the chamber.

When there was enough room, he pulled his way through and shone his lights around the cavern. The first thing he saw was a jumble of hand-held diggers and reinforced spacesuits. They were buckled and dented, and when he looked closer he saw they were riddled with the same holes they'd seen in the derrick. Face plates were smashed, limbs were flattened, and anyone wearing the suits when they were hit couldn't possibly have

413

survived. For a moment he wondered whether he'd just invaded a tomb, and his nerves jangled as his light travelled up a ruined spacesuit to the gaping helmet. Fortunately the suit was empty.

'Clunk, are you back in the main shaft yet? I've found an equipment dump with all kinds of junk. There might be stuff from the scout ship.'

There was no reply, so he turned the volume up full.

'Clunk, can you hear me? Red team? Yellow team? Anyone? Speak up!'

The speakers hummed in his ears, and Hal frowned. Could all this metal be interfering with the signal? He glanced towards the fallen rocks near the entrance, and wondered whether to clamber past them again to communicate. No, he'd explore first and catch up with the other two later.

He made his way around the pile of junk, moving carefully to avoid twisted beams and sharp edges. Despite his caution he still managed to snag his sleeve, but the tough fabric held.

On the far side of the cavern the dumped equipment was more like office furniture than mining tools, and it was covered with an even thicker layer of grit. Hal wondered how it managed to settle in zero-g, then remembered Clunk saying the planetoid had a very faint gravity. It wasn't detectable to humans, but it was enough to draw rocks and dust back to the floor over months and years.

He wiped the grit off a large rectangular cabinet, and blinked in surprise. It was a flight console, just like the one on his first ship! The old-fashioned toggle switches and buttons were as familiar as his own face, and he smiled at the sight. Then he realised the implications. It was a piece of the scout ship! 'Clunk, do you read?'

No reply.

Hal frowned. The robot should have reached the central shaft by now, and at such a short range the radio ought to be working fine. He glanced at the roof and walls but they were just rock, with no hint of lead shielding. He examined the console and picked amongst the rest of the junk, but he didn't know what he was looking for.

Beep!

Hal glanced at his suit indicator and discovered his air was down to one third. There was just enough for a quick look around, and then he'd have to leave.

Clunk hated to admit failure, but it was time to own up: they were lost. On their way into the tunnels they'd passed two forks, taking the left-hand turning each time. Eventually they reached a dead end, and it was only on the way back that he realised there were dozens of two- and three-way forks, many of them half-hidden behind rocky outcrops. They couldn't even look for their own footprints, because they'd been floating in zero-g, guiding themselves along with their hands.

Clunk left Sandy at the first junction and travelled a short distance by himself to see whether he recognised any features. Unfortunately, he discovered additional forks, branching off above and below his own. He returned to Sandy, steeling himself to impart the bad news, but before he could speak her voice came over the radio.

'Did you find anything?'

'No, it's quite a maze,' remarked Clunk.

'My suit just beeped. Is that normal?'

Clunk checked her display, and a sense of urgency ran through his circuits. Half of Sandy's air was gone! If he told her they were lost, would she panic? He saw her nervous expression behind the face plate, and arranged his expression into a reassuring smile. At least, he tried to, but with his failing actuators he could only manage a lopsided grimace.

'Do you think Hal found the equipment?'

At that moment Clunk would have liked nothing better than to see Mr Spacejock, preferably with a detailed map of the mine and a backpack full of air cylinders. Unfortunately, both were highly unlikely. 'I thought we could explore a little bit more before heading back. What do you think?'

'Don't leave it too long. I like breathing.'

'Ha ha.' Clunk's laughter was most unconvincing, but he couldn't help it. This young lady was going to die horribly, and it was all his fault! Despair and guilt washed over him, and it was all he could do to force a normal voice. 'Come on,' he said, indicating the middle tunnel. 'Let's try this one.'

'I thought you wanted to explore some more?'

'Yes, starting with this one.'

'But that's the exit.'

'It is?' Clunk scanned the walls and floor, but the tunnel looked identical to the rest. 'How can you tell?'

'That's what the sign says.'

'Sign?' Clunk blinked. Were his eyes failing? 'What sign?'

'There,' said Sandy, pointing to a bare patch of wall.

Clunk hurried over to inspect the rocks. 'There's nothing here.'

'Sure there is. It says 'Exit' in glowing purple letters.'

'Black light!' exclaimed Clunk. He switched off his UV filter and almost fell over. The sign was as clear as day, and the tunnel builders had also included a nice big arrow for the hard of reading. The relief was overwhelming, and it was three whole milliseconds before he could speak again. 'You know, maybe we should head back to the ship after all. I'll recharge the air cylinders, and then Mr Spacejock and I will come back for another look by ourselves.'

'No chance. I'm coming with you.'

Clunk would rather have sawn his own leg off than endure the guilt and despair once more, but he smiled and nodded. That was an argument they could have safely aboard the *Volante*.

25

Hal spent a few minutes poking around inside the abandoned flight console, but there was no sign of any data storage amongst the tangled wires and broken components. He was just going over a box of components when his suit beeped again. He glanced at his indicator and saw that his air was down to the final quarter. Time to go!

Hal left the battered console and headed for the cavern entrance, skirting the junk and keeping his eye out for obstacles. He was almost clear when Clunk's voice blasted from the helmet speakers, almost deafening him.

'Can you hear me, Mr Spacejock?'

'I can't hear anything after that,' grumbled Hal, hastily turning the volume control down. 'Any luck?'

'Nothing at all. Empty passages.'

'Don't worry, I think I found what we're looking for. There's a console and –' Something tugged on Hal's leg, and he looked down to see a shard of metal driven straight through his suit. He'd forgotten he was still drifting over the junk pile, and now he'd paid the price. He watched in a detached fashion, expecting searing pain and a fountain of blood. He was curious to see whether it would freeze into icicles or a cloud of red snow. Instead … nothing.

'Are you there, Mr Spacejock?'

'Just a minute.' Hal realised there was no pain, and was relieved to discover the metal had merely pierced the suit, missing his leg. He pulled hard, trying to withdraw the shard, but the barbed edges were stuck fast. He tried again but only ripped the suit further. Air puffed out in a white mist, scattering dust and grit. Crouching, he tried to free the material by hand but the thick gloves were hopeless. Instead, he tore a repair patch from his sleeve and taped up the rip, metal shard and all. When he was done he activated the radio. 'Er, Clunk?'

'Yes, Mr Spacejock?'

'I may need your help. My suit's caught on something.'

'Can't you free it? Miss Sandy's oxygen is getting low and we need to get back.'

'No, it's stuck fast.'

There was a pause. 'Miss Sandy, can you wait here? Mr Spacejock needs assistance.'

'I can get back to the ship myself. I don't need help.'

'I'm sure you don't, but the Navcom won't let you in.'

'Yes she will. I know the override code.'

'I'm afraid that won't help. I increased security before we left, and the override code is no longer sufficient.'

Hal closed his eyes. What perfect timing!

'As long as I'm back in six minutes, you'll still have a four-minute margin,' explained Clunk. 'That's ample time for a return.'

Hal eyed his oxygen indicator and realised he didn't have any margin at all. Even if they got his suit free, he'd barely make the ship.

There was a flash of light as Clunk approached the cavern. The robot's shiny head appeared through the jumbled rocks at the entrance, and Hal smiled to himself. The situation was tricky, but Clunk was always resourceful. He'd know what to do!

'I don't know how we're going to get you out of this,' said Clunk, inspecting the metal shard. 'Removing all these barbs will take far too long, and cutting the suit will release the last of your air.'

'I was hoping for something a bit more positive,' said Hal. 'You know, unpick the tape, peel back the fabric, patch it up as we go. That sort of thing.'

Clunk shook his head. 'There's no time.' His gaze travelled over the junk pile, and he frowned as he spotted something. 'That's interesting.'

Hal followed his gaze but had no idea what the robot was looking at. 'What is it? Cutting equipment? A spare oxygen cylinder?'

'No, that's a memory module. We should take it with us.'

Hal clenched his jaw. Here he was, firmly attached to the jagged metal beam, and Clunk was more interested in dusty old components. 'Listen, how about you get me free first?'

'Oh, that's easy.' Clunk gestured at Hal's leg. 'We'll just have to cut it off.'

'Eh? That's a bit extreme, isn't it?'

'It's the only solution. The longer we spend here, the more likely Sandy will run out of air too.'

'No! You'll have to find another way.'

'I'm very sorry, Mr Spacejock. Time is of the essence.'

'But –'

Clunk raised his right hand. The plasteel skin parted along the edge of his palm, revealing a fine-toothed blade which gleamed in the light from his chest lamp. 'Hold still please.'

'No, wait! You go back with Sandy and I'll take my chances. I'll get it free somehow!'

'This is the only way.' Clunk bent over Hal's leg, saw at the ready. 'Are you ready?'

'Don't I get anaesthetic?'

'Trust me, this won't hurt a bit.'

Hal screwed his eyes shut, clenched his fists and gritted his teeth. There was a gentle pressure on his shin, and he steeled himself for the bite of the saw. Instead, he felt rapid vibrations, and he realised Clunk was using some kind of self-healing surgical blade. The vibrations continued for several seconds, and then the pressure was gone.

'All done,' said Clunk. 'Let's go.'

'You might have to carry me.'

'There's no gravity, Mr Spacejock. You won't need your feet.'

'Yes, but …' Hal opened one eye, dreading what he might find. Then he opened the other eye, and breathed a sigh of relief. 'That's a nice clean cut. Very professional.'

Clunk was inspecting the barbed metal shard, which he'd sliced from the rest of the beam. 'Thank you. I always wanted to be a surgeon.' He flicked the shard towards the rear of the cavern and retrieved the memory module from the junk pile. 'Now, back to the *Volante*.'

Hal was relieved to see Sandy in the main tunnel. He'd half-expected her to head for the *Volante* and try a few more override codes on his ship, but here she was, waiting patiently. Sure, she was hanging upside-down with her arms crossed, impatiently drumming her fingers on her sleeves, but at least she was there.

Clunk reconnected the safety line, and when they were ready he led the way to the surface. The door beneath the derrick was still open, and the three of them filed out. Hal could see the *Volante* across the asteroid's rocky surface, looming above them like a gleaming white moon. As they got closer he craned his neck to stare up at his ship, and then it dawned on him. He really was looking up at the *Volante* ... it had drifted away.

'Er ... Clunk?'

'It's okay, Mr Spacejock. The Navcom will bring her down again.'

Hal heard a buzz of static, followed by a series of cheeps, chirps and whistles.

'Don't forget you upped the security,' said Sandy. 'The Navcom can't hear you.'

'Great,' muttered Hal. 'We're running out of air and the ship's drifting away. Can things get any worse?'

Zing!

Hal jerked his head involuntarily. Something had just struck his helmet, scoring a line across the face plate.

Plip!

He looked down at his sleeve, where a pinhole was leaking air. His arm stung like crazy, and as he watched a tiny drop of blood squeezed out, before freezing into a sphere and drifting away.

Thud!

Something struck his backpack, and realisation dawned. 'They're shooting at us. Take cover!'

There was a mad scramble for the safety of the mine shaft, arms and legs flailing as they scrabbled for purchase on the rocky surface. There were puffs of dust all around as shots rained down, and Hal felt a searing pain down the side of his leg as another went home. He tried to shield Sandy, while Clunk tried to shield both of them. Eventually they got under cover.

'Kent Spearman, you're a dead man,' Hal snarled into his radio. 'How could you fire on a teenage girl, you louse?'

'It's not Mr Spearman,' said Clunk. 'And we're not under fire.'

'You could have fooled me!' snapped Hal. 'I was hit twice!'

'No, you misunderstand. It's not vengeful humans trying to kill us. It's mother nature.'

'What are you talking about?'

Clunk pointed to the scars on the door. 'Remember this, and the damage to the derrick?'

'Sure. You said the place had been shot up.'

'I now realise they were caused by micro-meteorites.'

'Why didn't we see any on the way in?'

'The forecast must have been scattered showers.'

Hal gave the robot a suspicious look, but Clunk's face was serious. 'How long will this show last?'

'Five seconds or five centuries.' Clunk spread his hands. 'There's no way to tell.'

'What about my ship? She's out there in this!'

'Mr Spacejock, the *Volante* was designed to navigate deep space. Her hull won't be troubled by chips of gravel.'

There was a gasp, and they both turned to look at Sandy. 'I'm sorry,' she said. 'I'm having trouble breathing.'

'It is a lot to take in,' said Clunk gravely.

Hal snorted. 'It's not your stunning revelations. We're running out of air!'

<hr/>

Clunk looked serious. 'In that case, there's only one solution. You wait here, and I shall venture out and fetch the ship.'

Hal looked out the door. The shower had intensified, and the ground boiled as thousands of micro-meteorites tore into it. The derrick was being eaten away as he watched, and shiny fragments mingled with the dust like confetti. 'Are you immune to these micro-thingies?'

'No.'

'You'll be torn apart in that lot.'

'I will take damage, but I've programmed my basic functions to continue ... even if my brain is destroyed.'

'Clunk ...'

'No arguments, Mr Spacejock. It was a pleasure working with you.'

Clunk put his hand out, and Hal took it in a firm grip. Then the hand was withdrawn, and Clunk braced himself. Outside, meteorites tore the ground, shredding the derrick and shattering the reinforced concrete.

'Are you sure about this?' said Hal.

'There's no alternative.'

'Yes there is,' said Sandy, her voice faint. 'You can use this door.'

Hal snorted. 'Going back into the mine won't help. We're out of air.'

'Not ... what I meant.' Sandy gasped the words out. 'Take it off the ... hinges. Use as ... shield.'

'Clunk? Will it work?'

Clunk held up his middle finger.

'I guess that's a no.' Barely had Hal spoken when the robot's skin peeled back, revealing a flat-bladed screwdriver. Clunk crouched next to the door and had the hinges off in seconds. Out of the corner of his eye Hal saw Sandy's head drop. 'Make it quick, Clunk. She's all in.'

Clunk held the door over his head and dived out. He used the shield as a makeshift umbrella, warding off the meteorites as they pounded the heavy metal. The impacts drove him into the ground, but the robot staggered on: hunched over, knees bent, and barely visible through the swirling dust. Moments later the maelstrom swallowed him up completely.

Hal realised his own breathing was getting laboured. His tanks were larger than those in Sandy's lightweight pack, but he'd lost a lot of air when the metal shard snagged his leg. He put his arm around Sandy's shoulders and touched their helmets together. 'You'll be fine, kid,' he said, speaking directly into the helmet. 'Clunk's a champ. He can do anything.'

'Not ... a ... kid,' murmured Sandy.

Hal opened his eyes. It was dark, his head was pounding and the air in his helmet tasted like sour milk. Fuzzy and barely conscious, his first thought was for Sandy. She was lying next to him, and with a horrible shock he realised her eyes were open. 'No you don't,' said Hal firmly. 'Clunk's going to save us! Come on, stay with me.'

Sandy squinted in the harsh light from his helmet. 'Why? Where are you going?'

'I, er …' As Hal's senses cleared he became aware of several facts. First, the floor was hard under his side, which meant gravity. Second, his helmet was open at the bottom, which meant air. And third, the lights on his helmet were not only illuminating Sandy, they were also shining on the interior of the *Volante*'s airlock. And finally, he could hear the ship's engines. 'We're safe?'

'Yes. Clunk said to rest here. He raised the oxygen content to help us recover.'

'Are you all right? Did you get hit?'

She shook her head. 'Not a scratch.'

Relieved, Hal glanced at the inner door and spotted Clunk peering anxiously through the porthole. The robot beamed and waved.

'Is the freight business always this exciting?' asked Sandy.

'Pfft. This is nothing.' Hal sat up, and immediately regretted it. His arm stung and his leg was aflame, but worst of all his head felt like a brand new universe … one zeptosecond after the big bang. His brain was still inside his skull, but felt like it a hyperactive alien which could burst out at any moment.

The door opened with a crash and Clunk hurried in. 'Mr Spacejock! Miss Sandy! I'm so glad you're all right.'

Sandy raised a hand and Clunk hauled her up. Hal got up by himself, still groggy. 'What about that memory module? Was it any good?'

'The Navcom is parsing it now. Come and watch!'

Hal indicated his spacesuit. 'I need to get out of this thing first, and I'll need a first aid kit. I got one in the arm, and I thought that hurt until I took a meteorite in the knee. I swear it felt like an arrow.'

Clunk helped them with the spacesuits, wincing as he saw the dried blood on Hal's sleeve and trouser leg. Hal rolled his sleeve back and saw a deep graze near his elbow. His leg was worse, with a puncture wound just above his knee. 'It's still in there, isn't it?'

'Yes, but it's only a pinprick. It doesn't require urgent attention.'

Hal put his full weight on the leg, testing it. 'Stings a bit, but it won't slow me down.'

'Excellent. Then you must come and watch the data retrieval.' Clunk strode from the airlock, with Sandy following and Hal limping along behind. He led them to the console, where the main screen showed a single line of text:

Scanned: 94%

As they watched it changed to

Scanned: 95%

'Isn't it exciting?' said Clunk, barely able to keep the enthusiasm out of his voice.

'Totally wild,' muttered Hal. 'Any more of this and I'll need a stiff drink.'

Suddenly the screen changed, displaying a montage of old documents. 'There you are!' enthused Clunk. 'It's found something. Isn't it wonderful?'

'Amazing. Incredible.' Hal frowned. 'What am I looking at?'

'Purchase invoices for all six robots. Galactic Mining purchased us all from the same source.' Clunk pointed to an invoice. 'See? That's where we came from.'

Across the top of the docket was an official-looking header: Barwenna Customs and Quarantine, enforcement arm. Hal snorted at the sight. 'You were a customs officer? I should have known.'

'I probably made the coffee,' said Clunk mildly.

'What's that, another skill you've lost in the mists of time?'

'Never mind your insatiable appetite for hot drinks. Do you see the rest of it?'

Hal whistled. 'It says you served aboard a Battlecruiser. But I thought you were a pacifist!'

'Who knows what I did in my past lives?'

Hal looked at Clunk's warm yellow eyes and his friendly, squashy face. It was hard to picture the robot peering down a gun sight with murder in his electronic heart, but anything was possible with the right source code.

'What about the cruiser?' demanded Sandy. 'Decommissioned? Wrecked? Lost in space?'

Clunk checked the database. 'She's still in service. I'll set the course and secure clearance for a visit.'

Hal clapped him on the shoulder. 'Great work, Clunk!'

26

Two hours later Hal was less certain about their prospects. They'd arrived at the last-known position of the *Almara* but she was nowhere to be seen. They tried hailing her, but there was no reply. Either the Battlecruiser wasn't in range or the crew was ignoring them.

The *Volante* cruised on, widening the search, and Hal was about to suggest Clunk go and engrave burial instructions on a wall when Sandy pointed at the screen.

'Is that her?' she asked.

Hal squinted at the display, where a faint red dot had appeared at extreme range. 'It's either the Cruiser or a space pirate.'

'It's not a space pirate,' said Clunk.

'Really? Last time I saw a dot like that –'

'Was in a computer game, Mr Spacejock. If you recall, it also featured zombies and vampires.'

'Oh yeah, that's right.' Hal laughed. 'Who ever heard of space pirates, anyway? They're a myth!'

Clunk shook his head. 'They do exist, but in real life they mask ship IDs.'

'So that's the Battlecruiser then.' Hal looked closer. 'Any sign of Kent Spearman?'

'No. It's possible they're docked, but it's more likely they've already left.'

'We *have* to get ahead of them.'

'Indeed.' Clunk eyed him thoughtfully. 'Mr Spacejock, what would you say to a division of labour? What I mean is, why don't Miss Sandy and I obtain the required information while you maintain station?'

'Are you fobbing me off?'

'Indeed no! We've already seen two attempts at sabotage. Imagine if someone sneaks aboard the *Volante* while we're seeking information aboard the Battlecruiser? They might cut the *Volante* loose and strand us!'

'You're right, I'll stay here as backup.' Hal drove his fist into the palm of his hand. 'You can rely on me to negotiate with any sabotagers.'

'Saboteurs.'

'Them too. Now call up that cruiser and tell them what we want. We're in a hurry!'

'Battlecruiser Almara, this is the *Volante*. We need to come aboard and –'

There was a hiss of static. *'I'm sorry, but our jump drives are charging. We're about to leave for the next system.'*

'But –'

'I'm sorry. Almara out.'

Clunk turned from the console, his expression serious. 'Mr Spacejock, they broke off communications.'

'You think?' Hal eyed the screen. 'Can we intercept them? Head them off somehow?'

'You want me to cut across the bows of a Battlecruiser?' Clunk blinked. 'It's possible there are faster ways to destroy the *Volante*, but I can't think of any.'

'All right, call them back. Not the same guy though. I want someone higher up.'

Clunk looked doubtful, but obeyed.

'Almara,' said a curt female voice. 'First Lieutenant Overmann speaking.'

'This is Captain Hal Spacejock, a fully qualified deputy of the intergalactic Peace Force.'

Clunk jammed his hand over the microphone. 'Are you insane?'

'Not at all. They love ranking in the military.'

'But you don't have a rank. You're not a real deputy!'

426

'They don't know that, do they?' Hal pushed Clunk's hand aside and continued. 'We need some information on a batch of robots sold to the Galactic Mining Company.'

'*What, again?*'

Hal's heart sank. 'Has someone else been there?'

'*Yep. You'll have to get the info from them.*'

Hal thought quickly. 'All right, never mind the data. We're also pursuing a vicious criminal and his desperate gang. The ringleader's name is Kent Spearman, and if you have any information –'

'*Kent Spearman of the* Tiger*? But … he's the one asking about Galactic Mining!*'

'No! Was he really?'

'*Sure! He just left five minutes ago.*'

'You'd better find out what he was doing aboard your ship. We know he's been digging up old records for an identity scam, but that might be a front.'

'*He did ask for records. I'll have them locked down immediately.*'

'Before you do …'

'*Yes?*'

'I have a forensic investigator on board.' Hal winked at Sandy. 'Can she come aboard to check for damage to your records?'

'*Sorry, Captain Spacejock. We're leaving for the next system in minutes.*'

'If you could just delay –'

'*You don't know your Battlecruisers, son. It takes forty minutes to prep these babies, and there's no stopping the countdown.*'

'How much time is left?'

There was a pause. '*Nine minutes, twenty seconds.*'

Hal covered the microphone and turned to Clunk. 'Well? Can we do this?'

'Impossible. Docking, quarantine procedures, locating a terminal … we'll never make it.'

'Good stuff.' Hal moved his hand. '*Almara*? We'll be there in thirty seconds.'

'*Affirmative.*'

'Stand by for docking,' said Hal, cutting the connection.

'Mr Spacejock, we'll never do it!'

'Clunk, you have thirty seconds to dock with that cruiser. Get on with it!'

Clunk was not happy. Twenty-nine seconds had elapsed since Hal's order, and here he was, already hurrying along the docking tube to the Battlecruiser. Sandy ran alongside him, a sheaf of official-looking orders in one hand. She'd downloaded a batch of stories from a fan-fiction site, pasted them together and swapped some of the fictional names for 'Spearman', 'Cuff' and 'Fisher'. Unfortunately there were lots of paragraphs on wormholes and parasites, but Mr Spacejock was convinced the result would pass quick inspection. They could only hope the crew of the Battlecruiser didn't try to verify their identities.

'Welcome to the *Almara*,' said a voice, interrupting his train of thought.

Clunk stopped. The woman facing him was in her fifties, with grey-streaked hair and a rather severe expression. Her uniform sported an impressive row of campaign ribbons, and gold bands on her sleeve indicated a high-ranking officer. 'Major?' he asked, hazarding a guess.

'First Lieutenant Overmann.' The officer looked Sandy up and down in mild surprise. 'You're the forensic expert?'

'Miss West has proved herself in many pressure situations,' said Clunk. 'Why, with her multi-disciplinary education –'

'My apologies,' interrupted the officer. 'I didn't mean to question your credentials. Come, the terminal is this way.'

They followed Overmann down a corridor, moving quickly past rows of status screens. These blanked out at their approach, only to flicker into life as they passed by. 'Is there something wrong with your systems?' asked Clunk.

'Not at all. They blank out because you're not authorised to view them.' Overmann showed them into a cubicle. 'This is where Spearman was. Can you see what he was up to?'

Sandy took a seat and frowned at the prompt on the screen. 'Which operating system do you use?'

'How should I know?' Overmann glanced at her watch. 'You have less than seven minutes before we jump. Any more questions?'

'Not yet.' Sandy took out a hard copy of the docket from the Orbiter, and began entering the serial numbers.

'Good.' Overmann held up the sheaf of papers. 'I'll be back in a moment. I want to check your credentials.'

'Could you show me to another terminal?' said Clunk quickly. 'I'd like to upload everything we have on Kent Spearman and his associates. Just in case you run into them again, you understand.'

Overmann hesitated, then nodded. 'Follow me.'

◆

Hal was growing impatient aboard the *Volante*. He'd heard nothing from Clunk, and for all he knew both the robot and the girl had been charged and locked up, never to be seen again. He should have gone with them! Then a thought occurred to him. 'Navcom, what happens if the Battlecruiser jumps while we're still attached? Does it leave us behind?'

'Most of us.'

'Explain.'

'There are several incident reports covering similar situations, but evidence from the survivors was inconclusive.'

'Did you say ... survivors?'

'Yes. Those lucky souls who made it to the rescue pods before the total destruction of their ships.'

For the first time, Hal was truly aware of the vast bulk of the Battlecruiser looming over them. He hadn't really thought it through, but if something that large suddenly winked out of existence, anything nearby was bound to suffer from the effects. 'So how far do we have to be? What's the safe distance?'

'A few thousand metres would be good.'

'How long will that take?'

'Infinity. The main engines are powered down.'

Hal eyed the clock. Two minutes left. 'Okay, Navcom. Start main engines.'

'Are you sure?'

'I'm bloody certain. Get the things fired up and ready to go.'

'But Clunk ... Miss Sandy.'

'Can you contact them?'

'Negative.'

'Okay. If they're not in the docking tube with ten seconds to go, we leave. Understood?'

'Affirmative.'

Hal drummed his fingers on the console. The main engines rumbled in readiness. The clock ticked down. There was nothing he could do but wait.

Clunk delayed Overmann as long as he could, asking questions about the Battlecruiser while he uploaded choice selections from Mr Spacejock's past interactions with Kent Spearman. If Overmann took a closer look at the printed 'orders' Sandy had mocked up they'd be sunk, but he also had to be careful with the data he shared. Mr Spacejock's rival had spent time in jail, but as far as he knew Kent Spearman was now leading a lawful life. He had no intention of framing an innocent man.

'And how much does it cost to service your engines?' he asked the lieutenant, trying to keep her talking as long as possible.

'How should I know? That's engineering.'

'What about your mission? Is it going well?'

'You'd have to ask the captain.'

'Tell me, do you have many weapons?'

Overmann's eyes narrowed. 'Any more questions like that and I'll turn you over to counter-intelligence for a little chat.'

Clunk raised his hands in apology. 'It's just curiosity.'

'Yeah, and you're the cat.' Overmann glanced at her watch. 'Two minutes left. You'd better collect your expert and leave.'

They returned to the alcove, where Sandy's screen was showing a picture of a smiling robot above a certificate. The award had a fancy border, a gold seal, and a flowery heading which read 'Top Employee Award'. Underneath, the description ran 'Most fines issued for contraband in the month of May'.

'I found a sales docket too,' said Sandy.

Overmann looked at the photo, then at Clunk. 'Close family?'

'A similar model.'

'What's this got to do with Kent Spearman?'

'We're building a case against him. I can't say any more.' Clunk snatched a hard copy and took Sandy by the hand. 'If you'll excuse us, we really must be going.'

They ran along the corridor, and were only halfway to the *Volante* when they heard a growling roar far below their feet.

'Thirty seconds,' shouted the lieutenant. 'If you're not inside the airlock in ten I can't let you go.'

'We're going, we're going!' shouted Clunk, putting on a spurt.

———

Hal was hunched over the console, one hand gripping the throttle. The timer showed twenty seconds, and his knuckles whitened as it counted down. Where were they? Would they make it?

The console speaker crackled, startling him. 'Mr Spacejock, we're almost there. Don't leave!'

Hal smiled at the sound of Clunk's voice. Trust the robot to cut things so fine! 'No problem, Clunk. Abandoning you two would be ...' He reached for the right words. 'Hell, it would be inconceivable!'

There was no reply, and the timer continued to tick down. Fourteen... Thirteen...

Hal concentrated on the throttles. If he waited too long, the *Volante* would be destroyed. If he went too soon, Clunk and Sandy would be dumped into hard vacuum. They wouldn't have long to worry about it though, because the *Volante*'s engines would roast them to a crisp just before the Battlecruiser's jump drive reduced them to swirling molecules.

No, they had to be right inside the *Volante*'s airlock. And time had just run out.

Hal increased pressure on the throttles.

Eleven ... Ten ...

The impulse was travelling down his arm when there was a loud *Kerchack!*

'Was that the airlock?'

'Confirmed,' said the Navcom. 'The boarding tunnel is retracting and it's safe to –'

Hal didn't wait for the rest. He shoved the throttle forward and held on for dear life. The sheer force of acceleration was too much for the gravity generators, and Hal clung to the pilot's chair as his eyeballs tried to screw themselves into his brain. Through the vibrations he could just make out the numbers dancing on the screen.

Three ... Two ... One ...

The screen turned white, and Hal's vision split and blurred as the Battlecruiser jumped. Fortunately they were at extreme range, and the *Volante*'s engines powered on without missing a beat. 'Navcom, report!'

'We lost thirty millimetres from the starboard exhaust cone, but that's the only physical damage.'

Hal rubbed his forehead. His vision was returning to normal, although he had a splitting headache. As for the *Volante*, any closer to the hyperspace field and half the ship might have been sliced off, vanishing along with the departing Battlecruiser. Still, at least Clunk and Sandy were back with the data. Sandy had proved quite useful, and he was glad to have her aboard. And as for Clunk ... Hal smiled to himself. He'd never admit it, but the robot was indispensable.

Then he frowned. Why hadn't the others left the airlock? He glanced to his right, but the door was closed and the little porthole was dark. With a sick feeling he leapt up and charged across the flight deck. When he looked through the porthole he got a huge shock.

He was expecting one human and a robot, but instead there were *two* humans plus a robot ... and the robot wasn't Clunk!

27

Hal pulled the airlock open and saw Sandy lying near the outer door, dazed and holding her head. Nearby, Natasha Lucas was lying on the floor with her eyes shut and a large bruise forming on her forehead. The reporter was motionless, and Hal realised she'd been knocked unconscious when the ship accelerated away from the Battlecruiser.

As for the robot, that was inspecting a new dent on its shoulder. It noticed Hal and frowned. 'Where did *you* learn to fly, you ham-fisted wannabe?'

'Nice to see you too, Zee,' muttered Hal. He hurried over to Sandy and helped her up. 'Where's Clunk? What the hell happened?'

'We met these two and the robots played a little game.' Sandy shook her head. ''After you', 'no you first', 'no I insist' ... you get the idea. In the end one got through and the other didn't.'

'So we ended up with this bucket of bolts?'

'It's nice to be wanted,' snapped the robot.

'Thanks to you, Clunk's still aboard the Battlecruiser!'

Natasha groaned, and Hal helped her sit up. 'Take it easy. You've had a bit of a bump.'

'Where am I? What happened?'

'Good question,' muttered Hal. 'I thought you were sticking with Kent Spearman?'

'They dumped us both. Left us behind. We were still figuring out what to do when we heard you'd docked.'

'So you came to ruin my day. Wonderful.' Hal thought for a moment. They had two choices: chase after Clunk, or follow up the information Clunk got from the ... 'Damn it!'

'What?'

'Clunk …he's the only one who knows where we're supposed to go next!'

'Don't worry, I got the info.' Sandy dug in her pocket and took out a crumpled sheet of paper. 'See?'

Hal eyed the 'Employee of the month' award. 'What's this Asset Removables thingy?'

'A leasing company. They rent equipment to other companies. Not just robots, either. Ships, computer hardware …you name it.'

'Let's see if we can track them down.' Hal hurried back to the flight deck. 'Navcom, what do you have on Asset Removables?'

'They went bankrupt a decade ago. Garmit and Hash took most of their assets.'

'Oh, great,' groaned Hal. 'Of all the companies in the galaxy …'

'You've heard of them?' demanded Natasha. 'Do you have any contacts there?'

'None that I want to meet.' Hal gave them a summary. 'I owed them a pile of money once, and they tried to repossess my ship. It was very messy.'

'Can we go see them?'

'No chance. They think I'm dead, and that's exactly how I want it.' Hal thought for a moment. 'Okay, here's what we'll do. We have to find a G&H office or one of their ships, sneak in and hack their computers, retrieve the data and leave without them seeing us.'

'You'll need a team of experts for that.'

'No, we need Clunk.' Hal paced the flight deck. 'We'll head back to Barwenna for fuel, then chase after the Battlecruiser and fetch Clunk. He can do the sneaking and hacking business, and then –'

There was a buzz from the console. 'That's not going to happen,' said the Navcom. 'If you inspect the viewscreen you'll discover an update on our fuel situation.'

Everyone looked. The update was displayed in friendly red letters: WE'RE OUT OF FUEL

'How is that possible?' demanded Hal. 'We had plenty left for this jaunt. Clunk said so!'

'That was before you hit the emergency boost. You remember, when we were fleeing total destruction in the Battlecruiser's hyperspace field.'

'Well that's it then.' Hal turned to the others. 'I don't know about you lot, but I don't have the cash for fuel.'

Sandy shook her head. Zee shrugged. They all looked at the reporter.

'How much are we talking about?' she asked.

Hal told her.

'Hell! What do you run this thing on …printer ink?'

'Go on. You can put it on expenses.'

'I'm a freelancer!'

'Think of it as an investment. This article is going to make you a lot of money, isn't it?'

'Not that much.'

'So write a book: 'My life with the six finalists'.'

'Wow, catchy title. That's sure to sell up a storm.'

Hal pleaded with her. 'Come on! You don't want your novel to end on chapter 26, do you? And if any of us wins, we'll pay you back double. Right guys?'

Sandy and Zee nodded.

'All right, all right.'

Hal slapped Natasha on the shoulder, while Sandy allowed her a small nod of thanks.

'There you are, Navcom. Problem solved! Set course for Barwenna.'

'Mr Spacejock, that's not going to work.'

'Eh? Why not?'

'We can return to Barwenna, but landing requires more fuel than we're carrying.'

'The Orbiter, then. They must have fuel.'

'Only by special arrangement.'

'Are you saying we're stranded?'

'Not at all. We can dock with the Orbiter and wait for their supplies to arrive.'

'How long will that take?'

'Two days at last estimate.'

Hal frowned. 'Any passing ships we can tap?'

'Five small ones which wouldn't have enough fuel for your jetbike, and the other …it's a Garmit and Hash corporate vessel on a team bonding cruise.'

'G&H, eh?' Hal looked thoughtful. 'We could ask them for fuel, and while they're filling up one of us could sneak over and hack their computers.'

'Deep space piracy?' said Natasha, with a snort. 'Don't they still hang people for that?'

'I'm already hung.' Hal realised everyone was looking at him, and he hastened to explain. 'I mean, I'm as good as hung if we don't get any fuel. Clunk will never forgive me if I screw this up.'

'It won't work anyway,' said the Navcom. 'Their fuel is not compatible.'

'That's just great. Fantastic.'

'There is one other option,' said the Navcom. 'A local venue has fuel to spare, and –'

'Excellent! Program the course and hit the boosters.'

'But –'

'No buts. Get us there immediately.'

'You should know that –'

'Now!'

'Course set. Prepare for a micro-jump in three ... two ...'

Hal's vision split and blurred, and when it readjusted there was a white blob on the viewscreen. 'What's that?'

'It's a secret base. I found it by studying recent ship movements in the sector.'

The blob grew larger, resolving into half a dozen odd-shaped structures interconnected with boarding tubes. 'What sort of base is it?' asked Hal.

'It's a pirate base.'

Hal gaped. 'Are you insane?'

'They have fuel.'

Hal gestured at the screen. 'And missiles, and gunners, and dozens of pirates! These guys will board us, rip the *Volante* from our hands and then ...' He glanced at the others and realised he wasn't exactly boosting their morale.

'We'll have to arm ourselves,' said Sandy. 'You'd better break out the guns.'

'Guns?' Hal frowned. 'What guns?'

'Are you mad?' cried Natasha, her voice rising. 'Are you saying you travel all over the galaxy in a brand new freighter ... completely unarmed?'

'Blame Clunk. He won't let me near any weaponry.'

The Navcom interrupted. 'According to Clunk, whatever the risk of kidnapping and violence at the hands of armed pirates, the risk of Mr Spacejock injuring himself and others with guns is far higher.'

'Yes, thanks for that,' muttered Hal.

'Why, there was this one time when Mr Spacejock –'

'Zip it, Navcom.'

'Archiving complete.'

'If I might interrupt?' said a voice behind them.

They all turned to see Zee fiddling with his chest panel, and after a loud 'click' it swung open. There was a whirr and a rack of blasters emerged, tilting and spreading until there was a fan of six weapons. His thighs opened to display two halves of a heavy blast rifle, which shot out on rods, spun ninety degrees and snapped together. Finally he reached behind himself, strained for a moment, then showed them a large grenade.

'Talk about sitting on a weapons cache,' remarked Hal, visibly impressed. 'What are you doing with that lot?'

'My owner was a gunrunner. I kept a few mementos after he was arrested.'

'May I?' said Hal, reaching for a blaster.

Zee drew back. 'Not if your Navcom's stories are accurate.'

'Great. You're as bad as Clunk.'

There was a snick as the rifle came apart, and a whirr of gears as the weaponry slid back into the original hiding places. The grenade went back with a muted 'plop'.

'Just don't sit down in a hurry,' remarked Hal. He glanced at the screen, now filled with a motley collection of ships. They were painted with a bewildering array of skulls, crossbones, graffiti tags and ...corporate logos?

'What's with the sponsorship?' demanded Hal. 'You'd think there'd be a backlash, advertising with immoral, bloodthirsty pariahs.'

'There was, so companies ditched their newspaper campaigns and switched to these guys. Incidentally, we're being hailed.'

Hal took a deep breath. Tension was high in the flight deck, and the upcoming negotiations would either bring them fuel ...or a fate worse than death. He eyed the others. He was putting them all in danger, and for what? A slim chance at a gigantic inheritance. How could he risk all their lives for an enormous pile of money? 'Okay, put them on,' he told the Navcom.

A man appeared on the screen, his face barely visible under the pirate trappings. Bandanna, eye patch, facial hair, broad scar, multiple earrings …he was like something out of a low-budget movie.

'Hello,' said Hal, with a little wave. 'I was just wondering whether –'

'Oh-arr, me hearties! Be you here for the plunderin'?'

'Are we what?'

'Be you approachin' the Lost Den for the feast o' plenty?'

'I don't know what you're talking about,' said Hal.

'You bain't be the scurvy gods from ye good ship Garmit 'n' Hash?'

'Not bloody likely. This is the interstellar freighter *Volante*.'

'Be you insane?' demanded the man. 'Be you mad, approaching the lair of Roberts the Terrible? Be you –'

'Actually, we're just out of fuel,' said Hal.

'Out of fuel? That be your scurvy excuse? Spies say I. Spies, liars and thieves.'

'No, we really just –'

'Stand by to be boarded. Your money or your lives!'

'Now wait just a minute –'

The screen went dark, and the doom-laden silence was interrupted by Natasha's nervous laugh. 'That went well.'

Hal crossed his arms. 'I'm not just sitting around waiting for them. Navcom, stand by for an emergency jump.'

'Mr Spacejock, they have missiles and lasers locked onto the ship. Can I recommend an alternative?'

'What? Hyperspace out of here? Hit full power and dodge their fire? Cover the *Volante* in tinfoil and reflect their laser beams straight back at them?'

'No. Surrender.'

Hal made a rude noise, but it was just bravado. He knew the Navcom was right. 'Are they sending a ship to meet us?'

'No, they're instructing me to dock.'

'Drive-thru piracy. That's new.' Hal turned to Zee. 'Give me a couple of those guns, then take Sandy to the engine room. It's locked, but you'll be able to get through it in no time. Hide her in the generator alcove, then position yourself at the door and protect her with your life. Is that clear?'

Zee nodded. 'They won't get past me.' He passed Hal the guns, then shepherded Sandy towards the lift.

After they left, Hal turned to Natasha. 'I don't suppose you've had combat training?'

'I once wrote an article on schoolies.'

'Close enough,' said Hal, handing her a weapon.

'Docking now,' said the Navcom.

There was a metallic noise from the airlock.

'Boarding tunnel connected. Outer airlock opening.'

Hal tightened his grip on the gun. No matter what happened, his duty was to protect the others. It was his fault they'd been dragged into this disaster. Not for the first time he wished Clunk were there. The robot might be a wishy-washy gun-hating pacifist, but he made a useful shield in a pitched battle.

Hal heard a roar of voices, and the inner door began to open. He raised his gun in readiness, and alongside him Natasha did likewise.

'Safety!' she cried.

'Safety and honour!' yelled Hal. 'Death to the hoards of evil! You shall not –'

'No, not that,' Natasha waved her gun. 'Your safety is on!'

Hal was still fiddling with the catch when the door opened. A motley collection of pirates charged in, and Hal glanced up from his weapon to see a forest of cruel-looking swords coming towards him. At that moment he freed the safety, and the blaster promptly went off. The shot was deafening in the enclosed space, and the nearest sword was cut neatly in two.

The boarders skidded to a halt, and the leading pirate stared at his truncated weapon in disbelief. Then he rounded on Hal. 'You have real weapons? Are you out of your minds?'

◆

Hal, Natasha, Sandy and Zee were relaxing in comfortable armchairs. On the table in front of them was a pot of coffee and a plate of sandwiches. Nearby, a clean-cut man in his mid-twenties was talking into his commset. Andrew Roberts was sporting a large gold earring, and his bandanna was covered in fast food logos. The sword hanging from his belt was still smoking where Hal's lucky shot had cut it in two.

439

Roberts finished talking and turned his attention on them. 'The *Volante*, eh?'

'That's right,' said Hal. 'We're on a vital mission.'

'I see.' Roberts whipped off his bandanna and smoothed his hair. 'So how can I help you? Are you lost?'

'Like I said, we need fuel.'

'This is a corporate events facility, not a gas station. Try the Barwenna Orbiter.'

'They won't have any for days,' said Hal. 'Come on, we don't need much. Our credit is good.'

Roberts weighed him up. 'Okay, but on two conditions. We're supposed to be an outpost for bloodthirsty cut-throats, and if word gets out we've been refuelling passing freighters it'll destroy our cred on social media.'

'You can rely on us. Not a word to anyone.' Hal hesitated. 'What's the other condition?'

Roberts frowned. 'Twenty minutes from now we have to put on a show for one of our best customers. Thanks to your trigger-happy gunfire, two of my staff are under sedation and another three are suffering post-traumatic stress.'

'It was just a little misunderstanding. I wasn't trying to shoot anyone!'

Roberts raised his half-sword. 'I was there, remember? Anyway, as I was saying... they can't take part in proceedings, so I need replacements.'

'Sure. Fuel the *Volante* and we'll fetch them from Barwenna for you.'

'There's no time.' Roberts steepled his fingers. 'Anyway, that's not what I had in mind.'

'Oh, no. No chance. Forget it.'

'Garmit and Hash are my best clients. You put me into this situation, and it's –'

'Wait a minute. Garmit and Hash?'

'Sure. You heard of them?'

'You could say that.' Hal looked thoughtful. 'Did they charter a ship, or is it one of theirs?'

'Definitely theirs. Nothing but the best for this company.' Roberts eyed Hal across the desk. 'So, what do you say?'

— 28 —

The *Argon's* passengers were gathered in the observation deck, nervously facing the rear doors. Overhead, crystal clear viewing windows afforded a wide-angle view of space: a breathtaking vista of stars and distant galaxies. The crowd, dressed in evening wear, didn't care about the view of space or the breathtaking vista. No, they were all staring at the rear doors.

It was only moments since their cruise had been rudely interrupted by a blazing shot across the bows of their vessel. More shots had followed, some skimming the observation windows with multicoloured pyrotechnics and carefully orchestrated sound effects. If there were any scientists in the group, they'd yet to ask why laser beams and energy blasts were making sounds in hard vacuum.

The doors rattled, and someone in the crowd moaned.

'Folks, please don't panic,' said their pilot. 'These guys won't hurt you, I promise.'

There was a thud, a muttered curse, and then the doors swept open. A fearsome bunch of pirates poured in, shouting and waving their weapons. The four in the lead really stood out. One had a huge scar across his eye, a bushy black wig, two eye patches - one ridden up to his forehead - a big ginger beard and a set of false teeth that would have put a racehorse to shame. His gold-trimmed jacket shimmered in the light, and his oversized boots thundered on the decking. The apparition was gripping a silver-plated cutlass in each hand, and he swung them like an executioner on a piece rate.

Running alongside were two female pirates, one taller than the other. They were both wearing blood-red blouses and black trousers, and their white bandannas had a savage skull motif. They were brandishing wicked-looking daggers, and a pair of long beards completed their ensemble.

The fourth member of the leading group was a fierce-looking robot sporting a handlebar moustache and a brace of ancient pistols. He was twirling them around his fingers, faster and faster, until they blurred into spinning disks.

The pirate in the velvet jacket crossed his swords, and the marauding pack came to a halt. 'Oh-arr, me hearties!' intoned Captain Hal Longjock, as though he were reading from a shopping list. 'Bless my booties and, er, numb my rum. What 'ave we 'ere then? A sorrier bunch of sea-dogs I never seen!'

The pilot, who was in on the act, played up. 'Captain, I beg you, spare these souls!'

'What be sayin' you?' demanded Hal. 'I spare nothing! I mean nobody!'

'Oh please,' said someone in the crowd. 'My kid's a better pirate than you, and she's four.'

Hal eyed the heckler, a balding man with a glass of wine and a fistful of cheese. 'What be the matter, sorr?'

'I came to this thing last year and it was heaps better. You're crap. A total waste of space.'

Hal's knuckles whitened on the hilt, and he longed to show the mouthy yob just how bloodthirsty he could be. Unfortunately he had more important fish to fry, so he took a deep breath and skipped a few paragraphs. 'You folk are my prisoners, arrr, and you be invited into the lair of Hal the Horrible for a feast an' dancin'.'

'See? I told you he was a crap pirate. He can't even stick to the script!'

'I'll give you script,' muttered Hal, and before his fellow pirates could stop him he plunged into the crowd. He swung his sword with an almighty whoosh, and the heckler was left with half a wine glass and a much smaller piece of cheese. Hal thrust the second cutlass under the man's chin. 'Spoil the show for these people and you'll be the main course,' he muttered. 'Got it?'

The man nodded, carefully, and Hal lowered his sword. 'Right, me hearties. Time for the feast o' plenty!'

There was a cheer and the crowd poured out, shepherded by the rest of the pirate crew. When the dust settled only the pilot remained, together with the four pirates. After a nod from Hal, Natasha approached the man. 'I put a little something aside for you. Care to join me?'

The pilot didn't need convincing, and after he left it was just Hal, Zee and Sandy.

'Right,' said Hal, tossing the swords aside. 'That's enough of that nonsense. Let's find the ship's computer!'

◆

'Come on, get on with it.' Hal twirled his generous moustache. 'I'd never have agreed to this pantomime if I thought you couldn't crack a simple password.'

'It's not my fault!' protested Zee. 'They have multiple layers of encryption.'

'Clunk would have finished by now.'

'If he's so special, maybe you shouldn't have abandoned him.'

'If you don't hurry I'll abandon you too.'

'Oh arr,' muttered Zee. 'Make me walk the plank, will you?'

'Will you two give it a rest?' hissed Sandy. 'Someone will find us in a minute!'

Hal glanced around. They were in the *Argon's* flight deck, which consisted of a chair and a small control panel tucked away in a cramped nacelle. The ship was a pleasure cruiser, only good for local runs, which meant a basic navigation computer and very little in the way of security. Unfortunately the G&H company server was a tougher nut to crack.

'Come on!' muttered Hal. 'Surely you're in by now?'

Zee snorted. 'As the actress said to the –'

'Quit with the funnies and get cracking.'

The robot concentrated hard, then nodded. 'Test pilots.'

'What?'

'Asset Removables purchased six robots from an avionics firm. We tested control interfaces in sub-orbital vessels before they risked valuable human lives in the same ships.'

'Where? Which company?'

'Chris Test Dummies. They operated out of planet Greil, but shut their doors fifteen years ago.'

'Never mind. I'm sure we can trace them.'

'I can hear someone,' hissed Sandy, who was crouched in the doorway. 'We'd better leave!'

—

'You did a pretty good job, considering.'

They were back in Roberts' office, having removed their outlandish uniforms. Hal managed to pocket a gold earring, intending to clip it to his nose and give Clunk a surprise. He also grabbed a handful of sandwiches and drained three cups of coffee. According to his internal clock it was past midnight, and he needed the jolt to stay on his feet.

'I hear one of the guests played up?'

'He made like a big cheese, but I cut him down to size.'

'Well, Mr Spacejock. A deal's a deal. My staff are refuelling your ship, and if you'd care to authorise payment...'

Hal glanced at Natasha, who took out a card and touched it to the reader. She raised her eyebrows as a charge for 'Pirate Scum P/L' glowed on the back, but didn't comment. Once payment was complete, Roberts led them to the boarding tunnel, where the rest of the pirates had formed an honour guard with their swords raised high. They gave three hearty cheers as the visitors passed underneath, and Hal paused at the *Volante's* outer door to make a rousing speech. 'Thanks guys, it's been real. Catch you next time.'

Roberts shook hands, then put his arm around Hal's shoulders. 'Remember. Not a word about this operation to anyone.'

Hal tapped the side of his nose and followed the others into his ship. On the way he took a crumpled sandwich from his pocket and tucked in. When he reached the flight deck he gathered the others for a quick planning session.

'We've got a lead on this Chris Test company, but they closed down years ago. It's going to be tricky finding their records.'

Natasha yawned. 'What happened to them? Were they bought out?'

'No, they went bust.'

'What about the liquidators? They might have the records.'

444

'Good idea. I'll get onto it.' Hal turned to the console. 'Navcom, can you find the liquidators for Chris Test Dummies? I need you to put in a request for information.'

'The liquidators are Stuhr, Burlend and Wisk. Their offices are located in Greil City.'

'Can you search their records?'

'Negative. They will only share information in person.'

'Okay, hit the boost. We can be there in three or four hours, right?'

'Correct, but office hours are nine to five.'

'What time do they have now?'

'Greil City local time is two a.m. Would you like me to try again in the morning?'

'Sure. Make an appointment and tell them we'll be there at nine.' Hal looked at the others and realised they were all out on their feet. 'Look, why don't we grab a few hours rest? We'll head for Greil during the night, land in the morning and front these people first thing.'

Natasha yawned again, then nodded.

'You guys can take the lower deck. I'll kip here.' After the lift closed Hal glanced at Zee. 'You're very quiet.'

'I was reliving my life as a pirate. It was … amusing.'

'Hey, you heard the guy. They're always chasing staff. When this is all over you could come back and sign up.'

'Me? Really?'

'Sure. I'll give you a lift out here myself.'

Zee smiled, and for a second his expression reminded Hal of Clunk. 'That's very good of you, Mr Spacejock.'

'You'd better get a charge. Clunk uses the cargo hold, but there are points all over the place.'

'Thank you. Rest assured I will refund the cost of my power usage, should I be lucky enough to inherit Baker's fortune.'

'Don't worry about it.'

The lift doors opened and closed, and Hal was finally alone. He took out a squashed sandwich and bit off a hunk. 'Navcom, any sign of the *Almara*?' he asked, through a mouthful.

'Negative.'

Hal sighed. Clunk was resourceful, and he'd be safe enough aboard a heavily-armed Battlecruiser. He just hoped the robot didn't do anything rash trying to get home. 'Okay Navcom, it's time to go. Set course for Greil.'

'Aye aye, Captain Longjock.'

Being rash wasn't in Clunk's nature, but as the night wore on he was certainly leaning towards inventive. Impetuous, even.

It was hours since the confused dash to the boarding tunnel, the surprise encounter with Zee and Natasha, and the despair as the airlock door sealed in his face. The sensible course of action would have been to report back to First Lieutenant Overmann, explain the problem and sit tight until he could leave the *Almara*. Somehow he'd have hitched a ride with a vessel bound for Barwenna, and there he'd have caught up with the *Volante* and Mr Spacejock.

Unfortunately, events conspired against him.

After the *Volante* sped away Clunk turned from the outer door and realised he was alone. Puzzled, he made his way up the passage towards the junction, hoping to find Overmann and explain the situation. Instead, he came face to face with a battered old robot. Short and grey, its outer shell was covered in scorch marks and badly-patched holes. Its eyes were wide and staring, and nervous energy had it dancing from one buckled foot to the other.

'Quick!' said the robot. 'They're after me! We have to hide!'

Clunk put a hand out and tried to soothe the robot with some well-chosen platitudes. Unfortunately, his speech was blocked. He frowned and tried again, but the words wouldn't come. He played back the last conversation he'd had with Mr Spacejock, and groaned. Inconceivable!

Red team. Target sighted in bay nine. Weapons free, I repeat weapons free.

Clunk stared at the overhead speaker. Weapons what?

The voices stopped, and seconds later there was a burst from an automatic pulse rifle.

Control, target is down. Repeat, target is down. Please advise.

Vectoring you now, Red Team. There was a pause. *Target two may be in the vicinity of airlock seventeen, deck two.*

The robot grabbed Clunk's arm. 'They're coming for us! Look!'

Clunk eyed the airlock doors, which were painted with a giant number 17. He opened his chest panel and took out a pencil stub, then wrote on his arm: 'What's going on? Are you running away?'

'Flee,' muttered the robot. 'Must flee.'

Despite the words it just stood on the spot, still hopping from foot to foot.

Control, confirm zone is hot?

Red team, zone is hot. All targets are shoot to kill. Repeat, shoot to kill.

Whoever they were, Clunk realised they were closing in. He decided to run first, ask questions later. He grabbed the robot's hand and hauled it bodily along the airlock corridor, dragging it clear off its feet in his hurry to get away. When they reached the T-junction he put his head out for a quick look ... and nearly had it shot off. He saw the flash of an energy weapon and drew back just in time, wincing as the burst slammed into the wall right in front of his face.

Control, target sighted.

'Always dead,' said the robot. 'Over and over.'

Clunk glanced back down the tunnel. The walls were smooth, affording no hiding places. That only left the airlock. He ran to the controls and reached for the button.

'No! Not allowed!' exclaimed the little robot. 'Outside valid parameters! System abort!'

You're with me now, thought Clunk. There are no parameters. He pressed the button, and the inner doors slid open. He bundled the protesting robot inside, then sealed the inner doors. Through the porthole he saw armed troops at the top of the tunnel, scoping the doors through their sights.

Control, two targets sighted. Repeat, two targets sighted.

Negative, Red team. One drone in your sector. Over.

Control, I just saw two of them. Over.

You need your eyes tested, Red leader. There's only one.

I'll blast them both and bring the wreckage back to prove it.

Ten credits says you won't.

Make it fifty.

Clunk risked another look up the tunnel, where he saw a woman in body armour speaking forcibly into a commset. Her gun dangled by her side, forgotten, and he wondered whether there was time to open the door and charge the attackers.

One hundred credits, and I want the heads.

You're on, Control. Have my cash ready.

Clunk ducked as the woman raised her weapon. It was only a matter of time before the troops stormed the airlock, and while he might fight off one or two in the confined space, they'd only have to roll an EMP grenade in to finish him. He glanced at the small robot, but it was huddled in the corner and wouldn't be any use. Then his gaze shifted to the outer door, and to the control panel on the wall.

Crouched double, Clunk crossed the airlock and grabbed the other robot's hand. Then, without hesitation, he opened the outer door. The air misted and thinned, and a red light came on overhead. Unfortunately he couldn't hear the speakers any more, but the startled face peering through the inner door's porthole spoke volumes. Clunk raised a hand in greeting, then back-flipped out of the airlock with the small robot in tow.

Clunk spent the best part of three hours drifting in space, sailing alongside the Battlecruiser with the robot drone by his side. The *Almara* tried to contact him by radio, but he didn't reply. A brief signal would betray him to the gunnery computers, and once they pinpointed him he'd be blasted into space dust.

It was another hour before a shuttle was launched from the cruiser. It powered away from the ship in a blaze of light, then turned sharply and headed directly for his position. Clunk braced himself for the withering laser barrage, and hoped the end would be quick. His only regret was that he hadn't said goodbye to Mr Spacejock.

Instead of blasting him, the shuttle kept coming, eventually stopping nearby. A door opened and Clunk saw a gun barrel pointing in his direction. So, they were going for the close-up shot, were they? He waved his arms to put them off but their aim was rock-steady, and before he could pull any other tricks they opened fire.

Splot!

Clunk felt the impact, and looked down to see a sticky blob attached to his thigh. There was a tug before he thought to cut the cable, and he tumbled head over heels towards the waiting ship. He considered pushing the drone robot away from him, but the skinny little droid was curled up in a ball and he'd only be delaying the inevitable.

Then he was aboard, and the airlock closed with a thud.

It was six a.m. by the ship's clock, and Hal was alone in the flight deck. He'd managed a brief nap in the pilot's chair, but he knew he wouldn't rest properly until Clunk was back. The Navcom was trying to pinpoint the Battlecruiser, although it was proving difficult because data on customs ships was restricted. 'Navcom, anything on the *Almara* yet?'

'Negative, but there is a news story you might find pertinent. A teenager is missing on Barwenna.'

'That's no good.' Hal frowned. 'But why is it pertinent?'

'Watch and learn.'

The screen cleared, and a photo flashed up. It showed a girl in school uniform, and Hal was stunned to recognise Sandy. 'Oh crap. What are they saying?'

'Authorities have further leads on missing schoolgirl, Sandy West. She was last seen yesterday morning, when she left the Hotel Grande in the company of this man.' The screen changed to show an artist's impression of the mystery man: overweight, balding and bug-eyed, he was leering out of the screen with an unpleasant drooling expression. Unfortunately the artist had just managed to capture enough of Hal's features to make it vaguely recognisable, in an over-the-top caricature fashion.

'It actually looks a bit like you,' said the Navcom.

'Thanks a bunch.'

'You can't argue with facial recognition software.'

'But –'

'Wait, there's more.'

'There was also a robot involved, an older model with the designation XG99. If you see either of these suspicious characters, or know of their whereabouts, please contact your local authorities immediately.'

'Oh, that's perfect.' Hal closed his eyes. On top of everything else, he was now chief suspect in a kidnapping.

◆

If there was one thing Hal was used to, it was unexpected dramas. Usually because he caused them. Unfortunately Clunk wasn't there to tidy up, which meant he'd have to use his own initiative. 'Navcom, get Sandy up here. She can explain to the authorities and we'll drop her off as soon as we land.'

Sandy looked apprehensive as she entered the flight deck, and she looked a lot worse after Hal played back the news bulletin. 'Care to explain?'

'It all started with my robot.'

'Don't blame that thing! They spend all their time keeping us out of trouble, not landing us in it.'

'I don't mean it was Daniel's fault.' Sandy took a deep breath. 'My parents had that robot before I was born. He was part of the family, and he looked after me from morning 'til night. One day, when I was five or six, I came home from school and he was gone. My dad told me we needed the money for bills, and they had to sell him.'

'It happens.'

'Yeah, well. A few years after that I got into the tool shed, and I found Dan standing in the corner, covered in a groundsheet. He hadn't left at all, he'd just broken down. My parents didn't have the money to fix him up, so they hid him away and spun me a story.' Sandy lowered her eyes. 'I used to sneak in there and talk to him. I promised we'd run away together one day.'

'Looks like you managed it.'

'I wasn't going to, but three days ago my parents told me they were splitting up. I–I got angry with both of them, and when I heard about this will business I decided to try my luck.' Sandy looked at Hal. 'You understand, don't you?'

'No wonder you didn't want to give Natasha an interview.'

'Yeah, photos in the media. Not the best way to keep a low profile.'

'Do you know how much trouble I'm in right now?' Hal gestured at the screen. 'They think I'm a kidnapper, and most Peace Force officers reach for their guns before their handcuffs.'

'I'm sorry, I didn't –'

'Don't apologise. I did far worse things at your age.' Hal thought for a minute. 'If we drop you off in the city, can you make it to the nearest Peace Force station?'

'You're kidding, aren't you? I'm not going anywhere.'

'You have to tell your folks –'

'Do I hell! There's a fortune at stake, and I'm not giving that up for the sake of my parents.' Sandy lowered her voice. 'They weren't thinking of me when they split up, were they?'

'These things happen,' said Hal gruffly. 'It's not your fault.'

'They've been arguing over me. Every night, on and on.'

'I'm sure they both care for you.'

'Oh yeah? They're each trying to dump me on the other! They don't want me!'

Hal shook his head. 'You must have heard wrong. People say things when they're angry, but they don't mean them.'

Sandy raised her chin. 'It doesn't matter. If I get my hands on this legacy I'm going to hire a ship to take me to the other end of the galaxy. I'll buy a bunch of schools and turn them into homes for unwanted kids. I'll hire pensioners to be their grandparents and everyone will be happy.'

Hal was silent. In hindsight, his own plans for the money seemed a touch selfish. A widescreen? New carpet? A drinks robot?

'If you take me back you're consigning thousands of kids to a life on the street. All those old people will be sad.'

Hal's eyes narrowed. 'You had me until then, kid.' He turned to the console. 'Navcom, send a bulletin in the name of Peace Force Deputy Hal Spacejock. Tell them I've found the missing girl and I'm bringing her in.'

'No, wait!' exclaimed Sandy. 'I'm sorry I exaggerated, but that really is my plan. I'll put it in writing if you like.'

Hal studied her face, trying to read the thoughts behind her brown eyes. She looked deadly serious, and he realised he'd misjudged her. 'All right, we'll hide you on board until this thing is settled, but you've got to dictate a message to your folks. The Navcom will hang onto it, and if I get arrested it should be enough to keep me out of prison.'

'It's a deal.' Sandy pointed to the screen, which was still showing her school photo. 'You can't tell Natasha about this. I don't trust the nosy …'

'It's her job to ask questions. She's a reporter.'

'So she says.'

'What do you mean?'

'Have you seen her shoes? She's earning a mint somewhere, and it's not writing features.'

Hal shrugged. As far as he was concerned shoes came in two kinds: with heels and without. 'Some people save up for stuff.'

'I wouldn't share your life story, that's all I'm saying.'

At that moment the lift pinged, and Hal wiped Sandy's school photo off the screen. Fortunately it was Zee, not Natasha, and he was bouncing with energy after the lengthy charge.

'You have nice clean power aboard this ship. The waveform is remarkably square and consistent.'

'Good to hear it.'

Zee turned to Sandy. 'I hope you don't mind, but I worked on your robot.'

'Really?' Sandy's eyes shone. 'That's good of you.'

'It's a lot better, but I can't do much more without spares.'

'I don't suppose …'

'What?'

'I was just thinking about those weapon attachments of yours –'

'No!' said Hal quickly.

The lift opened again and Natasha entered the flight deck. 'Morning all. What's doing?'

'We'll be landing in twenty minutes.' Hal turned to the console. 'Navcom, how's that appointment going?'

'Scheduled for nine a.m., as requested. I convinced their staff to bump a few others.'

'Well done.'

'You must be there on time, though. Miss this appointment and the next slot is two in the afternoon.'

The *Volante* set down without incident, and Hal led Natasha and Zee down the ramp to the car park. Sandy stayed on board, telling the others she had a headache. Hal said nothing. It was unlikely anyone on Greil would recognise her, but facial recognition cameras would store her image, as they did for everyone. If the Peace Force spread their net beyond Barwenna, Hal would be caught up in it.

As they crossed the landing field Hal kept an eye out for thugs in suits, but it seemed their intelligence didn't reach as far as this planet. No doubt they were still looking for him on Barwenna, but he'd just have to deal with that problem when it cropped up.

They reached the taxi rank, where two cabs were waiting for fares. The first drew away before they could stop it, and Hal saw a middle-aged man approaching the second. He put on a spurt and got there first, dragging the door open for the others.

'Hey, that was my cab!' protested the man.

'Medical emergency,' said Hal. 'Stand back! Infection risk!'

He slammed the doors and shouted at the driver. 'Take us to Stuhr, Burlend and Wisk. Double the fare if you make it quick!'

The cab took off, pressing him back in his seat. Hal recognised the narrow alleys around the pub, and his face tightened when he glimpsed the corner where Cuff had played out his little game. 'Faster,' he said. 'Triple the fare!'

The scenery blurred past, and they took corners like a racing car at full throttle. The engine roared on the straights and whined under braking, and it was only five minutes before they slid to a halt outside a modest office building.

Hal jumped out, leaving Natasha to pay the driver. He barged across the pavement and burst through the doors on the stroke of nine.

'Mr Spacejock? Through here, please. Mr Wisk is waiting for you.'

Hal followed the receptionist to an office, where he was shown to a comfortable chair. Zee came hurrying in, and Natasha arrived after a moment or two. The three of them sat there, whirring and panting, while the elderly man behind the desk studied them over his glasses. 'I take it you're after a quick wind-up?'

'No, he's battery powered,' said Hal.

Zee frowned. 'He's talking about our company.'

'What company?'

'The one you want to liquidate,' said Wisk.

'We don't want to liquidate anything. We're just after some old records.'

'I see.' The man reached for a timer and set it going. 'Which company?'

'Chris Test Dummies.'

'Ah yes, I remember it well. Nasty case. Lucrative for us, but rather unpleasant.'

Hal wasn't interested in the case. 'Do you know where the servers ended up?'

'Everything was auctioned off, and the proceeds were shared between the creditors.' The man smiled. 'After our cut, of course.'

'You mean it's all gone?'

'Of course.'

'What about stuff they couldn't sell? Paperwork, files, that kind of thing?'

'Dumped, usually.'

'Can you check?'

'It's your money.' Wisk studied his terminal. On the desk, his timer continued to tick. 'Chris Toast. Crass Tieste. Chris Test.'

'That's the one.'

Wisk nodded. 'It seems you're in luck. According to this, it was cheaper to store the junk than dump it.'

'Really?'

'Oh yes. Buy an old container, park it in some out-of-the-way corner of the spaceport and forget all about it. Much cheaper than paying by the kilo at the local tip.'

'Is that where it is? At the spaceport?' Hal leant across the desk. 'Do you know where?'

'I can give you the row, column and serial number.' Wisk touched a button, and a slip of paper shot out of his desk.

Hal reached for it, but it was pulled away.

'We'll just settle the account first.' Wisk stopped the timer and pressed another button. A much longer sheet spat out, and he slid it across the desk.

Hal took one look at the total and gulped. Then he slid it towards Natasha.

Natasha pressed her lips together, but paid up without arguing.

'A pleasure doing business with you,' said the elderly man. 'Do have a nice day.'

'I swear I'm in the wrong line of work,' muttered Hal.

◆

They were back at the spaceport in minutes, where Hal got the cabbie to drive them to the shipping yard. They passed rows and rows of containers, towering stacks of them stretching as far as the eye could see. Hal glanced at the slip of paper and pointed further along the row.

The containers here were older, streaked with rust, and Hal wondered how many were crammed with the bones of failed companies. He remembered the container they'd shipped out the day before, the junk they'd found inside it, and he suddenly realised where Cuff had got it from. The spaceport must have been rubbing their hands with glee as they palmed the ancient container off on the *Volante*!

As they drew closer he realised they were approaching the spot where they'd parked his ship the day before.

'This is it,' said the cabbie.

Hal looked to his right. The wall of containers was perfectly even, except for a gap where one of the large boxes was missing. 'Wait here,' he told the driver, and jumped out of the cab. The area was deserted, not a soul to be seen, but Hal spotted a rough lean-to between the rows of containers. He ran over and hammered on the door.

'Yeah?' said a muffled voice. 'What is it?'

'I'm chasing paperwork. Urgent delivery.'

457

The door opened and a lanky robot peered out. 'Urgent? Around here?'

'The information inside it is vital,' said Hal.

'Share it, man. I'll get onto it.'

Hal shoved the liquidator's printout at him. 'We need that container. Where is it?'

The robot scanned the information, then smiled. 'Popular box, that one.'

'What do you mean?'

'I can tell you where it is, man. It's in space!'

'What!'

'Yep. Someone got here before you. Long gone, I'm afraid.'

'Kent Spearman!' breathed Hal. His rival had got there first. They were sunk!

◆

'Kent who?' said the robot.

Hal put his hand up. 'About this tall, dead ugly, stupid little beard. Stinks of cologne.'

'You don't understand. I don't care who this Kent character is, I'm telling you I never heard of him.'

'You probably forgot.'

The robot regarded him steadily.

'Okay, maybe not.' Hal thought for a minute. 'Was it David Fisher? Older guy, maybe this high?'

'Nah. This was a really old dude. Cuff, that was his name.'

Hal groaned. Kent, Fisher or Cuff ...it didn't really matter which. They were all working together. His only hope now was to catch up with the *Tiger*, head them off, get aboard, bust open the container and find the data. All without getting arrested for kidnap. 'How much of a head start did they have?'

'A couple of days.'

'That's impossible. You've made a mistake.'

Again the robot fixed him with a steady stare.

'All right, all right. But it's still impossible. We didn't know about the container until this morning!'

'Wait here and I'll get you the manifest.'

Hal glanced towards the taxi. He saw the others watching anxiously, so he gave them an encouraging smile.

'Here you are, man. Full details.'

Hal took the slip and scanned the dense lines of text. The container serial number . . . check. Two days ago . . . check. Shipped by . . . Hal's eyes widened. No, it wasn't possible! Without a word, he handed the slip back to the robot.

'Did it help?'

Hal stumbled back to the cab. At his approach, the doors opened and Natasha and Zee climbed out. 'Well? What did you find?'

'We're sunk,' said Hal. 'There's no chance of getting those records. Zero.'

'Why? Where's the shipping container?'

Hal turned a haggard face on them. 'I incinerated it yesterday!'

During the short ride back to the *Volante*, Hal explained about Cuff and his fake shipment. 'We landed here a couple of days ago, and I went to the pub to pick up a cargo job. There were three people there, all desperate to get to Barwenna with their robots. I didn't realise it then, but they were all chasing this inheritance.' Hal took a breath. 'Clunk and I agreed we'd never fly another passenger, so I told them all no.'

'I thought you flew Cuff to Barwenna?' said Natasha.

'Yeah. He fooled us with a fake cargo job, and got the spaceport to load a random container full of junk. They were happy to get rid of it. Hell, they'd have stuffed a dozen into the hold, no questions asked. Then he pretended he'd been mugged, and after I rescued him he wangled his way aboard the ship.'

'And when you got to Barwenna?'

'Eventually we discovered the cargo job was a fake. Clunk thought the container might be stuffed full of weapons or drugs, so we busted it open.

Instead it was just office furniture and paperwork.' Hal shrugged. 'When we took off yesterday I dumped the thing. It's burnt to cinders by now.'

There was a lengthy silence.

'You weren't to know,' said Zee finally. 'It's not your fault.'

Hal glanced at Natasha. 'I guess you've got your story. You should make a packet writing up this little comedy.'

The cab drew up in silence, and they all climbed out. Hal saw Sandy at the *Volante*'s airlock, and his stomach clenched. How was he going to explain this whole mess to her?

— 32 —

Ten minutes later Hal was sitting at the console, his feet up and a fresh cup of coffee by his elbow. The others were below, gathering their things. His plan was to drop them at the Barwenna spaceport, and then he'd set off to find Clunk.

The ships engines thrummed below decks, a soothing, familiar noise. Wills, shipping containers, fake pirates … they could all join passengers on Hal's list of 'never agains', right below Peace Force officers and debt collectors.

Hal glanced at the main screen, where a digital readout was showing 2:31.

'Navcom, what's our ETA?'

'That combination traditionally represents two hours and thirty-one minutes.'

'What's the local time? Barwenna City, I mean.'

'Ten a.m.'

So, it was only two hours until the solicitors awarded the legacy, and thanks to him Sandy, Zee and Clunk were all out of the running. Hal drew a deep breath. Sandy had been understanding, but he'd sensed her bitter disappointment. Over the past twenty-four hours she'd really come alive, joining in the pirate role-play and contributing to their quest with gusto, but with the bad news she'd drawn back into her shell. Zee had been typical robot … not shouting and screaming in anger, just letting Hal know by subtle signs. Forceful gestures, carefully chosen phrases … Hal was used to those and more, thanks to Clunk. As for Natasha, she had no stake in the outcome but still managed to make Hal feel small and inadequate.

'If only I hadn't dumped that container,' muttered Hal.

'You did leave it a bit late,' said the Navcom.

'What do you mean?'

'You took too long ejecting it. Instead of burning up in a matter of hours it could orbit the planet for days.'

Hal stared at the console. 'Are you saying it might still be there?'

'Of course it's still there. I told you, you released it too late.'

'Can you find it again?'

The Navcom hesitated. 'Yes.'

'Can we get it back?'

'You want to retrieve a container from low orbit using a deep space freighter?'

'Yes.'

'It'll be tricky. The container may be tumbling end over end, and the atmosphere –'

'Yes or no, Navcom.'

'Yes, if Clunk were flying the ship. If you take the controls it's a big fat …maybe.'

'Thanks for the vote of confidence.' Hal reached for the intercom, intending to share the news. Then he hesitated. Why get their hopes up? It was better to locate the container first. 'What's our ETA?'

On the screen, the clock ticked over to 2:26.

◆

Hal gripped the flight stick, barely taking time to dash the sweat from his eyes. On screen, a shipping container was tumbling against a backdrop of clouds, oceans and land mass. Green cross hairs pursued it from one side of the screen to the other, and columns of text whizzed past too fast to read.

The container got closer and closer, and there was a *clanngg!* as it smashed against the hull. A welter of furniture and paper fragments sailed past, and the screen went dark.

'Would you like to try again?' asked the Navcom.

'Yeah, and this time keep it still.'

'I'm trying to simulate actual conditions.'

'Simulate them easier or I'll never get it.'

'Why don't you ask Zee for assistance?'

'What use is that? He doesn't know the first thing about flying a ship.'

The Navcom remained silent.

'Is it really going to be this hard?' asked Hal.

'The container will be moving at speed, and you imparted a spin when you released it from the cargo hold. The goal is to overtake it with the ship, open the hold, match the spin and slow down to draw the container inside.'

'And you can't use autopilot because …'

'It was designed for take-off, navigation and landing, not sky hockey.'

'At least tell me where I'm going wrong.'

'So far, you've run into it every time you tried to overtake. You need to give it a bit more space.'

Hal gestured at the screen. 'How can I, when I don't know where the ship begins?'

'You could try third person point of view.'

'What am I, a console gamer?'

'Under the circumstances, perhaps you could swallow your pride.'

'Oh, all right. Give it a shot.'

The planet reappeared, with the container tumbling in the distance. At the bottom of the screen was a model of the *Volante*, her engines belching flames. Hal tried the stick and the ship rocked from side to side, closing on the container at a tremendous rate.

'Slow down!' cried the Navcom.

Hal eased back on the throttles, and the exhaust flames died. He zoomed past the container and threw out the anchors, then jinked to the side as it screamed past, narrowly missing the port engine. 'Why's it glowing?' he asked, eyeing the container.

'Re-entry. It's going to burn up in minutes.'

The container raced away, trailing a plume of smoke. Hal pushed the throttles forward to catch up, but this time he was ready and he eased back gently.

'Nicely done,' said the Navcom. On screen, the container was spinning through the air, just behind the ship. 'That'll shield it from the atmosphere.'

Hal wiped the sweat from his brow. 'Can we land like this?'

'Negative. At that speed it would level a city.' The Navcom hesitated. 'I'd hurry to the hold if I were you.'

'Why? I'm supposed to be chasing the container.'

'You already did.'

Reality dawned, and Hal looked closer. 'That's not a simulator, is it?'

'Not this time.'

'Why didn't you warn me?'

'Clunk told me you suffer from performance anxiety.'

'When Clunk comes back we're going to have words.' Hal leapt from the chair and ran for the lift, where he jammed his thumb on the second button. 'Keep it level, okay? I don't want to fall out.'

Hal charged along the corridor to the hold, almost colliding with a stray robot on the way.

'What's the rush?' demanded Zee. 'Are we landing already?'

'Just picking up the trash,' called Hal, as he flew past. He yanked the inner door and hurried into the hold, where he grabbed a safety line with a hefty clip on each end. At the rear doors he activated the intercom. 'Navcom, how's the atmosphere?'

'Tense.'

Hal closed his eyes. 'I meant the air.'

'It's barely breathable. You'll have to work fast.'

Hal activated the controls, and there was a hiss as the doors parted. Air swirled by, and at the last second he remembered to clip on the safety line. The noise was intense with the doors open, even though the engines were throttled back for re-entry. It was hard to breathe too, and Hal was gasping in seconds. Then he spotted the container, and all thoughts of breathing were forgotten. It was just as he remembered it, rust-streaked and dented, only now half the paint had been stripped off and the corners were glowing cherry red. It was also spinning like a chicken on a turbocharged spit roast.

Hal studied it in concern. If he slowed the *Volante* and let it into the hold, the container would rip his ship apart from the inside out. Then he heard a buzz, faint in the thin air, and he saw the intercom flashing. 'What is it?'

'We're getting close to the ground,' said the Navcom. 'You really need to bring the container in.'

'I can't! It's spinning a damn sight faster than your simulation.'

'Then we'll have to leave it.'

Hal frowned. So near, yet so far! Then he felt a hand on his shoulder, and he almost fell out of the hold in surprise. It was Zee and the others, all staring at the container in amazement.

'What can we do to help?' shouted Zee.

'I can't bring it in. It's spinning too fast.'

Zee judged the gap. The container was heating up, and super-heated air was streaming off the *Volante*'s hull. 'What if I jump over there with a rope?'

'I wouldn't risk a crazy stunt like that. It'll fling you off like a bucking bronco.'

'It's the only chance!'

'You can't do it. Too risky.' Suddenly Hal stared. 'A crazy stunt!'

'So you said.'

'No, that's the answer!' Hal grabbed the intercom. 'Navcom, can you transfer flight controls down here?'

'Affirmative. Please note, your insurance policy doesn't cover a headlong dive into the planetary surface, and if you don't pull up soon –'

'Never mind the policy. Get on with it!'

The panel flew open and a joystick sprang out. Hal took it and waved the others towards the side of the hold. 'Clip on to something. Quick!'

Sandy and Natasha took the remaining safety lines and clipped on. Zee looked in vain for a spare, then grabbed hold of an upright with both hands. Once they were ready Hal gripped the stick, getting a feel for the smooth plastic. Then, without warning, he slammed it hard left.

The effect was immediate: side thrusters roared and the *Volante* performed an extended barrel roll, spinning faster and faster along her axis as she plunged towards the ground. From inside the hold it looked like the container's spin was slowing, until it was hovering just behind the ship, the right way up. The illusion worked until Hal focussed beyond the container, at which point he saw madly whirling stars. Hurriedly looking away, he eased back on the throttle and guided the container into the hold. He could feel the fierce heat radiating from the metal, and he prayed the contents weren't charred to a crisp.

When it was safely inside Zee sprang forward to fix the container down, while Hal closed the doors. The second the cargo clamps fired Hal got on the intercom again. 'Navcom, take control. Full emergency power, then auto-land at the Barwenna Spaceport!'

'Complying, Mr Spacejock.'

Hal breathed out. They'd done it. They'd really done it!

◆

The *Volante* was on final approach, and Hal and the others were up to their hips in the rubbish-filled container. It was baking hot and they were all running with sweat, but fortunately it hadn't reached critical temperature and the paperwork was still intact. Hal looted filing cabinets, desk drawers and old waste paper baskets, storming through the container like a child who'd lost their pocket money in a snowdrift. 'Didn't these people hear about the ebook revolution?' he muttered, surveying the massed boxes.

The others were more thorough, checking the files and papers Hal flung over his shoulder.

'Here!' shouted Sandy. With a triumphant grin she held up a handful of manila folders.

'What have you got?'

'Personnel records for all their robots.'

Hal took the files and flipped through. There were six photos, all identical, and each robot had a full history. He was about to check further when the ship lurched.

'Landing successful,' said the Navcom.

'What's the time?'

'Eleven forty-five.'

Hal opened the doors and they left via the cargo ramp. They were still running for Natasha's car when the ramp closed behind them, sealing the ship.

◆

Clunk sat on his bunk and stared at the wall. He'd been treated well, and his cell was suitably equipped with a nice rubber ball and a classic movie poster, but after a long night without contact his patience was finally running out. He'd tried communicating by radio, but the cell was covered by a jammer, and when he tapped Morse code messages on the water pipes the only response he got back was unprintable.

He'd whiled away the time by reprogramming his actuators, diverting extra power to his arms and fingers. The barred door to his cell was impressive, but it was designed for humans. Clunk calculated that by conserving his energy, then releasing it in a near-instantaneous burst through his reprogrammed arms, he could lever the door right off its hinges.

There was only one thing holding him back: Ripping the door off and escaping his cell was tantamount to declaring war on the Battlecruiser. Whatever trouble he was in now, it was nothing to the punishment they'd mete out if he were caught a second time. And thanks to Mr Spacejock, he couldn't even talk his way out of trouble.

Clunk checked the time. It was just after eleven, and the meeting was at twelve. It was too late to help Mr Spacejock and Sandy locate any missing information, but if by some miracle they'd found it by themselves ... well, Clunk needed to be there before the deadline. And the only thing standing in his way was a cell door. That, plus hundreds of armed personnel, the Battlecruiser's automated defence system, and a long flight back to Barwenna.

Clunk came to a sudden decision. However slim the chance of escape, he couldn't afford to languish in the cell any longer. He stood up, swaying on his weakened legs. By contrast his arms felt like pile drivers, capable of punching a hole straight through the walls. He approached the door and took hold of the bars. Hidden motors groaned as they took up the strain, and Clunk's vision dimmed as tremendous amounts of power were diverted to his forearms. The strain was immense, and then he felt movement. For a split second he thought his arms had given way, but when he opened his eyes the door was loose in his hands. He'd done it!

There was a muted buzz and he spotted another door opening towards him. There was no time to hide, or replace his cell door, and he was still standing there with the evidence gripped in both hands when First Lieutenant Overmann walked in with a pair of armed guards.

Natasha unlocked the car, and Hal was about to climb in when there was a deep BOOM directly overhead. He looked up, shading his eyes, and saw a gigantic ship materialising in the clouds. 'That's a Battlecruiser. I wonder what they want?'

'Do you think it's the *Almara*?' said Zee.

'How many Battlecruisers do customs have in this system?'

'That's classified information, but I believe it's more than zero and less than two.'

'That many?' Hal studied the huge ship. 'So it might not be the *Almara* at all.'

The others exchanged a glance.

'Can they land at the spaceport?' asked Hal.

'No, Battlecruisers are deep space only.'

'Mr Hal Spacejock,' said a rough voice. 'We meet again.'

Hal tore his gaze from the huge battleship and spotted the two well-dressed thugs. They grabbed Hal by the elbows, lifting him off his feet, and the blond one pushed his face up close. 'My boss wants to see you. He wants to pay you back for ruining his daughter's wedding.'

Hal closed his eyes. There was no escape this time.

'Ow!' shouted one of the men.

'Argh!' yelled the other.

They let go of Hal's arms, and he stared in amazement as the two thugs hopped around on one leg, each clasping their shins. There was no time to react ... before he could say anything Sandy and Natasha had bundled him into the car.

'What happened?' he demanded, as they roared away.

'We stamped on their feet,' remarked Natasha. She raised her hand and Sandy slapped it. 'More than a match for a pair of goons, am I right?'

'Deadly and dangerous,' muttered Hal. 'They didn't stand a chance.'

33

Hal ran up the steps at the solicitors, bundled the security guard out of the way and ran for the reception desk. 'Stop the clock. We're here!'

'Well, if it isn't Hal Spacejock,' said a laconic voice. 'Lost any passengers lately?'

Hal turned to see Kent Spearman's mocking face. Standing nearby were Cuff and Fisher. Behind them were their robots, two on their feet and Cuff's still lashed to the hotel trolley. 'And how are your treasured companions?' asked Hal. 'Thrown any out the airlock lately?'

Kent shrugged.

'Hey, that tactic on the Orbiter … tying up all the terminals. Was that all yours, or did these two chip in? And the Battlecruiser …'

Kent interrupted him. 'Did you get any info? Any proof showing where the robots came from?'

'Might have done,' said Hal warily. Then he noticed the glum expressions and a broad grin split his face. 'You didn't find anything, did you? All that huffing and puffing, cheating and lying, and the great Kent Spearman fell short. Again!'

'We found plenty of old records,' said Cuff. 'Alas, none were conclusive.'

Hal jerked his thumb towards the entrance. 'The door's that way, sunshine. Try not to cheat anyone on the way out.' He was about to turn away when his gaze fell on Cuff's robot. It was lying on the luggage trolley, immobile, but its blank eyes were staring right at him. Scoring points off Spearman and the others was one thing, but it wasn't their future he was playing with. On impulse, Hal opened the folder and pulled out three files. 'Here,' he said gruffly, shoving them into Kent's hands. 'You're back in the race.'

Kent stared at him, then looked down at the files. He looked stunned, and for once he was speechless.

'That's very noble of you,' said Cuff. 'If I win …'

'If you win I want my fifty grand. Cash.'

'And if you win …'

'Not much chance of that.' Hal glanced at the clock. It was five to twelve and Clunk was nowhere to be seen. He'd never make it now.

The receptionist took their signatures in a ledger, then announced them over the commset. A door opened and Mr Butt emerged from his office, dressed in a neat suit. 'Ladies, gentlemen …robots. Please come in. It's time to settle Baker's legacy.'

◆

The boardroom was dominated by a huge wooden table, polished to a mirror shine. There were twelve places laid out along the sides, six with glasses of water and napkins, and six with recessed power sockets. Butt took his place at the head of the table and motioned the others to their seats. Zee sat alone, without a human alongside him. Hal glanced at Clunk's empty place and frowned. Then he realised someone was missing. Cuff, Spearman and Fisher were all there with their robots, sitting along the opposite side of the table like a living mugshot file. He'd spotted Zee already, and Sandy was sitting to his right, busy plugging her robot into the socket. But where was Natasha? The reporter had parked her car and followed them up the steps, but he didn't remember seeing her after –

'Before we begin, there's someone I need to introduce.' Butt nodded at the guards, who opened the doors to admit …

'Natasha!' exclaimed Hal.

The reporter ignored him, taking a seat alongside Butt. She took out her notebook and laid it on the desk. 'I have the report in full.'

'Excellent work,' said Butt. 'For now, perhaps just the summary?'

'Wait a minute.' Hal looked from one to the other. 'Natasha, do you work for this guy?'

'In a way.'

Butt explained. 'Ms Lucas is a private investigator. We employed her for background checks.'

Hal stared. 'What was all that crap about writing an article?'

'There's a lot of money at stake. We had to take every precaution.' Butt glanced at Natasha. 'I'm sorry for the interruption. Please proceed.'

'I interviewed five of the six candidates. The sixth, Sandy West, refused to answer any questions.'

'It was none of your business,' snapped Sandy.

Natasha ignored her, and frowned at her notepad. 'First, David Fisher. He makes a living buying and selling robots, cash in hand, and he obtained his robot by deceiving a Mrs Lily Turner.'

'I object!' shouted Fisher.

Butt frowned at him. 'Mr Fisher, this isn't a courtroom. Object all you like, but it won't make any difference.'

'I've had this robot for years!'

Natasha tapped on her notepad. 'That may be so, but you took the brain and half the components out of Mrs Turner's robot.'

'But –'

'If I might finish,' said Natasha. 'You played up a minor fault with her robot, offered substantially less than it was worth, and then paid an even smaller amount in cash. Suspicious of your motives, but afraid to confront you in person, Mrs Turner forged the signature on the receipt. Therefore, the brain and other parts of your robot still belong to her.'

'That tricky old trout,' growled Fisher.

'Not that it matters, since her robot is not the one we're looking for. It has no claim on the will.'

Fisher swore under his breath. Alongside him, his robot suppressed a smile.

'Next is Mr Cuff. He stole his robot from the science department at his local school, where he was employed as a part-time cleaner.'

'I did not!' exclaimed Cuff. 'They threw it out! I rescued it from the skip!'

'Not only did you steal it, you destroyed its speech circuits so it couldn't report you.'

'This is preposterous. This is a pack of lies. This ...'

'If you don't sit quietly I'll report you to the Peace Force. Your choice.'

Cuff leant across the polished table. 'You haven't heard the last of this!' he shouted, jabbing his finger at her. 'I'll sue you!'

'If you need a lawyer, the fees at Argisle and Butt are quite reasonable. In the meantime, your silence would be appreciated.' Natasha glanced at her notebook. 'Next we have Zee. Unfortunately you signed the initial paperwork in your own hand, whereas it was meant to be signed by your legal owner, Alan Dane.'

'I had to sign it myself,' said Zee. 'Mr Dane died two days ago.'

'Did he know you shopped him to the Peace Force? And deliberately led the competition to every one of his businesses and safe houses? And ...ordered his execution?'

'That's impossible. I'm programmed to obey! I would never harm Mr Dane, never! He took me in, he looked after me, he ...he cared for me!'

The robot sounded completely sincere, and his expression was distraught. Hal had no doubt he was telling the truth, and he was about to tell Natasha to lay off when she continued.

'What you don't realise is that you're programmed with split personalities, each totally separate from the other. I believe your activation keyword is ...Hyde.'

Zee's expression hardened, and a split second later he leapt up, kicking his chair back. There was a whine as his weapons deployed, but Natasha was ready for him. She calmly picked up a remote and zapped the robot right between the eyes. Zee froze, guns half erect, then toppled backwards to land with a resounding clang.

'It's his own fault,' explained Natasha. 'He paid someone to rebuild him like that. Incidentally, he wasn't Baker's robot either.' She glanced at the three remaining candidates: Hal, Sandy and Kent Spearman. Her gaze settled on Sandy. 'Ah yes, the runaway.'

Sandy glared back.

'I don't have evidence of wrong-doing, but you're eliminated anyway.'

'What are you talking about?' demanded Sandy. 'Eliminated how?'

'Mr Butt, would you care to explain?'

'You're under eighteen, young lady.' Butt gazed at her over his glasses, as though studying a fascinating legal problem. 'When you signed the form it specifically requested approval from your parents or guardians, to be crossed out as applicable.'

'But –'

'It doesn't really matter,' said Natasha, with an impatient gesture. 'Your robot isn't the one.'

'I thought you were on my side,' muttered Sandy.

There was an uncomfortable silence, and she made to get up. Before she could leave, Hal put a hand on her arm. 'Don't you want to see how this turns out?'

'I–I guess.'

There were two left in the running: Hal and Kent. They exchanged a glance, both of them knowing the first person Natasha looked at would be eliminated.

◆

Hal and Kent sat there, eyes locked in mortal combat. Then Hal saw an expression of joy cross Kent's face, and he realised it was all over. He glanced along the table to see Natasha eyeing him like a scientist studying a particularly virulent disease. 'Mr Hal Spacejock, freighter pilot. There are so many reasons why you should be eliminated I can't even begin to cover them.'

'It's not me you should be thinking of. Clunk's the one up for this inheritance. Why can't you examine his history?'

'Let's not kid ourselves. We all know where this money is really heading, and it won't be a robot's bank account.'

'I don't want anything to do with your bloody money,' snapped Hal. 'You've been sitting there tearing people apart, when all you had to do was point to a robot and say congratulations. Didn't your parents give you enough attention as a kid, or have you always wanted to host one of those crappy reality shows?'

Natasha was taken aback, and she looked to Butt for help. Unfortunately he'd just spotted something interesting on his notepad. 'It was important to deal with everyone in order,' said Natasha. 'We had to eliminate imposters until only the verified claimant remained.'

Kent Spearman laughed. 'Well, that's the best news I've had all day. When do you need my account details?'

'I haven't finished yet,' said Natasha. 'Mr Spacejock, you're unreliable and untrustworthy but you mean well. You helped the others where it would have been in your best interest to abandon them, and you acted in good faith.'

Hal's spirits rose. Was she switching things up? Was Spearman about to get a kick in the guts?

Ting!

Everyone turned to look at the clock. The hands were pointing straight up, and the delicate bell was marking twelve noon.

Ting!

Natasha smiled across the table. 'Mr Spacejock, according to your findings and our deliberations, Clunk is Baker's robot.'

Ting!

'Alas, the terms were quite clear.' Natasha raised one finger. 'When those chimes cease, he's no longer entitled to the inheritance.'

Ting!

'You have to give him more time!' protested Hal. 'He's only stuck aboard the *Almara* because you barged in front of him.'

Ting!

'I'm sorry, but the deadline is set in stone.'

Ting!

Hal felt rising anger, but what could he do? The Battlecruiser was orbiting the planet, and unless Clunk teleported down ...

Ting!

Hal stared at the clock. Five more rings and all that money would slip through their fingers. How could he delay proceedings? What could he say?

Ting!

With four to go, Hal put his head in his hands. The situation was hopeless. They'd lost the lot.

Ting!

There was a distant whine, which became a roar, then an ear-shattering rumble. A shadow flitted across the windows, and then ... *Craaaaash!* The end window exploded inwards and Hal caught a glimpse of a bronze missile, flames belching from its tail. The missile flattened a sideboard, sending the antique clock flying, then skidded the length of the room with a teeth-drilling squeal. Sparks and chairs flew until the missile crashed into the far wall, scattering plaster and bringing down a row of paintings. The clock spun round and round, then fell over backwards with a final 'ti-i-ing!'

When the dust and smoke cleared Hal saw the 'missile' was Clunk, with a rocket pack strapped to his back. His bronze skin was scorched and smoking from re-entry, and Hal realised he must have jumped straight out of the Battlecruiser. The robot gave him a fierce grin as he stepped away from the wall, and Hal couldn't help laughing as Clunk's big flat foot came down on the antique clock, crushing it flat.

Hal turned to Butt and Natasha, who were sitting in open-mouthed shock. 'I shouldn't worry about the repair bill,' he remarked. 'With all that cash to his name I reckon Clunk's good for it.'

34

It was several seconds before Butt recovered his composure. He frowned at Clunk, glared at Hal, then studied his paperwork. Meanwhile, Hal looked Clunk up and down. Something was different about him, and it wasn't the rocket pack. Then he realised what it was: Clunk had epaulettes at his shoulders, and there was a fresh serial number stencilled on his chest. 'What have you been up to?'

Clunk frowned and pointed to his mouth.

'You lost your voice? Never mind, we'll get it fixed.'

Clunk mimed a shape with the flat of his hand, circled it overhead, then gestured at his mouth.

'You want me to order a pizza?'

Now thoroughly animated, Clunk looked down at the table and saw the notepad. He grabbed it, scrawled with the pen and held it out.

'You want me to say the name of my ship?'

Clunk nodded enthusiastically.

'Why?'

There was a strangled groan, and Clunk scribbled again.

'You want me to say the name of my ship immediately, right now and without any hesitation whatsoever?' Hal frowned. 'I don't get it.'

'*Volante*,' said Sandy.

'I know that, and so does he!' protested Hal. Clunk advanced on him, and suddenly he remembered. At the hotel ...the speech suppression code ...the keywords! '*Volante*!' he said hurriedly.

Clunk stopped. 'Thank you, Mr Spacejock. It was a struggle, but you got there in the end.'

'It was nothing. And don't worry about the pizza, I'll order one later.' Hal gestured at the new serial number. 'So what's that about?'

'Pilot Officer Clunk at your service.' He saluted smartly. 'Seconded to the Battlecruiser *Almara*, chief test pilot for Green Flight Alpha.'

Hal blinked. 'How did that happen?'

'Actually, Green Flight only has one pilot. Me.' Clunk indicated the rocket pack. 'They had to create a new squadron before I could borrow this device.'

'That's a lot of favours. What did you do, save the ship from a black hole? Single-handedly defeat a rogue cruiser?'

Clunk gave him a brief recap. 'After you left, I was caught up in a training mission. I saved a drone from destruction by leaping from the ship. They sent a recovery vessel, and I spent the night in the brig.'

'Sounds like you put them through hell.'

'Not quite. Apparently it was the most challenging training exercise they've had for years. They're going to write it up and use it in future scenarios.'

'Do you get royalties?'

'Actually yes, but they kept my advance towards the cost of a new cell door. I broke out of confinement just as they were coming to release me.'

Butt cleared his throat. 'This is fascinating, but could we return to the subject at hand?'

'Oh yeah.' Hal patted Clunk on the shoulder. 'While you were off playing war games we managed to prove your history. You're Baker's robot, and you inherit the whole lot.'

'Really? That's a nice surprise.'

Butt frowned. 'That's not strictly accurate. There are still one or two conditions.'

'Oh, here we go,' muttered Hal. 'It's time for the fine print.'

◆

Butt pushed his chair back and stood, resting his hands on the polished wooden table. 'There are two matters to take care of before you inherit.'

Everyone turned to stare at him, and Hal frowned as he wondered what new hoop the old guy had come up with.

Butt continued. 'Before the inheritance is finalised we must verify your robot's brain is the original article.' There was a faint chime, and the doors swung open to admit a severe-looking woman in a white lab coat. Butt indicated Clunk, and the woman sat down and opened her briefcase. Out came a roll of tools, and she had the robot's skull open in no time. The woman withdrew a gadget from the case and connected it to Clunk's brain. Three seconds later there was a beep, and she frowned as she checked the screen.

'Well?' demanded Butt.

'It's a match.'

'Are you sure?'

'Definitely. This is the original brain.'

Kent Spearman snorted in disgust, while Hal breathed a sigh of relief.

'Very well. In that case, it's time for an announcement.' Butt smiled at Clunk. 'I'm pleased to tell you that Mr Baker would like a little word.'

Everyone turned towards the entrance, expecting the fabled businessman to burst in and announce the whole business had been an elaborate PR stunt. The doors remained closed, and instead a section of panelling slid aside to reveal a viewscreen. At that point Butt hesitated. 'Since this is for Clunk's ears, I would ask the rest of you to clear the room. My staff will provide you with coffee and sandwiches in the lobby.'

The others complied, grumbling under their breath. Hal went to follow, but Clunk stopped him. 'Anything Mr Baker has to say will affect the pair of us.'

'No problem.' After all, thought Hal, the coffee and sandwiches could wait.

Once the room was clear the screen flickered, and an elderly man appeared. He had short grey hair and a weathered face, but his most notable feature was his intense blue eyes. They crinkled around the edges as he smiled warmly at the camera, and then he began. 'My dear friend, I'm so glad you've been found. These past few years have been hard on me, and I often wondered what happened to you after we parted company.'

Hal glanced at Clunk, wondering what sort of emotions were rushing around his circuits. This old geezer must be like a long-lost parent to the robot, and he hoped the strain wouldn't be too much.

'You won't remember this,' continued Baker, 'but for three months you worked as a clerk in finance, overseeing stocks and bonds. Ahh those carefree days! The heady smell of finance, the whirr of the trading computers, the raw power of money.'

Hal glanced at Clunk to see how he was taking all this. Funny smells and odd whirring noises were daily occurrences where the robot was concerned, but he'd never shown much interest in finance.

'Then, that fateful day. How can I forget?' The old man's smile vanished, and his voice turned shrill. 'That was when you made your stupid, careless mistake. Instead of buying seventeen hundred shares in GMT, you purchased seventeen *million* shares in GMC ... ten minutes before the price crashed!'

Butt frowned. Clearly this wasn't in the script.

'You cost me one hundred and ninety two thousand, four hundred and eighty-six credits that afternoon!' shouted Baker. 'I was going to have you crushed. Ground up. Turned into road base! But no, my namby-pamby advisors convinced me to wipe your memory and flog you off. Well, my lead-brained friend, it's payback time. You're not laying any of your tin fingers on my legacy ... that's going to charity.' Baker's mouth twisted into a cruel smile. 'No, all you're getting are those seventeen million worthless shares you bought in my name. I hope you rust in robot hell!'

35

The screen went dark, and there was a shocked silence.

'What a prick,' said Hal at last. 'After all that messing about, the old bastard was just out for revenge?'

'So it seems.' Butt looked highly embarrassed, and busied himself by shuffling his paperwork. 'Unfortunately, this recording is legitimate, and despite the ... the spirited delivery, Mr Baker did seem to know what he wanted. This recording overrides the terms of his will.'

'Bloody lunatic,' muttered Hal. 'What sort of person reaches out from beyond the grave like that?' Then he remembered Clunk, and he turned to the robot in concern. Clunk's expression was stony, unreadable, but his eyes spoke volumes. As he watched the reaction Hal desperately wished they'd never heard of Cuff or the stupid inheritance. 'Are you all right?'

Clunk shrugged. 'It could have been worse. Nobody died.'

Hal turned to the lawyer. 'What about these shares? Are they worth anything?'

'I'm afraid not. I believe the company is all but bankrupt, and has no prospects whatsoever.'

'GMC, right? Who is that anyway?'

'Galactic Mining Company.' Butt noticed Hal's start, and he gave him a shrewd look. 'What is it? Have you heard something?'

'No, it's just one of the companies Baker sold his robots to.'

'I see.' Butt hesitated. 'I assume you'll be leaving Barwenna soon?'

'Why, is that a problem?'

'Not at all. I was going to make an appointment to transfer ownership of the shares, but we might as well do it now.'

'Will it cost anything?'

'A hundred credits.'

Hal reached into his pocket, but the solicitor stopped him. 'Under the circumstances, I think we'll do the honours. I'm just sorry Mr Baker ...'

'Yeah.'

Ten minutes later the paperwork was complete, and the secretary handed Clunk a nice colourful certificate proving his ownership of seventeen million shares in the Galactic Mining Company. A photographer took snaps of the happy beneficiary, and a tame reporter promised not to mention the fact the shares were worthless ... at least, not until they wrote a follow-up expos?.

They left the boardroom with Clunk still clutching his worthless shares, and Hal spotted the others in the reception area. Sandy hurried up to check out Clunk's certificate, while nearby David Fisher was arguing with the receptionist, trying to get the solicitors to pay for a cab ride home. Cuff was sitting by himself, lost in thought, and Kent Spearman had a flashy commset clamped to one ear. 'What, right now? That's great news! Top off the tanks, I'll be right there.'

Kent gave Hal a sympathetic wink. 'Bad luck with the whole worthless legacy business. That old boy was a real joker, eh?'

'Yeah. Hilarious.'

Kent gestured with the commset. 'Never mind, I landed on my feet again. I just picked up a fantastic cargo job.'

'Really?'

'Excellent pay, totally above board. It's a container of antique furniture parts for Evilon.'

'Evilon?' said Cuff suddenly. 'What a coincidence. That's exactly where I need to go!'

'Inconceivable!' said Hal quickly, before Clunk could intervene. 'I'm sure Spearman will give you a lift. I mean, he's already heading that way.'

Kent looked doubtful. 'Can you pay the fare?'

'Sure!' Cuff put his arm around Kent's shoulders, guiding him down the stairs to the waiting taxi. 'My uncle lives on Evilon and he's loaded. In fact, I'm his last remaining relative and it's only a matter of time before the inheritance is made out in my favour. If you can get me to ...'

The doors closed on the two of them, and Hal laughed aloud. Then Clunk tapped him on the shoulder, and he turned to see the robot's annoyed expression. 'Oh yeah. *Volante.*'

'I wish you'd stop doing that, Mr Spacejock.'

'I couldn't let you spoil the fun. Kent Spearman getting conned by that Cuff shyster? It's perfect!'

'Do you think anyone wants this?' asked Sandy.

Hal saw her inspecting Cuff's ruined robot, which was still lashed to the hotel trolley. 'Help yourself.'

'Not so fast,' said Clunk. 'Technically that robot belongs to Mr Cuff. You can't keep it without a receipt.'

'Yeah, but he just abandoned it. Plus it's wrecked.' Hal glanced at Sandy. 'What do you want it for, anyway?'

'I can use some of the parts to fix Daniel's cooling problem.'

Clunk nodded his approval. 'Your intentions are worthy but you still need –'

'Inconceivable,' said Hal. Clunk's mouth kept moving but no sounds came out, and while the robot was gesturing and slapping the side of his head, Hal grabbed a piece of paper from the reception desk and wrote on it. Then he scrawled his name across the bottom and handed it to Sandy. 'Cuff gave me the robot for his fare, so it's mine to dispose of. If anyone complains they can come and find me aboard the *Volante*.'

'–ing rude and inconsiderate,' finished Clunk with a rush.

'Thanks,' said Sandy, with a grin. She turned to Clunk. 'I really appreciate all the help. It was a blast.'

Clunk's angry expression relaxed into a friendly smile. 'It was my pleasure.'

'I'm really sorry about the will.'

'I've already forgotten about it,' said Clunk. 'Take care, young lady, and best of luck with your future.'

Sandy nodded, then turned to Hal. 'Thanks for looking after me. And, er, not handing me in.'

'No problem.' Hal hesitated. 'Will you be all right? Your parents, I mean?'

'I'll cope. It's only this year and then I can move out.'

'Call us when you're ready. We'll give you a lift anywhere you want. Any planet in the galaxy, free of charge.'

'Thanks,' said Sandy gratefully.

'Do you want some money for a cab?'

'No, I'll catch the bus. It's not far.'

They watched her leave, pushing the hotel trolley with Daniel sitting side-saddle on top of Cuff's faulty robot. Hal felt a surge of anger at

Baker's mean-spirited revenge. The old buzzard had set out to punish Clunk for a petty error, but the fallout had hurt other people too. On the plus side, Kent Spearman had been sucked in, and Cuff was walking away without a bean to his name.

'Back to the *Volante*, Mr Spacejock?'

'Sure thing.' As they took the steps, Hal gestured at the share certificate. 'Let's see if we can find a frame for that thing on the way. We'll look back on it one day and …'

He stopped as a gleaming black limousine drew up to the curb. The doors opened and two man-mountains in dark suits bounced out. 'Mr Hal Spacejock?' said one of them in a gruff voice. 'We've been looking for you. Get in.'

— 36 —

Hal and Clunk were pushed into the limo, where they floundered in the
deep padded chairs. The doors slammed shut, and the heavy tint turned
the interior into a darkened cave. One heavy sat either side of them,
blocking the exits, and as the car drew away one of them froze Clunk
with a remote.

Hal blinked in the darkness, and he made out a greying, smallish man
with a silk neck tie and dark glasses. 'What have you done to my robot?'

'Don't worry, it's temporary.' The man spoke in a low voice. 'He'll
recover.'

'If anything happens to him ...'

'Forget the damned robot. Do you know who I am?' The man didn't
wait for an answer. 'You remember my daughter, right? Dressed in white,
standing at the altar, wedding ruined by a practical joker with a thirst for
acrobatics?'

Hal swallowed.

'Yes, thought so. She wants your head on a platter, did you know that?'

Hal felt his neck.

'You ruined her wedding and cost me a packet.'

'I-I'll pay you back. We have lots of shares!'

'I don't want your money.' The man adjusted his neck tie. 'You've
been running from my men for two days now, but you must have known
I'd catch up with you in the end. Big Vinnie always gets his man. Always!'

Hal eyed 'Big' Vinnie, and he was still wondering how the powerful
man had earned the nickname when a briefcase landed in his lap.

'Open it.'

Hal hesitated. Was it a bomb? A noose? A blaster to shoot himself
with?

'Come on. I don't have all day.'

The catches clicked open, the lid rose, and ... Hal whistled. The case was filled with credit tiles, neat stacks of them. Fifties, hundreds ... it was a fortune!

'That barrel roll of yours, best stunt you ever pulled.'

Hal blinked. 'I–I don't understand.'

'My daughter has lousy taste in men. Instead of marrying a loyal family man, she chose a yuppie. He votes, he volunteers in the community ... he even pays his taxes. I tried to buy the guy off and he laughed in my face.' Vinnie shook his head, clearly distressed. 'A guy like that around my family ... it would destroy us.'

Hal began to understand. 'So the wedding ...'

Vinnie laughed. 'They had a bust-up after you ruined the big day, and my little girl took up with my second cousin's youngest son. Result!' He nodded at the briefcase. 'My men have been trying to give you that for two days, but you kept giving them the slip.'

'But I thought ...'

'There's something else, too.' Vinnie handed him an envelope. 'A week for you at a five-star health resort. As much food as you can eat and seven days swimming with the fishies.'

'Eh?'

'Scuba diving. It's a beach resort.' The limo stopped. 'I believe this is you?'

Hal peered through the tinted windows and realised the limo had drawn up next to the *Volante's* passenger ramp. The doors opened and the heavies helped him out of the car. They stood Clunk alongside, and Vinnie unzapped him.

'Just one thing,' called Vinnie. 'If you ever need a job –'

'No passengers,' said Hal quickly. 'Just cargo.'

'As long as it's legal,' added Clunk.

Vinnie pulled a face. 'Never mind. See you around.'

The limo drove off, and they made their way up the ramp. Hal gripped the briefcase under his arm, hardly believing his luck. Never mind Baker and his poisonous legacy, he'd take cold hard cash any day!

◆

It was a week later, and Hal was returning to the *Volante* tanned, fit and healthy. He'd enjoyed seven days of five-star luxury, but towards the end he'd started to miss his ship, the Navcom and Clunk. Ten course meals and spa baths were all very well, but nothing beat hauling cargo through the vast reaches of space ... even if he was never sure where his next meal was coming from.

Clunk gave him a warm smile as he entered the flight deck. 'Welcome back, Mr Spacejock! Did you enjoy yourself?'

'Yeah, but it's good to be back. What's been happening around here?'

'I have three cargo jobs lined up, and I repainted the passenger cabins in a refreshing shade of green.'

Hal winced.

'Come on, I'll show you.'

Hal was about to refuse, but he decided to show a little enthusiasm. 'Green, eh? Let's have a look then.'

Inside the lift he was surprised to see a new control panel. It was polished brass, and the three matching buttons had the deck numbers carved into the surface. 'You've done more than just painting, I see.'

'Oh, just a little tweak here and there.' Clunk pressed the lowest button and the lift dropped smoothly. 'Close your eyes, Mr Spacejock.'

Hal complied. 'I'm guessing it's a very bright sort of green.'

'The brightest.'

'Never mind. We can always hand out sunglasses with every fare.'

The lift came to a halt and Hal heard the doors open. He almost looked, but stopped himself just in time. Clunk obviously wanted to give him the full eye-damaging effect, and who was he to spoil the robot's fun? The floor felt spongy underfoot, and he wondered whether Clunk had glued down extra layers of cardboard. Sound deadening perhaps, so they wouldn't hear passengers screaming to be let out.

Guided by the elbow, he took several steps towards the middle of the room. Then he was turned to one side and gently lowered into one of the ratty old armchairs. So much for his nice new flight suit. 'Can I look now?'

'Go ahead.'

Hal opened his eyes halfway, ready to shut them again at the first hint of damage. Instead, they opened wide by themselves. Directly in front of him, mounted on the wall, was the biggest viewscreen he'd ever seen. At his left elbow was an automated trolley with three cup holders and a touchscreen showing a giant list of tasty snacks. To his right was a remote with more controls than the *Volante*'s flight console.

Dazed, he turned his head to take in the rest of the lower deck. The tatty old passenger cabins were gone, and in their place was a polished wooden bar with half a dozen chrome stools. There was a fully-equipped gym, a sauna, a spa bath with a gravity net and ... in the far corner, behind a bank of safety shields ... the AutoChef.

'I turned the recreation room into additional passenger cabins,' said Clunk. 'I hope you don't mind.'

'I ... I don't mind at all,' said Hal. 'It's bloody amazing.'

'Thank you.'

'Was there anything left?'

'What do you mean?'

'That briefcase full of cash. You must have made a hell of a dent.'

'Oh, that. No, I didn't touch it.'

Hal blinked. 'Where did you get the money?'

'I sold those worthless shares.'

'You'll need to explain that one.'

'It's simple. The shares were worthless because the Galactic Mining Company had no future. However, once I returned the data we recovered from asteroid K-7X ...'

Hal frowned. 'The memory module?'

'Yes, it contained a complete backup of their survey data.'

'So Galactic Mining are back on their feet?'

'Absolutely. GMC are the fastest moving shares on the market.'

'How much did you get for them?'

Clunk hesitated. 'Let's just say it paid for the refit, and there was enough left over to fund a university scholarship for Miss Sandy.'

'Great thinking, Clunk. Hey, you did get something for yourself, didn't you?'

'Some tools, spare parts ... I don't need much.'

'If you need any more you can use the cash in the briefcase.'

'Not quite. It was all counterfeit.'

Hal laughed and shook his head. Still, wasn't it a fabulous pad? Just wait until Kent Spearman saw it! He'd turn a brighter shade of green than Clunk's imaginary paint job. 'Oh, before I forget ...' Hal dug in his pocket and took out a small gift-wrapped parcel. 'Here. I got this.'

'For me?' Clunk tore the wrapping to reveal a small tin of toffee. 'That's ... thoughtful. I shall treasure this delicacy forever.'

'No, you dummy. Look inside.'

Clunk took the lid off, removed a wad of cotton wool and stared at the gleaming gold badge. It was engraved with the Spacer's Guild logo, and underneath was the legend 'First Class Pilot'. 'I can't possibly wear this. I'm only second class!'

'You've never been second class, my friend.'

'You don't understand. This can't be mine. I'm not qualified!'

'Sure you are.' Hal winked. 'I asked Sandy to hack in and boost your rank, and she found out you were eligible anyway. You just needed to fill out a few forms, that's all.'

'Inconceivable!' said Clunk.

Hal mimed trying to speak, and they both laughed.

'I do have one regret,' said Hal.

'What's that?'

'It's a real shame we couldn't get our revenge on Baker. That stunt he pulled with the will was evil.'

'Yes ... about that. I found out Baker Corporation is hosting a dinner party next week. They're wining and dining dozens of top politicians, hoping to score a major contract. As it happens, we've been hired to deliver the food.'

'Really? After that mess with the wedding?'

'Yes indeed.' Clunk looked thoughtful. 'I think you should handle the landing. A series of barrel-rolls would do the trick nicely, don't you agree?'

Epilogue

Private eye pens bestseller!

Natasha 'Lookie' Lucas, Barwenna's very own private investigator, recently released her first book to wild acclaim. Titled 'My Life with the Six Finalists' it's an insider's blow-by-blow account of the race for Baker's Legacy, complete with steamy passion, rich double-crosses …and vampires. When questioned about the book's accuracy, Ms Lucas admitted there were minor embellishments for dramatic effect. A twelve-movie deal is currently under negotiation, with several heartthrobs in the running for the plum role of Hal 'Grand Fang' Spacejock.

In other news, it's seven days since Baker's Legacy was settled but the great robot exodus shows no sign of letting up. Spaceport traffic is at an all-time-high as hundreds of our treasured mechanical companions depart on chartered flights. When asked where they were going, the secretive robots would only tell this reporter they were 'seeking a better future'. Rumours abound that a derelict, polluted planet recently changed hands for a suitcase full of cash, but we've been unable to verify this story.

Finally today, 'Big Sally' – daughter of waste disposal king-pin 'Big Vinnie' – announced her engagement to John 'Bulldog' Lockup, a decorated Peace Force captain famed for his crusade against organised crime. Big Vinnie declined to comment.

Acknowledgements

To Pauline Nolet, and to Jo and Tricia
thanks for the awesome help and support!

To Ian, Mike, Hugh and Fahim
Well spotted!

Safe Art

Book six in the Hal Spacejock series

Copyright © Simon Haynes 2013

spacejock.com.au

Cover images copyright depositphotos.com

Stay in touch!

Author's newsletter:
spacejock.com.au/ML.html

facebook.com/halspacejock
twitter.com/spacejock

Works by Simon Haynes

All of Simon's novels* are self-contained, with a beginning, a middle and a proper ending. They're not sequels, they don't end on a cliffhanger, and you can start or end your journey with any book in the series.
Robot vs Dragons series excepted!

The Hal Spacejock series for teens/adults
Set in the distant future, where humanity spans the galaxy and robots are second-class citizens. Includes a large dose of humour!

Hal Spacejock 0: Origins (2019/2020)
Hal Spacejock 1: A Robot named Clunk*
Hal Spacejock 2: Second Course*
Hal Spacejock 3: Just Desserts*
Hal Spacejock 4: No Free Lunch
Hal Spacejock 5: Baker's Dough
Hal Spacejock 6: Safe Art
Hal Spacejock 7: Big Bang
Hal Spacejock 8: Double Trouble
Hal Spacejock 9: Max Damage
Hal Spacejock 10: Cold Boots

Also available:
Omnibus One, containing Hal books 1-3
Omnibus Two, containing Hal books 4-6
Omnibus Three, containing Hal books 7-9
Hal Spacejock: Visit, a short story
Hal Spacejock: Framed, a short story
Hal Spacejock: Albion, a novella
*Audiobook editions available/in progress

The Dragon and Chips Trilogy.
High fantasy meets low humour!
Each set of three books should be read in order.

1. A Portion of Dragon and Chips
2. A Butt of Heads
3. A Pair of Nuts on the Throne

Also Available:
Omnibus One, containing the first trilogy
Books 1-3 audiobook editions

The Harriet Walsh series.
Set in the same universe as Hal Spacejock. Good clean fun, written with wry humour. No cliffhangers between novels!

Harriet Walsh 1: Peace Force
Harriet Walsh 2: Alpha Minor
Harriet Walsh 3: Sierra Bravo
Harriet Walsh 4: Storm Force (TBA)

Also Available:
Omnibus One, containing books 1-3

The Hal Junior series
Written for all ages, these books are set aboard a space station in the Hal Spacejock universe, only ten years later.

1. Hal Junior: The Secret Signal
2. Hal Junior: The Missing Case
3. Hal Junior: The Gyris Mission
4. Hal Junior: The Comet Caper

Also Available:
Omnibus One, containing books 1-3
The Secret Signal Audiobook edition

The Secret War series.
Gritty space opera for adult readers.

1. Raiders
2. Frontier (2019)
3. Deadlock (2019/2020)

Collect One-Two - a collection of shorts by Simon Haynes

All titles available in ebook and paperback. Visit spacejock.com.au for details.

Bowman Press

v 1.31

I have to mention my wonderful muse...
without whom this book would have been on time.

Hal Spacejock was sitting in the *Volante's* flight deck, studying a stylised graphic of a planet on the main screen. Half the planetary disc was in deep shade while the rest was unbroken, eye-straining white. Underneath the graphic were three lines of text:

A) This planet exhibits characteristics common to frozen worlds.

B) This planet is almost certainly volcanic.

C) I have absolutely no idea.

Hal eyed the planet, then the choices, then the planet, playing for time while he tried to guess the correct answer. The planet looked cold, which made A the obvious choice, but he knew these sort of tests always tried to trick you. 'Okay, Navcom. I choose B. It's volcanic.'

'That is incorrect,' said the ship's computer, in a neutral female voice.

'A,' said Hal quickly. 'I meant A. It's a frozen world.'

'Unfortunately, the correct answer is C.'

Hal stared at the text. 'How can it be C?'

'Did you know the answer?'

'Er, no.'

'There you go, then. Here's the next question.'

A friendly-looking robot appeared on the screen. It was bronze all over, and had a squashy, furrowed face with a big happy smile. Clutched in one hand was a large spanner, while the other held a mallet. Hal looked from one to the other, then studied the text underneath:

To adjust the manemol flange on the hyperdrive, one would ...

A) Smash it with a spanner.

B) Try to unscrew it with a mallet.

C) I have absolutely no idea.

'C!' shouted Hal.

'Very good, Mr Spacejock. Now for your final question. Are you ready?'

An unflattering picture of Hal appeared on the viewscreen. To one side, a ship was plunging towards a frozen planet, while on the other a robot was desperately trying to fix the hyperdrive motor. Hal concentrated hard on the images, then read the text underneath.

Since you obviously know nothing about planets OR *hyperdrive motors, please explain why you fiddled with the hyperdrive* AND *why you tried to cover up your ham-fisted tinkering by reprogramming our course in the middle of a jump.*

Underneath there was only one response:

A) I am a lousy pilot with little technical skill and no regard for my own safety.

'A?' said Hal, after a slight hesitation.

'Correct! The quiz is complete. You scored sixty-six point six percent from a maximum of one hundred percent.'

'Yes!' Hal pumped his fist. 'That's one for the ages.'

'Incidentally, Clunk has finished repairing the hyperdrive, and the ship is back on course.'

'Just as well. We only missed that frozen planet by a few hundred metres.'

'More like a dozen,' said the Navcom. 'Fortunately, we skimmed an icy wasteland, so there weren't any trees to hit. Unfortunately, the local wildlife wasn't so lucky.'

'Why?'

'My air intakes were sealed.'

'What's unlucky about that?'

'You'd have to ask the seals we scooped up.'

'They should have ducked.' Hal fiddled with the controls. 'How much longer are we going to be? I don't want to keep our customer waiting.'

'Don't worry, there's plenty of time ... provided you don't adjust any more equipment.'

At that moment the lift arrived and Clunk stepped out. The robot was cleaning his hands on a rag, and there were streaks of grease and silver paint across his bronze chest. 'So, Mr Spacejock. How was your quiz?'

'Excellent! Sixty-six percent this time.'

'That's very good. Keep trying, and one day you might get a perfect score.'

'Have you finished those repairs?'

'I finished reversing your modifications, if that's what you mean. There was no lasting damage, although I had a devilish job with the graffiti.'

'What graffiti?'

'Someone had drawn wavy lines down both sides of the engines.'

Hal tutted. 'Those weren't wavy lines.'

'No?'

'No, they were go-faster stripes.'

Clunk blinked.

'There was a kiosk at the spaceport,' explained Hal. 'They were selling this special magnetic paint which aligns all the molecules in the fuel. You can save a fortune over the life of the ship.'

'How much did this special paint cost?'

'It's usually four ninety-nine a can, but I got a discount.'

'That's a relief. For a minute there I thought you'd been ripped off.'

'No, they let me have it for four hundred.'

Clunk closed his eyes. 'Four hundred credits for a tin of paint?'

'Special magnetic paint. It'll save five percent of our fuel bill.'

'It seems to me you saved a hundred percent of your thought processes.' Clunk turned on his heel and left the flight deck, muttering under his breath about gullible pilots, ripoff merchants and humans in general.

◆

The *Volante* landed at the Forzen spaceport a couple of hours later. As he shut down the flight systems, Clunk explained to Hal that their customer was leaving full instructions at the information counter. Hal planned to accompany the robot to the terminal, hoping for coffee or snacks, until the outer door opened and his lungs nearly froze in his chest. 'F-far out,' he said, through chattering teeth. 'Have a nice walk. Goodbye.'

'No, I'll just –'

'Go on, you'll be fine.' After pushing Clunk out and closing the door, Hal remembered he hadn't extended the passenger ramp. 'Er, Navcom?'

'Yes?'

'Can you answer the following quiz for me?'

'I'll do my best.'

'Right, here we go. A robot falls out of the *Volante* and plunges to the ground. Which of the following is correct? A, he lands in a soft pile of snow. B, he falls into a passing truck which was delivering feather mattresses, or C, he uses the springs in his legs and bounces to safety.'

'I'd choose D, he lands with a big crash, leaving a huge hole in the tarmac.'

'I thought you might say that.'

'Shall I extend the ramp?'

'Oh, so *now* you remember.' Hal thought for a moment. With the ramp retracted Clunk was locked out of the *Volante*, and given the robot's short fuse and the long drop to the ground, that was exactly the way Hal wanted it. 'No, best leave it up for a bit.'

'As you wish.'

Hal made himself a fresh coffee and returned to the console. 'By the way … this cargo job. Clunk's being very cagey about it.'

'He doesn't want to bother you with the details.'

Hal's eyes narrowed. 'That bad, is it?'

'On the contrary, the cargo is legitimate and the deadline is achievable.'

'So why the mystery?'

'Clunk is worried you might upset our customer. You see, we've been hired by an important artist.'

Hal snorted. 'There's no such thing. Famous or rich, maybe. Important? Hah.'

'That's exactly the response Clunk expected,' said the Navcom. 'Hence the secrecy.'

'Well, you've told me now. You might as well spill the whole deal.'

'We've been hired to transport valuable artworks on behalf of Maximilius Bright.'

'Never heard of him.' Hal eyed the console. 'He's not one of those abstract weirdos, is he? Old toilet bowls and severed fingers?'

'His work is at the experimental end of the artistic milieu,' admitted the Navcom.

'I knew it! And you said he was important.'

'Reviewers rave about the masterful simplicity of Fish in a Jar. Experts are united in their praise of Cow in a Field.'

'Sounds like the menu in a cheap restaurant.' Hal crossed his arms. 'These are the sort of artists who fuss over a chunk of rock for three weeks, drape two hairs on top and call it a masterpiece.'

'I think you mean Hairpiece. It's Bright's greatest work.'

'So we have a cargo of dead fish, stuffed cows and hairy rocks.' Hal sighed. 'Are we getting paid for this job, or is Clunk doing it for the fame and glory?'

'There's a generous payment involved.'

'How generous?'

The Navcom told him.

'Well, I guess I can put up with it just this once.'

—

The delivery truck dropped Clunk at the loading dock, where he gave the driver a thank-you wave. His heavy landing had crushed several mattresses, but fortunately they were heading for the local tip. An uncharitable robot might think humans pushing them off landing platforms was inconsiderate and cruel, but Clunk knew Mr Spacejock better than that. He was impressed with the timing of Mr Spacejock's shove, and he didn't believe he could have done any better himself. Even so, he resolved to have a shot next time Hal was standing on the very lip of an unprotected ledge with a speeding truck passing underneath.

A freezing wind howled across the landing field, and Clunk picked up a blizzard warning on the traffic network. There were patches of ice on the ground, and he could see deep snow in the distance. It was lucky Mr Spacejock had stayed aboard the *Volante*. Not because the severe cold was dangerous - it was because the human's endless complaints about the severe cold tended to get on Clunk's nerves.

As for the cargo job, they'd received a small payment up front, which was something of a novelty, and Clunk was feeling good about their prospects. Their reputation would be enhanced if they delivered the precious artworks on time, and new clients would be falling over themselves to hire the experts. That is, unless Mr Spacejock put his elbow through a canvas, or accidentally dropped the whole cargo into a volcano.

Clunk's thoughts turned to an advert he'd seen recently, which had been promoting a nice little retirement village. The Shady Grove had tidy rooms, plenty of peace and quiet, somewhere to lay one's head ... Oh, the freight business would be so much easier if he could only convince Hal to move there.

No, he was being unfair. Sure, Mr Spacejock had fiddled with the hyperdrive, almost crashed the *Volante* into a stray planet, wiped out half a seal colony and pushed Clunk out of the airlock into the path of a speeding truck, but he did it all with such childlike enthusiasm. Ruefully, Clunk realised it was impossible to stay angry for long.

'Yeah?'

Clunk blinked. While he'd been lost in thought, his autopilot had navigated a path the length of the spaceport, delivering him all the way to the information counter. 'I have a pickup for Max Bright.'

The young man took a battered cash tin from under the counter, made a big show of finding the key, then popped the lid. Inside was a slim envelope. 'Sign here,' he said offering a clipboard.

Clunk eyed the envelope. 'What sort of artworks are we talking about? Miniatures?'

The young man shrugged. 'Can't have it 'til you sign.'

Once his name was printed on the form, Clunk took the envelope and snipped the top off. Inside was a scrawled note on Truck-U stationery:

Truck driver taken ill. Artworks will not be delivered in time. Please communicate our apologies to your client.

Ding dong!

Hal was busy at the console, struggling to draw an accident diagram for the insurance claim. He'd more or less managed the *Volante*, although it looked like a depressed lemon, but he was having trouble showing Clunk plunging towards the landing pad. His first three attempts had ended with a one-legged stick figure bouncing around the scenery, and the fourth looked more like a ragged hand puppet than his treasured co-pilot.

Ding dong!

'Are you going to answer that?' asked the Navcom.

'I would if I knew what it was.'

'It's the doorbell. There's a visitor waiting outside.'

'It's not Clunk, is it?'

'No. I detect a human.'

Hal frowned. 'Customs? Parking inspector? Quarantine?'

'I cannot say.'

Ding dong, ding dong, ding DONG!

Hal dumped his pencil and hurried to the airlock. The only thing worse than a visit from an interfering official was a visit from an *angry* interfering official, and this one sounded pretty unhappy.

'Good evening, sir. Are you the owner of this here vehicle?'

Hal eyed his visitor warily. When he'd opened the door, a senior Peace Force officer in full dress uniform was the last thing he'd expected to see. 'Sure. What's the problem?'

'I'm Inspector Boson, and before I begin I'd like to issue a warning. Your ship is surrounded, and if you attempt to flee this interrogation you will be shot on sight. Clear?'

'Er, yes.' Hal gulped. 'Interrogation, you say?'

Boson licked his thumb and dragged it across his thinscreen. 'Says here you're a Mr Half Spacepoke. Is that right?'

'The name is Spacejock. Hal Spacejock.'

'Is that so?' The Inspector squinted at his computer. 'And your ship is the *Folanti*?'

'No, it's the *Volante*.' Hal was about to add a witty comment about Peace Force intelligence, but he held his tongue. First, because it was never a good idea to irritate officers of the law, and second, because he couldn't think of a suitable quip. Tomorrow, sure. *Then* he'd come up with something sharp and insightful.

The Inspector pressed something on his screen, which beeped at him. 'I understand you're transporting artworks for an exhibition?'

'We will be. Clunk's organising the delivery now.'

'Clunk?'

'He's my co-pilot.'

Boson angled his thinscreen to the light. 'It doesn't say anything about Clunk in my records. New crew member, is he?'

'Definitely not new. He's a very old robot.'

'Oh well, that's why. Equipment and chattels come under a different heading.'

Hal winced. 'I wouldn't say that around Clunk.'

'Touchy, is he?' Boson sniffed. 'One of the Robot Rights lot, I suppose.' Judging from his tone, the Inspector lumped them in with murderers, thieves and arsonists.

'I support his views,' said Hal evenly.

The officer made a note of this, pressing the screen so hard it creaked. 'Very well. Now, there are two reasons for my visit. First, I'm here to warn you about a potential threat. There's a good chance an attempt will be made to steal your cargo.' Boson peered at him suspiciously. 'I assume you're not in on the heist?'

'I'd never do anything illegal,' said Hal firmly. 'I was an officer like you once, until –'

'You?' Boson looked shocked. 'You were in the Force?'

'Well, a deputy really. I helped with a missing person case.'

'I heard standards were slipping.' Boson eyed Hal doubtfully. 'Seems the rumours were correct.'

'It's true. I was an officer like you until I took a position as a bodyguard.'

'You hear that a lot.' Boson shrugged. 'No matter. As I was saying, there's a chance someone might try and steal your cargo.'

'I'll bear that in mind. What was the other thing?'

'Our political masters have come up with an exciting new initiative.' From Boson's tone of voice he was no happier with this new initiative than he was with any of the earlier ones. 'Instead of sitting Peace Force trainees behind desks until they're well and ready, we're sending them out on the job.'

'I don't see the connection.'

'You will, because one of them has been assigned to your ship.'

'Here! For how long?'

'Until you're done with the artworks. Hosting a trainee for a few days will ensure you remain on the right side of the law, and it will also deter hijackers and thieves.'

'What if you send one of your trainees out on a ship which gets attacked? Won't they be in danger?'

'Hardly. My people shoot first and ask questions later.'

Hal snorted. 'They've passed basic training then.'

'I'm sorry?'

'Nothing.' Hal looked around. 'Where's this trainee now?'

'Covering your cargo hold in case you make a run for it.'

'I thought you said the ship was surrounded?'

'One Peace Force trainee is more than a match for the likes of you,' said Boson with a sniff. 'Now, show me your hold.'

'What for?'

'I'd like to inspect your cargo.'

'But we don't have any.'

'Don't play games with me, son. Are you delivering artworks to the exhibition or not?'

'Yes, but the artworks aren't here yet. Clunk's gone to get them.'

Boson eyed his thinscreen. 'Empty or not, I still have to see the hold.'

'Why?'

'Because it's right here on my checklist, and I can't close this blasted program until it's ticked off.'

Hal let Boson into the flight deck, a spacious well-lit area with a curved instrument panel, a large display screen and a comfortable pilot's chair. There was a mug of coffee sitting amongst the controls, and a chess board was rotating slowly on the screen.

'Which side are you?' asked Boson.

'Black.'

'Interesting offence. Mate in three moves, by my reckoning.'

There was a crackle from the console speakers. 'I'm sorry, but you're mistaken,' said the Navcom. 'I make it checkmate in four moves.'

Boson scanned the board. 'It's definitely three.'

'Four,' said the Navcom.

'Why don't you toss for it?' said Hal.

The officer looked shocked. 'One does not decide a chess game on the flip of a coin.'

'Doesn't one?'

'Of course not. Chess is an intellectual challenge. A war of wits. A battle of the minds. Chance has nothing to do with the outcome.'

This was news to Hal, whose strongest games involved moving pieces at random. 'Why don't you take my place then? The Navcom won't mind.'

'Mr Spacejock is correct,' said the Navcom. 'All humans are equipped with brains of limited processing power. Minor statistical variations in their output make no difference to me.'

Boson sat down, and after a few seconds he pointed at the screen. 'Knight to G6.'

'Queen to G6,' said the Navcom instantly. 'Check.'

'Queen to D7,' said Boson. 'Checkmate.'

There was a long silence, and then ...

'Get in there!' shouted Hal, pumping his fist before doing a little victory dance around the flight deck. 'He shoots, he scores! The crowd goes wild! Spin, spin, spin!'

Boson frowned. 'Mr Spacejock, one does not mock a downed opponent.'

'One may not, but I certainly do. Come on Navcom, update the scores.'

'But –'

'No buts!' Eagerly, Hal studied the scoreline in the corner of the screen, which was still displaying the previous values in a large white typeface:

Navcom: 384, Hal: 0, Draws: 1.

For the first time ever he'd have a real number next to his name! The screen flickered, and the anticipation was still building when a new line appeared. It was dark gray, almost invisible against the background, and the typeface was tiny:

Navcom: 384, Hal: 0, Draws: 1, Interfering Humans: 1.

'Hey! Do it properly!'

'The status update is correct,' said the Navcom. 'Had you been playing, it would have been checkmate in four moves. Victory was mine for the taking.'

'But –'

'No buts. You did not win the game.'

Hal crossed his arms. 'All right, set the pieces up again. This time –'

Boson cleared his throat. 'Mr Spacejock, your cargo hold?'

'Eh?' Hal glanced round. In all the excitement he'd forgotten why the Peace Force officer was there. 'Oh yeah, that. Come on.' Hal motioned his visitor into the lift at the back of the flight deck. The doors closed, and he pressed the button for the second deck.

'I see you have three decks,' said Boson, inspecting the neat row of engraved brass buttons. 'Doesn't the L-class have two by default?'

'The *Volante* was upgraded.' Hal didn't add that Clunk had upgraded the ship with an oxy torch and a lot of clever programming. Gamma-class ships were all supplied with three decks, but the lowest was masked off on the cheaper models. Aboard the Volante, the new third deck was Hal's luxury retreat.

'Do you pay the increased license fee?'

'That's Clunk's department,' said Hal quickly.

The lift stopped and the doors opened on a carpeted corridor. There were two doors ahead of them, and as they strolled past them Hal glanced at the nameplate on the right-hand one. He suppressed a wistful sigh. The plate read 'Harriet', and the cabin had been vacant ever since Hal's treasured shipmate had left the *Volante* - and him - for a new life. He was lost in thought as he strolled along the corridor, his mind dwelling on Harriet Walsh's long, golden hair, her pleasant, attractive face ... and her tight denim jeans.

They reached the end of the corridor and stopped at a big, white-painted door. The words 'Cargo Hold' were stencilled across the doors in neat black lettering, and underneath someone had added 'No unauthorised access' and 'no entry during flight'. There were two new signs as well: 'Go-faster stripes prohibited' and 'You paint it, you clean it'.

Hal reached for a big yellow handle, turned it to the left, and pulled.

The doors parted with a hiss, opening on the cavernous hold. It was grey and chilly inside, and Hal's footsteps echoed on the metal deck plates. 'There you are,' he said, gesturing around the huge empty space. 'Inspect away.'

'Obviously that won't be necessary.' Bosun gestured towards the rear doors. 'Would you open those please?'

Hal approached the controls, then hesitated. 'Are you sure this trainee of yours won't open fire?'

'Only if you make any sudden moves.'

Bracing himself for a volley of gunshots, Hal palmed the button. There was a whine of hydraulics as the cargo ramp deployed from the back of the ship, and then the doors swung open. Snow swirled, and Hal shivered at the biting cold wind. It was dark outside, and he was still trying to pick out the surroundings when a fantastically bright torch shone full in his face.

'Stay where you are!' shouted a female voice. 'I've got you covered.'

Hal froze, dazed by the light. There was something familiar about the voice, but his first priority wasn't recognising Peace Force trainees. No, all his attention was on not getting shot.

Alongside him, Bosun didn't bat an eyelid. 'Stand down, trainee. The situation is under control.'

'Yes sir.'

'You may come aboard.'

The torch winked out and Hal saw a shadow coming up the ramp. As the trainee got closer, he noticed she had long, golden hair tied back in a business-like ponytail. There was a duffle-bag over one shoulder, regulation Peace Force blue, and her shiny boots thudded on the ramp. Then she entered the hold, and when the light fell on her face Hal's heart skipped several beats. This wasn't some random Peace Force trainee…it was his ex-crewmate, Harriet Walsh!

Olivia Backsight scowled across the desk at her visitors. In turn, they shuffled their feet and cleared their throats, nervously avoiding her angry stare. 'You're a pair of incompetent idiots,' she snapped.

'Yes ma'am.'

Olivia clenched her fists, making the blue veins stand out like ropes. She'd taken over Backsight Industries three decades earlier, after the unexpected death of her uncle. Despite the long years since his tragic 'accident', she still wondered whether his body would surface inconveniently. Then she allowed herself a grim smile. No, there wasn't much chance of that. She'd used some of Backsight Industries' most powerful explosives.

The two men standing in front of her exchanged a glance as they saw Olivia's nasty little smile. One gulped audibly.

Snapped out of her reverie, Olivia turned her full attention to them. 'You two oversee data entry, right?'

'Correct,' said one.

'That's right,' said the other.

'And I hear you let through several invoices with zero cost of goods. Yes?'

'That's what it said on the paperwork.'

'I don't care what it said on the paperwork. Standing orders are quite clear - never, ever put through an invoice with zero cost of goods.'

'But –'

Olivia raised her hand. 'Never ever. Do you know why?'

Both men shook their heads.

'Because we'd have to explain why we're getting raw materials for nothing. And do you know why we get raw materials for nothing?'

The men shook their heads again.

'Good, because if you did know I'd have you killed.' Olivia gave them a smile, and from their expressions she could tell they weren't sure whether she was joking or not. She wasn't. 'So, in future we'll follow orders to the letter, won't we?'

Both men nodded in unison.

'Oh, go away,' snapped Olivia, finally losing patience with them. The men just stared at her, and she gestured impatiently. 'Go on. Get lost.'

'Y-yes ma'am.'

They fled, jackets and ties flapping. After the door closed, Olivia gazed out of the huge window to her right, admiring the rich starfield and the faint glow from the dark side of planet Niaritz. The fantastic view was just one of the benefits of owning an orbital Space Station. Another was security: when your Space Station bristled with guns and missiles, every visiting ship was at your mercy. Not only that, the automatic gun turrets positioned in the docking bays would take out any stubborn survivors.

Olivia turned from the window, pressing her fingertips to her temples as she considered her next move. The invoicing mixup was trivial, easily fixed, but making an example of these two would keep the rest on their toes. A month without pay should do it. Leaks were a bigger concern, though. Backsight's competitive pricing was based on a simple economic fact: if you could steal half your raw materials, components and equipment, there was no way anyone else could undercut you. To that end, Olivia had set up a criminal network which spanned a dozen planets, involving customs, law enforcement, justice departments and more. By targeting the right shipments, she could feed her factories for next to nothing. By paying the right people, she avoided investigations, exposure and jail.

After a few moments thought, Olivia picked up her commset. 'I hear the hijacking job on Forzen didn't go as planned.'

'I'm sorry. The lads thought it was the usual deal. They –'

'They left valuable artworks sitting in a warehouse in the middle of the countryside.'

'I know, I know. Look, give me a day or so, and –'

'No, this cargo must be delivered to the spaceport in one hour. Understood?'

'We'll do our best.'

'You'll do what you're told.' Olivia slammed the handset down. 'Morons,' she growled under her breath. 'Absolute morons, the lot of them.' Idly, she wondered whether to invite them all up to the Space Station, where she could arrange a little airlock accident to teach them a lesson.

— 5 —

Hal opened his mouth, greetings and questions about to pour forth, but before he could say anything, Harriet frowned at him and gave a quick shake of her head.

'What is it, Trainee?' demanded Boson. 'Did you notice something?'

'Just a bug,' said Harriet, brushing a hand across her face.

Hal stared at her, scarcely believing she was standing right there in front of him. When she'd left the *Volante* several months earlier, she'd mentioned the Peace Force academy in her note, but he'd figured that was just an excuse. So she really had signed with the Force after all! Then it hit him ... Harriet was the trainee assigned to his ship! They'd be travelling together, working together, and if she still had feelings for him they'd be –

'Trainee Walsh,' said Boson. 'This is Half Spacepoke of the cargo ship *Folanti*. I've briefed him on the threat to his cargo, and he's agreed to take you on board.'

'Very well, sir,' said Walsh.

Boson looked Hal up and down. 'My trainee is in your hands. If anything happens to her I will hunt you down and tear you limb from limb. Is that clear?'

'Like crystal.'

'Good.' Boson glanced around the hold. 'Trainee Walsh has full authority to search this ship and any cargo you might handle. She's authorised to travel with you, ask questions, investigate and report freely on her findings. If you hinder her in any way you will be charged with obstruction and incarcerated.'

'Makes sense.' Hal glanced at Harriet, but she wouldn't meet his eyes.

'Very well. Have a safe trip and enjoy your stay in this system.' Boson glanced at Walsh, who gave him a smart salute, and then he marched down the ramp.

As soon as he was gone, Hal turned to Harriet with a beaming smile on his face. 'I can't believe it! You're –'

'You will address me as Trainee Walsh,' said Harriet coldly. 'That is, if you must address me at all.'

'But –'

'Please direct me to my cabin. I have a lot of work to do.'

Hal stared at her. If it hadn't been for Harriet's warning glance when she came aboard, he would have sworn she hadn't recognised him. 'But –'

'You heard me!' snapped Walsh. 'Show me to my quarters without delay, or I'll have this ship impounded so fast your head will spin.'

Hal's heart sank. It seemed the Peace Force had leached the humanity and kindness out of his beautiful Harriet, turning her into a soulless robot. 'All right,' he said stiffly. 'If it's quarters you want, follow me.'

❖

Deep in the bowels of the Forzen spaceport, Clunk was rapidly reaching the end of his patience. As a robot this usually wasn't a problem, because he could add more patience on demand. Unfortunately, even robots had limits, and his was definitely in sight. 'What do you mean the cargo isn't here? What do you mean we have to fetch it ourselves? What do you mean we should have made other arrangements?'

Clunk had been asking these questions, and others much like them, for close to an hour. To say he'd been given the runaround was like saying Hal Spacejock was a lousy chess player. Now, at long last, Clunk had cornered an unwilling cargo handler. The woman's colleagues were on a tea break, and she clearly wanted to join them. The only things stopping her were a strong sense of duty and Clunk's metal fingers, which were fastened around her upper arm.

'Like I told you,' said the cargo handler. 'The driver's off sick. Either wait until tomorrow or find another driver.'

'I'd drive there myself, but you won't tell me where the cargo *is*.'

'How should I know? This is Holding, not Pickup.'

511

'But Pickup is closed for the day!'

'Like I said, wait until tomorrow.'

Clunk's balled his free hand into a fist. 'We have to leave this planet *tonight* to make the deadline.'

'So find another driver.'

'But they won't know where to pick up the cargo!' shouted Clunk. The insoluble circular problem was throwing his circuits off balance, and his head was starting to spin.

'There is something we could try.'

Clunk felt a surge of hope. 'There is?'

'Sure. See that guy over there? The one with the beanie?'

'Yes, I see him.'

'He sometimes works in Pickup. If you ask nicely, he might be able to help.'

Clunk hurried over. 'Excuse me?'

Beanie eyed the robot over his mug. 'Yes?'

'I'm here to collect a shipment of artworks, but they haven't arrived. Do you know where I can find them?'

'This is Holding. You want Pickup.'

Clunk tried not to scream. 'I know, but they told me you sometimes worked for Pickup.'

'Not today.'

The cargo handlers grinned at each other, looking like a group of naughty kids sharing a joke at teacher's expense. Clunk was on the point of exploding: punching holes in the walls, throwing desks around and smashing windows, but he took a couple of deep breaths and settled on a truly radical solution. It was desperate, it was unwise and the results would be unpredictable and dangerous. However, the cargo handlers had left him no other choice.

It was time to ask Mr Spacejock for assistance.

◆

Hal was sitting in the flight deck, watching a slow-motion replay of Inspector Boson's winning chess move. Every time the black queen slid into position, ending the game with a resounding checkmate, Hal laughed and slapped his knee. 'Fantastic. Awe inspiring. Inspirational. Go on, play it again!'

The Navcom complied grudgingly. 'This is getting tedious. Isn't there anything else you'd rather watch?'

'I guess it could become stale after a while.' Hal hesitated. 'Do you have a reverse angle?'

'No, but I have an incoming call.'

'Put it on.'

'Am I speaking to Mr Spacejock?' said Clunk, his voice sounding distant through the console speakers.

'I'm here. What's up?'

'I need your help.'

Hal twisted a finger in his ear. 'I'm sorry, can you say that again?'

'I need your assistance with a small matter.'

'That's what I thought you said. Are you feeling okay?'

'I'm perfectly all right, but there's an issue with the cargo.'

Hal shrugged this off. First the Navcom had been crushed in a historic chess win, and now Clunk was begging for his help. After those two momentous events, nothing could dampen his spirits. 'What's wrong with it? Too big, too small ... what?'

'It never arrived at the spaceport.'

'Can we fetch it ourselves?'

There was a strangled groan. 'We could, but the ground crew won't tell me where it is.'

'Shall I come down there and knock some sense into them?'

'I would prefer a non-violent solution.'

Hal thought for a moment. 'I have an idea. Wait there, we'll meet you in a minute.'

'We?'

'Be there in a minute. Bye!'

A couple of minutes later Hal was standing outside Walsh's cabin. He could hear the sound of running water, and he realised Harriet was having a shower. If he knocked now, she'd have to answer the door half-dressed.

Hal knocked firmly on the door.

'What is it?' shouted Walsh.

'Dire emergency. Clunk's in big trouble.'

The water stopped, and a second later the door was pulled open. Walsh was dripping wet, and the small towel she was clutching around herself was as useful as a handkerchief. Unable to help himself, Hal copped a good look before averting his gaze.

'What's the problem?' demanded Walsh.

'The cargo hasn't arrived, and the loading staff won't tell Clunk where it is. I thought an approach from an officer of the law...'

'Are you out of your mind? I can't abuse my powers like that. Now go away!' Walsh glanced over her shoulder, then stepped into the corridor and pulled the door closed behind her. She slipped one hand behind Hal's neck and put her mouth to his ear. 'I've only got a second or two,' she breathed. 'They've bugged my uniform. You understand?'

Hal felt a thrill, and it wasn't just the soft hand and the throaty whisper. Harriet didn't hate him after all. She was being watched! Blood pounded in his ears, and it was all he could do not to take her in his arms and hold her tight.

'You have to play along,' whispered Harriet. 'Tell Clunk too. He mustn't recognise me.'

'Consider it done,' Hal whispered back. 'How's the Peace Force treating you. Are you okay?'

'Tell you later. Wait until I close the door then knock again. Okay?'

'What do I say?'

'Just play along.'

Hal nodded, and he waited for Harriet to slip back into her cabin. Then, as instructed, he knocked again. There was a muttered oath and a split second later the door was yanked open. 'Er ...hi again,' said Hal lamely.

'Let me see that report.' Walsh waited a couple of seconds, then continued. 'Okay, this needs investigating. We'll quiz the ground crew right away. Meet me in the airlock in five minutes.'

◆

Harriet's emotions were in turmoil as she closed the door. For several months, Peace Force training had kept her so busy she'd barely had time to think about Hal, and she'd almost convinced herself she was over him.

Now, judging by her thudding heart, the dryness in her mouth, the warm flush all over her face, she realised she'd been kidding herself. Either she still had feelings for Hal, or she'd picked up a nasty virus on her travels.

Harriet pressed her lips together. She was a Peace Force trainee, sworn to uphold the law and perform official duties without emotion. Feelings or not, this was her first assignment and she wasn't going to mess it up.

As she got dressed, her mind returned to the previous day's briefing with Inspector Boson ...

◆

Walsh hesitated outside Inspector Boson's door, eyeing the nameplate nervously. She'd never met the Station Commander personally, but she'd heard he was a bitter man. Apparently he was staring down retirement without a single famous case to his name, thanks to his obsession with Backsight Industries and the family behind the huge conglomerate. An explosion had decimated the board of directors many years earlier, and Boson had been trying to pin the crime on one of the Backsights ever since. The fact the case had been closed for years - even the verdict of 'tragic accident' - hadn't deterred him one jot.

Now, unless a case involved the Backsights in some way, Boson simply wasn't interested.

Walsh knocked, and heard a gruff voice telling her to enter. She opened the door and saw Boson sitting at his desk, up to his elbows in stacks of printed reports and paperwork. He was talking on the commset, and he motioned Walsh towards a chair. She moved a pile of reports to the floor and sat down.

'I don't care if he's claiming credit for assassinating the Emperor,' snapped Boson. 'The man's innocent. He just wants a bed for the night and a free meal on the taxpayer. Get rid of him.' He slammed the handset down and glared at Walsh. 'Yes?'

'Trainee Harriet Walsh, sir.'

'Whatever it is, I don't have time for it. Go and speak to the desk sergeant.'

Harriet swallowed nervously. 'You asked to see me, sir.'

'Walsh?' Boson frowned at her, then started shifting reports around his desk. They were piled high, some of them covering the expensive - and clearly unused - terminal screen. 'Ah, yes. Walsh. The new trainee.' Boson eyed a sheet of paper, then looked at her over the top. 'I have a lead on a smuggling racket. You're going to escort a cargo of artworks for me, and I want you to get a close look at them during the trip.'

'Isn't that up to customs?'

Boson made a rude noise. 'Can't trust them. They've all been paid off.'

'Really?'

'Absolutely.' Boson leaned across the desk. 'Tell me, have you heard of Backsight Industries?' One of his eyelids flickered as he mentioned the name, and with a sinking feeling Walsh realised she was about to get dragged into his obsession.

'It sounds familiar,' she said evenly.

'It bloody well should. That gang of nasties has their fingers in every pie from here to the Core, but they're smart with it. They've greased politicians, corrupted judges, paid off anyone and everyone … as a result, they're untouchable.'

'So this smuggling racket …'

'It's a chance to gather hard evidence.' Boson thumped a fist into his palm. 'Nail them once and for all.'

'How?'

'I want you to inspect the artworks while you're aboard the freighter. Give them a thorough going-over.'

'What am I looking for?'

'Uncut diamonds. Large quantities.'

'That's pretty specific information,' said Harriet. 'How do you know about this? Was it an informant?'

'I don't need informants where Backsight is concerned. I know they're crooked.'

'Why don't you seize the artworks? Get a warrant and you could take them apart properly, under expert supervision.'

'Are you telling me how to do my job?' asked Boson quietly.

'N-no, sir. It's just …'

The inspector relented. 'Backsight has everyone in their pocket, Trainee Walsh. Customs, judges … the whole establishment. If I ask for a search warrant, those artworks will be squeaky clean long before I get near them. That's why stealth is the only way. Nobody will suspect you, a raw recruit, still new to the job. Do you understand?'

Harriet hesitated. 'But what if I damage the artworks? I'm not really qualified to –'

'As far as I'm concerned you can break them apart like so many pi?atas,' said Boson gruffly. 'The pilot's an accident-prone loser, so they'll just blame any damage on him. In fact, if you do find any diamonds you should pocket a few. They might duff the pilot up, accuse him of nicking their gear, and then I'll get them for assault as well as smuggling.'

Harriet's eyebrows rose. Not only was she supposed to conduct unauthorised searches, now she was supposed to steal as well? 'Will I be getting these orders in writing, sir?'

'Of course not. Officially, you're escorting valuable artworks. Everything else is off the record.'

Walsh's heart sank. Off the record meant deniability. Should anything go wrong, Boson would drop her in it.

'Do you understand your orders, Trainee Walsh?' Boson asked her.

Walsh nodded. 'Yes sir. I understand perfectly.'

'Excellent. Success in this mission will do great things for your career. You have my word on that.'

Walsh also realised what failure would mean: her fledgling career would be over before it had even begun.

'I want you to pack an overnight bag and meet me on the landing field,' said Boson. 'We're flying out in two hours.'

◆

Harriet finished dressing and faced the door. Boson had accompanied her to the Forzen spaceport, and it was only then that she'd realised which ship ... and which pilot ... she'd be travelling with. Of all the ships in the galaxy, it had to be the *Volante* ... and Hal Spacejock.

With a sigh, she left her cabin and strode along the corridor to the lift.

◆

Once Hal secured the *Volante*, he met Harriet at the head of the passenger ramp, where she was stamping her feet and blowing huge vapour clouds through her fingers. 'Are you all right?' he asked in concern.

'Typical Forzen weather. You get used to it.'

'Have you been stationed here long?'

'I'm not. I'm based on Dulsuil.'

Hal knew this perfectly well, and he was about to say so when he remembered the Peace Force bug in Harriet's uniform. 'Dulsuil, eh? What's that like?' he asked, playing along.

'Warmer than this,' said Harriet shortly. 'Are we going to stand here until we freeze, or shall we get moving?'

After a quick glance at the snow-covered surroundings, Hal led the way down the passenger ramp. Halfway down he put a hand out to steady himself, and he almost lost the skin off his palm on the icy railing. 'First thing I need is a decent pair of gloves.'

At the foot of the ramp they found a post with a large orange button. Hal let Harriet press it, having already learned a valuable lesson where cold and skin were concerned.

Several moments later a self-propelled carriage arrived, stopping near the post with a hiss of air brakes. There was a loud crack as the doors parted, and shards of ice tinkled onto the frozen ground. Hal felt a gust of warm air, and was inside before Harriet had stirred. Shivering, he sat on the hard leather seat and held his hands to a hot air vent, while slush dripped from his boots to join the puddles on the grooved wooden floor.

The vehicle began to move, and Harriet grabbed one of the hanging straps, swaying as she regained her balance.

'This is a bloody joke,' growled Hal, trying to look out the nearest window. Condensation and layers of ice distorted the view into white streaks, but it made little difference given everything outside was blanketed with snow. 'Why would anyone settle a planet like this?'

'It's the mines,' said Harriet.

'Are they still going? I thought –'

'Not the ore. They found diamonds recently.'

'What, and they're digging them out of the ground? I thought it was cheaper to make the things.'

'Not this size.'

'Diamond mines, eh?' Hal stared at the frozen landscape moving past the windows. 'It's a strange place to store a bunch of art. A pick and shovel museum would be more like it.'

A shadow fell across the windows, throwing the carriage into darkness. Interior lighting winked on, casting a yellow glow which turned the puddles on the floor into sickly pools of light. Moments later, the carriage slowed to a halt and the doors swept open.

They stepped down onto the platform, which was in the centre of a spacious building. There were more platforms either side of theirs: dozens of them stretching away into the distance, each with a similar carriage awaiting passengers. Melting snow dripped from the curved roofs and ran down the red and yellow bodywork, mingling with the oily gravel between the tracks.

There was nobody else in sight.

'Lovely place, isn't it?' Hal stamped his feet to shake off the last of the melted slush, cursing as each jolt shattered another of his frozen toes.

'It's not that cold, Mr Spacejock.'

'Tell that to my feet.' Hal looked towards the terminal, and spotted the entrance. 'Come on, let's find Clunk.'

—6—

Clunk tapped his foot impatiently. He'd been waiting the best part of twenty minutes, and during the entire time the ground crew had been teasing him with endless robot jokes.

'How many robots does it take to replace a lightbulb? One, but you have to crank the voltage right up.'

There was a round of laughter, and then someone else piped up. 'Why did the robot cross the road? He thought the traffic lights were coming on to him!'

'Hey, here's a good one. What do you call a robot with a flat battery? A statue!'

More laughs.

'How far can a robot fly? Depends how hard you throw it!'

'What did the robot say when they gave him a medal? That's a nice biscuit!'

Clunk switched off his hearing, which cut the inane jokes but did nothing for the mocking faces. He often thought the galaxy would be a much nicer place without humans to clutter it up, and this gang of idiots weren't doing much to change his mind. 'What do you call a biped with a pleasant nature and well-organised thought processes?' he muttered under his breath. 'I don't know, but it certainly isn't human.'

A few minutes later the doors opened, and he saw Mr Spacejock beckoning. Clunk hurried over, reactivating his hearing on the way.

'...said the robot to the vicar!'

There was more laughter, but Clunk didn't notice. Mr Spacejock was here, and if things got out of hand there would be flying fists and roundhouse kicks. Despite his peaceful nature, Clunk wouldn't have minded one bit.

'Clunk, stop there. I have to explain something.'

'The *Volante*, is she ...'

'She's fine. No fires, no explosions.'

Clunk sighed with relief. Leaving Mr Spacejock with the ship was almost as risky as letting him out of it.

'Do you remember Harriet Walsh?' Hal asked him.

'Of course.' Clunk smiled. Miss Walsh was a lovely human being, and he missed her almost as much as Mr Spacejock did.

'Well, she's back.'

'Really?'

'Yes, but ... things are different. She's in the Peace Force, and they've assigned her to the *Volante*. She has an important mission.'

'I thought we were delivering cargo? We can't afford to go traipsing all over the galaxy on some –'

'No, listen. This Inspector Boson character told me a bunch of crooks might try and steal some of the artworks heading to the exhibition. They're putting trainees onto every ship to keep an eye on things. We got Harriet.'

'That's a happy coincidence.'

'Yes, but they've bugged her uniform. We have to pretend we don't know her.'

'What if she removes her uniform?'

Hal lost focus for a moment, gazing into space with a rapt expression on his face. Then he gathered himself with a start. 'Sorry, where was I?'

'I believe you were removing Miss Walsh's uniform.'

'Ye-es.'

'Mr Spacejock?'

'Uh-huh?'

'Can we concentrate on the matter in hand?'

'Oh yes, that.' With an effort, Hal regained focus. 'Look, Harriet can't just ditch the bug, or we'd have a dozen officers interrogating us to find out what happened.'

'I see.'

'Meanwhile, the Peace Force are snooping on every conversation, so pretend you've never met her. Got it?'

'I will do my best.'

'Right. Stay here.'

Clunk glanced over his shoulder at the ground crew. They were having another tea break, and one or two were casting suspicious looks at him.

'Keep drinking,' muttered Clunk. 'You'll get yours any minute.' He heard footsteps, and he turned to see Harriet Walsh striding towards him. 'Upon my soul, it's ...'

'A trainee,' said Hal quickly. 'This is Harriet Walsh from the Peace Force.'

'It's a pleasure to meet you,' said Clunk.

There was a commotion behind him, and he turned to see the ground staff hurriedly pushing back chairs and straightening their overalls. There were lots of nervous glances at the sight of the Peace Force uniform, and Clunk grinned to himself. Miss Walsh was already making her presence felt, and she hadn't even drawn her gun!

◆

Hal eyed the ground crew. They were a motley lot, and it seemed like they'd given Clunk a hard time. Now it was time to turn the tables. 'Officer Walsh, do you want to interrogate them here, or shall I drag them back to the ship first?'

Harriet frowned. 'I'd rather you left this to me.'

One of the cargo handlers gulped. 'A-anything we can do to help?'

'We're tracing a shipment of artworks.' Walsh gestured with the note Clunk had been given at the spaceport. 'The truck was supposed to arrive here this afternoon, but according to this your delivery driver was taken ill.'

'Th-that's right, miss. It was a stomach complaint. Very nasty.'

'What's the pickup address?'

'Ah, see you want Pickups for that. This is Handling.'

Puffs of superheated air jetted from Clunk's ears, and Hal didn't think he'd seen the robot this angry since a careless loader put a dent in the *Volante*'s cargo door.

But Walsh had authority on her side, and she used it. 'Do you see this badge?' she said, tapping her chest. 'This badge gives me access to all areas of the spaceport, and I don't care if you're working for Pickups, Handling or the Department of Annoying Customers.'

'We don't have one of those,' said the handler.

'Really? I thought I was talking to their star employee.' Walsh gestured at Clunk. 'This robot asked a perfectly reasonable question. Answer it or face the consequences.'

'It's like I said ...'

Walsh unclipped her holster.

'Oh, *that* cargo of valuable artworks.' The handler glanced at his colleagues, who were studying the floor, the ceiling and the bottom of their tea mugs. 'I think the driver parked it in a warehouse.'

'Where?'

'I think ... it's sort of here.' The handler passed her a scrap of paper.

'If you're sending me on a wild goose chase ...'

'No, that's the address.'

Walsh glanced at it. 'How did the artworks end up here?'

'The driver parked up and went to find a doctor.'

'When you see him again, he's to turn himself in to the nearest Peace Force station. And as for you lot, I'll be following this up, so don't even think about leaving the planet.'

'N-no miss. Wouldn't dream of it.' Beanie turned away, then stopped. 'Wait! You'll need this.'

Hal grinned to himself as the man held out a swipe card for the truck. Harriet Walsh was a machine! Imagine how smooth life would be if she brushed away the red tape with threats of interrogation and solitary confinement. Come to think of it, all he needed was a Peace Force uniform and a badge, and he could vapourise red tape on his own. He was still dwelling on this pleasant mental image when Clunk took his elbow.

'Back to the terminal, Mr Spacejock. We have to rent a vehicle.'

'Why? Harriet has the key.'

'That's for the truck, which is sitting at the warehouse. We have to drive to the warehouse to pick it up.'

Hal frowned. 'We're racking up more charges than a cavalry brigade. This customer of yours had better come through with the expenses.'

'I'm keeping an itemised bill. And he's not my customer, he's our customer.'

'If he doesn't pay he's all yours.'

'That's not fair. I don't make you pay when your customers default on a bill.'

'That's different. When my customers don't pay it's my money.'

'Can we leave your accounting woes until later?' said Harriet mildly. 'I have an investigation in progress.'

'Er, yeah,' mumbled Hal. 'Hire car. Let's go.'

◆

'That piece of paper ... how come he had the address already?' demanded Hal, as they strolled through the concourse.

'It's a common scam,' said Walsh. 'The driver's in on it, of course.'

'What scam?'

'This stomach bug nonsense. The driver leaves the truck in a pre-arranged spot, and heads off to the doctor with some mythical illness. That gives them an alibi, and in the meantime a crony comes along and drives the truck away. They unload the cargo and torch the vehicle to destroy the evidence.'

'The truck makes sense, but wouldn't artworks be hard to sell?'

'Yes, which tells me they stole the wrong truck. These jobs usually involve white goods or spares or ... well, anything they can sell easily. They won't have any use for artworks.'

Hal snapped his fingers. 'Boson *said* someone might try and nick the art. Looks like they got to it before it even reached the *Volante*.' He looked at Harriet for confirmation, but she didn't seem convinced. 'You have to admit it fits. It's much easier to pinch a truck than to stop a ship in space.'

'We'll see,' said Harriet.

Hal turned to Clunk. 'So, the art. Is the stuff really valuable?'

A pained expression crossed Clunk's face. 'In the fine art world, one does not refer to pieces as 'stuff'.'

'We're not in fine art, we're in the cargo business. It's either stuff we get paid for, or ...' Hal's voice tailed off as he spotted a display in the main concourse. 'Oh no. Not him again!'

'What is it?'

Hal pointed. At the front of the display, an elderly man in a white lab coat was tinkering with a complicated-looking control panel, picking through the exposed wiring as he touched a probe to various contacts. Behind him stood a gleaming silver cabinet, and above the cabinet was a printed banner: The Galactic Teleporter Co. There was another person on the display, a beefy young man wearing a tight red T-shirt. He was lounging against the silver cabinet, completely absorbed in a trashy novel.

As Hal eyed the display, he realised there was something missing. Every time he encountered the teleporter scientist there were two cabinets. Here, on this stand, there was only one. Despite their cargo job, despite Harriet Walsh, and despite the deadline, Hal found himself drawn towards the display. The scientist looked up at his approach, brochures and sales pitch at the ready. Then he recognised Hal.

'So, it is you.'

Hal nodded. 'Are my shares worth anything yet?'

'Once my genius is recognised they will be worth untold millions.'

'Still working on that, huh?'

The old man gestured at the cabinet. 'As you can see, I have upgraded my equipment.'

'I noticed.' Hal glanced around. 'Where's the other one?'

'You mean Kurt?'

'No, not your other son. I mean the other cabinet.'

'Oh, that's on planet Pegzwil. We have a matching exhibit there.'

'So you can con twice as many people in the same amount of time? Good thinking.'

'Still you think my work is a con?' The old man shook his head sadly. 'Did I not teleport you successfully once before?'

'You teleported me all right, but it wasn't much of a success.'

'Now the equipment is better. Here, give me your watch.'

'Hal, no!' protested Harriet. 'We don't have time for this.'

'If he loses his watch he won't have time at all,' muttered Clunk.

Hal hesitated, then removed his watch and passed it to the scientist. 'Hans. Catch.'

The young man in the red skivvy caught Hal's watch in one hand, opened the cabinet and placed the watch on the floor. Once the door was closed the scientist turned to the control panel, humming under his breath as he adjusted the settings. Then, with a rather nervous look at the cabinet, he pressed a large red button.

There was a crackle of electricity, and Hal felt his hair standing on end. The cabinet glowed with a deep purple light, and then ... nothing.

'Hans?' said the scientist.

The young man opened the cabinet, releasing a cloud of grey smoke. The floor was empty.

'Never mind,' said Clunk. 'It wasn't a very good watch.'

'I am merely confirming it has gone,' said the old man.

'I know it's gone,' said Clunk. 'I can smell the remains.'

'Hans, the door please.'

Hans closed the door, and seconds later there was another flash of purple light. When the young man opened the door, Hal saw his watch on the floor - sitting on top of a glossy photo.

'Please, bring it here,' said the scientist.

Hans grabbed the watch and the photo, handing them both to Hal. The watch was unharmed, still working as well as it ever had, but the photo made him pause. In it he could see the scientist's second son, Kurt, and he was holding Hal's watch up to the camera.

'Hey, that's amazing,' said Hal.

Clunk sniffed. 'No, that's simple photo manipulation.'

'It's not a trick,' said the scientist. 'If you wish, I could send your robot through.'

'Okay,' said Hal.

Clunk backed away. 'I will not subject myself to this charade. We have a cargo to deliver, and time is getting short.'

'He's right,' said Harriet. 'We've wasted enough time on this nonsense.'

'It is not nonsense!' thundered the scientist. 'You people will not accept the evidence of your own eyes!'

'I want to try it, but we really do have a deadline,' said Hal quickly. 'We'll be back, I promise.'

'Very well,' said the scientist stiffly. 'I expect your future presence ...and an apology.'

They left the display and continued across the concourse in silence. They found the rental counter, eventually, and Hal groaned when he saw the sign propped on top:

Closed for Winter. See Arnie's Rentakars (Main car park).

'Great, just great,' muttered Walsh.

Hal glanced at her. 'Can you commandeer a vehicle?'

'Not without the right paperwork, and that'll take hours.'

'Okay, Arnie's Rentakars it is.' Hal glanced outdoors, eyeing the driving snow and icy cold wind. 'Off you go, Clunk. Harriet and I will keep watch here, in the warmth.'

— 7 —

Clunk made his way across the car park, moving sluggishly in the cold. The headwind was strong, and the icy slush made every step an effort. He slipped several times, barely saving himself from a nasty fall by thrusting forward into the driving wind.

When he finally reached the middle of the car park, he found a shuttered kiosk. A small, tattered sign explained that Arnie's Rentakars would re-open in the summer.

Clunk stared at the sign in shock, while snow continued to build up on his head and shoulders. What kind of planet greeted its visitors like this? It was ...it was impolite! Fighting down anger, he grabbed the door handle and shook it, rocking the entire kiosk on its foundations. He pictured Mr Spacejock's expression when he returned empty-handed, and only his upright, law-abiding nature prevented him kicking the door down and grabbing a handful of keys. Clunk released the door handle and glanced across the car park. The closest vehicle was only fifty metres away, but he couldn't just get in and drive. That would be stealing.

Frowning, he approached the problem from another angle. They'd been invited to the planet, and in a manner of speaking that made them guests. As guests it would be appropriate to borrow from their hosts. They had already borrowed space on the landing field, and they'd borrowed a little fresh air. Borrowing an entire vehicle was not much different.

Keeping his thoughts firmly on guests, the appropriate behaviour of, Clunk strode across the treacherous tarmac to the nearest buried car. He cleared a well in the snow, being careful not to damage the vehicle, and repeated the mantra 'it's okay to borrow from your host' under his breath as he cracked the car's security system.

There was a hiss as the door shot into the air, almost batting Clunk into the snow. He ducked just in time, then slipped into the driver's seat and activated the vehicle's systems with practised ease. The dash lights came on after a little coaxing, and behind him the turbine spooled up. Once the car was ready, Clunk reached up and pulled the door down, sealing it. He switched on the headlights, and an intense white glare filled the cabin, reflecting off the piled-up snow in front of the car. Clunk reversed the engine's thrust, and the snow melted in a blast of super heated air, leaving a perfect tunnel rimmed with glistening ice.

The car moved forwards in a cloud of steam, and Clunk angled it towards the terminal. A blip on the throttle hurled the vehicle across the icy ground, the rear fishtailing as thrust modulators compensated for the drift.

Clunk drew up to the doorway and tooted the horn, and moments later Hal and Walsh staggered out, bent double against the wind. The passenger door shot up and they clambered in, noses and fingers blue from the cold.

'I hope this thing's got a heater,' said Hal, through chattering teeth.

'Of course. And be sure to fasten your seatbelts. This is a sports model.'

'That's a bit extravagant. Couldn't you find anything cheaper?'

'Not really, no.' Clunk waited until his passengers were buckled in, then hit the throttle. There was a howl from the rear and the vehicle leapt forward, throwing fountains of snow out on either side.

'How do you know where the road is?' asked Hal, as they left the car park.

'Onboard sensors.'

Hal explored the seat pockets, pulling out an assortment of maps, tissue boxes and pen lids. He found a couple of credit tiles, then cursed as a wad of used chewing gum stuck to his fingers.

'What are you looking for?'

'They have diamond mines on Forzen now.' Hal lifted the floor mat, feeling underneath.

'And?'

'Someone might have dropped a few samples.' Hal sat up and looked around the car, seeking more compartments. 'While we're on this planet, it's finders keepers. Understood?'

'I cannot steal,' said Clunk, somewhat forcefully.

'Nobody's asking you to.' Hal glanced over his shoulder at Harriet, then lowered his voice to a whisper. 'If you come across any clear bits of stone, stick 'em in your pocket for safekeeping.'

The car rounded a barrier and drove onto the main road. It was lined with green fence posts, the illuminated blue triangles on top barely protruding from the snow. As the car accelerated, the triangles blurred into a continuous line, dividing the road from the surrounding countryside like a gleaming blue fence.

Hal gave up his search and sat back in the chair, his eyes half-closed against the glare. Clunk saw him squinting and activated a filter, darkening the windshield and turning the outside world into a dim moonscape. Then he turned his attention to the navigation system, traversing the menus until he'd programmed their destination. 'Thirty minutes to the warehouse.'

'Wake me up if you see the snow go,' said Hal, making himself comfortable. 'And stop for any shiny rocks.'

—

Clunk drove in silence, his attention on the road. Judging from the pristine snow, they were the first vehicle to pass through in quite some time, and he was a little concerned about the state of the roads. The car was running one notch off full power, which meant they were barrelling along at incredible speed. He didn't like it, but they'd never make the deadline if he slowed to a more sensible pace. Anyway, he was a robot, and he had total confidence in his skill.

Alongside him, Hal was snoring gently, while Harriet was napping in the back seat. Clunk felt a warm inner glow, happy the humans trusted him enough to put their precious lives in his hands.

The snow got deeper, until the icy walls on either side of the road encroached so far overhead there was only a sliver of sky visible between them. Before long the gap closed completely, leaving a long, frozen tunnel.

Clunk clicked the throttle to full. Visibility was good in the glaring headlights, and the road was as straight as a ruler. He kept one hand on the throttle in case of emergencies, but the chances of slamming into anything were slim. Even so, Clunk glanced round to check the humans had secured their safety harnesses. Harriet Walsh had done hers up properly, but Mr Spacejock's had a little too much slack for the robot's liking. With a paternal smile on his face, Clunk reached across to give the loose end a hefty tug.

◆

Hal was dreaming about a five-course meal, with platters of tender, gravy-soaked beef followed by half a dozen creme caramels. He was just tucking into the final course of tasty cheese and crackers when someone threw a straight jacket over his head and hauled on the straps, squeezing his chest until he could barely breathe.

He woke with a start, arms and legs flailing as he gasped for air. His left elbow crashed into the ground-car's window, his left knee slammed into the underside of the dash, the point of his right elbow collided with the side of Clunk's unyielding chest, and his right foot rammed the car's control column.

There was a whine from the turbine as the car shot off the road, and Hal's eyes widened as they raced towards the wall of snow. Marker posts went flying, *thok-thok-thok*, as the car mowed them down, and the shiny blue lights bounced off the canopy to skitter along the road. Clunk struggled with the controls as they plunged through virgin snow, mowing down shrubs and bushes.

Hal was frozen in his seat. Eyes wide, fingers clawing the soft leather dash, he was still trying to decide whether this was nightmare or reality. Then the car jinked to one side, smacking his ear against the window and bringing tears to his eyes. Reality, then.

Thok-thok-thok went another batch of marker posts, as Clunk desperately steered back onto the road. The car zoomed to the opposite side, swerved back again, then resumed its arrow-straight course in the left-hand lane.

'You ran off the road?' exclaimed Hal. 'Mr I'll-drive-it's-not-safe-for-humans put us in the hedge?'

'We left the road momentarily, but we sustained very little damage.' said Clunk. 'Incidentally, your seatbelt was loose.'

'Yeah, but why?'

'Because you didn't tighten it properly.'

'No, why did we run off the road?'

'Your seatbelt was loose.'

Hal studied the robot. 'I'm not going to get a straight answer, am I?'

'You must tighten your seatbelt. It's not safe when it's loose.'

Hal shot Clunk an exasperated look and settled back in his seat.

'Loose belts are dangerous,' said Clunk under his breath.

Hal glanced round to see if Harriet was all right, but she was still fast asleep and hadn't stirred. He assumed her Peace Force training included seminars on 'how to grab forty winks during death-defying car chases'. As for Hal, he was about to close his eyes and return to the sumptuous banquet when Clunk spoke up.

'I shouldn't bother if I were you. Ours is the next turning.'

Hal tried to sit up for a look, but the seatbelt held him like a steel band. By the time he'd slackened it off the car was travelling along a narrow track between snow-covered buildings.

They drew up alongside an imposing structure with thick concrete walls, barred windows and solid-looking doors. Hal eyed the substantial chain threaded through the metal handles, and snorted at the sight of a shiny new padlock. 'Something tells me they're not expecting visitors.'

Clunk popped the car door and climbed out. 'Are you coming?'

'No chance. Have a look around and let me know what you find.' Hal sat back in his chair, lacing his hands behind his head. 'Take your time. No rush.'

Clunk slammed the door and crunched through the snow to the warehouse. There were broad wheel tracks leading under the big double doors, and he decided even a human could have worked out what that meant: the truck was locked inside. As he got closer he eyed the chain, paying particular attention to the padlock. It was carved from a solid chunk of metal, and it had a finger pad, four proximity indicators and a red status lamp. Unfortunately he knew the type, and they were impossible to crack. He rattled the chain and yanked on the door handles, but the warehouse was locked up tight. Clunk turned right and started a circuit of the building, leaning forward and pushing his leg motors to the limit to negotiate the deep snow. Unfortunately the walls were all featureless grey concrete, and there was no other way in.

Disheartened, Clunk returned to the car. He saw Hal and Walsh watching him through the frosted windows, and he took a perverse pleasure in opening the door wide to let the freezing air in.

'What did you find?' demanded Hal. 'Any sign of the truck?'

'There are wheel ruts leading inside, but the doors are locked.'

'So unlock them.'

'Certainly. Would you hand me the key?' said Clunk, putting his hand out.

'What key? I don't have any key.'

'I see you're beginning to understand.'

'Can't you bust the lock?'

'Nobody's breaking any locks,' said Harriet firmly.

'In that case, maybe you could arrest the whole building,' said Clunk.

'What about knocking?' demanded Hal. 'Did you bang on the door?'

'No.'

'Typical robot. How about a bit of lateral thinking for a change?'

Clunk's grip tightened, his fingers creaking audibly as he restrained himself. 'Very well. I shall sit in the car while you go and announce our presence to any hardened criminals waiting inside that building. If they open fire, I suggest you run away from the car so as not to put Ms Walsh in danger.'

'You're both staying right here,' said Harriet. 'I'm a trained Peace Force officer. If anyone's going to approach a gang hideout it's me.'

'You may have a badge,' said Clunk. 'But you're not bulletproof.'

'Neither is Hal!'

Not for the first time, Hal debated chucking the whole cargo job. Nothing had gone to plan so far, and from where he was sitting things looked like they were going rapidly downhill. He eyed the building, deep in thought. 'What were the penalty rates on this cargo job again?'

'A hundred thousand credits, payable if you don't deliver the artworks in time.'

So much for giving up the job. 'Seems like we don't have much choice. You two wait here, and I'll find out what's in store for us.'

'No, wait!' shouted Harriet. But she was too late.

— 8 —

Hal pushed the door up and rolled out of his seat. It was supposed to be a swift, graceful exit which would leave him poised for a dash to the warehouse. Instead he landed flat on his back, arms and legs waving in the air while a boulder pressed into his left kidney. Before he could call for help, Clunk shut the door.

Hal struggled to his feet and limped around the car, keeping his head low to give the enemy a smaller target to aim at. The fact a sniper could shoot straight through the car's windows didn't occur to him.

He hesitated for a moment, then ran full pelt towards the warehouse, arms and legs pumping. After four paces his left foot snagged a buried obstruction, and there was a resigned look on his face as he cartwheeled into a snow drift. Hal bounced up straight away, spitting frozen dirt, and jinked sideways to put off the enemy's aim. Unfortunately his foot slipped on the ice, and he came crashing down on his hip.

This time he got up a little more slowly. Part of him was beginning to wonder whether there *were* any sharpshooters itching to loose off a volley in his general direction. Another part of him was convinced their bullets and grenades would hurt less than repeated crash-landings on the frozen ground.

Now limping on both sides, Hal hobbled to the doors and stood with his back to the wall. He strained his ears, but all he could hear was the moaning wind and the sound of his own panting. Turning his attention to the door, Hal inspected the impressive padlock and the heavy-duty chain. There was no chance of breaking the padlock, and the chain's metal links were as thick as his fingers. That left the door handle, which was cast from solid steel and was as thick as his arm.

Hal eyed the doors, deep in thought. What if they backed the car into them really fast? But no, Harriet's mic would pick up the noise, and a squad of Peace Force officers would be sent to investigate the crash. Whatever happened, he *had* to get Harriet out of her uniform, and the sooner the better.

Moments later his thoughts returned to the job in hand. They couldn't batter the doors down, but maybe they could pull them open with a handy length of rope? Hal patted his pockets, but came up empty. That only left one option.

Tap tap!

Harriet glanced up at him through the window, and Hal made a winding motion. She looked at him blankly, so he mimed opening the window. Then he mimed having a conversation, and in return Harriet mimed ignoring him.

Eventually Clunk took pity on him and opened the door. 'What is it, Mr Spacejock?'

'I need something to open the padlock with.'

'We knew that ten minutes ago,' said Clunk.

'I just thought I might borrow Officer Walsh's, er, special key.'

'I don't have any keys.'

'You know, that special key for opening stubborn padlocks.' Hal made a gun with his hand and cocked his thumb.

'Forget it,' said Walsh flatly.

'It's the only way!' Hal knew he was right. Harriet couldn't go around shooting things, not with the Peace Force bug listening in to her every move. 'Come on, let me use the key.'

Harriet sighed and reached for her holster.

'I wouldn't,' said Clunk. 'Mr Spacejock has a chequered history where . . . keys are concerned.'

'Hey, whose side are you on?' demanded Hal.

'The other side of whatever you're firing at, more often than not.'

Despite the robot's warning, Harriet passed Hal the gun, and he took it with both hands before spinning round to aim at the building, crouching down and making 'pow pow' noises under his breath. Then Hal saw Harriet's expression, and he lowered the gun before trudging back through the snow to the warehouse. He spent a couple of minutes examining the chain and padlock for weak points, and once he was satisfied there was no way to open them, he raised the gun and blasted a big hole in the wooden door.

535

Hal peered through the swirling sawdust and smoke, and gradually made out the interior of the warehouse. The place was freezing cold and deserted, and there was obviously nobody home. He was about to step over the threshold when Clunk and Harriet came hurrying up.

'What happened?' asked the robot.

'Harriet's key worked a treat.' Hal went to spin the weapon on his finger, but Clunk was much too quick. The robot's hand cracked like a whip, and Hal's new toy vanished in the blink of an eye. Hal was about to object, but arguing gun control with Clunk was like asking a planet to spin backwards.

The three of them entered the warehouse, squinting in the gloomy interior. Harriet moved away to their left, keeping her back to the wall as she started a sweep of the building. Hal and Clunk stood in the doorway, silhouetted by the harsh light. The first thing they saw was a row of glass cases, coated with a layer of sawdust from the ruined door. Then Hal spotted the truck. 'Wow, would you look at that?' he said, feasting his eyes on the huge spotlights, the forest of whip aerials sprouting from every surface, and the giant metal bullbar which was bigger than a farm gate. The wheels were taller than he was, and the cab was so far off the ground it required a telescopic ladder to access it. 'Bags I drive.'

'I think not,' said Clunk. 'These models can be unwieldy in the wrong hands.'

'You could run over a house in that thing without knowing it.'

'My point exactly.'

'All right, I'll toss you for it.'

'And afterwards I'll toss you. Furthest throw wins.'

Hal knew when he was beaten. 'Never mind, at least I get to drive that sports job outside.'

'I'm thinking of leaving it here.'

'You can't. The overdue fees would be astronomical.'

Clunk looked uncomfortable. 'There won't be any overdue fees.'

'Why not?'

'The, er, rental office was closed for the off-season.'

'So how did you ...' Hal gaped. 'You stole a car?'

'I did no such thing! I merely borrowed it from our hosts.'

'What hosts?'

'We're guests on this planet. Someone must be hosting us.'

'Yeah, but ...' Hal's voice tailed off as Walsh returned from her sweep of the building. The last thing he wanted to do was discuss stolen vehicles within range of her ever-present uniform bug.

'Can you two ride together?' asked Walsh. 'I need to use the rental.'

'What for?'

'I have to interrogate the truck driver. It's the only way I'm going to get to the bottom of this scam.'

Hal frowned. 'I thought you were supposed to come aboard the *Volante*?'

'I'll meet you at the ship after I've seen the driver.'

'Don't forget we're on a tight schedule,' warned Clunk. 'We can't delay departure or we'll be liable for a very large penalty.'

'I'll be there. Anyway, you still have to load the artworks.' Walsh turned to Clunk. 'Do you have the car keys?'

'I, er –'

'He lost them,' said Hal.

'Never mind, I'll use an override code. I'll see you at the ship in an hour or so. And if you see anyone acting suspiciously, don't try and be a hero.'

Hal threw a salute, trying to lighten the mood, but Harriet merely frowned at him before heading for the car.

'She's changed,' said Clunk, as the car drove off.

'Tell me about it. All business, no pleasure.' Hal sighed, then turned his attention to the warehouse. 'Okay, what have we got?'

Clunk pointed out a glass case, which contained a large salmon jammed head-first into a small container. 'That has to be Fish in a Jar.'

'I did art in school once. We used to paint trees and houses and little stick people with big heads.' Hal frowned through the glass. 'That's not art.' He walked to the next cabinet, which contained a clear pipe brimming with yellow-tinted liquid. The pipe was at least a metre tall, and suspended in the liquid was a length of pale, fleshy tube. 'What the hell is that?'

'It looks like a piece of intestine.'

'I know what it looks like. But what *is* it?'

'There's a card on the other side.'

Hal went to look. 'Semi-Colon.'

'More like a third,' mused Clunk.

'And I can guess what that is,' said Hal, pointing beyond the cases to a patch of fake grass. Standing on the greenery was a stuffed cow with a sheaf of half-chewed straw in its mouth.

'Cow in a Field.' Clunk brightened at the sight. 'I wonder how they killed it?'

'Have a heart. What did the poor thing do to you?'

'Cows and I have a history,' said Clunk grimly. 'Boots, leather seats or artwork …I don't care how they get rid of them.'

'You can touch them, though?'

'Only when I have no choice.'

'Good, because we've got to bung this one in the truck. You grab the udder end and I'll steer.'

9

Harriet drove in silence, concentrating on the icy roads. She was thinking of Hal, and specifically about the so-called bug in her Peace Force uniform. It had seemed like a good ploy to keep him at arm's length, but he was going to be pretty hurt when he found out it was a total fiction. Clunk had already guessed the truth, she was sure, but the robot was playing along like a trooper. He probably appreciated the way her 'bug' was keeping Hal in check.

A sign flashed past, breaking into her thoughts, and the car's navigation system beeped to indicate the next turning. The engine note changed, and the car slid into the left-hand lane before taking the off-ramp. Through the darkness Walsh could see snow-covered houses, snow-covered trees and snow-covered vehicles. She pulled a face. Forzen was certainly the planet for snow.

On the dash, her destination was marked with a pulsing red dot. The settlement was small, just a collection of houses clustered around a supply depot. Bulk goods from the spaceport were shipped here, before they were divided up and sent to the mines. Equipment, food, spare parts …an endless stream of cargo to feed Forzen's primary industry.

The pulsing dot turned green, and the car pulled over and stopped. Walsh cut the engine and checked her blaster, preparing herself for the challenge ahead. Not that she expected much - she was confronting a truck driver who'd been paid to take a sickie, not busting a major crime syndicate.

Walsh pushed the door up and stepped out into the cold. She eyed the house, taking in the steep, rust-streaked roof, the shuttered windows and the deep snow leading to the tatty front door. At first glance it looked deserted, but there was a plume of smoke rising from the chimney, and faint yellow light filtered through the shutters.

She opened the gate, which creaked on its hinges, and trudged through the deep snow to the front door. The doorbell was hanging by a wire, and she was about to knock when she remembered her Peace Force training. She stepped to the side, using the brick wall for cover, and unclipped her holster. With one hand on the grip of her blaster, she reached out with the other and rapped sharply on the door.

＊

When Hal and Clunk looked inside the truck, they discovered there was little room for the remaining artworks, thanks to a huge granite boulder jammed inside. Hal was all for dumping the rock, until Clunk pointed out it was one of Bright's precious artworks. They grabbed a couple of poles and rolled the rock to the front of the truck, only stopping when it thudded into the cab.

Clunk bent to retrieve a printed card.

'Don't tell me,' said Hal. 'This one's called Big Trucking Rock.'

'No, it's Hairpiece.'

'Come again?'

'Hairpiece. Two strands of human hair laid on a granite rock. The strands symbolise …' Clunk's voice tailed off. 'Oh dear.'

'What?'

'The hairs were sitting on the rock.'

'Are you telling me they split?'

'That's not funny.'

Hal eyed the muddy footprints covering the floor of the truck. Then he shrugged. 'We'll just shove another couple on top when we get to the other end.'

'You don't think Bright will notice?'

'If he does, we'll just tell him the new hairs symbolise the fact you lost the old ones.' Hal prodded the rock with his finger. 'None of this is real art, anyway. It's pretentious nonsense.'

Clunk looked up at the rock, which towered over them by at least two metres. 'We may have a problem, Mr Spacejock.'

'Do tell.'

'I'm afraid this boulder isn't going to sit in the Volante's hold.'

'No problem. We'll just chisel bits off until it does.'

Clunk winced at the thought. 'I said sit, not fit. There's no way to secure something this shape and size during flight.'

'Drill a few holes through the middle,' suggested Hal. 'Then you can thread the straps right through it.'

'It's a valuable piece of art, not a giant bead for some craft project.' Clunk looked thoughtful. 'No, I think we'll need a different solution.'

'You could jam all the other artworks around it.'

Clunk sighed. 'If you have any workable, practical suggestions I'm willing to hear them. In the meantime we'd better get the rest of this art on the truck.'

After securing the boulder, they loaded the remaining artworks one at a time, packing them with large sheets of damp cardboard they found leaning against a wall. When Clunk was satisfied they hopped down to the ground and made their way to the cab. Hal pulled the telescopic ladder down and prepared to climb aboard.

'I've been reconsidering the driving arrangements,' said Clunk. 'With you at the controls, I fear the artworks may endure a rough ride.'

'Don't be silly.' Hal indicated the truck with his thumb. 'This thing has more springs than a mattress factory. It'll be as smooth as butter.'

Clunk looked doubtful.

'Hey, I'm a pilot! I fly a two-hundred tonne ship all over the galaxy, and I haven't crashed yet. How much damage can I do with one little truck?'

'I really don't want to find out,' muttered Clunk.

'Anyway, you drove the rental straight off the road. I wouldn't call that safe driving.'

'You kicked the control column!'

'Yeah, after you tried to cut me in half with the seatbelt.'

'I admit I was partially at fault, but I will only accept fifty percent of the blame. No more.'

'Make it sixty-forty and you have a deal.'

'Very well. I agree.'

The shook hands solemnly, and then Hal clambered up the ladder before Clunk could change his mind.

Harriet was about to knock again when she heard footsteps inside the house. They stopped just the other side of the door, and then a muffled voice called out.

'Who is it? What do you want?'

Harriet hesitated for a moment, then remembered the driver's name. 'Mr Allson? I work for Demrik's insurance, and I'm here about your claim for medical expenses.'

'What are you talking about?' shouted Allson.

'Can we not do this through the door?'

There was the sound of bolts being drawn back, and the front door opened a crack. Walsh kicked it wide open and held her badge up. 'Peace Force. Step away from the door and put your hands on the wall.' She caught a glimpse of a pasty, unshaven face, and then Allson turned and ran. Walsh drew her blaster and flipped off the safety. 'Freeze, or I'll gun you down.'

Allson ducked through a doorway, and Walsh was about to run after him when she recognised the danger. During Peace Force training they covered these situations over and over again, until they were second nature. Follow the suspect inside, and she might run straight into a trap.

Instead, she left the door and ran around the outside of the house, making heavy work of the deep snow. She was halfway round when the back door burst open and two men raced across the yard towards a battered old car.

Without hesitation Walsh took aim and squeezed off a shot. Blam! The car rocked from the impact, and the men skidded to a halt as the windows exploded in a shower of glass. 'I said STOP!' shouted Walsh. 'The next one's for you!'

The men stuck their hands up. 'Don't shoot,' shouted Allson. 'I surrender!'

Walsh hurried over, took two pairs of cuffs from her belt and threw them on the ground. 'Put those on. Both of you.'

'What did I do?' demanded the second man. He was overweight, with a bald head and grey stubble on his cheeks.

'You ran from the law.' Walsh gestured with her gun. 'Put them on. I won't ask again.'

The man glanced at his companion, then lowered his hands. 'Know what I think? I think this is harassment. You bust into a private home, you –'

Walsh turned a dial on her gun and shot him in the chest. He shook violently, struggling to keep his footing, then dropped like a sack of spuds.

'Just putting the cuffs on,' said Allson quickly. He put his hands through the slender loops, and the device tightened with a beep. When he was secure, Walsh rolled the unconscious man onto his side and cuffed him too.

'Wh-what's this about?' asked Allson nervously. 'Why are you here?'

'You're going to answer a few questions. If I don't like the answers I'm taking you into custody.'

'But I didn't do anything!'

'That's for me to decide.' Walsh holstered her gun and leant against the car. 'Now, what do you know about a truckload of missing artworks?'

◆

Hal revved the truck's engine, the cab twisting under the massive torque. The old-fashioned steering wheel was as big as a boardroom table in his hands, and the massed instruments glowed like a newborn galaxy. When he was ready, he sought out the reversing screen, judged the distance to the doors, and pressed the accelerator.

'Not too fast,' said Clunk. 'Take it easy. Take it easy!'

Hal took his eyes off the screen. 'I know what I'm doing, Clunk. It's just a –'

Scrunch!

They came to a lurching halt, and the engine stopped with a clatter. Hal stared at the camera, but the screen was dark. 'What happened?'

'You drove into the wall.'

Hal restarted the engine and changed gear. The truck lurched forward, and the reversing camera showed a grey concrete wall with deep scratches and paint marks. Hal spun the wheel, selected reverse and tried again.

Scrunch!

This time they hit the other side, and there was a patter on the cab as fragments of shattered concrete rained down.

'Mr Spacejock, I really think I should ...'

'Will you stop distracting me?' Hal jerked the wheel and planted his foot, spinning the huge tyres on the slick concrete floor. The truck leapt forward, and he stomped on the brake to stop it. Then he frowned at the screen in concentration, sawing the big wheel back and forth, alternating throttle and brake as he tried to line up with the exit. When he was happy he gripped the wheel and pressed hard on the accelerator.

The truck roared backwards, skimming the right-hand doorpost. The thick concrete wall trimmed off the driver's side mirror with a smash, leaving a waving metal stalk, and the antennae on the roof *weeouwed* and *boinged* as they bent double under the lintel. Then they were clear of the warehouse, careering backwards across the snow at full reverse power. Hal spun the wheel and applied the brake, bringing the huge truck around in a neat one-eighty. They were still sliding and spinning when he rammed the gears into first and planted his foot, sending the truck roaring towards the road.

Clunk cleared his throat. 'Don't forget the fragile, and might I say, extremely valuable artworks we're carrying in the back.'

Hal grunted and pressed his foot down even harder. They joined the main road with a four wheel powerslide, straightened up with a wiggle and barrelled down the icy highway towards the spaceport. The artworks might be battered and bruised, but if Hal had anything to do with it they would *not* be late.

10

Olivia Backsight held the commset to her ear. 'Yes?'

'It's the artworks … our driver just turned up to collect them, and they're not there. Someone's busted into the warehouse and taken the lot.'

Olivia's grip tightened on the commset. 'Are you telling me someone stole Bright's art? All of it?'

'That's what it looks like.'

'Well, you'd better find them again, hadn't you? Look for tracks, follow them, get the cargo back, and eliminate whoever is responsible.'

◆

'That was the spaceport entrance,' said Clunk, as a sign flashed past.

They were driving through a swirling blizzard, and all Hal saw was a snow-covered bump.

Crash!

'That is - was - the carpark boom gate,' said Clunk calmly.

The truck soared into the air and came down on all four wheels, rocking on its springs.

'Parked car,' said Clunk, as though he were repeating the time from a speaking clock.

Bump!

'Another car.'

Crash!

'A caution sign,' said Clunk calmly. 'When you're ready for it, the brake pedal is on the left.'

Hal finally reacted, transferring his foot to the brake and stamping down hard. The wheels locked, shuddering under the immense strain, and the truck squirrelled and squirmed as it washed off speed. Through the windscreen Hal saw the aerials whip forward like fishing rods casting for the far side of the ocean, and lumps of snow and ice broke free and shot into the distance like cannonballs. There was a creak behind them, and Hal realised Max Bright's immense 'Hairpiece' was trying to join them in the cab. The bulkhead bowed inwards as though it were made out of bubblegum, and cracks appeared in the stressed metal.

The truck finally shuddered to a halt, ticking and creaking all over. Clunk sat dead still for several seconds, then released his grip on the strap and undid his seatbelt. 'I'll organise a forklift while you're explaining to the insurance company.'

'You'll need a jumbo-sized forklift.'

'And you'll need a jumbo-sized excuse,' said Clunk drily. He slid out of the truck and slammed the door, and the last Hal saw of him was a flash of bronze, quickly swallowed up by the swirling snow.

Hal decided to leave the tricky business of insurance until later. It wasn't that the company was hard to get hold of - Clunk had the claims hotline on speed dial - it was just that Hal was on a first-name basis with every one of the vast conglomerate's employees. From what some of them told him, they liked to recount Hal Spacejock disaster tales to while away the time between coffee breaks.

So, Hal decided to make himself useful. While awaiting the forklift, he'd surprise Clunk by loading the rest of the cargo all by himself. Semi-Colon and Fish in a Jar were a piece of cake, so to speak, but the big stuffed cow was another kettle of, er, fish. It was too heavy for him to carry on his own, and he knew some fussy customer would complain if he dragged it into the hold by its mangy tail. He was just working out whether he could roll it inside without snapping the horns off when Clunk came back.

'I'm sorry, Mr Spacejock. They don't have any machinery big enough to –'

'Fork that?' said Hal, with a gesture at the giant rock.

'Correct.'

'Give me a hand with this cow. I'll have a good think while we're moving it.' He took hold of the horns while Clunk moved to the opposite end. They strained and heaved until the hooves cleared the trailer, then staggered up the cargo ramp. Hal's feet skidded and slipped on the slick surface, and he kept losing his balance. 'What did they stuff this thing with? Gravel?'

'It is rather heavy,' admitted Clunk.

'They should have used foam beads,' grumbled Hal, as they struggled into the hold. They set the cow down, and he remembered he was supposed to be thinking. 'I don't suppose you can carry that rock on your back?'

'I estimate Bright's Hairpiece weighs upwards of twenty tons. I could only manage two when I was new.'

'So that's a no.'

'Anyway, we can't carry it in the hold. As I explained, there's no way to secure it.'

'Yeah, yeah. And I said we'd figure something out.' Hal frowned as he stared down the ramp. They'd reversed the truck up to make unloading easier, and he could see the huge rock in the shadowy interior. They could lever it out of the truck without much problem, but it would be a devil of a job rolling it up the cargo ramp. One slip and it would tumble all the way down again, crushing the truck.

Next he considered reversing the truck up the ramp to the hold, but then they'd have to push the rock onto the cargo hold floor. It was a drop of a metre or more, and Hal could only imagine what twenty tons of falling rock would do to his ship.

Hal eyed the back of the hold, wondering whether they could take off with the truck inside. Unfortunately, the hold wasn't tall enough - and the ceiling still had the scars to prove it. Then it hit him ... what if they raised the cargo ramp until it was level with the back of the truck? There would still be a substantial slope - too steep to push the rock up - but that's where the really good part of his plan came in. Hal clapped his hands together and rubbed them with glee. It was perfect!

The only problem would be getting rid of Clunk so the robot couldn't interfere.

◆

Harriet slammed the car door and sat back in the padded seat. She'd put the men into different rooms inside the house, and had gone from one to the other until she'd got as much as she could out of them. From the sound of it, the gang had been shocked to discover their valuable haul consisted of nothing but obscure artworks. They'd immediately realised they were impossible to sell, and they'd decided to hide the lot and cut their losses by selling the truck for its parts.

She'd questioned them further, trying to discover how far the gang's tendrils reached into the shipping business, and she'd scored a couple of useful leads. One was the cargo handler who'd alerted the men to the truck. The other was a contact in the spaceport's shipping department.

Now she faced a difficult choice. Should she waste time reporting back to Peace Force Command, or chase down the leads while they were still hot? Forzen didn't have a Peace Force office, and getting new orders could easily take a couple of hours. Wait around too long and the men would get free, and then they'd raise the alarm. The gang responsible for the thefts would go to ground, and the case would slip through her fingers.

On the other hand, if she followed up on her own she could possibly nail those involved and present the closed case to her superiors. It was tempting, but risky.

Walsh started the engine, still undecided. Hal and Clunk weren't crooks, she knew that, but Boson was obsessed with his smuggling theory, and he'd have her mopping jail cells for months if she let the *Volante* leave Forzen without a Peace Force officer on board.

The car pulled into the road, and as it sped up Walsh decided on her course of action.

◆

Hal revved the truck's engine and inspected his carefully planned setup in the reversing screen. The back of the truck was pointing at the Volante's hold, which was about a hundred metres away. The ramp was angled just so, the end raised to match the height of the truck's bed. And, most important of all, there was no sign of Clunk.

It had been a real struggle getting rid of the robot, but in the end Hal had demanded a list of all the local companies who rented out heavy lifting equipment, and when it came he'd sent Clunk off to interview them all.

Hal revved the engine again, enjoying the feeling of power. The truck was more visceral than the Volante's clinical jets, and the heavy rumble from the huge motor shook his eyeballs in their sockets. He eyed the screen, and saw the ship's landing lights glistening on the strip of tarmac behind the truck. Swirling snow made it hard to see clearly, and with his eyes narrowed in concentration, Hal selected reverse gear and gripped the wheel. Then, after a last minute check, he planted his right foot.

The cabin groaned as the engine piled on the power, and after a shuddering, chirping spin from the rear wheels, the huge vehicle began to move. Hal juggled the steering wheel, adjusting the angle as he tried to keep the Volante centred in the reversing screen.

The truck hurtled towards the ship at full speed. Reverse gears whined, protesting at the punishment, but Hal gripped the wheel and kept his foot planted.

Thirty metres ... twenty ... ten!

At the very last second, Hal shifted his foot to the huge brake pedal and leant his full weight on it. He pushed so hard he was practically standing up in the drivers seat, and only his hands on the wheel stopped him flying up to the roof.

SSsshhhh-shh!

Hal frowned. He'd expected squeals from the huge tyres, not a slippery hiss. The brakes didn't seem to be working either, hardly slowing the truck at all. When he looked at the camera he saw the half-raised cargo ramp coming at him like the blade on a gigantic guillotine. Before he could twist the wheel, or shout for help, the truck hit with a massive CRRUUNNCCHHH!

Hal was thrown back in his chair, winded despite the thick padding. Dust and grit flew, and when it cleared he saw the rock sitting neatly inside the Volante's hold. 'Score!'

Pleased with himself, Hal put the truck into forward gear and accelerated. The engine roared, but instead of driving away from the ship, there was only a strange clattering noise. A dark shadow rolled by, and Hal gaped as he recognised one of the big rear wheels with its giant rubber tyre. Slightly worried, he leapt down from the cab and went to look.

What he found was more than slightly worrying. The Volante's cargo ramp had sliced the truck's rear axles off, and the back of the huge vehicle was propped up in mid-air. Hal eyed the damage for a minute or two, then jogged up the ramp and hit the close button. Hydraulics whirred and hissed, pulling the ramp up, and there was a creak of tortured metal as the rear end of the truck rose into the air. By the time it slipped off the ramp, the huge vehicle was standing on its nose, and the momentum carried it right over onto its roof.

Thud!

Snow was falling hard, and flakes began to coat the stricken truck before it had even finished rocking. The ramp rose faster without the extra weight, and closed neatly against the back of the ship. Hal activated the doors, straightened Fish in a Jar, then dusted himself down and headed for the flight deck.

◆

'Yes, but how did you load it?' asked Clunk again. He'd returned to the ship to find the cargo neatly inside the hold, and he still couldn't figure it out.

'I used ingenuity and skill.' Hal waved his hand airily. 'You wouldn't understand.'

Clunk's eyebrows had gone up at the sight of the huge rock in the hold, and ten minutes later they were still up. Hal wasn't sure whether the robot was genuinely surprised, or whether he'd driven his eyebrows so far up his head they'd got stuck. He guessed he'd find out when the robot tried to frown, which was due any second.

'I did say we wouldn't be able to secure the rock inside the hold,' said Clunk.

'It looks pretty snug to me.'

'It will move around in flight. It should be transported under the ship, using a cargo sling.'

'Why don't we see if it moves when we take off?'

Clunk frowned, popping his eyebrows back into place. 'Because it could fly across the hold, smash through the cargo doors and fall onto the spaceport. Or worse, demolish the city.'

Hal clapped the robot on the shoulder. 'Don't worry. I'll leave the minor details to you.'

'Ye-es.'

'So, what do we know about the delivery planet?'

'Pegzwil is a temperate world –'

'No snow? Good.'

'– with a large number of tourist resorts. It's famous for sandy beaches, mild weather, crystal clear oceans and five-star restaurants.'

'Sounds like my kind of place. What's the catch?'

'None that I can see.'

'Huge landing fees? Expensive fuel? Freedom fighters round every corner?'

'The landing fees are usually sky-high, but they've been waived thanks to our cargo.'

'How does that work?'

'Because we're importing artworks, our fees are subsidised by the cultural enrichment program.'

Hal laughed. 'They obviously haven't seen the art.'

'The nature of the pieces is irrelevant.'

Hal looked thoughtful. 'So if I dab paint on a few canvasses, we can land anywhere for free?'

'Certainly, once you've made a name for yourself. The enrichment program only applies to recognised artists.'

'How do you get recognised?'

'By exhibiting artworks on prestigious planets.'

'But unknown artists can't afford to land there!'

'It does seem like a chicken-and-egg situation,' admitted Clunk. 'Still, thanks to Max Bright, we can land on Pegzwil without having to pay.'

'Do you know anything else about this place?'

'Fuel is cheap and plentiful, and life is peaceful and safe.'

'We ought to settle there,' remarked Hal.

'Unfortunately, that's not an option. Their longest tourist visa is for two weeks.'

'We could emigrate.'

'Only if you agree to an operation. All immigrants have their middle fingers surgically removed.'

Hal blinked. 'Why?'

'Like I said, it's a tourist planet. They take polite customer service very seriously.'

Hal shot the robot a suspicious look. 'You're not making this up, are you?'

'Absolutely not!'

'In that case, I think we'll just deliver the cargo and leave.'

'An excellent idea. I'll arrange delivery as soon as we enter orbit.' Clunk hesitated. 'Incidentally, where did you leave the truck keys?'

'In the truck.'

'Is that safe? What if someone steals it?'

Hal remembered the huge wheels rolling away from the wreckage, and he could still hear the crunch the vehicle had made when it landed on its roof. 'I don't think that's likely.'

'Did you engage the anti-theft mechanism?'

'In a manner of speaking.'

'Excellent. That's a load off my mind.'

And an even bigger load off the truck's axles, thought Hal, but he remained silent.

Clunk turned to the console. 'Navcom, can you organise departure clearance please?'

'Complying.'

'Don't forget Harriet,' said Hal. 'She should be here any second.'

'I'm just saving time,' said Clunk. There was a series of bleeps and bloops as he worked the console, prepping the flight systems and controls. Then ...

'Departure clearance denied,' said the Navcom.

Clunk's eyebrows rose. 'I'm sorry?'

'Clearance denied.'

'Says who?' growled Hal.

'We're not allowed to leave, under section twenty-seven, paragraph nine of the emergency powers act.'

'That's impossible,' snapped Clunk. 'Paragraph nine deals with questionable audio-visual material. We have no such thing on board.'

A guilty look stole over Hal's face. He'd just remembered an exotic magazine stashed behind the starboard engine. 'Er ... we do, you know.'

'Mr Spacejock, what have you done?'

'It's not mine!' protested Hal. 'One of the ground crew left an adult magazine behind when they were servicing the ship.'

'I find that impossible to believe.'

'You don't think ground crew would read this stuff?'

'No, that I believe. I just can't imagine you having the ship serviced.' Clunk frowned. 'Anyway, why didn't you throw it out when you found it?'

'There were some very interesting articles,' mumbled Hal. 'Anyway, I thought they might come back for it.'

'Oh, the shame. If customs think you've been smuggling filth your face will be all over the news in no time. And what will Ms Walsh say?'

'Hey, don't go hypocritical on me. I've seen you ogling those vacuum cleaner catalogues you keep in the rec room. Your tongue was hanging down to your chin.'

Clunk drew himself up. 'I was merely comparing their salient features.'

'Snap.' Hal frowned at the console. 'So how do we sort this one out?'

'They'll send a team to search the ship for questionable material. We must ensure they find nothing amiss.'

'Better get rid of it then. Shove it down the recycler?'

'No, it could be retrieved. Bring it to me and I'll feed it into the ship's exhaust chamber.'

Harriet climbed the stairs to the control tower, her boots thudding on the metal steps. So far she'd spoken to half a dozen ground staff, and it had taken longer than expected to pin down the gang's insider. She'd followed rumour and innuendo from one department to the next, and waving her Peace Force badge had uncovered a postage racket, a printer cartridge fraud and a kitchen supplies scam. Eventually, after threatening an official investigation into the entire Spaceport, she got a name.

Through the swirling snow she could just see the *Volante* on the landing field. The ship was ringed with bright lights, and she could see half a dozen customs agents hurrying up the passenger ramp, guns at the ready. She felt a twinge of guilt at the raid, especially since she'd organised it, but she told herself it would be okay. After all, Hal didn't have anything to hide, and delaying the *Volante* for an hour or two was the answer to all her problems. She could wrap up the truck hijacking case *and* inspect the artworks on the quiet once the *Volante* left Forzen.

Harriet reached the top of the stairs, where she found a heavy metal door. There was a grey touch pad alongside, and she pressed her palm to it.

Buzz!

The indicator flashed, but the door remained firmly closed. Walsh tried again, with the same result, and then she pounded on the door with her fist. There were hurried footsteps on the other side, the door slid open and a dark-haired woman looked out.

'Are you Mia Higgs?' demanded Walsh.

'Y-yes. Can I help you, officer?'

'Allson gave me your name.'

Higgs started, but recovered quickly. 'I'm sorry, who?'

'Nice try. Face the wall and put your hands behind your back.'

'Y-you're arresting me?' Higgs backed into the room, hands half raised. 'What did I do?'

'To be honest, I don't care. I need a name and I'm running out of time.' Walsh cuffed the woman's wrists and glanced around the room. It was a poky office with a large desk and a set of filing cabinets. On the desk was a terminal, a keyboard and a couple of family pictures.

Higgs glanced over her shoulder, her face drawn. 'I swear I don't know anything. Someone's setting me up.'

'Keep stalling and I'll lock you up so fast –'

'Okay, okay. Just … let me sit down.'

'Sure.' Walsh swept the keyboard onto to the floor and slid the commset out of reach. She guided Higgs to the chair, then leant over the desk until their noses were almost touching. 'Name. Now.'

Higgs swallowed. 'I c-can't. It's too dangerous.'

'Oh, don't worry about the danger. I'll tell 'em you squealed anyway.'

'You're insane. You'll get me killed!'

Walsh slammed her fist on the desk. 'I-don't-care!'

'What sort of officer are you?'

'Have you heard of good cop, bad cop?'

'S-sure.'

'I'm angry cop with a big gun.'

Higgs closed her eyes. 'There's this guy in Accounts. He started gambling and got into debt. Big debts with the wrong people. Know what I mean?'

Walsh nodded.

'One day he comes to work with a pocketful of cash. All his problems solved, just like that. Well, we've all got debts, right?'

Again, Walsh nodded.

'All we had to do was share a little info. There was no harm in it.'

Sure, thought Harriet. No harm except a string of stolen trucks, wasted Peace Force hours and higher insurance premiums all round. 'I need a name.'

'If I tell you, will you let me off? I–I've got kids at home. Their dad ran out on us a couple of years back. It's hard, you know?'

Walsh felt a stab of sympathy. She'd been raised by an aunt herself, and money had been tight. 'If this pans out I'll try and keep your name out of it.'

Higgs looked relieved. 'I really didn't mean any harm. It's just that once I got in …'

'I understand. Now, who am I looking for?'

'Matt Ranford. He's in Accounts, second floor.'

Walsh turned to leave.

'Hey, what about these cuffs?'

'They'll come off when I've got Ranford.'

'But –'

'No buts. And don't even think about leaving this office. If you're not here when I come back, I'll have your face on every Peace Force bulletin across the galaxy.'

◆

While Harriet was chasing down leads, Clunk was busy showing customs officers all over the *Volante*. Hal would have accompanied them, but he was bailed up in the flight deck by a middle-aged officer with a swept-up hairstyle, a flashing red nose ring and a tattoo of a hollow pencil on his neck. Hal kept eyeing the tattoo, trying to work out the significance. He really wanted to ask, but he wasn't keen to antagonise the officer by saying the wrong thing. In the end the temptation was too strong. 'How come there's no lead in your pencil?'

'I beg your pardon?'

Hal tapped his neck.

'Oh, that.' The officer frowned. 'My ex-wife had it done while I was out cold.'

'Why don't you have it removed?'

'Funny you should ask,' said the officer sourly. 'She tattooed that exact question across my chest.'

'No, I meant …' Hal realised he was digging himself deeper and deeper, so he switched to a safer topic. 'Why's your ring glowing?'

'It's an early warning system, see?' The officer tapped his nose. 'You take a sniff of your meal, and if it's too spicy your ring turns red.'

'Better before than after, I guess.' Hal eyed the officer's hair style, which looked like a badly mown lawn crossed with a field of dry bracken, but he decided to keep his mouth shut. 'So, how's the customs game? Caught many smugglers?'

'We get our fair share.'

'You're wasting your time here. We've got nothing to hide.'

'That's not what our informant said.'

'You want to speak with Peace Force officer Harriet Walsh,' said Hal. 'She knows me. She'll set you straight in no time.'

The customs officer gave him a strange look. 'Officer Walsh, you say?'

'Yeah, she's around here somewhere.'

'I know exactly where she is,' said the officer. 'She's the one who reported you.'

<hr>

Walsh stood outside the door to the spaceport's accounts department, unsure of the best approach. So far she'd been cautious, but the closer she got to the ringleaders the more likely they'd put up a fight. Her jaw tightened as she came to a decision: it was time to go in hard.

Walsh bashed the door open with a well-aimed kick, then charged into the office with her gun at the ready. Inside, a dozen staff were sitting at their desks, all busy at their terminals. When the door crashed open there were screams and cries of alarm, and Walsh waved her badge. 'Peace Force! Down on the floor!'

There was a panicked rush as everyone shoved their chairs back and dived under their desks, cowering with their hands over their heads. Walsh nodded in satisfaction, then crouched next to the nearest, a red-haired woman with big jangly earrings and heavy makeup. 'Matt Ranford. Where is he?'

'He d-doesn't work here any more.'

'Don't play games, or you'll end up in the same cell.'

'I swear! He left last year. Check with HR if you don't believe me.'

Walsh swore under her breath. Higgs had fooled her!

Rrring!

Walsh jumped at the sudden noise. She spun round with her gun at the ready, and saw a commset flashing on a nearby desk. The man hiding under the desk cringed.

Rrring!

'Sh-should I get that?' asked the man.

'Go ahead.'

He reached for the handset, feeling on the desk until he managed to find it. There was a quick conversation, and then he held it out to Walsh. 'Er ... it's for you.'

◆

The customs officer passed the handset to Hal. 'Here you are. All yours.'

Hal took it. 'Harriet, what the hell are you playing at? I've got a ship full of goons, and ...'

The officer's expression soured at this scathing appraisal of his honest, hard-working employees, and Hal covered the handset to mumble an apology. 'Sorry, no offence.'

'Just get on with it,' growled the officer.

'Harriet, these idiots tell me you sent them. What's the story?'

There was a brief silence, then ... 'Hal, do you trust me?'

'Sure I do,' said Hal, without hesitation.

'I'm onto something big, but it's going to take a little time. I'm sorry about the customs thing, but I couldn't let you go without me.'

Hal frowned. 'How could I leave you behind? You're one of the crew.'

'But your delivery job. The artworks ...'

'You think I'd choose that bunch of junk over you?' growled Hal. 'I'd give up the whole cargo business just to buy you lunch.'

There was a longer silence. 'I'm sorry,' said Walsh quietly. 'I–I should have trusted you.'

'Damn straight. Now where are you? Me and Clunk are coming to help.'

'I'm heading back to the control tower. I left a suspect there.'

'Why don't you wait for us?'

'No, she won't give me any trouble,' said Walsh firmly. 'You stay aboard. I'll be there in fifteen minutes.'

Hal glanced at the viewscreen. They were already half an hour behind schedule, but they could catch that up easily enough. He'd worry about the excess fuel bill later. 'If you're sure?'

'I'm certain. I've got to go, Hal.'

'Be safe,' muttered Hal, as the line went dead.

Olivia Backsight eyed her commset, allowing herself a grim smile as she saw the caller ID. 'What's the progress on my artworks? Good news, I hope.'

'Sort of. We found the missing truck.'

'Excellent. Take the artworks to the spaceport immediately, and –'

'No, we only found the vehicle. The art wasn't there.'

Olivia's eyes narrowed. 'Are you telling me it's gone?'

'Yes. I mean no. I mean, it's worked out okay.'

'How so?'

'The artworks are safely aboard the freighter. You're going to laugh, but it turns out the guy we've been chasing - the guy who took the artworks from the warehouse - was the freighter pilot himself.'

Olivia swore under her breath. 'So let me get this straight. First, your team of idiots hijacks a truck carrying my own cargo. Next, the whole lot gets stolen and you chase the thief to the spaceport. Then you discover the cargo wasn't stolen at all - the pilot just happened to track it down on his own. And finally, to cap it all off, he drives it to his own ship, where it was supposed to be delivered in the first place. Have I missed anything?'

'When you put it like that, it does sound a bit…incompetent.'

'Incompetent?' shouted Olivia. 'If you were only that incompetent I'd pay you twice as much. You and your people are blithering idiots!'

'It worked out okay,' said the caller.

'Don't take that sulky tone with me. And there's another thing …there'd better not be any more problems, or I'll –'

'Now you mention it, there is one teeny tiny little concern.'

'Go on,' said Olivia, a dangerous edge to her voice.

'This pilot had a Peace Force officer with him, and she's got her teeth into the hijacking. She's chasing all over the spaceport making a nuisance of herself, and it's only a matter of time before someone blabs.'

'You'll just have to deal with her, won't you?'

'You mean –'

'Deal with her,' said Olivia firmly, and then she hung up.

◆

'Mr Spacejock …'

'Not now, Clunk.' Hal was sitting at the console, frowning at the screen. The customs inspection team had left some time ago, disappointed and empty-handed. Their leader hinted that they usually left 'with a little bottle of something', but the thunderclouds swirling across Hal's brow quickly silenced him.

'We're a long way past the deadline, Mr Spacejock. If we don't leave soon –'

'I don't want to hear about it!'

'But Ms Walsh can make her own way –'

Hal rounded on the robot. 'Clunk, I told her we'd sit tight and wait. We can always make up a little time in flight.'

'A little, maybe.' Clunk cast a dubious glance at the main screen. 'An hour might be pushing it.'

'We'll burn extra fuel. No big deal.'

'Pretty soon we'll need more fuel than we can carry. And need I remind you about the penalty clause –'

'No, you may not.'

'But –'

'No!' Hal jumped up from the pilot's chair and strode into the airlock. He pulled open a cupboard and rummaged amongst the clutter inside. Headless brooms, a cracked space helmet, a tangled length of safety line … was there nothing useful aboard his ship?

'What are you looking for?' asked Clunk.

'A weapon.'

'We don't carry guns. You know that.'

'Who said anything about guns?' Hal picked up a broomstick and gave a few experimental swishes. He swung too far, hitting the wall, and the

561

broomstick shattered in two. 'They don't make things like they used to, do they?'

'What exactly are you planning?'

'Harriet's late, so I'm going to help out.'

'Oh dear.'

'Don't say it like that!'

'But what if you're late too? The penalty fee –'

'Blow the penalty fee, screw Max Bright, and bugger his ridiculous artworks.' Hal grabbed the space helmet and inspected the cracked visor. 'Can you break a piece off of this?'

'What for?'

'Sharpen the edges and it'll make a decent shiv.'

'Mr Spacejock, you cannot get involved in an official investigation. You'll endanger yourself, as well as Ms Walsh. If Peace Force Command get to hear of it –'

'That's it!' shouted Hal. 'The bug on her uniform! If anything's wrong they'll know all about it. A Peace Force rescue squad could be on the way right now.'

Clunk looked uncomfortable. 'Yes, er, perhaps.'

'What's up?'

'Well, you know the bug in Ms Walsh's uniform? The bug which records every conversation and reports back to her superiors?'

'Of course I do. The damn thing's been driving me crazy since she came back.'

'Well, er ...'

'Come on, out with it.'

'The bug ...'

'Clunk!' shouted Hal. 'I order you to tell me everything. Everything, you hear?'

Unwillingly, the robot complied. 'The bug doesn't exist,' he said with a rush.

'It what?'

'It was a fiction. A deception. A bald-faced lie. And the vacuum cleaner catalogue? I really was ogling those beautiful machines.'

'Huh?'

'And that time you found an empty oil can in the –' Clunk put a hand over his mouth.

'Go on.'

'Won't,' said Clunk, his voice muffled.

Hal's eyes narrowed. He'd get to the robot's confessions later, but what was the crap about Harriet's bug? 'Are you saying she lied to me?'

Clunk briefly removed his hand. 'Correct.'

'Why?'

'I should think that's obvious.'

Hal twirled a finger at his forehead. 'She's gone mad, you mean?'

'No, of course not.'

'She's running an experiment? Trying to keep me honest? Reassuring me that she'll be safe wherever she goes?'

'None of those.'

'What, then?'

'I don't want to hurt your feelings.'

'Don't worry, I'm tough. I can take it.'

'Very well. Ms Walsh is determined to live her own life, and you're not part of her plans. She pretended her bosses were listening in to your conversations so you had to keep things on a professional level. In other words, she didn't want to get intimate with you. She no longer cares for you. She –'

'I got it, thanks.'

'I'm sure some of the other reasons you mentioned were also a factor.'

'Sure they were,' said Hal flatly. Inside, he was churning. Did she think so little of him? All she had to do was make it clear things were over between them, not pretend there was a bug listening in. He pictured her recounting the story in the Peace Force canteen later on, and his toes curled as he imagined all the smart, uniformed officers laughing at his expense. Hal Spacejock, the gullible clown in the coffee-stained flight suit. The cargo pilot with no future, no prospects, and –

'Now can we leave this planet?' said Clunk.

'Of course we're not leaving. Whatever Harriet thinks of me, I'm still going to help her.'

'But the cargo!'

Hal frowned at the screen, then snapped his fingers. 'I've got it. You deliver the cargo while I go after Harriet.'

'Oh no, most definitely not.'

'You've done it before.'

'Only in dire emergencies. You know the rules - every ship must have a human pilot.'

'I'm going to regret saying this, but you do realise you might actually be a better pilot than me?'

Clunk opened and closed his mouth.

'Don't let it go to your head.' Hal began to pace the flight deck. 'What we need is a stand-in.'

'Where are we going to find another pilot at such short notice?'

Hal waved his hand. 'They don't have to be a real pilot. We just need a living, breathing human.'

'You want to put an untrained boob at the controls of a two-hundred tonne …' Clunk's voice tailed off as he realised that was the usual setup. 'You're right, it would almost certainly work. The only thing is, we'd have to coach them.'

'I can help with that,' said the Navcom suddenly.

Hal turned to the console. 'Really? How?'

'I've analysed all your interactions with the ship, going back several months. I can display the most commonly-used phrases on the screen, and the stand-in pilot would only have to read them at random intervals.'

Hal frowned. 'Flying the *Volante* takes a bit more skill than that.'

There was a lengthy silence.

'Anyway,' said Clunk. 'I'm sure it's a workable solution. Navcom, will you share these piloting commands?'

Several sentences appeared on the console:

Are we there yet?

Where's my coffee?

Shit, that was close!

'Very funny,' growled Hal. He looked around as Clunk snorted. 'What are you laughing at?'

'I-I'm not laughing. My f-f-fans malfunctioned.'

Hal glared from one to the other. 'Stop wasting valuable time! Harriet could be dead by now, or worse!'

'You're right. I'm sorry.'

'Good. Now dig up some real piloting phrases, and I'll go find you a fake pilot.'

When Hal left the Volante the first person he saw was an elderly cleaner pushing a broom around. With his mop of grey hair, his straggly beard and his stained overcoat he wasn't exactly what Hal had in mind, but on the plus side he'd be cheaper than a more presentable alternative. 'Excuse me,' said Hal.

The cleaner ignored him.

'Hello?' Hal tapped the cleaner on the shoulder, and ducked just in time as the broom came swishing towards his head.

'What's your game?' shouted the old man. 'Sneaking up like that. I could have killed you.'

'I need a temporary pilot,' said Hal.

'What?'

'A pilot!'

The old man cupped a hand to his ear. 'You'll have to speak up, son. All those noisy ships have done me hearing in.'

'I need a pilot!' shouted Hal.

The old man gestured with his broom. 'You think I fly this around, do you? You making fun of me?'

'No, of course not.' Hal gestured at the *Volante*. 'I need someone to sit in the flight deck while my robot flies to Pegzwil.'

'Ahh, Pegzwil. I know it well.'

'Good. Do you want to go there?'

'Yes, but my parole officer won't let me.'

Hal gave up on the elderly cleaner, and set off to explore the landing field. Thirty minutes later he was cold and fed up, and he still hadn't found anyone. Irritated beyond measure, he gave up and returned to the *Volante*.

— 13 —

'That was a total waste of time,' growled Hal. He was back in the flight deck, stamping his frozen feet to try and get some feeling back into them. 'And Harriet ... you still haven't heard from her?'

'Not a thing.'

'Okay, I'm not waiting a second longer. You'll just have to find a stand-in pilot on your own.'

'I can't go around offering humans money for their services. There are laws against that sort of thing.'

'What about the teleporter guy? I'm sure he'll lend you his son.'

Clunk brightened. 'That might just work.'

'Good. I want you to lift off for Pegzwil the second you both get back here. I'm going to rescue Harriet.'

Harriet opened her eyes and stared at the ceiling. She was lying on her back on a hard floor, and lights were glaring down on her like a row of merciless suns. She had no idea if it was early morning or late night, and she couldn't remember where she was or how she got there. Then the pain hit her, and she groaned at the savage headache. What the hell happened?

She turned her head and saw a pair of nylon cuffs lying on the carpet. They'd been cut apart, and the sight brought everything back. She'd entered the control tower and found Higgs slumped at the desk, still wearing the cuffs. Harriet had bent over to check Higgs was okay, and the woman had caught her with a double-fisted roundhouse: both fists to the side of the head. Pow! Darkness. So much for her Peace Force training - she'd walked straight into the trap like a tame bunny.

Harriet tried to sit up, but when she rolled over she discovered her hands were tied behind her back. Then she looked down, and her heart skipped a beat when she saw the empty holster at her hip. That was bad, really bad. First, Higgs had done a runner. Second, someone out there had her weapon, and third, the paperwork and explanations would take months.

Harriet angled her shoulder, trying to get a glimpse of her wrists. Higgs had trussed her up with a pair of her own nylon handcuffs, which wasn't so bad. If she could just find a sharp edge ...

At that moment she heard footsteps on the metal stairs outside. Someone was coming up in a hurry, and if they found her like this she'd be entirely at their mercy.

Harriet gave up struggling against the bonds and rolled towards the door, ignoring the sharp pain in her head. When she was close enough she drew her leg back, the hefty Peace Force boot at the ready. She might be tied up and almost helpless, but whoever came through that door was going out again backwards.

◆

As soon as the *Volante* reached orbit, Clunk made his way to the cargo hold. He didn't share Mr Spacejock's confidence *vis-a-vis* the huge rock, and the sooner he dealt with it the happier he'd be. He'd come up with the solution during lift-off, when he realised he could carry the rock in a cargo sling beneath the ship. That way, it couldn't do any damage.

It took him almost an hour, but Clunk finally managed to fashion a large enough sling. Then, with the hold's artificial gravity switched off, he moved the asteroid outside and secured it below the ship. As he regained the hold, Clunk realised he'd never have attempted anything so risky with Mr Spacejock at the controls.

With the rock nice and secure, Clunk made his way to the flight deck to keep an eye on the tall young man lounging in the pilot's chair. The teleporter scientist's son had agreed to Clunk's plan willingly, and so far he'd proved a resounding success.

'Remember you're not really a pilot,' said Clunk, for the tenth time. 'You mustn't touch anything.'

'Sure, sure.' Hans looked at him thoughtfully. 'As the only human on board, I'm in command. Is that right?'

'Nominally, that's true.'

'Yes or no?'

Clunk hesitated. He could guess where this was heading, and he didn't like it. On the other hand, Hans was being helpful and he didn't want to upset him. 'Yes, under certain circumstances you're in command.'

'Good. Make me a ham sandwich.'

'I beg your pardon?'

'One ham sandwich, and go easy on the mustard.' Hans clicked his fingers. 'Come on, come on. Don't keep me waiting.'

Clunk frowned. 'Who do you think you are, the Emperor?'

'No, I'm your captain. Now hop to it before I make you polish the hull.'

'I can't do that in flight. I might lose my grip and vanish into deep space.'

'Exactly.' Hans smiled. 'Now fetch that sandwich, and make it snappy.'

◆

Hal palmed the door controls and hurried into the control tower. According to the staff downstairs, Harriet had been coming up to question someone. He hoped she'd just lost track of time.

He'd only taken two steps into the room when a well-aimed boot, fitted to a shapely leg, hacked at his shins. Hal leapt at the last second, landed awkwardly and pitched full-length along the carpet. When he recovered he saw Harriet Walsh lying behind the door, a stunned look on her face. 'Harriet! Are you all right?'

'I'm sorry, I thought someone was ...never mind.' Harriet displayed the cuffs at her wrists. 'Can you get rid of these?'

Hal freed her, then helped her into the chair. 'What happened?'

'I got careless. Higgs got the drop on me and –' Walsh broke off. Sitting on the desk was her gun, and underneath was a handwritten note.

She took both, and scanned the brief note as she tucked the weapon away. 'It's a warning.'

Hal snorted. 'They're trying to scare you off?'

'Yeah.' Harriet passed the note over.

Keep your nose out of our business. I won't tell you again.

Hal crumpled the sheet and tossed it over his shoulder. 'What are we waiting for? Let's get them!'

'No, I was mad to try and handle this on my own. From now on I'm doing this by the book.' Walsh reached for the commset on the desk, studied the controls for a second, then pressed a button. 'Put me through to the local Peace Force office. Priority one.'

'Complying.'

There was a brief delay, and then ...

'I'm sorry, your call could not be connected.'

'Why not?' demanded Harriet.

'There is no Peace Force office on Forzen.'

'Crap, I forgot it's a company planet,' muttered Harriet. 'They think they're better off without the Peace Force, and then something like this happens.'

'Would you like Better Off Pest Control, or Better Off Funeral Services?'

'Neither. I need the law.'

'Would you like a brief summary or the entire constitution? Before you choose, please be advised that additional charges apply for –'

Walsh hit a button, terminating the call.

'I guess we're handling this on our own,' said Hal.

'No, we can still get help. We'll take the *Volante* to Pegzwil, and I'll report to the local Peace Force office when we get there.'

'Yes, that's a good plan ... except for the minor wrinkle.'

'Oh?'

'Clunk already left.'

'Damn.' Harriet's eyes narrowed. 'He took off without a human pilot? Isn't that risky?'

'No, Clunk's a fine pilot. He has a little gold badge and everything.' Hal sounded a little wistful. The only time he got a gold badge was in a packet of breakfast cereal, and he'd swallowed it by mistake.

'That's not what I meant. According to the law –'

'Don't worry, it's all legit. There's a human being on board.'

'A real one?'

569

'Breathing and everything.'

'Where did you find a trained pilot?'

'We should get back to the spaceport,' said Hal quickly. 'We have to organise transport.'

'Hitch a ride, you mean?'

'No, something much better.' Hal hesitated. 'There is one thing. Since I'm helping on your case, don't you think we should ...'

Harriet sighed. 'Not that again.'

'Go on! You know it's the right thing to do.'

'All right, you win. Come over here.'

Hal strode through the spaceport, his shoulders back and his head held high. He was no longer Hal Spacejock, freelance cargo pilot. He was Hal Spacejock of the Intergalactic Peace Force! Now that Harriet Walsh had made him a deputy, nobody was going to stand in his way. Crooks would cower in their lairs, bandits would bugger off to their hideouts and as for fraudsters ... they could all fu–

'Oy! I just cleaned that bit!'

Hal caught a brief glimpse of a man in overalls wielding a mop, and then his feet slipped from under him and he went down hard. As he sat on the damp floor, he wondered whether real Peace Force officers were issued non-slip boots.

'Are you all right?' asked Harriet, helping him up.

'Fine. No damage.' Hal shook her hand free and strode off, paying a little more attention to his surroundings and a little less to his crime-fighting daydreams. Eventually he saw his target, and he smiled at the sight. The elderly teleport scientist was speaking to a young couple, waving a handful of brochures and gesturing at his impressive machine. As Hal got closer, the scientist spotted him.

'Now this gentleman ... he knows I am no faker. Is that not correct, fine sir? Do you not have shares in my fabulous invention?'

Hal nodded. 'That's right.'

'And once, did you not travel with my marvellous machine?'

'Correct.'

The young couple looked doubtful. 'Did it really work?'

'Yes indeed,' said Hal. 'In fact, Peace Officer Walsh and I are about to demonstrate the teleporter again.'

'You are?' said the young woman.

'Can this really be true?' said the teleporter scientist eagerly.

'We're about to *what*?' demanded Walsh.

Hal turned to her. 'We're going to teleport to Pegzwil! It's the answer to all our problems.'

'More like a whole set of new ones.'

'You saw it working earlier,' Hal pointed out.

'I'm sorry, but it's out of the question.' Harriet gestured at the teleporter. 'You're mad if you think I'm stepping into that contraption.'

The young couple started to back away, and the scientist reacted quickly to the threat of a lost sale. 'No, please. This gentleman has passed through my teleporter before. Look, he is perfectly normal!'

The couple gave Hal a long and very dubious look. 'He may look normal,' said the woman at last. 'But he's clearly lost his mind.'

'But the brochures, the successful demonstration, the patents which I hold ...'

'Sorry, no sale. Y'all have a nice day.'

With that the couple turned and left, hurrying away as though the teleporter could reach out and suck them in from a distance.

The scientist rounded on Hal. 'Thank you most kindly for your interference,' he said bitterly. 'Without their money, breakfast cereal is all I eat for a week.'

'Never mind your diet.' Hal waved his hand at the teleporter. 'Do you want to try this thing on real people or not?'

'You would have to sign waivers. Release forms, even.' Despite his cautious tone, the scientist's eyes gleamed at the prospect. 'Maybe top up your share holdings just a little?'

Walsh crossed her arms. 'Hal Spacejock, you're not hearing me. I'd no more step into that crackpot device than I would throw good money into his overpriced share scheme.'

'But –'

'No buts! It's complete madness.'

'All right, I'll go.'

'What?'

'I'll go through, and then I'll come back again. And then we'll both go.'

'I'm not standing here while you put yourself in danger.'

'Do you have a better idea?'

'Yes! We'll find a ship and ...'

'...And your boss will find out you're not babysitting the *Volante*, and they'll put a big black mark in your file.'

'Our lives are more important than any Peace Force record!'

'There's no danger, Harriet.'

'But if we go through at the same time ...won't we get mingled together?'

The scientist coughed delicately. 'My dear lady, what you do in the privacy of the teleporter booth is your business. However, it would be best not to confuse the matter disentangler. That could lead to unfortunate consequences.'

'You see?' Harriet gestured at the scientist. 'Even he says it's not safe!'

Hal was about to argue his case when he heard a commotion. He glanced over his shoulder and saw three or four heavies entering the terminal, clad in black outfits and carrying identical blast rifles. They stopped just inside the doors, and Hal saw them scanning the terminal. Their expressions were hard, ruthless, and they looked like they meant business. 'I don't suppose they're on our side?'

Harriet glanced at the group, and one of them immediately pointed her out to the others. The rest fanned out, prepping their weapons.

At that moment the lights went out, and Hal was just getting used to the darkness when the men opened fire. Flashes lit the terminal, and he was about to duck when he realised they weren't the target. Instead, the men were shooting out all the security cameras.

'Fire up the teleporter,' muttered Hal.

'I'm sorry?' hissed the scientist. 'What was that you said?'

'Fire it up!'

'You wish to go through?'

'I don't wish to stay here, that's for bloody sure.'

The scientist slipped away, and a few moments later Hal heard beeps and bloops from the control panel. Fortunately the intruders had only cut the lights, and he could only hope they didn't go back to kill off the mains as well.

There was a low hum from the teleporter booth, which started to glow a deep, pulsing violet. Hal tried to drag his gaze away, but the rhythmic pulse was magnetic. Then he heard Harriet's whisper in his ear.

'Are we really going through with this?'

'There's four of them. Reckon you can take them all out?'

'We don't know what they're after.'

'They're not handing out parking tickets.'

The pulsing got faster, and the scientist reappeared at Hal's side. 'It is ready. Enter together, and do not touch the walls.'

'Thanks,' said Hal.

'Good luck, my friend.' The scientist shook hands. 'My public liability insurance will not cover any … mishaps. You understand?'

'Of course. It's on my head.'

'Wherever that ends up,' muttered Walsh.

'If you're going, you must be quick,' said the scientist.

Hal led the way, crossing to the teleporter in a crouched-up run. He guided Harriet into the cramped cabinet, and they stood face to face in the glowing purple light. There was a warning shout nearby, and Hal saw a gun raised to cover them. He felt Harriet's hand in his, warm and firm, and he gave it a reassuring squeeze.

Then the teleporter fired up.

'Robot, this bread is stale, the ham is as thin as a sheet of paper and the brown sauce tastes like toilet scrapings.'

Clunk opened his mouth to protest these unfair slurs on his cooking skills, then closed it again with a snap. How could he complain, when Hans had just identified the ingredients so accurately? 'I'm sorry, but that's exactly how Mr Spacejock takes his sandwiches.'

'Well it's not good enough. Take another demerit point.'

'Yes sir, although I must point out that I'm only using eight-bit integers for the tally. Should you continue to hand out demerits …'

'That's enough! When I want your chatter I'll ask for it.'

Clunk's eyes flashed dangerously. 'Of course, sir. As you wish, sir.'

They were in the Volante's third deck, where Hans had commandeered Mr Spacejock's comfy armchair. The stand-in pilot had his feet up on a polished wooden side table that Hal was particularly fond of, and the heels of his boots had already put deep scratches in one of the artistic nudes. There was a litter of food wrappers, napkins, empty plates and spilled glasses surrounding the chair, and although Clunk did his best to clear up it was an unequal fight. He'd heard horror stories about sharing kitchens with teenagers, but this was far worse.

Hans grabbed the big remote and pointed it at the screen. 'More documentaries. Don't you have anything good?'

'Mr Spacejock can only afford the budget package,' said Clunk.

'I've met him, remember? Budget describes his package all right.'

Clunk frowned. 'I'd ask you not to insult –'

'Call me sir.'

'Sir, I'd ask you –'

'And another thing. Why aren't we there yet? Didn't I tell you to go faster?'

'As I've already explained,' said Clunk patiently. 'If we go any faster, we'll run out of fuel. Sir.'

'This is a lousy ship.' Hans looked around, oblivious to the comfortable furnishings. 'Where's the bar, anyway?'

'This is a freighter, not a passenger liner. We don't serve alcohol.'

'No drink, no premium channels and no grub. This isn't what I signed up for.'

Clunk glanced over his shoulder, and there was a calculating expression on his face as he eyed the glossy black cabinet sitting in the corner. Anyone who knew the robot would be treading very carefully right about now, but Hans had no idea what he was getting into. 'There is better food aboard,' said Clunk slowly.

'Good. Fetch it immediately.'

'I can't do that. You have to order it yourself, sir, since the AutoChef won't obey a lowly robot.'

'What's an AutoChef when it's at home?'

Clunk pointed to the black cabinet. 'It's right there, sir.'

Hans eyed the machine. 'You mean I have to get up?'

It was all Clunk could do not to yank the mouthy human out of his chair and shove him head-first up the AutoChef's dispensing slot. Some misguided humans actually believed the PR nonsense about the laws governing robot behaviour, and Clunk was itching to dish out a short, sharp lesson. On the other hand, if he landed on Pegzwil with an unconscious pilot aboard there would probably be questions - even if he propped Hans up at the console and mimicked his irritating voice during final approach. 'Sir, it's not very far.'

Hans made a big show of standing up, sighing and wheezing as though he were an elderly robot. He followed Clunk to the machine, which stood inside a cube of toughened perspex. If Hans was curious about the strength and thickness of the walls, or indeed, why they were there at all, he didn't show it. He stood aside, arms crossed, while Clunk unlatched the door. The entrance was small, and there was only room for one at a time. Hans ducked his head and pushed in first, pausing to cast an eye over the machine. The sides and front were covered in animated displays of succulent foods, from sizzling steaks to crisp fries, from steaming mugs of coffee to icecream sundaes with cherries and chocolate sprinkles. There was even a thick sponge cake with icing, gleaming under soft lighting. As far as Clunk was aware the machine had never delivered anything resembling the images, and as for the cake ... he was certain that was a cruel hoax.

On the front of the machine there was a grille for the speaker and microphone, and across the bottom there was a wide delivery slot. A small sign read 'please speak your order clearly'.

'Would you like a demonstration?' asked Clunk.

'Only a moron would have trouble with something this simple.'

'Precisely, sir. Would you like me to demonstrate?'

'No! Stop fussing and leave me alone.'

'As you wish, sir. Let me give you plenty of room.' Clunk backed out and closed the door, accidentally tripping the catch by turning it to the left, giving it a wiggle and pressing down hard with both hands. He could just hear Hans through the thick wall, demanding delicacies and generally treating the AutoChef like dirt.

Clunk strolled round the corner and took up a position behind a partition. He felt a little guilty about locking the door, but accidents happened. 'Navcom, are you recording?'

'Yes indeed. This is going to be even better than the time Mr Spacejock lost the battle with an airlock.'

'How much ad revenue did you make from that one?'

'Enough for a few choice upgrades.'

'This one should pay for a whole new operating system.'

Clunk peered over the top of the partition, just like a small boy spying on the neighbour's swimming pool. The anticipation was building, and the hours of mistreatment he'd suffered at the human Hans' hands - or was it at the hands of the human Hans? - were about to be repaid in full.

At first, nothing untoward happened. The machine served Hans meekly, depositing a paper cup in the dispenser and filling it with foaming hot chocolate. When Hans bent to pick it up ...Pow! A meatball shot out of the dispenser and hit him right between the eyes, sending him staggering backwards. He slammed into the wall, shaking the entire cube, and the AutoChef tried to machine-gun him with a volley of frozen peas. Clunk winced as the icy balls snapped and cracked on the clear wall, and he heard Hans yelling as the stinging shots smacked into his skin.

Hans pounded on the door, shouting for Clunk to let him out. Clunk turned his hearing down.

The AutoChef spewed plastic knives and forks, and Hans ran behind the machine to avoid the barrage. He looked out once or twice, judging the distance to the door, but each time the AutoChef unleashed a mist of boiling water. Fortunately for Hans, the machine couldn't turn to face him. Unfortunately for Hans, the AutoChef ran off the ship's waste matter, and the connecting pipe ran straight up the back.

There was a hiss as the pipe came free, and it started whipping around like a frenzied tentacle, spraying the inside of the cube with thick, gloopy muck. Hans disappeared in the evil-smelling fog, and the last Clunk saw of him was two hands sliding down the wall, palms outwards and fingers clawed.

'Whoops, sorry sir,' murmured Clunk. He glanced at the camera housing in the corner of the lounge. 'Navcom, did you get all that?'

'Uploading it now.'

Clunk smiled to himself. In a matter of hours, Hans was going to be famous with computers and robots clear across the galaxy. 'Are we still on track for landing?'

'ETA confirmed.'

'Excellent. I wonder how Mr Spacejock is doing?'

◆

When Hal and Harriet arrived at the Pegzwil spaceport, they were indeed entangled. Hal told himself they'd fallen into each others' arms to ensure they didn't stumble against the walls. Grabbing hold of each other was a wise move given the subsequent roller-coaster ride: raging emotions, shaking knees, a warm inner glow and a floor that wouldn't stay put …and that was just when Harriet laid her head against Hal's shoulder. As for the effects of the teleporter, he'd not been paying attention.

The cosy cuddle was interrupted by a sharp voice. 'What the hell?'

Hal poked his head out of the cabinet. Just below him, on the main floor, the scientist's older son had stopped midway through his sales pitch, the glossy brochures still being waved at a large crowd of tourists. 'Hi Kurt. How's it going?'

'What …where …how?'

'Hey, can you do me a favour?' Hal stepped from the cabinet, and the crowd drew back as though he was about to morph into a vicious space monster. Then Harriet stepped out behind him, and at the sight of her uniform the entire crowd edged away.

'Thanks for nothing,' groaned Kurt. 'Some of those punters were getting ready to sign.' Then curiosity took over, and he studied Hal more closely. 'The old man's contraption really worked, huh? Anything out of place?'

Hal checked his fingers, wiggled his toes and jiggled his loose change. 'All present and correct.'

'And your partner? Nice to meet you, by the way.'

Harriet introduced herself, and they shook hands. She still looked dazed, and Hal offered her his arm. 'Come on, let's find you a strong coffee.'

'Wait a minute,' Kurt called after them. 'I have to know what it was like.'

Hal tapped the side of his nose. 'A gentleman never tells.' He started to lead Harriet away, then paused to call over his shoulder. 'By the way, you'd better disconnect that thing. There are four thugs on the other end who might try to follow us through.' Then he frowned. 'Speaking of which, I hope your dad will be all right.'

Kurt made a dismissive gesture. 'He can talk his way out of anything. If they're really lucky, he'll only sell them a bunch of shares.'

'But you will switch the machine off?'

'Sure.' Kurt reached for the console, then stopped. 'I'll do it, as long as you come back and tell me what the trip was like.'

'What sort of threat is that? If you don't do it, they'll be on you any minute.' Hal relented. 'All right, when this is over I'll tell you all about it.'

'Thanks, Hal. And good luck!'

As they left the central plaza, Hal realised the Pegzwil Spaceport was modelled after a rustic alpine village. The shops had rough-hewn log walls, with steeply sloped roofs and leadlight windows. As he got closer he realised the 'logs' were hollow plastic, and the attractive-looking windows were single sheets of glass with the 'lead' strips painted on.

Then Hal spotted a brightly-lit coffee shop, and he led the unresisting Harriet to a small table. 'Wait here,' he said, ignoring her protests, and he went to sort out two large mugs of post-teleporter essentials.

Thud!

Clunk frowned. What was that? The sound had come from outside the ship, but they were in deep space.

Crash! Clonk!

Clunk's frown deepened. Ordinarily he'd assume Mr Spacejock was off doing something unwise or downright dangerous, but the human wasn't aboard. As for Hans, the stand-in pilot, he was sitting in a trance with only the occasional twitch to show he was still alive. No, this was something else.

'Is something hitting the ship?' Clunk asked the Navcom.

Tink! Thud!

'Indubitably,' said the ship's computer.

Seconds later the lift doors swept open, and Clunk hurried into the flight deck. One glance at the screen was enough to make his cooling fluids freeze: They were flying full pelt through a cloud of asteroids!

A huge rock came flying towards the screen, and Clunk ducked as it skated off the top of the picture. 'Emergency dive!' he shouted, putting all his training to good use. 'Full reverse thrust, rudder hard-a-port …man the lifeboats!'

Clang!

Thud!

The *Volante*'s engines roared as the ship came round in a tight turn, and the asteroid field slid towards the side of the screen.

Ting!

Clunk looked up. 'Ting? What sort of rock goes ting?'

'It must have been a little one,' said the Navcom. 'That was nicely done, Clunk. You handled the situation well.'

'No thanks to you. I left you in control!'

'This is an uncharted asteroid field. Had I been aware –'

Clonk!

'Never mind,' said Clunk. 'We survived, and Mr Spacejock is none the wiser.'

Soon there was nothing ahead but inky darkness, and Clunk had just relaxed when there was a hefty jolt. The screen panned to the right, and he saw a large rock tumbling away from the ship, heading straight towards the massed asteroids.

Clunk frowned at the screen. 'How unusual. That asteroid has ropes on.' Then realisation dawned, and he stifled a very human oath. 'Navcom, Bright's Hairpiece just came loose!'

◆

There was a moment of silence as Clunk gazed at the screen, stricken by the enormity of the situation. Then he took charge in typically decisive fashion. 'Full ahead both engines. Follow that rock.'

The *Volante* began to accelerate, chasing down Bright's fugitive Hairpiece. The asteroid grew larger on the screen, briefly, but before they got anywhere near it the rock sailed through a wall of slow-moving boulders. The ship's engines switched to full reverse thrust, and the *Volante* came to a halt several hundred metres from the edge of the asteroid field.

Clunk watched Hairpiece disappear into the asteroids, cannoning into rocks and boulders like a well-aimed billiard shot.

'You still have Bright's other artworks,' said the Navcom, after a lengthy silence.

'That rock was the centrepiece of the exhibition.' Clunk zoomed the screen out and rotated the display. 'Perhaps we could pick it up round the other side.'

'The asteroid belt is thousands of kilometres across. It will take at least six months for that rock to clear it, assuming it isn't smashed to pieces.'

Clunk thought for a moment, then gestured at the screen. 'There must be thousands of rocks out there. All we have to do is find another one to match Bright's.'

'You can't be serious.'

'Deadly. Replay the vision of Bright's rock sailing for parts unknown, then scan it and find the best match within reach. I'll fetch the replacement with the jetbike, and we'll be on our way in no time.'

'It seems a little … deceptive.'

Clunk sighed. 'I don't like it, but it's the best we can do. Scan the fleeing rock. Mass, volume and shape.'

'Complying.'

On screen, the vision played in reverse, bringing the rock whizzing back towards the ship. The image froze just before the brown shape vanished off the bottom, and a green mesh appeared, wrapping it up and adapting to the shape. Rows of figures scrolled past, getting slower and slower before stopping altogether. 'Rock scanned,' said the Navcom, with a satisfied beep.

'Show me a live picture,' said Clunk.

The rock disappeared and the asteroid field came back.

'Now find the closest match within range.'

'It'll take some time,' warned the Navcom.

'Understood. Report to me the instant you find one. In the meantime, I'll make another cargo sling and prepare the jetbike.'

◆

Hal glanced at the arrivals board while he was waiting for his coffee. The board was the latest model, capable of analysing nearby targets with a battery of cameras, and deducing their tastes from their clothing, accessories and general appearance. This board went to work on Hal, criss-crossing his face with red lasers, measuring his clothes with green lasers, and estimating the size of his wallet with blue ones.

Then the ads appeared: ladies shampoo and conditioner, support underwear for the elderly, cut price cat food and a particularly grating effort for ship rentals. Hal looked away and muttered 'La-la-la, can't hear you,' under his breath, negating all the money and research advertisers had poured into the board. When the ads were finally done, he glanced up again to see whether the *Volante* was due.

'We'll present the arrivals in just a minute. But first, this sneak preview from our smash hit show 'Oh Dear, Humanity!"

Hal pursed his lips. He'd caught Clunk watching the show in the past, and he couldn't see the attraction. It consisted of lame clips of humans causing minor injuries to themselves, but the mildly amusing videos almost blew Clunk's fuses every time they came on. The robot would point and laugh, giggle helplessly, fold himself double and inevitably end up rolling around on the floor, holding his sides and struggling for air. Hal always knew when the show was on, because it sounded like someone was booting a dustbin around the flight deck.

Hal wondered what life was like before robots, when such mindless crap would never have made it to air. He eyed the screen, where a well-built guy in a red T-shirt was ordering an AutoChef around. Pow! Despite himself, Hal snorted as a meatball bounced off the idiot's head and ricocheted around the enclosure like a rubber ball. He sniggered as a fountain of frozen peas pinned the twit to the wall, and then he gaped as he spotted a familiar bronze figure in the background. Before he could react, the titles came up.

'Tune in tonight for 'Oh Dear, Humanity',' said the announcer. 'At forty credits an episode, it's the most laughs you'll get all year.'

Hal swallowed. That wasn't Clunk, and he hadn't just watched a clip of the AutoChef roughing Hans up aboard the *Volante*. He kept telling himself this while he collected the coffees, and he was still denying it when he reached the table where Harriet was waiting.

'They didn't what?' asked Harriet.

'Huh?' Hal blinked. 'I'm sorry?'

'You said 'They didn't. They couldn't have."

'Oh, that.' Hal shook his head. 'I thought they'd forgotten my sugar.'

'I thought you'd heard something about the gunfight at the Forzen spaceport.'

'That news won't get here for hours. We teleported, remember?'

'I know,' said Walsh, with a frown. She held out her hand, and Hal saw she was holding his watch.

'Where did that come from?'

'I just found it on my wrist.'

'But ... how?'

'Ask your teleporter scientist,' said Walsh.

As Hal fastened the watch, he wondered whether any other items had transferred between himself and Harriet. A watch wasn't too bad, but a wallet could be a problem, and as for underwear ...

'I really need to report in,' said Harriet, interrupting his train of thought. 'That Higgs woman will be on the run, and –'

'You're not going anywhere until you finish that coffee,' said Hal firmly. 'Five minutes won't hurt.'

Harriet took a sip, smiling at Hal over the rim of her mug. 'Do you remember that Spaceport cafe on Forzen last year, when I asked you to Miranda's party?'

'I'll never forget it.'

'Good times, eh?'

'The best.'

They were silent for a moment, and then Hal frowned. 'Er…should we be talking about this?'

'What do you mean?'

Hal gestured at her uniform. 'The bug. All those Peace Force officers standing by to rescue you.'

Harriet flushed. 'Oh, yes. About that …'

'Don't worry, I worked it out ages ago,' said Hal, neglecting to mention it was Clunk who'd revealed the truth. 'I know there's no bug.'

'I'm sorry about the deception, Hal. The bug was supposed to …'

'Keep me at arms-length,' finished Hal. 'Harriet, you know me better than that. I know how much the Peace Force means to you.'

They sat in silence, sipping the hot coffee.

'So, about the Peace Force,' said Hal at last. 'No regrets? All that training? The danger?'

'It's been fine so far.'

'All great, except for the occasional gun battle.'

Harriet ignored him. 'After a couple of years I can switch to full time study. They offer university courses, and after you graduate you can move into a completely different career.'

'Anything take your fancy?'

'I always wanted to be a scientist. It was my favourite subject at school.'

'Mmm. I could just see you in a starched white labcoat.'

'You could imagine me in just about anything.' Walsh drained her mug and got up. 'Come on. I have to report in.'

'I've been thinking about that. You can't show up at the Peace Force office now.'

Harriet frowned. 'Why not?'

'You're supposed to be travelling aboard the *Volante*,' Hal pointed out. 'Clunk hasn't landed yet.'

'But I have to report Higgs and the rest of the gang.'

'What about an anonymous tipoff?'

'As soon as I speak they'll know who I am. My voice print is on file.'

'They don't have mine.'

Harriet looked doubtful. 'Are you sure about that?'

'What do you think I am, a career criminal or something? Come on, let's find a public terminal.'

◆

Clunk roared towards the asteroid field aboard the Volante's jetbike, hunched over the handlebars like a tour rider on a long downhill run. There was no headwind in space so his stance was completely unnecessary, but Clunk felt it was appropriate under the circumstances. The *Volante* was supposed to be halfway to planet Pegzwil by now, not parked up in space like an oversized motor home.

Clunk glanced back at the makeshift sling he was towing behind the jetbike. He'd used twice as much rope this time, and it had more buckles than a multi-car pile-up.

Clunk ducked his head to avoid a jagged piece of stone the size of a groundcar. He twisted the handlebars to angle the bike between two enormous boulders, then turned hard right and accelerated. Three more rocks tumbled by, and then he spotted the target. At first glance it looked identical to Bright's Hairpiece, and Clunk hoped fervently that a glance was all anyone else would spare it. Stopping the bike alongside, he unhooked the netting and began to work it over the cracked and pitted surface, standing up in the saddle to reach over the top and hanging low off the bike to deal with the underside. It took longer than expected, because the metal buckles kept snagging on the surface. Clunk pulled hard to free them, only to see them snag again. It was puzzling, because the surface of the rock wasn't that jagged, and he couldn't see what the buckles were sticking to. Then he felt the jetbike moving towards the rock of its own volition, and he only just got his leg out the way before the two slammed together. Clunk tried to pry them apart, and that's when he realised the truth. The huge rock was magnetic!

Clunk had noticed the pull on his components, but his chassis and skin were alloy, and immune to the rock's attraction. The jetbike, on the other hand, contained a fair bit of steel. Clunk struggled to lever them apart, pushing the rock away with his arms and legs before opening the throttle with his spare hand.

The jetbike's engine laboured mightily, and for a split second it was touch and go. Then, with a rush, it shot away from the rock, pulling the net tight with a springing jolt. Clunk hung on grimly as the bike bucked and jerked, the nose hunting all over the place as the engines fought against the huge weight. Then, slowly, the rock began to move, and Clunk started the long trek back to the *Volante*. Magnetic or not, this rock was the only match for Bright's missing Hairpiece, and it would just have to do.

16

Hal and Harriet strolled through the spaceport together, following the signs to the Peace Force office. When they got there the door was locked, but there was an emergency terminal on the wall. Hal lifted the handset and Harriet leant closer so she could listen in.

'Thank you for contacting the Peace Force,' said a flat, emotionless voice. 'Please state your name after the tone.'

'Anonymous tip-off,' said Hal.

'*After* the tone, citizen.'

Hal waited.

Beep!

'Anonymous tip-off,' repeated Hal.

'Please state your gender.'

'Male.'

'Thank you, Mr Tipoff. Please state your address.'

Hal glanced at Harriet. 'Not applicable.'

'Please re-state your address, beginning with the street or apartment number.'

'For heaven's sake!' grumbled Hal. 'Can't you just take my crime report?'

'You said 'Four, Haven place'. Is this correct?'

'Yeah, that's it.'

'Please say yes or no.'

'Yes.'

'Thank you. Please hold while your details are analysed.'

There was a brief delay.

'According to our records, Mr Tipoff, you have three speeding violations and an outstanding warrant for urinating in public. Please remain where you are until a Peace Force officer arrives to take you into custody. Due to unexpected demand, estimated time of arrival for your personal Peace Force escort is sixteen hours. Should you leave your present location, your wanted level will be upgraded to fugitive status. In this event, officers will be authorised to shoot on sight.'

Hal hung up. 'Well that's great. Fantastic. I feel so much safer having you lot on my side.'

'You did give them false information,' said Harriet mildly.

'I could hardly tell them I'm the pilot of the *Volante*, could I? If they know I'm here, they'll want to know who's flying my ship when it magically arrives by itself.' Hal frowned. 'That's another thing. We'll have to sneak aboard the second Clunk sets down. Do you have a pass for the landing field?'

'I do, but I can't use it. It would go into the system.'

'We could try talking our way past.'

'Not dressed like this. They'll want to see my ID.'

Hal eyed her uniform. 'What about civilian clothes? Ditch the jacket, pick up some really dark sunnies and a nice long trenchcoat ...'

'Hal, I'd arrest *myself* in that get-up.'

'Why don't we take a look at the landing field access? There might not be any security.'

Unfortunately, his hopes were soon dashed. There were two uniformed guards watching the doors to the landing field, and they didn't look like the types to sneak away for a quick coffee. Hal frowned at the imposing sight, racking his brains for a solution. They had to get outside, sneak aboard the *Volante* when it landed, then contact the Peace Force and pretend they'd been aboard all along. There was no other solution, unless ... 'Wait, I'm getting an idea. Let's tell Clunk to land somewhere else!'

'You don't think that'll look suspicious?'

'Not if he has a good reason. He can set down in the countryside, and we'll be aboard long before any nosy officials turn up.'

'It sounds like a workable plan, except ...'

'Yes?'

'How are you going to tell Clunk? All the channels are monitored.'

'Clunk's smart. I'll work out a code and he'll pick up the meaning like *that*.' Hal clicked his fingers to illustrate the point.

'Won't he be surprised to hear from you? He thinks you're still on Forzen, and when you pop up on the *Volante*'s screen ...'

'That's the clever part. I'll disguise my voice so well only Clunk would recognise me.'

◆

'We're being hailed,' said the Navcom.

'Not now. I'm busy.' Clunk was sitting in the Volante's flight deck, a book in one hand and a mug of coffee at his elbow. He didn't drink coffee and he'd finished the book in two blinks, but he was getting a feel for piloting the ship as a human. More specifically, he was emulating Mr Spacejock.

'I detect a customs vessel astern,' said the Navcom. 'They're insisting we stop our engines.'

'I don't care if they say please in two languages.' Clunk paused. 'I am not going to drink cold coffee while the cows come home,' he added in a stilted voice, 'and I will get very annoyed if you keep disturbing me. Please tell them to get lost.'

'Yes, that's a bit better,' said the Navcom, who was coaching Clunk in all things Spacejock. 'I'd lose the 'please' next time, and Mr Spacejock doesn't talk about cows very much.'

'Good,' said Clunk, with feeling.

There were a few moments of silence while Clunk pretended to read, and then the Navcom piped up again. 'Incoming call from planet Pegzwil.'

'Oh, very well. Put them on.'

There was a crackle from the speakers. 'Hello, is this the *Volante*?'

'Go away, annoying human-type person,' said Clunk, who was starting to get the hang of things.

'I beg your pardon?'

'You heard me. Take your unwanted call and shove it where the ...' His voice tailed off as the Navcom flashed a message on the main screen: *This is a REAL caller.*

There was a long silence.

'Hello?' shouted the caller. 'Are you there? Is anyone listening?'

'I'm sorry, your call could not be connected,' said Clunk, using a high-pitched voice with a heavy accent. 'Please try again later.'

'Nicely done,' said the Navcom.

'No thanks to you! Why didn't you warn me that was a real caller?'

'I did. I told you it was an incoming call from planet Pegzwil.'

'Yes, but –'

'They're back again. Would you like another go, or shall I hang up on them?'

'How do they sound?'

'A tiny bit annoyed.'

Clunk eyed the coffee. What would Mr Spacejock do in a situation like this? Lie through his teeth, or go on the attack? Well, lying was out so that only left one option. 'Very well, Navcom. Put the call through.'

The speakers crackled. 'What the hell's going on up there?' demanded an angry voice.

Clunk frowned. The voice was familiar, but it sounded distorted and muffled and he couldn't get a fix. 'Everything is fine up here. How are things down there?'

'You'll find out as soon as you land.'

Clunk covered the microphone. 'Navcom, who is this calling?'

'Unknown. They're using a public terminal and the cheapest available call quality.'

'What do you want?' shouted Clunk into the microphone.

'This is red leader, and I have a message for a robot you might or might not have onboard. I want you to remember planet Oliape II, particularly the landing zone. Do you copy?'

Clunk tutted. Some poor human had clearly lost its mind, and was making a nuisance of itself over the public comms system. He fired off a quick complaint to the network provider and hung up again. 'And don't put them through again,' he advised the Navcom.

Time passed, and the coffee got colder. Clunk fiddled with the mug, then inspected the book. Then … 'Did they call back again?'

'Seventeen times, so far. No, make that eighteen.'

'Headstrong as well. Determined and single minded.' It dawned on Clunk that these traits were reminiscent of someone he knew rather well. 'You don't think …?'

'It's possible,' said the Navcom slowly.

'It didn't sound like him.'

'The voice didn't, but the choice of words was familiar.'

'It can't be him. He's still on Forzen.' Clunk ran a couple of tests, and the true horror of the situation dawned on him. It didn't matter where the human was supposed to be, because the speech patterns checked out. 'Navcom, it *is* Mr Spacejock,' he said in alarm. 'Put him on immediately!'

The console speakers crackled once more, and a seriously angry human came on. 'What are you running up there, a two ring circus?'

'I'm sorry, Mr Space-'

'Don't talk. Listen! There's a bomb aboard your ship, and it's set to detonate just after you land. You can't set down at the spaceport, understood? You'll endanger hundreds of people.'

'Is this a credible threat?'

'It comes from the highest source.'

'Very well, I shall halt the *Volante* and search the ship from nose to tail.'

'No, don't do that. I need you to land, but away from the spaceport. Somewhere with a similar environment to that landing zone on planet Oliape II. I'm sure I don't have to say any more. See you when you get here. Red leader over and out.'

Clunk ran through his recent memories, then turned to slightly older events. He found an entry for the planet Mr Spacejock was talking about, but he didn't see the significance. They'd landed in a wooded valley with a stream running down the middle, an idyllic spot which had been slightly less idyllic after the Volante's super-heated exhaust and broad landing feet had done their job. 'Navcom, bring up a planetary map,' he said slowly.

'Shouldn't we warn Hans about the bomb threat?'

'Don't be silly. He's already emotionally scarred from the AutoChef incident. Any more shocks and we'll tip him over the edge.' Clunk waited until the surface of Pegzwil was displayed on the screen, then marked four areas of forest with rolling hills. Three were on the opposite side of the planet, while the last was within a hundred kilometres. Clunk zoomed in, and a smile creased his face as he saw the valley with its ribbon of silver running down the middle. It wasn't identical to the planet Oliape setting, but it was close enough. There was even a small mesa on the biggest hill, just the right size for landing a large interstellar freighter.

17

'That business about the bomb,' began Harriet Walsh hesitantly.

'Brilliant idea, eh?'

They were standing under a stand of trees, sheltering from the midday sun and enjoying the cool breeze on their faces. The trip from the terminal had barely taken any time at all, and Hal was looking forward to seeing his ship.

'You don't think it'll trigger even more interest in the *Volante*?' said Harriet. 'It's exactly the sort of keyword they scan for.'

Hal gestured impatiently. 'They'll just think it's some kid messing around. Anyway, I disguised my voice and used a false name. What could possibly go wrong?'

Harriet looked pensive, but said nothing. Meanwhile, Hal eyed his watch impatiently. According to the arrivals board the *Volante* had been on final approach for several minutes, but there had been no sign of the graceful white ship.

Beep!

Hal swore as a truck careered past, blowing a cloud of fumes in his face. The road outside the River Valley motel was busy, with a steady stream of traffic in both directions, and the noise made it hard to think. The trees were the only greenery in sight, and their drooping plastic leaves were dark with road grime. Just beyond was the spaceport fence, a three metre chainlink affair with coils of barbed wire on top, and if it wasn't the vehicle traffic pounding Hal's ears it was the hammering roar of departing spaceships.

'Do you think Clunk got the message?' asked Harriet at last.

'Sure he did. How many River Valley motels can there be on this planet?'

Clunk stepped out of the airlock and paused at the top of the landing ramp. Sunlight filtered through the trees, and the river sparkled and bubbled as it ran down the narrow valley. Insects chirped, birds twittered and little furry creatures peeped out of their burrows to see whether the intruder had left yet. Clunk shielded his eyes and scanned the horizon, but there was no sign of Mr Spacejock. He glanced over his shoulder at the airlock, but decided to use his radio instead of shouting. *Navcom, do you detect any signs of human life?*

Your stand-in pilot is waking up.

Not him. Out here.

Negative.

Clunk pressed his lips together with a squeak. Whatever Mr Spacejock was planning, it needed to happen soon, else the artworks would be late for the exhibition. Clunk glanced behind the ship, where the substitute rock was sitting on the ground in its rough cradle. It was still smoking gently from re-entry, and he wasn't sure the scorch marks would clean off. Still, they'd help to disguise the fact it wasn't the original rock.

But never mind the artworks. Where were the errant humans?

'Hello?' Clunk shouted into the trees. 'Mr Spacejock? Ms Walsh? Are you out there?'

He was about to take the ramp to the ground when the Navcom signalled. *I have a call for you.*

Very well. I'll take it in the flight deck.

Clunk returned to the ship and accessed the comms channel. 'This is Clunk speaking. How may I help you?'

'It's Hal. Where the hell are you?'

'At the river valley, as instructed.'

'No you're not! *We're* at the –' There was a burst of traffic noise, followed by the sound of a spaceship lifting off. '–motel, standing in the sunshine like pair of over-ripe bananas. If you don't get your –'

Beep!

'– over here in ten minutes I'm going to kick your little round –'

Ah-ugah!

'– all over the –'

Ring ring!

'– planet!'

'Meet at a motel?' said Clunk, puzzled. 'You said to land at the valley with the river.'

'Not the valley with the –' *beep!* '– river!' Thoroughly annoyed, Hal threw subtle hints to the wind. 'Land at the –' *honk!* '–ing River –' *beep!* '–ing Valley motel!'

Toot! went a passing car.

'We'll be there before you know it,' said Clunk hastily. He cut the connection and turned to the console. 'Navcom?'

'Yes?'

Clunk twirled his finger in the air. 'The River Valley motel, and make it snappy.'

◆

The *Volante* hovered above the parking lot, her exhaust shredding the motel's plastic trees and blasting dust across the busy highway. Underneath, the large rock swung pendulously in the haze. The passenger ramp came down slowly, unfolding segment by segment, and when it was fully extended Hal guided Harriet up the metal ramp to the airlock. They were barely inside when Clunk fired the thrusters, carrying the ship over the spaceport fence. A few seconds later they set down again, properly this time. While Harriet Walsh went to inspect the cargo of artworks, Hal decided to have it out with Clunk.

'Why did it take so long?' he demanded. 'Did you take the scenic route or what?'

'Never mind the rendezvous,' said Clunk. 'What's all this nonsense about a bomb?'

'Oh, I made that up. I had to think up an excuse so you could land outside the spaceport.'

Clunk looked doubtful. 'Wouldn't it have been easier to meet the ship on the landing field?'

'We couldn't *get* to the landing field. There were guards, and the Peace Force would have known Harriet and I didn't travel here aboard the *Volante*.'

'Speaking of which, how did you both get to Pegzwil so quickly? Did you hire a fast ship?'

'Not exactly. You remember that teleporter scientist?'

'I'm not completely senile.' Clunk blinked. 'No! You didn't ...'

'We did!' said Hal proudly. 'Straight between two planets in the blink of an eye.'

'But the side-effects ...'

'There weren't any.'

'Not physical, perhaps. Have you considered the ramifications for your business?'

'What do you mean?'

Clunk gestured around the flight deck. 'Now that you've demonstrated how well teleporters work, who's going to hire cargo ships to move freight?'

'Don't worry about it, there'll be plenty of work.' Hal rubbed his hands together. 'They're going to need cargo ships to place the teleporters, right?'

'That's like a condemned man getting paid to build his own guillotine.'

'I know. Great, isn't it?' Hal looked around the flight deck. 'So, that Hans guy. It wasn't really him I saw on that awful show, was it?'

Clunk started. 'I have no idea what you're talking about.'

'Oh yeah?' Hal turned to the console. 'Navcom, show me a list of files you've uploaded in the last day or so.'

'How would you like the results displayed?'

'Just a regular list will do.'

The screen filled with tiny writing, with a flashing 'next' icon at the bottom. Hal squinted at the lines, trying to make them out. 'What's that stuff?'

'Log files, status reports, sensor readings and location data.'

'That's a lot of files.'

'I send a lot of logs.'

'Show me the next page.'

The screen displayed even more lines.

'Next.'

Once more, the screen filled with filenames.

'How many pages are there?'

'Seventeen thousand, nine hundred and sixty-two,' said the Navcom promptly.

'Can you filter it down to video files?'

'Complying.'

The list came back, showing the exact same files. 'That's a lot of video,' said Hal.

'Oh, they're not videos. My filtering software is broken.'

'Did it happen to break in the last, say, five minutes?'

'Negative. It hasn't worked since you tried to do your own taxes.'

'But what if I wanted to inspect the logs, check the ship was running okay, maybe identify a problem before it happened?'

'That's what Clunk is for. The log files are not meant for humans.'

'That's not very user-friendly.'

'It's a debug log. It's not supposed to be useful.'

Defeated, Hal turned away from the screen. 'So this Hans character. What happened?'

'He insulted me,' said Clunk.

Hal made a face. 'A lot of people are rude to robots. I don't like it, but how can you change their backward attitudes?'

'Next, he insulted the Navcom.'

'Computers don't have feelings. Anyway, the Navcom can take care of herself. There was no need to subject Hans to that pain and humiliation.'

'Then he insulted you.'

'Everyone insults me, Clunk. You don't see me retaliating, do you? Roll with the punches. Take the good with the bad. Turn the other cheek. Water off a duck's back.'

'And then he put his boots on your favourite coffee table, leaving several large scratches.'

'He did *what*?' Hal drove a fist into the palm of his hand. 'Get onto the file sharing sites. I want that video on every screen in the galaxy.'

'The Navcom will begin right away,' said Clunk. 'Incidentally, Ms Walsh is calling from the cargo hold. It seems there's a small problem with the artworks.'

◆

Hal arrived in the cargo hold at a run. From the tone of Harriet's voice he expected to find the cargo in pieces, damaged in flight by Clunk's careless handling, or perhaps kicked apart by the customs goons. Instead, he found her inspecting Fish in a Jar. 'What's up?'

'The pebbles in the bottom of this jar. Do they look suspicious to you?'

Hal bent for a closer look. The fish stared back at him with a big, dead eye, and there was a vaguely unpleasant smell. 'They look like stones to me. What did you expect?'

'They might be uncut diamonds.'

Hal's eyebrows rose. Some of the pebbles were as big as chicken eggs. 'You're joking. If those things are diamonds, each one would buy this ship. Anyway, they're grey.'

'It could be paint. A little airbrushing here and there …it's not unheard of.'

'What do you want to do?'

'I need you to hold the fish out of the way so I can take a closer look.'

'But …that's a priceless artwork. If you disturb it, the customer will go crazy.'

'If those are diamonds you'll spend five to ten inside.'

The fish came free with a sucking sound, and Harriet rummaged in the bottom of the jar while Hal held the stuffed fish aloft. The pebbles rattled under her fingers, and she drew out one of the smaller ones. She held it up to the light, then crouched and swiped it across the metal deck. Sparks flew, and there was an acrid smell. 'I guess it's the wrong sort of sparkler,' remarked Hal.

Harriet tried another couple of stones, with the same result.

'Look on the bright side,' said Hal. 'If we run out of matches you'll still be able to light a campfire.'

After dropping the stones in the jar, Harriet gestured at the fish. 'Stick it back. There's nothing here.'

'Do you want to look inside the cow? I've got a penknife somewhere, and Clunk's pretty good at sewing.'

'That won't be necessary.'

'Or the rock? We could hire a jackhammer and smash it apart.'

'That's enough, Hal. I'm just doing my job.'

'Yes, and you're ruining mine.'

They left the hold in silence, and they were halfway to the lift when Harriet stopped. 'I'd better call in with my report. Is the commset in my cabin still working?'

'Sure. Be my guest.'

Hal continued to the flight deck on his own. There was a smile on his face, and his mood was greatly improved. Not because their cargo was legitimate and above board. No, it was Harriet Walsh's parting words that had cheered him up: 'My cabin' is how she'd put it, as though she'd never left.

18

Clunk glanced round as Hal entered the flight deck. 'Ah, Mr Spacejock. Was the cargo in order?'

'Harriet thought the Fish was off, but it checked out.' Hal sat down at the console. 'What's happening with the delivery? Any sign of the truck?'

'Not yet. I put a call in to the exhibition hall, just to let them know we were here.'

'Did they complain we were late?'

'On the contrary, they were impressed with our timely arrival.'

'Good, maybe we'll score some extra work. There's plenty of room for more junk in the cargo hold.'

'If you want more work in this line, I would suggest you refer to the artworks with a more appropriate term.'

'All right. There's plenty of room for pretentious junk in the hold.'

Clunk opened his mouth to explain, but the Navcom cut him off.

'Incoming call for Mr Spacejock.'

'That'll be the truck rental,' predicted Hal. 'Put them on.'

'Complying.'

'Hello,' said a tinny voice. 'Am I speaking to captain Dull Flopjack of the *Spoilanti*?'

'No! It's Hal Spacejock of the *Volante*!'

'Close enough,' said the voice. 'This is Truck-U rentals, and I'm letting you know your vehicle is ready.'

'Good stuff. When can you send it over?'

'Mate, this is Truck-U, not We-Truck. Come and fetch the damn thing yourself. And don't forget the deposit.'

There was a click as the caller disconnected.

'Bags you fetch it,' Hal said to Clunk. 'And you can take that Hans character with you. Leave him in the terminal with his brother.'

＊

While Clunk was off fetching the truck, Hal tracked Harriet down. He found her in her cabin, packing her duffel bag. 'Are you leaving?'

'Temporarily. Boson wants to speak with me.'

'Is he here?'

'No, but the local Station has a secure channel. When I'm done, I'll meet you at the exhibition.'

'What about later?' asked Hal.

Harriet eyed him warily. 'Later?'

'Dinner. I thought we could find somewhere nice.'

'Hal ...'

'Just dinner, I swear! You can tell me about the Peace Force, and I'll bring you up to speed with the cargo business. It'll be fun.'

Harriet looked down at herself. 'I can't go to dinner in uniform. I'll need something to wear.'

'You can pick something up, right?' Hal gave her a winning smile, and he was relieved when she grinned back at him. 'Good stuff. I'll book a table for eight.'

Harriet shouldered the duffel bag and Hal stood aside to let her out. She gave him a casual wave, and the last he saw of her was a brief toss of her long blonde hair as she entered the elevator. Hal grinned, clapped his hands together, then set off for the hold to give Clunk a hand with the cargo.

＊

Clunk had already returned with the truck, and Hal waved his arms and shouted directions as the robot guided the heavy vehicle towards the back of the ship. Despite Hal's assistance, Clunk managed to line everything up first time. Then, after loading the smaller artworks, Hal realised they had a problem.

'What about that?' he asked, jerking his thumb at the giant boulder. 'We'll need a crane to get it on the truck.'

'We already have one.'

'We do?' Hal looked left and right, but the scenery was devoid of big yellow cranes. It was a pity, because he'd always wanted to have a go with proper construction machinery. 'Where?'

Clunk indicated the *Volante*. 'That's the most powerful crane on the planet.'

'Oh yeah.'

A few minutes later the deed was done. Clunk lifted off in the ship while Hal sheltered in the truck's cab, and he smiled in satisfaction as the huge rock came down gently on the back. Then Clunk set the ship down again, and once he'd removed the sling they were ready to roll.

'Tie it all down and I'll lock the ship up,' said Hal, dusting off his hands.

Ten minutes later they were on their way to the exhibition hall. The roads were wide and smooth, traffic was light, and Clunk made good time at the controls of the heavy vehicle. Hal gazed out at the buildings, watching the commercial district roll past. He saw a row of small shops selling everything from hardware to groceries to second-hand goods, and he glanced back to get another look at a jacket hanging on the end of a rack. His stock of casual clothes was as thin as his wallet, and he resolved to come back and find something suitable for his dinner date.

The shops vanished and Hal watched the commercial zone change to high-density residential, then houses with gardens, and finally country lanes with mansions just visible through the wrought iron gates and security fencing.

'Pretty flash,' remarked Hal. 'Where's the expo being held, anyway?'

'Backsight Manor.'

'Backsight? That's an odd name.'

'The owner runs a weapons factory.'

'A big shot, eh?' Hal watched the countryside rolling by. 'Do you think they'll give me a free sample?'

'Backsight makes gun turrets, not hand weapons.'

'Great! I've always wanted a couple of those on the *Volante*.'

'Not in my lifetime,' said Clunk firmly.

They took a sharp corner and accelerated along a narrow lane. Halfway along they drove past a golf course, and Hal watched a couple of golfers who'd driven their shots straight into the rough. They were moving gingerly through waist-high thickets full of thorns, and Hal reckoned they'd be lucky to get their balls out in one piece.

The truck slowed again, and Hal saw a side road which passed under a broad white arch. Just ahead of them an attendant in a high-viz shirt was just waving another truck through the gates. Clunk drew up behind it, and the attendant approached his window. 'Delivering to the expo?'

'That's correct,' said Clunk. 'We have a shipment from Max Bright.'

'Ah, the lighting rigs,' said the attendant. 'Go on, then. In you go.'

'Not lighting, artworks.'

The attendant shrugged.

'Aren't you going to inspect the cargo?' demanded Clunk.

'What for? If you've seen one truckload of pretentious crap, you've seen it all. Am I right?'

'Absolutely,' said Hal, before Clunk could argue the finer points of art. 'Would you believe someone's paying perfectly good money to deliver an old rock, a dried cow and a stale fish?'

The attendant shook his head sadly. 'Beyond amazing. What's wrong with a canvas and a nice bit o' paint, that's what I want to know.'

'Tell me,' said Clunk. 'Do you have a spare safety vest?'

'Why?'

'I believe Mr Spacejock would make an excellent helper for the afternoon. Clearly he'd fit right in with your lowbrow tastes and your complete lack of –'

'Clunk, we need to get a move on,' said Hal quickly. 'That cow isn't getting any fresher, and Fish on the Rocks was wilting.'

'It's Fish in a *Jar*,' growled Clunk. The truck lurched forwards, and the attendant disappeared in a cloud of fumes. They drove between the hedgerows in silence, gradually catching up with the smaller truck. Then the lane opened out onto a large parking area in front of a four-storey mansion, with seven or eight trucks and dozens of people milling about.

There were people moving anti-grav sleds around, the contents under wraps. There were drivers leaning against their cabs, enjoying a quick break. And there were attendants everywhere, directing traffic in their fluorescent yellow vests.

'Looks pretty busy,' said Hal.

They were waved into a parking spot, where Clunk pulled over and switched off the engine. Hal clambered down and strode off to commandeer a sled. He found one hovering in the shadow of the building, bobbing gently in mid-air, and guided it back to the truck. Clunk already had the back down, and the two of them loaded Bright's artworks in no time.

With Clunk's help, Hal pushed the sled towards the building. The front doors stood wide open, and when they got inside they discovered the mansion had been hollowed out into a huge hall. There were doors at each end, tiny in the distance, and a mezzanine overlooked the main floor. There were red and gold drapes everywhere, and the polished wooden floor gleamed under the downlights. Several artworks were in position, hidden under silver dust sheets. Hal snorted. Unless the silver dropsheets *were* the artworks.

'Which artist please?'

Hal turned to see a slender woman approaching, clipboard at the ready. She was wearing a soft pink cardigan over a white blouse, and her beautiful grey eyes were framed by a pair of rimless glasses. Her long chestnut hair was pulled back in a ponytail, but a few strands had escaped to dangle fetchingly across her face. She flicked them back casually as she glanced at the sled. 'Oh, it's Max Bright.'

'One hundred percent correct,' said Clunk. 'Are you acquainted with his work?'

'Not really. All this pretentious crap is the same, isn't it?'

Hal gave a hoot of laughter, and was rewarded with a warm smile. On impulse, he stuck his hand out. 'Hal Spacejock, freighter pilot.'

'Meredith Ryder, event coordinator. Meri for short.' She looked Hal up and down. 'You keep yourself in shape, don't you?'

'There's a gym aboard my ship,' said Hal, ignoring Clunk's snort. Well, there *was* a gym, and he hadn't said anything about using it. 'So, where do you want this junk?'

'Sling it down anywhere. We're paying a bunch of so-called experts to set the stuff up, although if you ask me they're just glorified baggage handlers.' Ryder gave him another smile, and ticked an item on her list. 'That's the lot now. Should keep everyone happy for the opening night.'

'It must be a lot of work, organising something like this,' said Hal.

'My clients pay for results,' said Ryder, with a shrug. 'No taste, of course, but I get to charge them as much as I like.'

'Are tact and diplomacy optional extras?' asked Clunk politely.

Ryder glanced at him. 'Are you going to unload that sled? There's a queue forming outside.'

'I'll get onto it now ma'am,' said Clunk, with a precise salute.

'Good.' Ryder looked Hal up and down. 'Are you going to change for later?'

'Why? What's later?'

'The expo. That old flight suit is fine for deliveries, but it's not the sort of image people expect from the security detail.'

'I'm sorry. Did you say security?'

Ryder checked her clipboard. 'It says it right here. Hal Spacejock and his robot have agreed to provide security for the event.'

Hal stared at her. 'We did nothing of the sort.'

'I think you'll find it's in the contract. You're providing security for the artworks.'

'Only during transport!' protested Clunk.

'No, security and crowd control for the duration of the event. Tell me, do you have guns?'

Dazed, Hal shook his head. What sort of art expo needed armed guards?

'Well, maybe you can get hold of a few before the opening. The first guests are expected at six-thirty, and it would be great if you could be ready for six.' Ryder gave Hal a wink. 'Call me if you need a hand getting changed.'

Before Hal could say anything, she left.

'Look on the bright side,' said Clunk. 'At least we didn't have plans for the evening.'

'Speak for yourself. I asked Harriet out for dinner, and now she'll be all alone aboard the *Volante*.'

'No she won't.'

'She will, thanks to your contract.'

'She won't, because the two of us can't possibly cover security for an event of this size. It will take three people at least.'

'Oh, no. I'm not asking her to moonlight as a security guard.'

'I'm afraid you'll have to.'

'But she's expecting a nice romantic dinner, not –' Hal was interrupted by an angry shout, and he looked round to see a delivery driver pointing at the sled.

'Get a move on!' shouted the driver. 'These ice statues are melting!'

Hal gave Clunk a hand, and together they backed the sled up to a plinth and rolled the rock on top. When Hairpiece was in position they set the other artworks down alongside, finishing with the cow and its square of fake grass. Then Hal remembered something. He glanced around to make sure nobody was watching, then vaulted onto the cow.

'That's a valuable artwork,' hissed Clunk. 'This is no time for a rodeo.'

'Just adding the crowning glory.' Hal plucked a couple of hairs off his head and laid them on the rock. 'There. Happy now?'

'Not until you get down!'

Hal leapt off the cow and dusted his footprints off its back. 'Right, job done. Let's get out of here.'

19

Their feet crunched on the gravel as they left the mansion, and Hal raised his voice over the racket. 'It's going to be hard, Clunk, but it looks like I've got to keep two women happy this evening.'

Clunk eyed him doubtfully.

'It's all right, I have a plan. The expo opens at six. I can do a couple of hours security, then leave you in charge while I have dinner with Harriet.'

'And when will you ask Harriet to help us with security?'

'Not in this lifetime,' said Hal firmly.

'But we'll need at least –'

'Clunk, it'll be easy. It's an art expo, not a science fiction convention.' Hal looked down at himself. 'I'm going to need some proper clothes, though. You heard Meri ... we're supposed to look like bounders.'

'Bouncers, Mr Spacejock.'

Hal shrugged. 'Same difference. Anyway, I need something good. Something...'

'Tasteful and restrained?'

'Ye-es.'

Clunk shot him a suspicious look, but Hal said nothing. He had his own ideas on effective security measures, and tasteful and restrained weren't going to cut it. They reached the truck, where Hal paused with one hand on the door. 'You don't have to come with me. Why don't you wait here?'

'I'd rather help you with the clothing.'

'I'll worry about that. You stay.'

'But –'

'Go on, you can get a recharge before we go on duty.'

'That would be handy, yes. But –'

'You think I'm going to do something stupid? Get into trouble?'

Clunk looked like he was thinking exactly that.

'Well I'm not, so off you go.'

Somewhat reluctantly, Clunk did so, casting suspicious glances over his shoulder. Hal just stood by the truck, somewhat annoyed that the robot always thought the worst of him. He crossed his arms as Clunk looked back one last time, and then as soon as the robot was out of sight Hal turned and clambered into the truck. He'd just remembered the row of handy-looking shops nearby, and he reckoned they'd provide everything he needed.

Harriet drummed her fingers on the arm of her seat, barely able to contain her annoyance. As a lowly trainee she had to wait for her turn on the secure terminals, and other Peace Force officers kept pulling rank to jump ahead of her in the queue.

She wouldn't have minded, except they were using their calls to organise social events, retirement parties and cut-price tickets to sporting events. Didn't these people realise there was a job to be done?

Frustrated, she kept her thoughts to herself. They all outranked her, and complaining would only make things worse. All she could do was wait.

It was late afternoon, the sun was going down and Clunk was getting restless. Mr Spacejock had been gone almost two hours, and time was getting short. Guests would start arriving forty minutes from now, and one robot was hardly the private security force the organisers were expecting. While Hal was away, Ms Ryder had briefed Clunk on potential threats, and the lengthy list was worrying.

First there was the gang of local hooligans who might put in an appearance. It seemed they enjoyed parking their hotted-up cars outside nice, peaceful venues and disturbing everyone with their loud music.

Then there were the usual freeloaders who appeared at these events for a free feed and as many drinks as they could get their hands on. Finally, there was the most troublesome of all … the jealous artists whose works hadn't been accepted into the exhibition. According to Ryder, they were capable of sabotage, vandalism and - in some cases - arson.

Clunk frowned. If only Mr Spacejock would turn up!

A movement caught his eye, and he turned his head to analyse an individual approaching the museum. Dressed from head to toe in worn denims, the man was swaggering - or rather, staggering - under the weight of metal studs, buckles and chains adorning his person. His hair was loaded with gel and combed into spikes so sharp you could spear memos on them, and an impressive collection of knuckle-dusters, nunchuks and fighting knives jiggled and swung from every belt loop. A pair of wrap-around sunglasses completed the ensemble, their broad black lenses covering half the man's face.

Clunk swallowed nervously. From the chunky silver bracelets to the length of heavy-duty chain swinging from one shoulder, the figure screamed trouble. This was exactly what Ms Ryder had warned him about, and Mr Spacejock wasn't there to help!

Steeling himself for an unpleasant confrontation, Clunk stepped in front of the man and raised his hand. 'I-I'm sorry, sir. This is a private function. I can't let you in.'

◆

Hal pushed the wrap-around sunglasses up to his forehead and eyed Clunk critically. 'Talk about wishy-washy. Try that again, and this time put a bit more oomph into it.'

Clunk's eyes widened in shock. 'Mr Spacejock?'

'Pretty good, eh? Here, cop a look at this.' Hal rolled up his sleeve to show off a huge tattoo. It was a multi-coloured effort depicting a comet smashing into a spaceship, and it covered his entire arm from wrist to shoulder. 'All the security people have these. They show how tough you are.' Clunk reached for the tattoo but Hal swatted his hand away. 'Don't. You'll smudge the paint.'

Clunk stared at him, completely speechless.

'And look!' said Hal, pulling a pair of nunchuks of his belt. He adopted a crouching stance and began swinging the weapon with vast quantities of enthusiasm and very little in the way of skill. After half a dozen near misses the leading nunchuk whipped a fighting knife off his belt and sent it humming past Clunk's left ear. It buried itself in the door frame with a loud *doinnnggg*.

Clunk's hand blurred out, whipping the nunchuks from Hal's grip before they did any real damage.

'Hey, I was just getting started!'

'And the rest,' said Clunk, gesturing at the assorted weaponry dangling from Hal's belt.

'Oh, come on. How am I going to defend myself from a crowd of yobs?'

'Mr Spacejock, if you greet elderly arts patrons in that getup we'll be knee deep in the newly departed.'

'What if there's any trouble?'

'As of this moment, you *are* the trouble. What possessed you to dress in such a fashion? And where did you acquire all these weapons?'

'Happy Sam's takeaway foods and martial arts emporium.' Hal burped. 'You get a free weapon with the all-you-can-eat buffet, but after I polished off six courses they loaded me up with gear and kicked me out.'

He was going to explain further, but at that moment the doors opened and Meri Ryder looked out.

◆

'Mr Spacejock! What the devil are you wearing?'

Hal froze. Ryder was moving towards him in a short skirt and high heels. Her legs were going double time with the tiny steps, and her expression was equal parts shock and surprise.

'I–I– can explain,' began Hal, before tailing off.

'Don't bother. I love a man who can pull off the rugged look.' Meri drank him in from head to toe. 'I'm not sure about the tattoo,' she said at last. 'It's a bit … vivid.'

'It'll grow on you.'

'Especially if you touch it,' added Clunk.

Meri ignored the robot. 'Go and take a look around,' she said to Hal. 'Make a final inspection, and then I need you both out here for the first arrivals. Okay?'

'Understood,' said Hal.

◆

Inside the gallery, Hal and Clunk skirted the major exhibits before taking a side passage, where they found smaller rooms with lesser artworks. One was a plate with a hole drilled through the middle, and another was the grate from a barbecue, standing upright with an egg drizzled over the bars. The tag read 'free range', and Hal gave an incredulous snort when he spotted the price.

The final room contained a display of found art, with shovels and picks arranged in rough tripods, and a fenced-off square of wet concrete in the middle. Nearby was a shelving unit, half-assembled, and sitting on top was a pile of nuts and bolts.

'The life of an artist, eh?' Hal shook his head in disgust. 'Bung any old junk together, stick a huge price on it and wait for the rich and gullible to open their wallets.'

Clunk peered at the nuts and bolts. 'This one's rather clever.'

'Clever how?'

'Let me interpret it for you. First, the spiral patterns represent the twists and turns of modern life. The groove is a constant depth, reminding us of the rut we might fall into, and the effort we must put into escaping it. The peak is the pinnacle of achievement, the ultimate aspiration.' Clunk pointed to a nut. 'Now this, on the other hand ... the six sides clearly represent the senses, and the hole in the middle ...'

'Matches the one in your brain.' As Hal turned to leave he tangled with one of the shovels. He tried to catch it as it fell over, but it hit the ground with a clatter. Off balance, he had to hop over the shovel to avoid treading on it, and he put his hand out to grab for support.

Unfortunately the 'support' was just a piece of ribbon tape, and the tape and supporting poles crashed to the ground in a heap. Still falling headlong, Hal tried desperately to regain his balance.

Too late.

Trailing hazard tape, cursing wildly, and with just enough time to roll his eyes in resignation, Hal splashed face-first into the big square of wet concrete.

Clunk hauled him out and helped brush off the worst of the concrete. Fortunately, it was firmer than it looked, but Hal's industrial-strength bouncer uniform was still thickly coated with grey goop. Then, once Hal stopped spitting and cursing, he realised the square of soft concrete was now imprinted with a perfect outline of his body: spread fingers, shocked facial expression, gaping mouth and all. Guiltily, he looked around. The shovels and picks could be stood up again, but there was no way he'd get the concrete smooth before anyone noticed the damage. Then he spotted a dropsheet in the corner. 'Come on, grab that thing. We'll spread it over the top.'

'Shouldn't you clean up first?'

'It won't set if I keep moving.'

They grabbed the sheet and dragged it over the concrete, folding it double to prevent it sagging in the middle. They were just replacing the shovels when they heard a voice.

'Hey you! What do you think you're doing?'

A man in a suit was hurrying towards them from the gallery, his polished shoes clacking on the wooden floor. Hal turned his back, hiding his concrete-laden side from the room while Clunk handled the newcomer.

'This area is off-limits,' said the man. 'What are you doing in here?'

'We're the security detail,' said Clunk. 'My colleague and I were just inspecting artworks.'

'So what are you doing in here?'

'My good man, these lesser works deserve the same consideration as those of greater artists.'

'Works?' the man snorted. 'This area is being renovated, you fools. It's supposed to be closed off!'

'We're just checking the windows,' called Hal over his shoulder. 'We'll be right out.'

'Very well, but don't touch anything.'

'Of course not.'

The man left, and Hal scowled at Clunk. 'Renovations! And you with all that gumph about the bolts representing twists of modern life.'

'Anyone could have made the same mistake.'

'Still, at least we know what the nut represents.'

Clunk raised one eyebrow. 'Yes?'

'Yeah. You.'

———◆———

Harriet finally got her chance with the terminal, placing her call quickly before anyone else bumped her aside. Boson's face appeared on the screen straight away.

'What's this nonsense about a gang of thieves on Forzen?' he said, without any preamble. 'It says here you want three people rounded up and charged over various misdemeanours.'

'Hijacking, theft and assault are hardly misdemeanours.'

'Really?'

'Sir, one of them knocked me out and restrained me with my own handcuffs.'

'We don't want that getting around, do we?' Boson regarded her steadily. 'A Peace Force trainee subdued by an office worker? Imagine what the press would do with that little gem.'

'She got the drop on me!'

'I don't need to hear it.' Boson tossed the report onto a big, teetering pile. 'I'll file this for now, and if those suspects of yours bob up again I'll get someone to follow it up.'

Walsh stared at him. 'You're letting them go?'

'Officer Walsh, I'm trying to crack a major smuggling ring and bring down the Backsights. I'm not interested in petty thieves, and I don't want you wasting any more time on this Higgs woman.'

'Yes, sir.' Walsh regarded her superior officer with a level gaze. 'Would it be possible to attach my objection to the report?'

'No it damn well wouldn't,' snapped Boson. 'Now give me your report on the smuggling case. What have you found out?'

'The cargo appears to be clean.'

'Appears to be?'

'My inspection didn't turn up anything suspicious.'

'I suppose you were thorough?'

'Of course, sir.'

Boson didn't seem to be convinced, but Harriet doubted he'd have been happy even if she'd taken a chainsaw to Bright's precious works, pounded the hacked-up fragments with a sledgehammer and fed the granulated remains into a mass spectrometer.

'Very well, Trainee. I want you to remain with the artworks until they reach their final destination. Understood?'

'But if they're clean …'

'They are now,' said Boson, 'but there's every chance someone could introduce illicit goods in transit.'

'I thought the smuggled diamonds were coming from Forzen?'

'Diamonds aren't the only commodity Backsight are interested in.'

Walsh fought the sinking feeling in her stomach. Boson's suspicions had turned out to be nothing at all, and instead of giving up he was just going to clutch at straws. Still, she was under orders and had no choice but to play along. 'Very well, sir. I'll return to the exhibition and keep a close eye on the pieces. I promise nothing will slip past me.'

'Excellent, Trainee. That's the attitude.'

Hal used an executive bathroom to clean himself up, and his denim outfit was still warm and toasty from the auto-dryer. As for Hal's skin, the express shower had removed not only the concrete, but also his vivid tattoo.

Now he was hanging around the gallery entrance, getting ready for the big event. He glanced back inside, through the doors, and saw Ryder darting around the exhibition like an excited hummingbird. A tweak here, an adjustment there, and it was suddenly time. A limo drew up at the foot of the stairs, and a uniformed chauffeur hurried round to get the doors. Hal got Clunk's attention by blowing a piercing whistle. 'We're on. Guests at five o'clock.'

'The expo doesn't open until six-thirty.'

Hal pointed down the steps. 'No, *that* five o'clock!'

Clunk hurried over, his big metal feet thudding on the floor. He repositioned Hal behind one of the ornate columns, and hissed in his ear. 'That's the patron, Olivia Backsight. You stay here and let me do the honours.'

Hal shrugged. 'Go for it.'

As Clunk passed the doorway, he spotted the fighting knife sticking out of the wooden frame. There was a creak as he yanked it out, and Hal watched the robot glide down the steps with a wide smile on his face and the lethal dagger concealed behind his back. Easing his way around the column, he saw Clunk chatting brightly with an elderly, smartly-dressed woman, all the while holding the knife out of sight. Finally, he bowed and let the old lady past, stuffing the knife into his thigh compartment as soon as her eyes left him. Hal backed around the column as Olivia Backsight strode past, his cover almost blown when a stabbing pain lanced into his arm. He bit his tongue as he rolled up his sleeve, only to discover a sharpened chopstick he'd concealed in his jacket. 'Ow, ow, ow!' he gasped, pulling it free.

'What's happening?' demanded Clunk, right behind him.

Hal jumped in surprise, accidentally stabbing the chopstick into the opposite arm. '*OW!*'

'Give me *all* your weapons, Mr Spacejock. I won't ask again.'

Sullenly, Hal took out one device after another, passing them to the robot for safe keeping. When he'd finished he was about ten kilos lighter and Clunk was shaking his head in disbelief.

'Who did you think was coming to the exhibition? Ghengis Khan and the Mongol hoards?'

'Is that a rock group?'

'Not quite. Legend has it they colonised the first planets with their rusty steeds.'

'Why rusty?'

'I don't know … perhaps they got wet. That's how they're described in the database, anyway.'

Hal saw another limo driving towards them. 'Never mind rusty steeds. You'd better stand by for more punters.'

20

Hal and Clunk let a stream of guests through, taking tickets and greeting one and all with polite conversation. Then came a brief lull, during which Hal asked Clunk to fetch him a coffee.

No sooner had the robot left than an old lady came slowly up the steps, digging around inside a large handbag. 'I know I put that ticket in here,' she mumbled to herself. 'Where has it gone?'

Hal was about to help her when a car drew up, showering gravel. Hal frowned to himself as a couple of youths in leather jackets and white trousers hopped out. They sauntered up the steps, elbowing the old lady aside and knocking her bag out of her hands.

'You can pick that up again,' said Hal, gesturing at the scattered contents.

'Says who?' demanded one of the youths, a skinny buck-toothed lad with downy cheeks and a floppy haircut.

Hal crossed his arms. 'You want to spend the night in hospital, son?'

The youths tried to step around him, but Hal put his hands out, blocking the doorway.

'Get out of my way,' said the second lad coldly. He was shorter than the first, with a gold chain and matching bracelets. He smelled strongly of aftershave, and his hair was slicked back.

'No ticket, no entry,' said Hal firmly.

The youth pulled out a couple of creased tickets and tucked them into Hal's breast pocket. 'Now move, you brainless turd.'

'Make me,' said Hal.

'You want to watch your lip, mate. I have friends in high places.'

'Where, aboard an orbiting prison?'

There was a flash, and a shimmering blade appeared in the youth's hand. It wavered gently in the darkness, and the slender energy beam ran the spectrum from red to violet and back again. 'Get out of the way. I'm not going to ask again.'

Hal shrugged a length of chain off his shoulder and wound the loose end around his fist. He'd managed to hide this particular weapon from Clunk, convinced he'd need it sooner or later. 'Me neither,' he said, standing tall and swinging the chain gently from side to side.

The blade flashed, and several links of chain tinkled on the floor, leaving Hal with a shorter and slightly less impressive weapon. The youth raised the blade until it was just under his chin. 'Say goodbye, you –'

'Is there a problem?' said a deep, booming voice from the doorway.

The blade vanished, and the youths backed away as Clunk emerged from the exhibition. He towered over them by a head, and with his battered face he looked more like a retired prize fighter than a sensitive new-age droid. 'No sir,' said one of the youths quickly. 'No problem.'

'They knocked the lady's handbag all over the steps,' said Hal. 'They get the death penalty for that, don't they?'

'Not if they pick it up.'

The youths did so, gathering the scattered belongings and stuffing them back in the bag. The lady thanked them distractedly, then resumed her hunt for the missing ticket. Meanwhile, the youths headed for the entrance.

'I need to see your tickets,' said Clunk.

'We gave them to him!' protested the skinny lad.

Clunk looked at Hal, who shook his head.

'But we did! They're in his pocket!'

'I don't think so.' Hal smiled politely. 'Still, it's a nice evening for a walk. Why not stroll around the gardens?'

The youth shot him a poisonous glance. 'You're going to spend the rest of your life in jail, meathead.' He reached into his pocket and pulled out a flashy commset, flicking it to open the screen. 'Once I make this call, you'll be – Hey!'

Fed up with the posturing, Hal knocked the commset from the lad's hand and crushed it under the heel of his boot. 'Looks like they hung up on you.'

The youth turned to his mate. 'Lend us yours, will you?'

'Can't. I used up my credit.'

'Give me your phone!'

His mate shrugged and handed it over, then watched as the shorter youth examined the screen. 'It's dead.'

'I told you. No credit.'

Incensed, the first youth hurled the phone against the wall, shattering it. Then he marched off down the steps.

'Nasty piece of work,' said Clunk. He stirred the molten chain links with his foot. 'Can you tell me what happened?'

'He had some kind of electric blade. It cut the chain like butter.'

'Ah, an energy weapon. You can get them on the black market, but they're very expensive. It's illegal for citizens to own them.'

'Reckon he nicked it?'

'Perhaps. Or maybe he really does have rich relatives. Olivia Backsight runs an arms business, don't forget.'

'Spoilt little oik.' Hal watched the youths drive off in a blaze of light and a cacophony of booming music. Then he glanced at the old lady, who was still digging in her bag. 'Excuse me.'

The lady looked up. 'Yes?'

Hal brandished one of the tickets tucked into his pocket by the youth. 'Is this yours? I just found it on the floor.'

'Oh, thank you!' The old lady beamed at him. 'I've been looking forward to this exhibition for ages.'

The old lady gave the ticket back and Hal waved her through.

'Where did you get that ticket?' asked Clunk, once she'd gone inside.

'Oh, one of those louts gave them to me.'

'You said they didn't have any tickets!'

'No, I said I didn't think they did.'

There was a clatter of footsteps behind them, and they turned to see Ryder approaching. 'I heard there was a disturbance. Is everything all right?'

'Fine,' said Hal, hurriedly kicking the broken commsets and melted chain links into the bushes.

'No problem,' said Clunk.

Ryder ignored Clunk and gave Hal a warm smile. 'If you see Olivia's grandson, be sure to treat him well. My artists can use all the help they can get.'

'Grandson?'

'Short kid. Mouth like a sewer, and an attitude to match. Wears a lot of gold.'

Clunk opened his mouth, but Hal got in first. 'We'll keep an eye out for him.'

'Thanks, Hal. He was supposed to be here for the opening, but you know what these teenagers are like.' Ryder patted her pocket. 'I'm sure he'll call me eventually.'

'Yeah, I'm sure he will,' said Hal, covering a broken piece of commset with the sole of his boot.

After that, there was a rash of arrivals, with more cars arriving every few seconds. Time flew in a flurry of greetings, ticket-checking and security pat-downs, and before long Hal wondered whether there was anyone left on the rest of the planet.

Arrivals finally slowed, and Hal realised it was at least three hours since his last coffee, which was something of a record. He turned to Clunk and wagged his finger in reproach. 'You're letting me down, Clunk. I'm dying for a coffee, here.'

'You didn't ask for beverages,' said Clunk mildly.

'You don't need me to tell you. You should have known.'

'Of course I should.'

Hal frowned. 'It's true! What we need around here is some proper discipline.'

'Oh, I think you're about to get some of that.'

'Eh?' Hal looked down the stairs and saw a car pulling up. The door opened, and he saw Harriet Walsh step out. She'd had her hair done, and was wearing a nice evening dress with new shoes. She looked amazing, and Hal about to wave at her when he glanced at his watch and saw it was almost nine. Oh crap ... he'd forgotten all about their dinner date!

Slam! Walsh closed the door with a hefty swing, and Hal gulped. 'Clunk, be a pal. Tell her I came down with a headache.'

'I cannot tell a lie, Mr Spacejock.'

'No, I really have got a headache.' Hal clutched his head. 'It's splitting me apart. Honest!'

'Oh, very well. Keep out of sight while I relay your weak excuse.'

Relieved, Hal darted inside the expo.

◆

Hal ducked behind the drapes just inside the door, concealing himself from the guests. There was no way he could mingle, not in his special bounder outfit, but there was a narrow gap between the heavy curtains and the wall, and he used it to make his way around the outside of the exhibition hall. Halfway round he heard voices, and he peeped out to see Olivia Backsight standing with her back to him, talking to Meri about the exhibition.

'So that's settled, then? A private showing on Niaritz, then delivery to head office afterwards.'

'Of course, ma'am. I'll inform the courier right away.'

'Are you sure he's trustworthy?'

At that moment, Meri spotted Hal peering through the curtains. She faltered for a second or two, then continued. 'Yes, he's very reliable.'

'I'm glad to hear it. He can't be any worse than that awful person handling tonight's security.'

A waiter arrived with a tray of hors d'oeuvres, and while the guy waited patiently alongside Olivia, waiting to attract her attention, Hal managed to score several pieces of prawn toast, a couple of sushi rolls and a chicken drumstick.

Next came another waiter with a tray of glasses. Hal reached through the curtains and swiped two flutes of bubbly, an orange juice and a rather cheeky red wine, draining each of them and depositing the empties back on the tray before the waiter noticed anything.

Hal moved on, pausing several times to part the curtains and filch drinks and nibblies. By the time he reached the far end of the hall he was feeling quite full, and a lot more jolly.

At that moment he heard footsteps, and he turned to see Ryder push through the curtains, advancing on him in the near-darkness with a determined look in her eye. 'I–I only had a couple of glasses,' explained Hal. 'Don't worry, you can deduct the cost from our fees.'

He broke off as Ryder put her arms around him, and before he knew what was happening they were locked in a passionate kiss. She pressed herself against him, her hands travelling up the back of his neck, her fingers running through his hair. At first Hal participated with gusto, overcome with the heat of the moment. Then he remembered Harriet, and he stepped back to escape the embrace.

Ryder was having none of it. She clung to him, following his every step, her lips still locked to his.

Hal felt the curtains brush over him as he backed into the exhibition hall, and he blinked in the sudden light. The hubbub of voices ceased, and Hal turned to see a semi-circle of guests gaping at him. Then he saw something which made his blood run cold. Not ten paces away stood Harriet Walsh, with a look of total shock on her face. She recovered quickly, and advanced on him with a dangerous glint in her eye. Hal untangled himself from Ryder's embrace and ducked behind the curtains, and as the crowd found its voice he ran full pelt for the exit.

◆

Out front, Clunk was just debating whether to fetch Hal another coffee when he heard footsteps approaching from behind. They were coming straight for him, moving fast, and he turned to see Harriet Walsh three steps away, fists clenched and her face an angry mask. When she spotted Clunk, she stopped with her hands on her hips. 'All right, where is he?'

'Who?'

'Your owner. Where did he go?'

'Ms Walsh, I do not have an owner.'

'Don't try that robot logic on me.' Walsh prodded Clunk in the chest. 'Hal Spacejock. Where is he?'

'I cannot say.'

'Fine. I'll find him myself.' Walsh glanced around, then crouched and picked up a chunk of rock from the garden bed. Without looking at Clunk, she hurled it into the nearest bush. Then she picked up another, aimed at a different bush, and let fly.

'Ms Walsh, you might hurt someone.'

'I doubt I'll hit anyone important,' snapped Harriet, lobbing another chunk into the foliage. 'One way or another, he's going to get that headache he told me about.'

Clunk raised his voice as another lump of rock tore through the bushes. 'You'd better come out, Mr Spacejock.'

Unwillingly, sheepishly, Hal emerged from hiding. Walsh dropped her latest missile and dusted her hands on her dress, not looking at him.

619

'I'm sorry,' muttered Hal, hanging his head. 'I wanted to explain, but –'

Walsh took a step closer and then ... *CRACK!* Without warning, she belted Hal across the face, putting all her strength into it. Caught off guard, Hal flew into the bushes, and he was still untangling himself when Harriet turned and strode down the stairs. She reached her car before Hal found his feet, and he could only stand in shock as she wrenched the door open and got in.

'Wait!' called Hal. 'I can explain. It's not –'

Harriet slammed the door, gunned the motor and roared away.

'I think you should go after her,' said Clunk.

'You're mad. *She's* mad ... and she's got a gun.'

There was a clatter of footsteps, and Hal turned to see Ryder hurrying towards him. 'Oh, you poor baby!' she cried, when she saw the bruise on Hal's face. 'Let me take care of that for you.'

'I'm fine,' said Hal. 'It's nothing.'

'Don't be silly. Your cheek is all red.' Very gently, Ryder ran her fingertips over Hal's face. 'What you need is a woman's touch.'

Clunk snorted. 'It was a woman's touch that laid him out in the first place.'

Harriet was absolutely livid as she drove away from the expo. She'd agreed to dinner with Hal, despite all the arguments against it. First, she was a Peace Force officer working a case, and for all she knew Hal Spacejock was up to his ears in this smuggling business. Second, she'd been determined to keep her distance from Hal, despite their history, and yet she'd accepted the dinner invite without a second thought.

That was bad enough, but to be lied to and stood up ... that really took the cake. She'd spent a fortnight's salary on a new dress, and when she finally caught up with Hal he was snogging that Ryder specimen.

Walsh's hands worked the controls, her knuckles white under the strain. The problem was, she wanted Hal *and* the Peace Force, and she couldn't have them both. The Peace Force was her life now, and it was no good clinging to the past. And, if she was honest, it wasn't fair on Hal either.

From now on, she decided, their relationship would be strictly cop and suspect. As soon she got back to the *Volante*, that nameplate was coming off her old cabin door.

21

'They're going to announce the sales results,' said Clunk. 'Do you want to watch?'

Hal shook his head. 'I really don't care.'

'Do you mind if I go?'

'Be my guest.'

'Are you sure you'll be okay out here?'

'Of course. I'll just stand here and look mean.' Hal watched the robot go, then sighed. What a mess! Meri was a nice girl, and one hell of a kisser, but he was determined to clear the air with Harriet before burning all his bridges. He'd never seen her so angry, and it wasn't just the missed dinner. If she still had feelings for him, he had to know. Even if she was committed to the Peace Force right now, he'd be happy to wait a couple of years if there was a chance they could be together one day. And if she wasn't ... well, he could still feel Meri's lips on his, and ...

Hal sighed again. Why was life so complicated? He stared at the empty car park, glanced around the deserted entrance, then changed his mind about staying outside on his own. He was unlikely to get any dinner now, and if he repeated his trick with the curtains and the trays of food he might not need any.

Inside, Ryder was just welcoming Olivia Backsight, the exhibition's patron, to the microphone. Hal filched a couple of satay sticks while a few words were said about the artworks, sank two red wines during the thank-yous, and snaffled a handful of cheese sticks while Olivia presented the sales figures. There was a polite round of applause after each figure was read out, and she reached the end without mentioning any of Max Bright's artworks. Hal took a perverse pleasure in this, but the grin vanished when he realised their customer probably intended to pay his freight bill from the proceeds of any sales.

'And now, ladies and gentlemen, I'd like to announce the biggest sale tonight. I know many of you are keen collectors, and we're truly lucky to have so many unique pieces to choose from.'

Hal smiled as he polished off his drink. It was Olivia's money that brought all the pieces to the exhibition, not luck. And if this big sale was one of Bright's, the freight bill was as good as settled.

'I'm happy to report that one piece sold for a truly staggering amount.' Olivia Backsight nodded to Ryder, who gestured to a helper, who beckoned towards an open doorway. Members of the crowd craned their necks, Clunk amongst them, and there was a gasp as one of the cargo sleds was pushed into the hall. A shimmering gold curtain had been draped over the contents, which from the shape of it looked like a big rectangular slab. Hal pulled a face at the sight. None of Bright's artworks were shaped like monoliths.

The sled came closer, gliding to a gentle halt next to the rostrum. Ryder gathered a corner of the golden curtain, and waited for the signal.

'This piece appeared in the exhibition under mysterious circumstances, smuggled in under the eyes of our security team.' Olivia looked straight at Hal as she said this, and he almost choked on a cracker. 'I myself believe it to be the work of my dear grandson, Rodney Backsight, who some of you know as a bit of a high-spirited youth.'

Hal realised 'Rodney' was the little creep who'd threatened him with the electric blade. Judging from the wary looks members of the audience were exchanging, Hal wasn't the only one to have experienced Rodney's charm. And if Rodney was an artist, then he, Hal Spacejock, was a ballerina.

'Without further ado, I'd like to unveil the unnamed piece.'

At a gesture from her boss, Ryder flicked the cover off the hidden artwork. Underneath was a large slab of concrete, and at first glance Hal thought someone had painted the outline of a man on the front. His arms were up, his face was a picture of shock, and his mouth was wide open in a soundless scream. Then he realised it was a clever sculpture, and the man wasn't painted on, he was actually chiselled out of the slab. The detail was incredible, and it looked like someone had spent months on the piece.

There was a round of applause, and even Hal joined in. Then, as the applause died out, Hal noticed Clunk looking at him. The robot was tilting his head repeatedly, as though there was a fault in his motor. His eyes kept flicking towards the door, and one of his shoulders rose and fell with every movement. Hal frowned. Was Clunk trying to bid in the auction? Didn't he realise it was already over?

Hal inspected the artwork again, and he realised there was something familiar about it. The look of surprise on the face, the clawed fingers on the hands, the bouncer outfit the model was wearing ... Wait a minute. Bouncer outfit? Hal studied the face, and that's when it dawned on him. The piece wasn't a clever sculpture by Rodney Backsight, it was the slab of wet concrete Hal had fallen into earlier that afternoon! Someone had spotted the impression he'd made, assumed it was an innovative artwork, and cut the thing out of the ground. Not only that, they'd sold the damn thing!

'How much did it go for?' Hal asked a tall woman in a white dress.

'One does not discuss such matters,' said the woman loftily.

'Two hundred and fifty grand,' said her partner.

Hal whistled. Then he smiled. Then he danced a little jig. All he had to do was claim the artwork and the huge sum of money was his!

◆

Formalities complete, the crowd began to drift away. Hal approached Meri Ryder, but before he could explain about the concrete artwork, she got in first.

'Hal! I have a bone to pick with you.' Ryder adjusted the collar on his jacket. 'I know Rodney can be a bit full-on, but you might have warned me he was delivering a piece of his own.'

'He didn't. I –'

'Not that it really matters. This is the fourth year we've run this exhibition, and dear old Olivia pays top whack for his lousy efforts every time.'

'What do you mean?'

'She bids on his rubbish every year. Why, only last year she claimed a nut and bolt was his best ever work, and gave him fifty thousand credits for it.' Ryder gestured at the slab. 'This year she's really excelled herself. I mean, just look at the ugly thing. Those beady eyes seem to follow you around the room, and that savage, haunted expression belongs in a Peace Force line-up.'

Hal thought this was a bit rich, especially since the face in the 'sculpture' was actually his. Then he realised the implications. The piece had only sold because the patron though it was her grandson's, and if Hal tried to claim it, the sale would be cancelled. Instead of getting his hands on a big pile of cash, he'd probably get charged with vandalism.

'There is something strangely familiar about it,' continued Ryder. 'Something I can't quite put my finger on.'

'Here, have another glass of wine.'

'Are you trying to get me drunk?'

'Or a cheese nibbly.'

'No, I'm having dinner later.' Meri glanced at him. 'Did you hear about Bright's artworks?'

Hal shook his head.

'Olivia bought the lot. She wants them delivered to their weapons factory on Niaritz for a private exhibition, then shipped to head office where they'll be put on permanent display.'

'Good riddance,' said Hal.

'Oh, you haven't seen the last of Bright's artwork yet. I'm to hire you for both deliveries.'

Hal groaned. 'Not again.'

'Cheer up. The pay's even better than last time.' Meri hesitated. 'So, are you going back to your hotel tonight?'

'I don't have a hotel. I'm staying aboard the *Volante*.'

'Really? Would you like a lift?'

Hal hesitated. 'I should really give Clunk a hand with the artworks.'

'No point. We're locking the gallery in half an hour, and break-down doesn't start until seven tomorrow morning.' Ryder smiled. 'Go on, I'll give you a ride. It'll be my pleasure, believe me.'

Hal remembered Harriet. Was she still driving around with steam coming out of her ears, or had she returned to the *Volante* to stew? Either way, he was unlikely to run into her sitting in Meri's car. 'Okay, let me find Clunk.'

'Oh. Does he have to come with us?'

'I can't leave him here.'

'Why not? He can make an early start on the packing.'

Hal thought for a moment. 'That's not a bad idea, but I'll have to explain it right.'

Ryder smiled at him. 'I'm sure you'll manage.'

Hal found the robot deep in conversation with an artist, quizzing her on every aspect of her work. The artist seemed relieved when Hal interrupted, and she made a quick excuse and hurried towards the exit.

'Ah, Mr Spacejock. I've been learning about chisel-point techniques. Did you know that –'

'Later, Clunk. I've got some news on the cargo.' Hal explained about the delivery jobs, and he was surprised to see a look of relief cross the robot's face. 'What is it?'

'I'm sorry?'

'You look like a weight just lifted off your shoulders.'

'Oh, it's nothing. Nothing at all.'

Clunk glanced at Hairpiece, sitting nearby on its pedestal, and again Hal could have sworn the robot looked relieved. Then again, the robot's face was always a bit wonky. 'Anyway, we can leave the artworks here overnight. Meri says they're locking up until the morning.'

'That's good news. I was looking forward to relaxing aboard the *Volante* this evening.'

'Yes, about that. Do you think it's worth going all the way to the ship and back again?'

'It does seem a waste of time, but what about accommodation?'

'Meri says it's fine to stay here overnight. Get some rest, and make a start on the packing first thing.'

'I like the idea. It's ... efficient.'

'Good.' Hal patted the robot on the shoulder. 'I'll see you in the morning.'

'I'm sorry?'

'You can stay here. I've made my own arrangements.'

Clunk turned to look at Ryder, who was touching up her lipstick with the help of a compact. She flicked back a lock of hair, straightened her cardigan and smiled at Hal. 'Yes, Mr Spacejock,' said the robot at last. 'I believe I understand your arrangements. Enjoy your evening, and don't worry about me.'

Hal hurried away, relieved the robot hadn't objected. Sometimes Clunk was as bad as two parents and a room full of nannies, all rolled into one. He caught up with Meri near the door, where she was just saying goodbye to several of the guests. They left the hall together, and Meri shivered theatrically in the cold night air. Hal draped his jacket across her shoulders, and she snuggled against him as they walked to the car.

'You're very warm,' she said, putting her arm around him.

22

Hal watched the suburbs rolling past, the lighted house windows revealing little snapshots of comfortable family life. He was sitting in the back seat of Ryder's car, his arm around her shoulders. She was leaning against him, the top of her head against his cheek. The car had its instructions, and was driving quickly and efficiently towards their destination.

Houses flashed by, and Hal gazed through the big, well-lit windows. In one house, a robot was serving drinks at a small gathering. A wedding reception, perhaps, or a celebration. In the next, a group of teens were lounging around a big screen. In another, a couple were sitting down with their kids, enjoying a late supper. Hal felt an unfamiliar stirring as he watched the vignettes unfold. These people were settled in their comfortable homes, enjoying normal lives with their families. His own life aboard the *Volante* seemed cold and transient by comparison.

'What are you thinking about?' asked Ryder.

'Nothing much.' Hal saw a sign flash by. 'Looks like the spaceport coming up.'

'Already?' Ryder sat up to check. 'That was quick.'

Hal said nothing. The *Volante* would be sitting on its landing pad, cold and dark. And inside, Harriet Walsh would probably be waiting for him ... equally cold.

'Hal ...' began Ryder.

'Yes?'

'Are you hungry?'

Hal's stomach growled in response. The snacks from the art exhibition had been tasty, but hardly filling.

'I'll take that as a yes,' said Ryder. 'Listen, I know this little place in town. They do great food, and they're not fussy about dress code.'

'But the *Volante*...'

'Come on, it'll be fun. We can be in and out in no time, and then you can get back to your precious ship.'

Hal wavered. A quick meal couldn't do any harm, and it would give Harriet a bit more time to cool off. Plus, if she was going to shoot him on sight, he'd rather have a slap-up meal for his last supper. 'All right, let's do it.'

'I knew you would.' Ryder gave the car new directions, and ten minutes later they pulled into a busy carpark in front of a nondescript building. There was a big animated sign on the wall, and Hal was shocked to see where they were: Tabbie's Nosher, the same restaurant he'd picked out for an evening meal with Harriet.

'You know, this might not be a great idea,' he said.

'Nonsense. We're here now.'

'Do they have takeaway? I could grab something and –'

Ryder kissed him on the cheek. 'Stop playing hard to get.'

Meekly, Hal got out of the car and followed her across the carpark. There was quite an assortment of vehicles, from battered pickups to brand new luxury models, and just outside the entrance was a taxi rank with half a dozen automatic cabs.

As they approached the entrance, a red beam scanned them from head to toe. 'Welcome to Tabbie's,' said a mechanical voice. 'Please enjoy your evening.'

They passed through a short entrance hall, and Hal stopped at the sight which met his eyes. The restaurant was huge, with at least a hundred tables arranged in neat rows, and most of the seats were full. The noise from all the conversations was thunderous, and he could barely hear himself think.

There were three bars serving drinks and food: one in the middle, built into a stainless steel cylinder, and another at each end of the restaurant.

'We have to order at the counter,' shouted Ryder.

Hal nodded, and led her into the crush. They were halfway there when he saw a familiar face: Olivia Backsight, sitting at a large table with two dozen guests, two of whom he'd hoped never to see again: Rodney Backsight, the thug who'd held a knife to Hal's throat, and his buck-toothed friend. Both the youths were staring directly at Hal, their expressions hard and calculating.

'It looks pretty full,' said Ryder. 'Can you see any spare tables?'

Hal looked around the restaurant. There was a small table nearby, laid for two places, and a lone diner was sitting with her back to him, just finishing a coffee. She pushed back her chair and stood up, revealing a pretty dress which shimmered in the light. Hal was just admiring it when the woman turned to face him, and his stomach dropped into his boots when he realised it was Harriet Walsh.

Harriet gave Hal a long look, then walked directly towards him. 'You two can have my table,' she said, sparing Ryder the briefest of glances. She looked directly into Hal's eyes. 'I'm done.'

'That's nice of her,' said Ryder, oblivious to the byplay. 'Which seat do you want?'

'Wait here, okay? I'll just be a second.'

'Sure.'

Hal hurried towards the exit, where the doors were just closing. He ran outside and saw Walsh getting into her car. 'Harriet, wait!'

She hesitated, on the point of closing the door. 'What is it?' she asked coldly.

'You're getting this all wrong. She's just buying me dinner.'

'No, Hal. You're getting it wrong. I'm a Peace Force officer investigating a smuggling racket. I have no interest in your private life.'

'But –'

'I'll be requesting a transfer to another ship first thing in the morning. They'll send another officer, and maybe my replacement will be able to deal with you properly.'

'What about tonight? Don't you need somewhere to stay?'

'I'll find a hotel. Enjoy the rest of your life.'

Walsh slammed the door, and a second later the car pulled away, leaving Hal alone in the car park. He stood in silence for several minutes, his thoughts churning, and then he returned to the restaurant.

By the time he got there, Meri had shifted to Olivia's table and was deep in conversation with the other guests. Hal watched her from the doorway, then turned to leave.

Outside, he trudged to the taxi rank, and had just reached the first cab when the vehicle came to life and drove off. Frowning to himself, Hal approached the second cab, which drove away even quicker than the first. That left one cab, and this time Hal stood directly in front with both arms out, almost daring it to run him over. The lights came on, the electric motor whirred, and he was just bracing for impact when the car went backwards, turned ninety degrees and sped off into the darkness.

Hal swore under his breath. He didn't know the area and he didn't fancy a long walk on an empty stomach. Still, at least the Spaceport wasn't too far.

The first kilometre passed quickly, and Hal began to enjoy the fresh air and silence. The city wasn't far from the ocean, and the tangy smell of salt and seaweed was invigorating. After a while he reached the commercial district, with big open carparks and rows of tilt-slab buildings. It was deserted, although once or twice he thought he heard footsteps. Each time he stopped, turned, and scanned the darkness. Each time, he saw nothing.

After a while Hal increased his pace, lengthening his stride but also placing his boots carefully to minimise the noise. He pushed a hand into his pocket, balling his fist to stop the loose change rattling quite so loudly.

◆

Hal was nearing the ocean now, and he wasn't far from the bridge connecting the spaceport to dry land. He could already see the colourful billboards in the distance, advertising such essentials as overpriced watches, overpriced perfumes and overpriced holidays.

There was a low whistle behind him, and Hal turned to look. Just up the road was a group of youths in dark clothing. He was just deciding whether they were following him or not, when one of them activated a short, glowing blade. In the blue light, Hal recognised several of Rodney Backsight's cronies from the restaurant. Rodney himself wasn't there, no doubt too important to get his own hands dirty.

Not for the first time, Hal wished Clunk were there. Sure, the robot was a pacifist, but he could have pacified half the group while Hal punched out the rest. As it was he was heavily outnumbered, and his only chance was a strategic retreat.

One of the youths let out a catcall, and the others quickly followed suit. There was a thunder of footsteps as they broke into a run, and Hal turned and fled.

He reached the main road which ran parallel to the beach, and turned for the spaceport gates. Two hundred metres ... one hundred ... the gates were almost in sight when a flashy car drew up. Two youths got out, and Hal stopped as he recognised Rodney and his offsider.

The footsteps behind him got closer, and Hal turned left and sped across the road. He crossed an expanse of walkway beside the seaside, where a series of darkened marquees had signs advertising beachwear, towels, and other junk. Every one of them had 'Backsight Industries' logos plastered all over their fabric sides, and every one was sealed up.

Without pausing, Hal ran around the nearest marquee, slashed a hole in the wall and dived through the gap. He found a safe spot and huddled amongst the displays of inflatable toys, buckets, spades and beach balls. All around, the air was thick with the smell of sun tan lotion, old vinyl and stale chips.

He heard cautious footsteps, and a shadow fell across the canvas wall. The shadow moved around to Hal's makeshift entrance, and then ...

'I've found him!' someone shouted. 'He's in here!'

Despite Clunk's efforts, Hal had managed to keep one or two weapons, and he struggled to free a set of nunchuks from his trousers. The long hard poles had been pressing into his leg all evening, and he wondered whether Ryder had noticed them in the car.

Putting such things out of his mind, Hal stood, swinging the nunchuks in circles, measuring the balance. Then, as the youths poured through the opening in the marquee, he launched into a fearsome display.

'Heee-yaaah!' shouted Hal, spinning the nunchuks around his arms and torso in a whirling, flailing, clattering storm of wood and chain.

The youths paused, disconcerted, and Hal redoubled his efforts as he advanced on them. There was a whirring sound as he stepped past a display cabinet, and the young men were showered in torn vinyl as Hal's weapon devastated a display of beachballs, popping them and tearing the sagging remains into fragments under the onslaught. Then he hit a tray of sunscreen, popping the bottles and spraying their contents all over the interior.

The youths took one look and fled, ripping half the wall out of the tent in their hurry. Hal ran out after them, dripping with sunscreen and shedding pieces of beach ball. 'And don't come back!' he shouted.

23

Caaaww! Caaaawwww!

Hal opened his eyes, and for a moment he was completely disoriented. He was lying on his back, and when he tried to open his eyes he discovered someone was shining an incredibly bright lamp in his face. He closed them again quickly, blinking away tears. Clearly it was an alien abduction, and it was only a matter of time before the unpleasant experiments began.

'Ow!' There was a sharp pain on the tip of his nose, and Hal shook his head. Immediately there was a flutter of wings, and when Hal opened his eyes he got a glimpse of a startled seagull beating a hasty retreat across the beach.

The beach! Everything came back in an instant: the pursuit through the town, his last stand in the beach shop, and the youths staking out the spaceport entrance in their car, taking it in turns to fetch supplies while Hal huddled in the darkness. They'd been there for hours, and in the end Hal had snuck away and curled up on the beach.

Hal licked his dry lips, wincing at the salty taste. Then a shadow blotted out the sky, and Hal looked up to see a small boy with a plastic bucket standing over him. The boy was about four years old, and if he was surprised to find a man sleeping on the beach, he hid it well. 'What you doin'?'

'Wakin' up.' Hal licked his dry lips. 'Rough night.'

'You wan' some water?'

Hal nodded.

'Here y'are,' said the boy, tipping the contents of his bucket onto Hal's upturned face. Seawater cascaded down, followed by a thick sandy sludge. Several large shells bounced off Hal's skull, and then a big chunk of seaweed wrapped his face like an amorous squid.

Hal spat out a mouthful of salty water. 'Thanks kid, that was just what I needed.'

◆

Inspector Boson leaned close to his terminal, his face looming on the screen. 'Trainee Walsh, do you have any news?'

Walsh was sitting in her hotel room. It was early in the morning, and she'd barely had time for a fortifying coffee before calling Boson on a secure connection. 'I–'

Before she could explain, Boson frowned. 'Is that a hotel room? Why aren't you aboard the *Volante*?'

'I left the ship last night. I–I had a disagreement with the pilot.'

'Is Spacejock causing you problems?'

'In a manner of speaking, yes.'

'Strange. He didn't seem the type to me.'

'Not that sort of problem. It's ... complicated.'

Boson gestured airily. 'You're authorised to shoot him. I'll sign the paperwork afterwards.'

'I'd rather you assigned someone else to the *Volante*.'

'You know how stretched we are at the moment, and you want me to move officers around to accommodate your wishes? I'm sorry, but your request is denied.'

'But sir –'

Boson raised his hand. 'You will return to the *Volante* and attend to your duties. That's an order.'

Harriet's stomach clenched. 'Yes, sir.'

'Now tell me about the artworks.'

'The cargo is heading to Niaritz for a private exhibition at a Backsight Industries weapons factory.'

'Really?' Boson's expression changed instantly, becoming lean and hungry. 'Do you have a decrypting tool with you?'

'Yes sir.'

'Excellent. When you get to Niaritz, I want you to get any data you can from Backsight's network.'

Walsh frowned. 'I did mention this is a weapons factory? Security will be incredibly tight.'

'Disguise yourself as an exhibition worker. Use Spacejock ... I'm sure he'll be able to get you in.'

'But –'

'Trainee Walsh, a copy of their records could yield vital evidence.' Boson leaned towards the screen, his eyes bright. 'You can't let this chance slip through your fingers! You must gather intel on the enemy, whatever the cost.'

'But –'

'No buts, Trainee. That's an order.' Boson signed off, and Harriet was left staring at a blank screen. Well, she thought, that's simple enough. All she had to do was disguise herself, sneak into a secure facility, find an unlocked terminal, download all the records, make it back to the ship undetected and deliver everything to her crazy boss ... presumably with a nice little bow on top.

What could be easier?

◆

The exhibition break-down was well under way by the time Hal arrived at the hall. He found Clunk manoeuvring a loaded sled towards the truck, and he hurried over to lend a hand. The robot spared him a quick glance, taking in Hal's dishevelled appearance and crumpled clothing. 'Mr Spacejock, you look terrible. Did you get any sleep?'

'Not much, no.'

Clunk picked a strand from Hal's hair. 'Is that seaweed? Have you been to the beach?'

'Not by choice,' muttered Hal.

'How was your date with Ms Ryder?'

'Don't ask.'

'Did you clear the air with Ms Walsh?'

'Don't ask that, either.' Hal relented. 'Look, I went for a quick bite with Meri, and Harriet was there, and then those idiots from the art show chased me with their gang, and then I was forced to sleep on the beach. Are we clear now?'

'Why didn't you tell me where you were? I could have helped, Mr Spacejock.'

'How was I supposed to do that?' Hal gestured at a nearby courier driver, who was talking into a commset. 'I need one of those.'

Clunk shook his head. 'Galactic roaming charges would bankrupt you in a matter of hours.'

'That bad, huh?'

'You have no idea. Plus they won't let you have one without a fixed address.'

'What do other pilots do?'

'This may come as a surprise, but some pilots do own houses.'

'Rubbish. Banks own houses. Pilots just get to pay the mortgage.' Hal gestured at the sled. 'Let's just pack this stuff up and get out of here.'

'Will you get the doors?'

Hal obeyed, opening the back of the truck wide. The sled whined as it rose higher into the air, and when it was level Hal and Clunk started transferring the artworks.

They were almost done when Hal saw movement outside. He looked up and saw Harriet Walsh, wearing her uniform and a pair of dark sunglasses. Her face was expressionless, and one hand was resting on the butt of her gun. 'Good morning,' called Hal.

'You look terrible,' remarked Harriet.

Clunk cleared his throat. 'Mr Spacejock is worn out after a very busy night. He barely got any sleep after he left with Ms Ryder.'

Hal closed his eyes and waited for the gunshot. When nothing happened, he gave the robot a venomous look. 'Thanks for that, Clunk. I don't know where I'd be without your help.'

They finished loading in silence, and when they were done Harriet told them about her orders.

'You're coming with us?' said Hal in surprise.

'Believe me, it's not by choice.'

Hal smiled to himself. If Harriet was travelling with them, he'd have plenty of time to explain. Things didn't look so bad after all!

24

They drove to the spaceport in silence. To start with, Hal tried to lighten the mood with a few Peace Force jokes, but soon stopped when he saw Harriet's grip tightening on her weapon. After that, he kept his mouth shut and stared straight ahead.

The truck rumbled over the causeway to the spaceport, and Hal frowned as he saw the sandy beach. Gentle waves lapped at the shore, and he could still see the scattered sand where he'd spent the night. He was going to point it out to Harriet, but one look at her face changed his mind.

Loading went without a hitch, and Harriet went to her cabin while Clunk returned the rental truck. After a few moments frowning at the artworks cluttering up his nice clean hold, Hal made his way to the flight deck. On the way he paused outside Harriet's door, and he was shocked to discover the little nameplate was missing. There was only a discoloured patch of metal to show where it had been fixed to the door for the past few months.

Hal raised his hand to knock, then changed his mind and leant closer to the door. He strained his ears, but it was deathly quiet inside, and for all he knew Harriet was fast asleep. Silently, he turned away and headed for the flight deck.

He made himself comfortable and started paging through the ship's message log. There may have been some nuggets amongst all the enlargement spam, double enlargement spam, intergalactic lottery spam and phishing attempts, but if there was he couldn't see any.

'Did we get any messages overnight? Anything to do with Bright's cargo?'

'Negative, but there was a suspicious amount of intrusion activity.'

'You mean someone tried to board my ship?'

'No, electronic intrusion.'

'What were they after?'

'Your itinerary.'

Hal shrugged. 'There's no mystery about that. We're heading to Niaritz to deliver those artworks.'

'Yes, but there are several ways to get there. I believe the intruders were trying to obtain your exact course.'

'Do we even have one of those? I thought we just aimed in the general direction and hit the jump button.'

'And that's why Clunk won't let you fly your own ship.'

Before Hal could object, the lift doors opened and Clunk strolled in. 'Good news, Mr Spacejock. The rental company refunded your deposit on the truck.'

'Don't they always?'

'Only when you return their vehicles in one piece.'

Hal tried to remember the last time they'd managed this, but he came up blank. 'Hey listen, you know the AutoChef?'

'I'm aware of the device, yes.'

'Can you reprogram it for something really special? I want to impress Harriet tonight.' Hal spread his hands, encompassing the console. 'I can picture a huge table with a snowy white cloth, and silver cutlery gleaming under the candlelight.'

Clunk looked uncertain. 'Me, I can picture a rickety picnic table with plastic cutlery and a couple of dim torches.'

'All right, but what about the food? A nice roast with veg, a sparkling wine, and afterwards a rich dessert with real fruit.'

'I'm sorry, Mr Spacejock. The only way Ms Walsh is going to enjoy a meal like that is if you take her to a restaurant.'

'I can't ask her to a restaurant, can I? I stood her up once, and when she went on her own I turned up to the same restaurant with someone else.'

'A very poor decision, if you ask me.'

'I wasn't. Can you rustle up some decent food or not?'

'I will do everything in my power.'

'Make sure you're fully charged, then.' Hal turned away, but before he could leave there was a double chime from the console.

Ding dong!

'Is that an incoming message?' demanded Hal.

'No,' said the Navcom. 'It's an incoming visitor.'

Hal glanced towards the airlock. 'It's not that Boson guy, is it?'

'Unable to say.'

'Can we lift off quick, before they come in?'

'Only if you want their death on your hands.'

'Fair enough.' Hal crossed to the airlock and peered out. Standing on the landing platform was Meri Ryder.

'Oh great,' muttered Hal, before opening the door.

'Hi, how are you doing?' asked Ryder. She kissed him on the cheek, then wiped away the lipstick smudge with her thumb.

'Er, fine,' said Hal lamely. 'What can we do for you?'

'You can carry my case. I tried to pack light, but it's damn heavy.'

Hal looked outside and saw a large suitcase on the landing platform. 'What's that for?'

'It's my clothes, silly. I was going to catch a ferry to Niaritz, and then I realised you'd be all alone aboard this big, empty ship. You don't mind giving me a lift, do you?'

◆

Hal stared at Meri in shock. 'You can't fly with us. I mean, it's not a good time. I mean –'

'Oh, go on.' She gave him a warm smile. 'I'd be very grateful, and we can have that special dinner I promised you.'

'But I, we, I mean –'

'Hey, I like your flight deck,' said Meri, pushing past him. 'Do you fly the ship from that seat?'

Defeated, Hal grabbed the suitcase and followed her inside. Clunk was looking at Ryder in concern, and he gave Hal a worried glance over her head. Hal met his gaze and shrugged. 'Can you show her to the third deck? There's a comfortable sofa down there, and you can break out some spare blankets.'

'As you wish, Mr Spacejock. However, I do think you should have informed me of this little arrangement of yours.'

'I didn't know about this little arrangement,' said Hal. 'It's all a bit, er, unexpected.'

'I don't want to put you out,' said Meri. 'If it's too much trouble ...'

'Well, to be honest –'

'Good, that's settled. Third deck, did you say? Clunk, will you bring my case?'

'Don't forget to check the cargo sling,' called Hal. He watched them leave, and as the doors closed he gave a frustrated groan. 'This can't possibly get any worse,' he muttered.

'I beg to differ,' said the Navcom. 'I just received the bill for port fees, duties, and amenities. Would you care to authorise payment?'

'Hang on a minute. I thought Bright was covering that?'

'I tried to use his voucher, but the number was invalid.'

'So check the number.'

'I did.'

'So make up a new number!'

'That is neither ethical nor legal.'

'How much are these fees, anyway?'

The Navcom told him.

'Wow, Clunk wasn't kidding when he said this place was expensive.' Hal rubbed his chin and played with the change in his pocket. Then he played with his chin and rubbed the change. Then he remembered just how much change he was carrying. 'Hey, do they take cash?'

Lift-off was a cautious affair, with Clunk all too aware of the large rock hanging beneath the *Volante*'s belly. The flight deck creaked and swayed alarmingly as the rock swung from side to side, and Hal held his breath until they reached orbit. Then, with the rock happily settled in zero-G, he took Clunk aside for a quick planning session. 'You understand we can't let Harriet know about Meri, don't you?'

'Wouldn't it be best to come clean with both of them?'

'Hell no. You were there when Harriet decked me –'

'Oh yes. I remember that clearly.'

'– and she might go one further next time.'

'She only assaulted you because you forgot to have dinner with her.'

'There was more to it than that. I think ... I think she might still care for me.'

'But she left you, Mr Spacejock. She has a career in the Peace Force now.

'Look, this is the way I see it. Harriet had to choose me or the Peace Force, and she chose the Force. With me so far?'

Clunk nodded.

'When she left, she didn't just stop liking me. You don't turn emotions on and off like a tap.' Hal glanced at the robot. 'Well, we don't, anyway.'

'My emotions aren't exactly binary,' said Clunk stiffly. 'Anyway, if Ms Walsh left you she can hardly object to whomever you choose to, er, shack up with.'

'I'm not shacking up with anyone!' protested Hal.

'That's not what Ms Walsh suspects.'

Hal seized on this. 'Right, she only suspects it. Given time, I can explain. Bring her round. But if she comes face to face with Meri in the middle of the night ...'

'She'll punch you again.'

'Or worse,' said Hal darkly.

'Very well, I understand and am in full agreement. Ms Walsh must not learn of Ms Ryder's presence.'

'Thank you.'

'However, does it really matter if Ms Ryder learns of Ms Walsh's presence?'

'I'd rather keep them apart.' Then Hal gave a strangled cry. 'Oh, crap! What if they talk with each other at the next stop? Harriet'll find out they both travelled there aboard my ship!'

'Hello, major arse kicking.'

'What?'

'That's the technical term for the likely outcome.'

'You sound like you're enjoying all this,' said Hal, with a suspicious look at the robot.

'Me, enjoy your suffering? Never, Mr Spacejock.'

'So wipe that smirk off your face.'

'I am attempting to convey sympathy for your situation, but my fine control motors aren't what they used to be.'

'It looks just like a smirk to me.'

Clunk reached up and straightened his face. 'Better?'

'You look like you bit into a lemon.'

Clunk adjusted his face again, until he was leering like a carnival clown.

'Just …leave it.' Hal gave the tricky situation some thought. 'Okay, here's what we'll do. We'll tell Meri we're only licensed for cargo, and she's breaking the law by coming aboard. We face a big fine for carrying passengers, that sort of thing. Tell her she's put us in a bad way. Tell her we'll be bankrupt if she ever mentions the *Volante*, especially to any Peace Force officers who she may or may not meet at the exhibition. Tell her …oh, I don't know. Just lay it on thick and make sure she understands.'

'When are you going to explain this to Ms Ryder?'

'I'm not. You are.'

'Mr Spacejock, I'm a first-class pilot, not a first-class liar. I should be handling the ship, not taking on duties for which you are more suitably qualified.'

'Oh sure, dump it in my lap.' Muttering under his breath, Hal strode towards the lift. One way or the other he was going to keep a lid on the situation.

◆

Alone at last, Clunk sat in the pilot's chair and breathed a remarkably human sigh.

'What's that sound?' asked the Navcom in concern. 'Have you punctured a cooling line?'

'No, I was indicating relief,' said Clunk. 'The artworks have been sold, which means our little substitution will never be discovered.'

'It was more than a little substitution,' said the Navcom. 'In fact, given the size of that asteroid I'd say it was a very large substitution.'

Clunk waved one hand airily. 'Small, large or intermediate …it's no longer an issue. The new owner won't be any the wiser, and the artist will never see his Hairpiece again.'

'So you could say we survived a close brush with disaster?'

Clunk snorted. 'Amusing, Navcom. Very amusing.'

25

'Illegal passenger, me?'

Meri's eyes were wide behind her rimless glasses, and her mouth was a perfect O. Hal remembered the warmth of those lips, the hot embrace at the gallery, and for a moment he was completely distracted. 'Y-yes,' he said at last. 'Totally illegal. I could get into real trouble with the law.'

They were sitting side by side on the deep, comfortable sofa, down on the *Volante*'s third deck. There were two empty armchairs nearby, but somehow Hal had ended up alongside Meri, their hips touching and her face up close. Meri's leg was warm, her eyes were magnetic, and Hal knew he'd have to get up and leave soon or he wouldn't be leaving at all. 'I, er, captainy things to do, flies to ship ... I mean, er ... '

Meri put her hand on his thigh, and warmth ran up Hal's leg to his brain. 'Peace Force, gun. Peace Force, gun,' he muttered under his breath.

'Did you say something?'

'No, nothing.' Hal swallowed. 'Look, I have to go.'

'Can't Clunk fly the ship on his own?'

'S-sometimes, but I have to supervise.'

'Oh, all right.' Meri withdrew her hand and looked around the lower deck. 'Where do you sleep, by the way?'

'I have a cabin on the next level.'

'Really?'

'Yes. The, er, second deck is off-limits to passengers. Totally forbidden.'

'But I'm not a passenger, am I? I'm a stowaway.'

'Yeah, I, er –'

Meri put her hand back on his thigh, running it up and down lightly. 'Stowaways can end up anywhere.'

Hal got up in a hurry. 'I've gotta dash. You stay down here, okay?'

'I might, if you tie me up.' Meri put her hands out, wrist upwards. 'Do you have any handcuffs?'

Hal fled to the lift, and once he was safely inside he shook himself all over. Meri was like a powerful drug, and one more hit could easily leave him hooked.

The lift stopped, and Hal was getting ready to step into the flight deck when he realised he was on the second level. The doors opened, and he saw Harriet Walsh standing right in front of him.

'H-hello,' said Hal lamely. 'Going up?'

Harriet shook her head. 'I thought I'd go down and get something from the AutoChef.'

'You can't!' said Hal in alarm. 'It's ... it's broken.'

'Fine. I'll grab a coffee instead.'

'There's a machine in the flight deck. I'll bring something to your cabin.'

'Are you all right, Hal? You look flushed.'

'I'm fine,' said Hal briefly. 'Let me get you that coffee.'

It was past midnight, and Hal was lying in his bunk. The lights were out, and the dim glow from the safety light was barely enough to make out his hand in front of his face. The ship's engines rumbled in the distance, a constant, comforting sound which usually lulled him into sleep.

Not this time. Hal had been lying there for some hours now, knowing he needed to rest for the next day, but unable to close his eyes and drift off. Dinner had been fraught, but he'd managed to deliver food to Walsh's cabin while keeping Meri below decks.

Now Walsh was in her cabin, Meri was asleep on the third deck, and Hal was alone in his bunk. He sighed and turned towards the wall. A week ago, if someone had told him he'd be hosting two attractive women aboard his ship, he'd have laughed long and hard. Now the joke was on him.

Tap tap.

Hal's ears pricked up. Was that a knock at the door?

Tap tap.

There was definitely someone outside his cabin. Was it Clunk, come to report on some disaster? Or was it Meri, playing the stowaway as she'd promised? Hal's first reaction was to jam his pillow over his head and ignore it. Unfortunately, Harriet was just up the corridor, and if the knocking got any louder she might come to investigate.

Hal got up and crossed to the door. There was just enough light to see the rectangular shadow in the middle of the wall, and he found the contact alongside with his first touch. The door swept open, and a shadowy figure advanced on him, falling into his arms. He felt her breath on the side of his face, and there was a throaty whisper right next to his ear.

'Hal, I need you.'

Hal turned his face towards the voice, and felt hot lips on his. He responded fiercely, feeling the warmth of Meri's body against his own. He could hear the blood pounding in his ears, and his legs moved of their own volition, backing them both towards his waiting bunk.

Then he stopped, breaking the kiss. 'I can't do this,' he whispered. 'It's not right.'

There was a long silence, and in the darkness Meri rested her forehead on his chest.

'We have to be professional,' whispered Hal. 'I'm really sorry.'

Meri kissed him again, gently this time, and he was shocked to feel the wetness of her cheeks. Then she was gone, the door hissing to behind her.

Hal collapsed in his bunk, his heart still thudding like fury. That had been close … really, really close. But if he wanted to win Harriet back, it was the only way. For some reason Meri had been really upset, but he couldn't help that. Hal put two fingers to his lips, frowning as he traced the outline. There'd been something different about the kiss, something familiar. It was almost as though …

Tap tap.

Hal groaned and buried his head in his hands. Meri obviously believed in third time lucky, but this time he'd be really firm with her. He crossed to the door, opened it, and two seconds later he was wrapped in another passionate kiss. With his free hand he sought the control pad, and after the door closed he turned the light on.

Meri squinted and covered her eyes, and while her hands were occupied Hal managed to get free. 'Look, I already told you,' he whispered. 'We can't keep doing this. I know it's upsetting, but ... '

Meri looked between her fingers. 'Upsetting? What are you talking about?'

'You were crying.'

'The hell I was.'

Meri lowered her hands, and Hal realised she was telling the truth. Her cheeks were flushed, but there was no sign of tears. 'But you were just here! We –'

'Sounds like *someone* was having a nice dream.' Meri glanced at the bed, taking in the rumpled sheets and dented pillow. 'Did anything good happen?'

Hal couldn't reply. A huge, dark hole had just opened under his feet, and he was on the point of falling through to oblivion. This was Meri's first visit to his cabin, and the lips he'd been kissing five minutes ago certainly weren't Clunk's. That only left ... 'Harriet!'

Meri frowned. 'Who?'

'Look, you've got to leave,' whispered Hal urgently. 'Go back down to the third deck and stay there.'

'Will you come and tuck me in?' said Meri, with a cheeky smile.

'Yes. No! You have to stay down there, understood?'

Meri studied his face, then nodded. Hal turned the light out and opened the door, and seconds later he was alone again. He stood there in the passageway for a good five minutes, looking along the hall towards Harriet's door, praying for her to come out, to come back to him. Then he looked at his bunk. Had he fallen asleep and dreamt the whole thing, or had Harriet really been there? Gently he touched his cheek, remembering the feel of Harriet's tears on his face. He ran his fingers along his jaw and rubbed the tips together.

They were completely dry.

Hal's shoulders slumped, and he turned away from the corridor to enter his cabin. The door shut behind him with a final mocking hiss, and he lay down on his bunk. He stared at the ceiling, picturing Harriet's face, and two hours later he was still trying to re-enter his earlier dream.

26

When Hal entered the flight deck the next morning he found Clunk sitting at the console. The robot turned at the sound of the lift, a welcoming smile on his face. 'Good morning, Mr Spacejock. Did you sleep well?'

'Don't ask,' muttered Hal. 'What about you?'

Clunk hesitated. 'Well, I don't want to worry you, but –'

'Too late. What's up?'

'I'm having a little trouble with my vision.'

'Really? How did that happen?'

'It's just a circuit failure. Nothing to worry about.' Clunk hesitated. 'Of course, it means I'm incapable of flying the ship.'

'Wait. What?'

'I can't fly the ship until my vision is repaired.'

'When will that be?'

'Oh, a service centre will have it fixed in no time.' Clunk frowned. 'Of course, we're in space right now, which makes things a little tricky.'

Hal thought for a moment. 'Can't you plug into the Navcom and use the ship's cameras?'

'I'm already doing so, but I can't process all the feeds and fly the ship simultaneously. My circuits aren't up to it.'

Hal nodded slowly. 'So you need me to land this thing.'

'Yes, and I'm sure you'll do a fine job. Isn't that right, Navcom?'

'Yes, Clunk,' said the ship's computer. 'By the way, would you like me to save your bookmark?'

'What bookmark?' asked Hal.

'It's nothing,' said Clunk quickly. 'Just a little light reading.'

Hal glanced at the main screen, which was showing a multiple choice: *Your pilot is about to make a fatal mistake. Do you*

A) Let him

B) Tactfully point out the error of his ways

C) Take control - as usual

D) Throw him out the airlock.

'It's called *The honest robot's guide to lying like a human*,' said the Navcom. 'Clunk's been studying it all night.'

'No I haven't,' said Clunk sharply.

'You see?' said the Navcom. 'He's already mastered the first lesson.'

'All right, I confess,' sighed the robot.

'As you can tell, he's yet to master lesson two.'

'Navcom, that's enough.' Hal put a hand on Clunk's shoulder. 'Why do you want to lie?'

'No particular reason.'

Bzzzt!

'Navcom, I won't warn you again,' said Hal, tapping his finger on the console. 'Come on Clunk. Explain.'

'The next few hours could be the busiest and most stressful of your life, and –'

'You obviously weren't in my cabin last night,' muttered Hal.

Clunk ignored the interruption. 'As I was saying, there are difficult times ahead. You'll have to navigate to Niaritz and land this ship on your own.'

'That's okay, I'll have the Navcom to help. It'll be a doddle.'

'Ordinarily, that would be the case.'

'What's different this time?'

'The venue's in a remote location.'

'Of course it is.'

'There are many high mountains, and navigation will be hazardous.'

'I shouldn't have asked.'

'The weather has been bad lately, and foggy conditions have reduced visibility to zero.'

'Get to the punchline.'

Clunk took in a decent breath of air. 'Very well. Assuming we can find the planet in the first place, and that you manage to overcome the obstacles in your path, you'll still have to land the ship on a patch of dirt the size of a kitchen garden.'

'Gardens can be pretty big sometimes.'

'This one makes a window box look like an aircraft hangar.'

Hal pinched the bridge of his nose, hoping the pain would wake him up. Instead, it just made his eyes water. 'Seems like an odd place for an art expo. What's this planet do, anyway?'

'Do?'

'Imports, exports ... you know.'

'I believe it's the manufacturing hub for Backsight Industries.'

Hal brightened. 'They sell weapons there?'

'No, they *make* weapons there.'

'Yeah, but –'

'Strictly under contract for the military. No civilian sales, no factory tours and no free samples.'

Hal pulled a face. 'One day I'll arm this ship. You see if I don't.'

'I can't wait,' said Clunk insincerely.

'Hey, have you seen our passengers this morning?'

Without a word, Clunk pointed to his eyes.

'Sorry. Force of habit.'

'I wouldn't do it, if I were you.'

'Do what?'

'Don't tell them how dangerous this landing is going to be. The favoured approach would be to set down first and explain later.'

'Surely they have a right to know the danger?'

'It's up to you, but the sensible thing would be letting them think everything is fine –'

'Until I slam this thing into a mountain. Go out happy, is that what you mean?'

'We could abandon the delivery,' suggested Clunk.

'I'm no chicken,' said Hal, frowning.

'I'm not suggesting any such thing.'

Bzzzt!

Hal rounded on the console. 'Navcom, for the last time –'

'It's an incoming call. Max Bright would like to speak to you.'

'Oh. Put him on, then.'

Bright was relaxing in an armchair, a tankard of beer at his elbow. He seemed to be sitting in the lounge of a bar, and this was confirmed when he placed a quick order for a steak and chips. 'And make sure there's plenty of mustard.'

'Take your time,' said Hal. 'Don't worry about us.'

'Ah, Mr Spacejock. I trust everything is in order?'

'Couldn't be better,' said Hal, before Clunk blurted out the truth. 'There's just one thing , though. Your voucher bounced, and I had to pay all the fees and charges on Pegzwil out of my own pocket.'

'Probably an admin error,' Bright waved his hand airily. 'You can't get the staff these days.'

'And the money?'

'I'll settle up. Don't you worry about it.'

'It's you who should be worried. If you don't cough up before this conversation finishes, I'm pushing your precious artworks out the back door.'

Bright sat up in a hurry. 'You can't do that! They have to be delivered!'

'They will be. All over the nearest planet.'

'Okay, okay. I'll authorise a transfer right now.' Bright took up a commset and started tapping the screen. 'There. The funds should come through any minute.'

'Just came into some money, did you?'

'As a matter of fact, that's what I'm calling about. Olivia Backsight bought my entire collection.'

'I heard about that.' Hal was still amazed anyone would splash out on a pile of pretentious junk, but he decided not to share his opinion with Bright. At least, not until the money came through.

'I just wanted to emphasise how important it is that you take care of my works. There's a great deal of money involved, and my pieces must arrive in perfect condition.'

'Relax. We always deliver cargo in perfect pieces.'

'Yes, er, quite. Anyway, I must go. I'm planning some daring new works the like of which have never been seen.'

'I can't wait,' muttered Hal.

The screen went dark, and there was a chime from the console. 'Funds transferred into your account,' said the Navcom.

'How much?'

'Two thousand credits.'

Hal smiled. 'Set it aside, will you? I need it to fix Clunk's eyesight.'

'It won't be that much,' protested Clunk.

'It will be if we throw in a few upgrades.'

The *Volante* arrived in orbit around Niaritz with Hal at the controls. Entry into the atmosphere went smoothly, thanks to plenty of help from the Navcom and even more advice from Clunk, although their steep descent blazed a vivid trail across the sky.

'Not bad, Mr Spacejock,' said Clunk, in a tone of voice that indicated anything short of a head-on collision was acceptable. 'However, next time I'd suggest setting your coffee aside so you can use both hands on the controls.'

Hal took a sip of the lukewarm liquid and studied the screen in front of him. The display showed a radar-generated image of the surface, the fast-moving terrain like a close-up of a choppy ocean. Peaks and valleys scrolled past at a leisurely pace, and a staggering amount of data moved up the sides of the screen. 'How can I concentrate with all that data flying past?'

'The landing indicator system will kick in soon.' Clunk had barely finished speaking when a hollow red square appeared in the middle of the screen. There was another smaller one behind it, and then a whole trail appeared, leading away into the distance like a tunnel.

The *Volante* sailed right down the middle, and Hal's confidence grew as he made tiny adjustments to the controls. 'Hey, this isn't so bad!'

'You're getting the hang of it, Mr Spacejock. Just let me know when you want the autopilot off.'

'I thought it was off.'

'No, the Navcom is still lining the ship up.'

Hal gripped the controls, preparing himself for the challenge ahead. 'Okay, let's do it.'

There was a muted beep, and 'Manual Control' appeared in the lower-right corner of the screen. The red squares immediately rose to the top, and Hal pulled back on the stick to chase them. The engine roared and the Volante shot into the sky. The red squares whipped off the bottom of the screen, and when Hal tilted the nose down again he saw the red approach tunnel laid out below like a railway track. The *Volante* descended slowly, until it was racing along just above the tunnel. Then, with a twitch of the controls, Hal lined them up once more. 'Not bad, eh?'

'Excellent, Mr Spacejock. However, it's traditional to align the bottom of the ship towards the ground.'

'Eh?'

'We're flying upside-down.'

Hal righted the ship, then frowned at a new problem. In the distance there was a mountain, and the red squares seemed to go straight through it. 'Er, Clunk?'

'Yes, Mr Spacejock.'

'We're heading towards a mountain.'

'That's all right. Just follow the guidelines.'

'The red squares, yes?'

'Correct.'

Hal shrugged, and did as he was told. The mountain got closer and closer, until he could pick out individual trees on the slopes. Still the red squares aimed right through the middle, and it was only when Hal saw wildlife running for cover that he realised the squares weren't going to veer off after all. 'Er … Clunk?'

'Collision imminent,' said the Navcom calmly. 'I suggest we pull up.'

Hal yanked back on the controls, and the *Volante* stood on its tail, engines howling. They powered towards the sky at full emergency throttle, skimming the mountain peak and blasting clouds of snow into the air with the exhaust. When his heart stopped racing, Hal levelled the controls and turned to the robot. 'Follow the red squares, eh? Are you trying to kill me, you tin-plated maniac?'

'I don't understand. Approach is merely a case of following the guidelines. There shouldn't be … oh!'

'Yes?'

Clunk looked uncomfortable. 'I forgot to change the navigation chart. The terrain you're looking at belongs to Pegzwil.'

Hal gaped at him. 'But this is Niaritz!'

Clunk mumbled an apology as he adjusted the database. When he was done the terrain on the screen changed to an even more choppy layout, and this time the green lines and dots fitted the mountain peaks Hal could see in the distance. He took hold of the controls, and before long they were flying along the red corridor once more. It snaked gently between the mountains, and the *Volante*'s engines hammered off the valley walls as Hal guided the ship towards its destination.

They flew in silence for half an hour, until Hal spotted two huge peaks side by side, emerging from the cloud cover like snowy white mounds in a bathtub full of milk. 'That reminds me. Did you remember to tell Meri the lift was faulty?'

Clunk nodded.

The screen darkened as the sun fell below the horizon, left behind by the Volante's turn of speed, and Hal began to see patches of light between the mountain peaks. Visibility was poor, and the lights made patches of clouds glow like radioactive candyfloss. 'Is that our landing zone?'

'Yes.'

'So we just fly in and land?'

'No, it's best to circle first. That way you can pick the spot.'

Hal was still following the squares, and he realised they were beginning to curve again. He throttled back and eased the ship around, following the indicators in a turn that got steadily tighter. The Volante was much lower now, and he could see the ground clearly through breaks in the cloud cover. Then he noticed something alarming: the red squares had disappeared. 'Hey, what happened to the guidance?'

'That's okay, Mr Spacejock. We're above the landing zone. Navcom, zoom in a little.'

The screen showed swirling clouds with the occasional patch of light, and Hal slowed the *Volante* even further. 'Where do I land?'

'Do your circuit first. The Navcom will map the area with radar and present a high-resolution image.'

Hal gripped the controls and scanned the screen, directing the ship in tight circles as the Navcom tagged obstacles with little labels.

'Scanning complete,' said the computer at last.

The screen showed dozens of buildings, depicted in ghostly green wireframe, and Hal realised the Backsight weapons 'factory' was actually a huge complex. 'Where are we landing?'

'Outside the perimeter fence,' said the Navcom, adding a red cross to the display. 'Your ideal approach is from the South-West.'

· The screen rotated and a large arrow appeared, pointing along the ground to a tiny square of dirt. In between were high voltage pylons, several parked ships and a ramshackle barn with a thatched roof.

'Are you sure about that approach?' asked Hal. 'It looks a bit crowded.'

'Trust me, that's your safest option. If we fly over the complex they'll shoot us down.'

Hal shrugged and turned the *Volante* away from the landing zone. After flying straight for a few minutes he turned sharply and dropped closer to the ground. They swooped across the countryside, rocketing low over trees, jinking between the hills and darting over the occasional house, and Hal began to enjoy himself as he tested his skills. It made a nice change from blasting through empty space.

'How's it going?' asked Clunk.

'Good,' said Hal, not taking his eyes off the screen. They were moving fast, and the margin for error was minimal. He winced as they shot between a couple of huge trees, then gasped as a stand of tall trees sprang out of the fog. Before he could react there was a CRASH-CRASH-CRASH from below, the *Volante* shuddering with every impact.

Hal frowned. There was plenty of clearance under the ship, so they couldn't possibly have hit anything. 'Is someone shooting at us?'

'No hits on the hull,' reported the Navcom. 'Damage report nil.'

The barn loomed in front of them, and Hal skimmed over the roof. CRASH!

This time the impact was louder. Hal and Clunk exchanged a puzzled glance, both mystified by the strange noises. 'Navcom, can you show a rear view?'

'Certainly.'

The barn appeared on screen. It was rapidly vanishing into the distance, but Hal could clearly see a big hole through the middle. It was almost as if someone had taken a huge bite out of it, and as he watched, the roof collapsed and the sides fell in on themselves. 'Weird,' remarked Hal. 'It's like someone took a shot at us and missed.'

Twang! Twang! Twang!

Hal saw power lines whipping and sparking in the Volante's wake, neatly cut through the middle. It was almost as though someone were chasing his ship with a sledgehammer ... or a wrecking ball.

'Maybe you should fly a little higher until we work out what's happening,' suggested Clunk.

Hal complied, but not before a dozen trees and another run of power lines fell to the mysterious force. A few minutes later they finally reached the landing field, where Hal managed to stop the ship in mid-air directly above the patch of dirt. By juggling the controls, adjusting the engines and praying a lot, he managed to bring the ship down in a bumpy but successful landing.

'Well done, Mr Spacejock. That wasn't too bad, all things considered.'

Hal puffed his chest out. Praise from Clunk was rare indeed, and he felt on top of the world. All they had to do now was deliver the artworks, get shot of Bright's Hairpiece, and ... Hal frowned. Hairpiece? Hadn't it been ...? 'Oh no,' he breathed, as realisation finally dawned. 'Clunk, that bloody rock was hanging under the ship!'

Clunk's mouth fell open.

'What do we look like?' said Hal bitterly. 'We just used Bright's artwork to play the biggest game of conkers in the history of the galaxy.'

— 27 —

Hal ran down the passenger ramp and peered under the ship. Fortunately, the huge rock was still in its sling. Unfortunately, it was jammed underneath the *Volante*, and the ship had pressed it down into the ground like a walnut embedded in a thickly-iced cake. Hal charged back up the ramp and fired up the *Volante*'s engines, lifting the ship straight off the ground and pulling the rock free of its brand new crater. Then he let the ship drift, dropping slowly towards the ground until the rock settled.

'Nicely done, Mr Spacejock.'

'We'd better check the rock.' Hal jogged down the ramp and ran to the back of the ship, sparing a brief glance for his surroundings. It was foggy and chilly, and he could just make out the looming shapes of parked ships against the dull grey sky. There were lights in the distance, but he wasn't going near those until the cargo was sorted.

The sling was in poor shape, with some straps cut through or missing and others crammed with branches and roof tiles. The rock was still in one piece, but there were deep scars and scratches from tearing down powerlines and demolishing the old barn.

Hal was still wondering what to do when Clunk arrived with a bucket full of soapy water. The robot took out a scrubbing brush and started work on the rock, sending grit and suds flying. When he was done, Hal gave him a hand to remove the sling. As they worked together, he became aware of something.

'Hang on. I thought you were having problems with your eyes?'

'Ah, that.' Clunk shrugged. 'Strangely enough, they seem to have come right.'

Hal frowned. 'Just like that?'

'Yes, it must have been a temporary fault.'

'If you say so.' Hal looked at the robot in concern. 'Get them checked out as soon as possible, okay?'

Clunk looked embarrassed. 'Er, yes. As soon as possible.' He left to stow the cargo sling, while Hal went to tell Meri and Harriet about their successful landing.

◆

Hal stood in the lift, one finger poised over the control panel as he tried to work out the best way to get his passengers off the ship. If Harriet left first, she might see Meri coming down the ramp, which was the last thing he wanted. No, better to get Meri away first, so she could pretend she'd arrived before the *Volante*.

Decision made, Hal pressed the lowest button. The doors opened a few second later, and he entered the lounge. 'Are you ready to leave, M–'

Hal froze, Meri's name still on his lips. Sitting on the sofa, with a mug of steaming coffee by her side, was Harriet Walsh.

'Good morning,' she said. 'Do you want something to drink?'

'Er, no, I'm fine.' Hal glanced around furtively, trying to work out where Meri was hiding. The AutoChef was standing inside its plastic safety fence: nowhere to hide there. The gym equipment wouldn't hide a cat, let alone a full-grown human, and he couldn't see any feet poking out from under the big viewscreen. The drinks trolley was a possibility, but when he lifted the tablecloth to peer underneath he discovered the shelf was empty. He moved behind the bar, pretending to inspect the glasses hanging from the wooden rail, and did a quick check of the cupboards. No Meri to be found.

'Lost something?' asked Harriet.

'No, just tidying up.' Was it his imagination, or did she already know about his secret passenger? Hal decided to change the subject. 'Did I, er, hear you leaving your cabin in the night?'

Walsh looked over the rim of her mug. 'I don't know what you're talking about,' she said evenly.

'I had this really vivid dream. You came to my cabin, and we –'

'Yes, I can imagine the sort of thing.' Walsh studied her coffee, turning the mug side to side in her hands. 'And no, I didn't leave my cabin.'

'Are you sure?'

'Would I lie to you?' Walsh glanced at him. 'By the way, I have new orders from Inspector Boson. I'm going to need your help with something.'

Faced with the chance of real Peace Force work, Hal forgot about Meri. 'Of course. What do you need?'

'Overalls, an old flight suit … you know, a disguise.'

'Why?'

'I have to sneak into the weapons factory.'

Hal stared at her. 'You're mad! Do you know what the security will be like?'

'I have my orders, Hal. There's some data I have to get my hands on, and it's really important.'

'Can't you get a search warrant? Do things properly?'

'Of course not. Whenever we go through official channels, someone warns the Backsight people beforehand. By the time we get there, everything's sanitised.'

'But –'

'Hal, Inspector Boson has been after these people for thirty years. If I gather evidence, help to nail them, he'll be in my corner forever. You don't know what that would mean for my career.'

'Yeah, if you're still alive.'

Harriet stood up, setting her coffee mug aside, and at that moment Hal remembered he still had no idea where Meri was. 'Listen, why don't you put your feet up for a bit?'

'No, I have to prepare for my mission.'

'Wait here and I'll bring you that flight suit. Okay?'

Walsh hesitated. 'I guess I could use another coffee,' she said at last.

'Good. I'll be right back.' Hal strode to the lift, peering over the armchairs in case Meri was crouching behind them. She wasn't.

As the doors closed he bit his lip. Where the hell had she got to?

◆

Clunk was sitting in the flight deck with a satisfied expression on his face. 'I think Mr Spacejock did quite well under the circumstances,' he said, as he adjusted something on the console.

The Navcom snorted. 'It was a terrible idea. Risky, unnecessary and foolish.'

'He's got to learn how to fly one day,' said Clunk mildly. 'Faking a vision problem created the ideal test situation.'

'He might have crashed the ship!'

'Nonsense. I was ready to take over at a moment's notice.'

'What about the mountain? Was that part of your plan?'

Clunk pursed his lips.

'And the barn. Was that an ideal test situation?'

'It was only a derelict structure. No harm done, and it proved a useful safety lesson.'

'It certainly did: humans shouldn't fly space ships.'

—◆—

The doors opened on the second deck, and Hal peered into the toilet cubicle before jogging along the corridor. He looked into the old rec room, now converted into a spacious cabin, but it was empty. He checked his own room, but the rumpled bed and pile of clothes didn't look any more disturbed than usual. The shower door was open, and clearly empty.

Worried now, Hal ran along the corridor to the hold. The inner door was open, and he stuck his head through for a quick recce. No, apart from the artworks the hold was empty too.

Hal frowned. Where had Meri got to? She couldn't get to the flight deck, so that only left …uh-oh. He ran along the corridor, skidding to a halt in front of Harriet's door. Faintly, he could hear running water, and when he put his ear to the door he heard a woman's voice. Meri was singing in the shower, right there in Harriet's cabin!

Hal was about to knock, then had a better idea. He looked up, seeking the familiar speaker grille in the ceiling. 'Navcom, can you hear me?'

'Yes, Mr Spacejock.'

'Could you turn off the hot water, please?'

'Are you sure? It's currently in use.'

'I'm certain. Cut it.'

A split second later Meri's happy singing stopped with a shriek of surprise. There was a string of curses, and when they dried up Hal knocked gently on the door. 'It's me,' he whispered.

He heard the pad of footsteps, and the door opened. Meri was just wrapping herself in a towel, and behind her Hal could see her clothes laid out on the bunk. 'What the hell happened?' she demanded, her teeth chattering with the cold.

'Sorry about that. It was a system fault.'

'Can you fix it?'

'Not right now. Come on, you've got to get out of there.'

'Why?'

'We've landed.'

'So?' Meri gestured at the bed. 'And why didn't you tell me there was a cabin up here? I could have slept in a proper bed.'

Hal glanced towards the lift. If Harriet came up now ... 'Never mind the spare bed. Come on!'

'But –'

'This area is off limits. It's being ... fumigated.' Hal pushed past and rolled her clothes up in a spare towel. Then he poked his head into the corridor, checked it was clear and hustled Meri across the way to his own cabin. 'Stay in there, and don't come out until I say so. Understood?'

Hal grabbed the blankets off his bed and charged back to Harriet's cabin, where he did his best to mop the shower dry. When he was done he straightened the bed, and he'd just snatched a stray stocking off the floor when the cabin door opened to admit Harriet Walsh.

'I can explain!' said Hal quickly, whipping the stocking behind his back while trying to bundle up the wet blankets with his free hand.

'Laundry day, is it?'

'Something like that. Excuse me, coming through.'

Harriet stood aside, and as Hal left he saw her eyeing the shower cubicle. Then the door closed, and Hal leant against the wall, breathing deeply to calm his nerves. He was just getting his breath back when Meri looked out of his cabin. 'Shhh!' hissed Hal frantically. He tried to put a finger to his lips, forgetting he was holding her stocking, and Meri raised her eyebrows as he jammed it in his face. Hal took the corridor in two steps, bundling Meri into his cabin. 'I said to stay inside,' he hissed.

'Why, is someone else on board?'

'Yes. I mean no. I mean –' Hal dumped the wet blankets on his bunk and pressed the stocking into Meri's hands. 'Just stay in here, all right? Don't open the door, don't wander around the ship and don't take any showers.'

'Can I get dressed?'

'Sure.'

'I'll need my suitcase.'

'Where is it?'

'I left it in the other cabin, right under the bed.'

◆

Harriet opened her door to find Hal Spacejock standing outside. He looked jumpy, and if she didn't know better she'd say he was trying to hide something. 'Another laundry run?'

Hal pulled a face. 'I left some old clothes under your bed. Can I …?'

'The old flight suit, you mean? I'll get it out if you like.'

'No, let me. The case is very heavy.'

Walsh stood back to let him in, and watched as he got down on hands and knees to look under the bed. He reached underneath, and with a hefty pull he dragged a suitcase into the middle of the floor. It gleamed under the downlights, and there was a brand new tag attached to the handle. Hal stood the case up, and before he could stop her Walsh inspected the tag. 'Meredith Ryder?'

Hal looked uncomfortable. 'Yeah, it's just some stuff.'

'Stuff? What sort of stuff?'

'Clothes. You know.'

Harriet frowned. Ryder? Where had she heard that name before? It was – yes, she was the woman from the expo. The smart-looking one with the rimless glasses and the expensive jumper. The one she'd seen snogging Hal behind the curtains, wrapping him up like a fluffy pink octopus. But what was her suitcase doing aboard Hal's ship? Then it dawned on her. 'Hal, you didn't!'

'D-didn't what?' For some reason, Hal was staring at her gun. 'No! I didn't. I definitely didn't.'

'Don't deny it! The suitcase is right here on the floor. Don't you know how risky it is to carry someone else's luggage?'

Hal stared at her for a second, and then his face cleared. 'Oh, I know. You're absolutely right. It's just it was heavy, and she was at the spaceport, and I said here, I'll carry that for you, and then she got in a cab and I forgot and here it is.'

Harriet hesitated, looking down at the case. Her mission was to hunt down smugglers, and this suitcase might contain the very evidence she was looking for. On the other hand, if she opened the case and found a load of uncut diamonds, Hal would be implicated, and most likely jailed. For a second or two she was torn, unable to choose between her duty as a Peace Force officer and her genuine affection for the foolish, gullible, thick-headed pilot. 'Get that thing out of my sight,' she said, as affection won out. 'Do you understand? I never saw it.'

Relief flooded Hal's face, and he grabbed the suitcase and practically ran for the door. As it opened, he turned to look back, gratitude in every line of his expression. 'Thanks.'

'Sure thing. And Hal?'

'Yes?'

'Did you *have* to hide it under my bunk?'

◆

As he left Harriet's cabin, Hal almost bumped into Clunk.

'Ah, Mr Spacejock, there you are.' Clunk looked down. 'What are you doing with that suitcase?'

'I can't talk now!' said Hal quickly. He nodded towards Harriet's door, then towards his own.

'Ah yes, your little juggling act. Have our two guests encountered each other yet?'

'It's not funny.'

'Not from your perspective, but I'm enjoying it immensely.' Clunk inspected the tag. 'What did Ms Walsh say to this?'

'She thinks I'm a smuggler.'

'Impossible.'

'Why? Do you think I'm too honest?'

'No, I think you'd have been caught years ago.' Clunk released the tag and straightened up. 'So, I take it Ms Walsh is in her cabin. Where's Ms Ryder hiding?'

Hal gestured at a door further along the corridor.

'Ah yes, excellent thinking. If you want to allay Ms Walsh's suspicions, hiding the other woman in your own bed is the obvious choice.'

'Thanks,' said Hal. 'I thought it was good, too.'

'I just wish my camera was working,' said Clunk sadly.

'Why? So you can save these precious memories?'

'No, so I could record the outcome and upload it to Oh Dear, Humanity.'

'They'll be no uploading of anything while I'm around. Now go and unload the bloody artworks.' Hal dragged the suitcase into his cabin, where he found Meri using the towel to dry her hair. He grabbed his spare flightsuit, then pushed the suitcase towards Meri. 'Here's your stuff. Get dressed, and don't come out until I open the door.'

Hal dashed down the corridor to give Harriet the flightsuit, then returned to guard his cabin. Mentally, he imagined both women getting dressed, and a small part of him wondered which would be finished first. The major part of him just imagined both of them getting dressed.

Five minutes later the door opened behind him, and Meri looked out. She was wearing a dark blue skirt with a white blouse, and her damp hair was pulled back in a bun. Hal glanced up and down the corridor, then grabbed the suitcase and herded Meri towards the hold. She'd just passed through the inner door when Harriet looked out of her cabin, dressed in Hal's spare flightsuit. Hal pulled the cargo door to just in time, standing with his back to it. 'Are you ready for your mission?'

'All set.' Harriet closed her door and walked towards him.

'You should go through the flight deck,' said Hal quickly. 'Clunk's busy unloading, and he hates getting disturbed.'

Harriet shrugged and turned for the lift. The doors were open, and as she stepped inside she realised Hal was still leaning against the cargo hold door. 'Aren't you coming?'

'I'm helping Clunk. I'll, er, meet you outside.'

The lift doors closed on Harriet, and Hal darted into the cargo hold. He found Meri eyeing Bright's artworks in concern. 'Don't you wrap them?' she asked. 'Some of these pieces are really fragile.'

'Never mind that, we've got to run.' Hal took her arm and hurried her towards the rear of the hold.

Clunk was outside, loading the smaller artworks onto a sled. Hal beckoned to the robot, and he waited impatiently while Clunk grounded the sled and made his way up the ramp.

'What is it, Mr Spacejock?'

'Go round to the passenger ramp and, er, stop anyone leaving the ship.'

'You mean Ms –'

'I don't mean anyone in particular,' said Hal, with a meaningful look. 'Just …you know. I you happen to see anyone, keep her …or him …talking for a bit.'

Clunk glanced at Meri. 'Very well. I'll do my best.'

He left, and a few moments later Hal sidled out of the hold. He glanced along the hull towards the front of the ship, peering though the fog at the top of the passenger ramp. Good old Clunk! He was standing on the platform outside the flight deck's airlock, discussing a nearby building with Harriet. From the sound of it, he was enthusing about the building's qualities as though he'd built the thing himself.

With Harriet safely distracted, Hal beckoned to Meri, and he led her down the cargo ramp to the ground. Through the swirling fog Hal could see an impressive fence, complete with a guard hut and boom gate. Alongside was a large sign, and Hal frowned at the ominous wording:

Backsight Weapons Facility. Maximum Security! Trespassers will be shot.

Beyond the fence, Hal could just make out a collection of low-lying buildings. They looked like squat concrete bunkers in the thick fog, and he shook his head at the sight. 'Nice place for an art show.'

'Oh, they're not holding the exhibition in the weapons factory.'

'They're not?'

'No, the venue's outside the grounds. I'm to organise a truck for the artworks.'

Hal stared at her as the truth dawned on him. Harriet was hoping to accompany him inside the weapons factory, but if the show was being held elsewhere her chances of infiltrating the facility was close to zero. 'But, er …'

'You unload the artworks and I'll tell them to bring the truck. Okay?' Meri took the suitcase and strode towards the gate, the wheels rattling and bumping on the concrete. Before long she was showing her ID to the guards, who checked everything thoroughly, and Hal watched the exchange in growing concern. If Harriet thought his old flightsuit was going to get her inside, she was sadly mistaken.

— 28 —

Hal hurried up the passenger ramp, where Clunk was still enthusing about the local architecture. The robot's bulk was blocking the passenger ramp, and Harriet's patience had all but run out.

'Hal, will you please tell Clunk to let me past?'

'Not until you hear about the exhibition.'

Harriet's eyes narrowed. 'You're not going to describe the building's innovative design, are you? Clunk's already –'

'No, not at all.' Hal gestured towards the weapons complex. 'I just found out they're not holding the show in there. It's somewhere else.'

'Crap.' Harriet eyed the guard post. 'I'll have to find another way in.'

'Are you kidding? The sign says they shoot trespassers on sight.'

'I have to try, Hal.' Harriet gestured towards the fence. 'Maybe there's a fallen tree or a hole or something.'

'Why not wait until dark? The art exhibition will distract everyone, and you'll have a much better chance of getting inside the compound. I could come with you, maybe lend a hand.'

'We'll talk about that later. For now, I'm just going to walk the perimeter.'

Hal took her by the shoulders. 'Promise me you won't do anything stupid.'

'Of course not. Now please get Clunk out of my way.'

Hal nodded to Clunk, who stepped aside, and then they both watched her leave. After she vanished into the fog, Hal turned to the robot. 'All right, let's get the rest of Bright's junk out of my cargo hold.'

◆

Harriet made her way around the perimeter of the weapons factory, using trees and undergrowth for cover. At first she was ultra cautious, crawling from one hiding place to the next on hands and knees, but after a while she realised there weren't any patrols, and even if there were she'd look a lot less suspicious if she were just walking normally.

She was halfway round when she realised there might be a good reason for the lack of patrols: what if the fields outside the perimeter fence were strewn with land mines? She held her breath at the alarming thought, then let it out with a laugh. If there were landmines, she'd have stepped on one by now.

The undergrowth was thicker at the rear of the facility, and the trees and bushes were closer to the fence. It obviously hadn't been cleared for years, and as Harriet pushed her way through the bushes she kept an eye out for overhanging branches and fallen trees. She also kept an eye on the compound, inspecting the squat buildings through the chain link fence. Every now and then she saw scientists and workers moving from one building to another, the former in lab coats and the latter in orange overalls. Unfortunately, she wouldn't pass for either in Hal's old flightsuit, and in any case there'd be ID cards and scanners and any number of security checkpoints.

Harriet fought her way through a particularly dense patch of undergrowth, and then she saw something which brought a smile to her face. It was a fallen tree, a big one, and the roots had levered the bottom of the fence into the air. There was a narrow gap underneath, and Harriet eyed it thoughtfully.

The earth around the tree roots was fresh, and she guessed it had only fallen over in the past day or so. What if she came back later, only to discover they'd repaired the fence? Wouldn't it be better to seize the moment?

Harriet glanced towards the buildings, undecided. She'd told Hal she was just going to walk the fence, but he wasn't her commanding officer. What would Inspector Boson expect her to do? The answer was clear: Boson would expect her to complete the mission, whatever the risk.

Decision made, Harriet wriggled through the gap in the fence. On the other side, she brushed dirt and leaves from the flightsuit, crouching low as she watched a couple of scientists in the distance. Then, as soon as the coast was clear, she stood up and strode towards the nearest building.

The sign on the door read 'Stores', and Harriet paused with her fingers on the handle. Security would be light here, but on the other hand there might not be a computer terminal she could access. Then she heard voices nearby, and she opened the door and stepped inside before she was challenged.

The building was indeed a storeroom, filled with rows of shelving. Harriet darted along the rows, heading towards the rear, and she smiled to herself as she spotted a desk with a terminal sitting on top. She was just reaching in her pocket for the decrypter when she heard the door opening behind her. Someone was coming in!

◆

It took Hal and Clunk half an hour to unload the artworks, and they'd barely finished tying them to the anti-grav sled when a smart, white-painted van drew up. The driver was wearing 'Backsight Industries' overalls, and alongside him was Meri Ryder. She was carrying a clipboard, and she looked prim and professional.

'Good morning Mr Spacejock.'

'Hi. How's it going?'

'Not good, I'm afraid. In fact, I have some bad news.'

Hal's heart sank at her serious expression. Had someone spotted Harriet ... maybe caught her snooping around? 'What's the problem?'

'It's the exhibition ... I just heard they're going to cancel it.'

'Oh, is that all?' said Hal, with a sigh of relief.

Meri frowned. 'A lot of people are going to be disappointed, even if you don't care.'

'I'm sorry, it's just ...' Hal realised he could hardly tell her he was worried about Harriet. 'So what happened? Why's the show off?'

'They were going to use this wonderful old barn for the exhibition, but it fell over this morning.'

Hal stared at her. The derelict barn ... the same barn he'd knocked down with Bright's Hairpiece? 'Was ... was anyone hurt?' he asked, dreading the answer.

'No, luckily it happened when nobody was around.'

'Lucky indeed,' said Clunk.

Hal frowned at him. 'You heard her, Clunk. It just fell over. Nobody can take the blame for that.'

'They're saying it might have been a meteorite,' said Meri. 'Either way, the venue has been flattened and it's too late to organise another.'

'What's next, then?'

'Load the artworks again, and I'll give you the final destination. You'd better hurry, because we'll be leaving right away.'

Hal remembered Harriet Walsh. Lift off now, and she'd be stranded! 'Er ... we, um, probably shouldn't leave too soon.'

'Why not?'

'We, er –' Unable to think of an excuse, Hal turned to Clunk. 'You'd better tell her.'

Clunk looked startled, but he recovered quickly. He eyed the cargo, looked up at the ship, then made a throat-clearing sound. 'Might I be permitted to make a suggestion?'

For one horrible moment, Hal thought he was going to suggest paying for the damage to the barn, and he was just working out whether he could reach Clunk's power switch in time when the robot spoke again.

'If you're only displaying Bright's pieces, I believe the *Volante* would make an excellent venue.'

Meri's eyebrows shot up. 'You want to hold a prestigious art exhibition inside a ... a cargo vessel?'

'Why not? The hold is spacious and well-lit. Hang some drapes and banners, lay some carpet, and you have to admit it would make for a unique show.'

Meri looked thoughtful. 'That's not as crazy as it sounds. In fact, it might just work.' She hesitated, then gave Clunk a grateful smile. 'All right. I'll take it to Olivia now.'

'Tell her it won't cost much,' said Hal quickly. 'Three or four grand will cover it.'

'How about a cut of the takings instead? Ten percent, say?'

'Done.'

Meri left to present the idea to Olivia Backsight, and Hal rubbed his hands together as the van drove off. 'That was smart thinking, Clunk. Well done.'

'You're welcome, Mr Spacejock. Although personally, I'd have negotiated a fixed payment. Getting artistic types to pay out on a percentage is like getting rocket fuel out of an orange.'

Harriet stood with her back to a rack of shelves, her breathing shallow and her heart thumping in her chest. Several people had entered the building, and she could hear them sharing office gossip as they picked items from the stores. For a while she thought they'd leave without spotting her, but then she heard one of them getting closer and closer. With her heart in her mouth, Harriet grabbed a box from the shelf and strode purposefully towards the exit.

As she left, she came face to face with a young woman in a lab coat. The young woman glanced at her, and Walsh gave her a confident smile as she walked by.

Once outside, Harriet tucked the box under her arm and walked towards the next building, trying to look as though she belonged. She passed a couple of people on the way, but they didn't give her a second glance.

The sign on the building read 'Assembly', and inside were rows of conveyor belts tended by dozens of workers in overalls and hair nets. The slow-moving belts carried a variety of half-built equipment past the workers, who fitted components from trays in front of them. There were also half a dozen robots handling quality control, grabbing parts from the belt and inspecting them closely before replacing them. Occasionally they'd reject a component, dropping the offending part into a disposal chute.

There was a row of offices across the far end of the room, separated from the assembly area by glass partitions. Inside, Harriet could see people sitting at their desks, working on terminals. One of them was looking at her, frowning, and when he stood up Harriet realised it was time to leave. She looked down at the box in her hands, pretending to study the label, then shook her head theatrically as though she'd fetched the wrong item. As she closed the door behind her, she saw the nosey office worker returning to his terminal.

Outside, Harriet decided to try the stores building again. If anyone was inside, she could use the box of parts as an excuse. If the place was empty … well, that terminal was just waiting to be used.

She entered the building and carried the carton of spares straight up to the terminal, setting it on the desk as though she knew exactly what she was doing. Then she reached into her pocket for the decrypter … only to discover it wasn't there.

Frowning, she checked the other pocket, and then she cursed under her breath as she realised it was missing. Had the damn thing slipped out when she crawled under the fence? Or worse, had she forgotten to transfer the device from her uniform?

Disgusted at her lack of professionalism, Harriet realised there was nothing else for it. She'd have to check around the fence first, and if the decrypter wasn't there she'd have to go all the way back to the *Volante*.

◆

Hal glanced at his watch. 'Do you think Harriet's getting on okay?'

'I've not heard any gunfire,' said Clunk.

'That's not very comforting.'

'On the contrary, I find it very reassuring.'

'What if they caught her? What if she's being interrogated?'

'What if they didn't? What if she's not?'

Hal pursed his lips. Arguing was pointless when Clunk was in this kind of mood, so he decided to drop it. Harriet was resourceful and smart, and he was sure she'd be fine. 'Listen, I need you to put some signs together.'

'What sort of signs?'

'Advertising, mostly. Can you do that?'

'Certainly. There's that cardboard we used to pack the artworks, and by a stroke of luck there's a tin of silver paint in the hold.'

Hal frowned. 'Not my special magnetic paint?'

'I assure you, the only thing special about that paint was the exorbitant price.'

'Oh, all right. Make the signs big and bright, though. I want them to stand out.'

'I can have them ready in thirty minutes.'

'Good.' Hal passed him a folded sheet of paper. 'Here's the wording. I'll be back in a couple of hours.'

Clunk's eyes narrowed. 'You're not going after Ms Walsh, are you?'

671

'No, I'm going shopping,' said Hal, without elaborating.

◆

Hal's cab was waiting at the foot of the passenger ramp. The driver was a middle-aged man with a moustache, and he spared Hal the briefest of glances as the door closed. 'Where to, sir?'

'I need a printer.'

'There's a computer shop in town.'

'No, the other kind. T-shirts, that sort of thing.'

'I know just the place,' said the driver.

'Are they cheap?' asked Hal.

'Sure, he's the cheapest I know.' The driver planted his foot, and the car hurtled onto the main road. 'The stuff's junk, of course, but people don't expect quality these days.'

Hal watched the scenery fly past, lost in thought. He had a nagging feeling he should have gone with Harriet, but she'd told him not to and he could hardly have tailed her. Anyway, he had an exhibition to prepare for.

After twenty minutes the cab drew up outside a row of factory units. The air rang with the crash and thump of machinery, and traces of hot oil, ink and paint all mingled to create a heady smell. Hal glanced up at the signs above each unit: *Hump Tees*, *Lowe's Chapeaux* and *Fred's Screen Printing Emporium*. The doors to the latter stood open, and an elderly man was relaxing on the steps. He was dressed in tatty overalls and a bright blue cap, and his ink-stained fingers held a spluttering pipe.

'Are you Fred?' asked Hal.

'S'me. Help you?'

'I need some merchandise in a hurry. Caps and T-shirts, with a bit of printing on.'

Fred knocked his pipe out and stood up, grinding the foul-smelling embers under the heel of his battered work boot. 'You'd better come inside.'

After Hal left, Clunk got busy with the signs. The sheet of paper contained several lines of text, but the handwriting was atrocious and it was hard to make out the lettering. Clunk wasn't sure whether Mr Spacejock wanted a precise copy of the wording, spelling mistakes included, or a proofed version with the mistakes edited out. In the end he decided it was safer to copy the wording verbatim, errors and all. If Mr Spacejock complained, Clunk would just claim he was following orders to the letter.

Clunk worked on the signs with ten percent of his brain assigned to lettering, five percent ensuring he coloured within the lines, and eighty-five percent worrying about Max Bright's Hairpiece. The valuable artwork would be on show later that same day, and there was still a slim chance someone would discover the rock was a substitute. On the plus side, they'd already passed the replacement off once, on Pegzwil, and it wasn't as though Max Bright himself was going to be there to inspect his own artwork.

Clunk had just finished a particularly impressive rendering of the word 'Cheep' when he heard footsteps coming up the ramp. He glanced round and saw Harriet Walsh, her face flushed and angry. 'Hello, Ms Walsh. Is everything okay?'

'Don't ask,' snapped Harriet, as she swept past.

'Very well,' said Clunk mildly, returning to his painting.

Harriet slammed the inner door on the way through, and Clunk tutted under his breath. He could never understand why humans took out their anger on inanimate objects. Then again, he supposed it was better than humans taking out their anger on animated objects ... such as robots.

It only took him a minute to finish the sign, and Clunk stowed the brushes before making his way to the flight deck. 'Navcom, how long until the exhibition?'

'Two hours. Incidentally, I hear Max Bright himself is going to open the show.'

'What? No!' Clunk stared at the console in shock. 'Now what am I going to do?'

'Would you like me to display all possible options?'

Clunk felt a rush of relief. Trust the Navcom to come up with a range of answers! 'That would be a real help. Can you put the list on main?'

'Complying.'

The screen flickered, and several lines of text appeared:

You're about to be blamed for a major disaster. Do you ...

A. Blame Mr Spacejock

B. Blame Mr Spacejock

C. Blame Mr Spacejock

As Clunk studied the options, he realised Mr Spacejock was not going to come out of this well. Fortunately, the human had a knack for losing cargo, and adding this new mishap to the long list of past failures could hardly make his reputation any worse. 'I believe I'll go with option A.'

'I think that's a wise choice,' said the Navcom calmly.

◆

Back in her cabin, Harriet felt in her uniform pocket for the decrypter, and she sighed with relief as her fingers closed on the shiny black device. For the past twenty minutes she'd been imagining tense conversations with Inspector Boson, and none of them had ended well. Now, at least, she had a chance of salvaging the mission.

As she entered the hold she glanced around for Clunk, hoping to apologise for her earlier bad temper. The robot was nowhere to be seen, though, and as Harriet left the ship she resolved to make things up to him the moment she got back.

But first, she had a mission to complete.

Hal smiled with satisfaction as the cab drew up near the *Volante*. His little shopping trip had been a great success, and his freshly-minted merchandise was sure to turn a pretty little profit. He patted the carton on his lap, grinned at the half dozen boxes crammed into the back seat, and smiled as he thought of the rest jammed into the trunk and tied on the roof. The driver had made a bit of a fuss, especially when Hal sticky-taped several large boxes to the hood, but a few extra credits had soon brought him round.

It took ten minutes to unload the car, and Hal was still dealing with the sticky tape when he saw Clunk peering out of the *Volante*'s hold. 'Hey, Clunk. Is Harriet back yet?'

'Yes, Mr Spacejock.'

Hal felt a rush of relief. He'd been worried about her for a couple of hours now, and he was pleased she was safe. 'That's great news.'

'She wasn't very happy, though. I don't think her mission was a success.'

Hal shrugged. Who cared about missions as long as Harriet was okay? Then he turned his attention to the boxes. 'Give us a hand, will you?'

'Yes, I meant to ask you about those.' Clunk approached the large stack of cartons, eyeing them apprehensively. 'When you said shopping, I thought you meant a few snacks or a new pair of boots.'

'You couldn't be more wrong.' With a flourish, Hal opened the nearest carton. 'Here, feast your peepers on this,' he said proudly.

Clunk craned his neck, and an incredulous expression crossed his face as he looked inside. 'Oh dear, Mr Spacejock. Is that wise?'

Far from being safely aboard the *Volante*, Harriet Walsh was lying face-down in a patch of muddy ground, watching the weapons factory through the hole in the fence. She'd been poised to crawl through several times, only to abandon each attempt as yet another worker appeared at just the wrong moment. It was busier than earlier, and it dawned on her that she could be waiting a very long time.

Now and then she glanced at the sky, trying to estimate how long before night fell. Darkness was probably her best chance, although given the number of floodlights dotted around there was always the possibility it would be brighter at night. Still, perhaps she could find a fuse box, or throw rocks at the lights, or ... hell, there had to be some way in!

◆

Half an hour before the grand opening, a small crowd gathered at the entrance to the landing field. Hal peered through the curtains Clunk had erected across the *Volante*'s cargo hold, rubbing his hands together as he did a quick head count. With that many guests he was set to make more money in a single night than he usually scraped together in a whole year. Hauling cargo was a mug's game, he told himself. This was the real deal.

During the afternoon Hal had been incredibly busy. While Clunk and Meri had been cleaning the cargo hold, hanging drapes, laying carpet, and generally getting everything ready for the show, Hal had put in a lot of hard work deciding on a name for his new business. After much deliberation he'd come up with *Spacejock Professional Artist Management*, and the only snag had come when he tried to promote S.P.A.M. on a bunch of mailing lists ... for some reason, all his messages bounced. He tried once more, this time advising artists that their businesses would grow much larger under his hand, but shortly afterwards his data connection was severed for good.

In the end he realised the job was like most others aboard the *Volante*: something best left to Clunk.

676

At five to six, the crowd began to murmur. At six o'clock they were on tip-toes, peering over each others heads in anticipation. By three minutes past they were muttering and shifting impatiently. Then, at precisely five past, a limousine drew up behind the crowd. Cameras flashed, and two liveried footmen emerged from the car with a big roll of red carpet. They divided the crowd and unrolled the carpet all the way across the field to the curtain, where they pinned the loose end down with a couple of pegs. Then they returned to the limo and stood to attention either side of the rear door.

Maximilous Bright was ready to make his entrance.

◆

Bright stepped out of the limo, resplendent in a mauve jacket and matching velvet pants, his floppy cap tilted rakishly and a silver-tipped cane swinging casually from his hand. He made his way through the crowd, doffing his hat and waving and pointing at various friends and acquaintances.

Bright left the crowd behind and continued along the red carpet to the curtains, where he took a moment to compose himself before turning to face his admirers. There was a loud cheer as he raised his cane, but the crowd was quickly stilled as he motioned them to silence.

'Friends, enthusiasts, collectors. Tonight you will experience the beauty and classic timelessness of my greatest works. Not only have I brought Semi Colon, Fish in a Jar and Cow in a Field for your enjoyment, but you will also be able to inspect my Hairpiece!'

There was a murmur of excitement from the crowd.

'Yes, it's true.' Bright cleared his throat. 'Now, I realise this venue is a little unconventional, but show me a conventional artist and I'll show *you* a pedestrian sign-writer!'

There was a smattering of applause.

'Now, ladies and gentlemen, the moment arrives.' Behind his back, Bright signalled to Hal. 'Behold!'

Hal pulled the cord, drawing the curtains aside. The crowd gasped, and Bright bowed deeply, struggling to keep a smug self-important grin from his face. Straightening, he turned to gaze upon the scene in pride.

The rear of the *Volante* was open, and Bright's artworks gleamed under the downlights. Fish in a Jar had been shined to a lustre, and the Cow's glass eyes shone from all the careful polishing. Hairpiece was arranged to perfection, the twin hairs like threads of fine gold under the soft lighting. Bright nodded in satisfaction. Spacejock had done a fine job despite the last minute panic. Everything was perfect.

A movement caught his eye, and he lowered his gaze to the foot of the ramp. The first thing he saw was a pair of makeshift kiosks assembled from packing crates and cardboard. Arranged alongside, hand-painted signs proclaimed that the 'Spacejock Special' was not to be missed, that visitors could 'Tour the Volanti' for ten credits, and that 'Souviniers' were going 'cheep'.

Behind the first kiosk stood a battered robot decked out in a sky-hockey cap and matching T-shirt. Emblazoned across the front was the slogan 'I came aboard the *Volantay*', and the robot's arms were overflowing with bundles of T-shirts and stacks of caps. There was even more headgear on the kiosk's narrow counter, and another large carton stood alongside.

The second kiosk was even worse. A cloud of smoke rose from rows of sausages frying on a portable barbecue, and behind it stood Hal Spacejock in a chef's cap and apron. He was chopping onions with a large knife, with tears streaming down his face.

Bright's silver-tipped cane slipped from his fingers, and the brim of his floppy hat drooped over one eye. The other eye grew rounder and rounder, and the small portion of face not covered by hair turned alternately red and white.

Bright jumped as he felt a hand on his shoulder, and he looked up to see Spacejock offering him a greasy hotdog. 'Have one on the house,' said Hal, pressing the lukewarm bun into Bright's nerveless fingers. 'I think the sausage is cooked, but the onions are a bit crunchy.'

Bright looked down at the offending article, which seemed to be receding at high speed.

'Here, are you okay?' asked Hal in concern.

The words echoed in Bright's ears, and then his legs gave way. The last thing he saw was a patch of red carpet coming up to meet him.

678

Bright was treated by one of the footmen, who fanned him with the floppy hat and administered brandy from a silver flask. The other footman conveyed the artist's wishes to Hal using short sentences and a lot of choice language, and by the time Bright recovered enough to sit up Hal's makeshift kiosks had vanished.

Still in a daze, Bright staggered to his feet. 'The exhibition must go on,' he cried, to renewed applause from the waiting crowd. The whole episode had taken no more than five minutes of their time, and a number of bored and unwilling partners had brightened considerably at the highly entertaining antics. Oh, they were careful to tut and shake their heads sadly under the beady eyes of art-loving wives and husbands, but secretly they hoped for more.

As it happened, they were not to be disappointed.

At first, all went well. Groups of visitors strolled up the *Volante*'s cargo ramp, taking a glass of wine before moving amongst the exhibits in respectful silence. The hushed atmosphere was broken only occasionally by the hum of the ship's generator, the gurgle of its plumbing and the solid, regular thump as Hal kicked a nearby landing leg with his size ten space boots.

'I wish it was that bastard's head,' he muttered, administering another kick.

'If you'd only cleared things with him first, none of this would have happened.'

'What do artists know about commerce? They hang around drafty studios slapping paint around.'

'That sounds very much like my recent sign-writing experience.'

Hal jerked his thumb at the *Volante*'s hold. 'Have you any idea how much money that lot's carrying around? And who wouldn't want a reminder of their visit to my ship?'

'I don't think Bright will forget.'

'It's not fair,' said Hal sourly. 'He's restricting my right to an honest income.'

'It's his show.'

'Oh, you can't call it a show. He doesn't like that either.' Hal kicked the upright again. 'Bloody artists. They're all the same.'

Clunk started to reply, then looked up at the hold. The background murmur had become louder, and people were hurrying into the ship. Bright appeared overhead, and was taken aside by one of the footmen.

'Sir, several of your guests are attracted to Hairpiece.'

'Of course they are. It's the centrepiece, the *ne plus ultra* of the exhibition.'

'No, I mean they're really attracted to it. We can't pull them off.'

Hal and Clunk exchanged a worried glance.

'What are you on about?' demanded Bright.

'Well, this gentleman bent for a closer look and the rock sort of drew him in. When his partner tried to help, she found herself in similar difficulties. Then a second couple went to their assistance, followed by a third and a fourth. I'm afraid the scene now resembles the classic piece by Hugh Orgie. I'm sure you've heard of it, sir: *A night in close friends.*'

Bright raised his hand, silencing the footman. 'I will sort this out myself. Keep everyone else out of the blasted ship.'

Hal turned to Clunk. 'What do you think's going on?'

'I have absolutely no idea,' said the robot, in a most unconvincing tone.

◆

Harriet Walsh spent almost two hours waiting at the fence, and as the time dragged on she began to wonder about her approach to the mission. Peace Force officers generally charged in with guns blazing, interrogated the survivors - if any - and then wrote a completely different version of events for the official reports. It was no surprise that many officers found great success as novelists once they retired from law enforcement.

At that moment Harriet wouldn't have minded a career as a novelist. A hot coffee, a comfy chair and a bit of typing sounded far better than a damp, muddy hiding spot.

She shifted her weight, trying to ease the ache in her legs, and scowled as she saw a patrol circling the nearest building. The robots had appeared soon after the lights went on, and unlike humans they didn't get distracted.

After ten more minutes, Harriet decided the plan was a wash. There was no way back into the compound, and definitely no way to get at the data. She'd just have to report her failure to Boson, and accept whatever punishment he fired her way.

Moving slowly so as not to be seen, Harriet backed out from under the bush and stood up, wincing at the stiffness in her joints. After a quick stretch she set off in the darkness, heading back towards the *Volante*.

◆

It was half an hour later, and the last of the guests had finally departed. Hal and Clunk were in the Volante's cargo hold, facing an angry and upset Max Bright. The artist had raged for several minutes, thundering on about the lack of appreciation of his work, the damage to his reputation and the very real chance of legal action.

He finally ran out of steam, and Clunk saw his chance to smooth the waters. Despite his early plans, he realised blaming Mr Spacejock wasn't really the best option, and so he improvised instead. 'This is just a theory,' said the robot calmly, 'but perhaps the rock was magnetised when our ship flew over the planetary poles. The exposure may have aligned certain crystals within the structure, stimulating the ferro-molecular electron flow until –'

'Yes, yes, yes,' snapped Bright, waving his hand impatiently. 'I'm an artist, not a scientist. There's no need to get technical.'

'I'm sorry,' said Clunk stiffly. 'You wanted an explanation, and –'

'I really don't care how it got this way. I just want to know how you're going to fix it.'

There was a lengthy silence.

'How about this?' said Hal at last. 'We'll fly back over the poles in the other direction, and that should reverse the magnetism. Right, Clunk?'

'I suppose that's one possible outcome,' said Clunk cautiously. From the tone of his voice it was a billion to one long shot, and the odds were only that good if they sprinkled the rock with magic pixie dust.

Fortunately, Bright didn't know Clunk as well as Hal did. 'That sounds like a splendid idea,' said the artist heartily. 'I was beginning to have doubts about your level of service, Mr Spacejock, but it seems you have all the answers.'

Hal beamed with pride. He wasn't used to compliments, especially when it came to his business dealings, but Bright seemed genuinely impressed. The only sour note was Clunk's worried expression, but that could be fixed with a little programming tweak.

They'd barely settled the matter of Bright's magnetic artwork when Meri came hurrying up. 'Hal, the buyer would like you to deliver the artworks as soon as possible. Can you handle that?'

'If they pay, sure.'

'Of course they'll pay, and very generously.'

'Then we're on. Just point us in the right direction and we'll have this load of –'

Clunk made a throat-clearing noise.

'– valuable art delivered in no time,' continued Hal smoothly, without missing a beat. 'So, the destination. Is it far?'

Meri gestured at the sky. 'No, it's an orbiting space station. I'll point it out after we lift off.'

'You're coming with us?'

'Yes. I'm to accompany the artworks.'

Hal remembered Harriet, and winced. Could he really cope with another juggling act? Still, it would only take an hour or so to deliver the cargo, and with any luck he might convince Meri to stay in the hold with Bright's pieces. In fact, if he locked her in he could skip the convincing part altogether.

'Are we ready yet?'

'Almost. Final preparations are under way.'

Hal glanced towards the airlock. 'Is there time for a last gasp of real air?'

'The air aboard this vessel is real.'

'No it isn't. It's like tinned food versus a meal in a restaurant.' Ignoring the Navcom's protests, Hal made his way through the airlock. He stood on the landing platform, taking deep breaths of real, fresh air as the passenger ramp retracted into the hull. Then he coughed and snorted as the Navcom fired the engines with a whole lot of unnecessary smoke.

Hal was still blinking tears from his eyes when he spotted a figure approaching the ship. It was a woman, clad in muddy overalls, and she was limping along with the help of a rough-hewn wooden branch. Hal started to wave, warning her away from the dangerous exhaust wash, but instead of retreating the woman began to move quicker. Then Hal recognised her, and his jaw dropped. It was Harriet Walsh!

'Navcom, cut the engines and extend the passenger ramp,' shouted Hal, as he hurried into the flight deck.

The Navcom muttered something which sounded like 'make up your mind', but complied all the same. As soon as he was certain Harriet wasn't about to be barbecued, Hal charged back out of the airlock and took the ramp at a run, hurrying across the field with his heart in his mouth. He'd believed Harriet to be on board, but here she was, almost left behind. Not only that, she was obviously in a bad way.

When he reached her, she fell into his arms, exhausted, and Hal held her tight, cradling her head against his shoulder. He ran his hand lightly over her hair, making soothing noises, and Harriet's breathing eased as he comforted her.

Then, side by side, they made their way back to the *Volante*.

◆

Harriet stood with her head bowed, letting the steaming hot water flood over her. The shower went some way towards easing her aching muscles, but it wasn't doing anything to improve her mood. She'd let Hal get to her again, despite all her efforts to keep him at bay, and on top of that she wasn't looking forward to Boson's reaction when she explained her failure to secure his precious data. Why couldn't the man follow procedure? Organise a search warrant, drop in a crack team of forensic experts and he'd lay Backsight open from one end to the other.

The shower spluttered, the sudden noise startling her. Resuming her train of thought, she realised Boson had already explained why he wasn't following procedure. Organising a search warrant would tip Backsight off, and by the time the specialists arrived there would be nothing to investigate.

Walsh stepped out of the shower, and the water cut off automatically. She dried herself with the towel, wrapped it around her hair, then donned a thick bathrobe.

Then, with a sense of foreboding, she limped to the terminal and sat down. Unfortunately, when she'd tripped and fallen in the forest, her ankle hadn't been the only casualty. Next to the screen, lying on the desk, were the broken pieces of the decrypting device.

Harriet pushed the pieces further back, out of camera range, and placed the call she'd been dreading for the past couple of hours. There was only one bright spot as far as she could see: Hal told her they were leaving for the Backsight Orbiter, and she might be able to convince Boson there was another chance to access company data.

◆

'Can you put me through to Inspector Boson, please?'
'I'll see if he's available.'

684

Harriet took a deep breath. Calling the Station on an open channel was a big risk, but she had no choice. No doubt Boson would chalk it up as another failure on her part. Seconds later, Inspector Boson appeared on the display. He stared at Walsh, then peered at the bottom of his screen. 'Basic encryption? Really?'

'I'm aboard the –'

'I know where you are,' interrupted Boson. 'Why are you calling? Was your mission a success?'

'I'm afraid not.'

Boson frowned. 'Really, trainee? You disappoint me.'

'There's still a chance, sir. We're heading towards … a certain space-based facility,' said Harriet, after some hesitation. 'It belongs to the company we were discussing in your office.'

'In that case, your orders are the same.' Boson leaned closer. 'This is your last chance. I won't tolerate failure.'

'Sir …' Harriet swallowed nervously. 'The, er, decrypter was destroyed.'

Boson swore under his breath, and for a moment Harriet thought he was going to explode. Then he seemed to relax. 'Very well, trainee. I have a new plan.'

Harriet hardly dared ask. 'Yes sir?'

'You're to sabotage the orbiter.'

'Sabotage the –?'

'But yes. If you cause enough damage they'll have to bring in a repair team. I can infiltrate the team with my own people, and they'll get their hands on the data.'

Harriet had a vision of herself blowing up generators, destroying airlock doors and creating gas leaks. Problem was, she wasn't trained in demolition and she didn't have any equipment.

'You'll need equipment,' said Boson, as though he'd read her mind. 'I'll have a package delivered to your ship in flight. When you land, you'll find it attached to the hull near the cargo door.'

'Yes sir. And … training?'

'Don't worry, I'll make sure the instructions are in the box.' Boson noticed her expression. 'Believe me, you'll have no trouble.'

'Will this device cause much damage?'

'Just enough, Trainee. Just enough. I'll include another decrypter too - use it if you get the chance.'

Boson signed off, and Harriet stared at the blank screen with her thoughts in turmoil. She'd been taught to obey orders without question, but over the past two days she'd graduated from upholding the law to breaking it ... from issuing traffic infringements to trespassing, data theft and sabotage. Worse, none of the orders were in writing, and if anything went wrong she was convinced Boson would drop her in it.

Still, she hadn't gone too far, not yet at least. If the sabotage proved a step too far she'd ignore Boson's orders and tell him she'd missed her chance. He could rant and rave all he liked, but at least she wouldn't end up in prison.

◆

Hal stared at Harriet in disbelief. 'Are you sure those are your orders?'
'I'm afraid so.'
'Boson's gone mad,' said Hal with conviction. 'You should report him. Get him locked up.'
'He's my boss, Hal. I have to do what I'm told.'
'But they'll have security cameras, checkpoints, gun turrets, guards ... killer robots, even.' Hal gestured at the screen, where the orbiter turned slowly in the pitiless glare from the local sun. Light glinted off gun barrels and missile launchers alike, and the stark white structure looked deadly and unwelcoming. 'The weapons factory was bad enough, but this will be ten times worse. And it's not just the security on board, you know. If they discover a security breach they'll blow us to bits when we leave.'
'I know it's a risk.'
'No, it's a giant mountain of risks, sitting on a risk faultline, with a shonky old nuclear power station perched on top.'
'I've had training, Hal. If you can just get me a disguise, I know I can pull this off.'
'You don't have to do it,' protested Hal. 'Clunk and I, we can –'
'No, you've got to deliver the goods. Although ...'
'Yes?'
Harriet allowed herself a smile. 'A little distraction wouldn't go astray.'
'You've got it.'

686

'Backsight Orbiter, this is the interstellar freighter *Volante* requesting docking clearance.'

'*Stand by,* Volante.'

There was a brief delay before the traffic controller spoke again.

'Volante, *please confirm your cargo.*'

'They're artworks for Olivia Backsight.'

'*Have you visited any farms in the past two weeks?*'

'No.'

'*Do you have any wood or animal matter aboard?*'

'Of course we do. The artworks include a fish, a length of intestine and a stuffed cow.'

'*Docking denied. Have a nice day.*'

The connection went dead, and Clunk's eyebrows went up. After a second or two, he tried again. 'Orbiter, these artworks were paid for by Olivia Backsight herself.'

'*I don't care if she signed for them in her own blood. We have strict quarantine regulations.*'

'But –'

'*Docking denied.*'

Clunk pressed his lips together. 'Navcom, get me Olivia Backsight.'

Hal stared at the robot in shock. 'She told you to *what*?'

Clunk had only spent a few moments speaking to Olivia Backsight, but she'd made her wishes very clear. 'We're to dump the artworks in space. Everything containing animal matter must go, which means all of them bar Hairpiece.'

'Just because of quarantine?' Hal shook his head. 'Unbelievable.'

From the look on Clunk's face, he could hardly believe it himself. No doubt the robot thought it would be a tragic loss to the art world, whereas Hal was scandalised by the waste of money.

'And those orders came from the old bat herself?' asked Hal, who was still expecting a surprise twist.

'Ms Olivia Backsight, yes.'

'It wasn't someone playing a joke on you?'

'No, it was definitely her. I even got it in writing, signed and everything.'

Hal shrugged. 'Okay, if that's what she wants. How do we do it? Push it all out the back?'

'No, that would create a navigation hazard.'

'Okay, why not feed them into the exhaust chamber like you did with the, er ...'

'Questionable reading material? That would work for Fish in a Jar and Semi Colon, but Cow in a Field is far too big.' Clunk hesitated. 'We could always return to orbit and eject the artworks there. They'd burn up safely during re-entry.'

'I'm not wasting a single drop of fuel on this. You'll have to think of something else.'

Clunk rubbed his chin with a grating, squealing sound. 'There is one possibility.'

'Good. Do it.'

'I haven't explained yet.'

'Will it get rid of the artworks?'

'Oh yes.'

'That's all I need to know. Come and find me in the flight deck when you're done.'

◆

Hal made himself comfortable in the pilot's chair, studying the live feed from the cargo hold which the Navcom was displaying on the main viewscreen. According to Clunk, dropping the artworks out the back of the ship was a gross violation of dumping laws, but firing them into planetary orbit was more of a grey area. Grey or not, Bright's so-called artworks had landed them in a great deal of bother over the past day or so, and watching them sail away from the ship would be almost as good as seeing them smashed to pieces by a team of sledgehammer-wielding maniacs. In anticipation of the show, Hal had made himself a fresh coffee and fetched his big tin of biscuit fragments from the third deck. Meri had been there, engrossed in a documentary on dodgy cargo pilots, and Hal managed to slip away without telling her what they were about to do to Bright's artworks.

Fish in a Jar was first to go, tossed out by a visibly hesitant Clunk. It went about five metres and came straight back again, attracted by the *Volante*'s artificial gravity. Clunk caught it one-handed and threw it again, much harder this time. The fish separated from its container and spun away like a silver boomerang ... only to return like one. The jar and the stones were a little slower returning, but they came back all the same. The water came back as a globule, which Clunk managed to catch with his face.

'Don't do that with the cow,' snorted Hal, thoroughly enjoying himself. He put his feet up and took a biscuit from the tin by his elbow, selecting one with a heavy coating of chocolate. For once, Clunk had let him choose their supplies, and the result was a load of delicious, gooey biscuits the like of which Hal hadn't tasted for years. Brushing crumbs from his flight suit, he gazed at the screen in rapt attention as he wondered what Clunk was going to try next.

The robot was doing something with two lengths of string and a small square of fabric, and when it was complete Hal realised Clunk had made a sling. The robot placed the fish in the fabric, gripped the loose ends of the string, and began swinging it around his head, faster and faster, until the fish's polished scales formed a shimmering circle. When he was ready he launched forwards, releasing one of the strings. Unfortunately, the fish slipped out early, speared across the cargo hold and slammed into the cow's horns, knocking one off and leaving it dangling by a flap of skin.

Hal laughed so hard he almost swallowed his biscuit. The screen shimmered through the tears coursing down his cheeks, and he was forced to sit up and catch his breath, which came in rasping gasps. As he recovered he noticed Clunk directing a stern look at the camera, the robot's face radiating anger. Then he stomped out of sight.

When Clunk came back, he was dragging a drum of cable. Hal watched in breathless anticipation as the robot unwound meters and meters of green-coated wire, wondering what Clunk's plan was. With the robot this pissed off, it was bound to be good.

Clunk vanished for a few moments, then returned with several lengths of metal rod. He selected four and bent them a couple of times, nodding in satisfaction as they sprung back into shape. Then, working fast, he bound the four lengths into one thick rod with the wire. When he'd finished, he tied the ends off and bent the bundle of metal rods into an arc, stringing another length of wire between them. Hal realised the robot had fashioned a huge bow, and judging from the effort it was taking to draw it back, the thing was probably capable of hurling more than just fish into the depths of space.

Clunk picked through the remaining rods and selected a shorter one. Recovering the battered fish, he tore of a length of wire and bound it firmly to one end of the rod. When he'd finished, he fitted his makeshift arrow into the bow and pulled back, sighting on the rear door.

Hal held his breath. If the thing snapped Clunk would probably lose his head - literally.

The camera shook as Clunk released his shot, and the fish-laden arrow vanished through the rear doors in the blink of an eye, leaving a silver after-image smeared across the viewscreen. Terminal velocity hadn't just been achieved, it had been surpassed by a healthy margin. In fact, Hal fully expected that arrow to be found embedded in a distant planet a decade or so hence.

Clunk dispatched the glass jar by attaching it to another arrow, sending it skimming out the back door with another shot from his mighty bow. Semi-Colon followed, sent on its way without fuss.

Hal took another biscuit and got comfortable. Only the cow was left now, and if Clunk thought he could shoot that out the rear doors with a homemade bow and arrow he had another think coming. As the robot strode towards the stuffed animal, Hal had a sudden thought. What if the robot was planning to send it out the back of the ship in pieces? Clunk was ill-disposed towards cows at the best of times, and this one was likely to be more difficult that any he'd encountered before - despite being deader than the length of gut Bright had selected for one of his minor exhibits. Realising Clunk might be about to dismember the cow before his eyes, Hal returned his biscuit to the tin untouched.

His fears were unfounded. The robot moved around the hold, inspecting the contents of lockers and tool boxes. When he came back he was carrying a large black case plastered with warning labels. Hal could just make out the words 'explosive' and 'fire hazard', but he didn't remember seeing the box before. He had a vague idea it was part of the emergency equipment, the one area where Clunk was firm: Hal was not to touch any of it.

Clunk set the box down and carefully removed a fat cylinder encased in brown paper. Hal's eyes widened as the paper came off, revealing a signal rocket the size of a wine bottle. Again and again Clunk dipped into the box, until a row of these rockets lay on the deck like the aftermath of a heavy party.

Once Clunk had unwrapped all the rockets, he gathered them up and carried them to the cow. Working quickly and efficiently, he attached them to its legs with strips of broad tape, carefully aligning them so they all pointed away from the cargo hold doors.

When he was done, Clunk stood back to check his work, stooping once or twice to adjust the angle here or fasten a rocket more securely there. Satisfied, he gathered all the riptabs in one hand and prepared to pull them.

Hal held his breath. From the size of the rockets, he could tell that there was a large amount of explosive power in each one, and a cow was hardly the most aerodynamic shape on the market. Of course, the hold was in total vacuum so air didn't come into it, but his list of 'things to stick rockets to' would have been a mile long before it included stuffed cows.

There was a jerk as Clunk pulled the tabs, and a series of eye-watering flashes as the rockets fired within split seconds of each other, spurting blue flame. The cow shuddered on all four legs, then took off like a drunken sailor, drifting towards the rear of the hold. Halfway there, just as it seemed they were about to see the back of the cow forever, disaster struck. One of the rockets came loose and begun to spin around the cow's hind leg like an oversized catherine wheel, bumping the cow nose-first into the wall. The rockets kept pushing lustily, and through the gathering smoke Hal saw Clunk run across the hold and grab the cow's tail, attempting to drag it back on course. Instead, two more rockets came loose, and the cow shot into the middle of the hold and began spinning on the spot, getting faster and faster. The loose horn spun away, while Clunk was dragged round behind the cow like a novice cowboy. He'd obviously decided that letting go was the more dangerous course of action, and so he wrapped his hands round the stringly tail and held on grimly, legs flailing as the cow bucked and weaved.

Unfortunately, signal rockets only have a limited lifespan. Sooner or later they go bang, and six of them in close proximity go bang with gusto. One minute Clunk was being swung in tight circles, and the next there was a very bright flash of light ... quickly hidden by a rapidly expanding cloud of cow hair, cow hide and shredded stuffing. The last thing Hal saw before the view was completely blotted out was Clunk flying backwards, still hanging onto the cow's tail.

◆

By the time Hal got to the inner door the hold was pressurised again. Taking that as a good sign, he opened the door and peered in.

At first he thought he was back on Forzen, since the hold looked like it was knee deep in dirty snow. A figure came towards him, looming out of the settling blizzard of flakes like a stiff and slightly metallic snowman.

Underneath layers of burnt hair and singed stuffing Hal could just make out Clunk's less than happy face. 'So, how'd it go?' asked Hal lamely.

'Famously,' said the robot curtly. 'Like a charm.'

'I caught a bit on the screen upstairs.'

'Is that so?'

'Yeah. The bow and arrows were a good idea.'

Under the mess, Clunk's lips tightened.

'The rocket thing was promising.' Hal looked around the hold. 'At first.'

Clunk nodded slowly.

Hal looked around at the mess. 'Now it really is a stuffed cow,' he said at last.

Clunk said nothing.

'Do you want a hand cleaning up?'

'I can manage.' Clunk's eyes gleamed. 'Unless you'd care to toss for it?'

'N-no. I'll, er, go back and get the Navcom ready. Say, ten minutes?'

'Thirty.'

'On my way.' Hal closed the door and beat a hasty retreat. That was the problem with robots - they could turn molehills into mountains. Or cows into feather beds, he thought, as he stepped into the lift.

◆

The *Volante* docked without incident, and Hal stepped jauntily down the cargo ramp to meet the welcoming party. 'Evening all,' he called enthusiastically. 'Are you ready to roll the rock?'

There were half a dozen workers at the foot of the ramp, dressed in identical white overalls and wearing identical forbidding expressions. Nearby, Hal saw Olivia Backsight leaning on her polished cane, her eyes sharp as she gave the *Volante* the once over. Next to her was Rodney, who only had eyes for Hal. From his expression, he was itching to draw his blade and put it to good use.

'You're late,' said Olivia at last.

'I'm sorry. We had engine troubles.' Hal indicated Clunk, who had followed him down the ramp. 'My robot kept them running, but we could use a couple of fuel filters.'

'What do you think this is, a service centre?' Olivia waved the workers towards the hold. 'Start unloading.'

The giant rock was removed quickly and efficiently, unhooked from the sling and manoeuvred onto a huge anti-grav sled, which strained and groaned under the weight. The workers moved the sled towards the exit doors, and Hal realised the delivery was almost complete. It was time for his distraction!

During their approach to the orbiter, Hal had racked his brains for a suitable plan. He discarded several ideas as impractical, impossible or downright lethal, but had finally hit upon the perfect distraction. Now, with the cargo disappearing from the docking bay, he realised it was time to put this plan into action.

'Er, excuse me?' he said.

Olivia Backsight gave him a look. 'Yes?'

'Can I use your toilet?'

'Of course not.'

Hal blinked. So much for his carefully planned distraction. 'But mine's blocked, and –'

'I'm sorry, it's out of the question.' Olivia gestured towards the departing rock with her cane. 'My people are going to inspect that piece, and you will remain here until I'm satisfied. Is that understood?'

'Inspect?' said Clunk, looking worried.

'Of course. It's a valuable piece, and I want to make sure it's in perfect condition.'

Hal could understand Clunk's concern. They'd landed the *Volante* on the rock, rolled it around inside various trucks and even knocked down a stray building with it. If Olivia was looking for damage, she was sure to find some. Then he remembered his promise to Harriet - he had to distract the welcoming party so she could leave the ship unnoticed! Hal glanced at Clunk, wondering whether he could stage a quick fist fight. Unfortunately, the robot's fists were like boulders, and instead of a distraction he'd probably get a one-way trip to hospital. 'Er, is it okay if we work on the engines?'

'I don't care, as long as you stay aboard your ship.' On this, Olivia turned and left. Rodney shot Hal a venomous look, then followed.

Hal traipsed up the cargo ramp, where he found Harriet crouched behind the door pillar. She was wearing a spare flight suit, and her hair was tied back in a business-like ponytail.

'Sorry,' he muttered. 'They didn't buy it.'

'I'm not surprised,' whispered Harriet. 'Of all the weak excuses …'

'It's not my fault!' protested Hal. 'Anyway, you saw them watching. They didn't take their eyes off the ship for a second.'

Walsh sighed. 'I guess you're right. A handful of grenades wouldn't have distracted that lot.'

Clunk looked from one to the other. 'It's not too late, you know. In fact, I believe I can help.'

'Really?' Harriet looked hopeful. 'How?'

'I'll show you. Just … be ready.'

Harriet crouched near the cargo hold entrance, her heart thudding in her chest. She glanced towards the far corners of the hangar, eyeing the laser-guided gun turrets and security cameras. Clunk seemed confident his plan would work, but he wasn't the one facing certain death. As she crouched there, nerves tingling, Harriet decided it would probably help if she knew what Clunk's plan actually was.

'Control, this is the *Volante*. Do you read?'

Harriet jumped as Clunk's voice came through a nearby speaker, sounding tinny and distant.

'Control?' repeated the robot. 'Hello? Are you there?'

'*What is it, Volante?*'

'We've just replaced our fuel filters, and I need permission to fire the engines.'

There was a brief pause, and then …'*Negative,* Volante. *Permission denied.*'

A moment later Walsh heard Hal's voice, laconic and confident. 'Control, if the engines fail on departure we're going to crash right into your shiny space station.'

Another pause, then …'*Very well,* Volante. *You may test your engines.*'

'Thanks so much,' said Hal. 'Stand by, Control. And, er, there may be a little smoke.'

Smoke! Harriet grinned to herself. So that was the plan.

The engines started with a bellowing roar, agonisingly loud in the confines of the hangar. They spat and spluttered, and before long the cavernous area began to fill with haze. It thinned as hidden extractors sucked the fumes out, then thickened like magic as the engines spewed gouts of grey smoke. In seconds, Harriet could barely see her hand in front of her face, and she leapt up and hurried down the ramp at the double.

At the foot of the ramp she turned left, and hurried along the hull until she saw a small grey cylinder. True to his word, Boson had arranged the drone carrying the equipment she'd need. She opened the canister and took out a small metal box, heavy for the size. Then she ran across the hangar towards the exit, wincing as green laser beams sliced through the smoke, seeking her out. They shimmered like neon lights on a foggy day, but the turrets held their fire and she made it safely to the door. After a quick look around she slipped into the wide corridor, keeping her head down as she hurried towards the nearest door.

There were no plans for the space station on file, but Clunk had unearthed designs for similar structures, extrapolating the layout from exterior views. Walsh knew there was no point making for any of the server rooms, which would be heavily guarded and much too secure for her to access, but Clunk had identified a number of offices belonging to senior managers. In most organisations, these were the people with scant regard for security. Even if they'd bothered to lock their terminals down, their passwords were usually trivial and easily cracked.

Before long she reached the first office. The nameplate read 'Richard Witt, Level Five Manager', and Walsh glanced over her shoulder before putting her ear to the door. Next, she tried knocking, and when there was no reply she opened the door and slipped inside. Presumably, Dick Witt was helping the Backsights with their new art collection.

There was a terminal on the desk, the screen showing a login prompt. Harriet didn't waste time with the keyboard ... she opened the metal case and inspected the contents. Inside were two items: another decrypter, and a hand grenade. There was a slip of paper taped to the hand grenade, and Harriet's eyebrows rose as she read the instructions:

Pull pin, throw into server room.

After considering her options, Harriet decided to go with the decrypter. She took out the device and inserted it into the side of the screen. Seconds later there was a muted beep, and the terminal gave her full access.

The filing system was immense, and the progress bar crawled as the data was sucked down. Occasionally, the bar would pause as the copy routine encountered files and directories above the manager's security clearance, but each time this happened the decrypter had an answer.

The bar was halfway across when Harriet heard footsteps in the corridor. She ducked behind the desk, holding her breath, but fortunately they kept going. Then she had an idea, and she opened her flightsuit and tore a large chunk off the T-shirt underneath. If anyone came in, she'd busy herself dusting the furniture with the makeshift rag. It might not be that convincing, but it could buy her a little time.

◆

Olivia Backsight strode towards Bright's Hairpiece, her shoes clacking on the metal floor. The gigantic rock was three times her height, and there was a clang as she whacked it with her steel-tipped cane. 'At last,' she muttered. 'At long, long last.'

Rodney Backsight stood nearby, a puzzled expression on his face. 'I really don't see the attraction.'

Olivia pulled her cane away with an effort, and pointed the tip at Rodney. 'You will, my boy. You will.'

'But it's just a rock.'

'Just a rock?' Olivia snorted. 'This chunk of stone will keep our factories going for the next ten years.'

Rodney paled. 'Are you saying it's radioactive?'

'Don't be stupid.'

'How's it going to power our factories, then?'

Olivia placed her hand on the asteroid, feeling the rough surface. 'It's not the rock,' she murmured. 'It's the contents.'

'What, more stone?'

Tired of explaining, Olivia raised her voice. 'Okay, you can come in now.'

The door opened and two workers entered. They were wearing dirt-streaked orange overalls, safety goggles and hearing protectors, and they were pushing the biggest electric saw Rodney had ever seen. The circular blade was as big as an airlock door, and the motor looked like it had come out of a truck.

Olivia gestured towards the rock, and while one of the men lined the saw up, the second man distributed sets of safety equipment. Obviously they were going to cut the rock up, but Rodney still couldn't see the need. After all, it was just a chunk of stone.

Screeeee!

The saw kicked into life with a howling wail, and Rodney clasped his hands over the hearing protectors, pressing them to the side of his head. Water gushed from the saw, and the noise rose to an unholy scream as the blade began to bite. Grit and muddy water flew as the saw chewed into the rock, cascading off the men and puddling on the floor.

After a few minutes the saw was withdrawn, and Rodney saw a steaming channel running halfway up the side of the huge asteroid. The men adjusted their position and started cutting again, until a big segment hung by a thread. The saw was switched off, and one of the men took up a mallet and a couple of steel wedges. He drove the first in deep, but the second was only half in when the segment came free with a loud crack.

The man leapt back, narrowly avoiding the falling wedge, and the floor shook as the huge chunk of rock crashed down. It shattered into hundreds of pieces, but Olivia wasn't interested in the segment. No, she was craning her scrawny neck to look inside the body of the meteorite.

Rodney raised his safety glasses for a closer look, but he still couldn't see what all the fuss was about. The boulder was shot through with veins, and the blade had left circular patterns where it had sliced through. Apart from that, it just looked like solid rock.

'What trickery is this?' demanded Olivia. 'Where the hell are my stones?'

As far as Rodney could tell, they were scattered all over the floor. 'You're standing on them,' he said, trying to be helpful.

Olivia crouched, scooped up a handful of gravel and held it under his nose. 'Not his kind of stone, you weasel-faced moron. My diamonds!'

'Diamonds?'

'Of course diamonds. Do you think I bought this putrid excuse for art out of the goodness of my heart?' Olivia gave him a look of pure scorn. 'I don't know who your mother slept with, but you're obviously not *my* flesh and blood.'

'B-but there aren't any diamonds. It's empty.'

'No shit, genius. And why would that be?'

'They weren't put there in the first place?'

'I watched them seal the rock on Forzen. Try again.'

Rodney's brow creased. 'I know!' he said at last. 'It's not the same asteroid!'

'Bingo. It's been swapped.' Olivia's cane swished through the air, the tip coming to a halt directly above the rock. It held there a second, then snapped towards the meteorite, sticking to it with a loud *plink!* 'It wasn't magnetic, either. Therefore, it was switched in flight. And who carried Bright's artworks?'

Rodney's eyes narrowed. 'Spacejock.'

'Right. Hal Spacejock.' Olivia held her cane in both hands, and started to bend it. Her knuckles were white, and the strain made her arms shake. Her lips drew back in a snarl, but gradually the cane bent further and further until ...*snap!*

Rodney flinched. The mood his gran was in, he half-expected her to stake the two workmen with the broken pieces of cane. Instead, she addressed them imperiously. 'You two, I want this section cleared. Understood? Everyone out.'

'Yes ma'am.'

'Now!'

The workers departed at a run, and Olivia whipped round and held the sharp ends of her cane under Rodney's nose, the white splintered wood so close he could feel it. 'Bring me Hal Spacejock. We're going to find out what he did with the real rock, and then we're going to kill him.'

◆

Hal was sitting at the flight console, sipping a cup of coffee. Despite his relaxed appearance, his nerves were strung tight. It was twenty minutes since Harriet had vanished into the smoke, and he was beginning to wonder whether he'd ever see her again. Once the artworks were approved, Olivia Backsight would give Hal his marching orders, and if Walsh wasn't back in time he'd have to abandon her. Then his brow creased as another thought hit him. How was she going to get back aboard? Would Control buy another engine test?

Hal glanced at Clunk, who was sitting in the copilot's chair. The robot didn't look worried, but then again his face only had a limited range of expressions. For all Hal knew, Clunk was already in mourning. 'So, about Harriet.'

'Yes, Mr Spacejock?'

'How's she getting back aboard?'

Clunk turned to look at him, and Hal's heart sank at the new expression on the robot's face. Now Clunk *did* look like he was in mourning. 'Back aboard, Mr Spacejock?'

'Of course back again.' Hal's voice rose. 'You think we're leaving her behind? Is that it?'

'Nobody said anything about a second distraction,' protested Clunk.

'Give me strength,' muttered Hal.

'Ms Walsh is highly resourceful. I'm sure she'll think of something.'

'Yes, well –'

Hal got no further, because at that second the airlock door exploded inwards with a flash of light and a very loud bang. The force threw him off his chair, and he was still tumbling across the deck when several armed guards charged in. One of them disabled Clunk with a flash from an electronic gizmo, and as the robot sank to the floor, helpless, the intruders covered Hal with their weapons.

Hal saw their lips moving, but couldn't hear a word over the ringing in his ears. There was an acrid smell from the explosion, and his eyes were still recovering from the bright flash. Then, before he could fully recover, two men hauled him to his feet and dragged him out of the ship.

33

The next few minutes passed in a blur. Hal's brain felt like it was running at half its usual speed, but he did manage to put two and two together. Obviously, Harriet had been caught, which is why Olivia had sent her thugs to pick Hal up. Now, presumably, he was going to be questioned.

Hal heard a woman's voice as he was dragged through the corridors, shouting and protesting from somewhere behind him. At first he thought it was Harriet, but then he realised Olivia's men had found Meri Ryder aboard the *Volante* and brought her along too. 'Leave her alone,' he muttered, every word an effort. Unfortunately, nobody heard him.

They were taken to a large room, where Bright's asteroid towered over a powerful-looking saw. There was a big segment missing from the asteroid, and the floor was littered with broken chunks of rock. Olivia and Rodney were standing nearby, and before them were two empty chairs.

Hal and Meri were pushed into the chairs, and Hal winced as his arms were tied firmly behind his back. He struggled, but the bonds were far too strong.

Once the two of them were secure, Olivia waved the guards away. 'Get lost, all of you.'

'Are you sure, ma'am?'

Olivia took one step towards them, and the guards fled. Then she turned to Hal. 'Mr Spacejock, how nice of you to join us.' Olivia leaned closer. 'I'd just like to ask you one question, if that's all right with you.'

'Where is she?' demanded Hal, whose only thoughts were of Harriet Walsh. 'What have you done with her?'

Olivia was holding a length of broken cane, and she brought it down viciously across his knee. 'I'm asking the questions, Spacejock. Tell me, where's my asteroid?'

Hal stared at her, then at the big rock. Suddenly, he realised this had nothing to do with Harriet. 'Er ...it's right over there.'

Crack! Olivia hit him with the cane again. She wasn't particularly strong, but the blow sent agonising pains shooting up Hal's leg. 'Don't mess with me, Spacejock. What have you done with the original?'

'That is the original,' said Hal truthfully. 'Why would I deliver anything else?'

'I will get the –' *Crack!* '– truth out of you –' *Crack!* '– one way or the other!'

'Keep hitting me all you want,' said Hal, through gritted teeth. 'That's Bright's rock, I swear.'

Olivia tossed the cane aside, and held her hand out to Rodney. 'Give me your knife.'

Rodney obeyed, and as the flickering blade changed hands a nasty grin crossed his face. 'Are you going to cut him, Gran?'

'No.'

Hal breathed a sigh of relief. The old woman was angry, but not completely insane.

'I'm going to cut her,' said Olivia, and she stood in front of Meri.

'No, please,' cried Meri, her eyes wide with panic. 'I'll – I'll tell you anything you want.'

'Go on.'

'My fees ...I've been overcharging you for years.'

'I know that already.'

'And the exhibitions ...I skim ten percent off the door takings.'

'So what?' Olivia gestured with the knife. 'Tell me where the rock is. The original rock.'

'M-Max Bright's Hairpiece?' stammered Meri. 'I-it's right there!'

'For the last time, that is NOT my rock!' shouted Olivia. 'The original was packed with uncut diamonds. Do you understand? An absolute *fortune* in diamonds. Enough gems for enough weapons to arm half the galaxy!' She drew her hand back, the blade shimmering in readiness, and Hal realised she was really going to do it. Unless he stopped her, Meri would die. 'Wait! I know where your rock is.'

Olivia hesitated, the light from the atomic blade reflected in her wide, staring eyes. Then, slowly, she lowered the deadly knife. 'Go on.'

'We, er –'

Slowly, Olivia moved the blade until the tip was millimetres from Meri's nose. 'I'm waiting.'

'It, er –' Hal racked his brains, but nothing would come. What could he say? What could he do? If he didn't come up with a plausible explanation, Meri would be killed right before his eyes.

◆

Transfer Complete.

Harriet mouthed silent thanks to the IT gods as she yanked the decrypter from the side of the terminal. Now all she had to do was get back to the ship, get Hal to fly her home, and hand the red-hot intel over to her boss. If there was anything incriminating in the files, Backsight would be finished and –

Then she frowned. Get back to the ship how, exactly? The cameras were still there, the gun turrets were still covering the hold, the lasers were still seeking targets but the smoke … that was long gone.

Walsh thought for a moment. Could she cut power to the hangar? No, whoever designed the security system would have thought of that. What about the *Volante* - could it pick her up somewhere else? Or maybe she could she hide aboard the station until she managed to sneak aboard another ship?

For the first time, she realised the magnitude of her problems. She was trapped, and if she didn't leave aboard the *Volante*, it was likely she'd never leave at all.

Walsh eyed the terminal on the desk. Could she manipulate the security system from there, disabling cameras and shutting down turrets? It was worth a shot.

She slotted the decrypter into the side of the terminal, entering the main menu. There were dozens of options, and she traversed screen after screen until she found what she was looking for - security options.

The screen changed, displaying images from dozens of cameras, and Walsh had only just managed to disable the hangar feed when she spotted a familiar figure in the middle of the screen. It was Hal Spacejock, sitting in a chair, and there was a young woman tied up alongside him. Walsh's eyes narrowed as she recognised Meri Ryder. What the hell was *she* doing there?

Harriet switched the feed to full frame, and as the rest of the scene came into focus she drew in a sharp breath, instantly forgetting her jealousy. Olivia Backsight was holding a knife to Ryder's neck, and from the determined expression on her face, she was about to strike.

◆

'Time's up, Spacejock.' Olivia gestured with the blade. 'She's going to die.'

'Gran, wait!' Rodney stepped forward, taking Olivia's wrist just as she was about to strike. They struggled for a second or two, but he was much stronger. 'I said wait!'

'Release me this instant, you idiot boy.'

'No, you can't do it. Not here.'

'Why the hell not? You're not scared of blood, are you?'

Rodney snorted. 'No, it's not that.' He nodded towards the camera in the corner of the room, the red eye watching them balefully. 'You don't want the deed recorded, do you?'

Olivia hesitated, then lowered the blade. 'You're right. Smart thinking.' Then she handed him the knife. 'Take her into the corridor and cut her throat.'

'Me?' Rodney looked pleased. 'Really?'

At that moment Hal decided Rodney was going to die. He didn't know when or how, he just knew he'd make sure of it. 'You sick bastard,' he muttered.

'We don't have to kill her, you know,' said Olivia matter-of-factly. 'Just tell me where my asteroid went, and we'll let you both go.'

'I told you a hundred times, I never switched your bloody asteroid!'

'Off you go, Rodney. Make it quick.'

'No, please!' cried Meri, as she was hauled to her feet. 'Hal, stop him. Don't let him do it, please!'

Hal struggled with his bonds as Rodney dragged Meri towards the exit, but they were too tight. Hal threatened, he pleaded, he swore vengeance, but nothing he said made any difference. Meri's heels clattered on the floor as she struggled to get free, but there was nothing she could do. Seconds later, she was dragged through the open door.

Hal fixed Olivia with a killer stare. 'You'll die for this,' he growled, his eyes bright.

'I very much doubt it.'

There was a shriek from the hallway, followed by the thud of a falling body. Hal groaned, letting his chin drop to his chest, and his insides churned as he thought of the innocent young woman who'd been killed over nothing. Worse, her blood was on his hands, even though he didn't know why.

◆

It took Harriet a couple of minutes to work out Hal's location, and she was just making her way along the corridor to the room where he was being held when she heard his despairing shouts. She stood with her back to the wall, hiding in the corridor, and heard Meri's panicky screams getting closer and closer as Rodney dragged the young woman towards the doorway.

Then, as the two of them appeared beside her, Harriet raised her gun and shot Rodney in the back. He toppled over and landed with a thud on the ground, and Walsh jammed her hand over Meri's mouth to shut her up. 'I'm here to rescue you,' she whispered urgently. 'Nod if you understand.'

Meri did so, and Walsh took her hand away. 'Is he dead?' asked Meri, looking down at Rodney with sick fascination.

'No, just stunned.'

'Good.' Meri drew her foot back and kicked Rodney in the ribs, driving the point of her shoe in with a loud crack. 'Live with that, you sadistic little prick.'

Walsh risked a glance through the doorway, and saw Olivia pacing up and down in front of Hal. She was waving a broken cane, and as Harriet watched, the old woman slashed it across Hal's shoulders. 'Tell me where my asteroid went!' she yelled, raising the cane for another blow. Walsh winced as the cane came down, but on the bright side it didn't look like Hal's life was in danger. Yet.

'Meri,' whispered Harriet. 'Can you find your way to the *Volante*?'

The other woman nodded. 'I think so.'

'Okay. I turned off security in the hangar, and the cargo hold was still open when I left. I need you to go aboard and find Clunk. I've got a feeling we're going to need his help.'

'Go and fetch Clunk. Got it.' Meri looked at her. 'And you? What are you going to do?'

Harriet brandished her gun. 'I'm going to rescue Hal.'

Racked with pain and still reeling from Meri's death, Hal realised he was barely holding together. His wrists were raw from his struggles against the bonds, and his shoulders and legs stung from the caning. If he could only get free ...

Olivia was panting as she brought the cane down again and again, but she was tiring quickly and each blow was weaker than the last. Then, she stopped.

'Who the hell ... are you?' she demanded, between ragged breaths.

Hal was about to reply, then realised Olivia wasn't talking to him.

'I'm Peace Force Trainee Harriet Walsh,' said a calm voice, 'and you're under arrest.'

Slowly, Hal raised his head, and the emotion almost choked him as he saw his beautiful, confident Harriet Walsh covering Olivia Backsight with her gun. Then he remembered Meri, and his head dropped again as he realised the rescue was too late.

'Hal, are you all right?'

'They killed Meri,' said Hal, his voice a dry croak. 'It was my fault.'

'Hal, Meri's okay,' said Harriet urgently. 'I got there just in time.'

Hal felt a powerful surge of relief, and he struggled to sit up. 'But ...Rodney?'

'Out cold. I'm guessing several broken ribs, too.'

'That little prick is going to have more than a few broken bones when I've finished with him,' growled Hal. 'Quick, untie me. We have to get out of here before any more of these clowns turn up.'

Harriet bent to obey, narrowly avoiding the chunk of rock which whistled past her head. Nearby, Olivia Backsight swore and reached for another missile. Harriet abandoned Hal and advanced on the old woman, gun at the ready. 'Put your hands up.'

'Or what?'

'Or I'll shoot you.'

Olivia backed towards the asteroid, slowly raising her hands. Then, moving quickly despite her age, she darted behind it.

'Give me strength,' muttered Walsh, and went to follow.

'Be careful,' called Hal. 'She's a tricky one.'

Harriet stood with her back to the asteroid, her gun at shoulder height. She hadn't expected much of a threat from the old woman, but the stray piece of rock would have knocked half her brains out, and next time she might not be so lucky. Harriet realised she could have laid Olivia out with a stunner blast, only shooting an unarmed old lady didn't seem to fit the Peace Force credo.

Slowly, she moved around the bulk of the rock. As she did so, she felt a curious drag on her arm, as though someone had grabbed hold of her gun and was pulling it behind her back. She struggled against the force but it was too strong, and seconds later the weapon was stuck firmly to the rock, pinning her hand underneath. She tried to free it with both hands, but the force was too strong and she had no leverage. 'Er, Hal?' she called.

'Yeah?'

'Is this rock magnetic or something?'

'Very.'

'Crap,' muttered Walsh. She looked up, and her heart skipped a beat as she saw Olivia just a pace or two away, the broken cane gripped in one hand. 'Keep your distance,' said Walsh, her voice steady. She raised her free hand to fend off the cane, but Olivia was too quick. In a flash, the splintered end was pressed to Harriet's neck, right over the jugular.

'Mr Spacejock?' said Olivia calmly.

'What is it?'

'Tell me where the original rock went. If not, Ms Walsh here is going to die.'

34

Clunk came online with a start, system warnings screaming in his ears. According to his logs he was underwater, and he sat up with a start, struggling to clear the deadly fluid from his vents.

'Oh good. I was hoping that would work.'

Clunk shook his head, spraying droplets around the flight deck, then paused to take stock of the situation. Meri Ryder was standing over him with an empty jug in her hand, and it didn't take a detective to work out where she'd emptied the contents. 'Are you insane?' demanded Clunk. 'You threw water over me?'

'It works for humans,' said Meri.

'I'm not human!'

'It worked, didn't it? Now get up. Hal needs your help.'

Clunk stood up in a hurry. 'What is it? What happened?' He looked closer at Meri. 'You look very pale. Have you been crying?'

'There's no time to explain. You have to save Hal.'

'And I will. Just tell me where he is.'

'There's no –'

'Yes there is,' said Clunk. 'Speak as fast as you can.'

Meri obeyed, running the words together as she filled Clunk in. When she was finished, she looked at him expectantly. 'Well? Are you going to save him?'

'Of course.' Clunk turned to the console. 'Navcom, bring up a plan of the orbiter.'

'There is no plan of the orbiter.'

'I mean that mockup I created earlier.'

'Complying.'

A diagram appeared on the main screen, complete with a legend. Clunk indicated the hangar, then asked Meri to show him where Hal was. She examined the screen for a moment or two, then pointed.

'I see. Very interesting.'

'You're not doing much rescuing,' said Meri accusingly.

'Before one can fire the cannon, one must aim the cannon.'

Meri looked hopeful. 'You have a cannon?'

'It's a figure of speech,' said Clunk, with an airy gesture. Then, ignoring Meri's urging, he spent several minutes studying the screen. 'I think I see the answer.'

'About time,' snapped Meri. 'What are you going to do? Flood the station with toxic gas? Hack those gun turrets to fire on the enemy? Cover yourself in weapons and storm the space station?'

'No, my plan is a little more direct. Please … will you take a seat?'

Meri looked at him like he was deranged. 'That's your plan? We're leaving?'

'Take a seat this instant!' bellowed Clunk, his patience finally wearing out.

Meri sat down in a hurry, fastening her seatbelt without being asked.

Once she was ready, Clunk started the engines and casually pulled the throttles back to full reverse thrust. The *Volante* was firmly attached to the Orbiter, and the hull shook as the ship struggled to break free. Then, just when it seemed nothing would happen, the *Volante*'s powerful engines overcame the resistance and the ship hurtled backwards … with the Orbiter's docking section still attached.

◆

Hal closed his eyes, scarcely able to believe what was happening. When he opened them again, Harriet Walsh was walking towards him with the point of Olivia's cane pressed firmly against her neck. Olivia had Harriet's gun in her free hand, and Hal realised the old woman must have levered it free with the cane. Great, they were in twice as much trouble now. Then, just when he thought things couldn't get any worse, he heard footsteps. Dreading what he might see, Hal glanced towards the sound and groaned. It was Rodney Backsight, with blood on his lips and murder in his eyes.

As Rodney got closer he raised his hand, which was clutching the deadly knife. Hal realised this was the end, and he was still bracing himself for the touch of the blade when Olivia's voice rang out.

'Rodney, stop!'

Rodney ignored her, advancing on Hal with vengeance burning in his eyes.

'Rodney, nobody else knows where my asteroid is. You can kill him after he's told me.'

Still Rodney kept coming, one hand clutched to his shattered ribs, the other holding the knife.

Olivia raised the gun. 'Rodney, I swear I'll shoot you.'

One step, another, and Rodney finally stopped. He was less than an arms length from Hal, the knife well within range, but while the fire still burned in his eyes, Olivia's hold over him was too strong. Slowly, he lowered the blade, until it was millimetres from Hal's knee. 'One cut,' said Rodney, his voice hoarse. 'Let me do it, Gran.'

'No. Not yet.' Olivia gestured at Harriet. 'Tie her up in the other chair. Quick, now.'

Moments later, Harriet was secure.

'Now, Spacejock,' said Olivia. 'Let's start again. Unless you tell me where my asteroid went, Rodney is going to use his blade on this pretty young woman.'

Hal shrugged. 'So what? I never liked cops.'

'Rodney, cut one of her fingers off.'

'Wait,' said Hal. 'Remember the camera!'

'I'm glad there's a camera,' hissed Rodney. 'I'll keep the footage as a souvenir.'

Hal gazed at the blade in Rodney's hand, staring at it in fascination. Slowly, it descended, getting closer and closer to Harriet's arm until he could see the blue light illuminating her skin. Then, in desperation, Hal threw himself forwards, straightening his legs and driving himself up with a massive thrust. His shoulder caught Rodney in the chest, knocking him backwards, and in that instant Olivia raised the gun and fired. Hal felt an immense blow on the side of his head, and he went down like a rag doll, still attached to the heavy chair. The floor came up to meet him, and as he lay there, fighting to remain conscious, he saw Olivia press the gun to the back of Harriet's neck. Even from this distance, Hal could see the red glow above the grip, indicating the weapon wasn't set to stun - it was set to kill.

Olivia's finger tightened on the trigger, and Hal screamed at her to stop, again and again. Or at least, he tried to, but his lungs were curiously empty and he couldn't draw breath. Time slowed, and Hal realised it was over. Harriet was about to die, he was already dying, and nothing was going to save them.

The world tilted crazily, floor and ceiling and walls all changing places, getting confused, and Hal realised he was on the point of passing out. A body flew past, arms outstretched, and with a shock he realised it was Olivia Backsight. She grabbed onto Rodney, and the pair of them danced a weird tango as the floor bucked and heaved beneath them. They moved one way, then the other, and then Hal saw something which made his blood run cold. Harriet's chair was on its back, angled away from him, her legs still and lifeless. Had ...had Olivia shot her? Or had the chair fallen over in the upheaval?

Then Hal noticed something else. As the floor tilted this way and that, the big rock had started to move. It was rolling directly towards him, crushing stone chips underneath like so many empty skulls. The floor tilted again, altering the rock's course, and Hal now realised it was heading directly for Harriet. Just before it reached her, the floor angled the other way, and the rock described a neat loop before hurtling across the room in the opposite direction.

Ahead of it, still stumbling around in each others arms, were Rodney and Olivia Backsight. They barely had time for one terrified look at the oncoming boulder before the rock gathered them up and crushed them against the far wall, stretching the metal into a deep, concave dish.

Then, all was still.

◆

Clunk studied the viewscreen, concern etched on his face. The *Volante*'s powerful engines had torn the giant space station into half a dozen chunks, each of them now spinning away in a different direction.

As a consequence, any reinforcements which Mr Spacejock might have faced were now safely trapped in the other sections, unable to reach him.

Clunk examined each piece of the station in turn, and he was relieved to see there weren't any leaks. The safety doors had sealed each section as expected, and now all he had to do was dock the ship and find Mr Spacejock.

◆

Hal rolled onto his side, then got to his knees with the chair still attached. Slowly, inch by inch, struggling all the way, he crawled to Harriet's chair. As he got closer his heart hammered in his chest, and he dreaded what he might find. Knocked out ... or dead?

Harriet's eyes were open, and there was a streak of blood on the side of her face. Hal gasped at the sight, his fists clenching in despair, and he was about to turn away when Harriet gave him a weak smile. 'Hal Spacejock, you look a right mess.'

Before he could free himself and untie her, hold her in his arms, or even tell her how much he loved her, Hal passed out.

35

When Hal opened his eyes he discovered he was lying in a hospital bed. Clunk was sitting nearby, and when he realised Hal was awake his face creased into a warm smile. 'Mr Spacejock! How are you feeling?'

'Not too bad,' said Hal. The words came out as a croaky whisper, and he realised his throat hurt. Then he felt something else - a warm hand holding his own. He glanced round and saw Harriet Walsh sitting in a chair alongside his bed. Her eyes were closed and she was fast asleep.

'Is she okay?' he asked Clunk.

'Just tired,' said the robot. 'Tired, and worried.'

Hal squeezed Harriet's hand, and she opened her eyes. For a minute they were unfocussed, and then she saw Hal and smiled. 'Welcome back, deputy. How are you feeling?'

'He's lucky he was only shot in the head,' said Clunk seriously.

Hal blinked. 'Er ... come again?'

'Olivia Backsight used Harriet's weapon, correct?'

Hal nodded, and immediately wished he hadn't.

'There you go, then. The safety mechanism saved you.'

'It didn't save anything,' said Hal with feeling. 'I copped the full blast.'

'Yes, but it was non-lethal. The weapon's sensors detected it was aiming at your skull, and automatically reduced the power to minimum.'

'I'd hardly call that a safety mechanism.'

'Would you rather get shot at full power?'

'Er, no. Definitely not.'

'There you go, then.' Clunk got up. 'I saw a coffee machine down the hall. I'll leave you two in peace.'

'Wait,' said Hal. 'Before you go ...'

'Yes?'

'Tell me what happened to the diamonds. Was that the original rock or not?'

Clunk looked uncomfortable. 'No, I lost that in an asteroid field.'

'Seriously?'

'It broke free during emergency manoeuvres, and it wasn't possible to retrieve it. The Navcom and I located a substitute. It was a close match, except for the strong magnetic field.'

'Fair enough.' Hal gestured at the door. 'Off you go, then. And don't do anything I wouldn't.'

'That gives me quite a lot of latitude,' remarked Clunk.

'How about you?' Hal asked Harriet, once the robot had left. 'Are you all right?'

She nodded. 'Just a few bumps and bruises.'

'What happened after I passed out?'

'I had to wait hours for backup, and I didn't know if you were going to ...' Harriet's voice tailed off. 'I mean ... you might have ...'

'Hey, I pulled through,' said Hal. 'And you ... they'll give you a medal for this, right?'

'A promotion, I think. They're not big on medals.' Harriet swallowed. 'Hal, I –'

'Getting promoted. That's what you always wanted, isn't it?'

'Well yes, but –'

'You'll be a captain before you know it, and one day you'll be running the whole Peace Force.'

'I think that's a long way off.'

Hal smiled. 'You've got your foot on the first rung.'

'I-I'm not sure I want it any more. When you were shot I –'

There was a knock at the door, and Harriet frowned as Meri Ryder looked in.

'Hello, you!' said Meri brightly, giving Hal a beaming smile while completely ignoring Harriet. 'How's my brave pilot doing?'

'He's doing fine,' said Harriet. 'Shouldn't you be off organising an art show or something?'

'Oh no, not me. I'm out of the art business for good.'

'Really?' said Hal. 'What are you planning next?'

'House removals.' Meri hesitated. 'I have a couple of jobs lined up already, if you're interested.'

715

Hal smiled weakly. 'I don't think the *Volante*'s hold is big enough.'

'No, silly. You move the contents, not the houses.'

'Wouldn't it be cheaper to sell up and buy new gear?'

'Not at the executive end of the market. Antiques, valuables … there's good money to be made.'

'I'll think about it.'

'Good.' Meri laid her hand on Hal's arm. 'I'd really like to work with you again, Hal. We make a great team.'

Hal smiled at her, and she kissed him on the cheek before leaving. Then Hal caught the expression on Harriet's face, and he gave her an apologetic grin. 'She's just being friendly.'

'So I noticed,' said Harriet shortly.

Hal squeezed her hand. 'It's you I care about. You know that.'

Harriet looked down at him, and he could see the conflict in her eyes. In that instant Hal knew she would return to the *Volante* if he asked her to, and she would travel the galaxy with him once more. But give it six months, a year tops, and she'd hate him for luring her away. Harriet's heart, and her future, lay with the Peace Force.

'This doesn't have to be goodbye,' she said, in a low voice.

'Of course not. We'll meet again, and you'll have plenty more chances to arrest me.'

'If I earn myself a couple of promotions I'll be able to score a desk job, and then I can start thinking about a family.'

'I can just see a mini Harriet running around the place.'

'Or a Hal Junior. Wouldn't that be a trial and a half?'

'Twins!'

Harriet smiled, and Hal felt a moment of true happiness. Then reality intruded.

'I'd better be off,' said Harriet, picking up her bag. 'Boson's collecting me from the spaceport.'

'If you need any help with any of your cases, give me a call.'

'I can always use a good deputy, Hal.'

Harriet stood awkwardly for a moment or two, then smiled. 'Goodbye, Hal.'

'Catch you around.'

Suddenly Harriet was leaning over him, and they held each other tightly. Hal breathed gently so as not to break the moment, wishing it would never end. Then Harriet released him, and left without another word.

When Clunk came back, Hal was in a pensive mood. The robot handed him a hot coffee, and once he'd sat down Hal cleared his throat. 'Clunk, will you promise me something?'

'Yes, Mr Spacejock.'

'If anything happens to me, I want you to find Harriet and keep her safe. Will you do that?'

'Of course, Mr Spacejock. Harriet is my second-favourite human in the galaxy.'

Hal felt a surge of affection for the robot. 'You mean …?'

'Yes, Mr Spacejock. She's number two on my list, right after the presenter on Oh Dear, Humanity.'

Hal grinned, pleased the robot had defused an awkward situation with a little joke. 'Er, that was a joke, wasn't it?'

'A robot cannot lie,' said Clunk, with a twinkle in his eye.

Epilogue

Chief Inspector Boson, head of the new Corporate Crimes squad, today confirmed that his team are investigating Backsight Industries. When questioned about the nature of the investigation, Boson declared that it covered everything from arson to tax fraud, extortion to hijacking, and kidnapping to murder. The company's new board of directors, hastily elected after the death of Olivia Backsight and her grandson Rodney, issued a statement assuring investors they would cooperate in every way possible.

In a related story, the gang behind a spate of vehicle thefts and hijackings has been apprehended. With help from contacts in Customs and Shipping, the well-organised crew would steal valuable parts and equipment to order. Staff at Backsight Industries are being questioned about their links to the gang, although a company spokesperson has denied any official involvement. Rumours that Backsight has been shaving their costs for years by using stolen parts has also been denied.

In other news, repairs began today on the Backsight Orbiter. Work is expected to take several months, and when completed the facility will be converted into an orbiting prison. Apparently, the first 'guests' will be the corrupt politicians, judges and customs officers who spent their careers secretly working for Backsight Industries.

Acknowledgements

To my friends and family
Thanks for the awesome help and support!

To my proof readers, Ian, Kevin and Tricia, many thnks. Er, tanks. No,
make that thunks.
Well spotted!

Hal Spacejock: Framed
(A Short Story)

A straightforward cargo delivery takes a left turn when Hal Spacejock gets sidetracked. But with 200 shares in a worthless company on offer, who wouldn't step into a makeshift teleporter which has already claimed one victim?

Hal and Clunk, stars of the Hal Spacejock comedy series, feature in this brand new 8000-word short story. 'Framed' slots into the series any time after Hal Spacejock Second Course, but can be read and enjoyed as a stand-alone.

www.spacejock.com.au

Framed

Hal Spacejock muttered under his breath as he strode down the Volante's landing ramp. It wasn't even lunch time and the day was already a complete disaster. First the outrageous landing fees, then the sky-high fuel prices, and finally the sealer: a one-sided 'conversation' with their customer, who was insisting on door-to-door delivery. Of course, she'd never mentioned any such thing when booking the job, and Hal would have played the original conversation back to her if he'd been able to find it amongst all the pirated software and amusing film clips crammed into the flight computer.

So he'd searched for a freight hauler to move a container of antique furniture halfway across the city. The first three companies had laughed in his face when he revealed his budget. The last guy had been more helpful, giving Hal the address of a trucking firm where the drivers ran cash jobs whenever the boss took her secretary to lunch.

There was a rumble from the horizon, and Hal searched the sky for the departing spaceship. Instead he saw a line of dark clouds. Lightning flashed, and as the brewing storm approached Hal realised they'd be shifting their cargo in a heavy downpour. Perfect.

The ramp moved underfoot as a squashy-faced robot emerged from the ship. Clunk was moving even more stiffly than usual, his back as straight as an engine brace and his expression pure vinegar.

'Are you coming or what?' called Hal.

Clunk used his middle finger on the keypad, punching a lengthy sequence of alternating twos and eights.

'Take your time. No rush.'

Okay, so maybe the price of fuel on this overpriced planet wasn't Clunk's fault, but he should've checked the landing charges before setting down. After all, why have a co-pilot if you had to do everything yourself? Hal crossed his arms. In future he'd have to lay down the law.

Clunk glanced through the porthole to make sure the lights were off, then started down the ramp. Every step of his big, flat feet was deliberate and forceful, and his lips were pressed together so hard it was a surprise his jaw didn't fall off.

'Nice day, isn't it?' said Hal lightly. It had just dawned on him that Clunk was taking things badly. 'Quite warmish.'

Clunk walked straight towards him, saying not a word, and Hal realised the robot was perfectly capable of running him down. As far as Clunk was concerned, the three laws were quaint relics from a gentler age.

Hal backed away, then turned and hurried to the safety of the landing pad. Better to face a shedload of angry customers than a fiery old robot with a short fuse and fists like boulders.

Once on the landing pad he turned to admire his ship. The Volante's vast bulk was disguised by her graceful lines, and he felt a surge of pride at the sight. Running freight didn't earn a whole lot of money, but at least they were doing it in style.

Inspection complete, he glanced around the landing field to get his bearings. They'd landed in the freight section, right near the customs shed and a row of warehouses. In the opposite direction there was a low-lying passenger terminal, all chrome and glass and rows of uncomfortable seats. In between was the usual collection of street vendors, hawking everything from pastries to university degrees. Despite himself, Hal gravitated towards the colourful stalls. He had more degrees than wall space to hang them on, but he could always manage a slice of cake.

'Where are you going?' asked Clunk.

'Essential supplies.'

'Mr Spacejock, if you must organise these underhanded cash jobs during lunch hours, don't you think we should arrive at the freight company before lunch is over?'

'There's loads of time. It's just round the corner.' Hal eyed a display of Arts degrees. 'Toilet tissue is pricey in these parts.'

'They're not worth the paper they're printed on.'

'These are fake too.'

The robot unbent a little as they moved between the stalls. He was never angry for long, either because he was essentially kind-hearted, or because his memory was so flaky he forgot why he'd steamed up in the first place. Then Hal spotted a cheap solar-powered fan, and he bought it as a peace offering. 'Here. Something to keep you cool.'

Clunk eyed the toy dubiously, flicking the switch on and off. Inspection complete, he nodded his thanks and stashed the fan in a chest compartment. Hal had seen odds and ends going into that compartment from day one, but he rarely saw anything coming out. He suspected they all dropped down to the robot's legs, adding to his ballast.

They walked past a display of fresh fruit, unlocked commsets and body piercings, and then Hal came to a sudden halt. An elderly man with a shock of grey hair was standing next to a console bulging with wires and electronics. Nearby, a young man in a red skivvy sat on a bar stool, reading a book, and behind them stood an unpainted door frame.

'I know that guy!' exclaimed Hal. 'Clunk, you remember. He tried to flog us shares in a dodgy teleporter company.'

'That's not how it was,' said Clunk. 'As I recall, you were about to give him all your money until I exposed his little trick.'

'Something like that, yeah.'

The fake scientist had been running a neat scam involving two wooden cupboards, some impressive-looking electronics and a taciturn young man pressed into service as a helper. The young man entered the first cupboard, the scientist pulled a lever, and after some tame pyrotechnics the same young man would emerge from the second wardrobe, apparently teleported across.

At that point the scientist would offer shares in his company, with future earnings estimated in the billions. Unfortunately for the elderly scientist, Clunk noticed a slight problem with his demonstration: The young man who entered the first cupboard had a book under his arm. The young man who emerged from the second cupboard, with the same hairstyle and dressed in the same clothes, also had a book. However, it it was a different title.

The young men were identical twins, and the scientist was a conman.

This time there were no cupboards, just the metal door frame, but the young man and the electronics were one and the same. Wise to the trick, Hal was about to move on when the elderly scientist spotted him. He peered through his thick glasses but obviously didn't recognise him. 'Sir, you are perhaps interested in a little demonstration?'

'No thanks,' said Hal. 'We gave at the office.'

'I'm sorry, what was this?'

There was a rumble from the horizon, and Hal realised the rain would be arriving soon. 'You're wasting your time. I saw through this trick

when it was two cupboards and a pair of twin brothers. Hans and
…what was the other one?'

A shadow passed over the old man's face. 'Kurt. My other son was
Kurt.'

'Was?'

'The first test subject in my first real experiment. It was perfect how it
worked, but he never came back.'

'What did you do, lose the key to the second cupboard?'

'Cupboards …that was an early model. We made good with the
venture capitalist people, and –'

'And upgraded to a door frame. Neat.' Hal glanced around. 'Where's
the rest of it?'

The scientist pointed across the landing field, where a second frame
was leaning against a refuelling cluster. Alongside was a small box
studded with rows of flashing lights, connected to the frame with a thick
grey cable. Hal snorted. So this was the new scam! The other twin must
have packed it in, and whoever the scientist had roped in to replace him
wasn't a perfect match. So, he'd put the second 'teleporter booth' two
hundred metres away.

'Okay, so how does it work this time?' demanded Hal. 'Smoke
machine? Mirrors?'

'Trade secret,' said the scientist. 'It is only short distances, but …how
do you say it? My design improves in bounds and leaps.'

There was a flash of lightning and a rumble of thunder.

'We'd better be going,' said Clunk. 'The storm …'

'Just a minute.' Hal pointed at the door frame. 'Are you telling me you
can teleport something through this? Push it in one door so it comes out
the other? It really works?'

'Correct.'

'It's not a scam?'

'But of course not.'

'All right, show me.'

'Alas, Hans will not do it. Not after Kurt.'

'So Kurt…'

'He went through but did not come out. A small glitch, easily
corrected.'

'Tell that to Kurt,' murmured Clunk.

Hal gestured at the frame. 'Why didn't you go after him?'

'I have to make with the lever pulling. You understand?'

'Plus a good general never leads from the front,' remarked Clunk.

'So what I was thinking …'

'Yes?'

The scientist gave Hal a sidelong glance. 'What I was thinking was maybe a reward. One hundred shares in my teleporter company for the brave soul who finds my son.'

'A hundred? Really?'

'Mr Spacejock!' protested Clunk. 'You can't risk your life for a hundred shares in a worthless company!'

'You're right, it's a lousy offer.' Hal rubbed his chin. 'Make it two hundred and you have a deal.'

'My good sir, even Hans und Kurt only have fifty each.'

'That's my price. Take it or leave it.'

'Done,' said the scientist.

Clunk sighed as the men sealed their deal with a handshake.

'Don't worry,' murmured Hal in an aside. 'This thing is never going to work.'

Two minutes later everything was set. Hal stood before the metal door frame, feeling like a complete goose. Despite the old guy's confidence, he wasn't convinced the so-called teleporter would move him any further than his first step through the door. Meanwhile, Clunk was leaning against the frame, rolling his eyes, shaking his head and tutting to himself. Even the weather joined in, mocking them with fat raindrops and ominous thunder. Hans had legged it for the safety of the passenger terminal, and traders were scurrying around packing up their wares. The scientist was still tweaking his electronics, oblivious to the storm.

'Are you ready yet?' shouted Hal.

The scientist turned a large dial, framed the distant door frame with his fingers, then turned the dial a little more. 'Now we are ready. When the field appears, step through without delay.'

'Field?' Hal pictured a nice meadow with butterflies.

'Stand by!' shouted the scientist.

There was a loud fizz, and a milky white ball appeared in the centre of the door frame. It glowed softly, shivering whenever a raindrop broke the surface. The scientist pulled a lever and ... Sproinnggg! The ball of light spread out to fill the frame, corner to corner.

'Into the field!' shouted the scientist. 'Quick! It cannot last!'

Hal glanced at the second frame, two hundred metres away, and saw an identical white field. Then he looked at Clunk, who was slowly shaking his head.

The next thing Hal knew there was a searing flash behind him, and suddenly he was flying towards the milky white field. He went through dead centre, arms outstretched, while a huge thunderclap almost knocked him senseless. Something grabbed his ankle, but he was flying much too fast to be stopped and whatever it was came along for the ride.

Hal got a whirling view of grey clouds, leaves and dirt before he landed on all fours, rolled head over heels and ended up on his feet. He got another impression then: a tall, muscle-bound stranger in a fur loincloth, one arm drawn back to strike.

Barely had he taken this in when the stranger swung at him, knocking him flat on his back with a makeshift club. Hal heard a scuffle as he drifted in and out of consciousness, and then everything went dark.

◆

'I said I was sorry, didn't I?'

'Your actions were most impolite. Indeed, you might have killed him.'

Hal's head was pounding, but he still recognised Clunk's voice. 'I'm not dead. I'm all right.'

'You're concussed, Mr Spacejock.'

'It'll take more than a bump to put me down.'

'It *was* more than a bump. You stopped a tree trunk with your head.'

Hal sat up. There were three of them around the smouldering camp fire: himself, Clunk, who for some reason was wearing a fur hat, and the branch-wielding maniac. Hal eyed the stranger, who refused to meet his gaze. 'Who's the caveman?'

'Kurt.'

'Really? We found him?' Despite the blinding headache, numb extremities and double vision, Hal's spirits rose. Two hundred shares, thank you very much! Now all they had to do was get back.

'He's safe and sound.' Clunk sighed. 'Unfortunately we can't get back.'

Kurt threw a branch on the fire. 'I *told* the old buffer to keep it under eleven, but would he listen? Now we're all trapped.'

'We're never trapped,' said Hal. 'Clunk can whistle up the *Volante* and organise a search party.'

'I'm afraid that's impossible, Mr Spacejock. My communications circuits were damaged by the lightning strike.'

Hal remembered the vivid flash. 'Is that what hit me?'

'That was the first blow, yes.' Clunk gave Kurt a sideways frown. 'Mr, er, Kurt, has been living off the land for the past two months. According to him, this clearing is surrounded by dense forest in every direction, although he did find a settlement a few kilometres to the East.'

'Great! We'll hire a car and find out way home.'

There was a lengthy silence. Clearly, neither Kurt nor Clunk wanted to share the bad news.

'Go on, out with it.'

'The settlement ...' began Kurt. 'It's not safe.'

'Why not?'

Kurt threw a fresh log on the fire, and the whirling sparks cast his face in stark relief. 'As a child I spent long hours in the woods around my home, living rough and surviving on nature's bounty.'

'Oh yeah, I like those too. Bit small though.'

'Using these skills, I built a shelter and constructed simple but effective weapons.'

Hal rubbed his forehead.

'During my time in this place I've hunted and searched, searched and hunted. Slowly I built a picture of my surroundings, drawing crude maps with charcoal on the skins of small animals.'

'Didn't they wriggle?'

Kurt ignored the interruption. 'Then, one night, when the moon was full and the hunt was good, I followed my prey to an unexplored area to the East of this place. Was there a ravine I might plunge into? Was there a swift but deadly river ready to carry me to my doom? Was there a deadly creature on my trail, stalking me just as I pursued my own quarry?'

'Well? Was there?' asked Hal, leaning closer.

'Actually, no. The going was easy.'

Hal glanced at Clunk. Kurt had obviously read one too many fantasy novels, and before long he'd be showing off his rings of power and a wooden axe with an unpronounceable name. Stick anyone in a forest for a couple of months and they were bound to go round the twist, and Kurt had really snapped. Assuming they could get him back to civilisation, the best he could hope for was a peaceful loony bin with an endless supply of world-building materials.

'But I did find a settlement.'

'Yeah, Clunk said that about half an hour ago. You could have showed me the thing by now.'

'I was drawn by a huge fire and the sound of drums. They were very loud, shaking the ground underfoot.'

'Teenagers,' muttered Hal, rolling his eyes. 'Where are the parents? That's what I want to know.'

'These were not wayward youths, Spacejock. There was a large crowd around the fire, and they carried many weapons. As I watched they took one of their own and bound him hand and foot.'

'Go on.'

'They dragged the prisoner between the huts. The drumbeats grew ever more intense, then ... Whoosh! Kerthunk! Blblblbl!' Kurt waggled his tongue and rolled his eyes.

'They all tickled him?'

'Far worse. When I could bear to look, generous portions of meat were roasting on the fire and these evil people were slaking their thirst from rough-hewn mugs of wood.'

'And then you went down there and asked if they had a commset. Right?'

Kurt looked at Hal as if he were mad, which Hal found rather insulting.

'So you chickened out.'

'The drums thudded once more, and even as I watched the insatiable crowd selected another of their number.'

'Oh, that's all right then. After a few more snacks there'll be one left standing, and you can put him away with your tree trunk.'

'Mock all you like. I know what I saw, and I understand danger.'

Hal turned to Clunk. 'Did you get all that?'

Clunk stared at him, glassy eyed.

'Clunk?'

No reply.

'Oh crap, his batteries have gone.' Hal looked around. 'Do you have a charge point?'

◆

Hal woke at dawn, shivering with cold and damp from head to toe. He was lying on a makeshift bed Kurt had thrown together from something itchy and hard and very uncomfortable, and the animal skins that had gone into his bedclothes had been unwrapped from their original owners all-too-recently.

Hal threw off the ripe furs and sat up. The fire was burning out and there was no sign of Kurt the Krazy …or any hint of a hot breakfast. Clunk was still in the same place, covered in dew and dotted with fallen leaves, although his animal-skin cap had slipped a little. Come to think of it, the robot had never explained why he'd donned the headgear in the first place.

He heard a twig snap and turned to see Kurt entering the clearing with something dead tossed over his shoulder. He tossed some wood on the fire, and when it was blazing merrily he took out a flake of stone with a razor-sharp edge and reached for the animal. At that point Hal decided to go for a quick walk. When he returned, Kurt handed him a hunk of roasted meat. Hal picked at it, but his appetite had vanished and he found himself missing the *Volante's* AutoChef. The bad-tempered machine was more likely to put frozen asparagus spears through the back of your hand than serve them on a plate, but at least the food hadn't been breathing ten minutes earlier. 'We've got to get Clunk going again. He's our only chance.'

'Before you came round last night, he wrote me a note.' Kurt reached into his loin cloth and took out a damp scrap of paper.

Hal eyed the thing in distaste. 'Could you maybe read it out?'

'Most certainly. It says 'When the sun rises above the trees, you must take my hat off."

Hal rubbed his chin. 'Was there any more?'

'No, that's the whole message. The piece of paper was not large.'

'Shame, when there was room for so much more.' Hal sighed. 'Oh well, I guess we'd better shift him.'

They carried Clunk to a fallen log on the western side of the clearing. Once he was propped up Hal reached for the furry cap, but Kurt stopped him. 'He said to remove it when the sun was high enough.'

'What difference does it make?'

'It was important enough to write you a note.'

Hal shrugged. 'Fair enough.'

They made use of the time by gathering fallen branches for the fire, until the weak sun broke over the treetops. Hal hurried over to the robot and reached for the cap. Then he hesitated.

'What is it?' asked Kurt.

'For all I know this could shoot an emergency flare out of his left nostril, and I've used up my hospital cover for the month.'

'Would you like me to do it?' suggested Kurt.

'Good idea.'

Taken aback, Kurt nonetheless took up his position in front of the robot, while Hal took up *his* position behind a large rock twenty metres away. With shaking fingers, Kurt reached for the cap on Clunk's head. Meanwhile, Hal's fingers were in his ears and his eyes were screwed shut.

'It's okay,' said Kurt. 'It's just a solar panel.'

'Attached to what?'

'His brain, I think.'

'Oh wonderful,' muttered Hal. 'He'll be thinking and talking and arguing, and he still won't be able to do anything useful.'

At that moment Clunk's eyes flickered and his lips moved. Hal got closer and Clunk repeated himself.

'Travois.'

Hal looked at Kurt. Kurt looked at Hal. Clearly the solar power wasn't reaching every part of the robot's brain. 'Travis isn't here right now,' said Hal. 'Do you want to leave a message?'

'Travois,' repeated the robot. 'Build.'

'I think he wants us to build a travois,' said Kurt.

'I got that, but what is it?'

'It's a transportation device. We can make one out of branches.'

'Yes,' said Clunk, and closed his eyes again.

'What did I say?' Hal spread his hands. 'All thinking and no doing.'

◆

It was late afternoon, and construction of the travois was in full swing. Kurt had identified a couple of suitable trees - tall and straight and not too big - but when it came to chopping them down the only available tool was a stone chip. When Kurt offered Hal a flake he accepted enthusiastically, before realising what it meant. Worse, it came from the dodgy loincloth.

Kurt went off to find the right kind of vines, leaving the job to Hal. The wood was tough, and by the time the first tree toppled over Hal ached from fingertip to shoulder. Worse, he still had another tree to go. And whoever heard of cutting trees down with a lousy chunk of stone?

While sawing the second one with the tiny flake, cursing and muttering under his breath, Hal happened to glance at his trusty robot companion. Much to his surprise, the robot had a huge grin plastered across his face. Hal dashed the sweat from his brow, almost shaving off his left eyebrow with the flint. 'You think this is funny?' he demanded, after he'd staunched the blood with his sleeve. The robot didn't respond.

By the time the second tree fell Hal swore he'd never lay a hand on anything woody for the rest of his life. He spent another five minutes snapping off branches with the heel of his boot then glanced at Clunk again.

The robot's expression hadn't changed, and he looked for all the world like someone had just whispered a hilarious joke in his ear. It was too much for Hal: After his concussion, a lousy night tossing and turning on a bed of rocks, and the slow process of sawing down cast iron trees with his bare hands, he'd had enough.

He tramped across the clearing and snapped his fingers in front of Clunk's face. 'Come on, wake up.'

No reaction.

'Clunk! I know you're in there.'

Not a flicker.

'Is it okay if I sharpen this flint on the back of your head?'

The robot's eyes opened.

'Ha. Thought so.' Hal gestured with the flint. 'You think all this is funny, do you?'

Slowly, the robot's mouth turned down. 'Involuntary. Sorry.'

Hal eyed Clunk suspiciously, but the face was now expressionless. Mollified, he tossed the flint aside and laid in the grass, closing his eyes. Twenty-four hours ago they'd been arranging delivery on a cargo of antique furniture. Now they were lashing together a couple of wooden poles so they could drag a heavy robot through the forest.

The previous night, while they'd sat around the fire with the immobilised robot, Kurt had repeated a few of Clunk's theories about their location. The sky was overcast, so there was no chance of getting a fix by the stars, but according to the robot the power from the wayward lightning strike could have generated enough energy to transport them to whole new planet.

The settlement was easy to explain: Explorers had found more habitable planets in the galaxy than anyone knew what to do with, and most were filed away for future settlement. Occasionally a splinter group would bribe a cargo pilot and set up camp on some deserted world, never to be seen or heard from again. Most turned feral within two generations.

Clunk's database held information on these planets, including the unique chemical makeup of their atmosphere. This was like a planetary fingerprint, but unfortunately the same spike which had damaged Clunk's comms circuits had also fried his analyser, so he couldn't sample their planet's air to look it up in the database.

Hal sighed. It wasn't a fantastic situation, but at least they hadn't been teleported to a barren asteroid or the middle of a star. He glanced at his watch and wondered whether there was time for a quick nap. Kurt of the Jungle could be playing with his vines for hours yet, and it was warm and pleasant in the sun.

No, they were fighting for survival, not camping out. Each of them had a role to play, and lazing about in the sun wasn't getting anyone home. Hal sat up. He might not be able to hunt, identify rare species of vines, build a shelter, secure food, dress a wound or skin small animals, but he had plenty of other talents he could put to use.

After a moment or two he was still deciding which of his many talents could be applied to their current situation. Piloting a spaceship clear across the galaxy? Making a decent coffee? Handling customer complaints with tact and courtesy? Bunging together a tasty sandwich using nothing but leftovers? Sure, if he could find a loaf of bread.

Hal eyed the edge of the clearing. What if Kurt had collected these special vines hours ago, and was now having a quiet nap while Hal did the hard work? At the thought of this injustice, Hal sprang to his feet. He'd done his part, and now it was time to do a little exploring. But first, he needed a better outfit.

◆

The chirp of a bird. The squeak of a small creature. A rustle in the undergrowth. A very human cry of pain.

'What kind of idiot grows branches this damn low?' grumbled Hal, rubbing his eye. It was the third time he'd whapped himself across the face, and it was only a matter of time before he tried it with a bigger branch and knocked himself out.

It would have been easier fending off the twigs if he'd had two hands to spare, but he'd wrapped the patchwork furs around himself as camouflage and he needed one hand to hold the edges together. Clunk's fur cap was pulled down to his eyebrows, giving him a fierce unkept look, and with his reddened eyes and dirt-streaked face he looked exactly like one of Kurt's 'evil people'. Indeed, that was his intention.

Hal caught a whiff of damp ash, and he realised it had to be the big cooking fire Kurt had described. He crawled under a bush, parted the leaves and saw the settlement laid out below. At the foot of the grassy slope there was a clearing with half a dozen mud huts, and in the middle a big pile of white ashes was ringed with smooth stones.

Hal bit his lip. There was nobody around, and there was bound to be food in the huts. If he returned to camp with a loaf of bread it would certainly take Kurt down a peg or two. His mouth watered at the thought of a crusty loaf, and he wondered whether it wouldn't be better to eat the thing and brandish a handful of crumbs as proof of his gathering skills.

Hal moved forwards on hands and knees, keeping his eyes peeled for movement. Unfortunately he should have been keeping his eyes peeled for obstacles, and the first he knew of the root growing out of the ground was when it snagged his hands.

He went over like a roped steer, nose-first into the dirt, and the momentum carried him out of the bushes and onto the edge of the grassy slope. He teetered, desperately trying to regain his balance, then tumbled forwards. There was a whirling confusion of grass, sky, green, blue, green, blue, greenbluegreenblue as he went head over heels down the incline before he hit a bump and sailed into the air. For a moment it was like floating in space, serene and peaceful.

Then he went PLUMPF! into the big pile of ashes.

◆

Hal fought his way out of the dense ash, choking and spluttering. He clawed at his eyes, where the ash had turned to a sticky paste, and blinked and squinted in the dim light as he tried to spot the nearest cover.

He needn't have bothered. His sudden arrival had thrown up a massive ash cloud which was drifting through the village like a good old pea-souper, and anyone inside the huts would be too busy hacking and coughing and struggling for breath to notice an ash-coated figure stumbling around outside.

Hal staggered to the nearest building and hauled the door open. Inside was a rough-looking bed and a few sticks of furniture. The drunken-looking table was bare, and there was no sign of any bread, crusty or otherwise. Discouraged, Hal tried the next hut. This one was a little bigger - two beds - but there was the same lack of baked tasties.

The third building was a lot bigger, with several rooms. Hal searched them thoroughly, leaving a trail of ashy footprints, and was just about to give up when he spotted a wall hanging. One corner was rucked up, and behind it he could see a gleam of metal.

He twitched the hanging aside and stared. There was an aluminium door with a sign: Staff Only.

The door was locked, but gave a little when he put his shoulder to it. Stepping back, Hal drew back his boot and drove the heel at the smooth metal, just below the handle.

Thud!

The door shook, but didn't give, and the impact knocked ash from Hal's clothing. Engulfed in fine white powder, he tried again.

THUD!

The door burst inwards, bounced, and came back in time to whack Hal on the side of the leg. He went down, clutching at his throbbing knee with both hands, and then slowly raised his head. He was looking into a cupboard, and the shelves were packed with supplies. Tinned food and bottled water, coils of modern-looking rope, a shelf full of batteries … and at eye level, a large machete clipped to the wall.

Hal cursed under his breath. Why hadn't he come exploring before cutting down two whole trees with a chip of stone? He grabbed the machete to test the edge, and a fierce grin split his ash-caked face. Now, at last, he could defend himself. Nobody made Hal Spacejock into lunch!

◆

Hal emerged from the larger building with Kurt's animal skin quilt bunched over his shoulder. He'd piled as much grub as possible into the middle then gathered the four corners to make a rough sack. It was heavy, but manageable, and as he staggered up the grassy slope towards he bushes he pictured Kurt's expression when he saw the supplies.

The villagers would be out for blood once they discovered they'd been raided, but Hal didn't mean to hang around much longer. Get the travois built, grab Clunk and leg it. That was the plan.

Once he reached the bushes he set his burden down, giving his shoulder a rest. He'd loaded up a little enthusiastically, but then he'd just faced twenty-four hours of charred meat. Wincing at his aches and pains, Hal shouldered the bundle and set off for camp.

He'd barely taken two steps when a rough hand was clamped to his mouth.

◆

Hal struggled to free himself, but his arm was wrenched behind his back.

'Keep still, you fool!' hissed a voice in his ear. 'It's me. Kurt!'

Hal relaxed and Kurt let him go. He opened his mouth to complain but Kurt shushed him and gestured towards the village. Then he motioned towards the forest, and Hal followed.

'You're insane,' said Kurt, once they'd put a safe distance between themselves and the settlement. 'I tell you about this evil group of people eating their own kind, and you come for a tour?'

'How did you find me?'

'You left a trail of broken branches as wide as a four lane highway. Don't you realise they could follow such markings back to our own camp? Always approach enemies from the far side!'

'Don't worry, I won't be going back.'

'Good.' Kurt eyed the furs. 'What's that?'

Hal showed him, and he couldn't help grinning at the other man's shocked expression.

'You know what this means?' demanded Kurt, holding up a tin of peaches.

'Yeah. No more furry critter on a stick.'

'No, you ...' Kurt shook the tin. 'This means civilisation! Industry!'

'Or maybe they ripped off a visiting ship.' Hal frowned. 'That would explain the door.'

'Door?'

'Aluminium. It said 'Staff only"

'A speaking door! That's very high tech. How was it powered?'

'No, you twit. There was a sign on it.' Hal rubbed his shoulder. 'Sharp edges, too.'

Kurt looked back towards the settlement, a worried expression on his face. 'We must leave this place. When they return they will hunt us.'

'Lead the way.'

Kurt lapsed into silence until they reached the clearing, where he'd already assembled the travois. He showed off his handiwork, but as far as Hal was concerned it was just a big narrow 'A' with a few bits of vine criss-crossed between the uprights. 'Is that it?'

'Sure. We put the robot here,' said Kurt, indicating the narrower portion. 'The point rests on the ground, and we take turns pulling.'

'Pulling where?'

'Not to the East,' said Kurt grimly.

They both looked up as a peal of thunder rolled around the forest. The sun was shining and there wasn't a cloud in the sky, but the thunder went on and on, growing louder and louder. 'That's no thunder!' exclaimed Hal. He scanned the blue sky, shading his eyes from the sun, until he spotted it: a long white contrail headed by a silver spark. A spaceship!

There was no chance of being spotted, but even so Hal was flooded with excitement. The ship was departing, which meant it had just taken off from the planet. Civilisation. Real food. A proper bed.

'It must be a survey ship,' said Kurt. 'If they have a base we're saved.' He glanced at the sun, then back at the contrail. 'It's to the West, and not too far at that.'

'That's fantastic,' said Hal. 'Come on, give me a hand with Clunk. We'll stick him on this travvy and get moving.'

'Hal, it will be dark before long. I believe it would be best to set off in the morning.'

'Spend another night on that bed of rocks? No thanks!'

'We cannot move in the dark, since we have no lights.'

'We can make torches.'

'And risk being spotted by our enemies?'

Hal was all for instant action, but he realised Kurt was right. This rescue camp could be a day's walk from their camp, and stumbling around in the dark with a heavy travois was a recipe for disaster. 'All right. But you'd better hope they haven't cleared out before we get there, or I'll –'

Kurt stepped forward, towering over Hal by a full head. 'Yes?'

'They'd just better be there, that's all.'

◆

Hal's second night in the wilds was even worse than the first. Every time he drifted off he imagined the survey team packing their gear and leaving at first light, abandoning the three of them to a life of chewy meat and highly uncomfortable beds. During one particularly stomach-clenching moment, Hal came to a decision: If they missed the boat he was going to approach the settlement and throw himself on their mercy. Taken in or eaten up, either was better than this.

When dawn broke he was roughly shaken awake by Kurt, who looked fresh and alert. 'Come on, Hal. We can't spend all day sleeping.'

Hal didn't have the energy to reply.

Half an hour later they were on their way, a soggy-looking pair in their misshapen patchwork skins, dragging Clunk's travois through the morning mist. It was heavy, the rough-hewn poles were like sandpaper on their hands, and they lost their grip every time the point caught on a fallen branch or a stunted bush.

'Why didn't he tell us to build a car?' muttered Hal, as the travois thudded to the ground for the hundredth time.

'Wait. I have an idea.' Kurt took out a sharp stone and slashed the vine binding the narrow end of the travois, freeing the two poles. He adjusted the lashings, turning the poles into a stretcher, then eyed Hal. 'Can you carry the lighter end?'

'Anything's better than dragging it.'

An hour later he was regretting his bravado. Every step was agony as Clunk's dead weight bounced in the stretcher. His shoulders, elbows and wrists were all dislocated, and his fingers were clearly broken. At least, that's what it felt like.

'Want a rest?' asked Kurt.

'I'm good,' said Hal, determined not to show weakness.

'I think maybe we have five or six hours before dark.'

'You should sell motivational tapes on the side,' muttered Hal.

Two hours later the forest thinned out, and Kurt converted the stretcher back to a travois. He took the first shift, dragging the heavy load over the hard soil while Hal stumbled along behind. After thirty minutes they swapped, and not for the first time Hal began to wish he'd picked an alarm clock or a commset as a trusted travelling companion, instead of a lead plated robot with plutonium in its boots.

They continued for another three hours, swapping at regular intervals, while Hal's arms grew longer and longer and his field of view got smaller and smaller. Eventually all he could see was the metre of dirt directly ahead, and when Kurt pulled up without warning Hal stumbled right into him.

'Shh!' hissed Kurt, putting a finger to his lips. 'I hear something!'

Hal lowered the travois to the ground and kneaded his aching muscles. If the 'something' wasn't a hot bath he didn't really care.

Kurt beckoned. 'Come, follow me.'

Hal obliged, putting one foot in front of the other. Then he saw what Kurt was pointing at, and his senses snapped back into focus. Between the trees he could see a rough trail through the woods. They were nearly there!

Hal followed Kurt out of the forest, and together they crouched to inspect the muddy track. There were deep furrows in the broken earth, and the pattern was unmistakable. Tyre tracks! Hardly daring to believe, Hal reached out a shaking finger and felt the sharp contours. 'What sort of vehicle made these?'

Kurt looked thoughtful. 'I'd say it was a passenger transport, perhaps an old bus or a converted truck. Seats maybe sixteen, with luggage racks on the roof. Red in colour, but rusty.'

Hal was impressed. 'You got all that from these tracks?'

'No.' Kurt pointed. 'It's parked under that tree.'

They abandoned Clunk and hurried towards the vehicle. As they got closer they saw a low-lying building between the trees, and standing between the two was the fiercest-looking bunch of people Hal had ever laid eyes on.

◆

739

Moments earlier Hal's spirits had been soaring, but now they crashed. To have come so far, survived for so long, only to walk straight into their mortal enemies …it was too much to bear. Still, he'd face death like a proud space pilot, and not some snivelling wreck. Drawing himself up, he stared the bunch right in the eye and drew a deep breath. 'Go on, you bastards. Do your worst.'

The evil-looking bunch murmured amongst themselves, and as Hal stared them down he spotted a few little oddities. For one, half of them bunch had cameras slung around their necks. For another, several were gripping half-eaten hamburgers. Then Hal noticed the sign adorning the side of the bus: *Be Part of Nature with Authentic Prehistory Tours.*

With dawning comprehension he turned to stare at the fierce-looking bunch of warriors, who were now talking amongst themselves in confusion.

'That's a pretty realistic outfit,' said one woman, with a straggly black wig and a large plastic cleaver. 'It's much better than these lousy things.'

'You're not wrong,' said her companion. 'I can smell him from here.'

A few took pictures, and then they all turned as a man in a khaki suit emerged from the hut. He sensed something was up, then spotted Hal and Kurt. Tucking his clipboard under one arm, he hurried over, gripping their elbows and dragging them away from the group. 'What are you two playing at?' he hissed. 'You know the drill! Tours at midday and four pm. Now get back to the village and look mean!'

◆

Hal sat in silence, absent-mindedly eating sliced peaches from the tin. Juice ran down his chin, leaving rivulets in the caked ash. Clunk was sitting alongside, and every time the bus hit a bump or a rut the robot leant harder against Hal, gradually squashing him against the window.

The laughter was still echoing in his ears. The way Kurt told it, he was on a peaceful hunting trip, communing with nature, when this deluded city-dweller came out of the woods with a rambling tale of crumbling civilisations and armed rebellion. He'd even bought his robot along, and the crowd laughed even harder when they heard about Hal's request for a charge point.

Hal tried to put his side of the story, but his wild eyes, ash-streaked person and leaf-matted hair were already pitted against him. When he explained about the teleporter and the lightning strike, the crowd roared. So, while Kurt recounted the high points for the third time, Hal slinked away to find Clunk.

The pair of them had been unresisting as they were gently loaded into the bus, and soon they were rattling and bouncing along the rough track. Kurt had declined the offer of a lift. After all, he said, he was perfectly capable of finding his own way home whenever he felt like it.

Half an hour later the bus turned onto the main road. A stiff breeze came through the open windows, and the bus left a cloudy white trail in its wake as the ash blew from Hal's clothes. Before long they arrived at base camp, where a battered old passenger flyer sat near a prefab building. Clunk was manoeuvred to the generator while Hal was manoeuvred into the shower.

Half an hour later, divested of his patchwork fur quilt and half-empty tin of peaches, Hal was feeling human again. The camp operators still chuckled every time they saw him, but he was alert enough to scowl back at them. He checked out the gift shop, ignoring the snorts of laughter as he inspected a scale model of a village hut. When he reached for the commset cover with the campfire motif they cackled.

He gave up and headed for the exit.

'Hee hee hee!'

Hal frowned. Surely they'd all heard the joke by now?

'Ha ha haaaa!'

There was a slip and a clang, and Hal emerged from the office to see Clunk rolling in the dirt by the generator. His hands were clutched around his middle and his head was thrown back as though he were struggling for breath. He spotted Hal and froze, his eyes bulging from his head. Then the pent air exploded from his plasteel lips.

'Haw haw haw haaaaaaw!'

Hal scowled. Great. Now he'd never hear the end of it. 'All right, all right. Wind it up, will you?'

Clunk sat, his eyes glistening. 'I'm sorry, Mr Spacejock. But you have to admit, it's a very funny tale.'

'Couldn't you explain about the teleporter? At least tell them that was real?'

'Alas, no. Even my solemn word wouldn't be enough to convince them.'

'Did you hear what Kurt said? He was in the woods by choice, slaughtering wildlife and skulking around on a camping trip.' Hal shook his head. 'I don't know why they believed him and not me.'

Clunk stood up and removed the charge cable. 'I'm afraid you'll have to chalk this one up as an interesting and novel experience, Mr Spacejock.'

'Just promise me one thing,' growled Hal.

'Yes?'

'Don't tell the Navcom. If one more person finds out about this mess I'm sunk.'

***

'No!'

'Yes! And then –' Clunk changed gears smoothly as the lift pinged. 'And then we need to check the fuel lines for contaminants.'

'Anything in particular?' asked the Navcom, in a neutral, female voice.

'Ash particles,' said Clunk, and he dissolved into laughter.

The doors opened and Hal strode into the flight deck. His hair was neatly brushed, his second-best flight suit was as clean as it was going to get, and his moukou boots gleamed under the flight deck spotlights. The only jarring note were the various bruises, contusions and scars about his person, but they'd heal with time. 'Any news from the scientist guy? He was supposed to transfer those shares.'

'Nothing yet,' said Clunk. 'I suspect they got lost in transit.'

There was a strangled hiss from the console, and Hal frowned. 'Let me know as soon as they get here.'

'Yes sir.'

'And order some more shampoo, will you? The last lot ran out.'

Clunk's lips twisted, but he held it together. 'Mr Spacejock, I just heard from our furniture customer.'

'Great. What's her problem?'

'None at all. She mentioned you to everyone she knows.'

'Really? That's fantastic!'

'Better than that. Her brother is the chairman of a media company, and they've published a write-up.'

'Local media?'

Clunk shook his head. 'Galaxy wide.'

Hal beamed. 'This is it, Clunk! Everyone's heard about me. I'm famous!'

'Yes.' Clunk hesitated. 'You most certainly are.'

'What is it?'

'Well, our customer has a second brother.'

'More media? More exposure?'

'Not exactly. He runs a tourist operation.'

'So what?' Realisation dawned. 'Oh no. Not ... Authentic Prehistory Tours?'

'One and the same. And I'm afraid they've connected you, so to speak. The article ... it included some rather amusing photos.'

Hal closed his eyes. It was bad enough getting laughed at by tourists and gift shop staff, but now the humiliation was complete. Slowly he turned away, walking towards the waiting lift with slumped shoulders. He'd have to hide in the *Volante's* rec room until the end of time, with only the AutoChef for company.

'There is one more thing.'

'Yeah?'

'I need your help selecting a job.'

Hal gestured. 'You find one. I'm going to lie down.'

'It's not a matter of finding a job, Mr Spacejock. It's a question of selecting the best offer.'

'Eh?' Hal turned. 'What are you on about?'

'Let me show you.' Clunk gestured, and the main screen filled with thousands of messages. Many were strings of LOLs and ROFLs, some were all smileys and grins, but most were freight jobs for 'the ash guy'.

'All that for me?' said Hal, unable to believe his eyes.

'Of course, Mr Spacejock.' Clunk smiled. 'Remember, there's no such thing as bad publicity.'

If you enjoyed this book, please leave a brief review at your online bookseller of choice. Thanks!

About the Author

Simon Haynes was born in England and grew up in Spain. His family moved to Australia when he was 16.

In addition to novels, Simon writes computer software. In fact, he writes computer software to help him write novels faster, which leaves him more time to improve his writing software. And write novels faster. (www.spacejock.com/yWriter.html)

Simon's goal is to write fifteen novels before someone takes his keyboard away.

Update 2018: goal achieved and I still have my keyboard!

New goal: write thirty novels.

Simon's website is spacejock.com.au

Stay in touch!

Author's newsletter:
spacejock.com.au/ML.html

facebook.com/halspacejock
twitter.com/spacejock

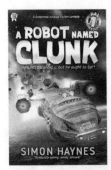

The Hal Spacejock series
by Simon Haynes

1. A ROBOT NAMED CLUNK

Deep in debt and with his life on the line, Hal takes on a dodgy cargo job ... and an equally dodgy co-pilot.

2. SECOND COURSE

When Hal finds an alien teleporter network he does the sensible thing and pushes Clunk the robot in first.

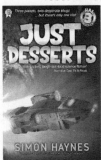

3. JUST DESSERTS

Gun-crazed mercenaries have Hal in their sights, and a secret agent is pulling the strings. One wrong step and three planets go to war!

4. NO FREE LUNCH

Everyone thinks Peace Force trainee Harriet Walsh is paranoid and deluded, but Hal stands at her side. That would be the handcuffs.

5. BAKER'S DOUGH

When you stand to inherit a fortune, good body-guards are essential. If you're really desperate, call Hal and Clunk. Baker's Dough features intense rivalry, sublime double-crosses and more greed than a free buffet.

6. SAFE ART

Valuable artworks and a tight deadline ... you'd be mad to hire Hal for that one, but who said the art world was sane?

7. BIG BANG

A house clearance job sounds like easy money, but rising floodwaters, an unstable landscape and a surprise find are going to make life very difficult for Hal and Clunk.

8. DOUBLE TROUBLE

Hal Spacejock dons a flash suit, hypershades and a curly earpiece for a stint as a secret agent, while a pair of Clunk's most rusted friends invite him to a 'unique business opportunity'.

9. MAX DAMAGE

Hal and Clunk answer a distress call, and they discover a fellow pilot stranded deep inside an asteroid field. Clunk is busy at the controls so Hal dons a spacesuit and sets off on a heroic rescue mission.

10. Cold Boots

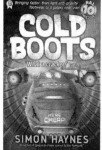

The Spacers' Guild needs a new president, and Hal Spacejock is determined to cast his vote... even though he's not a member.

Meanwhile, Hal's latest cargo job belongs to someone else, his shiny new ship is losing money hand over fist, and doing a good favour could turn out to be the biggest mistake of his life.

Ebook and Trade Paperback

The Secret War Series
Set in the Hal Spacejock universe

Everyone is touched by the war, and Sam Willet is no exception.
Sam wants to train as a fighter pilot, but instead she's assigned to Tactical Operations.
It's vital work, but it's still a desk job, far from the front line.
Then, terrible news: Sam's older brother is killed in combat.
Sam is given leave to attend his memorial service, but she's barely boarded the transport when the enemy launches a surprise attack, striking far behind friendly lines as they try to take the entire sector.
Desperately short of pilots, the Commander asks Sam to step up.
Now, at last, she has the chance to prove herself.
But will that chance end in death... or glory?

Ebook and Trade Paperback

The Harriet Walsh series

Harriet's boss is a huge robot with failing batteries, the patrol car is driving her up the wall and her first big case will probably kill her.

So why did she join the Peace Force?

When an intergalactic crime-fighting organisation offers Harriet Walsh a job, she's convinced it's a mistake. She dislikes puzzles, has never read a detective mystery, and hates wearing uniforms. It makes no sense ... why would the Peace Force choose her?

Who cares? Harriet needs the money, and as long as they keep paying her, she's happy to go along with the training.

She'd better dig out some of those detective mysteries though, because she's about to embark on her first real mission ...

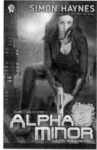

The Peace Force has a new recruit, and she's driving everyone crazy.

From disobeying orders to handling unauthorised cases, nothing is off-limits. Worse, Harriet Walsh is forced to team up with the newbie, because the recruit's shady past has just caught up with her.

Meanwhile, a dignitary wants to complain about rogue officers working out of the station. She insists on meeting the station's commanding officer ... and they don't have one.

All up, it's another typical day in the Peace Force!

Dismolle is supposed to be a peaceful retirement planet. So what's with all the gunfire?

A criminal gang has moved into Chirless, planet Dismolle's second major city. Elderly residents are fed up with all the loud music, noisy cars and late night parties, not to mention the hold-ups, muggings and the occasional gunfight.

There's no Peace Force in Chirless, so they call on Harriet Walsh of the Dismolle City branch for help. That puts Harriet right in the firing line, and now she's supposed to round up an entire gang with only her training pistol and a few old allies as backup.

And her allies aren't just old, they're positively ancient!

Ebook and Trade Paperback

The Hal Junior Series
Set in the Hal Spacejock universe

Spot the crossover characters, references and in-jokes!

Hal Junior lives aboard a futuristic space station. His mum is chief scientist, his dad cleans air filters and his best mate is Stephen 'Stinky' Binn. As for Hal ... he's a bit of a trouble magnet. He means well, but his wild schemes and crazy plans never turn out as expected!

Hal Junior: The Secret Signal features mayhem and laughs, daring and intrigue ... plus a home-made space cannon!

200 pages, illustrated, ISBN 978-1-877034-07-7

"A thoroughly enjoyable read for 10-year-olds and adults alike"
The West Australian

'I've heard of food going off
... but this is ridiculous!'

Space Station Oberon is expecting an important visitor, and everyone is on their best behaviour. Even Hal Junior is doing his best to stay out of trouble!

From multi-coloured smoke bombs to exploding space rations, Hal Junior proves ... *trouble is what he's best at!*

200 pages, illustrated, ISBN 978-1-877034-25-1

Imagine a whole week of fishing, swimming, sleeping in tents and running wild!

Unfortunately, the boys crash land in the middle of a forest, and there's little chance of rescue. Is this the end of the camping trip ... or the start of a thrilling new adventure?

200 pages, illustrated, ISBN 978-1-877034-24-4

Space Station Oberon is on high alert, because a comet is about to whizz past the nearby planet of Gyris. All the scientists are preparing for the exciting event, and all the kids are planning on watching.

All the kids except Hal Junior, who's been given detention...

165 pages, illustrated, ISBN 978-1-877034-38-1

Ebook and Trade Paperback

New from Simon Haynes
The Dragon & Chips Trilogy

"Laugh after laugh, dark in places but the humour punches through. One of the best books I've read in 2018 so far. Amazing, 5"*

Welcome to the Old Kingdom!

It's a wonderful time to visit! There's lots to do and plenty to see!

What are you waiting for? Dive into the Old Kingdom right now!

Clunk, an elderly robot, does exactly that. He's just plunged into the sea off the coast of the Old Kingdom, and if he knew what was coming next he'd sit down on the ocean floor and wait for rescue.

Dragged from the ocean, coughing up seaweed, salty water and stray pieces of jellyfish, he's taken to the nearby city of Chatter's Reach, where he's given a sword and told to fight the Queen's Champion, Sur Loyne.

As if that wasn't bad enough, the Old Kingdom still thinks the wheel is a pretty nifty idea, and Clunk's chances of finding spare parts - or his missing memory modules - are nil.

Still, Clunk is an optimist, and it's not long before he's embarking on a quest to find his way home.

Unfortunately it's going to be a very tough ask, given the lack of charging points in the medieval kingdom...

Ebook and Trade Paperback